FORT WORTH

Other books by Russell Hoban

THE LION OF

THE MOUSE AND HIS CHILD

RIDDLEY

Leonard Sanders

FORT WORTH

Delacorte Press/New York

Designed by Virginia M. Soulé

Copyright © 1984 by Leonard Sanders

Manufactured in the United States of America

First printing

Library of Congress Cataloging in Publication Data

Sanders, Leonard.
  Fort Worth.

  I. Title.
PS3569.A5127F6 1984   813'.54
ISBN 0-385-29360-7
Library of Congress Catalog Card Number: 84-7007

For Florene

Acknowledgment

With grateful acknowledgment to Jerry Flemmons, who graciously made information in his published works available to me; to my editor at Delacorte Press, Charles E. Spicer, Jr., for his unwavering, extraordinary effort, and for his many astute and valuable suggestions, and to my agent, Aaron M. Priest, for his initial and unflagging enthusiasm for this project.

FORT WORTH

A little rule, a little sway,
A sunbeam in a winter's day,
Is all the proud and mighty have,
Between the cradle and the grave.

John Dyer
Grongar Hill, 1729

God makes the country,
but man makes the town.

Captain Buckley B. Paddock
Editor
Fort Worth Democrat, 1873

BOOK ONE

Hell's Half Acre

After staying about a week at Johnson Station, we started in company with Major Arnold and command up Trinity River in search of a place to locate the regular United States troops. We passed through the Crosstimbers, crossing the different creeks as best we could, through a wild and beautiful country inhabited only by Indians, wild or mustang horses, innumerable quantities of deer, wolves and wild turkey.

> Simon B. Ferrar
> Mounted Texas Volunteers

I have located a new post on West Fork Trinity River. My address will be "Dallas, Dallas County," a town about thirty-five miles east of me.

> Ripley A. Arnold
> Brevet Major, 2nd Dragoons
> Founder of Fort Worth
> June 6, 1849

1

Dawn came slowly. Travis lay sleepless, rest-
less, as the first shafts of sunlight chased away wisps of low-lying mist and
the lingering horrors of the night. Behind him, in the clustered elms, a
colony of squirrels came to life and filled the river bottom with chatter.
Basking in the growing warmth, Travis clung to the comfort of morning
and its familiar sounds. A blue crane swooped low, landed on graveled
shoals downstream, and stood one-legged, leisurely fishing for minnows.
Calmly, Travis studied the dark shadows of the distant salt cedars, where
the headless major waited.

"You bloody Yank," he said aloud. "Why don't you tend to your own
affairs?"

His voice quieted the squirrels, but only for a moment.

Over a slow fire he boiled two duck eggs, a turnip, and an ear of corn.
The sun was an hour high when at last he rolled his blanket, shouldered
his pack, and walked on westward, his mind numb with clotted memories
of four years of war. Death hung around him like a pervasive fog.

All morning he dawdled, stopping often to bathe his bare feet in the
clear waters of the Trinity, pausing occasionally to nourish his parched,
war-shriveled soul with the rank greenness of the bottomland.

The war was over.

He was alive.

At noon he sat down to eat a few scraps of hardtack and jerky. He
then stretched out on a grassy slope and gazed upward through the
branches of a live oak to the great white clouds and fathomless blue of the
Texas sky. For a magic interval the soothing cry of a mourning dove, the
scolding of a bluejay, the joyous outpourings of a mockingbird muffled
even the cannons of Gettysburg. A small herd of white-tailed deer came
to feed in the sheltered cove. Around him, stirred by a soft breeze, the
grass sighed its timeless lament. Above, the trees whispered their ele-
mental truths.

Travis slept.

He awoke in midafternoon, alerted by a vague premonition. High overhead, a hawk ceased its primordial circles, folded its wings, and began a series of abrupt, measured descents. Travis sat up. Thirty yards away, at the center of the clearing, a baby cottontail nibbled at a clump of buttercups.

The deer had stopped grazing and stood with their flags aloft, rigid. Even the trees had fallen silent. The tiny rabbit was the only creature in the cove unaware of impending disaster. Spellbound, curiously unmoved, Travis followed the calculated plunge of the hawk until it reached the proper angle of attack, then dropped like a stone through the charged air.

The rabbit died in a bloody tumble, its final, pitifully weak bleat lingering for a moment among the living. The hawk seized its prey in crimson talons, cocked its head, and fired one-eyed challenges around the cove.

The enchanted interval ended. One by one, the deer lowered their heads to graze. The normal sounds of summer returned.

Travis was intimately acquainted with death. Indeed, he lived amidst a whole platoon of ghosts, led by the headless major. But for the first time since infancy, he was touched by the strangeness, the half-sensed potentialities of life.

A change came over him, a spiritual conversion as profound as baptism. Stunned by a hammer-blow of self-knowledge, he was moved to the depths of his soul. In awe, he spoke to the trees. "All my life, I've been like that little ol' scared rabbit. But by God, in the West, I'm going to be like that ol' hawk."

The sun was sinking into the upper branches of the scrub oaks. Still pondering the revelation, Travis again shouldered his pack. He resumed his walk westward.

Toward the end of that long day he waded a shallow creek and climbed the hill beyond to a small village poised on the edge of a bluff. In the glow of sunset he approached a scene of great desolation. At the center of the town square stood a half-built courthouse, fallen into ruins. Grass and weeds grew among the scattered stones. Around the square, unpainted clapboard buildings stood bleak and empty.

A summer storm loomed to the southwest. But swiftly the dark clouds fell apart, yielding only a dingy curtain of dust. The sky assumed the color of raw muslin spread over a fresh bayonet wound. Bullbats darted through the deepening twilight, circling, filling the air with their cries. Travis searched among the buildings for signs of life. He had begun to believe the village deserted when he saw an old man sitting as still as a statue on one of the chiseled stones. Homemade crutches leaned against his hip. An ancient black-and-white spotted hound lay at his feet. Travis walked toward him.

Otto Kretchmeir had seen so much of the world during his seventy-two years that he was seldom moved to pity. But as he studied the approaching boy, he was disturbed by an abundance of sad detail.

The boy was tall and gaunt, no more than a bundle of bones wrapped in loose-fitting trousers of Confederate gray and a ragged homespun shirt. His boots were in tatters. His knees and elbows moved in an aimless shuffle. The skin of his face, weathered nut-brown, was stretched tight over high cheekbones and a towering blade of a nose. His sunken button-black eyes seemed to look *through,* instead of *at.* He stood beneath a sooty hat, the crushed crown ventilated with a whole history of injuries. The limp, flaring brim was spread in tenuous anticipation of the slightest breeze.

On his back the boy carried a small pack that proclaimed his poverty more eloquently than words. On his right hip, in a display that shamed all other possessions, was strapped a huge .44 Whitneyville Walker Colt. When he spoke, his words came with great effort, as if there were a dislocation between mind and tongue. His voice was childlike.

"Mister, is this the West?"

Never before had Otto thought of west as being a specific place, as differentiated from a direction.

"Well, it's west of Dallas and a big part of the country. But it's east of an awful lot of nothing."

The boy looked toward the dying sunset, the distant scrub oaks, streams, rolling hills.

"What's out there?"

Otto spat into the dirt. "Comanches. Kiowas. Post oak. Scrub brush. Shinnery. Rocks. Sand. Buffalo. After about six hundred miles, El Paso del Norte, if you live to see it."

"Is that in the West?"

Alerted by the boy's intensity, Otto hesitated. "Why are you trying to put a brand on it?"

The boy's knees and elbows continued to jerk at discordant random. "Pa told me to find the West. Grow up with the country."

Otto had heard the expression. In fact, he had followed that advice himself, all the way from Mannheim, Germany. He studied the distant creek bottom, searching for movement. He could not believe that this helpless boy was alone.

"Your Pa didn't come with you?"

The boy shook his head. When he answered, his voice was devoid of emotion.

"He was buried at Chickamauga."

Otto saw the emptiness in the boy's eyes. He realized that the boy's mind had turned inward upon itself like an ingrown toenail. Otto had seen the phenomenon before in the shitstorms of war. He also realized that the boy's bone-thin gauntness was not from hunger alone, but from a deeper starvation, born of sleepless nights, long marches, and unrelenting terror.

"You were at Chickamauga?"

The boy did not answer. But the question stilled his jerking limbs. Gently, Otto prodded. "Where else?"

The boy's voice deepened. He looked into the distance and carefully shaped each syllable, as if speaking the language of a far country. "Missionary Ridge. Gettysburg. The Wilderness. Sharpsburg. Second Manassas."

"Lord God," Otto Kretchmeir breathed to himself. He closed his eyes. Once again he heard the roar of the Twin Sisters, the insidious sigh of grape, the screams of the Mexicans as they died in the mud flats along Buffalo Bayou. He himself had been a grown man at San Jacinto. Such things were beyond a mere boy.

The sun was gone. Dusk was deepening. Otto reached for his crutches. "I don't know where the West is. But you've come to the jumping-off place. You're in no shape to make it to El Paso. Not tonight, anyway. Come on. I'll treat you to supper."

Travis roused from his fitful doze to the crowing of roosters, the lowing of calves, the grunting of hogs in the peach orchard behind Otto's three-room house. Otto was still asleep, lying flat on his back, softly snoring. The hound Hector was draped across the foot of the bed. Travis lay for a time, examining his host in the dim light of dawn.

Otto was a large man, rotund and square-faced. His hair had thinned across the top. A full, unkempt white beard gave him the aspect of a grizzly bear. His eyes were deep-set and heavy-lidded. His habitual scowl, thick dark eyebrows, and a quick, unsmiling glance lent him a ferocious demeanor. But Travis sensed that Otto Kretchmeir might be the kindest man he had met since leaving Richmond. He reserved judgment. Three attempted robberies on his way west had taught him caution.

Otto stirred. Hector raised his head, yawned, walked off the bed, and trotted out the open door to raise a hind leg against an elderberry bush. Otto looked at Travis. "Couldn't you sleep?"

"Yes, sir," Travis lied. "I slept good."

He had no words to explain about the headless major.

Otto pulled on his trousers, slipped his feet into high-topped boots, reached for his crutches, and followed Hector, leaving in his wake the sweet-sour smell of nightsweat. He went to the other side of the elderberry bush.

Travis dressed. The woodbox by the small, flat-top, cast-iron stove was almost empty. During the night, going around the shack to piss, he had stumbled over a woodpile.

Moving steadily but unhurriedly, he found Otto's ax and chopped an armload of kindling. When he returned, Otto gave him an appraising glance.

"You may turn out to be as handy as a pocket on a shirt. How you like your eggs?"

For the first time in months, Travis was consumed by hunger. Soon the house was saturated with the aroma of eggs, smoked ham, biscuits, flour gravy, and steaming coffee. Travis ate, his appetite shoving courtesy and manners aside.

Afterward, he was ashamed. "I've no money," he said. "I'll pay you when I can."

Otto's scowl deepened. "Fret not thy gizzard. Frizzle not thy whirligig. We'll go out this morning and find some way for you to earn your keep."

Walking toward the town square with Otto, Travis studied the scattered small houses of Fort Worth. Most seemed deserted. The paint was peeling, the surrounding yards were knee-high in weeds. The streets, hardly more than wagon tracks, were straight, intersecting perfectly at right angles. Ahead lay the larger buildings around the courthouse square.

"This here's the old Fort Belknap Road," Otto said. "When the streets were laid out before the war, they named it Belknap Street." He pointed to a brick building in a nearby field. "Masonic lodge, only brick structure in town. Before the war, we had us a school there. Church services every Sunday. Now the floor's gone, ripped out to make looms so the women could spin clothing for the South." His gaze flicked to Travis. "Any of your people Masons?"

Travis remembered the cold gray day at Chickamauga. "Pa was. Mason words were said when he was buried."

Otto's gaze lingered on him. "That being the case, you'll probably be accepted into the lodge when you come of age, if you're of a mind."

Travis did not answer. His father had been secretive about the Masons.

"Remember this," Otto went on. "If you ever establish a town, build a good Masonic hall the first thing. You see, a lodge pulls everyone together. You'd think you'd want churches first. But churches divide a town something God-awful. I don't know why. Christians ought to work in harness. But they don't. They can go to war in a minute over the interpretation of a few words from the Bible. I've seen it happen."

They approached the square. A woman stood cutting roses from a scrawny bush in her yard and laying them in a basket on her arm. She waved to Otto. He waved back.

"Millie Latham," he said. "Husband's a doctor. Opposed secession. But he saw his duty. That's the way it was. Secession carried this county by only twenty-seven votes out of seven hundred polled. And within two months, the county raised ten companies of volunteers for the Confederacy. No one was left for conscription. The Lathams have a couple of pretty daughters, in case you're interested. Rebecca's just younger than you, I imagine. But my money's on the little one, Reva. She's going to be something. Smart as a whip."

Travis did not answer. He knew nothing about young women.

They paused to rest when they reached the square. Otto made for the fallen stones around the ruins of the half-built courthouse. He propped his crutches against his hip, arranged himself comfortably, and lit his pipe. Hector curled at his feet, lowered his head on crossed paws, and closed his eyes. Travis sank to the grass and waited.

"You wouldn't believe it now, but this county had seven thousand people in it before the war," Otto said after a time. "I saw this river bottom before there was anything or anybody. Came here with the Second Dragoons to establish the fort. June the sixth, in forty-nine."

The date held meaning for Travis. He searched for a moment before remembering the reason. "That was the day I was born."

Otto gave him an appraising glance. "Now that's something! A boy and a town born on the same day! Maybe your destinies are bound together."

Travis looked around the village. He saw nothing to encourage rapport. But the old man's rambling eloquence fired his imagination.

"We set up camp down there below the bluff. Spring rains drove us out. Mosquitoes thick as molasses. So we moved up here. Oh, nothing fancy. No stockade or breastworks. Never more than a parade ground and a few buildings. But we did our work." He pointed. "We sent patrols out to the west and north, cutting for hostile sign."

No battles were fought, Otto said. Every band of Indians that they found claimed to be hunting buffalo, then allowed under the treaties.

Conditions were so quiet that the principal concern shifted to keeping peace among the swarms of white settlers. With the protection of the soldiers, hundreds of farmers and planters soon infested the valley of the Trinity.

"The army moved on west in fifty-three. Set up a new line of forts. That was when I mustered out." Otto spat into the dust. "Hell, I left Germany to escape military conscription, and I wasn't in Texas six months until I was with Sam Houston at San Jacinto. I've fought in more border skirmishes than I can count. Punitive expeditions against Mexicans, against Indians. Then the Mexican War. All told, I've had twenty years of soldiering. That ought to be enough to do anybody."

Travis nodded agreement. His four years of war had been more than enough.

"When the army moved out, the civilians moved in," Otto went on. "Took over the buildings, lock, stock, and barrel. The barracks became a store, the stables a hotel. Lord God, but this place boomed! We had doctors, lawyers. I made harnesses, saddles. Couldn't keep up with the work. Three stage lines. Mail every day. A newspaper. Our own post office. Took the county seat away from Birdville. Good men died in that fight. But we won. Money was pledged to build this courthouse."

Otto said Fort Worth had been surrounded by plantations with a dozen new settlers arriving every day.

"Wealthy people, too. Families in fine carriages. All the way from Tennessee, Kentucky, Missouri. Most brought slaves, eight or ten wagon loads of property. We were on our way. Then the war came. Everything just fell apart."

Otto said his legs had been crushed beneath a freight wagon. Unable to fight for the Confederacy, he remained in Fort Worth and served as a sergeant in the home militia, guarding against Indian raids.

He pointed. "During the war, I saw Kiowas and Comanches several times right over there, sneaking along Marine Creek. A body wasn't safe between here and Jacksboro. We had some scary nights, we did."

Otto said Fort Worth had now dwindled to a tenth of its former size. Only women, children, and a few old men remained. All of the young men were gone.

"Most won't be coming back. Lord knows what'll happen to this town unless we get new blood. Young fellows like yourself."

Travis followed Otto across the square to the Deckman and Tucker Mercantile. Inside, five old men sat on a bench like a row of bedraggled blackbirds along a rail fence. On the wall hung a large map of the Confederacy, heavily marked with inks of various colors, the tracings of grimy hands. Otto pointed to it with considerable pride. He said that for four long years he and these other old veterans of San Jacinto, countless Indian battles, and the Mexican War had fought and refought the War Between the States as it progressed, reconstructing on the map the grand designs of the generals. Red circles marked battles where Tarrant County companies had fought.

"This here is Travis Spurlock," Otto announced. "He was at Chickamauga."

The old men fixed their flinty stares on Travis. One leaned forward. "You see our boys there?"

Travis looked to Otto for help. He found none. He shook his head. "No, sir."

"Seventh Texas?" the old man shouted. "You didn't see them? Didn't you see any of the fightin'?"

For one terrible moment, Travis again was among the rocks along Chickamauga Creek. He could hear the skirmishers, the slap, slap, of the bullets through the trees. He wanted to tell the old men how it had been, but the words would not come. His arms began to jerk. He could not stop them.

"He was there with Maney's Battalion," Otto said.

"On Johnson's left!" sang out another old man.

Travis nodded. He remembered talk of the Texans and their advance against Union artillery. He had heard the bombardment. He later saw the results.

"Where else, boy?" demanded the first old man.

Again, Travis could not speak. He stood, arms flailing, ashamed. He was consumed by a desire to weep—he who had not shed a single tear, not even at the burial of his father.

"He was at Gettysburg, Missionary Ridge, Sharpsburg, Second Manassas, the Wilderness," Otto said. "I don't know where else."

As if on command, the old men looked away. A silence fell. Otto reached for an earthenware jug at the end of the bench and removed the red corncob stopper. He handed the jug to Travis. "Robertson County whiskey. Nectar of the gods. It's said the primitive Baptists use it for sacramental purposes."

Travis managed several swallows. He could not control his trembling hands. Liquor spilled on his shirt.

Otto drifted toward the darkness at the rear of the store, where he stood for a few minutes talking with a huge man. He called and beckoned to Travis.

"This is Captain Seth Deckman," he said. "He needs some hired help. It'd be a way for you to earn your keep."

Captain Deckman was one of the biggest men Travis had ever seen

—a full head beyond six feet, and probably close to three hundred pounds. His dark eyes were unsmiling. "There's no money," he said. "But I can keep you and Otto in provisions."

Otto's eyes were averted, his expression neutral. But Travis did not resent the sudden introduction to a crafty side of Otto. He had learned in the war that every man sometimes had to do things that went against his nature. Travis needed work. He had no objection if Otto benefited.

"What you want me to do, sir?"

"You can tend the smokehouse fires before daylight. Keep the wood-box filled. Harness mules. Unload freight. Help butcher beef and hogs. Haul grain out to the mill. Otherwise make yourself useful, ten hours a day, six days a week."

The deal was sealed with a handshake. "I thank you, sir," Travis said.

Captain Deckman gave him the barest hint of a smile. "Better wait a few weeks."

Travis managed to remain awake through the next two nights. On the third, he slept. The headless major caught him unaware.

Again, he was lost, blindly fleeing the slaughter at Stones River. His company had disappeared into distant trees. The sky was leaden, drip-ping, the earth black gumbo, churned into a quagmire by three days of rain and the desperate maneuverings of two armies.

He had lingered too long, stripping food, powder, and lead from the corpses in the barren cornfield. He saw that he was alone. Frantic, he tried to run through the rows of stunted, dead cornstalks. Mud clung to his boots. Struggling in panic, he smelled the musk-laden approach of Yankees. Then, frozen with terror, he heard the stark reality of clanking sabers and farting horses.

Ahead lay a rank stand of trees. He looked back. Federals had reached the rock fence at the end of the field. Already the skirmishers were firing. Bullets hit the mud around him with ripe-watermelon thumps and passed near his head with dry-twig snaps.

A horse and rider cleared the stone fence in a graceful bound, floundered for a moment on the slick earth, then turned in his direction at a full gallop. Travis stood for an interminable moment spellbound, overwhelmed by the sheer, awful beauty of the Yankee officer's charge. Standing in his stirrups, the major was holding aloft a silver sword that sparkled and shimmered like the very gates of hell. Horse and rider were one, slipping and sliding on the wet ground, a macabre dance to the muffled thunder of shod hooves. The skirmishers ceased shooting as the officer entered their line of fire. For a few precious seconds out of all eternity, Travis and the charging major had a tiny portion of the battle-field solely to themselves.

Travis raised his rifle for a quick shot, involuntarily stepping back-ward to keep his balance. His foot caught in the mire. The bullet went wide. Helpless, his rifle empty, nauseated by the terrible shit-taste of fear, Travis knew he was only an instant away from joining the thousands of nameless, hollow-eyed corpses fertilizing the hedgerows and fields throughout the South. Desperately he raised his rifle in the forlorn hope of deflecting the saber blow.

For a timeless interval, the image of the charging Yankee hung suspended, as fixed and wrought with wondrous detail as a photograph. The major's eyes were alive with excitement and the pride of his own daring, his lips slightly parted with his exertion. He wore a meticulously trimmed and waxed moustache, the tips flaring like horns. His uniform was spotless, well tailored, and ablaze with decorations. The corner of a letter protruded from one breast pocket, as if hastily inserted at the alarm of foraging Rebels. His sorrel mare, a splendid animal, was broad in the chest and heavy through the shoulders and neck. Rider, horse, and saber posed a unity so awesome and exquisite that Travis marveled even as he stood on the abyss of eternity.

Then the air was split with the sigh of a passing cannonball. Looking up, Travis saw *two* dirt streaks arc through the leaden sky toward the advancing skirmishers.

The major's headless corpse remained in the saddle through three more strides, his saber still held on high, gore pumping aloft in a crimson cloud. The sorrel swerved to the left as she had been trained, providing a clear field for the saber slash.

The corpse left the saddle and slammed into Travis, carrying him deep into the mud, knocking all breath from his lungs, all rationality from his head. The corpse groped and clawed at him convulsively. In vain Travis fought to free himself from the sightless, senseless embrace. Half buried in the mire and gore, weighted by the twitching body, he heard the skirmishers approach. They gathered around him.

Travis was beyond fear. He awaited the bullet or bayonet that would free him from the restless, clawing terror. But the Yankee soldiers backed away in horror.

The Confederate cannons resumed their serenade. Another ball split the air. The Yankees scattered like quail, dashing for the shelter of the distant trees. Travis heard rifle fire from Rebel sharpshooters, the meat-ax sounds of bullets striking flesh.

Then silence fell. Travis and the major were left alone.

Travis lay all night on the field with the dead. At first light he crept away in the fog. Moving southeast toward Tullahoma, he searched in vain for his brigade. Behind him, all day long, he heard the stealthy step of the headless major.

For two days he wandered between the opposing armies, dodging bullets from friend and foe. At last he found the survivors of his company. He tried to tell them about the headless major, but no words came. His friends tied him to a wagonwheel to calm him. They cut away his encrusted uniform. That night, bound hand and foot in a wagonload of wounded, he was sent to the rear. Later he escaped and found his way back.

The headless major followed him throughout the remainder of the war and on the long trek west, lurking just beyond the reach of the campfire, awaiting the unguarded moment of sleep.

Travis awoke screaming. Otto fumbled about in the darkness. Hector fled howling into the night.

At last Otto flooded the room with the comforting amber glow of the lamp. Travis remained rigid in bed, the nightmare more real at the moment than reality itself. "Easy, boy," Otto said. He put out a hand, cautiously drew it back. "Everything's all right. You've just got the night terrors."

Travis sat up, blinking. Otto crabbed his way across the room and poured whiskey into a tin cup. "Night terrors are common," he said. "Used to have them myself. Still do, sometimes. Here. Drink this."

Travis drank the whiskey and shuddered, feeling the warmth spread through his stomach and into his limbs. He was ashamed, seeing himself as he thought Otto must see him, a child troubled by dreams. "I'm all right," he said.

Otto poured more whiskey, then fetched a cup for himself. He sat on the edge of the bed.

"After San Jacinto, a couple of Mexicans I killed bothered me right smart. There was another at Buena Vista. I used to wake up sometimes in terrible shape."

Travis could not stop trembling. He did not try to answer.

Otto went on in his rambling way. "I think part of the problem is that you have plenty of company in battle. Later, you have to face it alone. That's the way it was with me."

Again, Travis remained silent. He knew of no way to explain the headless major.

"It's a terrible thing to be alone," Otto said. "But I believe if a man has a good childhood, he can weather any storm. I think I see in you the marks of a fine family."

Otto waited.

Travis thought back to a mountain cabin and a tall, strong woman. "I don't know," he said. "Ma died when I was twelve."

Otto spoke cautiously. "She must have raised you well. You show certain refinements."

Travis heard the pride in his own voice. "Pa always said Ma was from one of the first families of Virginia. He said we would go back there some day, in style."

Gently, Otto pushed him deeper into remembrance. Calmed and relaxed by the whiskey, Travis began to talk.

Stumbling over the words, he told of the first days of the war, when his father met often with neighbors to discuss the wild rumors flying through the countryside. After reports of the Federal advance on Nashville were confirmed, the men felt they had no choice. They joined Maney's 24th Battalion of sharpshooters, Department of Cumberland, Army of Tennessee.

Haltingly, Travis described the winter he and his mother endured alone. Yankees drove away the livestock, emptied the grain bins. Half starved, heavy with child, his mother wasted away. There was nothing he could do. A neighboring widow came for her final hours. A boy baby, born alive, died a few hours later. Not yet thirteen, Travis set out to find his father.

He moved from one Confederate detachment to another, hunting Maney's sharpshooters. His long odyssey remained awash in confusion. He endured great battles, horrendous bombardments. Not until later did he come to know them by name. For a time he was a drummer. Later, he carried a rifle as a common soldier. Six days before Chickamauga, he at last found his father.

"He was shot the first day the Yankees tried to cross the river," Travis said. "Took him two days to die."

Travis was given his father's pistol, pocketknife, and Bible.

"That's all I have in the world," he said.

Otto sat silent for a time, then shook his head. "No, you've got more, Travis. Much more. You have everything your Pa and Ma taught you, all their expectations, their example. Believe me, boy. Many great men have started with less."

On a gray day in late November, as Travis returned to the square with buckets of water from the river, a man in a long frock coat stood on one of the fallen stones, speaking to a group of veterans gathered around him. Travis moved closer. The speaker was short and solidly built, with sharp, close-set eyes, and a flat nose that spread from cheek to cheek like an arrowhead. His compact body seemed charged with energy. His voice rolled over the square, rising and falling in melodious, thundering waves. Travis put down his buckets and stood transfixed.

"Listen to me, comrades," the man said, neatly clipping off each syllable. "We can no longer attenuate our circumstances! The worst is yet to come! Lee's surrender was not the harbinger of peace, as so deviously portrayed to us by the treacherous politicians of the North! I am here to tell you the truth! Before another year is out, we shall see the most villainous reprisals ever concocted by mortal man! Relentless persecution and bone-grinding poverty!"

Travis remained spellbound. He had never dreamed that words could be strung together in such marvelous fashion. He saw Otto in the crowd and drifted close. "Who's that?" he asked.

"Captain Tackett. One of the first settlers in Fort Worth," Otto said. "Commanded Company F, Waller's Battalion."

Building to his theme, Captain Tackett worked himself and his audience into a frenzy as he berated the heavy tax imposed by the U.S. Congress on medicinal quinine, sorely needed to combat rampant swamp fevers and malaria in the South, but hardly used in the North. His voice slipped into a deeper register and rolled across the square.

"For cold, cruel hatred and revenge, the quinine tariff far exceeds any law ever enacted by a government since the birth of Christ. Nero's persecution of the Christians, the Spanish decimation of the Moors and Jews, the massacre of the Huguenots in the time of Charles the Ninth, the genocide of Mexicans and Peruvians by Cortez and Pizarro, all pale before the transgressions of Thaddeus Stevens and his blackguards in the Union Congress! They are wreaking dire vengeance against their own kind! People who practice the same religion, who share the same lineage and homeland! They are guided only by their own perverse nature. Nothing like their heartless persecution of the South has happened in all recorded history!"

Travis stood fascinated. Through pace and inflection, the words transcended meaning and cast their own spell.

The captain concluded by admonishing the veterans for their laziness, for thinking they could rest, now that the war was over. He lowered his voice to a confidential whisper that rang across the square. "The fight has not yet begun! We must rebuild this town! We not only must restore it to its potentialities. We must move it forward to greatness, the fulfillment of all our aspirations. And I promise you, comrades. By so doing, we shall vanquish our enemies as effectively as we ever did in the field. We shall restore the peace and prosperity that is our God-given right!"

He stepped off the stone to resounding applause.

"How'd he learn to talk like that?" Travis asked.

"He's a lawyer," Otto said, as if that explained everything. "But he's

no bag of wind. No man in Texas knows more about legal matters. Even
Sam Houston used to shut up and listen when Captain Tackett spoke.
He's been everywhere and seen everything. Made the gold rush to Cali-
fornia in fifty-three. Said he saw beds of oyster shells on top of the Rocky
Mountains!"

In the days that followed, Travis found excuses to follow Captain
Tackett about town. Lurking within earshot, he doted on the unfamiliar
words, the rolling cadences, the dramatic pauses Captain Tackett imparted even to ordinary conversation. He tested the captain's eloquent
phrases on his own tongue.

One day he overheard Captain Tackett speaking to Otto. "Mr.
Kretchmeir, I've been wondering about that boy you've befriended.
Does the lad suffer from some grievous mental insufficiency?"

The two men had paused near the wagon Travis was unloading.
Travis knelt behind sacks of grain and listened.

"He's bright enough," Otto said. "He can read. Knows his numbers.
You never have to tell him something twice. He just has trouble working
his tongue."

"Could be he's a dreamer," Captain Tackett said. "If he ever awakes,
he may be one to watch."

By the time the first blue norther arrived, the gnawing worry in Fort
Worth was Reconstruction. Almost daily, small groups of dislocated Confederates passed by on their way west. They told of intolerable conditions
throughout the South.

The men of Fort Worth met on the courthouse square and night after
night debated what to do. Travis sat in the shadows of the flickering
bonfires and listened as Colonel John Peter Smith, Captain Tackett, and
other leaders shaped the town's future with skillful words. At last the
debates evolved a list of respected, elderly candidates—men who could
take the "ironclad oath" that they had done nothing to aid the Confederacy. Captain Tackett led a delegation to Austin. There they presented,
and received approval for, their slate of county officers. Thanks to these
clever leaders, Fort Worth escaped the terrible affliction of Reconstruction.

Throughout the long winter that followed, as Travis made his rounds
from pigpen to corral, from pasture to barn, he marveled over the way
Captain Tackett and Colonel Smith, a former schoolteacher, had swayed
the minds of men with the strength of their words. Again and again he
tried their ornate phrases on his own tongue. He pledged that some day
he would be their equal, worthy of respect and admiration.

One afternoon as he crossed Main Street, Rebecca Latham emerged from the Deckman and Tucker Mercantile with her father. Travis had seen her several times, but only from considerable distances.

The doctor steadied her hand as she stepped into the light hack parked in front of the store. Travis walked on toward them, sneaking covert glances at Rebecca, his senses reeling.

At close range, Rebecca seemed not flesh and blood but an inspired vision brought to life by some talented artist. She was tall and slim, yet totally feminine. Her abundant auburn hair cascaded in ringlets that rippled as she moved. Once seated, she turned soul-searching green eyes upon Travis.

The doctor spoke a greeting. Travis muttered a reply that was unintelligible, even to his own ears. He stumbled on the rough wooden sidewalk and almost fell. From the carriage came a suppressed giggle. Travis hurried on. He did not look back.

He felt like a fool.

That night he cringed with embarrassment at the memory. He vowed that never again would he allow himself to be humiliated in such a fashion, that the next time he encountered her, or any woman, he would know how to act.

During the days that followed, he carefully observed the manners of Captain Tackett, Colonel Smith, and other gentlemen in the presence of ladies.

Alone in a stable, or protected by the banks of a creek, he practiced their gestures and postures.

As the weeks went by, he tried to put Rebecca Latham out of his mind. He told himself that what she thought of him did not matter. Some day she would look at him and marvel. Someday he would walk with kings and queens.

Night after night he lay awake and dreamed of the man he would become.

He had not forgotten the hawk and the rabbit.

2

On a morning in the early spring of 1867, Travis awoke to a lowing murmur like distant thunder and the monumental aroma of cowshit. The odor clung mightily to the air, seeping into doorways and crevices with a cloying persistence that suggested it intended to stay for a hundred years.

Otto and Hector were up and gone. Travis dressed hurriedly and ran to the east edge of town, where an animated crowd stood watching a spectacular scene.

Thousands of Texas Longhorn steers ambled along in an orderly procession stretching away from the south. The lead steers were picking their way along Sycamore Creek. Three riders, slowly swinging coiled lariats, were milling the herd onto bed ground with practiced ease.

The cattle were like no other Travis ever had seen. Lean and gaunt, they were wild as deer, as fleet as antelope. They walked with heads lowered by the weight of wide, massive horns.

Otto was seated on a mesquite stump. He was filled with news. "There's another herd behind this one," he told Travis. "They're driving them straight north. They say the Missouri Pacific is already into Kansas!"

Travis watched the herd for a while, but soon had to hurry on to work. He found the square crowded with people. Excitement continued to mount around him throughout the day as the full meaning of the herds slowly dawned.

Before the war, cattle had been moved up the Shawnee Trail through Dallas. That route had been closed by the Missouri quarantine. Now, with the railroad already into Kansas, northbound cattle would be driven right through Fort Worth.

The herds had been on the trail several weeks. The drovers needed supplies for the long trek through the Indian nations. For two days Travis was kept busy, boxing and loading goods.

His imagination ran rampant. Otto said each Longhorn steer, practically worthless in Texas, would bring twelve or fifteen dollars at the Kansas railhead. Thousands of cattle roamed free over South Texas. Travis wondered if he had found his way to fortune.

He was unloading a freight wagon when he overheard one of the trail bosses talking with Captain Deckman. "My horse wrangler just quit. Leaves me a hand short. Know any young bucks who'd like to go up the trail?"

Travis lowered a heavy sack of beans. He thought of the graceful riders swinging their ropes, all the way through the Indian nations, to new places where interesting things probably were happening every day. Almost without thought, he spoke. "Mr. Hockstader, I'd like that job, sir."

Hockstader, tall and lean, gave Travis the calculating study he would give a wild steer. "Ever trailed cattle?"

"No, sir. But I know cows. I'm good with horses."

Hockstader exchanged glances with Captain Deckman. He turned back to Travis. "What would your folks say?"

"They're dead, sir."

"You got a saddle?"

"Yes, sir." Otto had given him an old Spanish rig.

"All right," Hockstader said. "The pay's twenty-five dollars a month. I'll be in town for the next hour or so."

"I might've known it," Captain Deckman said. "My best man quits on the busiest day of the year."

Travis stammered in embarrassment. He had not thought ahead to leaving Captain Deckman in the lurch. But the captain slapped him on the back and laughed. "Go ahead, boy. It's all right. Hell, if I was younger, I'd be going with you."

Travis pulled off his apron and started home, wondering how to explain his new plans to Otto.

"Good Lord, I've no claim on you, boy," Otto said. "I only want you to do me one favor. Come with me to see Captain Tackett and Major Van Emden. We've talked some about your future. I think you ought to hear us out before you go."

"I told Mr. Hockstader I'd be back in an hour."

Otto had worked all night repairing saddles, chaps, belts, and harness for the drovers. He tossed a strap onto his bench, wiped his hands, and reached for his crutches. "Mr. Hockstader will keep. The herd won't leave till morning."

They found Captain Tackett in front of his office, watching the milling traffic around the courthouse square. He gave a passing boy a penny to fetch Major Van Emden. Travis stood waiting impatiently, wondering what two of the most important men in town wanted with him.

After a few minutes the small, wiry figure of Major Kendall Van Emden crossed the square toward them.

There was an aura of mystery about Van Emden. He had arrived in town in early December, and spent several days exploring the Trinity River valley. Speculation had been high over what he might be seeking. The major was not just anybody. He had studied for the law at Franklin College. His father had served as Texas chargé d'affaires to the United States during the days when Texas was a separate nation, and had been the shoo-in candidate for governor when he died of cholera while campaigning in Houston.

The major had compiled his own illustrious record. He had been captured during the war, spent time in a Yankee prison, was exchanged, and fought on until felled by illness just before Appomattox. With his white goatee, piercing eyes, and calm demeanor, he held the respect of the whole community. He had bought a block in downtown Fort Worth, paying three hundred dollars spot cash. He already had moved his large family, various in-laws, and a platoon of servants from East Texas. He had let it be known that, after extensive study, he had concluded that Fort Worth with its choice location would prosper, and some day become a city of five thousand people.

The major exchanged greetings. Captain Tackett gestured toward Travis. "Young Spurlock here is on the verge of leaving town with three thousand Longhorns. Otto thought we should apprise him of that proposition we discussed the other day."

Van Emden nodded. "Clearly, there's no time to waste."

Travis was ushered into Captain Tackett's somber, cool office. A south breeze rippled the lace curtains. From across the square came the laughter of drovers in the saloon.

Tackett guided Travis to a big rawhide chair across from his desk. Otto perched on a horsehair sofa, his crutches resting against his knees.

Major Van Emden pulled a cane-bottom chair close to Travis. "Young man, we've been watching you for some time now. We've admired your industry, your intelligence. The four of us here have much in common. We've all endured the vicissitudes of war. I happen to know that you come from a fine family. You see, I've taken the liberty of writing to a friend in Tennessee who knew your father. I made inquiries about you, and your circumstances. I hope you don't mind."

"No, sir," Travis said, wondering why the major would go to so much trouble.

Van Emden placed a paternal hand on Travis's knee. "Young man, if you go up the trail with those cattle, you'll no doubt have a lot of fun. But

chances are you'll never amount to a plugged hat. That was *not* what
your father meant when he told you to go west and grow up with the
country. You don't want to squander your life. Son, you've got a head on
your shoulders. If you put your mind to it, you can *be* somebody. Fort
Worth needs young men like you."

Travis did not know what to say. He remained silent.

Captain Tackett rose, walked to a bookcase, and selected a volume.
He hunted through the text, then handed Travis the open book. "Read
the passage I've marked."

Travis turned the page so he could see the print in the dim light. The
words were strange. He stumbled through them. " 'There is a tide in the
affairs of men, which, taken at the flood, leads on to fortune. Omitted, all
the voyage of their life is bound in shallows and in miseries.' "

"Shakespeare. *Julius Caesar,*" Van Emden said. "What do those
words mean to you? Just give us your first thoughts."

Travis remembered axioms from McGuffey's *Readers,* drilled into
him by his mother. "Opportunity only knocks once. Take the wrong fork
in the road and you stray from righteousness. Strike while the iron's hot."

Captain Tackett and Major Van Emden exchanged glances.

"I've known eminent jurists who couldn't have restated the thought
better without lengthy consideration," said Van Emden. "Just as we
suspected, you have a fine mind, son. I'd regret to see it go to waste. Most
of those drovers with that trail herd can't read anything beyond the
brand on the rump of a Longhorn. You can thank God your family gave
you the start of an education. You've already got a jump on life. Use it!"

Captain Tackett leaned forward. "Travis, we want to help you. If you
can see your way clear to doing odd chores for me and for the major, I'll
grant you access to my law library, one of the finest in the state. We'll
direct your reading for the law, the most noble profession to which man
can aspire."

Otto broke into the discussion for the first time. "Travis, if you go
north with that herd, you'll just get busted up like me, and spend tho root
of your days a cripple."

Travis was confused. He still held the vision of himself tall in the
saddle, riding toward adventures as yet unknown. But Captain Tackett
and Major Van Emden had just created a dream no less clear—of himself
dressed in fine clothes, speaking powerful words before juries, before
multitudes, swaying the minds of men, admired and respected.

He knew which of the visions would have appealed to his father, and
to his mother.

He remembered the hawk and the rabbit.

But he could not see why one choice necessarily ruled out the other.
"I'd be back in a few months," he said.

Van Emden sighed. "Travis, reading for the law requires a great deal of concentration. You'll have to put your mind to it, totally, six days a week, for two or three years. Captain Tackett and I are offering our time to direct your reading, to examine you regularly and follow your progress. What we are offering is beyond monetary value. Understand this: your father was a Mason. The Masonic lodge requires of its members a strong sense of obligation, of brotherhood. Captain Tackett, Otto, and I are fellow Masons. We are morally required to assume the responsibilities of your father toward you, because he was our brother. Do you follow me?"

"Yes, sir," Travis said, although he only half understood. Throughout his childhood, his father had saddled a horse and ridden into town once a month to attend "lodge." Although his father never talked about it, he always seemed quieter and more thoughtful on those days. Travis also remembered that Confederate and Union soldiers who were Masons served their companies as traders, slipping into creek bottoms to swap Confederate tobacco for Union coffee, meeting in peace under what they called the Masonic "sign." Travis knew there was much more to Masonry than met the eye. He sensed the close-knit camaraderie of the three men facing him. He felt enveloped by the profound mystery they posed. But something else tugged at the back of his mind. "I'm beholden to you," he said. "But I promised Mr. Hockstader I'd go with the herd. Pa wouldn't want me to go back on a promise."

"Every footloose young man in town is dying to go in your place," Captain Tackett said. "Archibald Ledbetter and Timothy Oldfield have already spoken to Mr. Hockstader."

"I'll explain matters to Mr. Hockstader for you," Van Emden said. "Don't worry about it. He'll understand. You see, Mr. Hockstader's a Mason, too."

Travis quickly became so absorbed in his new routine that other considerations faded into insignificance. He filled woodboxes, chopped kindling, harnessed teams to buckboards, fed, curried, and saddled horses, tracked down witnesses, ran errands, trimmed and tended lamps, and read law far into each and every night.

Around him Fort Worth boomed. Although only a few more trail herds came through that spring and summer, anticipation remained high. Word came that the railroad had pushed across Kansas as far as Abilene. Travis listened quietly as Van Emden, Tackett, and other leaders and townspeople discussed prospects. They were optimistic. They agreed that with Fort Worth as the last supply outpost before setting out across the no-man's-land of the Indian nations, and the first encountered on return, prosperity was inevitable.

Fort Worth prepared. Supplies were freighted in until the walls of the stores seemed to bulge. Major Van Emden, although educated for the law, chose to open a general mercantile. Traveling from New Orleans to New York by rail, he purchased goods for delivery to the docks at Galveston. He transported the stock northward to Fort Worth by ox teams. Travis helped unload the finery.

Slowly, Travis worked his way into a new world. He remained busy throughout each day. His reward came after sundown, when he had the law office to himself. Night after night he sat up until dawn, reading with total understanding and a consuming fascination. He quickly absorbed *Hartley's Law Digest* and expanded into case law. He committed the precise wording of entire appellate decisions to memory, along with dissenting opinions, the names of the judges, attorneys, and key witnesses. And while he still stammered painfully in ordinary conversation, he found that the beauty and eloquence of legal language tended to free his tongue. He could quote page after page without a bobble.

Van Emden often dropped by to examine him on specific points. Travis soon suspected that although Tackett was craftier, and perhaps the better lawyer, Van Emden was better educated. Otto confirmed this impression. "Van Emden was graduated with highest honors from Franklin College at Nashville before the war," Otto said. "Gave his valedictory address in Latin."

One night Van Emden paused in his examination of Travis and closed the book he was holding. "Tell me, son. What is it about law you like best?"

Travis did not hesitate. "Words."

Van Emden smiled and nodded. "Travis, I believe you have a great gift. You have an astounding memory. You must put it to good use. The law is a noble profession. But when I was a boy, I was fortunate enough to hear some of the best orators this nation has ever produced—Calhoun, Clay, Webster. Those great men always seemed to look beyond law. If you're interested in public speaking, politics, you'll need to raise your sights. I'll bring you some books."

The next day he handed Travis a collection of Shakespeare's tragedies, a small volume containing the selected speeches of Daniel Webster, a King James version of the Holy Bible, volumes on Latin and Greek grammar, an English dictionary. He proved to Travis that the roots of a great many English words were derived from other languages. "In order to use English well, you must have an acquaintance with those languages," he explained.

Through spring rains, summer heat, and winter snows, Travis committed to memory great chunks of the Bible, Shakespeare, Cicero, Homer, Catullus, Virgil, and Webster. Eventually he exhausted the coveted libraries of Van Emden, Tackett, and John Peter Smith. Night after night he reeled to bed with his brain on fire. Seeking fuel to keep his mind stoked, he thought nothing of saddling a borrowed horse to ride fifty miles to borrow a book.

Van Emden and John Peter Smith praised his industry. As the months passed, they selected his reading. Under their guidance, he went on to devour Tolstoi, Balzac, and Hugo. He breezed through Dickens, Trollope, and Eliot. He argued Van Emden and the colonel to a standstill on the theories of Emerson and Thoreau. Such books as Jared Sparks's *Life of Washington* sent him into trances that lasted for weeks.

He also found a world even more romantic in the company of Sir Walter Scott, James Fenimore Cooper, Tennyson, Wordsworth, the Brontë sisters, and Elizabeth Barrett Browning.

Captain Tackett was not pleased with his descent into popular novels and verse. "Fluff!" he said. "You won't win cases by quoting poetry to jurors. Listen to me! Books are to be used in moderation, like whiskey. Don't be led astray!"

But the captain could not hide his pride. He often paraded Travis's peculiar knack of memory before visiting lawyers and judges. He challenged them to stump Travis on the most esoteric points of law. Travis obliged by citing chapter and verse of precedents for every specific case that they could mention.

Travis found he also possessed an uncanny aptitude for language. Van Emden had kept his exercise books from Franklin College. He grilled Travis almost nightly on Latin and Greek. Travis sailed through the basics. Soon he confronted the classics in their original languages. Familiarity led to even deeper understanding. Often he went alone into the surrounding woods and vented his oratory on trees. He tested his Latin on squirrels, his Greek on birds.

Those moments of stolen solitude provided the only childhood he had known.

In those precious, guarded interludes, through the glorious medium of books, he conversed and contended with the greatest minds that ever graced the earth.

On his errands for Captain Tackett and the courts, searching through the saloons for witnesses, lawyers, and jurors, Travis heard the stories told by drovers returning from Kansas. They described wild nights in the wide-open saloons, and deadly confrontations. Travis listened, fascinated. His imagination found it but a step from the days of Rob Roy and D'Artagnan to the newborn legend of the Texas gunfighter.

Gradually, he was drawn from his books by the vast transformations around him.

From early spring until late fall, trail herds were bedded constantly near town. Dust, the familiar odors, and the bawling of cattle hung in the air. The streets teemed with life. Saloons, dance halls, whorehouses, and shooting galleries sprang into existence, clustered around the southeast corner of the square. Heavy freight wagons pulled by ox teams brought in produce from the railhead at Monroe, Louisiana, or the docks at Galveston. Teamsters, drovers, buffalo hunters, and adventurers passing through on their way west kept the nights lively. Professional gamblers were as thick as fleas. Around the saloons and dance halls, cribs were built for the "soiled doves" who arrived to share the prosperity.

The section came to be known as Hell's Half Acre.

In the evenings, weary of his reading, Travis often went on long strolls through the acre. He liked the conviviality—the music, shouting, lighthearted laughter, and story telling. He felt that at last he had found a place where great events were an everyday occurrence. Fistfights flared nightly. Seldom a week went by without a shooting.

"You'd better stay the hell out of the acre," Otto warned. "You'll get knocked in the head over there. Or a case of the drip."

"What's the drip?" Travis asked.

"You'll know when you get it," Otto said.

Travis seldom had money, or immediate prospects of any. He occasionally exchanged pleasantries with some of the prostitutes. To avoid embarrassment, he usually implied that he had pressing, official business elsewhere. Yet, their constant teasing left him greatly disturbed. He watched the men they most admired. He set out to emulate them.

He combed his wild black mane into a dashing, stylish tumble. Otto made him a pair of high-topped boots. Travis kept them meticulously blacked and polished. He stuffed his trouser cuffs into them with studied abandon. Captain Tackett gave him an old but serviceable frock coat. Travis carefully placed it between his two tick mattresses each night to keep its character intact. He traded a blacksnake whip, braided from scraps in Otto's shop, for a broadbrimmed black hat, and decorated its leather band with an eagle feather. From cast-off saddle skirts he fashioned a black sheath for his .44 Walker Colt. He wore the weapon cavalry style, low on his left hip, the handle pointed forward for easy access in a cross-body draw.

Attired in his finery, he spent considerable time studying himself in the mirror.

He was not disappointed.

Several times each week he went into the creek bottoms to the west of town and practiced for hours, drawing and shooting his huge Colt until his hammer thumb bled. He became fast and accurate. Gaining confidence, he pitted his skills in friendly contests. Soon he acquired a reputation as one of the best pistol shootists in town.

Suddenly he noticed that he was no longer ignored. Men who never before had deigned to acknowledge his existence now spoke and nodded a greeting. Travis was surprised by their deference. With considerable practice, he developed an easy, elaborate gesture in removing his hat. He found that it reduced the ladies, especially the older matrons, to flustered blushes.

"Travis, you're becoming a good-looking young man," Captain Tackett said one day. "Don't become a dandy. You'll alienate juries."

For once, Travis ignored the captain's advice. In his new outfit, with his boots well polished and his Colt slung low, he felt like a man of the world, the equal of any in the acre.

Returning home late one night, he heard his name called from a dark doorway. In the shadows he recognized Ellie, one of the most popular girls. She claimed to be French, but there were those who said she merely had tainted blood.

"Why're you going home so early?" she whispered. "Come on up to my room. We'll make the moon spin."

Travis swept off his hat. "Thank you, but I have a busy day tomorrow, Miss Ellie. Perhaps another time."

From a block away came the music of a piano, loud laughter. Ellie stepped out of the doorway and into the light of a distant lantern. She put her hands to his lapels. Her voice came to him soft and husky. "Come on, Big Man. I promise you. For a dollar, you'll see fireworks like the Fourth of July."

Travis did not want to offend her. "Truth is, I got cleaned out at poker," he lied.

"How much you got left?"

"Two bits."

"All right. Two bits. If you won't tell anyone."

Travis felt trapped. The twenty-five cents in his pocket was all the money he owned. But he no longer was capable of resistance. Ellie was looking up at him with her lips parted, her tiny tongue rocking back and forth across her teeth. Her eyes were soft brown, and she was no bigger than a minute. A feverish desire grew within him.

"It would be my pleasure, Miss Ellie," he said.

He followed her up creaking wooden steps to a loft. Ellie undressed in the soft light of a lowered lamp. Her skin was the color of nutmeg. She tasted of cinnamon. She handled Travis expertly. The transaction was over almost before it started.

"You've been away from the well too long, Honey," Ellie said. "You come see me. We'll keep the edge worked off."

Travis left the loft feeling light and free, happy that another milestone was behind him, that one more mystery was solved.

Two months passed before he saw Ellie again. She appeared one morning before Judge Riley, along with several other women from the acre.

Travis sat with Captain Tackett, waiting for the opening of an important civil trial. The court usually dispensed with minor cases first. Travis felt Ellie's soulful brown eyes upon him. She gave no sign of recognition.

She was led before the bench. Mumbled words passed between the judge and Ellie's attorney.

Judge Riley rapped his gavel. "Ten days or ten dollars."

A short, dapper little man approached the clerk and paid Ellie's fine. She left the courtroom with him.

These scenes always disturbed Travis. He was now especially distressed at this ministering of "justice." He leaned close to the captain's ear. "I don't understand, sir. Everybody knows about the girls in the acre. Why do they allow them to work, and then arrest them?"

Captain Tackett did not seem to want to talk about it. "That's the way the matter is handled, son. Every so often one of those fallen angels is arrested and fined, so her identity can be made a matter of public record."

Travis persisted. "But why?"

Captain Tackett sighed. "Travis, society must be carefully structured. The fine, decent portion of the community must be separated, protected from what happens in the acre. We must keep a firm line of demarcation. A well-maintained public record is the proper way to draw that line."

Travis did not argue.

But he had felt uncomfortable with the duplicity.

He thought that in her own way, with her dignity, poise, and silence, Ellie had shown far more integrity than had the court.

Millie Latham saw Reva coming from far up the street, barefoot, pigtails flying. Leaping mud puddles, Reva darted through a weed-infested lot and bounded up the back steps into the house. The door slammed behind her.

Millie grabbed her by the shoulders and held her at arm's length. "Reva! Just look at that dress! It's absolutely ruined!"

Reva glanced down at her skirt in dumb incomprehension. She wiped tentatively at the mud and grass stains.

Consumed for a moment by irrational anger, Millie tightened her grip on Reva's shoulders and shook her. "Where have you been? I've had half the town out looking for you!"

Reva brought her arms up defensively. Tears sprang to her eyes.

Millie backed away, appalled at her own loss of control. As she had long feared, she seemed to be sinking to the level of her surroundings. She forced herself to speak calmly. "Where have you been all afternoon?" she asked again.

Reva began sniffling. "Over to Clem Berry's."

Millie sighed. "I should have known! How many times have I told you not to go over there? Do you remember my telling you why?"

Reva nodded. "You said they're trashy. But Momma, Clem's not. Really he's not."

"You let me be the judge of that! How did you stain your dress?"

Again, Reva glanced down. "Playing wolf over the river. I fell."

Millie had seen the young ruffians in the empty lots, bowling into each other like tenpins. "A boy's game!" she said.

Reva looked up at her through tear-dampened eyes. "Momma, girls play it too."

"Some girls," Millie said. "I'd always hoped most fervently it would never be a daughter of mine. Where's your sunbonnet?"

Reva put a hand to her head. She stood stricken, speechless.

Again Millie felt her anger flare. "The third you've lost in a month! Why can't you keep a bonnet on your head? It seems such a simple thing to do."

Reva turned to the wall, put her head in the crook of her arm, and began to blubber in earnest.

Millie sank into a chair and pondered what to do. At eleven, Reva remained a hopeless tomboy. The trait must have come from the Latham side. Certainly, nothing like it had ever occurred in Millie's family.

Reva was still sobbing. Millie fought down the grim apprehensions she harbored for her daughter's future. She pulled the child into her lap. "Reva, I know it's hard for you, growing up in a godforsaken town like this. But you must never, ever forget for a moment who you are. You were *born* a lady. You're descended from the finest families in the South. You simply must not play rough games like that!"

Reva wiped at her nose with the back of her hand. Millie handed her a lace handkerchief.

"And you *must* keep your bonnet on outdoors. Even if you're out only a minute. Some day you'll thank me. Believe me, you'll spend most of your life taking care of your complexion. The time to begin is now. Wear your bonnet! Do you hear?"

Reva nodded.

"And how many times have I told you never to run? Walk! Comport yourself as a lady. Always! You slammed the door just now. Suppose your father had been treating a patient?"

Reva mumbled into the crook of her arm. "I don't know how I'm supposed to remember everything. There must be a million rules around here. Don't go into the parlor during the day. Don't make any noise. Don't play with my best friends. Don't go downtown. Don't get my dress dirty." She raised her head. "What am I supposed to do? Stand in a corner all the time?"

Millie hesitated. Reva still was having difficulty accepting the return of her father after four years of war. His presence had altered completely the only life she had known. Moreover, there was a streak of independence in her that railed against the family's reduced circumstances. Where her sister Rebecca complied without protest, Reva questioned every restriction. Millie reached for her hand.

"Papa will only be using the parlor for a little while. Soon he'll have an office downtown. We'll have the house to ourselves again. Maybe we'll have an even bigger house, and you can have your own room. How would you like that?"

Intrigued with the idea, Reva quieted.

Millie turned the child around and unbuttoned the back of her dress. "Have Dulcie draw water for your bath. Go on, now. We'll have supper soon."

After Reva had gone, Millie sat alone on the back porch, toying with an idea that had been taking shape during the last few weeks.

She had assumed, when her daughters were born, that some day she would take them back home for their formal training, and that there they would make their debuts into society. But Rebecca was already fourteen, and had experienced only a smattering of the social graces. Reva was quickly becoming a little scamp, indistinguishable from the urchins in the shantytown she frequented along Sycamore Creek.

Millie thought of her relatives scattered throughout the South— Cousin Susan in Savannah, Cousin Rose in Charleston, Cousin Grace in Atlanta, and Aunt Zetta in Richmond. If she could take Reva and Rebecca back east for a leisurely tour, she could show them that there were things in the world other than life in a raw frontier village. The trip would not be expensive. The more Millie considered the idea, the better it seemed.

That evening she did not speak her thoughts to her husband until after supper, when he lit the kerosene lamp in the parlor, as was his custom, and sat reading a medical text. Millie took her needlepoint to the opposite chair to share the light. She waited patiently for an opportune moment.

In many ways her husband had returned from the war a different man. Gone were his high humor, gentle smile, and easygoing manner. He now was quick to anger, difficult to reach. He spent much of his time in morose contemplation. He would not talk about the war. What little Millie had learned of his experiences came in oblique ways. Once, stopping to consult a textbook before dispensing a drug, he remarked that it had been four years since he truly had practiced medicine.

"The Confederacy turned me into a hacksaw surgeon," he said. "I'll never forgive them for that. I'm now forced to learn healing all over again."

Later, Millie overheard him reassuring a trail driver whose leg had been crushed by a falling horse. "Young man, I performed hundreds, perhaps thousands, of amputations such as this during the war. Often twenty-five or thirty in a single day. Once the flesh begins to mortify, there's no other course. I may have been feared by my own troops, but I saved many lives. Your chances are far better here than on a battlefield."

Millie paused in her stitching to rethread her needle. When her husband at last put his medical book on the table and rubbed his eyes, she seized the moment.

She took a deep breath, let it out slowly, and plunged. "Bertram, I've been thinking about taking the girls east this summer, to visit Susan, Rose, Grace, maybe Aunt Zetta. I could show them a little refinement, give them a new outlook. I think it would help them immensely. We could go from Louisiana by rail. Surely it wouldn't be terribly expensive."

Bertram remained quiet so long that she began to think he had not heard. Since he had put aside his reading, and she had folded her sewing, he turned down the lamp to save the wick.

"I don't think you realize yet what has happened, Millie," he said. "The South as we knew it is gone. Perhaps forever. There's nothing left of most of the fine homes you remember. Only fire-blackened chimneys. You've got to understand this. Life there is even harder now than it is here. The South won't recover for another fifty years, if then. Even if it does, it'll be different. There are *no* social seasons now, no grand balls. I imagine you'd find most of your relatives in rags."

Seldom in her life had Millie received such a shock. She could not believe it. "None of their letters has even suggested such a thing!"

Again he nodded. "They're proud people. They put the best face on things. But the fact is that even quality folk went hungry during the war. And they're still suffering. With slavery gone, the economy will have to be restructured. The North is making that very difficult."

Millie had never been an admirer of the institution of slavery.

Dulcie, a tall, thin, coal-black young woman given to her as a child, was the only servant she had brought west. But Millie had long believed that slavery might be the Lord's design to take the heathen race out of darkest Africa and to introduce these people to Christianity.

Millie remained in shock. When she spoke, she heard the desperation in her own voice. "The girls are growing up! I've always intended for them to make their debuts in Charleston. What can we do?"

Bertram stared at his hands for a long moment. "We can face the facts. We can stop looking to the South for the answer to all our needs. We have to cut the cord. Except for the traditions that survive in us, the Old South is dead. Millie, no one is better qualified to train our daughters in the finer things of life than you."

That night Millie went to bed deeply disturbed. She lay awake for more than an hour, reflecting on what Bertram had said. She recalled that Cousin Rose had lightly mentioned in a letter that all of her Vienna Du Paquier chinaware had been stolen by the Yankees, that the huge old Flemish rosewood and ebony armoire Millie had so admired had been destroyed when foraging troops used it for kindling. Many other isolated, half-forgotten anecdotes came to mind. Bertram was right. Her cousins would be too proud to complain of poverty. They would couch their anguish in such trivial lamentations.

Millie's plans for the trip died slowly. But before she had gone to sleep that night, she arrived at a decision.

If she could not take her daughters to the South, she would bring the South to her daughters.

She offered up a prayer.

She told God that if it were His intention for civilization ever to flower in Fort Worth, then He could begin with her.

3

Travis filled the woodbox, stoked the fire, and was standing, poker in hand, when Captain Tackett shoved a twenty-dollar gold piece across his desk. "Take this and go get yourself fixed up. Buy a proper suit, all the trimmings. Van Emden will know exactly what you need."

Speechless, Travis suspected what was happening. But he did not want the disappointment of having jumped to the wrong conclusion.

Captain Tackett smiled at his confusion. "Meet me in Judge Riley's court first thing tomorrow morning. We may have a surprise for you."

Still dazed, Travis crossed the square to the mercantile. He had long dreamed of his admission to the bar. He could not absorb the fact that it was near at hand.

He would be one of the youngest lawyers in the state of Texas.

Major Van Emden was waiting. He looked Travis over with an appraising eye. "You have a flair for clothes," he said. "I recommend something striking, yet conservative and serviceable. How about this?"

Travis was pleased with the major's choice. The coat accented his narrow waist, then flared dramatically to his broad shoulders. The vest was lined with silk and decorated with tasteful stitching. The major's tailor worked through three fittings before everyone was satisfied.

The following morning, attired in his finery, Travis appeared in the newly completed courthouse. The entire legal profession of Fort Worth was in attendance.

Judge Riley gaveled for order. He crooked a long, bony finger at Travis. "Mr. Spurlock, you may approach the bench."

Travis felt as if he were sleepwalking. Around him the routine hum of the courtroom died away to a whisper.

Judge Riley looked down at him from the bench. "Travis Barclay Spurlock, you have read extensively for the practice of law. You have been examined exhaustively by Captain Tackett and Major Van Emden,

two of the most eminent attorneys in the state of Texas. You have been
found qualified. Do you desire admission to this court?"

Travis retained enough presence of mind to drop his voice into his
much-practiced deep bass. "I do, Your Honor."

"Then so be it." Judge Riley turned and spoke to his clerk. "Swear in
Travis Barclay Spurlock as an attorney and officer of this court. Please
show this was done on the court's own motion."

Travis thanked the judge. Then, with every attorney in Fort Worth
gathered around as witnesses, Travis raised his right hand before the
clerk and recited the oath.

One by one, his fellow lawyers stepped forward, shook his hand, and
offered their congratulations.

Judge Riley's gavel ended the brief ceremony. "Don't leave yet,
Counselor Spurlock. You now have a civic duty to perform. The court
hereby appoints you defense counsel for the State versus Mabel Gordon,
the first case to be heard on this morning's docket. You may have a few
minutes with the defendant to prepare your plea."

Travis accepted the papers from the clerk and glanced through
them. The specifications and charges were no surprise. Mabel Gordon
had been operating a sporting house in the acre for more than a year.
Travis knew her as Slewfoot. That was her name in the acre. She was
standing with the bailiff, eyeing Travis warily. She was short, square-built,
and muscular, with sullen eyes, a habitual scowl, and the hint of hair on
her upper lip. Travis had heard that she once chased two drovers through
the acre, brandishing a poker, before cornering them in a livery stable,
where she rapped their shins until they surrendered the four dollars they
owed her.

Travis escorted Slewfoot to the back of the courtroom. He had re-
hearsed the procedure so many times it now seemed natural. He opened
his fine new coat, put his thumbs in the armholes of his vest, stretched to
his full height, and looked out over the crowded courtroom. For the first
time in his life, he felt that he belonged. In that moment, all of his diverse
reading, daydreaming, mock practice, and posturing fell into place like
the alignment of the stars in the heavens. Confidence flooded through
him like heady liquor.

"Mrs. Gordon, do you know what's happening?" he asked.

Slewfoot gave him a withering glance. Her voice was as rough as a
man's. "Of course I do! They're going to fine me fifty dollars. They do it
every other Monday. And that's all the money I brought with me. I didn't
figure on no lawyer."

Travis patted her arm. "Don't worry about it, Mrs. Gordon. I've been
appointed by the court to defend you. And I will. You remain silent.

Leave everything to me. When the judge asks how you plead, tell him 'not guilty.' "

Slewfoot stared up at him. "I can't do that! They'd slam me in jail and throw the key away!"

Travis took her hands. "Mrs. Gordon, you've got to trust me. Simply do as I say, and I promise that you'll never have to pay another fine in Fort Worth."

Slewfoot looked at him doubtfully.

"Trust me," Travis said again. "I promise I'll get you off without a fine."

He walked Slewfoot back to the front of the courtroom. "The defense is ready, Your Honor," he announced.

Judge Riley read the charge. Specifically, Slewfoot was cited for the operation of a disorderly house.

"Mabel Gordon, how do you plead?" Judge Riley asked.

"On the advice of the lawyer you gave me, I plead not guilty," Slewfoot said.

Surprised laughter erupted throughout the courtroom. Judge Riley raised his gavel and left it poised in the air. High color came to his cheeks.

Travis spoke above the tumult. "Your Honor, the defense moves that the defendant be bound over for trial by jury."

Travis remained standing, his feet spread, his hands clasping his lapels. Captain Tackett tugged at his left sleeve, Mabel Gordon at his right.

"Travis, you only have to plead her guilty!" Tackett said. "Judge Riley appointed you as a simple courtesy, so you could earn your first fee!"

"You stringbean, snotnosed son of a bitch!" Slewfoot hissed. "You'll get me jailed!"

Travis ignored them both. He had never felt more confident. He had become a hawk instead of a rabbit.

Judge Riley pointed a long finger at him. "Young man—"

Travis interrupted. "May it please the court! Among the tenets I have learned from my esteemed colleagues is the fact that every accused is granted the right of trial by jury, under the United States Constitution and the statutes of the sovereign state of Texas. Have I been wrongfully instructed? Am I so woefully in error?"

Judge Riley pointed again, this time at Slewfoot. "Travis, this woman . . ."

The judge halted in midsentence, stricken with the knowledge that he was on the verge of uttering a prejudicial remark that would disqualify him in his own court. He took a deep breath, folded his arms on the bench, and glared at Captain Tackett. "Counsel for the defense has been well informed. Perhaps too well." He reached for the gavel. "Court will be in recess for thirty minutes. The defendant is hereby bound over to jury, for trial under the purview of this court."

A bailiff was sent into the courthouse square to round up a jury panel. Travis knew that within minutes word would be spread throughout Fort Worth that Slewfoot was on trial, with young Travis Spurlock as her defense attorney, trying his first case. He also knew that the news would be received with universal hilarity in saloons, gambling dens, dance halls, and legal circles. Slewfoot was the best-known madam in town. Every male above the age of twelve knew the location of Slewfoot's sporting house. Most also knew the names of her girls, their endowments and various skills.

By the time the jury was empaneled and spittoons positioned, no standing room remained.

Opening for the prosecution, County Attorney Hiram Westmore assured the jury that the state would prove the charges beyond the shadow of a doubt.

Adhering to his long-range strategy, Travis waived his opportunity for opening remarks. Laughter and several loud guffaws came from the benches behind him. Apparently his fellow lawyers thought he was losing his nerve. Slewfoot leaned close and whispered softly in his ear. "You bastard! When this is over, I'm going to kill you, so help me God!"

Travis gave her a reassuring smile.

Westmore called his first witness, Deputy Jake Hammond. Under the prosecutor's questioning, Hammond said that when he served the arrest warrant, he happened to observe several of Slewfoot's girls in various stages of undress. With sidelong smirks to the jury, Westmore pushed for specifics. Hammond's descriptions brought further laughter. Westmore guided Hammond into an admission that he also noticed a number of clients about the premises of Mabel Gordon's house. He testified that the house was well known as a place where the services of women could be purchased. With a final, self-satisfied glance at the jury, Westmore returned to his table.

"Pass the witness," he said.

Travis approached Hammond and stood without speaking. He waited in silence until Hammond shifted nervously in the witness chair, a trick Travis had learned from an obscure law book. In a slow, rumbling drawl, he asked his first question. "Sir, you speak of Mrs. Gordon's house with a great deal of familiarity. Was this the first occasion on which you were called upon to serve her with a warrant of arrest?"

Hammond grinned at the jury. "No. We've arrested her every other Monday for the last year."

"Mr. Hammond, you've testified that Mrs. Gordon's house is well known for providing men with feminine companionship. Tell me, do you know any of these alleged prostitutes?"

Laughter again rang throughout the courtroom. Hammond looked uneasily toward the judge.

"Answer the question," Judge Riley said.

"Some of them. Most of them. I guess just about everybody in town does."

"Would you call this an active house of prostitution? Is it open to the public twenty-four hours a day? Seven days a week?"

Hammond was again on familiar ground. "Yes, sir. I would call it very busy. Especially on Saturday night."

As he waited for order to be restored, Travis feigned puzzlement. "I don't understand. You've testified that Mrs. Gordon manages a well-known house of prostitution, and that it's open to the public around the clock, seven days a week. Yet, arrest papers are served only every other Monday. Why not *every* Monday?"

Hammond looked worriedly at the prosecutor. "I don't know."

"Why not Tuesdays?"

Hammond shrugged. "I don't know."

"Wednesdays? Thursdays? Saturday nights? Why not every day?" Travis leaned over Hammond and shouted at him. "You say this is a house of prostitution known to all the town. Known to every officer of the law! Why is it tolerated for thirteen days, but not the fourteenth? Why is Mrs. Gordon arrested every fourteen days, and every fourteen days only?"

"Objection! Objection!" Westmore was yelling. "Defense counsel is badgering the witness. Moreover, he's asking for opinion."

Travis wheeled and strode to the bench. "Your Honor, the prosecution qualified this witness as an officer of the law. Certainly it follows he is qualified to offer expert opinion on the administration of that law."

"Looks like he's got you there, Wes," Judge Riley said. "Objection overruled. Counsel will restate the question."

"Why is Mrs. Gordon arrested every other Monday, and every other Monday only?"

Hammond searched the room for help, and found none. "To set an example, I guess."

Travis nodded, faced the jury, and spread his arms toward Slewfoot. "Gentlemen of the jury, we have arrived at the core of the matter. Mrs. Gordon is here to serve as an example. Thank you, Mr. Hammond. Your testimony has been most enlightening."

Travis returned to his seat. Westmore called four ministers, one after the other. They gave identical testimony. Each stressed that while he had no firsthand information concerning Mrs. Gordon's place of business, he was prepared to describe at length the harmful effects of Mrs. Gordon's profession on Fort Worth's families. Each said several men among his congregation had confessed to patronizing Mrs. Gordon's establishment.

Travis did not cross-examine. He waited out the remainder of the prosecution's case.

Then Travis spoke. "The defense calls only one witness," he said. "Mabel Gordon."

In the general uproar, Slewfoot grabbed his arm. "Fuck you!" she hissed. "I'm not going on that stand. I won't do it! You can't make me!"

Travis leaned close to her ear. "Mrs. Gordon, you can do yourself and the community a great favor. Just trust me. All you have to do is go up there and tell the truth."

He cupped a hand under her elbow and led her to the stand. After routine questions to establish her identification, he dropped his voice to a soft rumble.

"Mrs. Gordon, the prosecution witnesses have stated that you operate a house of prostitution. Is this true?"

Slewfoot stared at him without answering.

"The truth, Mrs. Gordon. You only have to tell the truth."

Her reply was barely audible. "Yes."

"You can go ahead and say it, Mrs. Gordon. 'I operate a house of prostitution.' "

Slewfoot glared at the judge, at the jury, at Travis. "I operate a house of prostitution."

"I believe the specific charge against you is that you keep and maintain a disorderly house. Tell me, is your house disorderly?"

Slewfoot's indignation gave her voice strength. "The floors are mopped every day! I run a clean house!"

"I see. Perhaps the charge refers to your girls. Are they disorderly in their conduct, filthy in their habits, careless in their appearance?"

Slewfoot spoke proudly to the whole courtroom. "I keep only the finest girls. The doctor comes once a week! If a girl is sick, she doesn't work! Anyone will tell you I have the best-looking girls in town. The best-mannered."

"Perhaps, then, the prosecution might have meant that your visitors are disorderly. Do you take any precautions to maintain order among the clients?"

"There's a bouncer in the parlor all night. Two on Saturday nights. Officer Hammond usually works on Saturdays. Off duty, of course."

Travis waited for the laughter to subside. He allowed silence to linger before he asked his next question. "Mrs. Gordon, I'm amazed that the entire community is so familiar with what transpires in your establishment. I wonder, do you recognize anyone in the courtroom who has been a visitor in your house?" He quickly held up a hand, palm outward. "No names. Just answer the question. Yes or no."

Slewfoot hesitated. "Yes."

"More than one person?"

"Objection!" Westmore shouted. "Your Honor . . ."

"Counsel will approach the bench," Judge Riley said. He waited until Travis and Westmore stood before him. He stabbed his bony forefinger at Travis. "Young man, you're on extremely dangerous ground."

Travis nodded gravely. "I'm fully aware of that fact, Your Honor. I do not intend to pursue it further. I've established my point." He turned to Westmore. "Your witness, for the moment. I will redirect."

Westmore led Slewfoot into admissions that two shootings and a fatal knifing had occurred in her establishment during the last few months. He then passed the witness.

Travis approached Slewfoot slowly. He walked to the side of the witness chair and placed his arm protectively along the back. He spoke quietly.

"Mrs. Gordon, in effect we've established that we're all well acquainted here. One big family, as it were. Clearly you are among friends. I wonder, what inspired you to come to Fort Worth? Why did you come *here* to open your establishment?"

Slewfoot looked at him a moment before answering. "I heard that with the cattle drives, the buffalo hides, the town was booming."

"Let me understand. You felt the community had need of your capabilities in rendering the services that you provide?"

Slewfoot nodded. "Yes."

"Where were you before you came here?"

"San Antonio."

"And before that?"

"Baton Rouge."

"I see. You go where you deem a community has need of your capabilities."

"Yes."

"Mrs. Gordon, how long have you been providing communities with this service?"

Again, Slewfoot hesitated. "Twenty-two years."

"Twenty-two years," Travis mused. "I'm a gentleman. I would never ask a woman her age. But surely, Mrs. Gordon, you must have been very young . . ."

"I've been in this business since I was thirteen," Slewfoot snapped.

Travis feigned amazement. "Thirteen!" He glanced at the jury, sharing his discovery. He turned back to Slewfoot and sadly shook his head. "I wonder, what could bring a mere child to such circumstances? Did you run away from home?"

For a moment Travis thought she would not answer. She spoke softly, with the entire courtroom hanging on her every word. "My father died when I was eight. Times were hard. Ma was left with six little ones." Defiantly, she turned to the jury. "I have no apologies. I knew exactly what I was doing."

"And that is the reason you went into this way of life? To support your family?"

Again, Slewfoot faced the jury. "As God is my witness, I sent all I could spare to Ma, until all the little ones had left home and she was dead."

Travis let the statement hang in the charged silence. He then wheeled abruptly to Westmore. "The defense rests."

Westmore closed by stressing that every aspect of the charge had been proved. By her own admissions, the defendant did in fact operate a house of prostitution. Her establishment was a blight on the community, offensive to the sensibilities of every decent person. He demanded that the jury assess the maximum sentence accorded under law—six months in the county jail, a two-hundred-dollar fine.

Travis rose dramatically to his full height. He walked along the front of the jury box, turned, and faced the courtroom. With his hands on the lapels of his coat he posed like an actor on a stage. He waited until all attention was focused upon him.

He began slowly, feeling his way into his theme. He had spent two years preparing for the moment, and he made the most of it. Soon his vowels were rolling over the courtroom like the billows of an ocean. His shouts pierced the air like trumpet blasts. His words became as mighty as an army with banners.

"Gentlemen of the jury, the prosecution has told you at length of the defendant's terrible transgressions against society. Her sins have been enumerated for us with the utmost cold cruelty through the dispassionate wording of the law. But nothing has been said here concerning society's even more terrible transgressions against Mrs. Gordon!"

He walked to the defense table and Slewfoot's chair. Standing behind her, he placed his hands on her shoulders.

"Gentlemen of the jury, you see before you a fallen woman. Think what that means! Today, in this courtroom, Mrs. Gordon has been shorn of all respectability. The evidence so ably presented by the prosecution has pictured well her degradation and revolting condition. No longer can she walk in society with head held high. She must slink in the shadows, the object of scorn and reprobation from the entire community.

"But gentlemen! Is this of her own choosing? What has brought her to this sad circumstance?"

He left Slewfoot's chair and again walked near the jury box. "Gentlemen, once this woman was a babe in arms. She was pure, as is every baby born of woman. Mr. Ledbetter, you are the father of two precious young daughters, hardly out of the cradle. You well know the joy, the love, that childish innocence can engender in the human heart. Mr. Markham, Mr. Stockwell, you have known the tender feelings of a father for his daughter, the prayers and hopes that his child shall never know other than absolute purity, and love in its most wholesome form."

Travis spread an arm in a gesture toward Slewfoot. "Gentlemen, a father once lived who possessed such hopes and dreams for *this* woman. But—oh, most grievous day!—through tragic circumstance he died! Through no fault of her own, this innocent child was shorn of the love and security that only a father can provide! And what happened?"

Travis clenched his fists and shook them over his head. He shouted at the ceiling. "Oh, God! Where were the *men* in that community when that innocent child was forced to surrender her soft, virgin flesh to buy food, clothing, and shelter for her mother, and for her little brothers and sisters? I ask you, God! Where were her protectors? Hear me, God! I demand an answer!"

He stood for a long moment, looking upward, his clenched fists raised. All eyes followed his gaze. The courtroom was deathly quiet, waiting for lightning to strike.

And it did. Travis's right arm shot out toward the jury. "But in our deepest heart of hearts, we *know* the answer, don't we? The men in that community . . ." He stopped and shook his head. "No, I won't honor them by calling them men. They may have been of the male species. But they were not men. Not *one* of them would step forward to protect a thirteen-year-old child, who was sold into whoredom so that her younger brothers and sisters might live!"

Behind him, Slewfoot burst into tears. Travis paused, allowing time for the effects of her weeping to penetrate the consciousness of the jurymen.

He walked back and forth in front of the box, then leaned against the rail, hovering over the six men in the front row. "One of the state's witnesses said Mrs. Gordon was arrested to serve as an example. Gentlemen of the jury, no truer words were ever spoken. Mrs. Gordon sits today in this court as an example of the hypocrisy of this community. The prosecution proved that the nature of Mrs. Gordon's establishment is well known. We have learned that it operates twenty-four hours a day, seven days a week. If it is *so* offensive to this community, why is it not closed down? Why is there not an officer of the law on her premises, with an arrest warrant in hand, on Tuesdays, Wednesdays, Thursdays, Saturdays?"

He leaned closer. "I'll tell you why, gentlemen. Her establishment is allowed to flourish because this entire community profits from what transpires there! The trail driver who vents his lust between her perfumed sheets also buys his ropes, his clothing, his provisions in Fort Worth stores! The buffalo hunter, the freighter, the adventurer all come to Fort Worth because they know that this is a wide-open town. They know that in Fort Worth they can do anything they damned well please! And the entire community welcomes them!"

He walked back to the sobbing Slewfoot and stood gazing sadly down at her. "Are we such hypocrites that we will deny our own responsibility? No! I cannot believe it! We are men. We know that our sex was the cause of her ruin, and far, far more to blame than the woman that sits before you today. Gentlemen, women do not have the same willpower as men. They are not so constituted to resist wrongs done to them as are men. A woman, once wronged, grieves over that wrong a thousandfold more than a man. That is why the human race is so structured that man is not only woman's provider and helpmeet but also her protector!"

Travis faced the jury. "Gentlemen, while Jesus of Nazareth walked upon this earth, He rebuked kings and caesars. He spoke against the priests. He lashed out in wrath against the moneychangers. But never once did He utter one word of reproach against a woman of Mrs. Gordon's profession. No! Not once! Instead He said, 'He that is without sin among you, let him cast the first stone at her.' "

Travis paused so that the jury could ponder the import of all he had said. When he again spoke, his tone was soft, confidential. "We are mere men. We cannot hope to emulate the compassion of the Savior. But I do not believe we are such hypocrites that we can deny this woman justice. Gentlemen, the only verdict possible is one of not guilty."

The jury was out less than ten minutes. When acquittal was announced, the courtroom broke into sustained applause.

Travis gathered his law books and escorted Slewfoot from the room.

4

Travis waved a fistful of money over his head. "Another two hundred dollars says my filly's the best here today! Any takers?"

A hand shot up from the crowd. "I'll see fifty of that!"

"My esteemed colleague, Mr. Cowart, is down for fifty. Anyone else?"

A chorus of shouts erupted. Moving to the edge of the sidewalk, Travis accepted bets until the two hundred was covered. He then crossed the street to the starting barrier, opened his tote book, and assessed his outlay.

He was satisfied. Including the initial five-hundred-dollar purse, he now had a thousand dollars riding on the race.

Paisana stood at the starting post, tossing her jug head in anticipation. She was not an imposing horse, even for a colt. Her oversized, bulging jaw bordered on the grotesque. She was compact, barrel-chested, and almost two hands shorter than the Thoroughbred mare she was pitted against. No one in Fort Worth had seen her race. Even money had been plentiful. But Travis remained confident. Appearances were not everything.

He put an arm around his jockey. "Jimmy, don't let her swing wide at the turn. She can turn on a dime. She should gain a length at the pole."

Jimmy nodded. Small for his thirteen years, the wiry little Negro could stick to a horse like glue. But for insurance the seat of his trousers was smeared with blackstrap molasses.

The voice of the judge sounded over the noise of the crowd. "Horses ready, gentlemen?"

"Ready," Travis shouted.

He swung Jimmy onto Paisana's back and handed him the reins. "Use the quirt sparingly," he said. "Whipping will only distract her."

He led the filly to the post.

The two horses were to race down Main Street and into the open country beyond, circle a distant pole, and return to the starting point. More than two thousand people had gathered for the race.

Travis gave Jimmy one last admonition. "Don't jump the gun. She'll start fine. Just hang on."

He hurried back into the saloon and climbed to the second floor. A spot had been saved for him at the rail of the balcony.

At the starter's pistol the two horses broke even. Paisana gained a head in the first quarter but fell away by a length approaching the pole. As Travis expected, she made up the difference at the turn.

The two horses entered the home stretch neck and neck.

Travis held his breath. The horses raced toward the finish, the thunder of their hooves loud even above the cheering of the crowd. Paisana held her own for a hundred yards. She faded by a head, then battled her way past the bigger horse.

She won by half a length.

Moving through the congratulations and backslaps, Travis made his way down to the street. He was so proud of his filly he could hardly contain himself.

He knew he had seen the start of another racing legend.

"Give her a good rubdown," he told Jimmy. He tossed him a gold piece. "And here's your share of the take."

White teeth shining in a spectacular grin, Jimmy proudly walked the horse through the crowd toward the stables.

Travis returned to the saloon. "Set 'em up!" he called to the bartender. "The next round is on me."

Collecting his bets, and basking in the festive aura, Travis felt that his life was almost complete.

Two years had passed since the day he defended Mabel Gordon and, with his closing argument, became the legal champion of the acre. Now clients awaited him every morning at the jail and in the corner allotted to him in Captain Tackett's office. A team of matched bays and a light but fancy rig awaited his pleasure at the livery stable. He owned boots, suits, and coats for every day of the week, all of the latest fashion.

And today he was another fifteen hundred dollars richer.

In his search for excitement, he was spending more and more time in Hell's Half Acre. The saloons, dance halls, gambling dens, and sporting houses offered a ribald gusto lacking in the rest of the town. Poker amused him sufficiently to hold his interest. He usually won. He habitually strolled from saloon to saloon throughout each evening, sharing in the rampant conviviality. Seldom drunk, he was rarely sober. He slept more in bordellos than in his own bed.

He remained vaguely discontent. He felt that life should offer still more.

In his leisure moments he sensed that in some distant place, always somewhere other than where he was, the West existed, where tedium was unknown and magical things were an everyday occurrence.

He longed to be there.

"Travis," the attorney Cowart yelled from across the saloon. "I now have fifty dollars invested in your filly. For that kind of money I think I deserve to know where you got her."

"Sir, that falls under the statutes covering trade secrets," Travis yelled back.

"Come on, Travis!" someone called. "We want to know."

Travis turned his back to the bar and faced the saloon. The crowd hushed, expectant.

"I suppose it's no use," Travis said. "The little lady proved herself a champion. I confess. I bought her in Sherman. She's a direct descendant of Steel Dust, out of Fanny Wolf."

Cowart groaned. "I should've known! Those jaws!"

"She's small, but the blood tells," Travis said.

"I told you!" a man at the back of the crowd said to those around him. He pushed his way forward. "I saw Steel Dust race Monmouth in fifty-five! I could see the Steel Dust lines in your filly right off."

Travis bought the man a drink and encouraged him to talk. More drinks and stories followed. Travis reveled in the ensuing discussion of bloodlines.

Time slipped away. Travis was unaware that night was near until the barroom lamps were lit. Still he lingered, drinking, relishing the racing lore and camaraderie.

A sudden hush fell over the bar. Travis turned. A woman had entered from the side door. Her hair and eyes were shiny black, her skin as white as a magnolia blossom. Her lips met in a delicious cherry-colored pout.

Travis had heard about a new girl in town. Word was that her name was Jeanette, and that she came from the Bayou La Forche in southern Louisiana.

She was headed toward a table of gamblers when she saw Travis standing at the bar. She stopped. Her gaze moved slowly from his hat to his boots, and back again. She walked close and looked up at him from beneath half-lowered eyelids.

"Mister, you're pretty enough to send home to Momma."

Travis swept off his hat and gave her his best smile. He spoke in his courtroom bass. "Madam, gazing at you, I at last know the very essence of beauty."

"Oh, my!" Jeanette breathed. "I *do* have a weakness for sweet-talking gentlemen!"

Travis introduced himself. "I suggest we share a bottle of champagne to celebrate the inauguration of our acquaintance." He gently but firmly took her arm and guided her to a table.

She was as pliable and comfortable as soft suede. Soon Travis was lost in her beauty, hardly aware of what he was saying, alert to each movement of her pouting mouth, her darting tongue. She seemed enrapt with his every word. Her long, slender hand rested on his forearm. As she leaned near him to talk, her whispery voice seemed to waft its own perfume.

Travis ordered more champagne.

"Why don't we take the bottle to my boudoir?" she whispered. "We could get *much* better acquainted."

Travis walked her the two blocks to her room. Trembling artfully, she allowed him to remove her clothing. She feigned fear of his unbridled erection with playful, childlike innocence. Calling him her Texas stallion, she matched his soaring passion with her own, leading him to ever loftier plateaus.

Travis staggered home at dawn, spent, exhausted, shattered, aware that something new had entered his life.

For the first time, he was in love.

Travis was jarred from deep sleep. Otto made no attempt at quiet as he dumped coal into the stove. He set the scuttle down with a resounding thump and glanced at Travis. "Had a tomcat once, so crazy after it he wouldn't even take time to eat. Got down to skin and bones. Then he died. Fucked himself to death. Seems to me you might profit by his example."

Travis groaned, rolled to the edge of the bed, and put his feet to the floor. From the angle of the sun through the windows he knew he was late again. His clients would be waiting. Captain Tackett already had spoken sharply to him twice during the last week.

"Smells like a sporting house in here," Otto grumbled. "Poor old Hector slept outside last night. I could use a little fresh air myself."

Travis did not answer. His partying in the acre had become a sore point with everyone. But he could not help himself. For the last six weeks he had stumbled through each day eager for sundown, when Jeanette would be waiting. Each night they romped until dawn, her door barred against intruders, the outside world forgotten.

Hector whined outside. Otto let him in. Hector looked around the room, assessed the situation, then curled up behind the stove. He lowered his head onto his paws and closed his eyes.

"That's the prescription, Hector," Otto said, cleaning up after his breakfast. "Stick to the right tempo, and you'll never go wrong. Some people try to live life running as fast as they can. Then they wonder why they lose everything. Just proves that dogs are smarter than some people."

Travis felt weak and shaky. His head ached. "Some people don't know when to mind their own business," he said.

Otto paused to stare at him. "That could be," he said. With an abrupt motion, he snatched up his hat and coat and left for his work shed.

Travis rose and attempted to shave. His hands trembled uncontrollably. Twice he cut himself, leaving nicks that refused to stop bleeding. His stomach remained queasy. His muscles were sore from strenuous, marathon copulations. He struggled into his clothes, drank half a cup of bitter, lukewarm coffee, and set out for the office.

As he entered, Captain Tackett glanced up with a frown. No clients were waiting.

"I took the liberty of filing for continuance on your court appearance this morning," the captain said. "Also, you had two new clients. One was assault with a deadly weapon, the other public intoxication. I succeeded in obtaining a reduction of the assault charge to disturbance of the peace, and pleaded both guilty for minimum fines. You'll find the papers on your desk."

Travis thanked the captain, sank into his chair, and started leafing through the legal papers.

"I advise you to go home and get some sleep," Captain Tackett went on. "You're not in fit condition to be seen by your clients, or mine. I might add that when I pleaded illness for you this morning before the bench, there was general merriment among your colleagues. Your life seems to be an open book these days. When you've rested up sufficiently, we have some talking to do."

Travis felt beleaguered. Everyone was trying to run his life, making more demands upon him than he could fulfill.

"I'm ready now," he said.

"As you wish. Matters cannot go on in this fashion. This is a small town. People talk. I'll be blunt. You are the laughingstock of the community. If you can't straighten up and assume some shred of decency, then you can move out of this office. We'll terminate our relationship, and I'll have nothing more to do with you."

Travis fought back anger. He paused before speaking, a courtroom trick he used to keep tight control on his emotions. But his words came out twisted and mangled. He was appalled. He had not stammered in years.

"If I have problems, they're my own," he managed to say. The remark sounded wrong, but at the moment he did not care.

"Very well, I'll cite you chapter and verse. You have abused friendships, the trust everyone placed in you. Otto took you in when you were penniless and restored you to health. Major Van Emden, Colonel John Peter Smith, Judge Riley, and others have given you invaluable assistance and raised you to the profession you now enjoy. They fully expected you to honor their faith by taking your place in the community, by rearing a fine family, by assuming a position of leadership. Instead, you're throwing your life away, abusing all your God-given talents. I won't be a party to it. I've looked upon you as a son. But the course of dissipation upon which you are embarked is as common as pig tracks."

His anger mounting, Travis refused to retreat. "Just because people have helped me professionally gives them no right to run my private life."

"That's not the issue. The fact is that you have certain obligations you choose to ignore. I'm sure your parents would be devastated by disappointment. You owe a great deal to the brotherhood of Masonry. I had intended to put forth your name in the lodge when you come of age. But as you may know, a single negative vote by secret ballot is sufficient to bar membership. At the moment, your application probably would harvest more black balls than white."

"I won't be judged like this," Travis said. "No one understands."

Captain Tackett shook his head sadly. "That may be the problem, Travis. Everyone understands too well."

Travis saddled Paisana and fled into the rolling, scrub-brush prairies to the west, seeking solitude. He shunned the scattered settlements, the isolated houses. At night he spread his blankets under the stars and lay sleepless, contemplating his plight.

For days the battle raged within him as he roamed the lonely plains. Jeanette haunted his every moment. He doubted that he could give her up. But Captain Tackett's words would not go away.

Travis remained on the plains for six weeks.

When at last he turned back toward Fort Worth, he knew what he must do.

"Apologies will not suffice," Captain Tackett said. "You'll have to demonstrate to the entire community that you've seen the error of your ways."

They were seated in Tackett's office. The sun had set and the lamps were lit. An empty wagon clattered past the open window. From the distance came the lowing of cattle on the bed grounds east of town.

"I know I'm in a pickle," Travis said. "What can I do?"

Tackett rose from his desk and crossed to the window. He stood gazing for several minutes into the deepening twilight without answering. He then turned and looked at Travis. "If you wish to assess your situation honestly, and strive to put your life on the proper course, I'll help you. But you've been a bitter disappointment to me. I warn you. I'll not tolerate further erosion of our relationship."

Travis met his gaze. He knew he had to deal with the situation. "Captain Tackett, I regret beyond words that all of this has occurred. I wouldn't have hurt you for the world. Or Otto."

Again, the captain remained silent for a long moment. "What has happened can't be helped. Perhaps part of the fault is mine. I saw it coming. I should have spoken sooner. I knew you were in the clutches of that woman, and past all reason."

Travis thought of Jeanette, her steaming sexuality. At the moment he found the vision strangely unappealing. "Captain, I'm through with that life. I promise."

"Don't make rash pledges you won't keep. The matter goes beyond the specific to the general." Tackett paused, and frowned in thought. "All may not be lost. The sowing of wild oats is often tolerated. But youthful excesses must be followed by sufficient contrition."

"I'll consider anything you suggest," Travis said.

"First, you must get your thinking straight. Those people over in the acre are the dregs of society. They may have great reputations as gunmen, gamblers, fistfighters, or whatever. But they only hold the admiration of the ignorant. They are the scum of the earth. You're constituted of far better character, by breeding, education, moral judgment, any measure you choose."

"I know that, sir."

Tackett seemed not to have heard. "If you wish to be considered respectable, then you must associate with respectable people. This doesn't mean you can't keep your acquaintances in the acre. In fact, as an attorney catering to that clientele, it would serve your purpose to do so. But you must keep your professional distance! *They* will respect you for it. The *community* will respect you."

Travis nodded.

"Look around you. Study the way the decent people of this community comport themselves. Emulate their ways!"

Travis did not know exactly what he meant. "In what way?"

"Apply for membership in a church. That will require a public profession of faith. Stand up before the congregation and renounce the life

you've been living. Tell them you've seen the light, that you're out of the
sinning business. It won't be easy. But I'm confident you'll be received
with open arms. Every Christian loves a repentant sinner, for his own
faith is bolstered every time a fresh convert is brought into the fold."

Travis considered the suggestion. The thought of public confession
did not fill him with dread. In fact, a few eloquent, flowing phrases
already were springing to mind.

Tackett divined the direction of his thoughts. "But don't overdo it,"
he warned. "This won't be another occasion to practice your love of
strong effect."

Reva Latham sat rigid and motionless at the end of the family pew,
convinced that if Travis Spurlock did not cease speaking within the next
minute she would die.

Yet she did not want him to stop. Not ever. He stood tall and confident, so picture-book handsome he did not seem to belong in the same
world with other men. His deep voice filled the sanctuary as gloriously as
the celestial trumpets of Resurrection morning. As he talked and gestured, a thick curl of dark hair flopped back and forth on his forehead.
Reva found herself longing to brush it back into place. His gaze roamed
over the congregation and, for an interminable instant, rested on Reva.
She broke into a cold sweat.

She cringed, seeing herself as he must see her, a stringbean fourteen-
year-old in hand-me-down clothes, with arms and legs as lean as match-
sticks, hair wildly red and uncontrollable. She felt awkward, ugly, and
hopeless.

She risked a glance at Rebecca, the acknowledged beauty in the
family. At seventeen, Rebecca entertained gentleman callers every Sunday, and could pick and choose her escort to every social function. Rebecca sat with a slight, disinterested smile, as if Travis Spurlock were
speaking only light pleasantries. Her new, emerald-striped dress subtly
enhanced her recently acquired curves.

Reva fought a surge of un-Christian jealousy. When she had pleaded
recently for such a dress, her mother had laughed and said condescend-
ingly, "Reva, your time will come, all too soon."

Reva felt that her time would never come.

Looking at Rebecca, she knew she would never be as beautiful as her
sister.

Rebecca's long auburn hair was coiffed to perfection under her new
green-and-gold bonnet. She seemed totally composed. Only someone
acquainted with her every mood, such as a younger sister, would have

noticed the glint of excitement in her green eyes, the pinkish tinge at the tips of her ears, the high color in her cheeks.

Beyond Rebecca, Millie Latham listened with a slight frown of disapproval. At the other end of the pew, Reva's father stared thoughtfully at his hands, the way he did when other men discussed President Grant, the Yankee Congress, and the Republican administration.

Reva turned her attention back to Travis Spurlock as he made a point, his arms spread in supplication.

"I've long been a sinner working at his job," he said. "My sins are more than I can bear."

He paused. The congregation waited in silence.

"I've ignored God's commandments. On the retreat from Stones River, swept up in the spirit of battle, I bayoneted a defenseless Yankee boy." He lowered his head. "By the laws of man, perhaps my action was justified. It was an act of war. But I cannot absolve my mind of the knowledge that on this peaceful Sabbath morning, because of me, a mother somewhere grieves. I also remember a blue-clad boy on the banks of the Rapidan I killed by slitting his throat."

Gasps came from the congregation. Travis appeared to be so deeply engrossed in his confession that he did not notice.

"There were others. Many others. But those two rest most heavily on my conscience."

He said that although he was a gentleman, he had, on occasion and under extreme provocation, taken God's name in vain.

"I have known strong drink," he said. He lowered his voice to a whisper. "I also have known weakness of the flesh."

The congregation stirred. Reva was not certain exactly what he meant by that phrase, but Rebecca's ears flushed scarlet. Her mother's frown of disapproval deepened. Her father seemed totally lost in his study of his hands. Reva assumed that the phrase referred to the woman known as Jeanette. She had overheard whispered talk that Travis Spurlock was "throwing his life away on that woman." She had seen the woman once, emerging from a store. Reva thought her beautiful. But Millie had called Jeanette "cheap," the strongest word in her vocabulary.

Travis bowed his head and raised his arms. "The thorns I have reaped are of the tree I planted. They have torn me, and I bleed."

He described how, in his anguish, he had sought out Brother Stuart, who had led him to cleanse his soul through appeal to the One whose goodness is beyond all understanding.

"The tortures inflicted upon my immortal soul are at end," he concluded. "I stand before you today a repentant sinner. I humbly beseech admission to the fellowship of this church. And with God's help, I will walk in the paths of righteousness, forever."

A chorus of "amen" came from the congregation.

Brother Stuart stepped forward and led the congregation in a long, emotional prayer for the soul of the new convert in their midst.

Reva did not bow her head. She kept her gaze solidly fixed on Travis Spurlock, who stood tall, dark-browed, imposing, dominant, humble, and yet proud.

Solemnly, in the sacred aura of the sanctuary, Reva made a promise to God: If He would grant her that marvelous specimen of manhood, she would do His bidding, whatever He wanted, throughout the remainder of her life.

Five weeks later Reva stood nervously with her family as Travis Spurlock crossed the churchyard toward them. Each Sunday since his confession he had been invited to Sunday dinner by a different family. Today the duty fell on the Lathams.

Reva's father met him on the walk and shook hands. "Mr. Spurlock. We're so pleased you've accepted our invitation. I believe you've met Mrs. Latham. And our daughters, Rebecca and Reva."

Travis Spurlock swept off his hat with a slight bow. His eyes lingered on Rebecca, who had demurely lowered her head, yet was looking up at him with a frank, challenging gaze. Reva knew that Rebecca was flirting outrageously. She wondered why her father and mother could not see it.

"How nice to see you again, Miss Rebecca," Spurlock said. He turned to Reva. "And Miss Reva."

Reva knew she was flushing scarlet, and she hated herself for it.

"I see you have your own carriage, Mr. Spurlock," her father said. "If you'll follow our surrey, perhaps we'll have time for a cold drink on the gallery before dinner."

They walked toward the waiting carriages. Spring had given way to early summer, and the day was uncomfortably warm. Travis Spurlock came to help them into the surrey, first Millie, then Rebecca, and Reva. His hand on her elbow was light but firm.

Reva covertly watched him as he returned to his carriage. He seemed to move with an effortless grace as he shoved his matched bays back into their traces and snapped the trace chains onto the singletrees. He gathered the reins, stepped into his carriage, and nodded to Reva's father that he was ready.

Reva adjusted her parasol to ward off the sun. The surrey began to move. Rebecca leaned close to her ear. "Why didn't you say something when Mr. Spurlock spoke to you? Did you have to stand there like a perfect ninny?"

"At least I didn't make cow eyes at him," Reva said.

She found satisfaction in seeing that it was now Rebecca who was blushing.

"What do you mean?" Rebecca demanded. "Just because you don't know how to act—"

"That's enough!" their mother hissed. "If you two can't comport yourselves as young ladies, you can remain in your rooms while Mr. Spurlock is entertained. Is that understood?"

"Yes, Momma," Rebecca said.

Reva nodded. She could hear the hooves of Spurlock's bays close behind. She resisted the urge to look back. Instead, she watched the passing houses, offering Travis Spurlock a quarter profile. Three baby squirrels scampered down from a cottonwood tree and ran playing across the street, tumbling, tails flying. Reva laughed and, turning, caught Travis Spurlock's eye. He was smiling.

"Reva! Act your age!" her mother said softly.

Dulcie's son Jebulah, wearing his new swallow-tailed costume, was waiting in the drive to take the horses. Travis Spurlock left his carriage and stood looking at the new house, completed in early spring. The lumber had been brought from the sawmills in East Texas, the furniture from Charleston factories by way of Galveston. Both floors were surrounded by galleries. The roof had seven gables.

"Simply amazing, Doctor Latham," Spurlock said. "It's not only the grandest but also the loveliest house in town."

Reva's father took Spurlock's arm. "Come on up to the gallery. We'll have a cool drink while the ladies prepare for dinner."

Reva followed Rebecca and their mother into the house. She hurried upstairs to her room, where she could hear her father and Spurlock talking on the gallery below.

"Everyone says you're off to a fast start," her father was saying. "You plan on staying with the law?"

Hot with embarrassment, Reva stopped breathing. Already her father was questioning Travis Spurlock as if he were a prospective suitor. Had Rebecca's designs progressed further than she realized?

Spurlock answered easily, effortlessly. "Yes, sir. I trained for the law."

"You're a fine speaker. I thought you might have some ambition toward politics."

"No, sir. You see, I can't abide the way politicians are required to grovel for votes. I believe this electoral denigration of our leaders is one of the fundamental faults of democracy. No, sir. If I had anything at all to do with it, I'd prefer the role of kingmaker, like Mr. Van Emden."

"I see you have strong views on the subject," her father said. "Obviously you've thought about it considerably."

She heard Travis Spurlock's deep rumble of laughter. "Yes, sir. That I have."

Her father was silent for a moment. "I hope some day you may think better of it, Mr. Spurlock. I believe the time has come when we of the South must reassert ourselves politically. It'd be a noble enterprise for some young man like yourself."

"Perhaps I shall, sir. But it doesn't seem to be on the horizon at the moment."

Reva listened until she heard Dulcie come and take the men's empty glasses, signaling that dinner would be announced soon. Hurriedly she changed into her pink-trimmed white dress, even though she knew her mother would disapprove. It at least *suggested* she might have a few curves. In a final gesture of defiance, she slipped on her own heirloom gold locket, even older and more intricate than the one she knew Rebecca would be wearing. She had just found her shoes when she heard the soft tinkle of the dinner bell.

Before going downstairs, she lingered for a moment at the mirror to be certain that she had done all she could do.

Travis Spurlock was waiting with her father in the parlor. With casual diplomacy he offered both Reva and her sister an arm and escorted them into the dining room.

Although the dinner had been planned all week, her mother warned Spurlock in a flurry of chatter that he would have to accept pot luck. Reva knew that the baked chicken, early corn, new potatoes, and fresh spring vegetables all had been carefully prepared with her mother's family recipes. The table was set with candles, lace, the best silver.

While her father said grace, Reva took advantage of Spurlock's closed eyes to study his face.

Compared to other men he was like a colorful oil painting set amidst faded photographs. The thought sent shockwaves up her spine.

War, politics, religion, and commerce were forbidden topics at the Latham family table. That left precious little. Travis Spurlock kept them entertained through dinner with courtroom anecdotes.

Dulcie's succulent chocolate cake was served as dessert. Travis Spurlock lavished praise upon it. Apparently he mistakenly thought he was complimenting his hostess.

Reva's mother turned the praises aside. "Rebecca made the cake," she said. "Rebecca loves to bake delicacies. Sometimes I think she does quite well."

Reva was tempted to expose the barefaced lie. The truth was that Rebecca hated to cook and would never go into the kitchen if she could avoid it. But as Spurlock heaped further praise on the cake, and accepted another serving, Rebecca preened like a proud peacock.

After dinner, they returned to the parlor. Reva knew what was to come, and what was expected of her. The Sunday ritual for gentleman callers was as stylized as the Apostles' Creed. A suitor was required to invite the entire family to take an afternoon drive. Protocol demanded that, one by one, the family should decline, until only the eligible daughter remained to accept. Since the drive would take place under the eyes of the whole town, no chaperone was required. The rite served as a public declaration that the couple was interested in each other.

As Travis Spurlock proposed an outing in his carriage, Reva found herself unwilling to surrender him to Rebecca.

Millie took the initiative. "That is gracious of you, Mr. Spurlock. But Doctor Latham has had a difficult week, and I have a slight headache. Why don't you young people go on, and enjoy yourselves?"

Attention turned to Reva. She was fully aware of the awkwardness of her deliberate hesitation. She was grateful that she had prepared for the moment.

"I'd love to go," she said, and paused, savoring the stricken expression on Rebecca's face. "But I'm deeply involved in Edward Gibbon's *Decline and Fall of the Roman Empire*. Are you familiar with it, Mr. Spurlock?"

Apparently the stories she had heard about him were true. She was rewarded with a glint of interest in his dark eyes. "Of course, Miss Reva. A most remarkable work. But surely"—he hesitated, glanced at Millie, and chose his words with care—"Gibbon seems heavy fare for a young lady of your obvious sensibilities."

Millie and Rebecca sat aghast. Her father was studying his hands. Reva looked up at Travis Spurlock with a practiced, flirtatious gaze that would have done justice to Rebecca. "I disagree, Mr. Spurlock. Ben Jonson wrote that it is ignorance that is the natural enemy of art and, by extension perhaps, of the sensibilities."

Spurlock opened his mouth to reply, then seemed to reconsider. Again he glanced at Millie. "In that context, perhaps we *do* agree, Miss Reva. I'll look forward to learning your thoughts on Gibbon. He's difficult. I haven't met many scholars who have absorbed him in his entirety."

"The pleasure would be mine, Mr. Spurlock," Reva said.

Spurlock seemed to become suddenly aware that he had digressed from the ritual. He turned to Rebecca. "And you, Miss Rebecca? Would you care to go for a drive?"

Rebecca gave him that challenging glance Reva knew so well. "I would be most honored, Mr. Spurlock."

As they left the parlor, Travis paused at the door. "And we *will* continue our discussion of Gibbon, Miss Reva."

Millie waited until Travis Spurlock and Rebecca were scarcely out of earshot.

"Reva! What on earth possessed you? I never! Don't you realize that you put Mr. Spurlock in a most embarrassing position? Obviously you still have much to learn."

Reva did not bother to answer. Indeed, she *did* have much to learn. But she had won the opening skirmish. She hurried up to her room, opened Gibbon, and prepared for battle.

As the summer wore on, Travis found himself hopelessly entangled in an insidious web binding him to Rebecca as a suitor. Mrs. Latham frequently invited him to dinner, insisted that he stay for supper and, later, that he accompany the family to evening worship. Mentioning that she would be hostess for the Tarrant County Literary Society toward the end of July, she pleaded for him to be her guest of honor. "Captain Tackett and Colonel Smith often have spoken of your extensive knowledge of the classics," she said. "They say you're a walking library. I do hope you can come."

Not until after he accepted did he learn that he was expected to play Romeo to Rebecca's Juliet in selected scenes that would require extensive preparation.

"You and Rebecca can practice whenever convenient," Millie said. "You can use our parlor."

His practice sessions with Rebecca were intermingled with dinners and teas, suggestions and innuendos.

The reading before the Literary Society was a resounding success. Travis imbued Romeo with deep-voiced masculinity and calculated emotion. Rebecca's Juliet was tenuous, flirtatious, tearfully tragic. Praise was heaped upon them.

Throughout the evening Travis heard his name linked with Rebecca's, as if they were indeed star destined lovers.

As summer progressed, the whole town grew more and more engrossed in a romance that did not exist. Care was taken that Travis and Rebecca had time alone, and it was in these moments that the total poverty of the charade was fully revealed. Travis *liked* Rebecca. He even felt a certain fondness toward her. But something within him kept him from committing his heart. His intuition told him that if he did what was expected of him, and proposed to Rebecca, his entire life would be at a dead end.

Marriage seemed so ordinary.

He played the game, and did all the Lathams and the community expected of him. But he took great care never to commit himself.

As long as he remained single, all things were still possible.

On a night in August he found sleep impossible. The moon was full. Its soft light streamed through the open door. From Hell's Half Acre came shouts, Rabelaisian laughter. Travis groaned and sat up. Otto lay on his back, snoring. Hector lay full-length, panting in his sleep, his mouth open, his tongue resting on the plank floor.

Travis went out into the night and stood for a time pounding his fevered head against a cottonwood tree. He found no relief.

He knew the battle was lost. Dressing quietly, he walked over to the acre and began his search.

For an hour or more he walked quietly from saloon to saloon, buying an occasional drink, nodding his greetings to old friends.

At last he found Jeanette in the Bon Ton, drinking with two drummers from St. Louis. When she saw him, her expression froze, but only for a fleeting instant.

"Oh, look! Pretty Boy's back!" she shouted. "We heard you died and went to heaven!"

Travis smiled at the good-natured laughter. He had noticed that no one in the acre seemed to know how to take him since he had joined the church. He hoped Jeanette's teasing would remove some of the awkwardness.

"Drinks for the house!" he called out. "And a bottle of champagne for the lady, to celebrate the renewal of our acquaintance."

His night with Jeanette was much like the first one, only more delicious. Toward dawn, exhausted and spent, he sat up and took her hands in his own. The candle beside the bed flickered, sending his shadow dancing on the wall.

"Jeanette, I want to keep seeing you. But I can't come here to your room any more. If word ever got back to Captain Tackett, I'd be ruined. But I have a plan that might work."

Jeanette looked at him doubtfully. He paused, wondering how best to present his scheme. His only fear was of hurting Jeanette's feelings.

"I need an office over here in the acre. You know that place at the back of the Bon Ton on the sidestreet?"

Jeanette frowned. "Used to be sample rooms?"

Travis nodded. "I plan to set up an office there. In the evenings I'll pull the shades, unlatch the back door, and you can slip in. No one will ever know. If anyone sees you, he'll think you're going into the back door of the Bon Ton."

Jeanette's pout tightened. "I don't like sneaking around."

"But don't you see? It's the *only* way we can be together. I *must* keep up appearances. This way, I'll be with you every spare minute."

Jeanette gave him a long, hard stare. "Pretty Boy, I may not be much. But I'm not a toy you can keep in a box to take out to play with when you have nothing else to do."

"It wouldn't be like that at all," Travis insisted. "We would have long nights together. All to ourselves!"

She looked away and did not answer for a long moment. She sighed. "All right, Pretty Boy. Go over there with all your nice people and strut your stuff. Just don't forget where you get your best loving."

The next morning, Travis broached the idea of opening a supplementary office in the acre. Captain Tackett seemed pleased. Although the captain had never complained, Travis long had felt he had been concerned with the endless parade of riffraff from the acre trooping into his law office. The two locations would keep their vastly different levels of clientele separated.

That afternoon Travis went into the acre, leased and furnished the three-room office, and hung out his shingle.

During the next few weeks his practice more than doubled. Clients who had been intimidated by Captain Tackett's imposing quarters seemed to feel more at home in the hole-in-the-wall office back of the Bon Ton. Travis found himself working long hours in the new office.

Each evening he lingered until the street cleared. He then pulled the blinds, turned the lamp low, unlatched the back door, and awaited the soft click of Jeanette's high heels. Night after night they lay on the tired old sofa in the corner of the back room. For a time Travis almost recaptured the magic of his first nights with Jeanette.

But the old horsehair sofa lacked the allure of Jeanette's sheets, the vital smells of her room. Jeanette seemed ill at ease. Her delightful, spontaneous gaiety was gone.

Other obligations intruded. Travis could not abandon without explanation the weekly meetings of the Literary Society. His expertise with the classics had drawn him into the Shakespeare Club, the Arion Society. He was invited to join the church choir, an obligation that could hardly be refused. He spent each Thursday evening at choir practice. He was called upon to help establish a volunteer fire company. After the pumper and equipment arrived, Travis and his men spent each Saturday afternoon at drill. Time after time, circumstances forced him to send word to Jeanette that he would not be able to see her that evening.

Then Jeanette failed to keep trysts. For two nights in succession Travis waited hours for her in the darkened office, wishing one moment she would come, hoping in the next she would not.

On the third night she was late. She remained unmoved by his efforts to lift her out of a foul mood.

Her tears glistened in the candlelight. "If you really like me, why don't I see you more often?"

Faint sounds of revelry in the saloon next door penetrated the wall behind the sofa. Travis took her hands. "Believe me, I *do* want to be with you."

She shook her head. "Pretty Boy, we both know what you want. But let me tell you something. Money can't buy what you've had from me."

Travis lifted her shoulders from the sofa and held her in his arms. "Jeanette, can't you see that this secrecy is as much for your sake as for mine?"

She wept against his shoulder. He petted and comforted her, and for a while thought he had calmed her.

But as she dressed and prepared to leave, she turned to him. "I think we'd better not see each other anymore. This isn't making you happy. And it's killing me."

Travis thought she was complaining about the spartan sofa, the sounds next door. "I can't be seen going in and out of your room. But give me a day or two. I'll think of something else."

Jeanette gave him a long, withering look in the candlelight. "Pretty Boy, you can see me again on the day you walk me uptown, and twice around the square. That's my new price. It's gone up. Are you prepared to pay it?"

Travis did not know what to say. The silence grew.

Stifling a sob, Jeanette turned and fled into the night.

He did not follow.

Travis plunged back into his work, strangely relieved. He needed time alone to think.

He found himself resenting the constant demands Rebecca made upon him. Gradually he went out with her less and less, pleading the press of his work.

Christmas came and went. On a morning in late January, after a light snowfall, Travis arrived at the office and found Captain Tackett waiting at the door. Sheriff Martin Jessup and Dr. Granville Theikeld were seated in the inner office. Their demeanors were impressively solemn.

Captain Tackett gestured Travis into a chair. "I have bad news, son. One of the young women in the acre has committed suicide. She left this note, addressed to you."

Travis recognized Jeanette's elaborate scrawl, her graceful signature.

The note was brief.

Pretty Boy, I hope this causes no trouble for you. I only want you to know that you were the best thing that ever happened in my whole shitty life. I do love you.

Travis read the note over and over as his numbed brain battled to absorb it.

Dr. Theikeld cleared his throat before speaking. "The young woman cut her left carotid artery with a razor. She was found on the floor of her room, lying in her life's blood."

"I'm told she was a heavy user of laudanum," the sheriff added. "There seems to be something about the drug that makes them do away with themselves."

"Fourth one we've lost in six weeks," Dr. Theikeld said.

Travis sat remembering Jeanette's vitality, her laughing, teasing ways, her cries of joy as she clung to him in their lovemaking. He could not imagine her cold and dead, like the corpses along the fence rows during the war.

At last he found his voice. "What will happen now?"

Captain Tackett put a hand to his shoulder. "The sheriff and Dr. Theikeld have agreed that the note will remain confidential. It is nobody else's business."

"I didn't mean that. What about the funeral?"

The sheriff glanced at Captain Tackett before answering. "There were no letters or personal possessions to indicate she had a family."

"The county has provisions for pauper burials," the sheriff said. "A portion of the cemetery has been set aside."

Travis remembered the last night he had seen her. At the moment, he would give his life if he had followed her out that door. "I'll pay for the funeral," he said.

Captain Tackett's hand moved on his shoulder. "I'm sure that will be regarded as a commendable, Christian gesture. If you'd prefer, I'll make the arrangements."

"I'll do it," Travis said. "I owe her that."

Travis drifted through the remainder of the day in a fog of remorse. That night, the headless major returned. Travis awoke to stark terror, dark thoughts of rotting flesh, worms, and mortality.

At first light he sought out Brother Stuart. "My request may be improper," Travis said. "If you decline, I'll understand. But I'd be grateful if you'd conduct services for a young woman from the acre."

"We're all God's children," Stuart said. "How could I refuse?"

Sleepless, emotionally drained, Travis was moved to unburden his soul. "I wish there was some way I could make people understand how I came to be involved with her. She was a good person, Brother Stuart.

Generous. Honest. Caring. I don't know how she came to be what she was."

"Brother Spurlock, forgiveness is a fundamental tenet of Christendom. We can rest assured that her good qualities will be judged in paradise."

"She once mentioned a family in Louisiana. I wonder if I should search for them."

Stuart frowned. "I don't believe I would, under the circumstances. The news of her death probably would just add bitter gall to old wounds. The Bible tells us how the prodigal son was received after his profligate wanderings. But in our time, and in our society, there *is* no return for the prodigal daughter."

The next day, Jeanette was buried. The brief funeral procession circled the courthouse square twice before proceeding to Pioneer's Rest Cemetery.

Travis walked beside the coffin.

5

I've no money," said Elvira Nicholson.

Travis was disappointed. Elvira's tired gray eyes and tightly controlled face held unfathomed drama. He considered the situation carefully. He did not intend to allow the first murder case that had come his way to slip beyond his grasp over the simple lack of a fee.

"What about the farm? Is it clear of encumbrances?"

Elvira answered without expression. Her voice was level, her words precise, as if she were reciting in school. "I don't know. Sam always took care of those matters. He never confided in me."

Elvira's husband lay in Ed Livermore's mortuary, his skull cloven to the teeth. Travis had doubted from the first that the family had any cash on hand. He had seen the Nicholson farm, twenty miles out on the Grapevine Prairie. He remembered the clapboard, two-room house and its miserable furnishings. He had seen nothing there not dirt cheap. Elvira sat before him in a faded flour sack dress, still stained across the lap with Sam's brains. Her four children, now waiting at the hotel, were dressed in rags.

He carefully considered his tactics. "Before taking your case, I'll need something tangible to show. The bar association has requirements that must be met." He paused, to give her a moment of worry. Then he offered a solution. "I'll make out a promissory note for you to sign. Five hundred dollars, mentioning the farm as collateral. That'll satisfy everyone, and relieve you of immediate monetary concerns."

"That's all right with me," Elvira said without feeling. "Sam may have some money in the bank. His sister once told me there was an inheritance. I don't know anything about it. He never mentioned it."

Travis drafted the promissory note. After Elvira signed it, he carelessly tossed it into a basket on his desk, as if it were a troublesome, insignificant detail. He felt better. The note would serve as a hole card, no matter what happened. At least he was learning to protect himself.

"Mrs. Nicholson, I must ask you certain questions that won't be pleasant for either of us."

Elvira waited in silence.

"I understand you made a statement to the sheriff, confessing that you killed Sam."

"There was no need to lie about it."

Travis waited a moment. "Mrs. Nicholson, I want you to think back. What was in your mind at the moment you did it?"

Elvira frowned. "Nothing." She paused, thinking. "It was like I was floating. I just knew I'd die before I'd let him beat me again."

Travis felt a surge of hope. "He beat you? What with?"

"His fists, mostly. Sometimes with a horsewhip. Once with a trace chain."

"How many times did he do this?"

Elvira shrugged. "I lost count."

"Who knows about the beatings? Any of your family?"

Elvira shook her head. "I never told nobody."

"The children?"

"He beat them, too. We were deathly afraid of him."

Travis thought ahead to the trial. The eldest child was barely five years old, not exactly a prime candidate for a convincing witness.

"The bruises, Mrs. Nicholson. Did they show? Did anyone see them?"

She shook her head. "When company came, I kept to my room."

Travis hid his disappointment. He changed his tack. "Did he ever say *why* he beat you?"

"He said I was in cahoots with the devil. He thought I was letting men to the house while he was away. He said our children wasn't his'n."

The jury would find it difficult to believe that anyone would suspect Elvira could lure any male into her clutches. Thin to the point of emaciation, she had no flesh for anyone to desire. From her rough, mannish hands to her unwashed, tangled hair, Elvira Nicholson seemed woefully devoid of womanly charms.

"Did he give any reasons for this suspicion?"

Elvira considered the question at length. "Only once. The cows got into the alfalfa. I was afraid they'd bloat. A neighbor saw what'd happened and helped me drive them out of the field. Sam claimed I took down the fence on purpose, so the cows could get out and Mr. McMann would come over."

"Did Mr. McMann know about Sam's thoughts?"

"I don't think so."

"There were no other, similar occasions?"

"Sam was always saying he'd found ashes from a pipe, or smelled tobacco in the house." She shrugged. "He was crazy. I was scared to death of him. And there was no way I could get away from him."

"Mrs. Nicholson, I want you to consider this question carefully before you answer. When did you first decide to kill your husband?"

Elvira frowned. "Years ago, I guess. What I mean is, I knew it would come down to it some day."

"But when did you know, for a fact, that you were going to do it?"

Elvira thought for a moment. "I guess it was when I saw him turn off from the county road and start down toward the house. He was whipping the horses. I knew then he was in that crazy mood."

Travis spoke slowly, bearing down on each phrase. "Mrs. Nicholson, I don't want to hear you say those words again. Not in that exact way. Understand, I'm not asking you to lie. I wouldn't do that. But we must clothe the truth in suitable attire before we present it in court. All of us entertain dark thoughts at times, fantasies of violence we never would perform. You must not allow those fantasies to intrude upon the truth. And the truth is that you first feared you would have to kill your husband as he turned into the lane, when you saw that he was crazy mad, and you feared for your life and the lives of your children. Now, Mrs. Nicholson, isn't that the truth?"

"I guess so," Elvira said.

"From now on, I want every answer from you to be emphatic, either positive or negative. We must present a strong defense, with no doubts. Do you understand?"

Elvira nodded.

"I'll ask you again. Isn't that when you feared you would have to kill your husband?"

"I guess so," Elvira said again.

Travis sighed. Plainly, he had his work cut out for him. "That's all for now. Try to get some rest. We'll go over it again later."

He spent the next hour drawing up papers for Elvira's signature. When they were completed, he checked them for accuracy, then sat at his desk, his heart pounding with the very thought of the trial to come.

He had to win. If he was defeated, he might never again be trusted with a major case. He might spend the rest of his days as a small-town lawyer, serving small-town clients.

But victory in a sensational murder case could elevate him to an entirely new field of practice. The best criminal lawyers roamed not only Texas but even surrounding states. Their mere presence lent importance to distant courts. Newspapermen followed them like sheep. Top-notch defense lawyers were a rare, colorful breed, highly competitive, yet enveloped in a close camaraderie. Travis longed to be counted among them.

That afternoon he failed in his effort to arrange bail. But Elvira's youngest boy was a nursing infant. Judge Riley consented to Elvira's incarceration in a room at the hotel, with a matron in attendance.

Travis then walked across the square to the bank. As he entered, Pinckney Coffman rose from his desk. "Been expecting you, Travis. The sheriff and Hiram Westmore were here a few minutes ago. They done sealed Sam's account."

Travis was not surprised. County Attorney Hiram Westmore would be searching for every clue.

"As the widow's attorney, I believe I'm entitled to the particulars," he said.

Coffman handed him a sheaf of papers. "I've prepared a full accounting. Sam Nicholson had thirty-two thousand, three hundred fifty-six dollars and eighty-two cents in savings. In addition, he had another ten thousand dollars in gold coin in the bank safe."

Travis examined the figures, fighting to keep Coffman from seeing his surprise. He remembered Sam Nicholson's ramshackle, unpainted house, his wife and children dressed in rags.

Coffman smiled. "I may be telling tales out of school, but maybe you ought to know. Hiram was happy as a coon. He says he now has the motivation for the murder."

That evening Travis worked late, poring over precedents, mapping out his strategy. He felt as if he held a risky hand in an exciting poker game, and his opponent had just doubled the stakes.

When he was satisfied with his research, he reached for pen and paper and wrote a half dozen letters. He posted them at the stage office on his way home so they would go out on the morning mail.

That night he slept unusually content.

With the letters he not only had called Prosecutor Hiram Westmore's bluff but had also raised the stakes.

Reva halted at the top of the stairs, waited until her imagination filled the parlor below with people, gathered her skirts, and began her ritual descent, head high, trailing her free hand as she had been taught to do. The effect of her grand entrance was somewhat dampened by Rebecca's incessant sobs wafting down the stairway like an oppressive fog. Reva paused on the fourth step, nodded demurely to various acquaintances, then descended into the empty room. She curtsied to the guest of honor and turned to bestow a dazzling smile on Travis Spurlock.

"Reva, quit dawdling," her mother called from the dining room. "You know your father doesn't like to delay supper."

After a final check in the hall mirror, to make certain her mother would find nothing to criticize, Reva walked on into the dining room. Her mother was already seated. Her father waited impatiently by his chair.

"Where's Rebecca?" Millie asked.

"She won't be down," Reva announced. "She's still doing the Camille death scene."

"Reva! Never use honest emotion as a target for base humor. Your sister has just cause for her melancholy."

"I believe Rebecca's misinterpreting the situation," her father said. "Travis Spurlock is preparing for an important trial. He doesn't have much spare time."

"It would only take a minute to send a note," Millie snapped.

Dulcie entered the room. Conversation ceased. Family matters were not discussed in front of the servants, although Rebecca's frequent crying spells could hardly be a secret within the household.

As Dulcie served the soup, Reva studied her parents, puzzled. At first Millie had promoted Rebecca's romance with Travis Spurlock. Her father had resisted. Now Millie was criticizing him, and her father was pleading his cause.

Travis had led Rebecca on a long and not-so-merry chase. He had remained courteous and correct, but tantalizingly distant. Nothing Rebecca tried seemed to help. He had called on her less and less. When the scandal of Jeanette's funeral arose, after Travis paraded around the square beside her coffin, Rebecca had defended him, pointing out that he had many clients in the acre. But his interest in her apparently had continued to dwindle. Rebecca had not heard from him in two weeks.

Reva had guessed from the first that Rebecca's ambitions with Travis Spurlock were hopeless. How could a simpleton like Rebecca hope to hold the interest of such a man? Granted, most men did not expect women to converse on important subjects. But Reva sensed that Travis was different. She had seen the quick interest in his eyes when she had broached such topics. She suspected that he thrived on challenge. She intended to beard him at every turn, even though she was well aware of the dangers. Never should she allow him to consider her a rival in intellect. But she now had played Plato to his Socrates enough to know that he loved to instruct. She hoped to become his willing, lifelong pupil. She was reading every book she could find, laying the foundation.

Her other obstacles were far more serious.

Although the blessed curse had come upon her more than a year before, the long-promised changes had not arrived. Her breasts had turned tender but still remained the size of small plums. They showed no signs of growing larger. Her hips remained thin and boyish.

Nightly she prayed that the womanly changes would come, and

soon. And if the Lord helped those who helped themselves, she intended to do her part. Each night she applied a beauty cream of thirty-seven ingredients, concocted from a secret recipe handed down through her mother's family for five generations. The mixture, of such diverse material as oatmeal and wild sage, seemed to be working. The light sprinkle of freckles across the bridge of her nose definitely had faded. Under a light powder they were now almost invisible. She avoided the sun, never venturing out without parasol or bonnet.

In the privacy of her room she acted out every conceivable situation that might occur between herself and Travis Spurlock, practicing every inflection, every gesture. Facing herself in the mirror, she pretended to be only mildly amused by his courtly attentions, merely tolerant of his wit. Deftly she invented Byzantine plots to prevent their being alone a single minute. In her imagined social situations she succumbed to the charms of others while barely acknowledging that Travis Spurlock existed. She parried his every effort with incredibly complex obstacles.

"Reva, you're picking at your food," Millie said. "Can't you see your father is awaiting dessert? And how many times do I have to tell you? The blade of your butter knife should be turned *away* from you. Manners are not just for Sunday use. A true lady does these things naturally, without thought."

"Yes, Mother." Reva rearranged the butter knife. "Why don't we have a party and invite Mr. Spurlock? He might welcome the opportunity to see us again."

Millie glanced at her husband before answering. "I hardly think that would be apropos. I know you're fond of him too. But he does seem to be treating Rebecca with a calculated coolness. If that is his intention, we certainly wouldn't want to put him in an awkward situation. Or to place Rebecca in position for a refusal."

Reva's father started to speak, but at that moment Dulcie entered with the apple tarts. He waited until she returned to the pantry.

"Travis Spurlock strikes me as a young man in a hurry," he said. "He's not easily drawn out. But I suspect his ambitions reach far beyond Fort Worth. We may not be seeing him around here much longer."

Reva's heart skipped a beat. The first bite of apple tart turned to pasteboard in her mouth. The thought had never occurred to her that he might move on. But instinctively she knew it was a real possibility.

She endured the remainder of supper in a daze. As soon as possible, she asked to be excused, and returned to her room, her mind awhirl.

Somehow, in some way, she had to attract Travis Spurlock's attention before he turned his back on Fort Worth forever.

Early one morning a young man in eastern clothes entered the office and introduced himself. "Jonathan Eakin, from *Harper's New Monthly Magazine.* I have here a letter you sent to my editor."

Engrossed in pretrial preparations, Travis had almost forgotten the letters he had written weeks before. He rose to shake hands. "That I did. But I hardly expected he would respond with his most illustrious writer in person."

Eakin was a small man, with eyes as hard as flint. He was unsmiling, and he spoke with a clipped, harsh northern accent, in a tone that constantly bordered on sarcasm. He ignored the flattery. "If all you say is true, you may have a story here worth looking into."

"Rest assured, it's all true," Travis said. "In fact, I didn't tell the half of it. I'm aware of the reputation for exaggeration we Texans seem to have acquired in the East."

"Mr. Spurlock, I just arrived in Texas by way of El Paso. I traveled six hundred miles across West Texas in a stagecoach. At the moment I seriously doubt anything about Texas *could* be exaggerated."

That afternoon Travis introduced Eakin to Elvira Nicholson and her children. Eakin asked sharp, probing questions. Elvira described the crime, and her life with Sam. Eakin made extensive notes.

At last he folded his papers. "Mrs. Nicholson, I'm sending over an artist. I hope you don't mind if he makes a few sketches."

The next day's stage brought a writer and artist representing *Scribner's Monthly.* By the end of the week, *Lippincott's, The Nation,* and *Outlook* were also on the scene. Every aspect of Elvira's life, real or imagined, was examined to exhaustion.

Elvira complained. "I'm tired of talking about it, Mr. Spurlock. I don't care if they hang me. Just keep those newspapermen away from me."

Travis explained once again that the interviews were a part of his strategy. "We must cooperate with them. I took your case to win. I'm certainly not giving up now."

The first editions of the magazines containing Elvira's story arrived in Fort Worth a month before the trial. Travis turned through them in amazement. He hardly recognized himself, or Elvira. Page after page was devoted to Elvira and her plight.

"Ax murders are the height of fashion these days," Eakin said. "Ordinarily a self-created widow with four children would have received considerable space. The gold hoard takes it to the front ranks."

Travis marveled at the transformation of his client. What nature had omitted, the artists provided. In the exquisite woodcuts, Elvira's gauntness took on the fragile beauty of a Madonna of the Plains. She was rendered as ephemeral as a water sprite. Her blank, tired eyes assumed a haunted luster and a dark, melancholy cast. Her three older children stood hollow-eyed, stunned into insensibility by their sudden, semiorphaned state. Even the eyes of the suckling babe were wide in apparent contemplation of the horror of his situation.

With the opening skirmishes of the trial, the attention of the artists and writers shifted to Travis.

He did not shy away.

"We've about milked Elvira dry," Eakin said. "What about you? These hayseeds around here probably don't know the difference, but you stole Cicero blind in that opening statement. You're quite a talker. Where'd you get your education? What's your background?"

Under questioning, Travis admitted that yes, he had fought for the glorious Lost Cause. He enumerated the battles. He described his training for the law, his interest in classic literature and languages.

Eakin frowned for a long moment in thought. "An Abe Lincoln, backing up his words with a pistol. Reading law by candlelight and all that shit. It might work. We'll try it and see."

Travis was appalled by Eakin's cynicism. But he patiently answered Eakin's questions, and those of the other correspondents who came to call.

The next issues of the magazines that reached Fort Worth focused on Travis. The woodcuts depicted him dominating every courtroom scene. The artists seemed to compete in imbuing him with dynamism, his features conveying emotions worthy of Hamlet, as he meditated over the evidence. He was portrayed in the midst of an eloquent plea before the judge, his arms spread protectively over Elvira and her fatherless brood.

Eakin turned through the magazines and scowled. Travis now knew it was his way of hiding warmer feelings, such as pleasure. "Better dig deeper into your Cicero, counselor," Eakin said. "Before you gained national attention, you could've lost this case in this hick town and nobody would have been the wiser. Now you're in the spotlight. You've got to win. If you don't, you'll be a joke in every courtroom for the rest of your life. Personally, I don't think you've got a prayer."

As the trial progressed, Travis himself fell prey to depression. He was gambling on a single ploy. The stakes mounted each day, along with his doubts. The latest editions of the illustrated news magazines described with impressive detail the monumental tower of evidence amassed by the prosecution. The county attorney kept hammering away with his contention that Elvira plotted the murder of her husband in cold blood to steal his wealth. Ministers, farmers, and merchants trooped to the stand to testify that Sam Nicholson was a gentle, God-fearing man, the antithesis of a wifebeater.

Travis had no rebuttal witnesses.

As the state rested its case, the prospects for Elvira looked bleak.

Travis lowered his voice to his courtroom tone. "The defense will call only one witness. Elvira Nicholson."

The courtroom buzzed with surprise. The visiting lawyers shook their heads in dismay. He had not challenged the testimony of a single state witness. What evidence could Elvira offer, other than her pitiful story? Didn't he know that he would merely expose her to Westmore's brutal cross-examination?

The courtroom fell silent. Travis escorted Elvira and her baby to the stand. He made them comfortable, even returning to the defense table for the baby's sugar-water pacifier.

As Elvira held the baby, Travis led her gently through the routine opening questions.

Then he plunged directly to the heart of the matter. "Mrs. Nicholson, did you kill your husband?"

Elvira looked at the baby for a moment, then glanced up to meet the analytical stares of the jurors. He had coached her with care, and she performed admirably. "Yes," she said. "I killed him."

Consternation swept the courtroom. Judge Riley raised his gavel. But before he rapped for order the tumult ended. The courtroom waited breathlessly for the next question.

Travis glanced at the jury. He was attuned to the rhythm of the courtroom. He sensed total communication with the jurors. It was a feeling like nothing else in the world.

He turned back to his client. "Mrs. Nicholson, *why* did you kill your husband?"

Again, Elvira paused. She wiped a bit of drool from the baby's mouth before looking up at the jury. "He beat me. Whipped me. I was afraid for myself. For my children."

Travis patiently led her into a description of each beating, the circumstances, Sam's irrational jealousies. She told of the horrible pain, the wounds that required weeks to heal while she hid from the world in humiliation.

Elvira's testimony was flawless. She displayed a talent for pace and timing. Her responses were filled with small gestures that spoke volumes.

Under his soft questioning, she told of the terrible day she saw Sam turn from the road and drive his wagon down the lane, lashing his horses in the insane rage she knew all too well. Hesitantly, cuddling her baby, she told of her mind-numbing fear. She described her thoughts as she sent the older children into the pasture to gather the milk cows so they would not witness what she had to do.

Travis stood to one side, eyes half closed, so he would not distract the jurors from her testimony. "Mrs. Nicholson, I know this will be painful for you. But will you please tell the court exactly what then transpired?"

"Well, he jumped down off the wagon and came at me," Elvira said. She paused to adjust the baby's clothing. "I turned and ran to the cotton-wood stump, where we chop kindling. When he swung that whip back to lash me with it, I picked up the ax and ran at him."

She hesitated, and smoothed the baby's hair.

"I brought the ax down with all my strength." She rocked the baby in the cradle of her arms, and said no more.

"What did you do then?" Travis prodded.

"Well, I went into the house, got an old blanket, and covered Sam. I didn't want the children to see him thataway. Toward sundown, I went to a neighbor for help."

Travis nodded solemnly, as if the story he had just heard were the most natural in the world.

"Mrs. Nicholson, did Sam ever tell you that he had a considerable amount of money in the bank?"

Elvira shook her head. "Never. A sister of his once said something about an inheritance. But I never paid any attention. I thought it was a few dollars, at most. I never dreamed he had so much money."

"I see. Mrs. Nicholson, when was the last time Sam bought you a dress?"

She looked up at him, thought a moment, and shook her head. "Sam never bought me any dress. Not in the eight years we was married."

"He ever give you the *money* to buy a dress?"

"No. I always made my dresses out of flour sacks."

"What about the children? Did Sam buy them clothing?"

Again, she shook her head. "Sam said it'd be a waste, since they'd just outgrow whatever we bought. I made most of what they wore. Out of odds and ends."

"Mrs. Nicholson, you've described Sam's rages. You've told us of his jealousies. The irrational suspicions he entertained without the slightest foundation. Do you believe your husband was insane?"

Elvira considered the question for a moment while she bounced the baby. "No," she said. "He was just mean. Mean as a snake."

Travis turned away abruptly. "Your witness," he said to Westmore.

The prosecutor moved swiftly into his attack. He attempted to shake Elvira's story. She answered his questions calmly, distractedly, devoting most of her attention to the baby.

At one point, as Westmore ranted and raged, the baby became entranced with the bouncing, angry man who waved his arms so furiously. The baby cooed and reached out with his tiny fists. Westmore shouted a long, scathing question, replete with heated gestures. The baby gurgled his delight. Elvira smiled and tried to shush him, but the child continued to distract the attention of the jury while the questions of the prosecutor and Elvira's answers went unheeded.

Aware that he appeared to be contending with an infant, Westmore cut his losses by closing his cross-examination. As he returned to his seat, he nodded to the jury with satisfaction.

Clearly, he remained certain of victory.

Travis began his closing argument slowly. Patiently, he led the stern-faced jurors back over Elvira's testimony, step by step. For the first time, he challenged the prosecution's portrayal of Sam Nicholson as a model husband.

"Gentlemen of the jury, there is no way under God's heaven to dignify a skunk. No matter what flowery phrases you employ in his defense, a polecat remains a polecat. You can praise him to the stars, in the most illustrious terms of which the human tongue is capable, yet you still are left with a small, sly, skulking varmint, offensive to the nostrils and to every other sensibility. He'll clean out your henhouse in a single night, spilling blood for the sheer joy of meanness."

Travis walked close to the jury box and spoke softly.

"On the Sabbath day of October the fifteenth, eighteen hundred and seventy-one, while church bells throughout the land were pealing the faithful to evening worship, Sam Nicholson went to his home to flay the naked skin of his wife with a horsewhip. No matter how repugnant we find his purpose, we must face those facts. In fear for the lives of her children, Mrs. Nicholson sent them into the field to fetch the milk cows. In the defense of her children, she stood alone, armed only with an ax."

Travis spread his arms. "Gentlemen, I hesitate to relate the particulars my sworn duty now requires me to lay before you. My gorge rises at the thought! But gentlemen, there is no way to dignify a polecat. Our mutual duty *demands* that we consider Sam Nicholson. What kind of man was he?"

He lowered his voice. "While Sam Nicholson imparted false, pious phrases to his neighbors, to preachers, to merchants—and you have heard here how well he had them fooled—he showed a different countenance to his wife and children. What was he to them? Gentlemen, I'll tell you! He was a wifebeater! A childbeater! He was a miser! While he hoarded his gold in a bank, his children went into the winter winds in rags pieced together by his devoted wife. While he gloated in his greed, his family went to bed hungry. They were kept alive only by the bare scraps of sustenance made palatable by his devoted wife."

Travis walked to Elvira and placed a hand on her shoulder. "And how did Sam Nicholson repay that devotion? Gentlemen, I'll tell you. He flayed her naked flesh with a horsewhip! His diseased, depraved mind accused her of infidelities and sins too grievous to mention." Travis turned his head in profile to the jury box, and fixed the jurors with one steely eye. "Gentlemen, let's not dignify the polecat here today. Sam Nicholson was not a man. He was a skunk! Mrs. Nicholson has told us she killed him. The only question before us is, *Was she justified in killing him?* And gentlemen, my answer is *yes!*"

Again, Travis walked near the jury box, turning first one eagle eye, then the other. His voice thundered. "If I had been present at the Nicholson farm on that day, in full possession of the facts as we now know them, and witnessed the events as they transpired, I would have stepped in front of Elvira Nicholson and killed Sam for her. Gladly! I would have relieved her of that onerous, repulsive chore in the twinkling of an eye. I would have blown Sam Nicholson's brains to the four winds. I would have placed my ear to his breast and listened with consummate satisfaction as his yelping, sniveling soul clawed its way through the gates of hell! Any of us would have done the same! Sam Nicholson was not a man! He was a skunk! An animal that deserved killing!"

Travis returned to the defense table and placed a hand on Elvira's shoulder. "The prosecution has attempted to cast doubt on the facts as Mrs. Nicholson has related them. They say she lied. But gentlemen, we know better! We have seen the horrendous circumstance of this family, dressed in rags, eating scraps from the table, while in his gluttonous, swinish greed Sam Nicholson acquired more and more gold for his hoard."

Gently, Travis lifted the baby from its mother's lap. He walked with the child to the jury box, slowly unwrapping the folds of the blanket.

"Gentlemen, I ask you. Could you, or anyone, tell an untruth with this precious bundle on your knee? Could you lie to the Savior while clutching an angel to your heart?"

He held the baby aloft so all the jurors could see its beatific face. The baby cooed on cue and gave the jury a wide smile. Travis continued to hold the baby high. It kicked, waved its arms, and bubbled with joy.

"Man never stands as close to God as in the presence of such innocence," Travis said softly. "We know that when Elvira Nicholson testified that she killed Sam out of fear, she told the truth as God loves it. Straight and untarnished. We now know the facts. We know that Elvira killed Sam Nicholson to protect her angels."

Lowering the baby, Travis kissed it and handed it back to Elvira. Slowly, almost reluctantly, he again turned to the jurors.

"Gentlemen, Elvira Nicholson is on trial here today because she kept watch over God's littlest angels. Can we do less? Can we leave here with conscience absolved, unless we grant this woman full justice? No, gentlemen. Sam Nicholson *needed* killing. This community stands in her debt. We can repay a portion of that debt by declaring her not guilty."

The jury was out less than twenty minutes.

Elvira was found innocent on all counts.

"Travis Spurlock could make roses bloom on a blackjack stump," said Captain Tackett. "I've never heard the like."

The hour was late. The celebration in the Bon Ton had been long and glorious. Captain Tackett had entertained the visiting lawyers and news correspondents with stories of Travis's past courtroom oratory.

"Lord, but that trick with the baby was risky," said Higginbotham from San Antonio. "If it'd been me, that baby would've bawled all the time Elvira was testifying. He'd have howled bloody murder when I delivered my summation. And when I held him up before the jurors, he'd have pissed like a fountain."

"There was never any danger of that," Travis said.

"Come on, Travis. How'd you do it?" asked Morehead from Austin.

Travis shook his head. "Professional secret."

With a roar, the visiting attorneys begged for the explanation. Travis grinned. "Gentlemen, one never knows when the opportunity may knock again. In some future years, trying a crime not yet committed, I may again employ the technique to good advantage."

Travis endured another chorus of groans and good-natured catcalls.

Full of himself, he laughed. "All right, gentlemen, I'll tell you the secret. Throughout the trial, that baby wore britches sewn from a double fold of wagon sheet, stuffed with absorbent cotton. During the proceedings today, he rested secure in the arms of Bacchus. His mother wasn't in on it. I switched bottles on her. The baby's sugar water was laced with the best whiskey to be found in Hell's Half Acre. Gentlemen, I suggest we now have another drink out of the same jug."

The next issue of *Harper's New Monthly Magazine* devoted eight pages to Elvira's acquittal. A full-paged woodcut depicted Travis holding the baby aloft before the jurors. His closing argument was published in full under the headline: *Declared Innocent With the Corroboration of*

God's Littlest Angels. Similar stories appeared in *Scribner's, Lippincott's, The Nation,* and *Outlook.*

In the months that followed, Travis found his life changed irrevocably. He no longer could pretend enthusiasm for minor local cases while delicious murder trials beckoned in distant courts. His law practice expanded. Departing amicably from Captain Tackett's quarters, he engaged a suite of second-floor rooms overlooking the square. He hired two bright, eager young men as assistants.

Otto's house seemed to shrink as Travis brought in more and more finery. Travis proposed building a new house for them on the west side of town, but Otto did not warm to the idea.

"This is my home," he said. "I'll live out my days here."

Reluctantly, Travis moved into a suite at Andrews Tavern. He soon discovered that he liked the atmosphere. After supper each day, in the quiet hours of evening, he would sit on the gallery and converse with men from all walks of life—drummers, visiting lawyers, adventurers, entrepreneurs, land speculators, army officers, merchants, government officials, cattlemen, gamblers, promoters.

Each had his own story. Travis bought them drinks and drew them out. He learned of conditions in faraway places and compared them to his own. He listened to their dreams of empire.

Some had traveled extensively in West Texas, and described what they had seen. They said that beyond the Brazos were countless thousands of square miles of open rangeland, available for the taking. To the northwest lay the Llano Estacado, great plains so vast and flat that a horse and rider could be distinguished as far as the eye could see, where men navigated by star and compass as if on the boundless ocean. Travis listened to these romantics and dreamed with them. They said that someday on these plains and prairies great cities would rise, as populous as those along the eastern seaboard or the ancient capitals of Europe. They said that someday railroads and stage lines would crisscross this vast expanse, linking these great centers of commerce into an amalgamation of activity beyond all contemplation.

One evening Travis met a tall, impressive adventurer who introduced himself as Captain Buckley B. Paddock. He affected a cane and top hat, a colorful cravat, and a fur-lined collar on his well-tailored suit. He wore a cookie-duster moustache. His coarse dark hair was parted down the middle and swept into wings on each side that bobbed as he talked. His eyes were calm and thoughtful. Travis could see that he kept much inside himself.

Over the course of two evenings Travis learned they had much in common, even though Paddock was born a Yankee. Early in life, from the reading of many books, Paddock had determined that any and all hope for the nation lay with the South and its traditions of aristocracy, chivalry, and culture. On the outbreak of war, he left his home in Wisconsin Territory and, at seventeen, cast his lot with the Confederacy as a private soldier. His demonstrated valor lifted him from the ranks. At eighteen he held the rank of captain. He was prominent on the field at Shiloh, Corinth, and Vicksburg. He commanded a daring raid against a Union ironclad on the Yazoo, a feat celebrated throughout the South. Travis remembered talk of it.

Paddock now had come to West Texas to examine its prospects for the future.

"I'm convinced that during the next hundred years this nation will see the greatest accomplishments of man since the days of the Roman Empire," Paddock said. "The dreams, the men, the land, the raw materials are here. I'm further convinced that Fort Worth will be a mighty center of this expansion. I'm looking for a way to get my feet wet."

"What line are you interested in?"

Paddock hesitated. "I've been thinking of starting a newspaper."

"The man you need to see is Major Van Emden," Travis told him. "If you'll come along with me in the morning, I'll introduce you."

Van Emden was a fortuitous trader. Often the uses of the merchandise he acquired were not readily apparent. Travis happened to know that a few months earlier the major and a few friends had swapped a wagonload of wheat for an old Washington press. They had been unable to find anyone capable of operating the equipment.

As Travis anticipated, Van Emden and Paddock warmed quickly to each other. They struck a deal. Paddock was named editor and publisher of the *Fort Worth Democrat*.

From the first, Paddock infused the newspaper with energy. He constantly exhorted the people of Fort Worth to fulfill their own expectations. He was lively, articulate, full of ideas. Travis enjoyed his company immensely and spent considerable time with him. They idled away nights poring over maps, coordinating all they had learned of commerce in Texas and other states. They determined to their satisfaction that because of its providential location, Fort Worth was destined to become a major metropolis in the Southwest, linking the High Plains of the Panhandle, the ranch country of West Texas, the Piney Woods and lumber mills of East Texas, and the seaports of the Gulf. Paddock devised a map, depicting the future railroads, stage lines, and wagon trails, spreading outward from Fort Worth like the legs of a giant tarantula. To the east, Dallas was no more than a kneejoint on one hairy leg.

The drawing, emblazoned on the front page of every edition of the *Fort Worth Democrat*, became known as *"The Tarantula Map."* Wherever he went, Travis carried a copy in his pocket, prepared to demonstrate on a moment's notice that in Fort Worth all things were possible.

6

The Jacksboro courtroom was packed. Travis stood near the hall door, swapping jokes with his colleagues. Judge Simpson's voice rose above the din.

"Mr. Spurlock, the state has filed a petition for continuance of your client's case until tomorrow morning. Do you at this time wish to present valid argument why this request should not be granted?"

To the contrary, Travis felt a wave of relief. The drinking and story telling the night before had continued into the early morning hours. His head throbbed. His tongue was dry. He spoke from the rear of the courtroom. "Continuance is agreeable to the defense, Your Honor."

Judge Simpson cupped a hand to his ear. "Speak up, Mr. Spurlock. The court can hardly hear you."

Travis raised his voice. "That's all right, Your Honor. I can barely *see* you."

The courtroom erupted with laughter, led by the assembled lawyers. All knew that the judge had been in as bad shape as anyone.

Judge Simpson did not offer the hint of a smile. But there was a glint of humor in his eyes. "The court may tolerate contempt, but never ridicule. Be apprised, Mr. Spurlock."

"I said continuance is agreeable to the defense, Your Honor."

"Then continuance is hereby granted. However, it is not the purpose of this court to deprive the fair metropolis of Jacksboro of the wit, eloquence, and learned services of Mr. Spurlock for a single day. Therefore the court hereby appoints Mr. Spurlock attorney for defense in the case of State versus Elmo Reaves, assigned to this afternoon's docket."

"Thank you, Your Honor," Travis said. He was not surprised. Attorneys unexpectedly idled by circumstances often were given court assignments to help with the added expenses of the road.

"A case involving grand larceny, I believe," Judge Simpson added.

"You may confer with your client this morning. I expect to hear the case first thing this afternoon, Mr. Spurlock."

Feeling the need of fresher and cooler air, Travis walked from the courtroom into the marbled hall. Newt Nippert from Sherman followed him.

"Well, Travis, that'll teach you to bait the judge," Nippert said. "Elmo Reaves doesn't have the chance of a junebug in a henhouse. John Hawkins will mop up the floor with you."

Hawkins was the county attorney. He seemed to be jealous of Travis. He and Travis had been sniping at each other all week. So far, Travis was ahead.

"I don't believe I'm familiar with the case," Travis said.

"I didn't think you was, since I didn't hear you protest. The facts seem to be that Elmo was caught branding forty-six cattle that weren't his. The sheriff and two deputies caught him at work with a running iron. He'd been busy. He'd already branded the forty-six. Twenty-two more were waiting in a dry wash he had jury-rigged as a corral."

"In that case, I'd better get busy myself," Travis said. "I'd sure hate to see such an industrious man hanged."

He walked down the hall to the county attorney's office and asked to see his client. A deputy was sent to fetch the prisoner from the jail.

After a few minutes he returned with a pencil-thin, red-haired cowman who stood at least six feet, four inches tall, bowed into a question mark.

"This is Elmo Reaves," the deputy said. He gestured toward a door. "Y'all can talk in that corner room."

Travis was guiding Reaves into the room when he collided with County Attorney Hawkins, emerging from a side door. Hawkins glanced at the prisoner and sized up the situation immediately. He smirked. "Mr. Spurlock, you'd better give your client your very best advice. He'll be needing it."

Travis did not answer. There were few men he disliked instinctively. Hawkins was one. Most county attorneys resented the close camaraderie of the defense lawyers traveling with the circuit court. With Hawkins, animosity was an obsession.

Travis turned his back on Hawkins and followed Reaves into a small room, bare except for a table and cane-bottom chairs. The second-floor windows looked out on the square, now jammed with wagons, hacks, and horses. Circuit court always drew a crowd to town. The day was hot, and the windows were open. Travis motioned Reaves into a chair.

"The court has appointed me as your lawyer," he explained. "I'll be happy to serve, and I'll do my best for you. But there's one thing I require. You mustn't lie to me. Just tell me what happened."

Elmo Reaves was a slow, thoughtful talker. Travis listened with sinking heart as he told of stealing the cattle, corralling them in a gully, and working with a branding iron for two days.

"I didn't hear the sheriff coming until he was right on top of me," he said. "He had the drop on me. There wasn't a damned thing I could do."

"Ever been in trouble before?"

Reaves nodded sadly. "I stole a wagonload of hogs over by Denton. Served time on that. Two years."

Dirt-dauber wasps were building a nest near the corner window. One flew into the room. Travis waved a hand and encouraged it back through the open window.

"Reaves, I can't offer much hope for your chances," he said. "The judge is fair. He probably won't hang you. But with a prior conviction on the books, you can look forward to at least ten to twenty at hard labor."

"That's about what I figured," Reaves said.

Travis saw a commotion out on the street. A heavy, four-seat buckboard was pushing its way through the traffic around the square.

Travis spoke quietly. "See that stage? It's on its way to Graham and Albany. It'll be stopped at the hotel for about ten minutes while they change horses."

Reaves looked at him, frowning in puzzlement.

"My advice to you is to get the hell out of Jack County, and never come back," Travis said. "In fact, if I were you, I'd quit the state of Texas."

Reaves sat with his mouth open.

"I've developed a powerful thirst sitting here," Travis rambled on conversationally. "In a minute, I'll step out into the hall for a drink of water. I wouldn't be surprised if a few dollars don't fall out of my pocket. It's only a few feet to the ground. If I were you, and I broke both ankles jumping out that window, I'd still make it to that stage."

Reaves managed to speak. "Why are you doing this for me?"

Travis stood, peeled two tens from a roll of bills, and dropped them to the floor. "Let's just say I don't see a chinaman's chance for you in this court, and I can't abide losing cases. Especially in Jack County." He paused at the door. "There's just one thing more."

He waited until he had his client's full attention. "If you're dumb enough to get caught, you'd better not say one word about my part in it. You won't live to hang. I'll shoot you dead."

Travis walked out into the hall. The public water can was wrapped in wet burlap. Several tin cups were attached to it with light chains. Travis found the water moderately cool, as if from a deep cistern. He lingered in the hall outside the county attorney's offices. Aside from two clerks busy at their desks, the offices were empty.

When he returned to the corner room, Reaves and the money were gone. Travis arranged a chair, tipped it back, braced his boots against the window sill, and lit a cigar. For the next two hours he watched the dirt-dauber wasps ply their trade.

Noon came and went. Travis was dozing when the deputy knocked at the door.

"Come in. It's open," Travis said.

The deputy stepped into the room. His eyes widened when he saw only Travis. "Where's Reaves?" he asked.

Travis feigned surprise. "I thought he was in jail. Didn't you come and get him a while ago?"

The deputy's mouth worked futilely. No sound came. He hurried off.

A few minutes later he returned with Hawkins and the sheriff. Hawkins searched wildly around the room, as if unable to accept the fact that Reaves was truly gone.

Travis caught his eye. "Mr. Prosecutor, I gave my client my very best advice."

Hawkins stared blankly at him, then fled. A half hour passed before he returned. "Judge Simpson wishes to see you in his chambers. Be apprised that I'm preparing formal charges against you, Mr. Spurlock, for aiding and abetting the escape of a known criminal."

"Mr. Hawkins, I'm surprised at you," Travis said. "I remind you that Mr. Reaves is not yet convicted. I'm not prepared to accept the claim that he is a criminal."

Travis, Hawkins, and the sheriff filed into the chambers allocated to the visiting judge. Simpson studied Travis coldly. Gone was the easygoing, voluble man Travis had known on the road. "This situation is most serious, Mr. Spurlock," he said. "Mr. Hawkins is of the opinion that you somehow assisted the prisoner in his escape."

"Your Honor, this whole matter is a most unfortunate comedy of errors," Travis said easily. "I had finished conferring with my client, and stepped into the hall for a drink of water. When I returned, Reaves was gone. Naturally, I assumed that the deputy had returned him to his cell. Otherwise, I would have raised an alarm."

Judge Simpson gave Travis a long, calculating stare. "And I understand you spent the next several hours in that room alone."

"Your Honor, due to the state's request for continuance in the Lauderdale murder case, I was idle. As you may understand, I was somewhat the worse for wear after an evening of conviviality. I'm afraid I slept, sir, until awakened by the deputy a few minutes ago."

"And you know nothing about the prisoner's escape?"

"I have absolutely no knowledge of the prisoner's present whereabouts, Your Honor. As far as I know, he still resides in the county jail."

If Simpson noticed the evasive answer, he gave no sign.

"Am I to understand you didn't suspect for a moment that the prisoner may have jumped through the open window?"

Travis raised his hands. "Your Honor, the room is on the second floor. It's a considerable distance to the ground."

Hawkins snorted. "Less than ten feet. A child could jump it."

"Mr. Hawkins inferred considerable meaning in your statement that you gave your client your very best advice," the judge said. "What exactly did you tell your client?"

Travis hesitated. "Your Honor, I hardly think it my place to point out to the court that what passes between a duly constituted counselor and his client is one of the most sacred domains under the sovereign protection of the law. I know of no precedent where this confidentiality has been breached."

"Your point is well taken," Judge Simpson said.

Travis pushed on. "Allow me also to cite the fact that the prisoner was not in my custody. If he were, I might have exercised more diligence."

The judge frowned in thought. "That's a fine technicality, Mr. Spurlock. Granted, a prisoner remains in custody of the county until the moment he is brought into the confines of the court. However, as an officer of the court, you certainly should have demonstrated a greater sense of responsibility."

Travis sensed that the time had arrived for a conciliatory gesture. "Yes, sir. I can see that now."

"However, you can hardly be charged with the omission. The court considers it incumbent upon itself to warn the prosecutor that the burden of proof in the charges he is contemplating must rest with the state. Unless the prosecutor has further pertinent information to add, the court sees no convincing evidence to warrant such charges."

All eyes turned to Hawkins. He spoke with obvious reluctance. "I have no further evidence, Your Honor."

"Then the court hereby reprimands Travis Spurlock for his carelessness, and cautions him to be more observant to his duties in the future. I trust this will end the matter."

"Thank you, Your Honor," Travis said.

By the time Travis returned to the boarding house, word had spread. No one seemed to have the slightest doubt as to what Travis had done. For the most part, the traveling lawyers were a tightly knit group, arrayed against the local prosecutors. Dislike of Hawkins was general. The victory Travis had scored was considered a masterstroke. As he moved through the handshakes and backslaps, Travis merely smiled and said nothing. He knew that despite what Judge Simpson had said, the matter was not ended.

Newt Nippert from Sherman put Travis's thoughts into words.

"You'd better be on your toes tomorrow. Hawkins will be laying for you."

The courtroom was unbearably hot and oppressive, the air clammy and muggy from the brief summer shower that had fallen just before noon. As Travis droned on with his final argument, the members of the jury seemed unable to stay awake, much less to concentrate on his words. The courtroom windows were open. The noises from the street tended to drown out his voice.

Sweating profusely, Travis described in lengthy detail the argument that led to the fatal shooting. Repeatedly Hawkins objected to his tedious repetitions. Usually the judge overruled, supporting Travis in his contention that the jury should be fully informed.

Charged with murder in the second degree, Arnold Lauderdale was alleged to have shot his partner, Harley Flippins, after the two fell into disagreement over the division of profits from the sale of a small herd of cattle. The shooting occurred behind a livery stable. The defendant was the only surviving witness. His sole defense rested on his contention that Flippins came at him with a knife. But no knife was ever found. When the hand of the deceased was opened, it held nothing but a small metallic pencil that now lay on the exhibits table.

Travis droned on, elaborating each minute detail. "The herd in this dispute consisted of four six-year-olds, eight three-year-olds, five four-year-olds, seven five-year-olds, sixteen two-year-olds, and thirty-six year-lings."

He described the various markings and the condition of the cattle. He kept his voice flat and monotonous.

The case for the defendant seemed hopeless. All morning Hawkins had presented solid evidence. Lauderdale sat at the defense table contrite and hangdog in appearance. Reluctantly, Travis had decided not to put him on the stand.

Droning on, Travis saw that one juror was nodding off to sleep. Another was fighting to keep his eyes open.

Slowly pacing the floor, Travis walked by the exhibits table. Allowing a hand to drag along its surface, he surreptitiously palmed the metallic pencil.

He strolled to the opposite side of the room from the jury box. "Mr. Lauderdale believed the six-year-olds were worth twelve dollars each. But Mr. Flippins had figured them at ten. Overall, a difference of two hundred and sixteen dollars."

Facing away from the jurors, Travis suddenly stopped talking. He rolled his shoulders like a man in the midst of a seizure. He made loud gasping sounds deep in his throat. Abruptly, he turned, his face transformed into a grotesque mask he had practiced for hours in front of a mirror. With a shriek, he charged the jury box, coattails flying. He held his right hand high, swinging the pencil as if it were a knife. Still yelling, he leaped the jury railing, slashing wildly at the air.

The jurymen scattered, scrambling and falling in their haste to get out of the way. Two bailiffs leaped across the room and grabbed Travis. He shrugged them off.

The courtroom was in an uproar. Judge Simpson gaveled for order.

Travis waited until calm had been restored. Smiling, he walked to the front of the jury box. "Gentlemen, all I have here in my hand is that little ol' pencil from the exhibits table." He held it up for them to see. "You thought I was coming at you with a knife, didn't you? If you'd been armed, you might have shot me! Now that is exactly what happened to the defendant. When his partner shouted in anger, and came at him with upraised fist, Arnold Lauderdale thought, just for a single, fleeting moment, that Mr. Flippins had a knife in his fist. In that moment of self-preservation, he shot the man who had been his beloved partner for more than five years. He regretted his action instantly. He still regrets it today. But gentlemen of the jury, it is our solemn responsibility to assess Arnold Lauderdale's actions in that fearful moment. I submit to you that he acted as *any* reasonable man would have, under the circumstances. He acted just as you might have acted rashly against me a few minutes ago."

Lauderdale was acquitted.

The celebration that night was spirited. Travis was toasted repeatedly for his victories. Even Judge Simpson warmed to the occasion, and shared the laughter over the panic in the jury box. Travis was satisfied.

Of such courtroom prowess were legends born. He knew that his exploits were being recounted wherever lawyers met. He was earning the respect and friendship of some of the most influential men in the state.

Someday he would put that friendship to good use.

"I hope you'll forgive me," Travis said. "The truth is that I've been occupied, on the road most of the time."

Rebecca Latham smiled and knelt to examine a rose. "It *has* been a while." She laughed lightly. "We were beginning to wonder if you had moved on."

They were in the garden behind the Latham home. The other members of the family had withdrawn, leaving Travis and Rebecca alone. The late afternoon sunlight played in gentle patterns along the ground. Soft lint from the cottonwoods filled the quiet air.

"I had not intended for our friendship to suffer," Travis said. "I should have dropped you a letter. I apologize. It seems that when I'm involved in my work, I tend to concentrate on it completely."

Rebecca tugged at the stem of the rose. Travis offered her his penknife. Selecting each blossom carefully, Rebecca gathered a bouquet. Travis stood waiting.

"Much has happened since last I saw you," she said without looking up. "The Shakespeare Club has several new members. On Easter Sunday, the church had dinner on the ground at Cold Springs. I'm sure you would have enjoyed it."

Travis half listened as Rebecca went on chatting. So many of his earlier pursuits now seemed shallow. He no longer had the slightest interest in the dinners, parties, balls, and entertainments that clearly were Rebecca's whole life. He had missed her company, and that of the other young ladies, but only in random idle moments.

Rebecca completed her bouquet and returned his penknife. She held the flowers close to her face as she strolled to the wrought iron bench in the center of the garden. Travis joined her on the bench while she continued her description of the social season he had missed. He tried to concentrate on her words. He hardly knew some of the younger people she mentioned.

At last she paused and looked at him. "One other thing has happened. I'll tell you as a friend. Wilbur Howard has asked me to marry him."

Buffeted by a mixture of conflicting emotions, Travis did not react immediately. Overriding all other feelings was a strong sense of relief. Close behind was a painful awareness of loss. He had been drawn to the stability and stature of the Latham family. The doctor reminded him of his own father. Mrs. Latham possessed the same gentility he remembered in his mother. Reva, with her warmth, wide-ranging interests, and rapier-sharp mind, was a little sister anyone would treasure.

He knew he should consider his situation logically. Rebecca was lively, good-natured, witty, honest, beautiful—all that any man could desire in a wife.

Her ploy in telling him of the proposal was oblique, but obvious. He was certain that his own proposal would take precedence. He had seen the evidence in Rebecca's eyes.

But he could not bring himself to make the commitment. He had watched his friends marry, one by one, and settle into a family life with children and myriad other responsibilities.

He still felt that, somehow, life should offer more.

Rebecca was waiting. His courtroom training came to his rescue. He kept his face expressionless. Then, calculatedly, he offered her a troubled frown. He owed her that. "Have you given him your answer?"

"No," Rebecca said. She searched his face.

Travis knew he was in one of those rare moments that alter one's life irrevocably. In his state of heightened awareness, the scene burned itself indelibly into his memory—the glint of sunlight on Rebecca's eyelashes, the song of a distant mockingbird, the cottonwood lint in the air, the intimate smells of magnolia, roses, and Rebecca.

He knew he might be making a mistake he would live to regret. But his response came from a faculty deeper than logic. "I'm pleased for you, Rebecca," he said. "Wilbur's a fine young man. I hear he has an excellent future. I'm sure you will make the right decision."

In truth, Travis was not well acquainted with the prospective bridegroom. He only knew that Wilbur was a cotton buyer, involved in commerce.

Rebecca showed her true breeding. "Yes, I'm honored that he has asked me," she said lightly. "I probably will give him my answer soon." She paused. "I really should place these roses in water."

Travis followed her back into the house. The rest of the family were seated in the parlor. From the carefully controlled expressions of Doctor and Mrs. Latham, Travis knew they had divined the outcome of Rebecca's ploy.

Only Reva seemed oblivious. "Oh, Mr. Spurlock, I've been wanting to ask you something. I'm reading Emerson, and I'm so confused! His Transcendantalism doesn't sound anything like what I remember from Kant's *Pure Reason!*"

Travis welcomed the diversion. "Miss Reva, I'm not sure that Emerson ever acknowledged the usual interpretation of Kant. You see, he adapted Kant's philosophy to his own purpose, more in keeping with the views of Coleridge and Wordsworth."

"And Thoreau!" Reva said. "How does his work relate?"

Travis had hoped that the discussion might lighten the moment. But he saw that Rebecca was close to tears.

"Miss Reva, I'm afraid it's quite complicated. I hope we can discuss it at length some time. But right now, I really must go. I have a brief to prepare before leaving for Jefferson in the morning."

"Mr. Spurlock, surely you'll stay for supper!" said Mrs. Latham.

"I'm sorry, but duty calls."

The elder Lathams seemed relieved. Doctor Latham rose and escorted him to the door. Glancing back, Travis saw that Reva's lower lip was trembling, that she also seemed in the grip of strong emotion. He wondered if she had sensed the awkward situation and had posed the literary questions as a gambit.

He did not know.

She was a puzzling child.

Travis remained low in spirits throughout the evening. He knew he had crossed a Rubicon and there was no turning back. He had set inexorable events in motion. Rebecca and Wilbur would be wed, and in a sense he was the molder of their marriage. He had disappointed Doctor and Mrs. Latham. And perhaps Reva. His relationships with them were no doubt ended.

He walked the streets, wondering why he could not be content with the ordinary life that seemed to satisfy other men. Surely there lay something deep within himself that he did not understand.

He strolled into Hell's Half Acre. Five trail herds were bedded down along the Trinity. The warm, sweet smell of moist cow manure hung over the town like honeysuckle.

The acre was lively. Travis moved from one saloon to another, shaking hands, nodding his greetings, seldom lingering long enough to finish a drink. He was invited to join several poker games. But he felt too restless. He moved on.

On his way back to the tavern he stopped by the Silver Lode. The saloon was untypically quiet. Three cattlemen stood at the end of the bar, closing a deal. Two buffalo hiders hovered over dominoes at a back table.

Travis spoke to the bartender. "Everyone seems to be down at the Bon Ton tonight, Jay Jay."

Jay Jay muttered an oath. "This saloon is dying on a green vine, Mr. Spurlock. And there's no sense to it. I keep telling the owners. We could have the busiest place in town here. Way things are going, we'll be closed in six months."

Travis was intrigued. Fort Worth was booming. How could any saloon be losing money? "Why?" he asked.

Jay Jay was a large man, bald as an onion, with a nice smile. His full name was Junius James Gibson. Everyone in the acre called him Jay Jay. He wiped the bar and leaned closer. "Whiskey alone just isn't enough these days, Mr. Spurlock. The customers expect more. Most of them have been off to themselves three, four months, maybe a year, herding cattle, hunting buffalo, whatever. They're tired of each other's company. They know more about each other than they ever wanted to know. They need something else to talk about during their next stretch alone. Almost anything will do. A red-hot poker game. Conversation with a good-looking woman. A dancer who'll make them wake up with a stiff prick for the next six months. A good roll in the hay. Anything they can josh each other about, day after day, week after week. That's what they want. Whoever packages that in one saloon in this town will get rich."

Travis felt a rush of interest. He knew that Jay Jay was not making idle talk. "Why don't you do it yourself?"

Jay Jay shrugged. "Money. It'd have to be done right, a big splash right from the start. Huge grand opening. Something they'd talk about all up and down the trail. I used to run a place in New Orleans. I know people who could supply all I'd need—girls, dancers, musicians, card sharps. I've made drawings of the way things ought to be arranged. I've figured the materials right down to the board foot. But I just don't have the money to do it right."

Travis's excitement flared. He kept his voice calm. "Jay Jay, I happen to have some cash available at the moment. Why don't we get together and explore your idea? We might come to an agreement that would be mutually profitable."

A week later, after Travis returned from trying a murder case in Jefferson, Jay Jay came to see him. They spent the afternoon poring over Jay Jay's drawings and figures. By sundown they had come to an agreement.

Jay Jay would build and operate an establishment to be known as the Red Lantern. Travis would advance all necessary money. His participation was to remain a secret between them. They would divide the profits equally.

Ostensibly acting as Jay Jay's legal agent, Travis purchased an entire square block on Fifth Street. With the tendency of Hell's Half Acre to expand southward from the courthouse, Travis estimated that within a year or two, the Red Lantern would be in the middle of the acre.

Lumber was ordered and freighted in from the sawmills in East Texas. As the huge structure began to take shape, Travis found it impossible to remain at a distance. Cautiously, he dropped hints that frequent visits to the site were necessary to clear up various legal obstacles for Jay Jay. The ruse was unnecessary. Construction of the Red Lantern became the talk of the town. Spectators gathered every day. Nothing of comparable size had ever been built in Fort Worth.

The cluster of structures covered the block. On the north, facing town, the barnlike main building rose three stories high. Inside, magnificent chandeliers hung from a high ceiling. At the end of the huge polished dance floor a proscenium arch provided a platform for performers. Hardwood bars stretched the length of each wall. Stairs at each corner led up to a horseshoe-shaped gallery, where spectators could look down upon the festivities.

Behind the building, rows of cribs encircled a courtyard. During the summer months—the peak of the trail driving season—the outdoor plaza would be used as a second dance floor. Each tiny crib was equipped with the basic necessities—coal oil lamp, cot, water pitcher, and basin.

Not everyone in Fort Worth looked upon the Red Lantern with favor. Travis heard that a few ministers and some of their followers were setting up an organization to voice opposition.

Concerned, he arranged quiet meetings with community leaders. Carefully explaining that he was speaking as Jay Jay's attorney, he asked their views. The consensus seemed to be that if kept within reasonable bounds the Red Lantern would be a great asset to the town.

Relieved that he had strong civic support, Travis helped Jay Jay prepare broadsides to be posted along the full length of the Chisholm Trail. As a further personal investment, he acquired more property to the south and east of the Red Lantern.

At last opening night arrived. Riders came from vast distances. Eight herds were bedded down close enough for drovers to attend. Scores of buffalo hunters and freighters were in town.

Travis strolled among the throngs that jammed the Red Lantern, somewhat frustrated that he was unable to take due credit. He hid his pride as he greeted his friends and enjoyed the sights. Every half hour, dancers from New Orleans kicked up their heels and showed their bottoms beneath flared skirts. Forty-six girls guided men around the dance floor and took them to the cribs out back. Twenty bartenders kept the liquor flowing. Seven musicians managed to make themselves heard above the uproar.

Fort Worth had never seen such a night, not even in Hell's Half Acre.

Toward midnight, Jay Jay took Travis aside. "I can't believe it. We're taking in money five times as fast as I'd figured. And this is just the start. Wait till word spreads about this place!"

Opening night never ended. The saloon continued to operate around the clock, seven days a week. Riders came from hundreds of miles around to see the largest bar in Texas, perhaps the world.

By early summer the Red Lantern had more than returned the initial investment. And still the profits rolled in.

Problems arose. Occasionally drunken tempers flared. Shootings and stabbings were frequent. After the more serious incidents Travis was usually visited by a delegation of businessmen. He was urged, as Jay Jay's attorney, to ask that the festivities be toned down for a while. Travis would convey the word.

After a few weeks, on signal from Travis, Jay Jay would slowly lift the lid again.

Travis thus found himself functioning as the moderator of morals for the community. He did not feel comfortable with the situation.

But never for a moment did he dream that his new role might hold great anguish for himself and for his descendants in generations to come.

7

W e're here to explore the practicality of bringing our railroad on past Dallas to Fort Worth, and making this our westernmost terminal," said Colonel Scott.

Aware that the three distinguished visitors were carefully studying his face, Travis put his full attention on buttering his biscuit. "I can't conceive of your selecting any other site, Colonel Scott," he said. "I'll be most happy to serve as your guide, answer any questions you may have, and introduce you to the leaders of our community."

"Excellent," Scott said. He turned to his assistants. "This is a most fortuitous encounter. We've hardly started, and already we have half a day's work done."

From the quick, overly effusive laughter of Scott's two companions, Travis understood that Scott was the man to sell. He was the stud duck. The other two were lackeys.

Travis was tired. He had returned late the previous evening from Austin, where he had spent a week pleading a case before the Texas Supreme Court. Exhausted from the two-day return trip, he had overslept. On descending for breakfast, he had found the three strangers alone in the dining room. They wore hand-tailored suits of the finest cloth, silk cravats, diamond stickpins the size of buckshot, and soft-leather, high-buttoned shoes. After they invited him to join them, he quickly learned that Scott was president of the Texas & Pacific Railway Company, advancing deeper into the state from East Texas.

Travis placed his napkin on the table. "If you gentlemen will excuse me a moment, I'll send for my carriage, so it'll be ready by the time we finish breakfast."

He went into the parlor and wrote a hurried note to Major Van Emden, apprising him of the situation. He then gave one of the tavern boys a nickel to fetch Jimmy and the carriage and to deliver the note to Van Emden.

After breakfast he drove the visitors to the north side of the square and halted at the edge of the bluff. April had just arrived. Spring was heavy in the air. The prospect from the bluff, far greener than usual, was even more impressive. "Denton is thirty miles over yonder," Travis said, pointing. "Decatur over there about the same distance. Jacksboro and Graham are somewhat farther out. Weatherford's a day's ride to the west, and Dallas the same to the east. All thriving county seat towns."

Scott smiled at the reference to Dallas. "It was my impression that your neighbor to the east may have greater pretensions. The people over there assured me I wouldn't find anything of interest in Fort Worth."

"There's a bit of good-natured rivalry, sir," Travis said. "But as I'm sure you know, it's Fort Worth, not Dallas, that's the supply point for the Chisholm Trail."

Scott pointed to the northwest. "What's the land like out there? Some maps still label it the Great American Desert."

"They're wrong, sir," Travis assured him. "I've traveled across the width and the breadth of it. Some of the soil is as rich as any in Alabama, Georgia, or Tennessee. As soon as the Indians and buffalo are gone, it'll fill up with settlers."

"Farm country?"

Travis hedged. He suspected that Scott knew the answer, and was testing him. "I'd say most of it is more suited to cattle."

"And what do you believe Fort Worth has to offer us that Dallas doesn't?"

Travis gestured to the west. "You're looking at it, sir. Someday Fort Worth will be one of the largest cattle shipping centers in the nation. It's inevitable."

He drove the visitors down Main Street to the open prairie.

Scott pulled out a hand-drawn map. "According to our preliminary information, the town is bordered on the north, east, and west by streams. That would seem to leave this the only accessible direction in wet weather."

"Yes, sir," Travis said. He and Editor Paddock long ago had determined that the best site for the railroad yard was a mile to the southeast of the courthouse.

"Well, I've seen enough," Scott said. "I'm prepared to talk to your city leaders."

Travis drove them to Major Van Emden's office. Paddock, the major, Captain Tackett, and Colonel John Peter Smith were waiting.

After introductions, Scott outlined the situation. "We're favorably impressed with Fort Worth," he concluded. "But as you may imagine, we have certain requisites."

"What, exactly?" Van Emden asked.

Colonel Scott had not achieved his high position by mincing words. "We will require three hundred and twenty acres within the city limits, on the south side of town, free and unencumbered. If you can guarantee that, we'll proceed toward Fort Worth with the railroad as rapidly as humanly possible."

"That may take us a little while," Van Emden said.

Scott hesitated. "We can wait a month for your answer. But no more."

"Sir, you misunderstand me," Van Emden said. "I was speaking in terms of two or three hours."

Her mouth was deep red, her eyes a luminous green, and her hair the color of wild strawberries. She stood framed by the stained-glass windows of the church, leading the choir in the old hymn "Amazing Grace."

Travis sat mesmerized, wondering whether he had been around Reva Latham for years without truly seeing her, or if she had burst forth overnight in some miraculous transformation.

Hasty calculation told him that she was barely fifteen. But in the months since he last had seen her, she had grown taller than her sister Rebecca. She was slimmer, but the pale green dress she wore clung gently to delicious curves.

She looked in his direction and smiled as her voice soared as clear and pure as mountain air. The congregation sat hushed, drinking in her beauty.

As she sang the final verse, Travis was overwhelmed by sadness. Circumstances had placed her beyond his reach. After the way he had treated Rebecca, he doubted that her parents would tolerate his court-ship of a second daughter.

The hymn ended. Reva primly resumed her seat. Travis sat through the sermon hardly listening, acutely aware of Reva, the changes in her.

Afterward he followed the congregation out the church door. In fair weather most families lingered on the church lawn to exchange pleasant-ries before driving home to Sunday dinner. The Latham family was standing at the edge of the walk. Travis could not easily avoid them. He shook hands with Dr. Latham and the new son-in-law, Wilbur Howard. He spoke to Mrs. Latham and Rebecca, then turned with calculated casualness to Reva.

"You gave us a splendid rendition of that glorious old hymn this morning, Miss Reva. You are to be congratulated."

The emerald eyes, the rosebud smile flickered at him. "Thank you, Mr. Spurlock. You're most kind."

She turned to speak to other well-wishers. Travis was left standing awkwardly. He said good day to the other Lathams and waved for Jimmy to bring his carriage.

As he drove away, he looked back. Reva Latham was stepping into a smart black-and-red buggy driven by Larkin Evans, a young man hardly beyond adolescence.

Travis was seized by an irrational pang of jealousy.

He had intended to treat himself to a leisurely dinner at the tavern before returning to his office to work through the afternoon and early evening. But dissatisfaction welled within him. The perfect spring day seemed wasted.

He remembered the pleasures of outings in the company of lively, witty, bright young women, their smells, their occasional touch, their enticing mystery.

Reluctantly, he conceded to himself that he may have been too preoccupied with his career in recent years.

Already he was far wealthier than he ever dreamed possible. News of the coming of the railroad had spread throughout the Southwest. Every day more emigrants swarmed into town to share the bonanza. Building could not keep pace. A thousand people were now living in tents on the fringes of the city. Travis had sold some of his property at fabulous profits and bought more on speculation. He had added three more young men to his staff. Still his office remained inundated with the legal paperwork from the boom. Money continued to flow in from the Red Lantern. Most nights not even standing room at the bars could be found. The girls were kept so busy they now seldom left their cribs.

Moreover, his stature continued to rise in the community. Only last week a delegation had asked him to be principal speaker at this year's Fourth of July celebration. Traditionally the community invited some prominent orator, usually one from another state. Travis knew that his selection was a singular honor.

Yet his wealth and status had not brought satisfaction.

He returned to the tavern, dined on quail, and retired to the gallery, where he smoked a meditative cigar, staring into the distant blue of the Texas sky.

That evening he labored over his Fourth of July speech. The work did not go well. Vague disturbances nibbled at the corners of his mind. Reva's glorious soprano voice still caressed his ears. Her emerald eyes and tantalizing smile haunted him.

He sat staring at the wall, wondering why he was so miserable.

"Wilbur is such a nice young man," Millie said. "I know Rebecca had her heart set on Travis Spurlock, but I'm glad now that didn't work out."

Reva sat motionless in the parlor, listening to her mother and father on the gallery. Engrossed in her reading, she had been paying little attention until mention of Travis Spurlock. Her father's reply was too low for Reva to hear. But he must have said something in favor of Travis, for Millie felt obliged to take issue.

"I suppose there's nothing *wrong* with Travis Spurlock. He seems gentle and kind. His manners are perfect. But I've always had the feeling there's an underlying *brashness* about him that might crop up some time in the most unexpected way."

"Brashness?"

"A hardness."

Reva heard her father's rocking chair creak as he leaned forward to his spittoon. "Travis Spurlock saw a lot of the war, Millie. I have no doubt it affected him."

"All the same, Wilbur's much less complicated. I believe Rebecca will be more satisfied with him in the long run."

Her father did not answer. Quietly, Reva closed her book and slipped up the stairs to her room.

Lying full-length on her bed, she gazed up at the ceiling and reviewed the events of the day.

Her intuition told her that she now had Travis Spurlock intrigued. While singing, and afterward, she had observed the way his gaze lingered on her.

She had been surprised at the changes in him. The last few months seemed to have aged him by years. The lines in his face were more pronounced, his dark, brooding eyes even deeper-set. He had seemed troubled. By what, she could not guess.

When she stepped into Larkin's buggy, she had risked a glance in his direction. He had been looking back, watching.

She felt certain he was rising to the lure.

She was prepared. She intended to devote her every moment, her very life to her campaign. No illustrious military general, no conquering monarch of history would match her for single-minded effort.

But her innate gifts of reasoning told her to bide her time. For the moment the best strategy was to let her quarry fret.

Reva heard her parents go into their room and retire for the night. The house grew still.

She lay awake, concocting extravagant plans.

"You look like you've been rode hard and put away wet," Otto said.

Travis sank into a chair. Hector came and lay at his feet. Travis reached down and rubbed the dog's ears. Hector whined his pleasure.

Travis had not visited Otto in months. Now he had need of a good listener. "It just seems that every once in a while life catches up with me," he said.

Otto poured whiskey and passed Travis a cup. "I thought you had the world by the tail these days."

Travis tried to explain. "I suppose I've just grown tired of turning murderers loose. I've had my fill of prostitutes, gamblers, and drunks. The drummers at the tavern all sound alike. I've lost interest in the church. Same sermon every Sunday. The same people, the same shallow talk." He paused. "Maybe you should have let me go on up the trail, years ago. I might've been a cattle baron by now."

"Or sleeping in a shallow grave," Otto said. He sipped his whiskey and paused to light his pipe. "Travis, everybody gets blue occasionally. Hell, you're young. Wait till you're an old fart like me."

Travis had taken off his coat and vest in deference to the heat. He unbuttoned his shirt. "I'm more than just blue, Otto. I no longer know for sure where I'm headed."

"Maybe you set your sights too low. You started out to become a wheelhorse lawyer. You've accomplished that in short order. Maybe you need a breather before taking your next step."

"I don't know what that will be."

Otto sat for a time, working with his pipe. "I thought you had your course all mapped out to Austin, maybe Washington. You could do it, you know. You've got enough piss and vinegar in you to do anything you put your mind to."

Travis did not answer.

Otto rambled on. "I think the trick to life is knowing early what you want and going after it. Cast yourself in a mold created by your own imagination. Too many people just drift, like I did. I received a good education, far as it went. Came from a good family. But my mind never fastened on anything. I never cared about the trappings you admire. Fine clothes, expensive cigars. I never knew *what* I wanted. Still don't. Not even now, when it's too goddamned late anyway."

Travis thought back to what was in his mind when he started reading for the law in Captain Tackett's office. "Money was only a part of it," he said. "What I always wanted was to know all there is to know. I used to think that if I could read enough books, talk to enough people, I would find contentment. I no longer believe that. The more I learn, the more I want to know."

Otto gave a gentle chuckle. "Travis, I think what you need is a good woman."

"No!" Travis said emphatically. "Thank God I at least know I'm not constituted to be a family man. For me, the confines of marriage would be stifling."

"I always figured the benefits would more than outweigh the short-comings."

Travis did not answer immediately. Again he was consumed by the feeling that somewhere other than where he was grand events were occurring. "Maybe I should leave Fort Worth," he said. "With the railroad coming, I could sell out for enough to go anywhere, do whatever I want."

Otto shook his head. "If I've learned anything in life, it's that running away is never the answer. The same set of problems will be waiting for you, no matter where you go. Usually you're just set back a notch. You've made a good start here. Hang on."

"I'm tired of smelling the hog wallows in the streets."

"Paris was once a small village with pigs in the streets. So was Athens, Rome, London. This town will develop. Give it a few centuries."

"A lot of towns fall by the wayside," Travis said. "What makes you think Fort Worth will succeed?"

"It has as good a chance as any. Depends on the people. Those living in it now, and the generations to come."

Travis thought of faraway places he had never been, of grand sights he had never seen. "I'm not sure I want to hitch my wagon to this town."

"You've got to start somewhere. You said something a while ago about turning murderers loose. Does that bother you? Maybe that's sticking in your craw."

"Courtroom law is only a game," Travis said. "Like poker. I don't worry about it."

Otto gave him a long, searching look. "You probably know more about these things than I do. But it seems to me there's something in us that drives us to grow, to mend, to build. I've thought about it a lot. Because of me, there are horses and oxen working in good harness all over North and West Texas. I'm satisfied with that. But I think it'll take a lot more to satisfy you, Travis. A hell of a lot more. I doubt that a family would be enough. But it might be a start."

Three nights later Otto died in his sleep. He was found by a neighbor who heard Hector's pitiful whining. The news reached Travis in Denton, where he was trying a case. He returned in time for the funeral.

Otto's handwritten will left his house and possessions to Travis. Since there was no one else to take care of Hector, Travis moved back into the house. The hound refused to eat, and paced day and night in a relentless, doomed search. Two weeks later he died.

Through long nights of grieving, Travis wondered why his own restless spirit lived on.

Travis strolled back to his pavilion in Cold Springs Park, pleased with the reception accorded his Fourth of July speech. For more than two hours he had lectured the crowd on the contributions of the founding fathers of Texas and of the nation. He had been interrupted throughout by applause. The entire speech had been delivered without a bobble, and without a single scribbled note to aid his memory.

Yet he remained troubled.

He had not reached the one person he secretly had hoped to impress. Seated in the first row of folding chairs, Reva Latham had seemed lost in her own daydreams. She had looked at the sky, the children running and playing in the distance, anywhere but at Travis. He had hardly been able to take his eyes off her.

She seemed more beautiful each time he saw her.

Jimmy was waiting beneath the canvas pavilion. He helped Travis take off his sweat-soaked frock coat. "That was sure something, Mr. Spurlock. Suh, where'd you learn to talk like that?"

Travis laughed, recalling that he once had asked the same question on first hearing Captain Tackett speak. "It's a gift, Jimmy. But one that requires considerable application."

"Yessuh," Jimmy said. He helped Travis remove his boots.

Across the meadow the band struck up "Dixie." The crowd cheered. Travis sank onto a canvas chair, certain that he had helped to launch one of the best Fourth of July celebrations in the town's history.

The tent was filled with trapped heat. Travis peeled off his vest and shirt. Jimmy poured a basin of water. Travis washed away the accumulated sweat and dust. Jimmy laid out the costume for the jousting tournament.

"Suh, why do they call the riders knights?" Jimmy asked.

Travis was puzzled for a moment, until he realized the boy had confused "knights" with "nights". He hesitated, wondering how to explain the concept of medieval gallantry to an illiterate former slave. "This is a different word, Jimmy. In olden times, there were men across the seas who rode around, doing nothing but good deeds. They rescued women in distress, saved travelers from highwaymen, and protected the circuit preachers of that day. They had to be good with sword and lance. They practiced their skills at tournaments."

"Yessuh," Jimmy said with a frown, obviously interested, but clearly not understanding.

Travis was glad Jimmy did not pursue the question. He himself did not fully understand the sudden preoccupation of Texans with jousting. Perhaps in part it was because in Texas the 1870s were a barren time for young men of a romantic nature. The windup at Appomattox had ended thirty years of constant fighting for Texans, against Indians, Mexicans, Yankees and—all too frequently—each other. Now the hot-blooded young cavaliers had no war. Colonel Ranald S. Mackenzie and his buffalo soldiers were mopping up the last ragtag bands of Kiowas and Comanches out on the High Plains to the north. Juarez and his followers had overthrown and executed Emperor Maximilian to the south. For the first time in living memory peace reigned on all borders.

The passion for jousting, with roots more solidly in the works of Sir Walter Scott and Sir Thomas Malory than in history, had spread across Texas like a prairie fire. Within months every town had a jousting course and its own champion. Fort Worth was no exception.

Travis had practiced hard for the tournament. He now felt wildly impulsive.

He fully intended to risk his entire future on the outcome.

Carefully, he began to dress.

The black trousers were tight in the Mexican fashion, the legs stuffed into high-shinned boots. The white shirt was heavily layered with lace, emulating a weaving of mail. Heavy in the shoulders, tapering into a short waist, the black bolero coat also was decorated with mailed lace, in imitation of armor.

A trumpet sounded, summoning the knights to the jousting. Travis paused before his mirror to check every last detail of his costume. He then buckled on his wide, flat-bladed sword, picked up his gloves and helmet, and stepped out of the tent and into the relative coolness of the summer day.

His red-and-green guidon was whipping sharply in the breeze before his canopy. His shield, emblazoned with a fancied family crest, hung at the entrance. Up and down the line of gaily colored pavilions the other knights were emerging and preparing to mount. Travis looked across the meadow to the jousting course. Three small rings hung from a horizontal pole twenty-five feet long. The grandstand, decorated with colorful pennants and banners, was now filled with people. Crowds also were gathering at each end of the course.

Jimmy brought Paisana to the front of the pavilion. Travis pulled on his gloves and visored helmet. He mounted, took his lance from its stand, and trotted toward the grandstand.

Although he had drawn the third number, he could not rest easy.

He might be preempted, his impulsive plans wrecked.

The band broke into a spirited version of "The Yellow Rose of Texas." The crowd cheered. Every male Texan knew that the song had been composed in celebration of a high yellow slave named Rose, who had so fascinated the Mexican General Santa Anna that Sam Houston literally caught him with his pants down at San Jacinto. The tune had been a favorite with Hood's Texas Brigade during the war.

Travis and the other knights lined up before the grandstand. The band concluded "The Yellow Rose" to lusty applause. Judge Riley walked to the speaker's stand to assume his role as ruler of the tournament.

"First knight," the judge called out in his high, reedy voice. "What fair damsel do you champion?"

Jesse Farrar rode forward and dipped his lance. "Miss Sarah Langton, sir," he shouted.

With a flurry of pageantry the court attendants escorted Sarah Langton to one of twelve empty chairs in front of Judge Riley. Sarah smiled, pulled off her left glove, and tossed it at her feet. Farrar rode forward, exchanged whispered words with her, picked up the glove, and placed it in his belt.

"Second knight," Judge Riley called. "What fair damsel do you champion?"

Conrad Brinson rode forward. "Miss Ruth Allen!" he called.

Travis almost laughed aloud in relief. He waited patiently until his turn.

"Third knight. What fair damsel do you champion?"

Travis rode forward and dipped his lance. On cue, Paisana curtsied as she had been taught. The crowd applauded. Travis waited for full attention.

"Sir, I champion, and hope to bring honor to, the fairest of the fair, Miss Reva Latham."

A surprised murmur swept through the crowd. Customarily, young ladies were named by aspiring suitors. His choice bordered on a public declaration. The fact that he was the oldest of the knights and she barely fifteen added zest to the revelation. No doubt most of those who knew her still considered her a child.

Reva seemed composed and regal as she was escorted to the row of princesses. Travis waited until she dropped her glove. He rode close to the grandstand.

Her emerald eyes smiled down at him. "Mr. Spurlock, you do me honor, both by naming me, and by the pretty words."

"Pretty words, perhaps. But not empty words."

He picked up her glove and placed it inside his shirt, next to his heart.

The extravagant gesture made Reva laugh. Tilting her head mockingly, she spoke with calculated exaggeration. "Upon brows more worthy could a wreath of chivalry never be placed."

Travis bowed and walked his horse backward, conveying with a smile his recognition of the line from *Ivanhoe*. But he was troubled and mildly offended.

Her tone had conveyed vaguely mocking gaiety, not sincerity.

The first knight snared two rings. The second missed all three. When his turn arrived, Travis swung his horse close to the crowd, allowing the longest possible approach.

He had learned from extensive practice that while most riders tended to hold their horses to a gallop, a full-out run was best. Not only was the faster pace more spectacular, but it also provided a smoother ride. By blending himself to the horse's movements, he could keep the tip of the lance steadier.

Spurring Paisana into a run, he aimed for the first ring, turning slightly in the saddle to cradle the lance firmly with forearm, elbow, and rib cage. The crowd cheered at his unexpected speed. He snared the first ring and the second but missed the third by the breadth of a hair.

Disappointed, he trotted back to the grandstand and lowered his lance. Reva removed the red-ribboned rings from the tip. She seemed amused. "It was the wind, Sir Knight. I saw the last ring move just as you struck."

Travis nodded his agreement. He backed his horse and returned to the tournament.

By the end of the first run only three knights remained—Travis, Farrar and Medford. Each had speared two rings.

The trumpets sounded for the second run. Farrar circled his prancing horse nervously, estimating the distance. A hush fell over the crowd.

Charging, Farrar lowered his lance, its purple and gold streamers rippling behind him. Unerringly, he snared the first, second, and third rings to a roar from the spectators. Raising his visor, he proudly trotted to the grandstand to present the trophies to his lady.

Travis waited while new rings were affixed to the pole. He walked Paisana in a circle, calming her. Then, with a firm touch of his spurs, he again charged down the course, aiming his lance with total concentration. At a dead run he snared all three rings.

He trotted back across the field to the applause of the spectators. He lowered his lance. Reva removed the rings from the tip. She said something to him that he could not hear over the noise of the crowd.

Medford speared only two rings.

Travis and Farrar were left alone on the field.

The heated competition on the course had paled before the battle raging within Reva's own heart.

Had she overplayed her hand?

She knew that Travis Spurlock was a proud man. Too much levity and feigned disinterest might predispose him against her. She must keep him intrigued. And confused. But not angered.

On his last approach to the grandstand she had seen a disturbance, perhaps even irritation, in his eyes.

She sensed that the time had come to change her tactics.

If she was not too late.

His pride made him vulnerable. If he lost the tournament, he would be beyond reach. The outcome was crucial.

Reva held her breath as Jesse Farrar prepared for his run. She felt her heart pounding. Travis waited off to one side, calmly watching.

Gathering his reins, Farrar trotted his horse in two quick circles, then galloped down the track. He plucked the first and second rings. For an instant, Reva thought he had snared the third. But then she saw that she was mistaken. He had struck it a glancing blow, sending it high into the air, spinning around the pole.

The crowd applauded. Farrar came across the grass to the bandstand and presented the two rings to his lady. He glanced back at Travis, grinning an unspoken challenge.

Travis and the crowd waited while new rings were affixed. The crowd grew quiet. The suspense mounted. Still Travis hesitated. He looked toward the grandstand, to Reva, as if seeking a source of strength.

In a sudden communion of spirit she did not fully comprehend, Reva understood that Travis was tormented by some agonizing need that only she could provide.

Overwhelmed by the rampant emotions welling within her, she rose from her chair and did something she later could not account for, even to herself.

She blew Travis a kiss.

Around her, spectators burst into shocked, surprised laughter and applause.

Reva held her head high. She knew her mother would be prostrate with anger. Her sister might never speak to her again. Her father would be morose and troubled for weeks.

At the moment she did not care.

Travis dipped his lance to her in an elaborate, sweeping gesture, and made his horse do its little curtsy.

Then, lowering his visor, he prepared his equipment, made his long, slow circle near the grandstand, and again charged down the course.

Reva heard no sounds other than the thundering of the horse's hooves as Travis bore down upon the targets. The tip of his lance was as steady as a rock.

The first, second, and third rings disappeared from the pole to a sustained roar from the crowd.

Travis trotted back triumphant, holding the rings high, the crimson streamers rippling in the breeze.

Making no effort to hide her excitement, Reva accepted the rings.

When the crowd quieted, Judge Riley spoke. "Honored Knight Travis Spurlock, having vanquished the field, it is now your duty, as well as your privilege, to name the fair lady who will reign over today's festivities as the Queen of Beauty, Honor and Love. You have championed the fair Lady Reva Latham, but it is your undoubted prerogative now to confer this crown on whom you please. Raise your lance."

Judge Riley leaned forward and placed the ornate metal crown on the tip of the lance. Travis walked his horse backward a few paces, then turned and rode back and forth before the grandstand as if searching for a beauty worthy of the prize.

The crowd laughed, delighted with his teasing. Reva felt a blush rising to her cheeks. She was certain he would give the crown to her. But when he paused several times, as if in indecision, her fear grew that he might yet take revenge for her earlier lightheartedness.

At last he rode before her and lowered the crown. She removed it from the tip of the lance. Attendants took it from her and placed it on her head.

Judge Riley escorted her down the steps to the front of the grandstand for the final ceremony. Travis handed his reins to his groom. He drew his sword and knelt at her feet, holding the handle out to her.

Reva took the sword and placed the blade on his shoulder. She did not have to be prompted on the proper words. They were engraved in her heart. "Gallant knight, I declare thee exemplar of valor and chivalry, most worthy of the title Champion of the Tournament."

Travis rose, acknowledged the applause, sheathed his sword, and escorted her back to her seat. He leaned close. "Fair lady, after sundown, would you do me the honor of accompanying me on a walk along the river?"

Reva hesitated only an instant. Her previous, carefully laid strategy demanded that she remain aloof. But intuition now told her that this day must be perfect, an ever-fixed beacon in the trials of love Travis Spurlock would suffer in the days ahead.

She looked up at him in the way she had so often practiced but had not intended to employ until much, much later. "Sir Knight, such gallantry cannot be refused."

Travis returned to his pavilion, adjusted the flaps to admit the breeze, and lay down to rest on his cot. He had no interest in the wrestling matches, sack races, or other sports that would consume the remainder of the afternoon.

Reva Latham remained a puzzle to him. She had been distant, whimsical, even frivolous. Yet before the entire town she had blown a kiss to him—a public act that would have been considered improper even between a couple betrothed.

And in that last moment she had looked up at him with such naked adoration that his blood froze.

He did not know what to make of her.

And while he remained confused by her motives, he was even more mystified by his own. He still felt no inclination toward marriage. But Reva intruded constantly on his thoughts. He kept remembering her graceful walk, the regal way she held her head, the warm caress of her quickest glance.

Eventually he dozed.

He dreamed of Reva.

8

Travis watched the ripple of moonlight on the water. "I hope you didn't consider me presumptuous this afternoon," he said.

"I hardly knew what to think, Mr. Spurlock," Reva said. "It happened so suddenly."

They were strolling along the tree-lined riverbank, faintly illuminated by distant lanterns and the full moon. Across the meadow the Trinity Valley String Quartet was playing "Annie Laurie."

"I should have spoken to you sooner. The truth is, I was not as impetuous as it may have seemed," Travis said. "I would like permission to call upon you. May I speak with your father?"

Reva hesitated. "Mr. Spurlock, perhaps it would be best if I deferred my answer. Mother is very angry with me at the moment. She feels— quite rightly, perhaps—that I may lack the maturity to receive gentleman callers."

Travis could well imagine Millie's anger. No doubt the town gossips were already at work, deploring the forwardness of the Lathams' younger daughter.

"To the contrary, I consider you unusually precocious," Travis said. "I flatter myself that I may have some influence with your mother. Do I have your permission to speak with her?"

"If you like."

The first skyrocket went up, signaling that the fireworks display would begin in five minutes.

Travis walked Reva back toward the grandstand. He found a spot to one side of the crowd and spread a ground cloth as the fireworks exhibition opened.

Reva pointed. "Look! A shooting star!"

The meteorite streaked from the southwest corner of the sky to the northwest. At first it was mistaken for part of the fireworks. After the

error was recognized, the crowd laughed and applauded nature's participation in the celebration.

"Did you make a wish?" Travis asked.

Reva looked at him with that tantalizing smile, so childlike, yet
knowing. "Of course," she said.

"What?"

"I shan't tell you. If I did, it wouldn't come true."

Travis sat pondering the significance of his own impulsive wish,
hurriedly made as the star faded.

He had wished that Reva would become his bride.

After the display ended, he walked her to the Latham carriage. Her
parents were waiting. They greeted Travis with a polite coolness.

Reva turned and offered her hand. "Mr. Spurlock, I thank you for the
honor you have paid me. Truly, it has been a perfect day."

Travis handed her into the carriage. "I do believe that in naming the
fairest of the fair, we should not be dishonest. And thank you. I've never
enjoyed myself more." He turned to her parents. "Doctor, Mrs. Latham,
I hope I may call upon you soon."

Millie answered with a trace of iron in her voice. "At your earliest
convenience, Mr. Spurlock. I believe we have matters to discuss."

For the sake of propriety, Travis waited two days before calling at
the Latham home.

Dr. Latham ushered him into the parlor, where Millie was waiting.
As Travis had expected, Reva was not present. Dr. Latham closed the hall
door.

As soon as they were seated, Millie got right to the point. "Mr.
Spurlock, surely you understand our concern over the public attention
you paid our daughter at the celebration."

Travis nodded solemnly. "Mrs. Latham, the fault is entirely mine. I
hope you'll not blame Miss Reva in the least. There was no collusion on
her part."

Latham sat to one side and remained silent. His wife glanced at him,
then turned back to Travis.

"We're concerned, Mr. Spurlock, because Reva is so young. You're a
worldly man. Surely you recognize her innocence. She isn't prepared for
the disappointments of life."

Travis knew she was alluding to his rejection of Rebecca. He was
prepared. "Mrs. Latham, I wouldn't hurt Miss Reva for the world. I hold
nothing but the highest esteem for you and your family. As you know, I
was one of Rebecca's greatest admirers. But the truth is, I felt that our
temperaments were not of accord. That she is now happily married to
another, and no doubt glad of her good fortune, confirms my judgment.
I've looked upon Reva with favor for many months. If I've caused a

breath of scandal, I want to put it to rest by public demonstration of my sincerity. I request your permission to call on your daughter Reva."

Millie again glanced at her husband. He did not respond. She turned back to Travis. "Mr. Spurlock, we also hold you in high regard. If Reva were a year or two older, we'd be pleased to receive you. We don't want to place her in situations beyond her competence."

Travis dropped his voice into courtroom tones. "Mrs. Latham, I promise that I'll attend her under only the most circumspect of circumstances. I'm sure you've observed that Miss Reva is most intelligent, and unusually mature in thought. I'm confident you can depend on her good judgment."

Latham stirred, and spoke for the first time. "She's headstrong."

Travis smiled. "She has spirit, Dr. Latham. I've long observed that."

Once again, Millie glanced at Latham. This time she apparently received some signal that Travis missed. She hesitated. "We don't want to deny our daughter the enjoyment of your good companionship. We're gratified to know that you share our concern that Reva is so young, yet so advanced in other ways. I'm glad we had this discussion, Mr. Spurlock. You've put our minds at ease. You have our permission. We'll place our trust in you."

Dr. Latham opened the parlor door. Millie called up the staircase. After a moment, Reva slowly descended, one hand managing her skirts, the other trailing behind her for balance. The soft glow of the hall lamp darkened her hair, sent delicate shadows playing along the contours of her face. She paused on the fourth step and gave Travis a dazzling smile before entering the parlor.

"Mr. Spurlock is here to call on you, Reva," Millie said. "He has your father's permission. If you and your father will entertain him for a moment, I'll go see what is keeping Dulcie."

As Dulcie served coffee and cake, Millie filled in the silence. "Dr. Latham mentioned that you've been in Austin recently, Mr. Spurlock. Did you have a pleasant trip?"

"As pleasant as could be expected," Travis said. "Conditions are still somewhat unsettled down there."

Dr. Latham stirred. "What chance do you think Governor Davis has for reelection?"

The question put Travis on familiar ground. "I believe he's on his way out, sir. But we're in for a stormy time until the election."

With the readmission of Texas to the Union and removal of the ironclad oath at the polls, the Carpetbag elements at last had been ousted from the legislature. But Davis, the Reconstruction governor, still held office.

"You see any chance of doing away with the State Police?" Latham asked.

Travis considered the question. Davis had reorganized the Texas Rangers into the State Police, to enforce his Carpetbag government.

"Not until Davis is out of office, sir. I believe he'll veto everything the legislature does."

"We've never stood in greater need of effective young men in Austin. Have you reconsidered the matter?"

"I really haven't had the time, sir. My law practice more than keeps me busy. But I believe the situation in Austin is improving without me."

Millie adroitly shifted the conversation to church activities and local events. Travis followed along with half an ear. His eyes seldom wandered far from Reva's face.

When he rose to leave, she looked up at him with the same naked adoration she had revealed at the Fourth of July celebration. "I'm so glad you came, Mr. Spurlock."

Travis left the Latham home that evening quite confident that he only needed to play out his cards and Reva would be his for the asking.

He was surprised and confused two days later when his note inviting Reva to a Saturday afternoon playparty was returned with regrets and a single handwritten line, "I'm sorry, Mr. Spurlock, but I have made previous plans."

"Did she say anything?" he asked Jimmy.

"No, suh," Jimmy said. "She just kinda laughed, and wrote down what I brung you."

Her refusal left Travis deeply disturbed. But after much consideration, he reasoned that perhaps she *had* made previous commitments before he had declared himself.

His conclusions seemed confirmed with her acceptance of his next invitation, to the volunteer fire company picnic. Throughout the afternoon she remained cheerful, warm, friendly, often smiling at him as if they had some shared secret.

When Travis took her home that evening, he again felt that all was right with the world.

Then she politely declined his next two invitations.

He learned that she was receiving other gentleman callers; apparently his performance at the July Fourth celebration had focused attention on her eligibility.

Travis became so preoccupied with her that he found himself neglecting his law practice. He turned down two murder cases in distant towns because he could not bear the thought of being away for any length of time.

Day and night he thought of nothing else. He doted on their every moment together, every word spoken. Her image remained constantly in his mind's eye. He lived for the moment he would see her again.

Reva was tired. It had been a long, exciting day. The sun was poised on the western horizon, half hidden by post oak and mesquite. "We'll not make it home before dark," she said, her tone conveying more of her concern than she intended.

"The fault is mine," Travis said. "If your parents are angry, I'll take the blame."

Reva watched his large hands on the reins, holding the bays in check. The horses had maintained a steady trot for more than an hour. Their flanks were sleek with froth and they were blowing in a sustained rhythm. The steel tires of the buggy hummed steadily along the hard-packed caliche road.

"I only regret causing them worry," Reva said.

She estimated that they were still six miles or more from town. Although the memory of the last Indian raid remained strong, she was not frightened. Travis was wearing his pistol. A rifle lay nestled at their feet, next to the dashboard.

They had attended the races near Flower Mound in Denton County. Travis had entered three horses in the various heats. Two had won. All three were trotting along behind the buggy. Travis's black boy Jimmy was curled up on the saddle blankets in the boot. The last Reva had looked, he had been asleep.

Travis was deep into one of his mysterious, brooding silences. Reva did not attempt to jar him into conversation. She had become comfortable with his moods, even though she did not understand them.

Jackrabbits had come out to graze in the coolness of late afternoon. Reva entertained herself by catching sight of them in the distance, then watching them hop away at the approach of the buggy. Occasionally she saw coyotes, seldom more than a flick of gray disappearing into the brush. A patch of white to one side of the road attracted her attention. As they drew near, she saw that it was a pile of scattered bones. The skull of a Longhorn lay on the ground, the horns still attached, the dark, hollow eyes staring at her. Reva shivered.

"Cold?" Travis asked. "I'll have Jimmy hand up another blanket."

"No, thank you," Reva said. "I guess someone just walked over my grave."

"We should be there about an hour after dark," Travis said. "We'll have a full moon in a little while."

Reva would have been content if the trip lasted forever.

She had decided to drop all pretense. Throughout the last six months she had led him on a merry chase. But she knew that even the best-hooked fish can slip the barb before it is netted. She did not intend to dally. In three more months she would turn sixteen, and not even Millie would object to her marriage.

Darkness came, and for a time they rode in starlight. Then the moon rose, huge and red-tinged in the eastern sky.

As they entered town, Reva grew apprehensive. She saw that it was quite late. Most of the houses were dark. When she arrived home, she was not surprised to see the hall and parlor lamps lit and her father sitting in the shadows on the gallery.

"I'm afraid I'm in for it," she said. "Father will be furious."

"Let me talk to him," Travis said. "I think I can convince him the fault is entirely mine."

"I'd rather have him angry at me than at you."

Still half asleep, Jimmy came to the front of the carriage to hold the team. Travis helped her to the ground. With dismay she saw that her father had left the gallery and was walking toward them. She was preparing her first words of explanation and apology when she saw his face in the moonlight and realized that he was not angry, but upset. His expression was the one he wore for days after the death of a patient.

He put a hand on Travis Spurlock's shoulder. "Travis, something bad has happened back east. Jay Cooke and his national banks have failed. I don't know the particulars, only reports from the people on the late stage from Dallas. They said the whole country is in an uproar."

Reva was affected more by her father's manner than his words. It was the first time she had heard him address Travis by his Christian name. His comforting hand on Travis's shoulder was the most personal gesture she had ever seen him make toward another man.

"What will it mean for the railroad?" Travis asked.

"I don't think that has been determined yet. A group has gathered in Major Van Emden's office. I've just come from there. I stayed up awhile to give you the news."

"Thank you," Travis said. "Perhaps it isn't as bad as it seems."

"I hope not. The major sent a boy to Dallas, to wire his informants in the East for details. We should know considerably more tomorrow."

Reva did not fully understand the import of the news. But she saw forebodings of tragedy in her father's face, in Travis Spurlock's quick withdrawal into himself. He abruptly said good night and drove away.

She walked up the front steps with her father. "I don't understand, Papa. How could something in the East affect us so?"

"It might stop the building of the railroad. If it does, our boom will collapse. Everyone who has invested in Fort Worth's future will lose his shirt. The newcomers will leave. We'd be just another country village again."

"But the *Democrat* said the railroad has already built past Dallas!"

He held the door open for her and blew out the hall lamp. "If construction stops there, twenty-six miles short, it might as well be twenty-six hundred as far as we're concerned."

Reva went upstairs to her room. She undressed in the dark, put on her nightgown, and sat at her window, looking out at the full moon.

Slowly, she began to understand that she herself might be a principal victim of Jay Cooke's misfortune, even though she had not a dime invested in the national economy.

Major Van Emden scanned through the sheaf of telegrams just delivered from the railhead. Travis was jostled as the crowd pressed closer. "I'm afraid it's even worse than we've feared," the major said. "Apparently Jay Cooke's empire has collapsed like a stack of cards. Banks throughout the East are closed. Prices on Wall Street plummeted so badly yesterday that trading was halted. Some of the nation's largest institutions have closed their doors."

Van Emden continued to leaf through the telegrams. Travis could not understand how a man as rich as Cooke could go broke. He had financed the Union throughout the war, and was now building the Northern Pacific across the nation.

"Is there any word about our railroad?" Travis asked.

Van Emden sighed and held up a scrap of paper. "I have here a message from Mr. Scott of the Texas and Pacific. He offers his regrets but informs me that he has ordered his men to stop laying rail until the situation clears."

The construction crew was at Eagle Ford, a few miles west of Dallas. "If they stop now, Dallas will become the railhead by default," Travis said.

Van Emden nodded. "I'm not optimistic. I happen to know that the financing for the Texas-Pacific is marginal."

"At least we still have the cattle drives and buffalo hide traffic," said one of the newcomers behind Travis.

Van Emden frowned. "My Chicago informant tells me that the price of beef has already fallen dramatically there. I'm sure it'll be only a matter of days before the effect will be felt at the Kansas markets. The downturn has assumed the stature of a national panic. I doubt that the market for buffalo hides will continue to flourish."

Silence reigned as the men in Van Emden's office absorbed the news.

"Then our boom is over," Travis said.

Van Emden tossed the stack of telegrams onto his desk. "That's about the size of it," he said.

On a morning in early spring, Travis grew restless. He had not been out of the house in weeks. After scrambling eggs for breakfast, he set out for the Red Lantern.

He walked through the muddy streets, his mind hardened to the desolation around him. On all sides, houses stood bleak and vacant, the hollow windows staring like eyeless corpses. He passed the square. Most of the buildings were boarded and shuttered. He glanced to the north. Dark gray clouds heralded another approaching cold snap, with its promise of more wind and sleet.

Van Emden's words had proved prophetic. The tent city around Fort Worth had disappeared. The lawyers, doctors, merchants, and myriad speculators who had arrived in anticipation of the railroad departed almost overnight. Most had moved to Dallas and the new railhead. The warehouses and commercial enterprises that rightfully belonged in Fort Worth had taken root in Dallas. The cattle market in Kansas had evaporated. For the first time in six years the Chisholm Trail had remained empty through the driving season.

The winter had been the worst in oldest memory. Snow, ice, and vicious northers had kept everyone indoors. For a time the gnawing worry over the economy had been supplanted by a universal concern for bare survival. Texas had been swept by the most devastating blizzards in history. Foundation herds had been destroyed as far south as the Rio Grande. Some of the most prominent ranchers in Texas were broke.

Months had passed before Travis began to realize the full effect of the Panic on his own situation. Every cent he owned was locked into real estate—scores of lots, a dozen buildings, and several thousand acres in the surrounding countryside. Slowly he came to realize that he could not sell any of his property or, at the moment, even give it away. In fact, he did not have the cash to pay the taxes. Nor did he have prospects. The Red Lantern was barely meeting expenses. His law practice had dwindled to nothing. He had kept the office open until further pretense became ridiculous. He had been forced to sell his horses and carriages for a tenth of their worth, keeping only Paisana.

Once again he had sought refuge in books. He read through the long winter nights and slept through the quiet afternoons.

He found small comfort in the thought that matters could be worse. When the Panic struck, he had been on the verge of asking Reva to marry him.

Now that possibility seemed beyond reach. He had no money, no profession, no prospects.

Jay Jay was alone at the bar, reading a New Orleans newspaper. He glanced up at Travis with unconcealed amusement. "Good Lord, I mistook you for a grizzly bear."

Travis had grown accustomed to the teasing about his beard. "Any customers today?"

Jay Jay poured him a glass of bourbon. "Three fellas came through on their way to California. They were looking to drink on credit. I sent them on their way."

Travis looked at the dusty balcony, the curtained stage. The cribs behind the saloon were boarded and nailed, the prostitutes gone to greener pastures. Jay Jay now served drinks from the forward end of one bar in the barnlike building. The ghostly echoes in the cavernous interior cast a deadly pall. Fort Worth, once the liveliest town in the West, was a tomb. The Red Lantern, the eye of the hurricane during the town's grandest nights, was now its saddest sight.

"Hear the new Dallas joke?" Jay Jay asked.

"Which one?"

"Remember Cowart?"

Travis nodded. After the Panic struck, Cowart had closed his law office and moved to Dallas.

"He says Fort Worth is so dead he saw a panther asleep on the courthouse steps at high noon."

"He could be right," Travis said.

"Maybe so, but that's a hell of a way to treat your old friends. They quoted him in the *Dallas News*. I hear everybody over there's laughing about it."

Travis sipped the whiskey and felt its warmth spread. "Jay Jay, if you want to close this place and move on, I'll understand."

Jay Jay shook his head. "From what I hear, conditions are bad all over. I'm getting by. The wife and kids are still eating. I'll hang on awhile longer."

"I can't promise you anything," Travis warned.

Jay Jay folded his arms on the bar. "Hell, this town may come back yet. I damned sure want to be here if it does."

Travis finished his drink. He left the saloon, heading toward the Latham home, a friendly game of cooncan with Dr. Latham and, if he was lucky, a glimpse of Reva.

Although he still daydreamed from time to time of leaving for some distant place where exciting events were daily occurrences, he consoled himself with the thought that he was now in a temporary period of retreat. Eventually he would emerge triumphant.

But above all else was one overriding concern that held him to Fort Worth: he could not find it in himself to leave Reva.

He could not win her.

But neither could he leave her.

Through three long years Reva watched the disintegration of Travis Spurlock with a heart so aching that she expected it to burst any day. Persistent rumors came that he was losing his mind. His neighbors reported that he read through the nights and slept through the days. They said he often roamed the streets, talking to himself.

Living from day to day, Reva wondered how long she could endure her suffering. Travis visited two or three times a week, ostensibly to play cooncan with her father. He seemed so desolate. He sat at card games for hours, casting such sad glances at her that she often went to her room to weep.

But she had quickly learned not to invite him to stay for supper.

His pride would not tolerate charity.

He now treated her as a sister. On the rare occasions when he took her for long walks along the river, he spoke of everything but love. Reva knew the truth: he would never propose without prospects. It did not matter that she happily would live in a sod shanty out on the treeless plains, if it meant living with him.

Other suitors still came to call occasionally. She quietly discouraged them, one by one. Travis continued to hang around the house like a faithful, morose old hound.

As the years passed, Reva also saw deterioration in herself. The secret beauty formula, handed down through five generations of her mother's family, gradually yielded to Texas sun and wind.

As her nineteenth birthday approached, Reva Latham felt ancient. She was certain she was doomed to die an old maid.

9

Travis was deep into the translation of an eso-
teric passage of Epictetus when he heard the knock at the door. He was
appalled to find Major Van Emden on the front porch. He invited the
major in even though the house was in shambles.

The major seemed not to notice. "Travis, we can't go on this way," he
said, dropping into Otto's old rocker. "When I look back over the last
three years, I wonder how we've survived. The time has come for us to do
something."

"What?"

"I have a plan. A few days ago I telegraphed Mr. Bond of the Texas
and Pacific Railway to let me know when he next would be in Texas. I've
just received a reply. He'll be visiting Marshall this week. I want you to go
with me to see him. You are a most persuasive speaker when you put your
mind to it."

Travis thought of his lack of clothes and money. "What do you hope
to accomplish?"

Van Emden paused. "I want to convince Mr. Bond that his company
must build the railroad on into Fort Worth."

"I read his statement in the *Democrat* last week," Travis reminded
the major. "He said the railroad has no money."

Van Emden nodded. "But suppose the people of Fort Worth should
offer to underwrite the construction. What do you suppose he would
say?"

For a moment Travis wondered if the major had lost his mind. His
doubts must have shown on his face. The major explained.

"Property here may be without value now. But with the promise of a
railroad the picture would change dramatically. If we can receive assurances that the railroad will build the final twenty-six miles, I believe I can
obtain sufficient mortgage loans to cover the costs of construction."

Travis immediately grasped the major's desperate plan; the town in effect would place itself in hock to pay for bringing in the railroad. He hesitated, uncertain what to say. If the railroad could be built, the boom of early 1873 would return.

Again he would be a wealthy man.

But the risks would be enormous. He thought of the sheer physical feat of grading the path for a railroad through twenty-six miles of hardwood timber and uneven terrain. There would be rocky hillsides to level, numerous creeks and streams to ford. He also thought ahead to legal problems that might be insoluble.

The T&P's right-of-way grant from the state was only a few months away from expiration.

"We wouldn't have much time," he said.

The major nodded. "I know. I've made transportation arrangements for us to leave tomorrow."

The Fort Worth delegation was received by Frank S. Bond himself in his office at the end of his private railway car. He rose, shook hands, and graciously gestured his visitors into chairs facing his massive desk. Overwhelmed by the magnificence of the railcar's appointments, Travis sank into a red velvet bergère and looked at his surroundings. The walls were dark-paneled, the furniture of heavily carved giltwood. The brass spittoons gleamed like gold. Over the desk hung a huge painting of a train, heavily loaded, pulling a long grade, with black smoke pouring from its wide funnel. A few hundred feet in front of the train, most improbably, a construction crew was busily laying track. Behind the train, even more improbably, a small city was bustling with activity, smoke rising from the chimneys of factories. Farmers were tilling lush green fields at the city's edge. A brass plate on the picture proclaimed its title: *Westward the Course of Empire Makes Its Way.*

Travis turned his full attention back to his host.

Frank S. Bond was well over six feet, broad of shoulder, and heavily muscled. His weathered, deeply lined face betrayed much exposure to the elements. As he passed around a box of cigars, Travis saw that the other four members of the Fort Worth delegation were also taking Bond's measure.

Travis was tired. He, Van Emden, Paddock, John Peter Smith, and James Jarvis had left Fort Worth before midnight, boarding the train in Dallas shortly after dawn. The hundred-and-forty-mile trip to Marshall had been accomplished in eight hours. His new suit, bought on credit, restored much of his old confidence. He had carefully trimmed his beard and wore a new black hat that stopped just short of a Mexican sombrero.

Bond took a cigar for himself, bit off the end, and replaced the box on his desk. He waited until all cigars were lit and the office had assumed a blue haze. "Gentlemen, I'm most honored by your visit. What can I do for you?"

Major Van Emden took the question. "Mister Bond, we're here to find out when you're going to carry out your promise to extend the railroad on into Fort Worth."

Bond smiled. "Surely you know the condition of the present economy. Unfortunately, financing simply isn't available."

"You don't expect the situation to improve?" Van Emden asked. "You have no plans to begin construction soon?"

Bond shook his head. "Not in the foreseeable future."

"But aren't you able to buy rails on credit?"

Travis recognized the question as a trap. Bond walked into it still smiling. "We can buy *rails* on credit, Mr. Van Emden. But you see, there's no money for grading the roadbed. That's a short-term commitment. We don't have the available cash."

Van Emden sprang the trap. "Mister Bond, we're prepared to undertake the contract for grading the road. We'll accept your note, due in a reasonable length of time."

Bond stared at Van Emden for a long moment. He glanced at his other guests, then burst into laughter. "Major, you can't be serious! Do you know what is involved?"

Travis spoke for the first time, lowering his voice into its old, familiar courtroom resonance. "I assure you, sir, the major is not being facetious. You'd do well to attend us. Your railroad stands to profit a great deal from our enterprise."

Bond's lingering smile faded. "Gentlemen, my apologies if I've offended you. But you're businessmen. Not railroaders. You just don't realize what a tremendous amount of labor this entails."

"I assure you that we do," Travis said.

"Your proposal is unprecedented," Bond insisted. "The building of a railroad requires specialists. Surveyors. Engineers. Trained laborers. Special equipment."

"Understand us, sir," Travis said. "We'll obtain the necessary equipment. We'll organize a construction company and hire the specialists. All we need from you is a contract, under terms mutually agreeable."

Bond frowned in thought, then shook his head. "Preposterous. Young man, you're talking about twenty-six miles of railroad. Our land-grant arrangement with the state expires with this term of the Texas Legislature. We have it on good authority that we'll not be granted an extension. Without that arrangement, further construction is impossible."

"We're well aware of the time limitation," Travis said. "That's why we must have our answer today."

Bond bridled like a startled colt. "You certainly drive a hard bargain, Mr. . . ."

"Spurlock," Travis said, stressing each syllable. "Travis Barclay Spurlock."

Travis saw the name register. Bond gave him a long, hard study. "I assure you, Mr. Spurlock, that if I committed the railroad to such a venture, I'd be laughed out of the company. I've been building railroads for more than twenty years. I've never heard of an arrangement such as you propose."

Travis rose and crossed to the map. "Mr. Bond, I'm sure you agree that the economy won't be down forever. Indeed, it's already showing signs of recovery. When that happens, with your railroad terminating in Dallas, and loss of the right-of-way on west, you'll be missing more than half the commerce you might enjoy in that region. If the terminus were here, in Fort Worth, you'd be supplying the Chisholm Trail, the greatest cattle enterprise ever envisioned. You'd be one day's travel closer to the burgeoning ranch country here to the west. Fort Worth is connected by stage to county seat towns in every direction, an aggregate population of more than twenty thousand people. Buffalo hides from the High Plains would be placed closer to your railroad, making Fort Worth a more practical loading point than those in Kansas now served by the Missouri Pacific. Knowledgeable persons say the day of the Longhorn is numbered. Already, shorthorn cattle are breeding in the ranch country, cattle that can't be driven long distances without grievous loss of weight. For the first time, rail shipment will be more economical than trail driving. The railroad that first enters Fort Worth will be in command of this vast market. Mr. Bond, if your railroad misses this opportunity, it will forever be a mere branch line, rather than a transcontinental trunk."

Bond listened to Travis with a troubled frown. "Mr. Spurlock, you present a convincing argument. I can see that there's much in what you say. But the risks are simply too great."

Travis spoke quietly. "Mr. Bond, the five gentlemen before you today are risking everything acquired in a lifetime, the security of families, friends, our very future. Yet we're willing to take that risk for your railroad, because we have every confidence in the outcome."

Bond studied Travis through a lengthy silence. "How do you propose to finance your company?"

Travis saw the opening and plunged. "We presently have capital stock of twenty-five thousand dollars pledged. With your promise of a contract, we'll be fully organized and at work within the week."

"What about experienced men?"

"Because of the present economic situation, many good engineers are out of work. We've talked with several. They're awaiting our word. One of our directors will be Mr. Jesse Zane-Cetti, who settled in Fort Worth after your railroad stopped building at Eagle Ford."

Bond seemed impressed. "A good man."

"We've negotiated a tentative contract with Roche and Tierney for the grading. They're ready to start to work."

Bond could not conceal his surprise. Roche and Tierney was one of the largest construction companies in Texas. He looked at the map and frowned. "What terms do you propose?"

After three hours of negotiation, the contract was completed. Under the agreement, the Tarrant County Construction Company would prepare the roadbed. The Texas & Pacific Railway Company would lay the track.

Bond agreed to accompany his chief engineer to Fort Worth the following week. "Remember, the first train must enter Fort Worth before this session of the legislature adjourns in Austin," he warned. "Time is of the essence."

Van Emden reached into his coat pocket. "I have here a telegram, already prepared for dispatch by your telegrapher. A boy and a fast horse are waiting in Dallas to carry the word to Fort Worth. Mr. Bond, machinery will be in motion by daylight tomorrow."

Fort Worth awoke from its three-year sleep. Travis saw the changes immediately on his return from Marshall. Anticipation hung in the air.

Within days Van Emden arranged mortgages with a consortium of state bankers. Property owners trooped in and signed, converting the money to shares in the construction company.

In apparent defiance of its new, heavily indebted state, the town burst into activity. Paintbrushes appeared. Soon the clapboard buildings around the square assumed a new look. The first construction crews arrived and moved their families into long-vacant houses. Each morning long trains of wagons left with men and equipment for the work camps. In the evening they returned with reports of remarkable progress, of formidable obstacles overcome. The town's bootstrap project received heartfelt prayers in the churches, spirited toasts in the bars.

Travis worked far into each night, clearing titles, processing deeds, and legalizing various partnerships and enterprises. In the acre, Jay Jay peeled the boards from the cribs and hung the mattresses out to air. He polished the long bars and restocked the shelves. At night he wrote letters to various portions of the country, disseminating the good news.

Within days extra stagecoaches and hacks were required to bring passengers from the railhead in Dallas. The new arrivals were a curious lot. Lawyers, doctors, and prosperous merchants shared coaches, hacks, and buggies with prostitutes, gamblers, and confidence men. Dumped en masse in front of Andrews Tavern, they wandered the streets, as cautious as stray cats, until they found their own kind and took up their new lives.

Soon every building on the square was occupied. Again tents appeared on the fringes of town. Hammers sounded from dawn to dusk. Blocked on the north and east by the river, the town expanded to the south and west.

Totally immersed in his work, Travis did not allow himself to think about Reva.

He recognized that his situation was now even worse.

Before, he had merely been broke and without prospects.

He was still broke, and now everything he owned was mortgaged. If the railroad construction scheme failed, he would not only lose all but would have to work for years, perhaps the remainder of his life, to pay off his debts.

Moreover, he was plagued by dark premonitions. The legislature was nearing adjournment. Time was running out on the construction crews as they met a succession of obstacles—streams flooded by spring rains, delays in delivery of equipment, strata of solid rock that had to be removed by tedious blasting. Costs were escalating, and no more money was available.

Night after night, Travis lay awake, worrying.

When at last he fell into an exhausted, deep sleep, he once again was visited by the headless major.

Reva was confused. She had assumed that with the return of prosperity Travis would renew his courtship. But to her bewilderment and dismay, he no longer came to the house to visit, not even to play cuonican with her father. Each Sunday in church he nodded politely, told her how lovely she looked, and moved on, leaving her to ride home with her parents like an old maid.

The entire town was alive with excitement over the coming of the railroad. Each time she went downtown she saw new stores, new people. She learned that Travis had reopened his law office and was so busy that he had added two assistants. Once, emerging from a store, she saw him approaching on the sidewalk. Abruptly he turned, crossed the street, and disappeared into the crowd around a land office. The incident left her shaken. She was certain that Travis had seen her and purposefully avoided her.

Hurt, angry, and at the end of her patience, she could not decide whether Travis had lost interest in her or was merely taking her devotion for granted.

"Travis Spurlock is careless with his affections," Millie told her. "Remember how he treated Rebecca!"

"I wonder if I've done something to offend him," Reva said.

"Nothing except to give him three years of your life," Millie said. "You've made a doormat of yourself. Who has respect for a doormat?"

After thinking the matter through, Reva felt there might be something in what her mother said.

She grew more infuriated with Travis each passing day. On a bright Sunday morning, as Travis approached her on the church lawn to perform his ridiculous ritual, her anger took charge. As he swept off his hat and opened his mouth to speak, she turned her back and strode away toward the carriage.

Not until later did she realize she had created a scene the town gossips would relish.

But she was beyond caring. Her mother was right. It was high time she considered her own feelings.

"We're in trouble," said Major Van Emden. "Bad trouble. Mr. Darnell is gravely ill in Austin, perhaps on his deathbed. The legislature is preparing to adjourn."

For a moment Travis was revisited by the dark forebodings that had plagued him for weeks. Without Tarrant County Representative Nicholas Darnell's presence on the floor, there would be no way to block adjournment of the legislature. And if the railroad did not reach Fort Worth before adjournment, the Texas & Pacific would not receive sixteen sections of land for each mile of track completed. Shorn of that inducement, the company would be forced to abandon the project.

"Has the legislature set a date?" Travis asked.

The major shook his head. "The particulars I've received, all confidential, suggest that the remaining legislation will be cleared within days. The motion for adjournment is expected before the middle of next week."

Travis groaned. The T&P tracks were now ten miles short of town. At the present pace, the construction crews would need at least another month.

"It seems we should be able to do something," Van Emden said.

"I'll put my mind to it," Travis promised.

That evening, unable to concentrate on his work, he went home early. He sat for hours, seeking a solution to the problem. And as he pondered, he grew angry, remembering the way the Panic of 1873 turned his wealth to ashes in a single night.

Now the three long years of waiting had cost him Reva. Apparently her heart had hardened against him. He cringed at the humiliation of her turning her back on him before the whole congregation of the church.

But he was helpless to do anything about it—not while faced with the prospect of spending the remainder of his life in servitude, paying off monumental debts.

He thought again of the hawk and the rabbit.

Somehow, he must find a way to bring in the railroad on time.

He wrestled with the problem throughout the night and emerged with three possible solutions. The first was precarious. There was little likelihood of forcing new bills onto the floor of the legislature so late in the session. The second possibility was beyond mortal control. Representative Darnell either would or would not die. He might live long enough to stay adjournment. That matter was in God's hands.

Only one avenue lay open to avert disaster: somehow, the construction must be speeded to an astounding degree.

After daylight he hurried to Van Emden's office. "What's our population now?" he asked.

Van Emden considered the question. "From a low of about three hundred and fifty souls right after the Panic, I would guess we have now fifteen hundred, perhaps two thousand people."

From merchandising Van Emden had expanded into banking. His estimate was probably the best available.

"And every one of those two thousand people has a vested interest in the completion of the railroad," Travis pointed out. "That gives us a veritable army."

Van Emden smoothed his silvery goatee. "Travis, I can tell you with authority that almost everyone in town is strapped. All significant capital is already invested in the project."

"I'm not thinking of capital," Travis explained. "I'm talking about labor. I'm remembering that in numbers the Chinese can move mountains, a bucket of dirt at a time. We don't have millions of Chinese, but we have two thousand people who might be willing to do the work."

Van Emden remained silent, thinking it through. "At least we'll determine how badly the people of this town want a railroad," he said.

By noon of the following day the community was organized. All the able-bodied men and boys were equipped with hoes, picks, shovels, axes, plows—any and every tool capable of moving earth, brush, and rocks—loaded on wagons, and moved off to the construction site. The women and girls drew assignments to help prepare and cook food for transportation to the work camps. Every kitchen was put to use. Children were called in from play to snap beans, shuck corn, shell peas, peel potatoes.

Under the pressure of the emergency, the social structure gave way. Gamblers rolled up their sleeves and worked beside bankers and lawyers. Prostitutes who had almost forgotten their family names toiled beside matrons who had never seen the inside of a dance hall or saloon. Every nonessential store and office in town was closed, and the clerks and storekeepers went out to work on the railroad.

Travis assumed charge of the timber-clearing operation. With axes and whipsaws his crew removed the trees and heavy tangles of brush. The remaining stumps were blasted out with dynamite. Mule teams dragged all rubbish to one side, where it was piled and burned.

Close behind his crew came mules and heavy draft horses pulling graders and slip-scrapers, leveling the ground, slicing through hillsides, and filling in ravines. Impacted rocks were removed by shovel, pick, mules, and muscle.

After the roadbed was smoothed, graveled, and tamped, the ties and rails were laid by work gangs from the Texas & Pacific. With darkness, lanterns were lit and work continued far into the night. Every man was expected to remain at his duties until he dropped. Cots were supplied to allow each man a few hours of sleep before returning to his job.

By the end of the second day Travis was in despair. None of his crew was accustomed to such hard physical labor. Blisters, tired muscles, and aching backs were taking a heavy toll. On the first day they advanced no more than a quarter of a mile. On the second, even less.

"At this pace, it'll take us forty days," he told Van Emden. "We must move faster."

"The spirits are willing, but the flesh is weak," Van Emden said. "Don't worry, Travis. They'll toughen in a few days."

Word spread through the camps that Fort Worth's desperate effort was causing considerable hilarity throughout the state. Crews hauling the rails brought newspapers from Dallas containing cartoons and humorous stories making fun of the town that had closed down to go out and work on the railroad. On Sunday, sightseers came from as far as fifty miles away to witness the spectacle. Dallas residents drove out, picnicked on the hillsides, and watched Fort Worth's labor with amusement.

By the fifth day, blisters were turning into calluses. Muscles were growing firm. The rails advanced a full half mile.

For the first time, Travis grew optimistic. "We're getting the hang of it," he told Van Emden one evening. "At this pace, we'll be into town in fifteen more days."

"That may not be soon enough," the major said. "I've received word from Austin. Motion was made yesterday for the legislature to adjourn. Nicholas Darnell was carried into the House chamber on a stretcher. He cast the sole dissenting vote."

Travis knew vaguely that a unanimous vote was required for adjournment. But he did not know if escape clauses existed in the rules. "How long can he keep them in session?"

Van Emden looked toward Fort Worth, still eight miles away.

"As long as he lives," he said. "His doctors now believe that may be only a matter of hours."

Riding high in the back of the heavy farm wagon, Reva grabbed a tub of boiled potatoes just as it started to slide toward the endgate. "Please be more careful!" she shouted to the driver. "We don't want to dump this food on the ground!"

The driver grunted his acknowledgment. But he had his own hands full. They were now descending a steep hill over rough, rocky terrain. The wagon tipped dangerously. Standing with his feet braced, the driver pulled back on the leaders with all his strength and fought to keep the teams in their traces. Reva clung to the sideboards for support and held her breath. Slowly the wagon righted and eased down the hillside into a flat, graveled wash.

Reva wiped perspiration from her forehead. She had never worked so hard in her life. Each day she arose hours before daylight to perform all kinds of unaccustomed tasks—peeling potatoes, culling beans, washing pots and pans, and laboring over a wood cookstove in the summer heat. All over town, women were working in the kitchens alongside their servants, preparing mountains of food to be delivered to the churches, where it was assembled and loaded onto wagons. The younger women took turns accompanying the meals out to the work camps. Reva was on her first trip. Despite the heat and heavy work, she wore one of her favorite dresses—the green one that Travis Spurlock twice had commented upon favorably. Although she had heard much talk about the chaotic conditions at the construction site, she hoped desperately to see him, if only from a distance.

She also had news to deliver. Major Van Emden had received a late message from Austin. Miraculously, Representative Darnell still lived. Each day for five days he had been carried into the House chamber in Austin to cast his vote against adjournment. Prayer services were being held for him twice each day in Fort Worth churches.

The driver rose to his feet again and pointed. "They's just ovah that hill, Miss Reva. You can see where they's burnin' brush, and raisin' dust. We'll be there directly."

Blinding heat shimmered off the limestone hillside. Reva stood in the jolting wagon, grasped the sideboards for support, pulled her bonnet lower to shield her eyes from the glare, and stared at the rising cloud of dust. Suddenly the sharp concussion of an explosion buffeted the air. She screamed.

Her driver laughed. "Blastin', Miss Reva," he said. "They's blastin' out tree stumps."

The four horses struggled their way up the next steep hill. As the wagon reached the top, the breathtaking panorama of the construction site came into view.

More than five hundred men swarmed over the hillsides like ants. In the foreground, work crews and teams were clearing away timber. Several hundred yards behind them, six-, eight-, and ten-mule teams were working with huge road graders, cutting a deep slash into a hillside. Another crew was building a wooden bridge over a ravine. Farther back, men and teams with slip-scrapers, picks, and shovels were leveling the roadbed. In the distance a locomotive backed along the completed track, pushing a flatcar loaded with ties and rails. Reva searched, but she could not find Travis Spurlock in the swarming activity.

"They's set up some tables over yonder in the shade," her driver said. "The men come in about a hundred at a time to eat."

He drove down the hillside to a shady glade. Strong hands helped her from the wagon. She immediately set to work, directing the unloading of the food and its placement on the tables.

More than two hours later she at last turned away from the empty tables, exhausted, sodden with perspiration. She walked down a grassy slope to the nearby creek, wet a cloth, lifted her hair, and sponged her face and neck. When she looked up, Travis Spurlock was standing on a small wooden bridge over the stream, ax in hand, watching her.

Perhaps in that moment she would have remained silent if she had not sensed pain in his expressionless gaze. As he abruptly turned away, she called out to him. "Mr. Spurlock, I would speak with you."

He hesitated, studied her for a moment, walked to the end of the bridge, and carefully picked his way down the steep embankment.

Never before had Reva seen him without coat and tie. He now wore only soiled trousers, boots, and a thin undershirt. But no one, ever, could have mistaken him for a common laborer. His bearing, his quiet, commanding presence bespoke power. Reva was momentarily distracted by the sight of the rock-hard muscles rippling under tanned, naked skin. Dark, corded veins stood out on his arms. As he came near, she was engulfed for a moment by the mingled smells of sweat, raw earth, green trees, and maleness. He shifted the ax to his left hand and swept off his hat. He smiled. "Miss Latham. How nice to see you again."

Momentarily taken aback by the pointed avoidance of her first name, Reva regretted the impulse that made her call to him. She did not know what to say. And in that instant, all planning, pretense, and convention fell away.

"Mr. Spurlock, we seem to have become estranged," she said quietly. "I want you to know that I regret this. If the situation came about through some fault of my own, I apologize. I have ever valued you as a friend, and shall continue to do so."

Travis looked at her for an interminable interval without speaking. Almost as if the sight of her were too much to bear, he gazed into the distance, his face still expressionless.

He turned back to her and spoke in the rich, resonant voice that had so long haunted her sleep. "Miss Reva, I assure you that I hold no living person on this earth in higher esteem. And let me further assure you that you have done nothing to give me offense." He paused, as if uncertain how far to go. Rivulets of sweat flowed from his temples, across the high cheekbones, and into the neck of the thin undershirt.

"The fault is mine," he went on after a moment. "The truth of the matter, Miss Reva, is that I am not yet prepared to speak my thoughts to you. I hope and pray that opportune moment will yet arrive. But until then, I'm uncomfortable in your presence. Driven to speak, I constantly must hold my tongue."

At first, Reva did not understand. Then she remembered the man's monumental pride. Common sense should have told her that restoration of his wealth played a major role in his intentions toward her.

She felt a rush of color to her face. "Mr. Spurlock, I've overstepped. Now *I'm* uncomfortable."

He smiled. A shout came from the top of the knoll, meaningless to Reva, but apparently of urgent significance to him. "You haven't overstepped," he said. "In your wonderful way, you've said exactly the right thing." He glanced to the top of the knoll. "I must go. Good-bye, until later." He replaced his hat and, light as a cat, jumped the small stream and moved swiftly away.

Seized by a desperation she did not fully understand, Reva again called to him. "Mr. Spurlock?"

He stopped and turned. "Yes?"

"When you are prepared to speak your thoughts, perhaps I shall be inclined to speak my own."

A transformation of awesome proportions swept over his face. The dark, impenetrable eyes softened, the stern, expressionless countenance changed. For a moment Reva felt she was looking directly into the depths of his soul. Even in the bright sunlight he seemed surrounded by a celestial aura. Across the small bubbling brook, separated by hardly more than their arms' lengths, they exchanged silent communication of such unbounded adoration that Reva felt she might swoon.

The next she knew, Travis was climbing the steep bank of the stream, his tight trousers revealing the powerful muscles of his thighs and buttocks. He topped the rise and disappeared.

Reva stood in the creek bottom, trembling, appalled at her outspoken defiance of all convention. Yet she was filled with a calm, inner peace.

She returned to the wagon with a firm resolve to say nothing to her mother, or anyone, of what had just transpired.

She intended to keep the blessed moment a secret until she was carried to her grave.

Breaking through a tangle of underbrush, Travis wiped the sweat from his eyes and looked westward. Fort Worth lay on the horizon, less than two miles distant. He sank to the ground, exhausted.

One by one, his crew came out of the post oak and sprawled on the hard, rocky ground. They closed their eyes, rubbed aching muscles, and strained for breath in the sweltering heat. The waterboy had said that the thermometer at camp registered a hundred and six in the shade. Travis had no doubt the air on the open hillside was closer to a hundred and twenty.

He heard shod hooves on the rocks below. Chief Engineer D. W. Washburn had left the survey crew, and was picking his way across a shallow draw. Staggering to his feet, Travis strode down the slope to intercept him.

Washburn nodded a greeting and swung down from the saddle. He stood holding the reins as Travis approached.

"Mr. Washburn, my men are beat," Travis said. "I don't think they'll make it through the remainder of the day."

Washburn regarded Travis with hollow eyes. Travis knew the engineer had suffered as much as anyone.

"I've just talked with the major," Washburn said. "We agreed we must do something. Word came a while ago. Darnell still lives. But he's now slipping in and out of a coma."

Travis removed his hat and wiped the sweat from his forehead. Each day for fourteen days, save Sundays, Darnell had been carried into the House chamber on a cot to cast his vote to block adjournment.

Now the goal was in sight. But if Darnell went into a coma and could not speak, the town's marathon project would yet end in disaster.

Now Travis felt that the stakes were far greater than merely losing his life's savings and being saddled with horrendous debts.

He stood to lose far more.

He remembered the way Reva had looked in the creek bottom, telling him in so many words that if he asked, she would marry him.

He gazed at Fort Worth in the distance. "So near, and yet so far."

Washburn nodded. "We can't hope for Darnell to do more. He may have given his life as it is. Major Van Emden has proposed that we make one last effort. Tonight at sundown we'll conduct a rally. The major said to tell you to be in good voice."

"We're still almost two miles short," Travis said. "At least three days. What can we do?"

Washburn pointed across the distant washes and creeks. "The agreement with the state only calls for us to lay track and to run a train into Fort Worth. The exact wording doesn't say how it should be done, Mr. Spurlock. I don't know about you, but I fully intend to have a train into Fort Worth by noon tomorrow."

Lanterns flickered in the surrounding trees. Standing in the bed of a wagon, Travis looked down on the faces of more than five hundred exhausted men. He knew he must keep his speech brief, but effective.

"Remember how the people drove out from Dallas two weeks ago, looked upon our labors, and laughed?" he asked. "They were of the opinion that we would fail. I'm telling you tonight that we will succeed!"

A few cheers and rebel yells came from the crowd. Travis waited until the sound died away.

"Texas is unique," he went on. "The people of Dallas have forgotten that fact, if they ever knew it. When we Texans set our minds to it, we can accomplish the impossible. This state possesses a record as wild, romantic, and heroic as any on the face of the earth! No minstrel's lay ever told of deeds more daring than those at the Alamo, where fewer than two hundred Texans battled an army of thousands to a standstill for thirteen glorious days! Then there are the sanctified fields of San Patricio, Agua Dulce, Refugio, Goliad, San Jacinto. I need not enumerate all the illustrious battlefields of Texas to you men. You know them as well as I. No castle hall of yore ever resounded to such deathless legends as Texas possesses. They are ingrained in our very souls!"

Again, Travis was interrupted by yelling and cheering, this time stronger. He waited for quiet. "Most of us here have done our duty in battle. But gentlemen, the time of the soldier is over. Today we face new and perhaps even graver challenges."

He raised his voice. "Gentlemen, I predict that we here tonight shall go down in legend as the builders! We here tonight have been ordained by God to come forth into this wilderness to found great cities! Where but a few short years ago the naked savage held dominion, we have constructed homes, churches, schools, commercial enterprises of great scope and import. Gentlemen, *that* shall be *our* legend! Let us live so that in future years our children, and our children's children, shall look back on our time and marvel. Let us resolve tonight that we shall not fail them."

Travis let the applause build, then held out his arms for quiet.

"Mr. Washburn, our chief engineer, has proposed that we change our method. Instead of laying permanent track we shall, from this moment on, concentrate solely on taking the first train into Fort Worth. Mr. Washburn believes that if we work all night, we can accomplish our task by noon tomorrow. I say we can do it *before* noon tomorrow! I say let's get to work!"

Travis leaped from the wagon to a thunderous response. He picked up his ax, seized a lantern, and set off into the darkness.

In the first hour after dawn the tracks emerged from the woods and entered the final mile. With his work completed, Travis and his crew dropped back to help prepare the roadbed.

Washburn gave Travis only minimal instructions. "Just take care to keep the road level," he said. "Don't worry about drainage or rough spots. We can fix those later."

By midmorning the tracks reached Sycamore Creek.

"We don't have time to build a bridge," Washburn said. "Let's make a crib of lumber and ties. That'll do."

Once past the creek, the roadbed was forgotten. Ties and rails were laid on the hard rough ground and anchored with stones.

At 11:23 A.M. on July 19, 1876, the first train chugged into Fort Worth, a plume of black smoke pouring from its stack, its whistle screaming amidst the constant gunfire.

Its arrival ignited a celebration of monstrous proportions. The railroad crews were paid off in Fort Worth, instead of Dallas, upon promise that no arrests would be made for public drunkenness.

Each portion of Fort Worth celebrated in its own way. Prostitutes who had labored over cookstoves and laundry tubs for two long weeks continued their civic duty in the cribs. Bartenders who had gone weeks without sufficient sleep laid aside their picks and shovels to preside over their professional domains. The doors of every church were opened for prayer services, and thanks were given to God for Fort Worth's deliverance. Neither the accidental fire that destroyed the courthouse during

the celebration nor the astounding news of the disaster on the Little Big
Horn dampened spirits.

Three weeks later, in a fitting climax to the festivities, Travis Spurlock and Reva Latham were married. They boarded an eastbound train
for a long honeymoon in New Orleans.

BOOK TWO

A Bunch of Wildness

The railroad brought its evils as well as its benefits. For several years Fort Worth was the clearing house between the legally constituted society of the East and the free and untrammeled life of the West. Here the currents of humanity met, and in the swirling vortex that ensued could be found every class of mankind.

> Buckley B. Paddock
> *Fort Worth and Northwest Texas*
> Fort Worth, 1922

In Fort Worth, there was an 11th Commandment: Thou Shalt Not Mess With J. Frank Norris.

> Alf Evans
> Fort Worth newspaperman

10

The coming of the railroad transformed Fort Worth into a city as exotic as Baghdad. Travis often walked the streets, savoring the strange sights, the unaccustomed smells. The railroad men with their peculiar speech and greasy overalls often were left with hours to kill before starting their eastward runs. They drifted into the bars and swapped stories of floods and washouts, deadly curves, cannonball straightaways. Buffalo hunters with their large-caliber rifles, long skinning knives, and remarkable odors told of the whimsical wanderings of the great buffalo herds and described the slaughter of hundreds of animals from a single stand. Army troopers came in from Forts Belknap, Griffin, and Concho, accompanying supply trains on their way to and from the rail terminal. They gathered in the saloons and talked of desperate Indian fights, waterless forced marches, and brave comrades long dead. Civilian freighters, with their long blacksnake whips snapping like gunshots, lined up their six- to eight-yoke ox-drawn wagons at the depot, and loaded and unloaded commerce from the farthest reaches of West Texas. The railroad could not keep pace. Soon the bales of buffalo hides awaiting shipment covered six acres around the terminal, in stacks higher than a man's head.

Entertainment in the acre became ever more plentiful. Secure in his role as moral overseer, Travis visited all the attractions. He saw Madame Rentz's Female Minstrels introduce that Parisian sensation, the cancan, at the Theatre Comique. Each hour on the hour a tightrope walker performed over Main Street. Every saloon had its own band, which sporadically marched through the acre to drum up business. Variety shows, touring dramatic productions were common.

Residents of Dallas and other Texas towns were offered cut-rate rail excursions, allowing the curious to visit the spot where the panther once slept. Cockfights, dogfights, shooting matches, and horse races kept even the most jaded entertained. Almost every saloon nurtured a world's

champion bareknuckle fighter and posted a hundred-dollar prize to anyone who could whip him.

Travis did not lose out on the accelerating prosperity. He and Jay Jay
opened three more sporting palaces and two bars—the Waco Tap and the
Panther City Saloon, which housed a live mascot. A hundred-dollar bill
dangled in the center of the panther's cage, a prize for anyone with the
courage to stick a hand through the bars. Maimings were frequent.

Stagecoach traffic tripled. Fort Worth became the eastern terminus
of the longest stagecoach line in the world—fifteen hundred and sixty
miles to Fort Yuma in seventeen bone-jarring days, if not interrupted.
Soon the passage was cut to thirteen days, allowing the passengers even
less relief. "The coyotes beyond the Concho could not afford to wait that
long for their mail," Editor Paddock explained to his readers.

Travis saw other changes around him. With the arrival of the railroad
and accompanying telegraph wire, accurate time became a universal
obsession. Suddenly every man had to have a watch. Long accustomed to
casual glances skyward and rough estimates that the day still had "about
two hours by sun," even the most rustic townsman began regulating his
days in minutes, even seconds. The whistle of each approaching and
departing train sent every male fishing for his watch, to keep himself
informed if the trains were truly running on time. Even the younger
children could rattle off the rail schedules all the way to St. Louis. Train
engineers became childhood heroes. Travis was amused to see small boys
striding about the streets in overalls and billed caps, imitating the train-
man's habitual spraddle-legged walk.

In keeping with its worldly status, Fort Worth introduced civic innovations. Travis helped to form a transportation company to build a trolley
line down Main Street. A car pulled by a mule regularly serviced the
mile-long run from the courthouse to the rail depot. Streetlamps were
installed, fueled by gas from a central carbide plant. Hotels became
plentiful—the Transcontinental, the Virginia House, Peers House, the
Pacific, the El Paso, and the Clark House. All offered the most modern
conveniences available. The Peers House was noted for its "female waiters." Editor Paddock tested their services and was moved to write an
editorial. He informed his readers that they were "exceedingly useful."

With the constant influx of new residents, Travis again found his law
practice expanding. Soon he had six assistants. The railroad and its rapid
transportation proved to be an open sesame to an expanded practice in
other states. His reputation as an orator also grew. He was soon invited to
serve as keynote speaker at many distant conclaves.

The Masonic lodge, almost moribund while the town drifted in the
doldrums, was revived. In solemn ceremonies Travis at last was inducted
as an entered apprentice. His prodigious memory readily absorbed the

elaborate rituals and recantations of ancient mysteries. He was soon received into fellowcraft and raised to the third degree fully instructed in secrets dating back to the building of King Solomon's temple. He learned to recognize brother Masons wherever he might go by speech, grip, and sign. He found the brotherhood to be of far more benefit than he ever dreamed. If he ran short of funds in a distant city, he had only to stroll into the nearest bank, search for a Masonic lapel pin, explain his predicament, and offer the grip, along with a few signal phrases. Local judges and attorneys who might ordinarily resent a defense counsel from out of state mellowed noticeably when they recognized Travis as a fellow Mason.

With the vast amounts of money rolling in from the acre and his legal practice, Travis soon felt cramped in the small house he had purchased after he and Reva returned from their honeymoon. It seemed inadequate for a man of rising national influence. He summoned a builder from Galveston.

"I want the biggest, the finest, the most ornate home in North Texas," he explained.

The builder, a small man named Ridley Jamieson, adjusted his pincenez, opened a portfolio, spread a stack of drawings, and selected one. "Something like this?"

Travis glanced at the sketch of a small cottage, hardly larger than the one he owned. "Sir, you misunderstand me," he said. "It's far too small. I want the grandest home west of the Mississippi. If you can't build it, I'll find someone who can."

The builder went through the stack of sketches. Travis rejected them, one by one.

"These are all I have with me," Jamieson said. "If you'll give me an idea of what you have in mind, perhaps I can devote a couple of days to preparing a sketch."

Travis described a house in which he was bivouacked in Atlanta, before the town was burned. Jamieson took notes.

Two days later he returned and spread his new sketch. Travis gazed in awe at his dream home, materialized on paper. The house was exactly as he remembered, a big box structure three stories high, hollowed out inside to soaring ceilings. Jamieson had even detailed the grand staircase, leading up to a horseshoe balcony around the second floor landing. Wide galleries framed the house on all floors. Soaring Doric columns supported the front.

"That's it," Travis said. "I'll want to discuss these plans with Mrs.

Spurlock. No doubt we'll suggest minor changes. But I believe you have the basic idea."

Jamieson fiddled nervously with his pince-nez. "Mr. Spurlock, I feel I must point out that a house of this size, with all the special carpentry required, would probably be the most expensive home in Texas."

Travis turned his profile to Jamieson and gave him an amused stare. "Sir, provide me with what I want, and expense will be no object."

After careful search Travis selected a site at the top of a hill to the west of town. The rear galleries would look down upon the Clear Fork of the Trinity and the open country to the west. The front galleries would offer a view of downtown Fort Worth, the railroad station and, in the distance, the cattle herds waiting to ford the river.

For eight months Travis devoted every spare moment to the house. He arranged for Reva to consult with Jamieson on the arrangement of the kitchen and closets, but he attended to every other detail. The white marble for the entry hall and grand ballroom was brought from Italy. The wood for the dark paneling came from Africa, the chandeliers from France, the rugs from Persia, the drapery from Ireland.

One evening Travis sat reviewing the builder's drawings, asking Reva for her opinions.

She seemed unusually distracted. "When does Mr. Jamieson expect to have the house completed?"

"By late February or early March," Travis said. "I suppose we could move in earlier. But I want it to be in readiness, so it will be perfect from the first day."

Reva did not respond. She picked up her embroidery and worked for a time in silence. Travis studied the interior design of the parlor, wondering if the granite facing of the fireplace should be rough-cut stone or quarried and polished.

Reva spoke so quietly he almost did not hear. "February may not be soon enough."

The remark jarred his train of thought. "Soon enough for what?"

Reva was looking at him with a peculiar expression, partly amused, partly defiant. "I visited Dr. Feild today. He agrees with my first suspicions. He believes we will be needing the nursery by January."

Travis slipped to his knees beside her chair. He took her hands in his. "A baby?"

Reva seemed cool, distant. "As they say in your world, the jury is still out. But in my mind there's little doubt."

Travis was ecstatic over the news, yet disturbed that matters of such importance could be transpiring in his own house without his knowledge. "When did you first suspect? Why didn't you tell me?"

Reva's face remained devoid of expression. "You were in St. Louis. I thought it best not to trouble you with matters you couldn't help."

"You were ill? And you didn't let me know?"

"It was only a few days of discomfort. There was nothing you could've done."

Travis knew, from his association with experienced men, that women tended to exaggerate their female difficulties. Despite his concern he felt he should not indulge the weakness. He squeezed her hands. "Reva, I'm so pleased. You're all right now?"

Reva did not smile. "I'm fine," she said.

The next day Travis offered Jamieson a sizable bonus to complete the house by early January.

The longer Reva knew Travis, the more she loved him, and the less she understood him. He kept her locked out of his world. He never shared his work, his worries, his thoughts, his dreams. When she asked questions, he answered in generalities. He was driven by forces she could not fathom.

When they were married she assumed that by starting a family and building a new home he planned to settle down. But as the months went by he seemed to welcome every opportunity to spend time away from her. She began to feel as if she were nothing but chattel, kept to serve his occasional whims, while he was principally occupied elsewhere.

His energy left her amazed. He charged from one place to the next as if he never had enough time for all he had to do. She saw so little of him. Even when he was in town he was awake and gone at first light. He invariably returned late for supper and urged her to go on to bed, saying he had further work to do that would not wait until morning. Often he did not return until long after midnight.

Reva was undaunted by the responsibilities of running the household. Indeed, her mother had trained her well for such an eventuality. But she was not prepared to rear a family alone. The prospect left her numb with apprehension.

The matter came to a head one evening after supper. Casually Travis announced that he would be leaving the following day to try a murder case in Marion, Ohio. He said he probably would be gone two or three weeks.

Reva had entered her seventh month. She spoke out of fear. "And what am I supposed to do while you're gone?"

Travis seemed genuinely puzzled. "What do you mean?"

"I'll not stay in this house alone. Especially not with a baby on the way."

"But you're not alone. Your family is right here. You have Dulcie. And Jimmy."

Her mother had insisted that she take Dulcie, who had been with the family since birth. And Jimmy slept in a tackroom behind the stables.

"That's not the same," Reva said. "I want a husband. I'm alone now like I've never been before."

Travis did not answer immediately. His troubled frown deepened. "Reva, obviously you can't go with me, in your condition. It's an arduous journey. And it would be the same if you *were* along. I'll be working long hours, examining witnesses, building my case for the defendant."

"I don't *want* to go with you," Reva said. "I want you to stay *home!* Especially now! I don't understand why you have to be gone so much."

Travis sighed. "Reva, I thought you knew my profession, what it involves. I must go wherever I'm needed. It's our means of livelihood."

Reva looked at him for a long moment. "I understand that. I'm prepared to make some sacrifices. But it seems to me you take advantage of every opportunity to be gone. Why do *you* have to be the speaker at every convention in the country? What does that have to do with your profession?"

Travis reached for her hand. "Reva, I know it's difficult for you to understand. But my public speaking is a part of the whole. The heightened recognition attracts the major cases. I'm constantly meeting and conferring with men whose acquaintance will be greatly rewarding some day."

"I'd gladly trade a little future happiness for more in the present."

Travis did not answer. He remained silent and morose through the remainder of the evening. At last he urged her to go to bed, saying he would go back to the office for a while, as he had more work to do.

That night Reva cried herself to sleep.

When she awoke the next morning he was gone.

"Well, he's *your* friend, Travis," said Judge Tackett. "We were hoping you could do something with him."

Travis faced the delegation gathered in his office. "What seems to be the trouble?"

Tackett glanced at Van Emden and at John Peter Smith before answering. "It's a matter of the proper proportion," he said. "Our new marshal is perhaps a bit too enthusiastic in enforcing the law."

"The fact of the matter is that the trail drivers are now avoiding Fort Worth," said the major. "More of them are going up the Western Trail."

"I hadn't noticed any falloff," Travis said.

"This year's total drive will be more than twice last year's," Paddock said. "I figure it at about three hundred and twenty thousand Longhorns. Sure, we've had increased traffic. But a third of the market is going north by way of Fort Griffin and Doan's Store. That trade also should be coming here."

"Fortunately, we still have a few loyal friends," Major Van Emden said. "Captain King alone is sending up thirty thousand head this season. And rail traffic is picking up. We have sixty thousand shorthorns awaiting shipment. But make no mistake, Travis. The word is out among the drovers to avoid Fort Worth."

Travis allowed silence to linger. He had just returned home. The Ohio trial had been long and taxing. But he had kept in contact with his Fort Worth office. Apparently his satisfaction over the election of his friend Jim Courtright as town marshal had been premature.

"What's Jim doing wrong?" he asked.

Paddock explained. "If anyone gets out of line, he raps them over the head with a pistol and throws them in the dungeon. Awakening in that hellhole has turned more men away from whiskey than the pledge."

Travis laughed. Drunks often were tossed into the dank, pitch-black cellar beneath the jail to speed sobriety. "What do you want me to do about it?"

"Just talk to him," Tackett said. "Show him the error of his ways."

Only reluctantly did Travis at last agree.

He found Courtright sitting with friends at a table in the White Elephant Saloon. He caught the marshal's eye. "Jim, could I see you a minute on a personal matter?"

Courtright followed him to the rear of the saloon. Standing at least two or three inches above Travis's six feet two, Courtright possessed a bearing that demanded attention. Only the most dense cowhand would assume that the two pistols tucked into the red Mexican sash at his waist were decorative.

Travis had known Courtright for several years. The man was not talkative, but over many drinks and poker games Travis had learned that he was a native of Illinois. Only seventeen at the outbreak of the war, he had served as scout with Wild Bill Hickok and Buffalo Bill Cody in the Union army under General Alexander Logan. In keeping with the style affected by the scouts, he wore his hair shoulder-length, curled inward slightly at the ends.

In Fort Worth he was known as "Long Hair Jim."

After the war Courtright had remained in the army, perfecting his skill as a sharpshooter. While stationed in Arkansas he met and married Betty Weeks. She was barely fourteen. Jim often said he believed in marrying them young and raising them right.

Betty also learned to shoot. After Jim left the army the couple trav-

eled for a time with medicine shows, vaudevilles, and circuses, performing feats of marksmanship. In Virginia City, Jim was partially blinded by
wadding from a blank cartridge. While his eye healed, he and Betty
drifted to Fort Worth. Jim had tried to farm for a while. Betty opened a
shooting gallery. Jim decided he was unsuited for the farm. He was well
liked, and Travis had been among those who had urged him to run for the
office of marshal. Jim had outpolled the ten other candidates on the
ballot.

"What's on your mind?" Courtright asked. He kept his pale blue eyes
fixed on a group of drovers at the bar.

Travis raised a hand to signal for drinks. "I'll not beat around the
bush, Jim. A group of town leaders has asked me to talk to you. They feel
you're doing too good a job. They think you're running off their trade."

Courtright smoothed the ends of his drooping moustache. "Travis, I
hear it from the other side, too. A lot of ministers, church people are
begging me to do something about the acre."

"Reformers are like the poor," Travis said. "They'll always be with
us. We're talking about the merchants that put the bread on our table."

Courtright adjusted the two Colt pistols in his sash. "Travis, what the
shit do they expect me to do? In the last week alone I've seen Ben
Thompson, Clay Allison, John Wesley Hardin, King Fisher, Bill Longley,
and Sam Bass, all right here in the acre. Don't the people here know that
if I don't enforce the law, there won't *be* any law?"

"They believe you can keep the peace, yet not get in the way of
anyone having a good time."

"Sam Bass robbed the Weatherford stage last week at Mary's Crossing. I don't have the evidence, but I know it was him."

"I don't believe it," Travis said.

"Travis, you're too goddamn trusting with people. Those fellows I
mentioned would just as soon part your hair as look at you. If I let them,
the scum from the acre would take over this town. You heard what
happened to Lucille Nelson, didn't you?"

Travis shook his head. Lucille Nelson was a spinster who lived with
her aged, deaf, and half-blind father.

"Guess it happened while you were on one of your trips. A couple of
cowhands were up on the square. One of them saw Lucille and thought
she was a whore he had fucked the night before. He put his arm around
her, slapped her on the flank, and was trying to haul her off to the acre
when Lucille fainted. Old Major Nelson was headed for the acre with a
Navy Colt when I caught up with him. That's what we'd have if I allowed
it. Decent women wouldn't be safe on the streets."

Travis conceded the point. "All right, we can keep their hell raising confined to the acre. Hell, Jim, these cowhands don't want much! What's the harm if they get drunk, shoot their pistols in the air a few times?"

"It isn't my place to tell a lawyer that there's an ordinance on the books that prohibits firing a gun within the city limits. Correct me if I'm wrong, but I think it's called disturbing the peace. It sure as hell disturbs *my* peace. Sometimes I have to get out of bed a half dozen times a night to see if the shooting is a gunfight or a bunch of drunks riding up and down the streets shooting at signs. And those cowboys stick together. If I don't iron one of them out now and then, they gang up and whip my deputies. I can't allow that!"

"Perhaps there's a better way," Travis insisted. "Why don't you just put on a good-natured demonstration every two or three days with those pistols? That'd give those cowhands something to think about. I don't know of anything that would be more conducive to proper deportment."

Travis knew he had scored in his appeal to Courtright's vanity. Travis had seen him shoot the pips from the five of spades at thirty paces, emptying his revolver so fast the gunfire sounded as a solid roar. He had seen him hit a dime tossed into the air, and split a card set on edge.

"All right, I'll try it," Courtright said. "But only as an experiment. I don't think it'll work."

In early January of 1878 Travis and Reva moved into their new home. From the first, Reva called it Bluebonnet because the scrollwork and gingerbread around the galleries and eaves reminded her of the popular Texas flower.

On a cold, wet night three weeks later, Reva went into labor. Dr. Theodore Feild arrived and hurried upstairs. Travis sat in the parlor for hours, sipping brandy as he listened to the bustle of the servants, the rattle of sleet against the windows. Toward dawn the sounds stilled and Travis thought he heard the cry of a baby. He remained uncertain until Dr. Feild descended the long staircase, smiling. "It's a healthy young lady, Travis. Congratulations!"

Travis rose to his feet to accept the doctor's handshake. "And Reva?"

"Tired, but well. Everything went comparatively easy."

Travis offered the doctor a brandy. A few minutes later they went upstairs to visit the mother and child.

Reva lay with her head sunk deep into a pillow. Lines of exhaustion cast fragile shadows in the lamplight. She smiled at Travis and reached out a hand. Beside her, the baby looked up at Travis with deep-set Spurlock eyes.

"Have you selected a name?" Dr. Feild asked.

"We will call her Zetta, after Reva's maternal aunt," Travis said. He leaned over and grasped the baby's tiny fingers. "This little lady is a good omen, Doctor. She keeps peace in the family. We hadn't yet agreed on a name for a boy."

Reva smiled at him. She knew that he had wanted a boy and was hiding his disappointment.

The baby was healthy from the start, and soon the household revolved around her. But Reva recovered slowly. She spent long hours in bed and seemed listless. She remained weak and did not regain her usual healthy color. Travis worried about her for weeks. At last he went to see Dr. Feild.

"Travis, there are some aspects to birth we don't understand," the doctor said. "I don't know why, but it's not uncommon for young mothers to be overcome with sadness for a time. Most recover in short order."

"My mother died of childbed fever," Travis explained. "The memory of her suffering preys heavily on my mind."

"Reva is basically a healthy woman," the doctor said. "I'll give her some laudanum. That should lift her out of her despondency. I do believe it'd help if you could arrange your schedule to devote more time to her through the next few weeks."

Fortunately, Travis had made no firm commitments. He declined a case in Nashville he might otherwise have accepted, turned down a speaking engagement in Chicago, and skipped a convention of the bar in Louisville.

He spent long evenings at home. For a time he felt that he and Reva were recapturing the magic of his early courtship. Each night after the baby went to sleep they talked softly for hours, reliving the past, anticipating the future. Gradually Reva regained her strength and her humor. They laughed at the antics of the baby, the complications she had brought into their lives. They slept through the nights entwined in complete communion. For a time Travis knew contentment.

The baby was barely six months old when Travis received a note one afternoon from Dr. Feild, asking him to step over to his office. The doctor's face was grim.

"Travis, after giving the matter considerable thought, I concluded that I should inform you first. Reva is with child again. It's too soon. With her slow recovery from her first birth, I'm somewhat concerned about her."

Travis was stunned. Once again he thought of his mother, the cold nights in a cabin on the side of a Tennessee mountain. "Reva doesn't know?" he asked.

"She suspects. But there's little doubt. The symptoms are plain. However, I put her off until tomorrow, until I could talk to you."

Travis remembered that Major Van Emden had lost his first wife after four babies in quick succession.

"I should be horsewhipped," he said.

"Who are we to question the ways of the Lord?" Dr. Feild asked. "And who knows? Another child may be exactly the right prescription. I'm also concerned about you. I know your apprehensions. That's why I called you here. I don't want you conveying your fears to Reva."

"Then there's no danger?"

Dr. Feild hedged. "The second baby is usually easier than the first. Physically, Reva is not as strong as I'd like. But at this point I foresee no reasons for complications."

Reva visited the doctor the following day. That evening, she broke the news to Travis. He successfully feigned surprise, and enthusiasm.

"I feel certain that it will be a boy this time," Reva said. "I'll relent. You can name him."

"We have plenty of time to think on it," Travis said.

Dr. Feild insisted that Reva take long rests each day. Travis hired two more servants to help Dulcie with the huge house, freeing her to take care of the baby. He hurried home each evening and sought to keep Reva entertained by reading to her from newspapers and books.

Reva went into labor early one afternoon in late March of 1879. Travis was summoned home from his office.

As Dr. Feild had predicted, the delivery was easier. Before midnight Reva gave birth to a baby boy.

"I hope you've agreed on a name for him by now," Dr. Feild said.

"There was never any real question," Travis said. "We'll honor Reva's maternal grandmother's family, and call him Durwood."

Reva beamed her happiness. "There'll be others," she said to Travis. "We'll get around to all branches of the family."

To the surprise of everyone, Reva was back on her feet within days. She quickly resumed charge of the household. She doted on the babies and was with them constantly. She set up a cot in the nursery and slept there, to be near if she were needed.

To Travis's unpracticed eye, Durwood seemed unusually frail. He mentioned his concern to Dr. Feild.

"It's probably hereditary," the doctor said. "Does your family tend toward thinness?"

"My parents were thin," Travis said. "I was. But everybody was, during the war."

"The boy seems healthy. I don't believe it's anything to worry about," said the doctor.

With Reva constantly tending to the babies, Travis again felt excluded from the life of his own household. Reva seldom came to bed.

Remembering Major Van Emden's first wife, who died after four babies in quick succession, Travis was relieved. He did not intend to impose further demands upon her.

Quietly, he built and furnished a room behind Jay Jay's office at the Red Lantern. There he received newly arrived women, before they went to work in the acre. The solution seemed practical. He obtained relief without interfering in Reva's newfound interests or endangering her life with further pregnancies.

As the months passed, he spent less time at home, where he no longer seemed needed.

Other matters demanded his attention.

The Texas & Pacific announced plans to build on westward. Fort Worth no longer would serve as the terminal. Travis, Van Emden, and Paddock met to decide what to do.

"We haven't been overburdened with luck," Paddock said. "If the Panic of 1873 had come three months later, we would've been the metropolis and Dallas would've been nothing more than a small county seat town. Now Dallas has gained the jump on us. We must do something quick if we're ever to recover."

"The Tarantula Map," Travis said.

"Exactly. We can't possibly thrive as a mere waterstop on a single railroad. We must become a crossroad."

"I have contacts," Major Van Emden said. "I'll determine what can be done."

A few weeks later the major learned that the Santa Fe Railway was planning to complete a route from Chicago and Kansas City to Houston and the Gulf. The Santa Fe board was debating whether to build through Dallas or Fort Worth.

"We must preclude any offer from Dallas," Van Emden said. "Through a friend on the board, I've determined exactly what the railroad will require as an incentive."

The town's merchants were called into an emergency session. The doors were locked, and no one was allowed to leave until the seed money was pledged.

A few weeks later the Missouri-Kansas-Texas was lured into Fort Worth by a similar ruse.

The issue of Courtright's law enforcement flared anew. A rancher complained that two of his men were pistol-whipped so severely they were unable to continue up the trail. He told the city council he would never again bring herds past Fort Worth.

"Hell, I'm quitting," Courtright told Travis. "If those sons o' bitches want a wide-open town, that's exactly what they're going to get."

He said his former commanding officer, now a U.S. senator, owned mines and ranches in New Mexico Territory. "He's being robbed blind out there. He wants me to put a stop to it."

Even though Travis still considered Courtright his friend, he was relieved to see him go. With less enthusiastic lawmen in office, control in the acre quickly became much easier.

As Travis assumed increasing responsibility for the administration of law in the acre, he never thought for a single moment that he was acting for his own interests rather than for those of the city. Indeed, he never considered the interests any different.

Nor did he dream that anyone ever would.

11

Again Durwood fled from his sixth birthday gift in tears. Exasperated, Travis walked back across the lawn to Reva. "This is ridiculous. He *will* ride that pony. It's as gentle as a lamb. No harm could possibly come to him."

He reached for his son. Wailing, Durwood circled behind Reva and clung desperately to her skirts.

Reva made no effort to corral him. She spoke calmly. "Why don't we go back into the house and wait until another time?"

"Because the way to fight a fear is to face it," Travis said. He caught Durwood by the arm, picked him up, and carried him, kicking and screaming, across the lawn.

Jimmy stood by the pony, head bowed, gaze averted. The hand-tooled saddle was in place and cinched tight.

Travis swung Durwood astride. The boy went as rigid as a board. He sat with eyes squeezed shut. He held doggedly to the saddlehorn. His sobs changed to the sound of a mewing kitten.

"Travis, please!" Reva called from the lawn.

"Reva, this is no time to discuss it," Travis said. He forced Durwood's feet into stirrups. "Now just sit up there and hold on. Jimmy will lead you."

Jimmy walked the pony slowly down the drive toward the street, Durwood screaming with each step. Travis walked beside him. As they reached the street, Durwood's yells showed no signs of abating. Neighbors were watching.

"All right," Travis said to Jimmy. "I guess his mother's right. We'll try it some other day."

"Yassuh," Jimmy said, his gaze still averted.

Travis pulled Durwood off the pony. He saw with disgust that the boy had wet his pants. Carrying him on his hip, he walked back to Reva.

Zetta had come out of the house and now stood beside her mother. She watched the pony as it was led away. "Papa, I'll ride him," she said.

"The pony is Durwood's gift, not yours," Travis said.

"But if he's afraid of horses, and I'm not, why does he get the pony?"

Travis glanced at Reva before replying. "Because Durwood will be a man some day, and men must learn to ride." Durwood again ran to cling to his mother's skirts. Travis knelt beside him. "That was a fine spectacle for the servants to see. I never thought a son of mine would be afraid of horses, dogs, guns, and cats."

"He isn't afraid of cats," Zetta said. "He just doesn't like them very much."

Durwood turned and ran up the front steps and into the house.

Reva's face remained devoid of expression. "Travis, I think you should go in and talk to him. He needs the confidence that only you can give him."

Travis shook his head. "I don't know of anything to say to him that I haven't already said."

Zetta pulled at his hand. "We could play dominoes."

Travis felt that he no longer was good company. "Go on in, if you want. I think I'll sit on the gallery awhile. I'll come on into the house after dark."

He settled into his big rocking chair and lit a cigar. The sun was low across the Trinity, and Bluebonnet cast a long shadow. From his high vantage point he could see across town to the open pastures beyond. The 5:25 eastbound train stood at the station, gathering steam. The sweet, cloying smell of honeysuckle hung heavily in the air. Nighthawks darted among the houses at hardly more than rooftop level, filling the hillside with their cries. From the next block came the sounds of a group of children at play. Cicadas sang in the mimosas.

Travis knew he should go inside the house and whip his son for cowardice, but he could not bring himself to do it.

He could not imagine where he had erred as a father.

There had been so little time.

Zetta was clearly the strong one. She was quick-minded, firm and unwavering in her beliefs. Aside from a streak of stubbornness, she was the perfect child.

But Durwood was weak. Travis could not deny the fact. He had tried every way he knew to put some backbone into the boy, without success. To a large degree he blamed Reva. She seemed to want to keep him a baby. She catered to his every whim. The boy was spoiled rotten.

The problem had caused the first major rift in their marriage. Reva blamed Travis and his long absences for Durwood's timidity.

"He has no one to look up to," she said each time the subject arose.

"He knows that other boys have fathers home every night. He feels different."

"My absences haven't hurt Zetta," Travis pointed out.

He could not make Reva understand that his traveling was necessary. Gradually he was building a strong political base. Already his influence reached deep into both houses in Austin. He had the ear of the governor. He had acquired considerable power in Washington. He now saw a clear pathway to achieving all he had dreamed.

The struggle had been long and arduous.

He had been elevated to the thirty-third degree of Masonry and now attended conclaves throughout the country, building friendships that mattered. He had been a founder of the Confederate Veterans. He served as a steward to the Southern Baptist General Convention. He was a director of the National Bar Association, and had been elected to the National Committee of the Democratic Party. He also sat on the national boards of the Moose, the Elks. Often he begged Reva to travel with him. She invariably declined. He usually took his mistress of the moment along, discreetly, in a separate portion of the train.

And his work had become ever more demanding. He now received annual retainers from some of the largest ranches in the state. Representing them, he had been instrumental in passage of the leasing act, which made fence cutting a felony. The fight had been bitter. The advocates of free grass had taken their battle to the verge of civil war in West Texas. Travis had won a compromise. The new leasing act required that at least one gate be placed in every three miles of fence.

Through his connections he had invested heavily in the building of new railroads, now spreading across the state like cracks in a shattered mirror. His wealth was accumulating. Someday he would be recognized as a kingmaker who selected his own politicians and placed them in seats of power.

He had been successful in every endeavor excepting that of a family.

Travis sat and brooded in the gathering dusk.

He did not know how he could have acted differently.

He heard movement in the darkness. "Who's there?" he called.

"It's Jimmy. Suh, there's a man out at the stable, says he wants to see you."

Travis left his rocking chair and walked to the edge of the porch. "A man? What does he want?"

"I don't know, suh. He won't say."

"Stay here. I'll be right back."

Travis went into the house, strapped on his pistol, and lit a lantern. He followed Jimmy out to the stables.

Jimmy pointed. "He's out there in the trees, right over yonder."

Holding the lantern high, Travis walked toward the riverbank. A shadow moved in the darkness.

The shadow spoke. "Travis, it's Jim Courtright. I'd take it as a personal favor if you'd put out that light."

Courtright stood at the edge of the lantern's throw. Travis would not have recognized him. His clothes were torn. His long hair was matted. He did not remotely resemble the dandy who had left Fort Worth.

Travis raised the hood of the lantern and blew out the flame. He was not especially pleased to see the man. "What the hell are you doing back here?" he asked.

Courtright came out of the brush. "Travis, I'm in a bit of trouble. There's a thousand dollars on my head. I don't know if you've heard anything about it, but I've been indicted on two counts of murder out in Soccoro."

"The newspapers here mentioned something about it. You jump bond?"

"Bond hell. We broke jail. Jim McIntire's with me."

Travis knew McIntire as a sometime railroad detective and hired gun, perhaps a cut beneath Courtright. "Where's he now?"

"Waiting across the river. We hoped you'd be able to help us."

Travis wanted nothing to do with the matter. "Jim, my advice to you would be to go back and face the music. You've got friends here who'll testify to your character."

"Hell, no! Travis, you don't understand. This is a political deal. We'd be walking right into a noose. We figure if we can just lay low for a while, it'll all blow over."

"I wouldn't count on it. How're you fixed?"

"We're flat. We barely got out of New Mexico. We've been riding the river bottoms ever since."

Travis considered what to do. With Courtright gone, the Fort Worth political scene had achieved a delicate balance. Travis knew he was acting against his better judgment, but he could not refuse help to an old friend. "I guess we can hide you out in the brush back of the cemetery a few days. I'll make inquiries in New Mexico and see what I can do. I'll bring you some provisions. Keep out of sight. Don't take any chances."

"Don't worry about me," Courtright said. "I'd rather be in Fort Worth, dead in a pine box, than alive in any other town."

Zetta lingered behind the rest of her school class, hoping the teacher would not see her. Every time the class went on a field trip, the teacher assigned her to help maintain order. The burden separated her from friends, caused the others to call her names, and robbed her of the pleasure of the outing. It was not fair.

"Hurry along, children!" the teacher called. "Don't dawdle."

The class filed through the train station and lined up in ranks on the loading platform. Zetta pushed her way into a back row.

The train crept into the station with a fearsome rumbling and clatter. The engine passed, steam rising from beneath the wheels. The bell over the cab turned flips as it pealed its warning. Zetta put her forefingers in her ears to block out the sounds. The baggage cars passed. The first passenger cars appeared, the people inside staring out the windows with the superiority of travelers, gazing down at the local mortals as if from a great distance. The train shuddered and came to a squealing stop.

"Wait now, children! Wait till I tell you to board!"

Zetta and her class, traveling only thirty miles to Dallas, stood waiting to board their car. Zetta watched the adult passengers come out of the station. For a moment she thought she caught a glimpse of her father, but she was not certain. She knew he was leaving sometime during the day for Boston. She slipped to the end of the back row for a better view.

Travis was standing behind a baggage cart. Impulsively, Zetta threw up a hand and started to call to him. But something about his stance, his demeanor, made her hesitate.

A woman walked up beside him. She was blond, well dressed, and as pretty as any picture Zetta had ever seen. The woman said something to her father. Furtively, he glanced over his shoulder, as if to ascertain that they were screened from the other adults by the baggage cart. They conferred briefly. Then Travis handed the woman something. She squeezed his hand, turned, and walked toward a nearby car.

Glancing around once again to see if they had been observed, Travis walked rapidly toward the Pullman cars at the front of the train.

Zetta suddenly felt sick to her stomach. Apparently the dirty stories were true. Only last week her best friend Agnes had heard her parents discussing a rumor that Travis Spurlock had been seen in Cleveland in the company of a woman from the acre. Agnes had conveyed the details with obvious relish. She said her parents believed that Travis and the woman traveled together to every one of his speeches. She said her parents had speculated over whether poor Reva knew about it.

Zetta stood stock still as the woman prepared to board the car in front of her. The woman paused, and happened to glance in her direction. Their gazes met. The woman smiled brightly at her, then stepped onto the train.

Zetta was certain the woman did not know her. She had only seen a homely child, staring at a pretty woman boarding a train.

"Zetta!" yelled Mrs. Sparrow. "Where have you been? Come here and help me!"

Trapped, Zetta moved to the front of the class.

"We'll board now, children. One at a time. Careful! Zetta, stand by the steps. Make sure no one falls."

Zetta waited while her classmates boarded, one by one.

She could hardly see them for her tears.

Travis kept Courtright hidden behind the cemetery almost a month. He wired New Mexico Territory for particulars. The reply was not encouraging. He drove out in a hack to give Courtright the news. "It looks like they've got an airtight case against you," he said. "Two witnesses claim they saw you shoot those two men in cold blood."

Courtright nodded. "I told you I was being railroaded. It didn't happen that way at all."

"Keep out of sight and give me a little more time," Travis said. "I'll find out a little more about those witnesses. We might be able to build a case."

Three days later Travis caught sight of Courtright walking along Main Street, shaking hands, greeting old friends.

"Are you crazy?" Travis demanded. "There's a thousand-dollar price on your head."

Courtright laughed. "Don't worry. I don't have an enemy in this town. My friends will let me know if the Rangers are on the way."

Within another month, Courtright was back at work as a deputy marshal. Travis went to the city administration and attempted to point out the possible legal complications of an escaped murder suspect serving as an arresting officer. No one seemed concerned.

"Some of those people over in the acre are kind of sudden," said Dill Rea, the new marshal. "When my deputies call them down, they go on the prod. But they listen to Jim. I need him."

Courtright's network proved effective. On three separate occasions Travis heard that New Mexico officers had arrived in town in the company of Texas Rangers. In each instance Courtright was notified in time to disappear. He seemed to regard the whole affair as a joke.

Months passed. Then Marshal Rea received a wire from the Albuquerque chief of police, asking permission to obtain Courtright's help in identifying some photographs. Travis warned Courtright that the request sounded like a trap.

"Hell, I doubt it," Courtright said. "They knew all along that those

two witnesses were lying. The whole thing has probably blown over by
now."

Courtright met the visitors at the station. That night he entertained
them lavishly in the acre. Travis had a few drinks with them. All seemed
to be in order.

The next afternoon Marshal Rea telephoned Travis in panic. The
new gadget was now more than a novelty, but Travis still disliked using it.
The line seemed even noisier than usual. Travis had difficulty making out
the marshal's words. "Travis, I'm at the Ginnochio. The Rangers are
holding Jim upstairs in one of the rooms. There's a mob forming out front,
and they mean business. There's going to be bloodshed unless we do
something quick."

"Why call me?" Travis asked. "What the hell can I do?"

"Those people out there know and trust you. Maybe you can talk to
them."

Rea said that while Jim was in the officers' room at the Ginnochio,
concentrating on the photographs, the Rangers got the drop on him.

"They're waiting for the next southbound train," Rea said. "The
mob's not about to let them take Jim. There's talk about storming the
hotel."

Travis rang off and hurried down to the Ginnochio.

If anything, Rea had understated the situation. More than a thousand
men had gathered. They were armed with rifles, pistols, and shotguns.
They milled in front of the hotel, shouting at the Rangers, demanding
Courtright's release.

Marshal Rea and his men had set up a command post in the hotel
lobby. The city officers seemed uncertain as to which side they were on.
They admired the Rangers. But they loved Courtright.

Sheriff Maddox arrived. He offered a suggestion. "If we could divert
the crowd for a minute, we could slip Jim out the back way and up to the
county jail."

Marshal Rea liked the idea. "Travis can do the trick."

They devised a plan. Travis waited until the sheriff positioned a team
and rig in the alley behind the hotel. He then crossed the street to the
railroad ticket office and climbed onto a ledge over the window. Accustomed to speaking to the farthest reaches of convention halls, he soon
had the mob's attention. "Jim Courtright is safe!" he shouted. "You all
know that Jim is one of my best friends. I wouldn't lie to you. I assure you
that both our county and city officers are looking after his interests. . . ."

Over the heads of the crowd, he saw the rig leave the end of the alley
and turn northward toward the county jail. At the far edge of the mob a
shout was raised. "There they go!"

The mob turned in time to see Courtright, the Rangers, and Sheriff

Maddox disappearing up the street. An angry roar erupted. Travis waved for quiet and tried to speak. He was shouted down.

A rock was thrown. It hit the building behind him. Glass shattered.

Travis scrambled down from the ledge. City officers rushed to screen him from the mob. He was pushed into a hack and driven away.

That evening Jay Jay came to see him. "Travis, I thought I should warn you. There's a lot of bad feeling in the acre over your part in this. Some people think you were in cahoots with the Rangers from the start."

For a moment Travis was consumed by self-righteous anger. "That's not so, and you know it. Jim doesn't have a better friend in town than me."

"Tempers are high," Jay Jay said. "No one's thinking straight. There's going to be trouble unless some one can put a stop to it. And there's only two people I know of who can keep the lid on the acre. Jim Courtright and you. Now you're both out of the running."

Travis knew that Jay Jay was right. He had lost the respect of the people—and control of the acre. He was worried. If matters got out of hand, and erupted into a riot, the backlash from town might close the acre for good.

If that happened, his investments there would become worthless overnight. Many of his friends would suffer.

"Put out the word that no one should do anything foolish," he said. "Promise everybody that we'll work something out."

Travis spent most of the night deciding what to do.

The next morning he hurried across the square to the courthouse and took Sheriff Maddox to one side. "If we let them take Jim out of town, we'll be sending him to his death. He'll hang for sure. We can't let that happen."

Maddox shook his head. "Travis, the Rangers have extradition papers signed by the governor. There isn't a goddamned thing I can do."

"See if you can delay them," Travis said. "I'll arrange something."

Maddox advised the Rangers that since the weekend was at hand, they should await the peace of the Sabbath before attempting to move Courtright from the jail to the depot.

The officers agreed.

On Sunday morning all was calm. The Rangers felt safe in taking their prisoner across the street to the Merchants Restaurant for breakfast. Nothing unusual occurred. At noon they took him to Sunday dinner at the restaurant without incident.

Through Maddox, Travis learned that the Rangers planned to take Courtright to supper at five before boarding the six o'clock train for Austin.

He made preparations.

The restaurant was almost full when Courtright and the officers entered. Only one table remained vacant. Travis sat in a corner, dining with friends. He was pleased to see that waitress Caroline Brown adroitly managed the seating so that Courtright faced the door to the kitchen.

A few minutes later Caroline managed to attract Courtright's attention through the small, diamond-shaped glass in the door. Through hand signals, she conveyed to him the fact that two pistols were secreted under his table.

Never altering his expression, Courtright slowly turned and glanced at Travis. With a brief nod, Travis confirmed Caroline's information. Maintaining his poker face, Courtright winked at Travis, then turned back to his plate.

Travis found himself admiring Courtright's ironclad nerve. Glancing only occasionally at the clock on the wall to his left, Courtright ate a leisurely, sumptuous supper.

At a quarter to six Travis heard the faint rumble of the southbound train, passing a few blocks away. He knew it would spend only a few minutes at the station.

Courtright dropped his napkin. He turned to the Albuquerque police chief. "Mr. Reynolds, would you mind picking up my napkin for me?"

"Pick it up yourself," Reynolds snapped. "I'm not your goddamned slave."

Slowly, Courtright jackknifed his long frame and reached under the table.

"Look out! Move back!" came a yell from across the room.

All three officers glanced toward the diversion. Courtright stood up so fast that his chair went sailing across the room and into the wall behind him. He held two cocked pistols.

The three officers froze. More than twenty pistols had been drawn. All were pointed in their direction.

Travis stood with his own .44 in his hand.

Courtright gestured to the officers with a pistol. "Take your time, gentlemen. Go ahead and finish your supper. I've got a train to catch."

He carefully backed out the door. A moment later, Travis heard gunshots as Courtright cleared the way in his dash for the depot.

The Ranger captain gazed at the pistols pointed at him. "All of you men are in serious trouble," he said. "Aiding and abetting a prisoner in his escape is a penitentiary offense."

Travis walked toward him, ostentatiously holstering his pistol. "Captain, you misunderstand," he said in his most soothing courtroom tones. "Don't you see? We drew our guns to come to your assistance. We were not about to allow any harm to come to you. Only the fact that we faced two cocked pistols, and our own intimate knowledge of Mr. Courtright's deadly accuracy, prevented our intervention in his escape."

The captain's face slowly turned an interesting shade of red. Dark veins corded at his neck and temples. But he knew when he was licked.

"I've always heard that Fort Worth is a lawless hellhole," he said. "Now I know it's true."

Never revealing to anyone the pain in her heart, Reva often went into a closet, secure from the prying eyes of the servants, and wept for her children, for her husband, and for herself.

Travis remained blind to the realities in his own home. She could not bring herself to confront him on the subject. Zetta was now in her eighth year. Reva could not find in her the slightest trace of the celebrated beauty of the Collins women. Instead the perversities of fate had given her the monumental nose, jutting jaw, and dark, fierce, hawk eyes of her father. Those features, so handsome on a man, seemed grotesque on the face of a girl child. Reva knew that Zetta had been subjected to the taunts of other children, and often she had seen glances exchanged between adults.

She remembered her own agonizing childhood, growing up in the shadow of Rebecca's beauty. But her own blemishes had been the common afflictions of adolescence. In time, nature had healed them. Zetta's defects were basic.

With the satisfaction of a father who sees his mirror image, Travis continued to think of Zetta as a lovely child. Reva did not have the heart to tell him otherwise.

Their quarrels over his treatment of the children were bitter enough. He insisted that self-discipline should begin early. He was too demanding. Citing his own example, he set high standards and expected the children to conform. What praise he offered was tempered with sharp criticism. Before each injury to their egos healed, another was inflicted. Perhaps because he never had a childhood of his own, Travis could not see the harm in what he was doing. The house remained filled with tension, relieved only during his trips out of town.

During the brief, relaxed atmosphere of his absences, Reva became acquainted with the true natures of her son and daughter. Driven by hunger for their father's approval, both had become perfectionists, but in different ways. Zetta devoted illogical, consummate attention to flawed trifles—a hem that did not hang in the proper way, an errant lock that defied the comb. She devoted hours to elaborate rituals. Her shoes must be shined in a certain manner, with attendant concentration over polish and cloth. A pleat ironed carelessly sent her into tears of outrage. Her room, her desk were arranged just so. If a single item was moved out of place, she would shout her dismay to the whole household.

Around other children Zetta stood silent and defiant. She seemed to avoid the emotional entanglements of personal relationships.

Durwood worried Reva even more. She would not have breathed it to a soul—she hardly admitted it to herself—but Durwood seemed to have inherited the femininity that Zetta lacked. She searched in vain for signs of the irrepressible male gusto she so treasured in Travis.

Although Travis never said a word, Reva often saw puzzlement and disappointment in his eyes.

Gradually he had shown his disapproval by ignoring Durwood. With helpless anguish, Reva had watched her son retreat into a shell, narrowing his world to the few things he did well. He worked at his arithmetic for hours at a time, filling page after page in his tablets with neat rows of figures. He performed his schoolwork to the letter, but never went one step beyond. If a lesson in geography called for the listing of the chief exports of Brazil, Durwood memorized the statistics. But he had not inherited the curiosity of his father. He was not moved to locate Brazil on the map, or to learn of its people and language. He assembled facts like dry cordwood and presented them to his teacher in exchange for a precise row of A's on his report cards.

In December of that year, Zetta was selected to play the Virgin Mary in the school pageant. Reva, Zetta, and Dulcie spent days making her costume—a floor-length white robe, topped by an elaborate tinsel-wrapped halo of cloth-covered cardboard. Zetta practiced her lines until she could recite them perfectly.

A cold norther struck in the afternoon before the performance. By nightfall heavy sleet was falling and the ground was covered with a glaze of ice. As usual, Travis arrived home from the office more than an hour late. "Bundle the children well," he said. "I'll have the carriage brought around to the front door."

Travis first took Zetta's costume out to the carriage and supervised its stowage. Jimmy helped, but the horses were skittish in the wind and sleet. Jimmy climbed back onto his seat to hold the team. One at a time, Travis led his family out to the carriage over the ice, first Durwood, then Zetta, then Reva.

When they arrived at the school, and Zetta's costume was unloaded, Travis discovered that he had sat on Zetta's halo.

It was crushed beyond repair.

In the school corridor, crowded with people, Zetta burst into tears. "Everything's ruined," she wailed. "I can't go on stage without it!"

Travis took her into one of the empty classrooms. He seized her by the arms. "Nonsense, Zetta!" he said. "You would look more the part in rags! What do you think Joseph and Mary were wearing in that manger?"

"But we had it all planned," Zetta sobbed. "I can't be Mary without a halo!"

Travis knelt beside her. "Listen to me. Either you go on as if nothing has happened, or I'll tan your hide good when we get home. You understand?"

The threat shocked Zetta into silence. Reva helped her into her costume. By the time she left to go backstage with the other children, she seemed to have recovered.

But during the nativity scene, leaning over the Christ Child, Zetta again burst into tears. She blubbered her way through her lines. The audience was mystified. Reva heard the buzz of whispered exchanges.

Travis was furious. On the way home he remained silent. He took Zetta into the parlor and gave vent to his anger. "Don't you ever again make such a spectacle of yourself in public. Do you hear me? You're a Spurlock! If you can't control your emotions, you can stay home!"

Reva wanted to intervene, but she knew that would only make matters worse.

At that moment of Zetta's supreme humiliation, Reva happened to glance at Durwood.

In the soft lamplight, his eyes glinted with a smug satisfaction. His hint of a smile conveyed sly, secret knowledge.

With a chill, Reva remembered that after placing the costume in the carriage, Travis had taken Durwood over the ice first. Durwood had remained alone in the carriage while Travis returned to the house for Zetta. He easily could have tossed the halo into the darkness of the seat, knowing that Travis, wearing a heavy overcoat, would not notice when he lowered his weight onto it.

Reva quickly pushed the suspicion from her mind.

But in the weeks and months that followed, the memory flowered anew each time Zetta became upset over some possession that had been misplaced, moved, or broken.

Reva was never able to catch Durwood in the act, but her conviction grew that he was responsible.

At last she came to accept what she long had felt in her heart.

She pitied her daughter.

And she did not like her son.

"Travis, I'm *not* mistaken," Jay Jay said. "I heard him right. He's demanding ten percent of the take. For protection."

They were seated in Jay Jay's upstairs office, with the doors closed, the sound of the German marching band below muffled. "What protection does he plan to offer?" Travis asked.

"He won't say. But he's cutting himself in for ten percent of the gross. He's made the same pitch all over the acre. Even to Luke Short."

"What'd Luke say?"

"Luke told him to go to hell."

Travis carefully considered the situation. He still found difficulty believing that Jim Courtright could be so stupid. True, ever since his return from exile six months ago, Jim had done some odd things. But this was the worst. It was a hell of a way to repay old favors.

Travis had sent money to Courtright throughout the year he and his family had remained in exile in Seattle. Quietly Travis continued to work on the murder charges in New Mexico Territory. With encouragement, one key witness became hazy on details. The other died a natural death. Travis had sent word to Courtright and McIntire that conditions were ripe. They surrendered, stood trial, and were cleared of all charges.

Courtright had returned home triumphant—met at the station by a huge crowd and paraded up Main Street behind a brass band. Since then he had opened his own detective agency. Now his purpose seemed clear. He intended to set up a protection racket and milk profits from the whole acre.

Travis thought the problem through. Conditions in the acre had seldom been so unsettled. A citizen's group had met several times at the courthouse during the last few weeks to discuss ways to establish law and order in the acre. The group had passed a resolution encouraging officers to enforce the law.

Travis could not fathom what was in Courtright's mind. "I think we'd better walk over and see Luke," he said.

They left the Red Lantern and walked up Main Street to the White Elephant, where Luke Short was in partnership with a man named Johnson. Travis did not know Luke Short well. Few people did. He handled the gambling side of the White Elephant operation, while Johnson handled the saloon itself. Travis had learned that Short had managed similar ventures in Dodge City, Tombstone, Denver, Deadwood, Leadville, Gunnison, Trinidad, Silverton, Aspen, and Hayes City. He was known as a fast man with a gun. In Tombstone he had shot and killed the gambler Charlie Storms, who had enjoyed a considerable reputation as a gunman while alive. Short had let it be known around Fort Worth that he was a close friend of Bat Masterson, Virgil and Wyatt Earp, and Doc Holliday.

Short and Johnson were standing at the front of the White Elephant Saloon. The afternoon was quiet. The saloon was practically deserted.

Short was a small man, but compact and muscular. He was dressed in dapper fashion, with a three-piece suit, stiff hat, and a gold watch chain with ornament affixed.

Travis spoke to him in lowered voice. "Jay Jay here says Courtright has approached you with a proposition. It doesn't sound like Jim. I wonder if there isn't some misunderstanding."

"He was plain enough when he put it to me," Short said. "I've heard since that he's said some hard things about me. I don't like it one damned bit. If Jim's your friend, you'd better tell him to back off."

"Luke, I think we'd better get this straightened out before something happens we'll all regret," Travis said.

Short nodded. "Hell, I've always considered Jim my friend. I gave him money a few months ago so he could go to New Mexico and get loose from those charges. And this is the way he's repaid me."

"Speak of the devil," said Johnson.

Travis followed Johnson's gaze. Jim Courtright and his partner in the detective agency, Charles Bull, were walking past the saloon. Without a word Johnson went out the open door and hailed them a few steps down the sidewalk, in front of the shooting gallery.

"I hope Jim listens to reason," Short said. "I don't want trouble."

A shoeshine boy entered the saloon. Short called him over, raised a pant leg, and placed his boot on the stand to have it blackened. Travis and Jay Jay stood watching Johnson and Courtright. Johnson was doing most of the talking. Courtright stood listening, his face expressionless. They talked for several minutes.

Then Johnson gestured for Short, Travis, and Jay Jay to join them. Short tipped the shoeshine boy. Travis and Jay Jay followed Short out onto the sidewalk, where Johnson, Bull, and Courtright stood waiting.

Johnson spoke to Short. "Jim said he's only offering us a service. He said he regrets it if you've misunderstood and if you're disturbed about it."

Courtright towered over the smaller man. Short stood with feet spread, his thumbs hooked in the armholes of his vest. "What kind of service? I don't think I misunderstood you, Jim. Of course I'm disturbed. Haven't I always treated you right?"

"You've been a friend," Courtright said. "But I've since heard some things I don't like."

"So have I," Short said. "But I don't pay attention to everything I hear."

Short released his thumbs from his vest and brought his hands down. Courtright took a step backward. "Luke, don't you pull on me!"

"I have no gun here," Short said. His hands moved, spreading his coat.

Recognizing the danger, Travis stepped to one side, out of the line of fire. Courtright's hand went for his gun. Short's arms were a blur as he moved to one side, drawing a .45 Colt.

Short's gun roared. Courtright stood, pistol in hand, his eyes wide in surprise. He staggered backward toward the shooting gallery, still holding the pistol.

Short fired four more bullets into him.

Courtright fell to the sidewalk and lay still.

For a moment the scene remained frozen. Then Travis rushed to Courtright and rolled him face up. Courtright looked up at Travis and tried to speak. Then his eyes glazed over.

He still held his pistol in his hand. The hammer was not cocked. Travis saw that Courtright's hammer thumb had been blown away, apparently by Short's first bullet.

"It was self-defense," Short said behind him. "You men saw the whole thing."

Travis rose without answering, the reality of the moment more strange than any hallucination.

"Travis, you saw it, didn't you?" Short asked.

Travis nodded. Now that the shooting was over, people were gathering to stare at the body.

"I want you to defend me," Short said. "You can be both my witness and my lawyer, can't you?"

"I don't think it'll come to that," Travis said.

At the courthouse, they all made statements as to what had transpired. Travis quietly advised no mention of Jim's protection racket. "It'd only confuse the issue," he explained.

The county attorney agreed that self-defense was clear-cut. He said Short would not be prosecuted.

Before the day was out, Travis heard several versions of the shooting. Some said that Courtright's gun jammed. Others said Short masked his draw with the gesture of spreading his coat, and had his gun in hand before Courtright saw the danger. One rumor had it that Short was in love with Courtright's wife. That story came from Betty Courtright. But she also said Jim was shot in the back, and Travis knew that was not true.

Travis realized that he had witnessed the start of a legend, of the kind that filled the pages of Dime novels. Long Hair Jim Courtright had been regarded as perhaps the fastest gunman in Texas. Only Clay Allison and John Wesley Hardin were ever mentioned in the same breath. Even the greenest cowhand knew that Courtright ranked above Masterson, Holliday, Ketchum, Virgil Earp, Bill Longley. Travis knew that during the next few years the shooting would be discussed to exhaustion at every saloon, cowcamp, and waterhole west of the Mississippi.

He had been there.

And even he remained uncertain as to exactly what happened.

Two weeks later, Jay Jay also was dead, not in an epic gunfight but in another of the senseless killings that had become all too common in the acre. Travis did not see it. He received the story from witnesses.

Jay Jay had relieved the bartender for supper. The saloon was nearly empty. Three trainmen were hunched over a table, arguing about the merits of their union. A card game was in progress at the back. Old Harley Presnell stood at the bar, soaked to his ears. Fumbling with his whiskey, he dropped his shot glass, grabbed for it, and almost fell.

Jay Jay walked over, picked up the glass, and repeated the sad litany of bartenders since time immemorial. "You've had enough, Mr. Presnell. You'd better go on home."

"Just one more," Presnell pleaded.

"You've had enough," Jay Jay said again. "Go on home."

Presnell stepped away from the bar and raised his hands in a fighter's stance. "Nobody tells me when to go home."

The bouncer was out back, policing the cribs. Jay Jay saw no need to summon him. Harley Presnell was well past seventy. Forty years of unsuccessful farming had worn him down to the nub. He earned his keep as a sometime carpenter and handyman.

Jay Jay seized him by the collar and marched him out the front door.

The three trainmen left. Jay Jay took another round of drinks to the card players. He washed and polished the used glasses, and was stacking them behind the bar when he heard footsteps on the plank floor. He turned.

Harvey Presnell stood with feet spread. He held a twelve-gauge, double-bore shotgun, the barrels swinging in an arc, as if searching for a bird on the wing.

Then the shotgun centered on Jay Jay.

"God damn it, nobody tells me when to go home," Presnell said.

He fired both barrels. The eighteen slugs of double-ought buckshot removed the top of Jay Jay's head and showered the shelving behind the bar with his brains.

"Now I'll go home," said Harvey Presnell.

No one stopped him.

When officers went to arrest him, he was asleep. The next day he remembered nothing about killing Jay Jay.

Travis went through the funeral in a daze. He did not know which way to turn. Their long partnership had been so enmeshed in trust that few papers existed. He had used Jay Jay as a blind so long that he could find no way to unravel the situation.

Jay Jay's widow Isobel was even more confused. "He once told me that you had put up the money for the business, and that it belonged to you. He said that if anything ever happened, I was to go to you."

"I put up the money, but everything was half his," Travis explained. "If you're agreeable, I'll buy your share."

Isobel seemed overwhelmed by the amount he offered. She could not rid herself of the misapprehension that he was acting out of charity.

Eventually, only half convinced, she accepted the money, signed the necessary papers, and moved back with her family in Louisiana.

For the first time, the property in the acre was brought out from behind the secret partnership. Travis managed to hide the transactions to some degree through escrows and powers of attorney. But he could not escape a few public records.

Quietly he selected managers to replace Jay Jay. He swore each to secrecy.

For a time he was worried that his ownership of the businesses might become general knowledge.

But the flow of money continued. Nothing seemed to have changed.

Eventually Travis ceased to worry.

12

On a morning in the early spring of 1894, Reva was tending her flowers in the side lawn, weeding the irises. The Flower Parade was only a few weeks away, and she had decided that at sixteen Zetta was old enough to take part. A two-day soaking rain had just ended. Strong morning sunlight had restored a lush greenness to the lawn and to the bordering flowerbeds. Reva was thinking ahead, itemizing what blossoms would be available for the Flower Parade, when the sun suddenly turned dark and the world spun around. She sat down heavily in the grass and sank into blackness.

She awoke to Dulcie's panicky ministrations with a washcloth. "Miss Reva! Miss Reva!"

"I'm all right," she said. "I must have fainted. I don't understand it."

That afternoon she hurried to see Dr. Threadkeld. After an examination and pertinent questions, he smiled. "You're in fine health, Reva. In fact, every sign points to a budding pregnancy. This time I foresee no difficulty."

Reva remained in a state of shock. She long ago had abandoned all hope of more children. "But I'm thirty-six!" she heard herself say. It was hard to believe the good news.

Reva returned home in a daze, never for a moment questioning the diagnosis. The familiar symptoms were too plain. Moreover, she was certain she knew when she had conceived. There was no doubt it had happened on the trip to the Democratic Convention in Chicago. Something about trains seemed to bring out the erotic side of Travis.

"There's no better combination on earth than a sweet woman, a good Pullman berth, and a rough track," Travis had said.

Shocked, yet amused, Reva had giggled her way through a stretch of especially rough track on the Santa Fe line, southbound out of Chicago.

She waited that evening until Travis was in bed and spoke lightly. "You'd better use your high connections to get that rough track on the

Santa Fe repaired. It looks as if I'll be derailed for the best part of nine months."

Reva had suspected that he would be overjoyed, but she was unprepared for his reaction. He turned on the lights, danced around the room, and shouted his joy until Reva laughingly quietened him, fearing he would rouse Zetta and Durwood. He insisted on opening a bottle of champagne.

Before they went to sleep, Reva mentioned one of her minor worries. "How will we tell Zetta and Durwood?"

Travis laughed. "Why tell them at all?"

Reva waited until she became concerned that Zetta might guess. One afternoon after school she called them into the parlor and closed the French doors. She faced them, still not certain how they would take the news. Durwood remained small for his fifteen years, thin and fidgety. A teachers' darling, he seemed to have no interests other than schoolwork. He scrupulously maintained a straight-A average.

Zetta had grown tall and awkward, with broad shoulders and long, bony arms. Almost as a gesture of defiance she wore her hair pulled back into a severe bun. She sat looking at Reva with frank puzzlement.

"I thought I should tell you something that affects you, all of us," Reva said. "You're soon to have a little brother or sister."

Durwood seemed to retreat deeper into his shell. His eyes turned opaque behind his spectacles. Anyone who did not know him would have assumed that he had not heard.

Zetta gasped. She turned so pale that her freckles seemed to stand out from the flesh. "A baby!" she managed to say. "Another brother?"

Reva tried to turn it into a joke. "Or sister. I haven't made up my mind. Which would you prefer?"

Zetta spoke with the full disdain of her sixteen years. "Neither! Mother, I think you're positively indecent!"

Reva burst out laughing. For a moment she could not control herself. But she saw that Zetta was angry. She reached for her hand. "Zetta, I'm sorry. I'm not laughing at you. I do respect your feelings. It's just that if what you said is true, then there are many indecent people in the world."

Zetta jerked her hand away. She spoke with such naked hatred that Reva felt cold chills at the nape of her neck.

"I'd have thought that with your luck so far, you'd have had enough sense to quit."

Reva sat for a moment, stunned speechless. Then she slapped Zetta across the face with all her strength. Her voice quivered with anger. "Don't you ever, ever say anything like that again!"

Zetta burst out crying and fled upstairs.

Reva did not follow. Shaken, she went to her own room.

The next morning Zetta remained aloof. Durwood was merely indifferent. The incident was never mentioned.

But Zetta's words lingered in Reva's mind throughout her pregnancy. Deep in her heart she knew that her daughter's outburst bore a hard kernel of truth.

Night after night Reva lay awake, wondering if she were bringing even more unhappiness into the world.

From the first moment she saw Clayton Barrett Spurlock, Reva knew that at last she had produced a fitting heir for Travis. Even as the nurses wiped and dried Clay's husky little body, he gazed upon the world with such calm authority that she never doubted his strength of character.

From the day he learned to point, he bossed the household.

He was in his sixth month when the smallpox scare hit. A Negro who worked in one of the downtown hotels was the first victim. He died on the fourth day of illness. By then, six more cases had been confirmed, and rumors were flying that diseased travelers, evicted from other communities, had been seen alighting from incoming trains.

Overwhelmed with fear for her baby, Reva phoned her father.

"Isolate yourself," he advised. "Take Zetta and Durwood out of school. Keep them home. Ask Dulcie to sleep in until this is over. Let your other servants go. Travis may be a problem. He has to deal with the public. But convince him that he must stay away from the baby. Don't buy fresh vegetables. Boil everything you eat or drink. Don't receive visitors. You needn't be rude. Just say you're concerned about the baby. They'll understand."

"What about vaccination?" she asked. Groups were being formed to pass the cowpox strain from one person to the next, using the serum from skin lesions.

"It's too risky. You're liable to contact a carrier. I believe it'd simply be best to go into seclusion."

Reva put her father's suggestions into effect. Zetta, in her first year at Fort Worth College, and Durwood, a senior in high school, were reluctant, but their objections ended when the schools were closed. Within two weeks, forty-two patients had been moved to the pesthouse south of town. The epidemic was termed the worst in thirteen years.

Two weeks later Millie phoned with the news that Reva's father was seriously ill. "It's smallpox," she said. "There's no doubt."

Reva's first thought was to see him.

"That's out of the question," Millie said. "You have your own family to consider. Besides, he was moved to the pesthouse this afternoon. I'm gathering my things now. I'll go out tonight to take care of him until he's well."

Reva had heard many horror stories about conditions at the pesthouse. She could not imagine her parents in such a place. "Isn't there something else we can do?"

"Reva, your father has sent many patients out there. He won't hear of not going himself. Besides, it's the law."

"Let me be the one to go take care of him," Reva begged. "I'm younger—and stronger."

"My place is with him," Millie said. "Your place is with *your* family. Don't worry about me. I'll look after myself. Your father grew careless. After working through several epidemics, he thought he was immune. Obviously he wasn't. If you want to help, you can wire your sister. But tell her not to worry. Your father has weathered many a storm. He'll weather this one."

Rebecca and Wilbur had moved to Memphis, where Wilbur was attempting to become established in cotton trading. That afternoon, Reva sent Rebecca a telegram that included Millie's optimistic outlook.

Two nights later Millie did not sound so confident. "Your father has the sledgehammer strain. His lesions have already begun to hemmorhage."

By the next evening her father was dead and Millie herself was ill. "We put her to bed this morning," said Dr. Calloway. "She now has a fever of a hundred and four, which usually signals the fulminant strain. We'll do our best, but I'm afraid I can't offer much hope."

Reva was devastated. Never in her life had she felt so helpless.

"I simply must go out there and take care of her," she told Travis. "There's no one else. Rebecca couldn't possibly get here in time, even if she's inclined, which I doubt. I can't leave Mama to die alone!"

"I won't hear of your going," Travis said. "You think Millie would want her grandchild to grow up without a mother? She understands. She would be the first to tell you."

The argument was ended by Dulcie, who came to Reva with tears streaming down her ebony face. "Miss Reva, I've knowed Miss Millie since she was borned. She needs me now. I had the pox when I was just a little tyke. They tell me that once you've had it, you don't need to worry about getting it again."

So Dulcie sat at Millie's bedside during her last two days on earth.

Since public gatherings were banned, Travis arranged for private graveside services. Only Reva, Travis, Zetta, and Durwood attended. It seemed such a futile gesture, for the bodies were already in the ground, the graves raw and ugly.

During the next few weeks Reva stumbled from day to day, enveloped in a grief that would not go away. Moreover, she was faced with the disposition of her girlhood home and all its contents. Although her father had named Travis as executor of his estate, every agonizing decision fell on Reva. Each insignificant knickknack was burdened with memories.

Complications arose. Somehow Rebecca developed the idea that she was being cheated out of her rightful inheritance, that Travis and Reva were absconding with the bulk of the estate. Her letters, at first full of complaints, gradually turned mean and vicious. The smallpox epidemic ended, but still Rebecca refused to come to Fort Worth to discuss the estate. Reva suspected that Wilbur lacked the money for her travel expenses.

For the first time in her life Reva felt alone, abandoned. Eventually the estate was settled, but she knew that the breach with Rebecca would never be healed. Too much had been said in their letters. Their relationship was doomed to dwindle to cool, polite notes each Christmas season.

Travis offered little comfort. He seemed even more preoccupied than usual. He sat reading newspapers for hours at a time and frequently left on brief trips to Austin.

Reva was nursing the baby one afternoon when he came home early from the office. His eyes were animated, and he seemed as if he could hardly contain himself. "I think we both need a change of scene," he said. "How would you like to live in Washington for a while?"

Reva stared at him blankly. She could not imagine leaving the comforts of Bluebonnet. "Why Washington?"

Travis laughed. "I suppose you've heard that the old senator is dead."

"Yes," Reva said, puzzled. The news had been displayed prominently in the newspapers.

"The governor has appointed me to fill the remainder of the term, and I've accepted. The announcement will be made tomorrow in Austin."

Reva felt as if she could not survive one more disruption in her life. She spoke from her heart, without thought. "Do I have to go?"

The pleading tone in her voice brought Travis up short. He sat beside the bed and looked at her. "I suppose not. It won't be for long. Just over a year. I could take bachelor quarters, travel back and forth. But it would be a disappointment. I had so anticipated having you with me."

Reva felt tears start. She could not stop them. "Did you have to accept?"

Travis frowned. "It's a matter of responsibility, Reva. The party needs me. You see, the governor wants the post himself. And we want him in Washington. But he can't resign now and allow the lieutenant governor to appoint him, for the lieutenant governor is a weak man. The party would fall into disarray in Austin before election."

"It seems you could think of me! Your family!"

Travis did not answer for a moment. "I've thought of little else. Time after time I've turned down requests that I seek public office. I've agreed now only to fulfill the unexpired term, then step aside and support the governor in his bid. It seemed so simple. We could close Bluebonnet while we're gone and take a furnished place in Washington. I *was* thinking of you! I want to show you off at the grand balls. And a year in Washington would mean so much to the children."

Reva saw the hurt on his face. She realized that she was being selfish. Of course the children would benefit from the new experiences, from having a United States senator as a father. She spoke quickly. "Travis, it's just that I'm overwhelmed! At least give me a few minutes to absorb the idea. I've never once thought I'd ever be the wife of a U.S. senator! Of course I'll go with you."

Travis laughed his pleasure. He leaned over the bed and kissed her. "That's my little lady," he said. "We have a whole week to pack. But pull out your best dress. The reporters will be out here the first thing tomorrow morning."

Travis rose to his full height and faced the chairman. "Will the senator yield?"

Vice President Adlai E. Stevenson gaveled for order. "The chair recognizes the distinguished senator from Texas. Does the floor yield?"

Senator Gorman of Maryland bowed. "I yield to my respected colleague from Texas."

Travis turned and faced the gallery. The reporters were waiting, expectant, sensing that what he was about to say might be news. His stand on the Cuban issue had been a matter of speculation for days. Several senators who had started to leave the chamber were returning to their seats. Travis paused, allowing time for the stir to cease. He then spoke in practiced, lowered tones, gradually building his volume.

"Mr. President, esteemed colleagues, I stand before you today clothed in sorrow. I had hoped, before the events of last evening, that the leaders of my party would choose the right course. But clearly, that is not to be. The momentous events of our time demand that we rise above partisan politics."

Again he paused, allowing his audience to adjust to the fact that he was bolting the stated position of his party.

"Last week, when President Cleveland invoked the Monroe Doctrine against Great Britain in that country's dispute with Venezuela over the borders of British Guiana, I applauded the action. He effectively brought Great Britain to heel. A potentially dangerous situation was averted. But now, after the horrendous atrocities in Cuba, with the proof accumulating in every daily newspaper, I must ask a question: If the Monroe Doctrine is alive for Great Britain, why is it dead for Spain?"

Shouts of approval and disapproval rang throughout the chamber. Vice President Stevenson gaveled for order. Travis raised his voice.

"This august body has the responsibility to advise and consent on foreign policy. We as a nation have a responsibility to protect the weak, to confront aggressors. Cuba lies ninety miles from our shores. We have fifty million dollars of investments at risk in that country, one hundred million dollars in annual trade. Why do we stand here and quibble, when events are leading us inexorably toward war?"

The word had been assiduously avoided in the debates. Travis was gratified to see that it had the desired effect. He waited for the reaction to cease.

"Yes, gentlemen, I said war. Why do we shy away from plain facts? If we fail to stem the current progression of events, war with Spain is a certainty."

Shouts of dismay interrupted him. Travis glanced toward the press gallery. Several reporters had dispatched runners to telephones, to alert their city desks.

"Our course is clear," Travis resumed. "Once again we must prevail on the President to recognize the insurgent forces in Cuba and to offer our services for arbitration. I submit that no one in this chamber has seen more of war than I. No one wishes war less than I. Gentlemen, unless we act boldly, quickly, and decisively, that is exactly what we will have."

Travis resumed his seat, content that he had put the cap on one of the stormiest days in the U.S. Senate. The seats in the press gallery were practically deserted.

The debate droned on. Travis sat, only half listening, as he thought ahead to the ramifications of his speech.

His role in the Senate was peculiar, in that although he was a newcomer to Washington, he had held high office in the Democratic Party and had firm connections throughout the capital. During his first six months in office he had remained quiet, feeling his way. Now he had concluded that he must take a stand. His bold declaration that the President's policies were leading to war would make banner headlines and no doubt would be the major topic of discussion in Washington for days.

The Senate adjourned. Travis moved toward the door, accepting the proffered handshakes. Vice President Adlai Stevenson descended from his chair and confronted Travis in the aisle. The other senators moved aside to give them room to confer, yet lingered within earshot.

Adlai Stevenson was a tall, handsome man, despite his baldness. His eyes were deep-set and intelligent. A gray cookie-duster moustache lent his countenance gravity. His grip was firm. "An eloquent speech, Senator Spurlock. But most surprising. It almost seemed as if you wish to drive the party further away from the administration."

Travis spoke loud enough to be heard by the surrounding eavesdroppers. "To the contrary, Mr. Vice President, my purpose is to bring the President back to the party."

He walked on out of the chamber, confident that his message to the President would be delivered.

Life in Washington provided a rare opportunity for Reva to see her husband at work. She watched his performances at social functions with amazement. He moved among titled foreigners, administration officials, and the more famous politicians with a supreme confidence. She was impressed by the deference he received, even from those far older and more experienced. Somehow he had managed to envelop himself in mystery. She saw that others also sensed his hidden depths. They were intrigued, just as she had been since she was fourteen.

The parade of receptions, balls, and formal dinners was ceaseless. Travis also entertained, carefully orchestrating his political ploys. Thoroughly trained by Millie, Reva found herself adept at complying with even the most abstract rules of Washington protocol.

She worried about Zetta, who remained in the background and refused to participate, and about Durwood, cloistered in his first year at William and Lee. Life in Washington had not improved family unity, as she had hoped. In fact, it had driven them further apart. But Travis clearly was in his natural element. She remained astonished at his unbounded energy. Toward the end of his term in the Senate she was not surprised to find that she was again pregnant.

They lingered in Washington several weeks after the congressional session ended. Then, although she was in her fifth month, Reva felt well enough to accompany Travis to the Democratic National Convention in Chicago. There he led the fight to block routine endorsement of President Cleveland's administration—the first time in history that a political party had disassociated itself from its own president.

He headed the Texas delegation, and quietly organized support for a party platform advocating moderate, sane monetary policies. He moved tirelessly among the delegates, using anecdotes, jokes, argument, and confidences to sway votes.

But the unruly element on the convention floor prevailed. When Reva heard William Jennings Bryan deliver his Cross of Gold speech to unrestrained applause, she knew that Travis had lost. On a high tide of emotion, the convention selected Bryan as the Democratic nominee. Shorn of his major weapon, the speaker's platform, Travis could not assemble enough votes.

"There's no denying the appeal of the man," Travis said of Bryan. "But he has wrecked the convention. He can't make that speech at every polling place. His policies are not popular. The Republicans now can win with any candidate they choose."

But when the gold-policy Democrats bolted the convention to select their own candidates, Travis refused to go out with them.

"When you lose a battle, you don't quit the field," he said. "We'll be back to fight another day."

With the final portion of her pregnancy falling during the late summer months, Reva suffered from the heat. Temperatures rose well over a hundred day after day. Even the nights were hot and sultry. Reva moved into the southwest bedroom on the upper floor to catch as much breeze as possible. Zetta spread wet towels over the windows to cool the air.

The delivery was difficult. Reva was depleted of strength. But with her first glimpse of her new baby boy, all memory of her suffering and sacrifice faded.

From his first days, Malvern Jennings Spurlock habitually wore a winning, beatific smile almost impossible to resist. His features were soft, like Reva's own. He quickly laughed and cooed his way into everyone's affections.

While Reva recuperated, Zetta took charge of the household with a firm hand that brooked no interference. Travis attempted to show his appreciation. Zetta rebuffed his compliments with a vehemence Reva found puzzling.

"Zetta's turning into a perfect shrew," she said to Travis.

"It's just a phase," he said. "She'll grow out of it."

But Zetta had her hands full. Clay was an active child and required constant watching. As soon as he learned a peculiar, prancing toddle, he ran full tilt into furniture, doors, and walls with reckless, fearless abandon. Often cut and bruised, he seldom cried. Reva sometimes wondered if he were senseless to pain. He seemed to regard his baby brother as his new toy, and was fierce in his possessiveness.

Only Durwood remained immune to Vern's charms.

It was with Vern's arrival that the atmosphere of Bluebonnet changed. Tension left the air like dust in a summer rain. Not even Zetta's constant Greek chorus of complaint penetrated the peace that settled over the household.

At last Reva felt she had achieved contentment.

13

Zetta dressed slowly, taking pains with the gown made especially for the Flower Parade. It was of white linen, with a full-length skirt ironed to perfection, a high, blue choke collar, and bloused sleeves with ruffled cuffs. The belting was a blue silk sash, perfectly matching her ornate, flowered hat. She carried a white parasol with a blue silk fringe. Before she left her room, she checked her ensemble one last time. She was certain this would be the most important day of her life.

She descended the stairs. Auggie and Dulcie were alone in the parlor. Auggie rose to his feet. "Zetta, you look absolutely wonderful," he said. "Picture perfect!"

"Don't she?" Dulcie said, a little too effusively, clasping her hands in excitement. "Honey, your Papa and Mama done gone on. They said to tell you they'd see you after the parade."

Auggie escorted her to his carriage. He was small, and delicately built, but possessed a serious intensity Zetta liked. His forehead was high, his copper-colored curls hidden beneath his bowler. Of his features, she liked his eyes best. They were soft brown, somber, and thoughtful. His gray suit was neat and well cut. His mouth was firm, his face thin and angular. Zetta watched his sensitive, strong hands as he picked up the reins and guided the horses out of the drive.

"I told the Van Emden girls we would drop by their lawn party after the parade," he said. "Is that all right?"

Zetta hesitated. She did not want to put Auggie into an awkward situation, but neither did she wish to anger her father, especially where Auggie was concerned. "I'd love to go, if we can stop by Bluebonnet for a few minutes on the way. You see, some of Father's friends are here for his speech. I really should put in an appearance."

Auggie drove for a time in silence. "I might not fit in. That's not exactly my crowd."

"If you're a registered voter, you'll fit in. They're only politicians."

"I might not be welcome."

She shushed him. "Of course you'll be welcome. Don't you ever think otherwise."

They moved downtown at an easy trot. Auggie seemed unusually preoccupied. Zetta remained quiet, studying him.

She had known from the first day she met him that Augustus Porthouse offered the only chance she would ever have for happiness. She also was certain he had only awaited spring, and the romance of the Flower Festival, to declare his intentions.

She had entertained other gentleman callers during the three years since her family's return from Washington, but Auggie was the only one who had gone beyond the required courtesies. Only Auggie made her blood race.

True, he was divorced. He had explained once, in a passing reference, that he had married young, and badly. Zetta did not know the details, only that he had gone to Mexico on his honeymoon, and that some incident there had ended the marriage. She sensed that he had been hurt badly and was now looking beyond surface appearances in a bride. They had much in common. He seemed to appreciate the depth of her knowledge in the arts. He appeared to value her opinions.

But to her dismay, Travis disliked Auggie. Only Reva's intervention had prevented Travis from discouraging him. Auggie had been the subject of several stormy scenes.

"The man has no money, no prospects," Travis had said. "Apparently he has no ambition."

"He intends to become an artist or a writer," Zetta had explained. "He hasn't decided which."

"Zetta, a man who takes on the burden of a family must be practical," Travis had warned. "Painting and writing are pleasant and rewarding diversions. But a man has the responsibility of providing for those he loves."

There the matter had been standing for months. Auggie came each Sunday to take her for a drive. On one or two evenings each week he escorted her to a play or musical program.

Reva had suggested several coy maneuvers to force Auggie's hand. Zetta refused to use them. She felt that their relationship was exceptional, beyond the traditional ploys of courtship. She placed her faith in honesty.

Auggie parked the carriage and they found seats on the reviewing stand in front of the new red granite courthouse. The parade consisted of marching bands, and more than a hundred vehicles heavily decorated with fresh-cut flowers, carrying young ladies attired in elegant gowns.

Family retainers, togged out in elaborate costumes, walked beside the horses.

After the parade Travis delivered his speech from the platform in front of the courthouse. Preoccupied with Auggie and his solemnity, Zetta did not pay much attention. She only knew it had something to do with the sinking of the battleship *Maine* and the war fever that was sweeping the country.

But Auggie was impressed by the speech. On the way back to Blue-bonnet, he was even more somber. "The senator's right," he said. "This war will make America a world power."

For once Zetta was unable to hold her acid tongue. "That's a blessed poor reason to have a war," she snapped.

Auggie seemed not to have heard. "As the senator said, there's much more involved. How did he put it? The shift of power from the Old World to the New. The passing of the torch."

Zetta fell silent. Reva had warned her many times that she must never push herself into the male domain.

When they arrived at Bluebonnet, the driveway and street were crowded with carriages. In the parlor her father was surrounded by politicians. Talk was of the spring primaries, the coming war. Zetta and Auggie sampled the punch, made light conversation, and left within the hour.

They drove toward the lawn party at the Van Emden home. But as they drew near, Auggie suddenly turned into the park drive. He found a quiet spot and pulled the horses to a halt.

He sat for a time without speaking, as if collecting his thoughts. He then wrapped the reins around the brake, reached for her hands, and turned to face her. "Zetta, this is probably not the right way to do this. But there's so little time. So I'll just ask right out. Will you wait for me?"

Alarmed by the husky emotion in his voice, Zetta hesitated. She was confused. "Wait?"

"I've made up my mind. I'm enlisting. I doubt it'll be a long war. But it'd be easier to go, if I knew you'd wait for me."

Zetta felt that once again the world was slipping beyond her grasp. She could not block the anger in her voice. "Enlisting? Why, for God's sake?"

Auggie released her hands and looked into the distant trees. "Zetta, I don't know how to explain the way I feel. It just seems like something I must get behind me, before I can go on in life. As the senator said, this is our test as a nation, both as individuals and as a people. I feel it's my duty."

Furious, Zetta tossed her mother's warnings aside. "I couldn't dis-agree with my father more! I think the war with Spain is the ultimate in stupidity. What does the fighting on that miserable little island have to do with us?"

Auggie shook his head. "I was hoping you'd understand." Again he reached for her hands. "Zetta, I know you're a wonderful person. Honest, witty, intelligent, charming. I couldn't ask for more in a wife. I want to spend the rest of my life with you. Please try to see that this is something I simply must do."

Zetta opened her mouth to speak, then paused, uncertain what course to take.

She had just received her first proposal. She was twenty, and might never hear another. She loved Auggie. Spending her life with him was everything she wished. She shoved every other consideration aside. "Of course I'll wait for you," she said.

As Auggie kissed her, Zetta reminded herself that the odds were heavily in her favor. Auggie was of frail build and constitution. He might not pass the physical examinations. If he managed to enlist, he might not be sent overseas.

Travis ushered Auggie into the inner sanctum of his office complex and attempted to put the young man at ease. "Drink?" he asked. "Spot of bourbon?"

"No thank you, Senator," Auggie said.

Gesturing toward a chair, Travis sat at his desk and regarded his prospective son-in-law with a critical eye. Apparently Zetta was sold on the young man, but he had hoped for more. Auggie was small, thin, and nervous by nature. He had a good steady eye and an honest demeanor. But Travis could not imagine a man reaching twenty-seven years of age without accomplishing something in life. He assumed that Auggie was approaching him for help in obtaining employment, or perhaps a political appointment.

"What's on your mind this fine day, Auggie?" he asked.

Auggie clenched his hands, examined them for a moment, then looked up to meet Travis's gaze. "I came to tell you, sir, that I'm planning to enlist for service in the war. I've spoken to Zetta, and she has promised to wait for me."

Travis was surprised. He could not imagine those soft hands wielding a bayonet or firing a rifle or machine gun. The thought came to him that perhaps there was more to this young man than met the eye. "I think that's very commendable, Auggie. And I'm pleased with Zetta's response."

Auggie smiled. "You see, sir, if I'm going, I don't want to waste my time. I want to get right into the thick of it. I was hoping that with your connections, you might be able to help me do that."

For the first time since he had known Auggie Porthouse, Travis felt a rush of empathy. He understood Auggie's wish perfectly. In fact, if he were not almost fifty and burdened with family, he would have attempted to enter the war himself in some capacity. "I'll be glad to do what I can. What kind of situation would you prefer?"

"I think the cavalry, sir."

Travis thought of Durwood and his fear of horses. Auggie might be lacking in physical attributes, but he had spirit.

Travis remembered an item in the morning paper that had stirred his own blood. "Perhaps I *can* be of help. Does the name Theodore Roosevelt mean anything to you?"

Auggie frowned. "The New York police commissioner?"

Travis nodded. "More recently, assistant secretary of the Navy. A Republican, but a splendid fellow. He has just resigned his Navy post to organize a volunteer cavalry outfit. He's in San Antonio right this minute recruiting. If I'm any judge of character, he'll make his way into the thick of the fighting."

"That sounds wonderful, sir. How do I go about it?"

"If you'll take the six o'clock train, you'll be able to catch him in San Antonio. He'll be at the Menger Hotel, recruiting in the bar." Travis reached for a sheet of letterhead stationery. "I believe a letter from me will provide all the introduction you'll need."

He wrote a hurried note, including the comment that he believed Roosevelt would find the applicant tougher than he appeared. Travis signed the letter, sealed and addressed it, and handed it to Auggie.

"If there's anything else I can do to help, I'll be happy to oblige."

"You've already done more than enough, sir. Thank you."

Travis walked him to the door and put a comradely hand on his shoulder. "Good-bye, and good luck. And I want you to know that we're proud of you. Let us hear from you. We'll be looking forward to welcoming you into our family when you return."

Travis watched Auggie walk away and wondered how the fragile young man would fare in the rough world of the cavalry.

There was one certainty.

If anyone could make a man of him, Teddy Roosevelt would.

Although Travis continued to follow politics, he discovered that he had neglected business too long. With the proliferation of railroads to virtually every small town throughout the state, revenues gradually declined. The operations of two railroads in which he owned major interests became marginal. After service in the Senate and the higher reaches of the Democratic Party, he felt he no longer should represent murderers. He turned almost exclusively to civil practice, a specialty he had too long neglected. He had invested considerable money in a meat-packing venture, but the techniques of refrigerated rail shipment were not yet perfected. The effort was underfinanced and ill-managed. Travis lost heavily.

With the closing of the Chisholm Trail, income from Hell's Half Acre also declined. The rambunctious portion of town shrunk, and the respectable population expanded. Travis tried to sell his property in the acre, thinking to invest the proceeds elsewhere, but he had chosen the locations too well. They lay within the tainted district, and there was no market for them. Eventually Travis abandoned the effort. As other revenues dwindled, the rentals and blind partnerships in the acre became the bulk of his income.

A month after Auggie left, Travis received a brief note from Roosevelt, thanking him for sending a recruit, and devoting a full paragraph to praise for Auggie's diligence and dedication. Auggie sent frequent letters to Zetta, but she seldom commented on their contents.

In late June, newspaper accounts reported that Roosevelt and his Rough Riders had landed in Cuba. A few days later they participated in a major battle at La Quasima. On the first day of July, as a part of Shafter's movement on Santiago, the Rough Riders were cited for an impetuous and daring charge on foot up Kettle Hill in the battle for San Juan.

Auggie's letters to Zetta ceased. She waited each day for the postman, then retired to her room, not even emerging for the family meals. Reva took food up to her on a tray. Zetta refused to eat.

Travis telegraphed contacts in Washington, but was unable to obtain any information.

In late July an envelope arrived, bearing Roosevelt's familiar bold scrawl. Travis opened it with trepidation. He found another envelope inside, addressed to Zetta, and a few hurried lines addressed to himself:

> *I suppose by now you have been notified of the death of Lieutenant Porthouse from yellow fever. Unfortunately, he did not live to participate in the action during the Battle of Santiago. However, he distinguished himself with his gallantry and bravery in the fighting at La Quasima. I have recommended his posthumous decoration. You have my deepest condolences in your loss of an outstanding prospective son-in-law. Under separate cover, along with my personal note, I am forwarding a letter found in Lieutenant Porthouse's possession at the time of his death, and addressed to your daughter. Lieutenant Porthouse*

was a fine young man, and a splendid soldier. He will be missed
by my entire command.

Travis was grateful that the weeks of silence had prepared Zetta for the worst. He took the letter home and went up to her room.

She was seated in the corner by the open windows, a book open on her lap. She looked up, guarded, wary. He seldom came to her room.

"Zetta, I'm afraid I'm the bearer of very bad news," he said. "I think you know what it is."

He handed her the letter, including the covering note from Roosevelt. He sank onto an ottoman and waited as she read them.

She cupped a hand over her mouth and made a choking sound. But when she spoke, her voice was devoid of emotion.

"I've known since his letters stopped. I think I knew even before he left."

"Zetta, I can't tell you how sorry I am," Travis said. "I was wrong about him. He was a fine young man."

Her voice remained flat. "I hope you and Colonel Roosevelt are satisfied. The war has been glorified. Colonel Roosevelt has been glorified. You and your speeches have been glorified. Auggie has been glorified. I only have one question. What about the life Auggie and I planned together? What about the children we'll never have? Who'll glorify them?"

Her total lack of emotion worried Travis. He feared she was in a state of shock. "Zetta, we all grieve his loss. Maybe this isn't the time to say this, but you're young. You have a long life ahead of you. There'll be other men."

Zetta made a helpless gesture. The book slid from her lap to the floor. "Papa, I'm twenty—an old maid. There were no men in my life before Auggie. There won't be any now. You want to know what the boys called me in school? *Horseface!* I'm ugly! Don't you know that?"

Travis picked up the book. It was a volume of poetry by Emily Dickinson. "Zetta, that's not true! You're overwrought."

"It *is* true. Mama knows the kind of life I have ahead of me. I see her pain every time she looks at me." Zetta waved the letter. "This is my death notice too. I died with Auggie in that stinking little town in Cuba."

Travis thought she was out of her head. He tried to calm her. "Zetta, you're alive. You're a lovely girl. Of course there'll be other men. But we'll talk about that later. This isn't the time—"

"There's no better time," Zetta snapped. Her eyes narrowed in anger. "If it hadn't been for you and your selfish, inflated, vainglorious patriotism, Auggie'd still be alive!"

Travis did not understand. "Selfish?"

"You don't care about me, Mama, or your family. I know about your other women. You think only of your own pleasure, your own ego."

Stunned, Travis groped for the first words that came to mind. "Zetta, maybe you've heard some rumors, but . . ."

"Spare me the lies. I've seen you!"

Travis remained silent for a moment, wondering how much she knew. "Does your mother know?"

Zetta looked at him with undisguised hatred. "If she does, she didn't learn from me. *I'm* not heartless."

Travis groped for the right words. "Zetta, there are many things about life you don't understand."

"If they're as gross as I think, then I don't want to know them."

Travis rose to his feet and handed her the book. "Anyway, I'm sorry about Auggie. I wouldn't have had it happen for the world. But you're wrong to blame me. Auggie was a man, and he made his choice."

Zetta remained in her room for days. When she emerged, she wore black.

The color was apt. In the months that followed, Zetta became a dark presence in Bluebonnet, forever voicing the somber view, foretelling tragedies, criticizing every imperfection, serving as the family conscience. She seldom appeared in public. On the rare occasions when she attended musical or dramatic performances, she took care to arrive late, after the lights were dimmed. Quietly, she devoted much time to charities and helped to underwrite the Fort Worth appearances of Enrico Caruso, Eleanora Duse, Lilly Langtry, Edwin Booth, Harry Lauder, Sarah Bernhardt, Dustin Farnum, Douglas Fairbanks, and the Barrymores. She championed avant-garde art and refused to compromise with the bluenosed and fainthearted. Accepting the budget problems of the fledgling public library as her own, she hounded the city council and county commission until adequate funds were granted.

Travis observed her accomplishments with mingled pride and dismay.

Apparently Zetta had decided that if she were forced to live as a spinster, she would perform the role with a vengeance.

With the turn of the century, the nation entered a period of disorienting transition. Travis watched the changes with growing apprehension. His long battle for a meat-packing plant ended as Swift & Company absorbed the troubled local firm and expanded operations to envelop a large portion of North Fort Worth.

Armour & Company was not far behind. The city began the most dramatic period of growth since the coming of the railroad. Acres of corrals blossomed on the North Side to hold livestock for shipping, slaughter, and exchange. The air was laden with an array of new odors.

Wherever Travis went he felt like a stranger. At home Reva devoted most of her attention to young Clay and Vern. His relationship with Zetta eventually settled into an armed truce. Durwood finished college and began work as a bookkeeper in a bank. He became immersed in photography. His interest was not with portraits or landscapes but with pictures of abstract light patterns. Travis could not make head or tail of them.

To escape, Travis again turned to poker. He felt that an ex-senator should not frequent open saloons, so he patronized the private rooms. There he found a more genteel clientele.

One afternoon, in search of a good game of five-card stud, he wandered into the room over the White Elephant. Four men sat at a corner table. The rest of the room was deserted.

"Senator! Come on over and take a hand," said one of the men.

Travis had entered from the bright sunlight of the street. Slowly his eyes adjusted to the gloom. He recognized the men. They were a witty, lively bunch. He had played poker with them several times.

"I hope you're playing no-limit," he said to the one he remembered as Jim Lowe. "I feel especially lucky today."

Lowe laughed. "We've had some luck ourselves lately. Maybe we can accommodate you."

Travis pulled up a chair. Lowe seemed to be the wheelhorse of the bunch. He played a mean game of poker. Money seemed to have no meaning for him.

His friend Harry Place was a more conservative player. But his quietness could be misleading. An opponent never knew what he was thinking.

The third man was named Bill, the fourth, Ben. Travis could not remember their last names.

He had seen them in the acre several times and was curious about them. They would be gone for months at a time, then reappear for marathon parties. They dressed well and seemed to have an inexhaustible supply of money. Travis once asked their line of work.

"We're in speculation," Lowe had said.

The others laughed as if it were a private joke.

Travis did not inquire further.

Travis won consistently through the afternoon. Toward sundown he was more than five hundred dollars ahead.

Lowe looked up at the clock. "We're just warming you up for a killing, Senator. But our timing is off. We're due at a party."

They cashed in their chips. Lowe bought a final round of drinks.

"Fact is, Bill here is getting married," he said. "We're giving him a send-off. Why don't you come on along?"

Travis offered the groom his congratulations. On impulse, he agreed to accompany them to the party.

Leaving the White Elephant, they walked down Main Street to a rooming house known as Maddox Flats. There the party was in progress.

Travis was introduced to Lily, the bride. With a jolt, he realized that she was a veteran of Fanny's sporting house. Glancing around, he recognized several other girls from Fanny's. Growing uncomfortable, he walked across the room to Lowe, intending to make excuses and leave.

"Senator, meet Etta," Lowe said. "Etta, entertain the senator."

Travis had never seen the woman before. She was tall, with soft brown eyes and a sensuous mouth. She wore a trim, well-tailored black dress. Clearly, she was a cut above her companions. She had an air of mystery about her, of a compact, strong character.

Her voice was low and throaty. "Are you really a senator?"

"Former senator," Travis said. "I just dropped by to wish the bride and groom my best."

Place and Lowe were now half drunk and roughhousing. They scuffled, trying to wrestle each other to the floor. Lowe tripped Place, then turned and ran out of the room. Their footsteps clattered down the stairs.

"I doubt those two will ever grow up," Etta said.

"I take it you know them well," Travis said.

She looked at him for a half beat before answering. "Harry's my husband," she said.

Travis was of two minds. He wanted to continue his talk with this fascinating woman. But he remembered where he was and who he was with. He could not have it get back to Reva—or Zetta—that he was seen in a public rooming house, cavorting with prostitutes.

"I really must be going," he said. "If I miss seeing Mr. Lowe on the way out, tell him I said thanks for inviting me."

As Travis walked out into the street, Lowe was trick-riding a bicycle back and forth in front of the building. The prostitutes were leaning out of the second-floor windows, cheering him to feats ever more reckless.

On a busy afternoon several months later Travis sat at his desk, compiling an appeal in a landmark railroad case. His secretary interrupted to announce a Mr. William Pinkerton.

The name was familiar. But not until the man entered did Travis make the connection to the Allan Pinkerton who had founded the detective agency. "I've read your father's books," he said. "What can I do for you?"

Pinkerton opened a portfolio and handed him a photograph. "I only need you to help me with some identifications, Senator. Do you recognize these individuals?"

Travis not only knew the men, he remembered when the photograph was made. On the day of his last poker game with them, Jim Lowe, Harry Place, and their friends had joked about their trip over to John Swartz's studio for a formal group portrait. Pretending to study the photograph, Travis considered his answer. He felt a vague loyalty to Lowe. Yet he had to remember his own position.

"I assume this interrogation is of a confidential nature," he said.

"Of course."

"I've played a few games of poker with these gentlemen."

"What did they call themselves?"

Travis pointed. "This one was Jim Lowe. This one was Harry Place. These two I knew as Ben and Bill. I don't recall the other gentlemen."

"And when was this?"

"About late June, maybe early July. They had a party at Maddox Flats."

Pinkerton handed him another photograph. "Was this woman with them?"

Travis had no difficulty remembering. He nodded. "She was introduced to me as Etta. She said Harry Place was her husband."

Pinkerton retrieved the photographs and thanked Travis for his cooperation.

"Would you mind telling me the nature of the case?" Travis asked.

Pinkerton smiled. "Lowe is better known as Butch Cassidy. Harry Place is Harry Longbaugh, alias the Sundance Kid. Any money you won in that poker game probably came from the Winnemucca Bank job."

"I hope you don't want it for evidence," Travis said. "I imagine I've either spent or deposited the cash."

Pinkerton shook his head. "Their next take was forty thousand dollars in unsigned bank notes from the Great Northern Express Company. That money's much easier to trace. They brought it back here, and the whores down at Fanny's spent two days forging the signatures. A bank cashier in Dallas spotted some of the notes. That's what put us on their trail."

"And the woman?"

"That picture of her was made at the old Mathew Brady studio in New York. She went there with Cassidy and Longbaugh. They partied for a while before quitting the country. The three of them are now robbing banks and trains and raising hell all over South America."

Long after Pinkerton had left, Travis sat in a meditative silence, thinking of Etta, her delicate beauty, and her profound mystery.

Never before had he been so impressed by anyone on such a brief encounter.

He could not shake the feeling that somehow their lives were entwined, and that they were destined to meet again.

14

The brisk April wind had grown even colder in the hour since sunrise. Travis turned up the collar of his sheepskin coat and leaned forward to control his high-strung horse. "We're ready now, Mr. President," he said. "When we jump the next wolf, the three of us will take the lead. The rest of the party will follow."

President Theodore Roosevelt nodded his understanding, stood in his stirrups, and attempted to see over the next rise. He turned to Travis. "Shouldn't we have more dogs?"

Jack Abernathy was only a few yards ahead, unleashing the three hounds. "Jack says he only needs enough dogs to turn the wolf into a fighting stance," Travis explained. "The dogs are trained to keep the wolf at bay, not to fight."

Abernathy moved forward at a trot. Travis and the President fell in close behind. The hounds fanned out in the thick, knee-high grass ahead, keeping their noses to the ground, crisscrossing in search of wolf sign.

Travis glanced behind. The rest of the party was advancing, about two hundred yards to the rear.

As unofficial host for the President's visit to the Big Pasture, he felt a huge responsibility for the conduct of the hunting party.

Ahead, one of the dogs stopped, moved in a half circle, gave voice, then broke into a run. The other hounds took up the cry. All three disappeared over the crest of the hill. Abernathy put spurs to the big horse he called Sam Bass. Travis heard the slap of the President's quirt, and they were off at a full-out run to keep the dogs in sight.

As he topped the rise, Travis caught a glimpse of the wolf, no more than a quarter of a mile away. Abruptly, the wolf changed direction.

"He's heading for rough ground!" Travis yelled.

Roosevelt did not answer, but again quirted his horse. Riding a few yards behind, Travis marveled over the way Roosevelt moved as if he and the horse were one—no mean feat for such a large man. The horse was a dove-colored stallion, the best of the blooded string at Tom Waggoner's D Ranch. Travis was astride a dun from Burk Burnett's 6666. Both were range-wise, adept at dodging the small boulders often hidden in the waving grass.

Travis saw why the wolf had turned. The animal was racing through a large prairie dog town. Holes dotted the prairie, posing deadly hazards for a running horse. Travis tightened his reins, assuming that the President would slow to a trot, as any sane man would do.

Roosevelt did not hesitate. He swung his horse into the mounds of fresh-tossed dirt at a full run, skillfully guiding his horse around some holes, leaping others.

Travis had no choice. The safety of the President was his responsibility. Abandoning caution, he put spurs to his horse.

The wolf was still in sight, running toward a distant ravine. Travis held his breath as the President's stallion plunged across a prairie dog mound and stumbled. Roosevelt shifted his weight, helping the horse to recover. They rode on.

Once clear of the prairie dog town, Travis glanced back. No other rider was in sight. They had left the remainder of the party far behind.

Travis and Roosevelt were thundering down a draw when, far ahead, the wolf turned to face the dogs. First one hound then another lunged, feigning an attack, keeping the wolf at bay.

Abernathy arrived at the scene, pulled Sam Bass to a halt, and leaped from the saddle. He ran toward the wolf on foot. The dogs continued to circle, snapping, lunging, keeping the animal busy.

Travis and Roosevelt rode to within thirty feet of the drama and stopped.

With his right arm before him as if to ward off a blow, Abernathy advanced. Snarling, the wolf seemed confused by the unexpected threat of a man on foot. He feinted toward Abernathy, then retreated, fangs bared. Again Abernathy moved forward.

Almost too fast for the eye to follow, the wolf lunged, his fangs going for Abernathy's throat. The pudgy cowboy slashed at the wolf with open palm.

Then Abernathy stood grinning up at the President, holding the kicking wolf free of the ground by its lower jaw.

He had captured the wolf using only his bare hands.

"Bully!" Roosevelt shouted. He leaped from the saddle. "Travis, did you see that? Good golly! I wouldn't have believed it!"

The wolf was still struggling. Travis was worried that it might get loose.

The President did not seem to share his concern. Roosevelt walked close and examined Abernathy's grip on the jawbone. "Has the wolf hurt you?"

"No," Abernathy said, raising the wolf higher for the President's inspection. "You see, there's not much power in his jaws. A wolf doesn't chew his food, like some animals. He just tears with his canine teeth. If you can manage to grab him back of those fangs, you've got him."

Roosevelt circled Abernathy, examining the kicking wolf. The remainder of the hunting party arrived. Most were on horseback. Some rode in surreys. Comanche Chief Quanah Parker, three of his wives, and one of his babies rode in one hack. In another were ranchers Burk Burnett, Tom Waggoner, and the President's physician, Dr. Alexander Lambert.

A camera was set up. Roosevelt and Abernathy were photographed with the catch. Other members of the hunting party gathered around, and more pictures were made.

A stick was slipped into the wolf's jaws. Abernathy removed his hand. The animal was muzzled and loaded into a cage on the back of a wagon.

"This is bully sport," Roosevelt said to Abernathy. "I'll tell you what. The next wolf we raise, I'll try to nab him. You can advise me if I go about it wrong."

Abernathy looked to Travis in silent appeal.

"It's also dangerous sport, Mr. President," Travis said. "I've seen several men attempt it. Abernathy is the only man I know who can do it without harm."

"A wolf always goes for the throat," Abernathy explained. "If he gets me, we're just out one Texas cowboy. But we've only got one president."

Roosevelt laughed. "Mr. Abernathy, I've been handling congressmen for years. They always go for the throat."

Dr. Lambert had overheard the exchange. He left his hack and approached the President. "Teddy, I'm responsible for your health. A wolf's fangs are capable of ripping out your jugular in the twinkling of an eye. If that happened out here on the prairie, there wouldn't be a thing I could do for you."

Roosevelt slapped Lambert on the back. "Alex, you have a talent for convincing argument. All right. I'll leave it to the expert. But some day I want to learn that trick, Mr. Abernathy."

As the group moved on westward, Travis felt a wave of relief that they had been able to talk the President out of attempting to subdue a wolf with his bare hands.

Before starting his speaking tour across the country, Roosevelt had written Travis, saying he had heard stories about a Texas cowboy named

Jack Abernathy who caught wolves with his bare hands. The President said that if the stories were true he would like to see the feat performed.

Fortunately Travis had the right connections. Years before, he had met Quanah Parker when one of the chief's fathers-in-law had asphyxiated himself in a Fort Worth hotel by blowing out the gas lamp. Travis had been instrumental in convincing the victim's suspicious family that Quanah was blameless. In appreciation Quanah had taken Travis into the tribe as a blood brother, and retained him to represent the Comanches before the Bureau of Indian Affairs. It was a simple matter to obtain from his old friend permission for the President to hunt on Indian lands. Travis also had done considerable legal work for two of the state's largest spreads, owned by Burk Burnett and Tom Waggoner. The ranchers helped to organize the hunt, supplying horses and equipment.

Before Roosevelt's speech in Fort Worth, Travis had entertained him at Bluebonnet. He then escorted him by train across the Red River, where the hunting party awaited. Soldiers were patrolling the borders of the reservation, turning back newspapermen and the public.

That afternoon they raised two more wolves. Abernathy captured one. The other escaped.

"This is the life," Roosevelt told Travis. "I've seldom had such fun."

On the way back to camp the President suddenly leaped from his horse and flailed at the ground with his quirt. Travis rode toward him, arriving in time to see Roosevelt finish killing a large diamondback.

The snake was sacked and preserved for the Smithsonian.

That evening, in deference to the teetotaler President, the day's exploits were toasted with grape juice before a roaring campfire.

The next morning the presidential party boarded the train at the small town of Frederick, Oklahoma Territory. While his aides tended to the baggage, Roosevelt took Travis aside.

"I've not only had a grand time," he said. "I've also found the type of men I admire. You'll be hearing from me."

A week after Roosevelt returned to Washington, the newspapers announced that Jack Abernathy had received a presidential appointment as United States marshal to Oklahoma Territory.

On the same day, Travis was summoned to the Roosevelt home at Sagamore Hill on Oyster Bay, Long Island, for briefing on his appointment as a special presidential envoy to Europe.

"What I want you to do is to dip your toe, and let me know the temperature of the water," Roosevelt said. "Ostensibly, you'll be my emissary, with a private message for each person on your list. But it goes beyond that. I want you to talk to them. Look them in the eye. Tell me what you think."

Travis did not answer. He had just seen the list. He remembered his long-ago vow that some day he would walk with kings and queens.

He was seated in the North Room at Sagamore Hill, surrounded by memorabilia of Roosevelt's life. Two buffalo heads flanked the tall fireplace. On the opposite wall the President's Rough Rider sword, hat, and revolver hung from the wide antlers of an elk. The large room—at least thirty by forty feet—was decorated by high Ionic columns that added dignity to the rustic, reddish-brown woodwork. A high ceiling added to its sense of spaciousness. The large windows on the west wall were framed by bookshelves.

"King Edward is the lynchpin," Roosevelt went on. "As you probably know, he's related to most of the crowned heads of Europe, corresponds with them constantly, sees them often. I'm convinced that he alone has prevented war thus far."

"I've heard he dislikes Americans," Travis said.

Roosevelt nodded agreement. "He's a snob. He considers us crude. Perhaps by his standards we are. But at the same time, he's greatly impressed by erudition, manners, and ideas. He has several American friends. I believe you and he will hit it off fine."

"I understand I'm to travel with my family, as if on a long European tour. That may mislead the press. But it won't deceive everyone. What'll be my relationship with the embassies?"

Roosevelt laughed. "Cordial, I hope. You'll encounter some resentment. But I'll do what I can to pave the way. I want you to spend a couple of weeks in Washington before you leave. You'll receive thorough background information from the State Department."

Travis debated how best to phrase his next question. "Mr. President, I've read all the material. But nowhere do I find the answer. What is the underlying purpose of my trip?"

Roosevelt gazed out the west windows, toward the setting sun. "Travis, we must serve notice on Europe that the time has come for us Americans to assert ourselves in world affairs. They haven't yet awakened to the fact that we're an international power. Too much is at stake. Trade, immigration, all aspects of our national life are affected."

"I quite agree, sir. I've often said as much on the floor of the Senate, and elsewhere."

Roosevelt nodded. He spoke slowly, stressing each syllable. "There's another facet to your trip, one that's seldom acknowledged in diplomatic circles. Before any formal talks between countries, there must be informal contact, a meeting of minds on the subject outside routine diplomatic channels, with nothing in writing that might compromise us later.

Your mission is such a quasi-official probe. I hope you understand the delicacy, especially with King Edward. If your mission is successful, more talks will be conducted, to put a formal countenance on it. But you are responsible for the beginning."

"I understand," Travis said. "I'm to convey your views, listen to his, and make no commitments."

"Exactly. You see, Edward holds a unique position not only in Europe but within his own government. No English monarch of modern times has been granted such sweeping powers in foreign affairs. The devotion of his public is almost total. We *must* let him know where we stand."

They talked a while of specific issues, Roosevelt's views, and the logistics of Travis's trip.

Afterward, Roosevelt walked him down the hall to the front gallery, where a carriage awaited to take him back to Oyster Bay. On the front steps the President gave him a farewell handshake and put an arm around his shoulder. "Travis, you have an uncanny ability to reason with other men, to read what's on their minds. I've seen you at work on the floor of the Senate, in the political arena, on the treeless prairies. This won't be much different."

Travis spoke with a tone he hoped conveyed total confidence. "Mr. President, I'll do my best."

Travis examined his new suit in the full-length mirror. The knee breeches and high stockings felt tight, the frock coat too loose. He brushed the ruffled lace on his chest in an attempt to make it lie flat. "I feel like an absolute fool," he said.

Reva giggled. "You wore a costume much like that at the jousting tournament, and you didn't seem to mind."

"That was thirty years ago, and all in fun," Travis said. "I've enough on my mind without feeling like a clown to boot."

"You look dashing, and charming," Reva said. "I'm laughing only because you seem to have stepped out of the wrong century."

Again Travis wondered why King Edward VII, who had made fashionable such innovations as the Norfolk coat, dinner jacket, and homburg hat, remained so inflexible on formal dress. The king still insisted on knee breeches and the frock coat, and was known to rebuke, publicly, anyone who deviated in the slightest. For safety, Travis had commissioned his suit with the king's own tailor.

He had no doubt as to the importance of the evening. During his two weeks in London he had managed to see the king only once. His personal letter from Roosevelt had been accepted by Francis Knollys, the king's private secretary, and Travis was dismissed after a brief, innocuous exchange with the king. There had been something odd about the whole affair.

For more than a week Travis had expected an invitation for a private audience. While waiting, he had toured London with his family. Anticipating word from the palace any day, he had not dared venture outside of London. Through his clubs in America he obtained reciprocal privileges at White's, Boodle's, and St. James's, and whiled away his evenings at cards with titled gentry. But he had heard nothing from the palace. At last, growing desperate, he allowed the embassy to let it be known to the press that he was in town. He received a dozen newspaper reporters in his family suite at Claridge's, supplied them with background press clippings, and answered their questions concerning his experiences in the American West. The resulting stories were accompanied by fanciful illustrations of his Civil War exploits, his Indian tribal ceremonies, his forays on the plains buffalo hunting, and his wolf hunt with Roosevelt.

The invitation to a Buckingham Palace reception had arrived four days ago. Travis had immediately recognized it for what it was.

The king wanted to look him over.

If he passed muster, he might yet gain the king's confidence and live up to Roosevelt's expectations.

"I'll probably swoon in this corset," Reva said. "Keep your penknife handy. It may save my life."

"You look ravishing," Travis said.

Her hair was swept up in the bird's nest made fashionable by Paris courtesans and the heroines of Charles Dana Gibson. Her gown was of pearl-colored silk, appliquéd with lace, cut to stress her narrow waist. She wore the pearl collar he had given her on their silver anniversary. The necklace was especially striking above her off-the-shoulder décolletage. Travis knew that her complaint about the corset was not an idle remark. The hourglass waist had become such an obsession that some women resorted to surgery for removal of their lower ribs.

Zetta came in to help her mother with last-minute preparations. "Don't forget that the queen is almost deaf, Mama. Remember to raise your voice and speak directly to her. She's lame, and terribly sensitive about it. Try not to notice."

"I doubt we'll have much opportunity," Reva said.

Travis checked his watch. "The carriage will be waiting. We mustn't be late."

Zetta accompanied them downstairs, fussing to make sure Reva had all her accessories. Reva remained enveloped in her habitual calm.

They were driven into Buckingham Palace through the Marble Arch, taking their place in line. As their carriage drew up at the entrance, liveried footmen scurried to help them alight. They were ushered inside, their wraps were taken, and they joined a queue in the foyer.

As they stood waiting to be announced, a voice boomed behind him. "Ah, Senator, good to see you again!"

Travis turned. Richard Burdon Haldane stood immediately behind them. After meeting him one evening over cards at Boodle's, Travis had checked on his background. He learned that although Haldane was a leader in the imperialist wing of the Liberal Party, he recently had been named to the War Office, usually considered the grave of the ambitious.

Haldane was alone. Travis recalled that he was unmarried.

Haldane raised himself on tiptoe in an effort to see into the ballroom. "It'll no doubt be a sticky evening, Senator. I wager His Majesty won't be in the best of humor."

Haldane's voice had once been compared to that of a beast in pain. The other guests either smiled or pointedly ignored him.

Travis thought briefly of stepping out of line on some pretense but quickly reconsidered. Haldane was one of the staunchest supporters of the king in Parliament. One might do worse than to be seen in Haldane's company.

He introduced Reva. "Why should the king be unhappy?" Reva whispered. "Has something happened?"

Travis spoke softly. "An interview with the king's nephew, the Kaiser Wilhelm, appeared today in the *Daily Telegraph*. He was quite uncomplimentary about the English and about King Edward."

"He said we English are as mad as March hares," Haldane said. "Took full credit for our victories in the Boer War. Claimed he sent the queen all our battle plans. You never heard such rot."

Travis and Reva were announced. As they entered the ballroom, Travis recognized several gentlemen he had met at the clubs. The reception was small by diplomatic standards, hardly more than three dozen couples. He saw no deviations from the prescribed knee breeches and frock coats. In contrast, the ladies were elegantly gowned in the most modern fashions.

Travis felt tension in the air. He remembered Haldane's prediction.

King Edward and Queen Alexandra entered a few minutes later, passing quite close to Travis and Reva.

The king had the blotchy coloring of a seriously ill man. He was corpulent in the extreme, and wheezed from the simple exertion of walking. He was of slightly less than average height, and almost bald, his head sleek and shining under the crystal chandeliers. His well-trimmed beard was gray, blending into his full, darker moustache.

The queen seemed much younger than her years. Tall and willowy, she moved with a graceful glide that almost masked her stiff knee, the result of rheumatic fever early in her marriage. She wore her short, reddish hair in ringlets swept high, enhancing her long, angular face. Her dress was of dark silk chiffon, low-cut, with frilly half sleeves. A strand of pearls was wrapped around her throat five times, in the fashion she had created.

A reception line formed and moved rapidly. Soon Travis and Reva were presented.

Travis saw the king studying him from head to foot, no doubt looking for imperfections. Travis bowed deeply as Reva curtsied.

"Good evening, Senator," Edward said. "Sorry I didn't have time to chat more the other day. President Roosevelt wrote that he thinks most highly of you."

"The President does me honor, Your Majesty."

Edward's appraising gaze lingered. He nodded almost imperceptibly, as if in approval. Travis moved on.

The reception was a curious affair. Although a small orchestra played softly at one end of the room, there was no dancing. Sideboards offered a sumptuous array of food, too substantial to be termed hors d'oeuvres, yet short of a full supper. The king moved to the buffet and acquitted himself well. Travis noticed he seemed to have a weakness for Viennese pastries.

The guests assembled in small groups and talked. Across the room Travis saw Whitelaw Reid, the American ambassador. They acknowledged each other's presence with exchanged nods.

Travis and Reva drifted into a circle where Haldane was holding forth, describing a humorous incident during a shooting party at Sandringham. Busy studying the faces of the guests, Travis paid little attention until Haldane spoke his name. "Senator Spurlock, I understand you had a jolly adventure with your indefatigable President. Won't you tell us about it?"

In a moment of insight, Travis suddenly understood the situation. He had been kept at arm's length out of caution during the last few weeks, while his credentials were checked in America. Gregarious by nature, Edward had been embarrassed by scandals throughout his life. His close friends and trusted associates had involved him in paternity suits, divorce proceedings, and other licentious escapades. Older, he now had grown cautious. Travis guessed that Haldane, an *intime* of the king, had been specially assigned to draw him out. Perhaps their meeting at Boodle's had not been accidental. Travis recalled that while backgammon and baccarat were played at other tables, Haldane had insisted on contract bridge, the king's current passion.

As Travis told anecdotes of the wolf hunt, Edward drifted closer. Travis felt the king's analytical gaze on him as he related the incident of Roosevelt killing a large rattlesnake with his quirt.

"One might think your President would carry a bigger stick," Edward said.

The group laughed in appreciation of the king's wit.

"I've read about your herds of buffalo," Edward said. "They must have provided considerable sport."

Travis described the great buffalo slaughter, the resulting commerce. A question was asked about the effect on the Indians. Travis told of his visits to the reservations, the efforts of the government to turn the Indians into productive citizens.

Concerned that he was being too loquacious, he searched for a way to turn attention from himself.

Haldane came to his rescue. "I think we English have forgiven you for the loss of the colonies. After all, we still have India, quite troublesome enough. But I suspect we'll always retain some jealousy over your experience in the opening of the American West. We'll always wonder how the Apaches and Comanches would have fared against the British square. Now we'll never know."

A few minutes later the king and queen withdrew, and the festivities ended.

Two days later Travis received a handwritten note inviting him to a quiet evening of cards. He recognized the address. It was the home of Alice Keppel, the king's mistress.

His long wait had ended.

"Now the game begins," he told Reva.

The first thing Travis learned about King Edward's card playing was that he could not abide losing. Although Alice Keppel remained in good humor, the king's moods swung with the run of the cards.

Travis was paired with Donald Wallace, the *Times* expert on Russia and a close friend of the king. Mrs. Keppel and Edward were partnered. George Keppel was nowhere in evidence. Travis had heard that Keppel held a remarkably feudal view on sharing his wife with his sovereign.

Edward was an intense but mediocre player. Alice Keppel was adept, but careless and indifferent. Soon Travis and Wallace were far ahead. Travis grew uncomfortable. They were wagering moderately high stakes. After two hours of play, a rift flared between Alice and the king over their confused signals in bidding.

"Why did you bid two no trump?" Edward demanded of Alice. "You should have said two clubs."

Alice arrayed her dummy hand. "You didn't have to stay with no trumps," she said. "You could have come back with your strong suit."

Travis studied the tabled cards. From his own hand, the clues of

Wallace's bidding, and Alice's cards, he could not see how Edward could be holding anything resembling a strong hand. Clearly the king again had overbid.

Edward led with the ace of hearts. As his mind leaped ahead three plays, Travis decided he would sacrifice his high cards in the hope his generosity would not be noticed.

It was imperative to keep Edward in a good mood.

Wallace picked a card, hesitated, and changed his mind. Edward impatiently drummed his fingers on the table. Alice put a fresh cigarette into her long holder. Travis offered her a light.

He now had spent three long evenings at the card table with Edward. Thus far, no confidences had been exchanged.

Wallace played a jack. Travis surmised that Wallace also had made the decision not to contest Edward's hand. Edward fed a card from the dummy hand. Travis made his contribution.

Edward seemed happy with the way the cards were falling. "I believe I'm cutting my losses, Senator. I knew the cards would improve eventually."

"Perhaps I should stick to poker," Travis said.

Edward won the hand. With earlier coups by Alice, the two swept the final rubber. Edward bent over pad and pencil and totaled the score. He glanced at the tall clock in the corner. "Much later than I thought," he said. "Senator, I've imposed on you, hoping to recover my game."

"Not at all, sir," Travis said. "I often stay up late."

Edward rose and clapped his hands to awaken his dog, asleep on a rug before the fire. "All the same, I'll give you a lift to your hotel. I believe you're staying at Claridge's?"

Travis thought the offer might be a signal, but he was not certain. "That isn't necessary, Your Highness."

"It isn't out of the way," Edward said. "Only take a moment. Come along, Donald. We'll drop you off."

As they prepared to leave, the king's long-haired fox terrier came bounding across the room, barking. Edward shushed him. "Caesar, you naughty, naughty dog. You'll have Mrs. Keppel's quarters raided for gaming. Wouldn't that be a pretty kettle of fish?"

Alice laughed. She took Travis by the arm and escorted him to the door. "Do come again, Senator. It's been a pleasure having you."

Edward's driver was waiting in the royal Daimler at the door. Travis, Edward, and Caesar crowded into the back seat of the car. Wallace rode in front with the driver. The top had been erected and the windows buttoned against the pelting rain. Travis noticed that the damp night air seemed to aggravate the king's bronchial condition.

Edward remained silent until Wallace had been delivered to his door. As they pulled away from the curb, he spoke. "Does President Roosevelt plan to stand for reelection?"

The bluntness of the question took Travis by surprise. He answered with total candor. "I don't know, sir. I doubt that he's yet made up his own mind. At least, he hasn't confided in me."

"I hope he does. We need him. I truly believe he's the strongest American president since Lincoln, perhaps since Washington, and the greatest moral force of his age. The Algeciras conference and the Treaty of Portsmouth were diplomatic victories of the first rank. The world stands in his debt."

Again Travis was surprised. Roosevelt tended to be remembered chiefly for his heavy-handed policies in Panama and his statement about speaking softly and carrying a big stick. Few remembered that in 1905 alone he had helped avert a war between Germany and France, forced the Russo-Japanese War to the treaty table, and received the Nobel Peace Prize.

"He's one of your greatest admirers, Your Majesty."

Edward did not answer for a moment. A light splatter of rain was blowing into the car through the crevices in the window flaps. Edward moved Caesar to the floor to get him out of the draft. "What do you want to talk to me about?"

Travis took a deep breath. "Concern is growing in America over the policies of your nephew, the kaiser. The President has become alarmed over the situation. He fears that the kaiser is providing England with false assurances of peace while he continues to build Germany's naval fleet."

Edward's voice was deep and husky. His answer came so quietly that Travis had to strain to hear him over the rain and the noise of the Daimler. "You can tell your President that Wilhelm has given me no assurances. Absolutely no assurances at all. Every time I've raised the question he has refused to discuss the matter."

Travis knew he had scored a diplomatic coup. Edward and the kaiser had met several times on the Continent for private talks. Very few persons in the British government knew what had transpired.

Travis had made many drafts of the core of his message. He spoke from memory. "President Roosevelt is most desirous of arriving at some understanding with the British government concerning the European situation, perhaps in an informal way. Sentiment in America is strongly against the kaiser. If England is drawn into war, there is a chance that America could offer armed assistance."

Again, Edward spoke quietly. "If Germany persists in her present course, war is inevitable."

"President Roosevelt is of the same opinion."

"Will America be prepared?"

Travis hesitated. He knew of Edward's battle to build more battle-ships and to enlarge the British army by several divisions. Strong opposition had formed in Parliament, where the popular belief had flowered that if England disarmed Germany would follow suit. Travis found it significant that armament seemed to be Edward's chief worry.

"The Spanish-American War, Indian fighting, and various Mexican border incidents have helped us to maintain a standing army," he explained. "But it is antiquated. We would need time to build a modern, mechanized fighting force."

The driver braked the Daimler to a stop at Claridge's. A doorman hurried out. Edward halted him with an upraised palm.

"You can inform your President that through our mutual trust I believe we can arrive at an informal understanding. I think that would be best, rather than to create a formal alliance that would complicate our other relationships. If he is agreeable to this position, I recommend that we pursue the matter as soon as possible."

Edward left him at the curb and drove away. Travis hurried upstairs to his suite. He spent the remainder of the night drafting a long report to Roosevelt for inclusion in the next diplomatic pouch to leave London. He quoted the entire conversation, word for word. He further added his observation that Edward was seriously ill.

"He eats enough to kill any man, not to mention brandies and wine," he wrote. "He smokes at least a dozen cigars a day, and two dozen cigarettes. After a walk of more than twenty feet, he wheezes. He has a chronic, nasty cough and sometimes clutches at his heart as if in pain. I find it astounding that the English remain unaware of his true condition."

He deliberated at length over his concluding line. He did not want to give the appearance of lecturing the President, but he felt moved to underscore the gravity of the situation.

"His death would alter the delicate balance in Europe overnight," he wrote. "I do not know how the English would fare without him. But on his death, war would become a certainty."

The remainder of the trip was anticlimactic. After a tour of England, Scotland, and Ireland, Travis took his family on to Germany. He obtained an interview with the kaiser, but it proved unproductive. The Spurlocks then made a leisurely tour of France, Switzerland, Italy, Spain, and Portugal, and a side trip to see the pyramids and the Cairo Museum.

In Egypt Travis saw that his family was tired and homesick. Durwood was on leave from his job at the bank, and had written twice, asking for extensions. Travis knew his younger sons should be returned to school.

At last he went to the steamship office and booked passage home.

15

Malvern Spurlock huddled against the cold north wind as the aviators tinkered with the engine of the small yellow flying machine. Around him the crowd waited impatiently. After several more minutes the aviators backed away from the monoplane and launched another kite. The crowd groaned.

"They've got to test the air currents," Ormer Locklear explained. Since Vern's return from Europe three years ago, Ormer had become his best friend. Ormer had read every article he could find on flying machines and knew all about such matters.

Clay, almost seventeen, spoke from the conviction of seniority. "They're all gutless wonders," he said.

Vern was moved to speak in their defense, but he could never win arguments with Clay. He remained silent, watching the kite rise in the swift breeze over the driving park. He knew that the International Aviators were not cowards. He had read the glowing accounts of their performances at the first international air show a few weeks earlier at Belmont Park in New York. Later, one of the aviators, John B. Moisant, had been killed in a performance in New Orleans. The Swiss flier Edmond Audemars, now standing beside the yellow Demoiselle, had survived several aeroplane crashes. Vern had gone with Ormer down to the rail depot to watch as the machines were unloaded and assembled under the careful supervision of the aviators. He had recognized each of the International Aviators from the woodcut drawings and posters. He felt he knew them all.

The kite danced toward the south. From the many hours he had spent flying his own kites, Vern knew that the aviators were searching for crosscurrents and downdrafts.

After a time the group on the field reeled in the kite and returned to the plane. Audemars climbed into the cockpit.

"Looks like they're going to try again," Clay said. "Anybody want to make any bets?"

The crowd quieted, expectant. Fort Worth's first air show had attracted fifteen thousand people. They had been kept waiting in the cold wind more than two hours. So far, not much had happened. They had seen only kite flying and several false starts.

René Simon spun the propeller. The engine caught and roared to life. Audemars advanced and retreated the throttle, making the engine backfire. With Fool Flyer Simon holding one wing, and the French aviator Roland Gerros guiding the other, Audemars aligned the aeroplane and pushed the throttle wide open. The small yellow Demoiselle began to roll.

Simon and Gerros ran beside the flying machine until it gathered speed. Bouncing, it rolled faster and faster. Vern could feel the tension of the crowd.

As the aeroplane reached the grandstand it lifted off the ground for several feet, hesitated, then slowly settled back to earth.

The crowd groaned.

"If I couldn't do better than that, I'd stay home," Clay said.

"Audemars was hunting for an updraft," Ormer explained. "He couldn't find one."

"He needs guts, not wind," Clay said again. "Once he got off the ground, why didn't he go on up?"

Overcome by his own disappointment, Vern remained silent. The flying machine was pushed back to its starting point. Audemars shook his head to the others on the field, apparently explaining some difficulty. An argument seemed to flare. Gerros walked away, toward his own plane.

"Gerros is going to try," Ormer said hopefully.

Simon ran toward Gerros and grabbed him. The two men stood in the middle of the field shouting, waving their arms. Fool Flyer Simon apparently was attempting to talk Gerros out of risking his life.

"It's just an act," Clay said. "They know the crowd's about to give up and go home."

Gerros pulled his arm free and walked to his red monoplane, *The Statue of Liberty*. He climbed into the cockpit. A mechanic helped him start the engine.

Gerros seemed troubled by something. He motioned a mechanic closer. They talked for a moment, and an adjustment was made on the powerful engine. Gerros opened the throttle again and seemed satisfied. He raised his left hand to the crowd. The little red monoplane began to trundle forward.

As the aeroplane neared the grandstand it rose several feet into the air. But instead of again settling to earth, as the crowd expected, it buzzed along for several yards just off the ground, canted slightly against the wind. Then, trembling delicately in the gusts that swept the field, it rose magically and swiftly, climbing gracefully.

The crowd burst into excited applause, then quieted abruptly.

To the absolute amazement of everyone, the flying machine kept climbing. It went up and up, soaring into the sky until eventually even the throbbing of the engine faded away.

Vern kept his gaze locked on the tiny speck as it grew smaller and smaller.

He attempted to imagine what the earth looked like from up there. Several summers before, he had tied a box camera to a kite, rigged a thread to trip the shutter, and sent it aloft. But every picture had been blurred. He often had lain on hillsides, watching hawks sailing hundreds of feet high, and wondered what they saw below. Never in his life had he envied anyone as much as Roland Gerros.

Around him, speculation was rife that Gerros had lost his direction and would not be able to find his way back. Vern did not believe the talk, for his imagination also had taken wing. He could visualize the French aviator flying along, buffeted by the wind, feeling the vibrations of the powerful engine through the control stick and the seat of his pants, gazing down in disdainful amusement at the roofs of barns and houses, the tops of trees, horses, and cattle, the tiny ribbons of roads and cowpaths.

At that moment Vern would have given his life for two minutes in the cockpit.

"Here he comes," Ormer said, pointing. "He's turned back."

Vern searched for a moment before he found the tiny red speck against the blue sky. As the aeroplane took shape, the crowd again burst into applause.

Gerros brought the flying machine directly over the driving park, no more than a hundred feet in the air. The crowd exclaimed in alarm as the aviator's peril became evident. The tiny craft was tossed like a leaf in the strong gusts. The wings rocked violently as Gerros swerved to meet each blast.

When he turned at the end of the field, the craft plunged straight toward the ground. Women screamed. Gerros fought the currents and regained control. The flying machine steadied. The rubber-tired wheels alighted gently in almost exactly the same spot where they had left the earth a few minutes before.

The crowd went wild. Bursting through the police barrier, the mob swarmed onto the field.

"Come on," Ormer said. He and Clay raced down the bleachers two at a time.

Vern did not follow. On the field, Audemar and Simon helped Gerros from the cockpit. They pounded him on the back and lifted him to their shoulders.

Vern turned away.

He was not yet sixteen, and the first aeroplane flight in Fort Worth's history had already been made.

"Where've you been?" Ermatine demanded. "You said you were coming right over."

Clay tossed his jacket over the back of a chair. "Vern wanted to go see that damnfool aeroplane show," he said. "I had to go with him."

He sat on the chair and pulled off his boots. Ermatine came close and put a hand to the bruise on his cheek. Her slightest touch still filled him with excitement, even after two years.

"Don't lie to me," she said. "You've been fighting again."

"That's from yesterday," he said. "Arnie Hopkins got smart with me. I busted his ass."

Ermatine giggled. Standing in front of him, she clenched both hands behind his head and pulled his face into her breasts. "You baited him," she said. "I've heard you taunting those boys into fighting you."

It was true. He had called Arnie a sissy. He did not understand why he was driven to prod other boys into fistfights. But with an older brother who was afraid of horses, the town joke, he had to do something. And he could not go hunt lions in Africa, or tigers in India, as his father was doing at the moment.

Ermatine began unbuttoning his shirt. "Come on," she whispered. "We've got to hurry."

That was part of the game. Ermatine's husband worked at the ice plant. He usually arrived home about five fifteen. The threat of discovery added to the fun. Sometimes they were still coupled when her husband's boots clomped up the front steps.

Clay peeled out of his trousers and stood naked. Ermatine tossed off her robe and tumbled onto the bed.

"Let's do something different," she said. "How'd you like it like this?"

Clay poised over her, savoring the moment. She was much older, maybe even as old as forty—he had never asked. Her thick dark hair was gathered behind her head. She was looking up at him hungrily, her deep brown eyes narrowed and smoldering as they always did when she really wanted him. Her full, red, sensuous lips were open, waiting for him.

Holding back, as she had taught him, he began working, teasing her, as she writhed in ecstasy. They built the pace to a crescendo.

"Now! Now!" she shouted.

Ermatine had shown him various tricks. Now he performed them. They collapsed in a shuddering heap.

Then, like an automobile shifting into a higher gear, she began again.

Clay often fantasized the scene of her husband stepping into the bedroom just at the final moment. In his fantasy he would rise, erection still intact, and beat the man insensible before returning triumphant to Ermatine.

The fantasy would never be realized. Her husband, "Bull" Durham, was so big he had to move through most doors sideways. All day long he lifted hundred-pound blocks of ice with no more effort than most men would devote to a loaf of bread. Clay had seen him shoulder a two-hundred-pound chunk and carry it up a flight of steps.

"Now! Now!" Ermatine cried.

Eventually Clay lost count. They reached that plateau of delicious terror they sought, sweating, panting, listening.

And then came the sounds at the front door.

Wildly, Clay was tempted to fulfill his fantasy. He clung to Ermatine for a long, desperate, convulsive moment.

Then the horror in her eyes sent him rolling off the bed. He grabbed his clothes and boots, and fled through the kitchen onto the back porch. Easing open the door, he slipped out naked into the back yard.

Screened from neighboring houses by shrubbery, he ran to a lilac bush and hid behind it. With bare buttocks scooting on the cold ground, he wrestled into his shorts and trousers.

A few minutes later he was fully dressed, shivering, when Ermatine signaled from the kitchen. He ran to the back fence and cleared it in a vaulting leap.

Then he began the long walk home.

He searched idly for someone to fight. Seldom had he felt more full of himself. Only the exquisite excitement of bareknuckle battle was better than being with Ermatine. He loved the smooth, solid beauty of a well-delivered blow, delicious pain shooting up his arms, the ultimate satisfaction of an opponent humbled.

Because of his reputation, and the reluctance of anyone to fight him, he had become adept in the subtleties of challenge, a ritual as stylized and elaborate as an Oriental religion. Although a fight might be over in five minutes, the verbal preliminaries could exhaust half an afternoon. He had learned to maneuver his victims into untenable positions. Once affixed, the labels "coward," "sissy," or "son of a bitch" allowed no retreat. A direct challenge to manhood brooked no compromise.

Truly he did not understand Ermatine. She knew he did not love her, and she gave no indication that she loved him. They had nothing between them but sex, and crazed, edge-of-the-cliff shared excitement.

He had asked her once why she invited him into her house that day so long ago, when it all started.

"Boredom," she said. She had raised up on one elbow and looked at him. "Clay, remember this. Plenty of women in this world are ripe for adventure. You only have to give them the chance. Most men look at women's fronts, or their rears. It'll pay you to watch their eyes. You can see if a woman's hunting, even when she doesn't know it."

She said there was one important thing about women that most men did not know. "Men will preen and strut, and think they're the cock of the walk. But let me tell you something. The weakest woman alive has more sexuality than any of them."

She had demonstrated that fact so thoroughly, and so many times, that Clay's education was complete.

He was not quite seventeen. And already he was searching women's eyes.

For two days the drill had been pounding deeper into the earth, the bailer bringing up shattered chips of limestone and shale. But now the tailings had changed. Clay moved forward and dipped his hand into the dark, mysterious mound of dirt. He felt moisture.

"Yep, we're getting close," Purvis said. "Another twenty or thirty feet should do it."

"How deep are you now?" Clay asked.

The driller checked the cable. "About a hundred and ten feet, thereabouts."

Clay had watched the entire drilling operation with total fascination. The old water well at Bluebonnet had played out. Purvis blamed rusted casing and other debris plugging the well from the bottom. He had recommended a new well, thirty feet south of the other. He had claimed that the old well had missed the best source of water.

Purvis gave a signal. The crew began feeding the bit back into the hole.

"How'd you know the water would be there?" Clay asked.

Purvis glanced up to check the position of the sun, pulled his watch from his pocket and looked at it, and spat into the dirt. "You develop a feel," he said. "I can't explain it. You just get so you *know* where water is. Some drillers use dowsing rods, all kinds of tricks." He tapped his temple with a forefinger. "But it's really up here."

Clay had been told that Purvis was a Cajun from Louisiana, but he spoke with an East Texas drawl. Small in stature, he was wiry of limb, and kept his black, coarse hair well greased. He told Clay he had been drilling water wells for thirty years or more.

Clay loved anything mechanical. As a boy his first ambition had been to become a railroad engineer. Later he had fallen in love with steamships, suspension bridges, steam tractors, bicycles, horseless carriages, and motorcycles. But never before had he realized that a water well held its own fascination.

The walking beam drove the bit deeper. Again Clay felt of the mysterious moist dirt, pulled to the surface from a depth of more than a hundred feet.

"What's down there?" he asked.

Purvis looked at him for a moment and took out his pipe. He spoke as he poured tobacco into the bowl. "Not many people ask that question. They just want water and don't care about the rest." He tamped the tobacco, struck a match, and drew fire into the bowl. "Fact of the matter, the whole history of the earth is down there. Layer after layer, over millions of years. We're down now to strata formed long before man ever walked the earth."

Clay rolled the dirt over his fingers, thrilled by the knowledge that he was the first person ever to touch it. "You mean you always find the same rocks at the same depth?"

Purvis blew smoke and shook his head. "Not that simple. Sometimes formations are pinched out. You may run into an igneous intrusion—the top of an old lava flow—that'll wear out your bit, and there's nothing to do but pull the stem and start over somewheres else. But generally you run into certain layers consistently in certain sections of the country."

"With all the layers of rock, how'd the water get that deep?"

Purvis put one hand over the other to demonstrate. "Trapped," he said. "Rock formations, one on top of the other, like this, can keep it deep, sometimes under pressure. I've had water come in with such force that it'd lift the drill stem right out of the hole. There's underground streams and rivers, lakes, maybe even waterfalls down there. Great caverns man'll never see. I've had drill stems drop a hundred feet. You never know what you'll run into. No two wells are ever the same, even if they're ten feet apart."

"How deep can you go?"

"With this rig, I'd hate to go more'n two or three hundred feet. I've drilled to better'n twenty-five hundred with a rotary."

"How deep do you find oil?"

Purvis grinned. "Don't ever forget this. You find oil where it is, and noplace else. I've had good show at a hundred and fifty feet, up in Clay County, over in Brown County, down by Bexar. About fifteen years ago I was hired by the city of Corsicana to go deep for warm artesian water. We hit oil at about a thousand feet and had to set casing to block it off. We drilled on to almost twenty-five hundred feet before we reached water, but oil kept seeping down the outside of the casing and ruined the water. The city people were mad as hell."

Clay remembered the excitement over Spindletop when he was six years old. Several sections of Oklahoma were now in the midst of oil booms. People were becoming millionaires overnight. "Why don't you drill for oil?" he asked.

"To make money on oil, you've got to find a lot of it, all in one place," Purvis explained. "Otherwise the find isn't commercial."

"Do you think there's more oil in Texas?"

Purvis tapped the spent tobacco out of his pipe. "Hell, yes! There's plenty of oil, deep, all over Texas. Almost anywhere you go you hear about seeps. Water wells ruined, scum on creeks and lakes, Indian medicine springs. You find people using it to grease wagon wheels, drinking it as a curative, or spreading it in their henhouses to kill redbugs. And that's only the oil that finds its way close to the surface. The real play is farther down. Maybe thousands of feet, deeper than man has ever gone before."

The crew stopped drilling and began pulling the stem. Purvis left to direct the bailing operation. Clay sat and watched more dirt, dark with moisture, rise from where it had lain for a span of time that staggered his imagination.

Automobiles had become common. Many people in Fort Worth had even sold their horses and carriages, so great was their confidence in the machine age. The internal combustion engine had found use in aeroplanes, electrical plants, water pumping stations, and even in railway locomotives. Clay had read that the demand for oil would soon surpass every present expectation.

Slowly, Clay saw the future in its true perspective, with automobiles filling the land, replacing the horse as standard transportation. He had no inkling as to how enough gasoline might be manufactured and distributed in sufficient quantities. But he understood clearly the scope of the oil discoveries that would be required to fulfill the demands of the machine age.

Gradually he realized that at last he had found his life's work.

If oil was there to be found, he would find it.

Travis was sitting in his office, reading the afternoon newspaper, when his secretary knocked tentatively on his door. The secretary—a young man studying for the law—spoke with a puzzled frown.

"Senator, there's a young woman to see you. Her name is Eunice Gray."

The name meant nothing to Travis. "Show her in," he said.

When she entered, she was smiling, as if at a secret joke. He stared, momentarily stunned. Although he had seen her only once, her face was as familiar as his own.

She seemed amused at his reaction. She offered her hand. "My name is Eunice Gray."

He remembered Pinkerton's visit, the wanted posters, the woman called Etta.

"Of course," he said. "Eunice Gray. How are you?"

Instead of answering, she walked around his office, examining the photographs of Travis with royalty, senators, presidents, ruins, Indian chiefs, and dead elephants, lions, and tigers. She arranged herself in a leather chair and leaned back to look at him.

She had not changed. Her dark brown skirt and jacket were exquisitely fitted, her white blouse ruffled and feminine, with a wide bow at the throat. Her hat was jaunty yet formal. She picked up a letter opener from his desk with long, tapering fingers. Her skin was well tanned, her complexion remained flawless. Her soft brown eyes, her sensuous lips seemed to be mocking him.

"Senator, . . ." she began.

He held up a hand and interrupted. "Travis, please."

She rewarded him with another smile. "Travis, then. I need your help. You see, I've recently returned to Fort Worth, and I need introductions to the prominent men of the community. Men who will appreciate the type of services I have to offer."

Travis stared at her for a moment, not quite believing his ears. Surely she knew he would not pimp for her. He could not fathom her game. While he hesitated, forming his reply, she palmed the blade of the letter opener, stroked it, and put the tip to her lips.

"I only need introductions," she said. "I'll do the rest. And there's a great deal in it for you. I believe we understand each other."

Travis laughed in appreciation of her audacity. For a moment he thought of the hatred in Zetta's eyes the day she told him she had seen him with a woman. But he remembered that even kings had mistresses.

"Yes, Eunice Gray. I believe we understand each other."

She waited, relinquishing control of the conversation.

Travis thought for a moment. He could find no obstacles to a plan forming in his mind.

"Miss Gray, perhaps this isn't the time nor situation to explore the matter. As it happens, I must leave tomorrow night for St. Louis and a three-day bar convention. Why don't you come along on the trip, traveling separately, of course. There we can become better acquainted and discuss the matter at our leisure."

Eunice rose from her chair, handed the letter opener to him, and walked to the door, where she stopped and turned. "That was exactly what I had in mind," she said.

Before Travis could reply, she was gone.

Wrapped around the handle of the letter opener was a note bearing the name of her hotel and her room number.

The Reverend Mr. J. Frank Norris spent the night on his knees, alone in the sanctuary of the First Baptist Church, praying for guidance.

Not in all the years of his ministry had he faced such a problem.

He asked God if he should go forward or retreat. The possibility of a middle ground never entered his mind.

In his life there had been no room for compromise.

Reared on a hardscrabble Hill County farm, he had witnessed his father's slow destruction through self-inflicted alcohol.

At fifteen he had been shot by horse thieves. For three long years he lay paralyzed. The doctors gave up all hope. They said he would never walk again.

Then came a miracle, transporting J. Frank Norris forever from the depths of despair into the restless realms of religious ecstasy. Through his saintly mother's marathon prayers and the holy intervention of a rural preacher, the paralysis was lifted.

In gratitude, with rapturous surrender to Jesus Christ, Norris pledged his life to the ministry.

Eventually he walked again.

The second miracle of his life he performed himself. Somehow the penniless, almost unlettered youth earned his way through Baylor University in those difficult times, so completely swaying administrators with his fervor that rules were bent and concessions made.

In those days he did not know the meaning of rest. The Gospel lay like a glowing coal in his chest. He was so impatient to start his ministry that in his freshman year he wandered into the surrounding countryside, found an abandoned schoolhouse serving as a shelter for goats, cleaned it, and started his own summer revival among the farm workers. He preached for thirty-one nights in succession and won forty-one converts to Christ.

His bootstrap ministry helped pay his tuition. Impervious to summer heat or the snows of winter, he preached at many rural churches, often riding all night to fulfill his commitments and returning the next night to attend his university classes, all without sleep.

Graduated with the highest honors the university accorded, he won a scholarship to the Southern Baptist Theological Seminary in Louisville.

There he completed the three-year course in two years and again was valedictorian of his class. He returned to Texas as one of the most accomplished theologians in the Baptist Church.

In recognition of his accomplishments he was named editor of the *Baptist Standard,* the largest denominational newspaper in Texas and the most influential church publication in the South. His zeal, combined with his inflexible nature, quickly brought Baptist politics in Texas to a boil. He conducted a fervent campaign to outlaw racetrack gambling in Texas. The resulting furor caused bitter battles within the church and created headlines in newspapers statewide. Pressures were brought to bear in Austin. He made many enemies, but his campaign was successful. He then began a movement to separate Baylor Theological Seminary from Baylor University—a highly emotional controversy that split Texas Baptists right down the middle.

Eventually Texas Baptists agreed on one thing: J. Frank Norris was so inspired that the church might not survive him.

He was asked to resign his editorship.

Church authorities urged him to consult with God and to rethink his ministry. They suggested that he go to a secluded place and research his soul.

In keeping with this advice Norris had accepted a quiet pastorship in Fort Worth.

For three years he had conformed. He had preached gentle sermons that disturbed no one. He visited the members of his affluent congregation and saw that they lived among platoons of domestic servants, shining horseless carriages, secretaries, fine clothes, expense accounts, and vacations. Even worse, he too became accustomed to these conveniences. He met all of the expectations of his congregation: he larded his sermons with jokes, mild discussions of the ethics of Christianity, and passing comments on current events.

He walked among his flock so quietly that no one dreamed of the war raging in his soul.

Self-loathing was eating him alive. While he preached complacent sermons to an unconcerned congregation, sin romped unfettered a stone's throw away. Everywhere he looked he saw the devil's handiwork. As he tossed and turned in his bed the din of Hell's Half Acre could be heard all night long. Drunks roamed the streets, often shouting profanity. Prostitutes accosted men on the sidewalks. The smell of liquor hung heavily in the air. From his privileged perspective as pastor he knew of husbands and fathers led astray, of young women deflowered, of mothers with broken hearts.

Norris knew he had it within himself to cast down the temples of sin.

He knew he could shore up community weaknesses with his own moral strength.

Then there had come a sign, as clear-cut as the lifting of the paralysis. But for a while Norris did not recognize it as a sacred message.

The Ministerial Alliance, composed of Fort Worth pastors of all faiths, had taken up once again the problem of Hell's Half Acre. Norris had paid little attention. The acre was an old, tired subject within the alliance. But this time someone suggested the hiring of a detective to investigate ownership of the brothels, bars, and gambling halls. Norris endorsed the measure without thought. To his mind, the saloonkeepers and whore-mongers were faceless entities, mere minions of the devil.

Private Detective George Chapman was hired. His extensive report a few months later came like a bombshell. Not one of the pastors had bargained for such devastating revelations.

Through tax rolls, deeds, and other various legal documents, George Chapman had determined that ninety percent of Hell's Half Acre was owned by ten pillars of the community—men well known and respected throughout Texas and the nation.

All were prominent in church work. Three were deacons in J. Frank's own church. One held high offices in the Southern General Convention, the Democratic Party, and had served as a United States senator.

Before the names were known, the pastors had solemnly agreed to read from the pulpit whatever the report contained.

After they received the report, the other pastors had hesitated and backed away.

Each knew that ten wagonloads of dynamite would cause less of an uproar in the community than George Chapman's report.

No one wished to light the fuse.

Now J. Frank Norris prayed for guidance. He knew that if he took up the challenge, he faced the greatest fight of his life. Powerful forces were at work. The devil had formed a great alliance. Norris knew that if he spoke his mind the resulting cataclysm would place his ministry at stake, perhaps cause an irreparable rift in the Southern Baptist confederation.

He raised his voice in prayer in the empty sanctuary. "Lord, I'm the most knocked-down, run-over, chewed-up, fired preacher in the world," he said. "Like You wrote in the Scriptures, 'Better that he had never been born.' I'm drawing a big salary, wearing tailor-made suits, preaching in the midst of a city of over a hundred thousand people, none paying any attention to me. I'm not causing a riffle. My moisture has turned into the drought of summer, my soul is poured out like water. I've been unfaithful to my heavenly committed trust. Lord, if I'm not worthy, just tell me. But if You want me to do Thy work, I will do it if it sets the world on fire."

In this fashion, Norris prayed the whole night through.

Then, just before dawn, as first light penetrated the east windows of the church, J. Frank Norris felt the hand of the Lord on his shoulder and he heard God speak.

16

Stepping over patches of ice and frozen slush, Travis hurried across Main Street, late for a called meeting of the church board, his mind still lingering on tantalizing, inscrutable Eunice Gray.

The trip to St. Louis had not solved her mystery. She was a courtesan unique even to his experience. Not since the days of Jeanette had he known such erotic abandon. His speech to the bar association had gone well, but most of his time had been spent with Eunice. He suspected that his absence had been noticed at some convention programs.

He had learned nothing of her background. She had parried every question. When he mentioned Jim Lowe and Harry Place, she only smiled. She talked familiarly of New York, Chicago, Denver, and San Francisco. Only once had she mentioned South America.

In the Pullman compartment on the way home he had suggested that she might find suitable accommodations in an apartment house he owned. She had thanked him, neither accepting nor rejecting the offer. There the matter stood.

Hurrying into the church, Travis tossed his overcoat and hat onto a pew and walked through the sanctuary and into the conference room. He was the last to arrive. As he entered, the other members of the board looked up. The Reverend Mr. J. Frank Norris gave him a brief nod but did not speak.

Circling the table to his accustomed seat, Travis felt a tension in the room that immediately put him on guard. Only one or two of the deacons returned his greeting. The others seemed to have difficulty meeting his eyes.

Something was wrong. All of the men in the room were supposed to be his friends. He took his seat at the end of the table, facing Norris.

The preacher was a tall, lean, hungry-looking man. He sat now unsmiling, his frown permanently fixed. There had always been a burning, troubled intensity about his eyes. But this morning he seemed self-satisfied about something. "Now that we're all here, I'll open the meeting," he said. "Have you all seen this?"

He opened the Saturday edition of the *Fort Worth Record* to a double-page advertisement. The newspaper was passed down the table. Travis gave it a quick examination.

The advertisement welcomed out-of-town visitors to the state convention of the Texas Liquor Dealers Association, just opening in the North Side Coliseum. The names of many Fort Worth men were listed as sponsors. His name was there, along with two other deacons seated at the table—Art Shipley and Wilmer Mooreland. Travis vaguely remembered being asked to serve as a local sponsor. He had donated five hundred dollars.

Travis passed the newspaper on without comment. Shipley and Mooreland seemed puzzled and disturbed. They looked at him questioningly.

J. Frank Norris waited until the offending advertisement made a full circle of the table. He rose to his feet, shook his head as if in sorrow, and read the text of the advertisement aloud. His tone had a graveyard hollowness. He moved on to the list of names, giving stress to Spurlock, Shipley, and Mooreland. Then he spoke directly to Travis.

"This type of conduct by the deacons of this church cannot be permitted. The leaders of the church are expected to be above reproach. I will give . . ."

For a moment Travis was caught in the grip of blind anger. He spoke through a red haze. "Just a minute, Brother Norris! You've tried and convicted, without hearing a shred of evidence. If you want to discuss this in a reasonable manner, I'll be glad to do so. I'm not here to be lectured."

"Senator Spurlock, this is God's house. Not a court of law!" Norris raged back. "When you openly support a wicked, perverted enterprise such as this, there's no room for discussion. As I was saying before I was so rudely interrupted, I'll give you a choice. You three can resign from the governing board of this church, or I'll go before the congregation at worship tomorrow morning and request that you be expelled from membership."

Travis rose to his feet with every intention of striking Norris in the face. Years of courtroom control interceded. Slowly he fought back his anger. He wished in one moment that he was armed and was glad in the next that he was not. He considered a counter motion to remove Norris from the pulpit. But when he glanced at the other deacons, he saw surprise on the faces of only two—Shipley and Mooreland. Clearly the preacher had organized his support before calling the meeting.

Travis saw that he was playing against a stacked deck. But he could not let the matter pass. "Preacher, who in hell do you think pays your salary? If we three walk out that door, a good percentage of your church budget goes with us. And so help me God, if you persist in this quixotic behavior, I'll see that you lose the bulk of your financial support for this church."

"There's no need to blaspheme in the house of the Lord," Norris said quietly. "I'm in the right. I'm immune to threats."

"You have my resignation from this board as of this moment," Travis said. "But I warn you! This isn't the end of it."

Norris gave him the ghost of a smile. "On that we agree, Senator. You don't know the half of it."

Travis stormed out. He heard Shipley and Mooreland trailing in his wake. He grabbed up his overcoat and whipped through the front door. Behind him Mooreland called his name. Travis did not stop. At the moment he did not trust himself to speak.

That evening he told Reva what had happened. He attempted to place little import on the incident. "Preachers come and go," he said. "It'll blow over."

Travis was considering the transfer of his membership to another church when a note arrived from Norris:

Senator Spurlock:

The topic of my sermon this Sunday will be *The Ten Biggest Devils in Town and Their Records Given.* I invite you to attend, and I will give you the opportunity of reply.

J. Frank Norris

Travis did not mention the note to his family. But when they arrived at the church the following Sunday, the topic of the sermon was emblazoned on a red banner across the entrance. Travis had difficulty finding seats. By the time Norris mounted to the pulpit the sanctuary was packed.

After the opening hymn, Norris began his sermon with a tirade against Hell's Half Acre. He offered graphic descriptions of husbands, fathers, and impressionable young men whose lives were destroyed by diseased women and hard liquor. He told of the lust of men in the taverns, the exploitation of innocent young bodies, the souls lost to eternal damnation.

The congregation was stunned into absolute silence. The acre was seldom mentioned in polite society, and never in mixed company.

Travis felt that the fare was far too strong for many tender young ears. For a moment he thought of walking out with his family. Only the memory of the note held him.

Warming to his theme, Norris gave statistics concerning the population of Hell's Half Acre—eighty houses of prostitution, more than seven hundred prostitutes, forty-six bars, sixteen gambling halls, five vaudeville theaters.

At first Travis wondered where the preacher had obtained his figures. They seemed vastly inflated. But he realized that much investigation had been done by someone. He suspected where the sermon was headed. He tensed, waiting for Norris to reach his point.

He did not have long to wait.

"And who owns these citadels of Satan?" Norris shouted, waving a fist in the air. "I'll tell you! The ten biggest devils in town! And who is the biggest devil of them all? I'll tell you! Travis Barclay Spurlock! A deacon of our own church!"

Travis felt all eyes upon him. He managed to keep his face expressionless.

Rapidly, item by item, Norris described every piece of property Travis owned in the acre. He told how many prostitutes resided in each rooming house and whorehouse, the number of cases of liquor served each year in each bar. The inventory was far more complete than Travis could have given himself.

He glanced at his family. Reva was white with shock. He reached for her hand. It was cold to his touch. Zetta was staring at the preacher, color high on her cheeks. Beyond her, Clay was listening with obvious amusement. Vern's eyes were wide in astonishment. Durwood sat without expression, as if he were listening to dry figures at the bank.

At last Norris finished with Travis. He went on down his list of devils.

Travis knew them all. They were his friends.

The congregation sat oddly subdued.

"There are other devils in our midst!" Norris concluded, pounding the pulpit. "But *these* are the ten biggest devils in town. I invited each of them to the services today, and offered them the opportunity of a reply. Only one is here. Travis Barclay Spurlock. Senator, do you wish to respond?"

Reva pulled at his hand, urging him to remain seated. But Travis rose to his feet. He paused, as was his habit, for dramatic effect, then filled the tabernacle with his courtroom voice, raised in self-righteous indignation.

"I do indeed. It is no secret that I own property in various sections of Fort Worth and throughout Tarrant County. The records are on the tax rolls for all to see. But if your list of my realty had been complete, Brother Norris, you still would have enumerated but a paltry portion of my worldly riches. You forgot to mention my wealth of friends, many of whom are present. You forgot to mention my family, whom you have publicly embarrassed by your intemperate and unreasonable performance. You forgot to mention my reputation, prized beyond value."

Again Travis paused, in full control of the charged atmosphere.

"I will not reply to your charges, Pastor. I consider them beneath notice. If I'm a villain, then I'm a villain, and I'll work that out with my Maker when the time comes. I do not need your judgment. I only wish to offer a word of warning to this congregation."

Turning his back to the pastor, Travis spoke to the upturned faces. "My friends, under this man's direction our church, as we have known and loved it, is headed for the shoals of hatred, petty jealousies, and character assassination. Family will be turned against family. Christian against Christian. All to serve this man's personal ambition. I'll not be a party to it. I hereby withdraw my membership from this congregation. But my heart bleeds for my church, for I have loved it. I leave my church, but I do not leave my friends. I still love you all. I walk out those doors harboring no animosity toward anyone."

The congregation watched in silence as Travis escorted his family up the aisle. As he approached the front doors he heard whispered conferences behind him, the shuffle of feet, and the reassuring sound of others following.

On the way home Reva asked only one question. "Is what he said true?"

Reva, Zetta, and his sons looked at Travis, awaiting his answer. "It's true," he said.

Reva went to bed and stayed there. For three days she refused food.

Travis sat down beside her bed one evening and told her how his ownership in the acre came about over a long period of time until even he was amazed by the scope of his involvement.

"But why?" she asked. "Why did you do it?"

He tried to explain. "There was a feeling that if outside interests came in they would take over, that the acre would get out of hand and wreck the community. We thought that by local ownership we could keep a lid on things."

"You men actually discussed it?"

"Nothing formal," he said. "But it was generally understood."

After a time Reva resumed her household duties. But she refused to go out in public.

Zetta marched about the house, a black figure of wrath. She would not speak to Travis or look at him.

Even Durwood lashed out one morning at the breakfast table. "You've ruined my life," he said, his thin lips trembling. "I was to be named chief cashier and vice president next spring. Now everyone in town knows my father owns brothels."

"He means whorehouses," Clay drawled.

"Clay!" Reva said. "If you can't speak decently, you can leave the table!"

"I'd rather own whorehouses than be a sissified, thirty-three-year-old stick-in-the-mud, like some people I could mention," Clay said.

"Clay! That's enough!" Reva said.

Clay left the table, but not before one last shot. "Where does he get off, anyway, middle-aged and still living at home, criticizing the money that sent him to college, that buys his clothes and food?"

"I pay my own way!" Durwood shouted.

"Sure you do," Clay taunted. "You've worked in that bank twelve years and you still don't make as much as a grocery clerk."

"I suppose you'll do better!"

"If I don't make ten times what you make by the time I'm twenty-one, I'll shoot myself."

Reva threw up her hands and burst into tears. She left the table and fled to her room.

In the silence that followed, Travis looked at his children, one by one.

"I don't want this scene repeated," he said. "From now on you can stay off the subject, especially in front of your mother. If there's a problem over my holdings in the acre, it's *my* problem. Every tub stands on its own bottom. No one will blame you."

"They *do* blame us," Zetta snapped. "There'll be whispers everywhere we go."

Again Travis looked at his children. Now thirty-four, Zetta had grown steadily into a waspish crone. At thirty-three, Durwood was weak, and dull as dishwater. Clay, now eighteen and in his second year at Fort Worth College, was wild and unpredictable. Vern, seventeen and in his final year of high school, was more like his mother—a dreamer, a romantic.

"Listen to me," Travis said. "People will put just as much credence in this affair as *we* give it, and no more. If we go on about our daily lives and pay no attention, the matter will simply go away. For your mother's sake, for your sake, I'll sell the property in the acre, gradually, quietly, and in a businesslike manner. That's my last word on it."

Fifteen families followed Travis out of the church that Sunday, while many more sat in indecision.

Within hours the scandal within the First Baptist Church was known throughout Fort Worth. Members of other denominations were amused, unaware that the conflagration would soon engulf their own churches, the whole community.

Of the nine hundred members on the church rolls the day Travis departed, six hundred left during the next few weeks, taking most of the church's financial support with them.

"I believe the man has lost his mind," Reva said.

"He's crazy like a fox," Zetta snapped. "Money couldn't buy this kind of attention."

Zetta's words proved prophetic.

Thousands of people came, eager to learn what J. Frank Norris would say next.

He did not disappoint them. For years he had been disgusted with the hypocrisy he saw at every turn. He named names and spared no one. His sermons grew more and more sensational. Each Sunday he portrayed Travis as the greatest whoremonger in town, the biggest hypocrite.

Gradually he enlarged his attack to encompass the entire city administration. Determined to close the acre, he managed to get the wet-dry issue on the November election ballot.

One Saturday night two shots were fired through the window of his study as he prepared a Sunday sermon. The bullets narrowly missed his head.

The following week his church was burned to the ground. Norris himself was indicted for arson. Witnesses testified that Norris burned his own church for the purpose of sensationalism—and for the insurance money to build a larger tabernacle to accommodate his rapidly growing congregation.

After an emotion-packed trial, Norris was acquitted.

A few days after the verdict the district attorney who prosecuted him was killed in a head-on collision with a streetcar on the Paddock Viaduct. The DA's mistress, riding in the front seat of the car, also died in the wreck.

Norris told his congregation that as he probed among the debris he found a broken whiskey bottle, containing liquor and the shattered brains of the district attorney.

With the grisly trophy resting on the pulpit, he preached a stirring sermon on the miracle of God's vindication.

In the following weeks he located a large circus tent that had been used by Sarah Bernhardt on her national tours. He filled it night after night in a marathon summer revival.

The town was torn asunder. Some thought J. Frank Norris was a saint. Others believed him to be the greatest calamity to hit Fort Worth since the Panic of 1873.

The mayor called a meeting in the North Side Coliseum, inviting all males over the age of twenty-one. He publicly offered his opinion that if there were fifty red-blooded men in Fort Worth, a preacher would be hanging from a lamp post by sunup. Norris sent a male stenographer to the meeting. Every word spoken was printed in his church newspaper, *The Searchlight.*

His parsonage was burned. Norris and his family fled into the snowy night, barely escaping with their lives.

City officials chopped down his tent, declaring it a fire hazard. Norris preached in the open air to congregations of thousands.

J. Frank Norris envisioned the Hell's Half Acre scandal as the beginning of a mighty crusade.

For Travis it seemed to be the end.

At sixty-two he was becoming an impoverished old man.

The scandal came close on the heels of a series of bad investments. The bulk of his railroad stock had been rendered worthless by competing lines and resulting bankruptcies.

As the year wore on, his legal practice steadily declined. Clients who routinely forwarded an annual retainer found excuses to go elsewhere. One by one his associates moved out and opened offices of their own.

Gradually Travis closed his properties in the acre. He was unable to find buyers. Income dwindled to a trickle, then stopped.

With nothing else to do, Travis visited Eunice Gray often, not for sex but for her common sense and good company. Now the courtesan of a select few among Fort Worth's wealthiest men, Eunice was acquainted with community gossip. But she did not speak of the Norris scandal until one evening when Travis broached the subject.

"I don't understand it," he said. "My holdings in the acre weren't that secret. I'm sure many knew, or suspected. Now everyone treats me as a pariah. I'm still the same man I was when they sought my advice and attention. I still think the same thoughts. What has changed?"

Eunice smiled sadly. "If you were a woman in my position, you'd understand. This nation is hopelessly immature. You and I may be living a hundred years before our time."

In the fall a touring opera tenor was scheduled to perform selections from Gounod's *Faust* at Greenwall's Opera House. Reva and Zetta were among the sponsors. Immediately following the performance a reception was planned in Major Van Emden's home. The Spurlocks were expected to attend.

The commitment had been made long in advance. But Reva had not appeared in public since Norris read Travis's name from the pulpit. She did not want to go. Travis insisted. They argued. At last Travis convinced her that since they held tickets, her absence would be more conspicuous than her presence.

The tenor's performance was better than the usual fare. The audience emerged in a good mood. Travis, Reva, and Zetta drove the tenor to Major Van Emden's home for a reception. There he was entertained for an hour before his train for Austin.

After his departure the party continued, as was the custom.

Travis was gratified to see that Reva seemed to be enjoying herself. No references were made to J. Frank Norris. Everyone was warm, friendly. Gradually, Travis relaxed.

But as he stood talking with Van Emden he heard the strident voice of Allegra Conard rising behind him. One of the town's best-known busybodies, Allegra invariably spoke before she thought. Her knack for saying the wrong thing at the right time was legendary.

Allegra's high voice rose in argument. "No, Justine! I don't think Faust is allegorical at all! Men probably sell their souls to the devil more often than we know! Look at Travis Spurlock!"

In the wake of her ringing voice, there fell one of those awkward silences when no one is able to think of anything to say. Stricken by her own indiscretion, Allegra searched the faces around her, making fishlike movements with her mouth.

Travis felt sympathetic eyes upon him. His first inclination was to let the moment pass, leaving Allegra to stew in her own conversational juice. But he then realized that he would never have a better forum to state his case. Virtually every influential person in Fort Worth was within earshot.

He spoke conversationally, as if to Allegra, but he imbued his voice with courtroom resonance that carried to every corner. "Mrs. Conard, you bring up an interesting point," he said. "I think Gounod, like Goethe, conceived Doctor Faust as perfectly encompassing the concept of the duality of man."

Allegra stood poised, staring at him, uncertain whether she had been rescued or cast into deeper trouble. "What do you mean, Senator?" she asked.

"Why, Goethe's concept of two souls warring within the same breast," Travis said. "His idea that within every man is a little of the devil, and a little godliness. I believe that's the basis of our fascination with the Faust legend. He knew the best of himself and the worst of himself. Wouldn't you agree, Mrs. Conard?"

Allegra was in far over her head. "Perhaps," she said.

"You see, that's what Frank Norris can't understand," Travis went on. "With his narrow mind, he's incapable of grasping the fact that most of the men who visited the acre over the years were basically decent. They went on to found families, build homes, raise fine children, establish

schools and churches. But on their visits to Fort Worth, if for only a night
or two, they explored the other side of their nature. Their lives were
enriched, because forever after, they knew a bit more about themselves,
had a better grasp on reality."

Allegra—and the entire room—stood entranced. The whole town
had been waiting for Travis to answer Norris. And now they were witnesses.

"Those men built this country," Travis said. "I don't know what we'd
have done without them. When I came to Fort Worth, there were not
more than two hundred and fifty people here. There was a blacksmith
shop, a flour mill, a cobbler, a general store. There was no post office. Not
even a saloon. We built a city where there was nothing but wilderness
infested by Indians and poverty. We saved Fort Worth from the Carpetbag rule suffered by the rest of the South. We supplied the drovers who
took the cattle up the Chisholm Trail and brought prosperity back in
their saddlebags, to enrich all Texas. And with these hands I helped bring
the first railroad into Fort Worth. God, but I'm proud of that!"

He tilted his head in the calculated pause that had held the attention
of countless juries and audiences.

"Think of it, Mrs. Conard. Cities erected across half a continent,
interlaced with transportation and commerce, all within our lifetime!
Thousands of miles of wilderness tamed, and turned to the plow and the
domesticated animal! There has been nothing like it in the entire history
of the world!"

He lowered his voice to the confidential tone he habitually used on
juries. "I saw a phrase in the newspaper the other day that saddened me.
The writer used the term 'The myth of the West.' Wouldn't it be a terrible
thing, Mrs. Conard, if all we accomplished were relegated to the realm of
myth? I can't think of a greater tragedy. It all *happened!* I saw it! At
random moments over a half century, at various places over the American continent, all the elements of that myth occurred in reality. And I'm
here to tell you that most of them occurred right here in Fort Worth!"

He studied his audience and was gratified with the enrapt attention.
He turned back to Allegra.

"I want to thank you, Mrs. Conard. You've helped me to understand.
I've been approaching the end of my life regretting that perhaps I didn't
use my God-given talents to best advantage, that I didn't try for the
presidency as some urged me to do. But Mrs. Conard, I now see that my
most significant accomplishments are right here. That 'myth of the West'
writer kept talking about cow ponies and cowboys. I can tell you, they
were horses and men!"

He smiled. "No, Mrs. Conard, we weren't saints. But neither were
we complete sinners, as Frank Norris seems to think. If we'd been saints,

we wouldn't have known the trail drivers, railroad men, freighters, buffalo hunters, land speculators, prospectors, soldiers, hide buyers, Indian fighters. And you would never have known the comfortable city you now enjoy. We did what we had to do. And we built this city, this country. I have no apologies to make. I don't expect everyone to agree with me, but as far as I'm concerned, J. Frank Norris and his ilk can go straight to hell."

He turned to his wife. "Reva, I think it's time we went home to see about the children."

Travis was gratified by the look of pride his wife gave him across the crowded room. "Of course, Senator," she said.

She walked toward him, smiling as if she did not have a care in the world.

BOOK THREE

The Boom Years

I don't do these things because I want to run the risk of being killed. I do it to demonstrate what can be done. Somebody has got to show the way. . . . I am convinced that someday we will all be flying and the more things that are attempted and accomplished, the quicker we will get there.

Ormer Locklear (1891–1920)
Interview, 1919

The Dallas–Fort Worth rivalry has been overstated. They're both good towns. Fort Worth is progressive and modern. It has outstanding leadership and fine people. Of course I never go over to the goddamned place.

Dallas businessman
to James Farley

17

Whenever Vern Spurlock wanted something, he became impossible to ignore. When word came in the late fall of 1915 that the entire U.S. Army Aero Squadron was scheduled to land in Ryan Pasture on the edge of town, Vern laid siege.

As usual, he did not reveal the complete scope of the plot hatching in his mind.

The aero squadron—the nation's total flying armada of seven planes—was en route from Fort Sill to Mexico to chase Pancho Villa. The pilots were to be entertained overnight by Fort Worth business leaders. Travis was among them.

Vern went to work seeking an invitation.

"I'm sorry, son," Travis said. "But it's a small group, a private dining room. Besides, Mr. Carter is the host. It just wouldn't be proper for me to ask."

Vern refused to allow the issue to drop. In the four years since the Roland Gerros flight he had been obsessed with flying machines. He and Clay had helped the Locklear brothers in the construction of a glider. Using railroad trestles and riverbanks as launching platforms, they had sailed for seconds at a time, usually rebuilding the frail craft after each flight. They had been among the crowd of ten thousand people in Ryan Pasture when Calbraith Perry Rodgers landed his Vin-Fiz Flyer, the first aeroplane to arrive in Fort Worth under its own power and the first to fly across the continent.

Now Vern actually had a chance to talk with aviators.

"I don't want a dinner. Just put me in a corner," he begged Travis. "I won't say a word. No one will know I'm there."

"Son, I can't," Travis said. "Now, that's the end of it!"

"Fix it up for me to be a waiter," he pleaded. "I just want to hear what's said."

"Absolutely not!" Travis thundered. "I don't want to hear another word!"

But as always, the constant, sad hunger on Vern's face did its work. At the last moment Travis relented.

"My youngest son is crazy about flying," he explained to Amon Carter. "He wants to become an aviator. Perhaps the exposure will satisfy his curiosity and remove the idea from his mind."

With his invitation secured, Vern then proceeded to edge his way into the periphery of the welcoming committee.

Vern knew he was living in dramatic times. With the war in Europe a patriotic fervor was building. His father blamed Taft and Wilson for not averting the war. In 1912 Travis had bolted the Democratic Party and backed Teddy Roosevelt's Bull Moose campaign. Now President Wilson was promising he would keep the United States out of the war. But doubt was growing that he could.

The reception committee drove out to the field an hour before the planes were scheduled to land. The cool, crisp November day was overcast with gray but unmarred by the solid clouds that mean turbulence aloft. The northwest wind was brisk but steady. The pasture was level and free of stones. The dried brown grass was shin-high, providing a firm carpet.

Wearing his best dark suit, Vern waited quietly with his father and other dignitaries on the edge of the marked landing strip. As the crowd grew, Fort Worth police kept it behind rope barriers to prevent a repeat of the debacle with the Rodgers Vin-Fiz Flyer. On that day four years ago the mob had rushed onto the field before the plane reached earth, and tragedy had been averted only by the aviator's skill. Rodgers had pulled his plane back into the air, circled, and landed in a different portion of the pasture.

"There they are!" someone yelled from the crowd.

Vern searched the leaden sky to the north. At first he could not find them. Then he saw the specks far in the distance.

Travis checked his watch. "They're a few minutes early."

"They had a good tailwind," Vern said.

A cheer went up from the crowd. The seven aeroplanes grew steadily in size. Slowly losing altitude, the bi-wing Jennys passed directly over the field to an enthusiastic ovation.

Then, one by one, they landed on the brown grass of the pasture, spun around at the end of the field, and taxied back toward the crowd. They were aligned and tied down in perfect military fashion.

Vern walked a few paces behind his father as the welcoming committee moved onto the field. A tall, lean captain stepped out of the nearest plane. He peeled off his flying helmet and goggles, stowed them in the cockpit, and retrieved a broadbrimmed campaign hat. He jumped the final three feet to earth, advanced to meet the welcoming committee, and saluted. "Captain Benjamin Foulois, gentlemen, at your service."

Vern felt shivers down his spine. He was thoroughly familiar with the exploits of Captain Foulois. As an officer in the Signal Corps, Foulois had taken delivery from the Wright Brothers of the very first plane purchased by the U.S. Army. Fifteen minutes of instruction were included in the deal, and Foulois had become the first military aviator in United States history. He was outspoken and a champion of flying machines. His published statements continually kept him in hot water with the military commanders in Washington.

Foulois moved down the line of the welcoming dignitaries, shaking hands, cupping his left ear to hear the introductions. Vern had read that the roar of the engines and wind tended to make aviators slightly deaf.

As Foulois approached, Vern studied the man he long had admired more than any other.

The captain wore high-topped tan boots and olive-colored jodhpurs. The pockets of his neat, tight-fitting military blouse were stuffed with maps and papers. His dark hair was close-cropped, and he was smooth-shaven. His face was deeply creased. He seemed to be making a special effort to remember names as he moved along the receiving line.

"And this is my youngest son, Malvern," Travis said. "He has developed a great interest in your profession."

Foulois shook hands and gave Vern an appraising glance. Vern stood as straight as he could, matching Foulois in height and military bearing. But he knew his face must appear callow and woefully unmarked to a man like Foulois.

"Good," Foulois said, tightening his grip. "We'll be needing new aviators badly before long."

Vern glanced at his father, anticipating a frown of concern. But Travis had turned and was leading the guests toward the automobiles that would take them to their hotel.

That evening Vern sat quietly through the dinner. Amon Carter and Travis offered brief remarks, welcoming the group to Fort Worth, and Captain Foulois rose to respond. His calm, self-assured demeanor told Vern that sparks were about to fly.

"I first want to express our appreciation for your hospitality," he said. "Your interest in aviation is encouraging to me, and I'll tell you why. During the next few years, the army will be forced to spend more than a hundred million dollars for the development of air power. Frankly, we need your help."

A murmur of surprise swept through the room. Foulois seemed not to notice.

"America is in poor shape, militarily," he went on. "Our little army today would be wiped out in the first good fight we had."

Vern saw concern, even shock, on the faces of the Fort Worth men.

"Captain, isn't that putting it a bit strong?" asked old Major Van Emden.

Foulois shook his head. "Major, we wouldn't be ready to fight if war were declared today. We wouldn't be ready in a year. Nor would we be ready in five years if our condition wasn't better than it is today."

He pointed in the direction of Ryan Pasture. "The highest number of any of the aeroplanes out yonder on the field tonight is fifty-three. That figure means that many aeroplanes have been owned by the United States Army in the last six years. Gentlemen, that many machines are being shipped to Europe every day. That many are being *destroyed* in Europe every day."

He urged the Fort Worth men to appeal to their congressmen and demand that something be done.

"Tonight, one of you quoted a Texas congressman as having said that military preparedness is all graft. Five years ago I was sent to San Antonio with the only aeroplane in government service. I had to teach myself how to fly, and the government allowed me a hundred and fifty dollars a year to keep the machine up. In the first year I spent three hundred dollars out of my own pocket on it. I don't think you could have called me a grafter under such circumstances."

"Captain, what threat do you see to America?" someone asked. "Surely we can take care of Mexico if the need arises."

"Our next war will be with Germany," Foulois said. "It's almost here, and we're sadly unprepared."

Vern heard exclamations of dismay and disagreement from around the table. Several of the men in the room were first generation German-Americans.

Foulois did not retreat. "If Germany comes out victorious in the war now being waged, she will have the strongest army in the world. If Germany cares to take issue with the United States after this European war, she could land troops anywhere she pleased along the Atlantic Coast and take every munitions factory we have. At the moment, they're all located along the eastern seaboard. We could stop her only with a large, well-trained aero corps."

"How could aeroplanes prevent such a landing?" Travis asked. "I thought they were used only for artillery spotting and reconnaissance."

"You're right, Senator. At the moment, they're limited to that role in this country. But in Europe machine guns are being installed on aircraft.

Aviators are now using their machines to shoot down other aeroplanes, to strafe troops and military targets on the ground. Experiments have demonstrated that small bombs can be dropped with considerable accuracy. The role of the aeroplane in future warfare is unlimited."

After the dinner concluded, the men spilled out into the hotel lobby. Small groups stood discussing the captain's startling views. Vern saw his chance. Travis was involved in a conversation near the hotel desk, his attention diverted. Captain Foulois seemed tired. He said good night to the men around him and started for his room.

Vern approached him at the door to the elevator. "Sir, how would I go about enlisting in the aero squadron?"

Foulois stopped and shook his head. "I wish I could offer you some encouragement, son. But I can't. You heard what I said tonight. We're limited to a small number of planes, only a few aviators. They're all volunteers from the Signal Corps, experienced men with considerable army service. There's a long waiting list. You might enlist in the army and volunteer. But your chances would be remote."

Vern knew his disappointment registered on his face. "I understand, sir."

Foulois put a hand on his shoulder. "If war comes, or if the country wakes up to the danger and expands the aero squadron, the situation will be vastly different. Growth of the flying corps will be rapid. If that happens, write to me, and I'll do everything I can. We badly need young men like you."

Vern thanked him and turned away.

Fortunately, Travis had not seen the exchange.

During the next few weeks Vern walked through his classes at Fort Worth University in a daze. He devoured every word in the daily newspapers. Most of the news columns were consumed by the oil excitement sweeping West Texas. But he found reports describing the aero squadron's role in the pursuit of Villa. Army generals were high in their praise of the usefulness of aircraft for locating the enemy troops.

In Europe the land war had entered a stalemate. Both sides were attempting new techniques to break the deadly trench warfare. They had introduced poison gas and massed bayonet attacks. Occasionally news correspondents now described aerial "dogfights" in which armed German and British observation craft attempted to shoot each other out of the skies.

Vern found a brief item buried on a back page of the *Fort Worth Star-Telegram* revealing that, for the first time, the Royal Flying Force was accepting United States citizens for pilot training in Canada.

It was the chance he had been seeking. He was determined to go from the moment he finished reading the few lines of type.

His only indecision arose over how to make his departure. If his mother, father, and sister learned of his plans, they would stop him. But he could not bring himself to run away without explanation, and his feelings were too complex to put into a letter.

The next day Clay bought a new Maxwell. He came by and invited Vern along to try it out. They cruised the streets in it for a while, then took it into the country to see how fast it would go.

Vern waited until they were on the open stretches west of town. He then told his brother that he planned to enlist.

"You're crazy!" Clay exploded. "You'll just go over there and get yourself killed!"

Clay pulled the automobile to the side of the road and stopped. "Look, why don't you stay here? Throw in with me and we'll hunt for oil. We'll both get rich and have more fun than a barrel of monkeys."

"Nothing you say will change my mind," Vern said. "This is something I've got to do. Besides, we'll be into the war before long. I'm just getting in on the ground floor."

Clay looked at him for a long moment, then shook his head in disgust. He started the Maxwell forward again and shifted gears to cross Mary's Creek.

For a time they sped along a wagon track lined with sunflowers. "Maybe war's inevitable," Clay said. "But your going off to get yourself killed isn't." He freed one hand from the wheel and grabbed Vern's arm. "Look! What are all those tanks, aeroplanes, trucks, ships going to need? Oil! You can do more for your country right here in Texas. You'd be draft exempt. Essential to the war effort. And getting rich!"

Vern felt frustrated. He knew he never would be able to explain the way he felt, not even to Clay. "That's your way of life," he said. "Not mine."

"It'd be a hell of a lot more profitable than flying around in a mess of canvas, sticks, and baling wire."

Vern was puzzled by the remark. "I'm not doing this for profit."

They passed the recreation and dance pavilion at Lake Como, with its weekend jam of people. Clay turned his head to look for unattached women and wandered off the road. He struggled to get the car back onto the gravel surface. "I don't think you've thought of what this will do to Mama and Papa," he said. "Mama will take to her bed again. Papa will pull every string in Washington to get you back. In irons, if necessary. Zetta will flay everyone in sight. I won't be able to go near her for months. Durwood's the only one who won't give a shit."

"I know," Vern said. "That's why I'm telling you. I want you to explain why I'm doing it this way. I want to spare them—and me—the long good-byes."

Clay grinned. "You're just afraid they'll stop you."

"No. I'm going," Vern said again. "My mind is made up."

Clay used a straight and level stretch of road to push the Maxwell past fifty miles an hour. The engine settled into a steady roar. Grass sped along under the wheels. The wind whipped at Vern's jacket.

He found himself wishing the Maxwell had wings.

The next morning Clay helped slip Vern's luggage out of Bluebonnet, past Zetta and Reva, even past the servants. His emotions were mixed. He did not want Vern to leave, but he felt Vern had the right to do whatever he wanted.

That evening he drove Vern to the railroad station.

Although he had always felt that he and Vern were closer than most brothers, they had never been demonstrative. But while Vern bought his tickets, dark ruminations swept through Clay's mind. He was jolted by the thought that he might never see Vern again.

When they at last stood beside the train, and the time came to say good-bye, Clay gave way to impulse. He put his arms around Vern and gave him a farewell hug. As they separated, he saw that Vern's eyes were glazed with tears.

"God damn it, Clay, I thought I could depend on you not to make a scene."

Clay attempted to laugh. "You just take care of yourself."

The train whistle signaled. The conductor called his warning. Clay walked Vern to the steps.

At the last moment, they again embraced.

Then Vern climbed into the coach. He did not look back.

Clay also left town that evening, not telling anyone where he was going. For a week he drove through the most remote rural regions of West Texas. He spent his days seeking oil sign.

He had kept up with the news on West Texas oil exploration. Successful shallow wells had been drilled near Petrolia and Henrietta, but so far efforts to expand those pools had resulted in dry holes. Northwest of Wichita Falls, rancher W. T. Waggoner had attempted to drill a water well on his ranch and struck oil. Disgusted, he sank four more wells and found only salt water and oil. His cattle remained thirsty, but word of his discovery spread. The resulting boom town was named for his daughter Electra. Less spectacular play had been found in other West Texas counties.

Clay avoided them.

He wanted his own field.

Prowling the feed stores, blacksmith shops, and tin-top roadhouses, he struck up conversations and led the topic around to oil. In Abilene he met a drifter who told him that only a few miles to the south ranchers and farmers had found damp gas in their water wells. The man said he had seen oil floating on Hog Creek—so named because many hogs grazed on acorns along the creek banks. Clay spent two days walking the creek, sniffing the water, and burning countless matches over suspicious cracks in the ground. He found nothing.

Then he drove to a farm a hundred miles to the north, where seepage had been reported in a water well. He learned that exploration already had been done nearby, without success.

Travel in those remote regions was difficult. Often he drove for miles over roads that were little more than wagon tracks. Bridges were few. Streams could be forded only at low water. After the slightest rain the roads turned into mud. He often had to go fifty miles out of his way to find a bridge over a swollen creek or river.

Stranded by rain for two days near Petrolia, he spent his time in the bars, drinking with the roughnecks, tool pushers, and drillers, studying them, listening to their talk.

He learned that he might be on the wrong course. Many oilmen now believed there was little correlation between surface sign and a successful well. They told of countless places where rich seeps had led only to dry holes, or wells of minuscule production. The prevailing theory now was that most oil pools lay deep within the earth, and that only cracks or fissures allowed small amounts to find their way near the surface.

In Wichita Falls he wandered into a bar near the freight yards and struck up a conversation with an oil field driller who introduced himself as Pete Pierson. Small and wiry, with curly, copper-colored hair, Pierson walked with a bowlegged, rocking motion and talked incessantly. Clay guessed he was in his early thirties.

Clay prodded him with a string of questions. At last Pierson put down his beer bottle and looked at Clay with suspicion. "What kind of work you do?"

"I'm thinking about going into the oil business."

Pierson hooted. "They're building a nuthouse out on the edge of town. Maybe you'd better go check in."

"I need to talk to somebody with field experience. It'd be worth money to me."

"Now I hear you much better," Pierson said. He spread his right hand on the bar. Two fingers were missing. "That finger there's at the bottom of a hole at Drumright, Oklahoma. I lost this one at Heavener."

They moved to the back of the bar. Clay asked him questions for more than three hours.

At last Pierson threw up his hands. "This ain't no goddamn good. You can't just talk about it. I've got to show you. Hell, come on out to the well. About time I was getting back anyhow."

They drove to a drilling rig fifteen miles northwest of town. For three days Clay followed Pierson around the derrick floor, asking questions. He listened closely to the answers. He knew he was obtaining information that had not yet found its way into any textbook.

Each night he drove back to town, bought beer, iced it down, and drove it back out to the crew. When the bit was working in soft strata, they might go all night without having to make a trip—pulling the drill stem to change a worn-out bit. On these quieter nights, they sat around, drank beer, and talked.

Clay soaked up the oil field lore. He watched the way Pierson handled the men, mixing with them but always keeping a slight distance. Pierson seemed to get the most work out of every man. He had a wealth of tricks and was forever leading, shaming, praising, or pleading. He was tireless; he thought nothing of climbing the derrick twenty times a night to check the traveling block.

"This one's going to be a dry hole," he confided one night. "We're down to twenty-three hundred and we haven't had a sniff. You get a feel for it. Over at Petrolia we got so we knew what kind of formation we'd hit next. It was like boring a hole through an onion, layer after layer. Usually we'd hit gas first and let the well blow. If we were lucky, there'd be oil behind it. At Electra the formations weren't quite as consistent. But we always knew when we were getting close."

On the last night Clay walked Pierson to one side. "You ever thought of drilling a well on your own?"

"Seldom think of anything else. But I'm not made of money."

"Money might be found. You know of any good sites?"

"Maybe."

"I'm going into this game with both feet," Clay said. "But I want to do it right. My plan is to go where no wells have been drilled, and hunt for another field."

Pierson made a face. "Lone wolves seldom make big money. They drill too many dry holes. And when they hit, word usually leaks out before they can sew up the leases around them. If they send their partners a telegram, or wire for equipment to complete the well, they might as well put an advertisement in the newspapers. Half the telegraph operators up and down the tracks sell the information that goes out over the wires."

"How would you go about it?" Clay asked.

"Why the shit should I tell you?"

"Because we're going to be partners."

Pierson laughed and slapped his knee. "I guess that's as good a reason as any. Well, there's only one way to make consistent money in this game. Let the *other* fellow go to the expense of exploration. Keep your money handy, ready to jump. Always know where there's a rig or two available. Set up your own spy system—telegraph operators, roustabouts, bartenders, anyone who might hear something. When you get wind of a major strike, you move fast. The first thing you do is lease equipment. If the strike is really big, every rig in Texas and Oklahoma will be sewed up within twenty-four hours. You get to the discovery well the quickest way you can and sign up every lease in sight. You can't lose money. Leases that sell for two or three hundred dollars will bring a thousand in a week. You spud in as fast as possible and make hole around the clock, hoping to bring in one of the first big producers. The oil companies will have men on the scene to buy a certain number of wells so they can control the market. If you're late, you get the hind tit, and it might take you two or three years of production to make any real money. If you hit a good well and sell out, you're in good shape for the next go-round."

"You really think there'll be more oil booms?"

"When they start, they'll go off like a string of firecrackers. That's the way it was in Oklahoma. And if Texas doesn't have more oil than Oklahoma, I've never pissed beer."

Clay liked Pierson. He doubted he could find a more knowledgeable and suitable partner.

They agreed that Clay would lay the groundwork for their partnership while Pierson completed his contract.

On his return to Fort Worth, Clay drove to the Fort Worth Club and phoned Travis.

"Where in hell have you been?" Travis demanded.

Clay told him. Travis did not draw a breath before asking the next question.

"Did Vern go with you?"

Clay hesitated. "Vern's all right. He left town a few days ago."

"Where is he?"

"He's all right," Clay said again. "Look, I'm at the Fort Worth Club. Why don't you come over? I'll buy you a drink and tell you what I know."

Clay only had time to order a drink before Travis strode into the dark paneled bar. He came straight to Clay and sat down facing him. With remarkable self-control he exchanged amenities with the waiter and ordered his drink. Not until the waiter had left did he turn to Clay.

"Where is he?"

Until the moment he saw the depth of concern in his father's eyes, Clay had not fully realized his responsibility in Vern's caper. "Vern swore me to secrecy," he said. "Two weeks ago he left to join the Canadian Royal Flying Corps."

Cold fury came into Travis's eyes. A deadly pallor spread over his face. "And you let him go?"

Clay lowered his head. "Look, it wasn't my place to stop him."

"It *was* your place. And if you weren't man enough, you could have come to me!"

Clay let the insult pass. "Papa, he only told me because he wanted to tell *somebody*. There was nowhere else he could turn."

The drinks arrived. Travis left his untouched. He sat for a time without speaking. Clay waited, knowing what was to come.

"This will just about kill his mother."

"I'll talk to her," Clay said. "I'll try to explain what was in his mind."

Travis looked at him as if seeing him for the first time. "You will *not* talk to your mother. You've done enough. You've probably let your brother go off to his grave."

"Now wait just a goddamn minute," Clay said. "Don't you saddle me with this! It's not my fault Vern couldn't come to you and tell you what he wanted to do with his life. He knew you wouldn't even consider what *he* wanted. You'd only think about what *you* wanted. He knew you'd have the President and maybe the Prime Minister of Canada on the phone an hour after he left town."

"You're right," Travis said. "That's exactly what I would have done, because I care. What worries me—frightens me—about you is that you *don't* care."

Clay thought of the scene in the train station. "I love Vern as much as anyone."

Travis gave him another long, searching look. He rose from the table, his drink still untouched. "I think it best you not come by Bluebonnet for a while," he said.

Travis could not remember a time in his life when he had been so angry—at Clay, at Vern, and at himself for not foreseeing the situation.

But he was also afraid.

Judging from the news accounts, the battles in Europe seemed bloody even by the standards of the War Between the States. Along the western front, trench fighting continued in a long, devastating stalemate. Machine guns, grenades, mortars, artillery, and poison gas were taking terrible tolls. Neither side could move without horrendous losses.

In his worst nightmares, Travis still remembered Cold Harbor.

There, allowed a few hours of grace before the battle, the Confederates constructed deep, zigzagged trenches. General Grant had hurled his entire Army of the Potomac against them along a six-mile front, driving toward the Chickahominy and Richmond. Seven thousand federal troops died in eight minutes. Travis had seen the slaughter. He later walked among the corpses. He had no illusions concerning trench warfare. He had participated in its birth.

And he remembered the balloonists who sometimes wafted accidentally over the lines, helpless targets for enemy sharpshooters.

He held faint hope of Vern's return from the war.

Although he had always recoiled from the thought of playing favorites with his children, he could not deny that Vern had always held a special place. Each of the other children was flawed—Zetta with her bitterness, Durwood with his weak ways, and Clay with his recklessness.

Only Vern had seemed perfect, with a gentle personality that everyone loved and respected.

Reluctantly, Travis went home and broke the news. As he had anticipated, Reva was devastated. She went into her darkened bedroom, so distraught she could not discuss the matter.

Zetta's reaction was similar to his own. She blamed Clay.

"He could've told us," she said. "At least he didn't have to leave us frantic with worry for two weeks. I'll never forgive him for that!"

Even Durwood seemed disturbed. "And to think we were on the verge of going to the police! When Clay knew all the time!"

Bluebonnet fell into premature mourning, as if Vern's demise were foretold. With Reva confined to her darkened room, and Zetta's constant lamentations, even the servants spoke in subdued tones.

Travis escaped to the comfort of Eunice Gray's apartment.

"I don't understand why those two boys acted so callously toward their parents," he told her. "Vern for doing what he did. Clay for not telling us."

Eunice hesitated before answering him. "Travis, they're not boys. They're men. You don't own them anymore. You'll have to learn to turn loose."

"Vern is not yet twenty. Clay is barely twenty-one."

Eunice raised up on one elbow. "That's a time of testing," she said. "They have to leave the nest, to see how well they can do on their own."

"Vern's too young," Travis insisted. "He's too sensitive, vulnerable."

Eunice smiled. "Vern's the dreamer. But don't sell him short. From what you say, I wouldn't be surprised if he isn't the toughest Spurlock of all."

During the next few days everything fell rapidly into place for Clay. Pierson completed the dry hole, left his contractor, and came to Fort Worth. Clay took a room at the Metropolitan and they spent many hours poring over maps and charts.

Clay devoted a night to penciling in every known major discovery in the Southwest. "Everyone's been thinking too small," he said. "Look here. What do you see? There's a pattern, from Paola, Kansas, down through Bartlesville, Tulsa, Drumright, Chandler, Seminole—all the Oklahoma fields—to Petrolia and Electra. A strip about sixty, maybe eighty or a hundred miles wide, from northeast to southwest. Maybe it goes on into the middle of Texas!" He pointed to the map. "I was told there's an oil seep right here, along this creek south of Ranger. I walked it, but I couldn't find a trace."

"A seep may not mean a damned thing," Pierson said. "But you may be right about the pattern. There could be a sand formation, or maybe a series of sands, right across here in the bed of an old sea."

"A sea? Here?"

"Hell, yes! I've brought up sea shells and shark's teeth from two thousand feet. Turds turned into rock, shit long before anything resembling man ever existed. Bones of animals we can only imagine. Hell, all of this country has seen swamps, deserts, forests, mountains, seas, down through millions and millions of years. How the hell else could all of those different formations have got there?"

Clay had obtained county surveyor's maps. He and Pierson spent several nights studying them. One evening Pierson pointed to a spot in western Wichita County. "This may be it right here. I remember that country. There's play to the northeast. Nothing spectacular, but solid production. And more back over this way a few miles. I can't find any evidence of this land under lease. Why don't we take a run up there?"

Two days later they arrived in the rugged, mesquite-infested country northwest of Wichita Falls. They toured the potential sites, and Clay received his first lesson in oil field diplomacy. "Let me handle it," Pierson said. "When oil's mentioned, people tend to get excited. Some ranchers hate oil people worse than Republicans. Others tend to get feverish and think they'll be rich by noon tomorrow. They're one way or the other. There doesn't seem to be any middle ground."

They found terrain Pierson liked. It lay on a ranch that was small by Texas standards. The owner was listed as Lester Denwoodie. Clay and Pierson found him at the ranch house on a crisp October morning, about an hour after sunrise.

He was as lean and weathered as a bois d'arc fencepost. He led Clay and Pierson down the porch steps, away from the house, and fixed them with slate-gray eyes as unyielding as flint. "What you fellas want?"

Pierson was friendly but not effusive. "We're what you might call oil prospectors. We've been studying this country pretty close. From what we've found, the northeast corner of your place might be a good spot to test."

"You mean drill?"

"That's right."

Denwoodie turned his head and looked off toward the scattered barns and corrals. "What's in it for me?"

"If we drilled, and if we found anything, one-eighth of all that comes out of the ground. If you'll ask around, you'll find that's standard. In addition, we'd expect to take the whole place under lease, at whatever we agree on. I think most of the land around here is going at a dollar an acre."

"What if you don't find nothing?"

Pierson allowed a long, slow grin to creep across his face. "In that case, you've got a hole in the ground, a road across a corner of your place, and a couple of thousand dollars for your trouble. And me and my partner will be scratching to find the money to drill somewhere else."

Clay thought he saw a flicker of humor flare briefly behind Denwoodie's poker face. But he was not certain. "I don't want my land messed up," he said.

"We'd cut a road in from the section line," Pierson said. "We wouldn't bother you here at the house. You'll never know we're on the place. Aside from the road, we'd only need a couple of acres around the well for our equipment, a small pond. I've never seen a well cause any problems with cattle, but if you'd like, we'd fence it off."

"A pond? Sounds like you're going to mess up my land."

Pierson hesitated only a split second. "I won't lie to you. If we decided to drill, we'd play hell with a couple of acres. Outside of that, a good spring rain would wash away all signs we'd been here."

Denwoodie glanced back toward the house. A woman stood in the door, two small children clinging to her thin housedress. "I don't know," he said. "Give me time to think about it."

"We're looking at some other sites around here," Pierson said. "We'll be back in three or four days."

Pierson waited until they were back on the road, headed for Wichita Falls. "He's hooked."

Clay had seen no such evidence. "How do you know?"

"If he wasn't, he'd have told us to get the fuck off his place in the first five minutes. He only wants to be sure he won't get skinned. He'll talk to his banker, maybe to a lawyer. I think he'll go for a dollar, maybe a dollar and a quarter."

Pierson was right. A few days later the lease was signed.

"What are the odds we'll find oil?" Clay asked.

Pierson seemed irritated by the question. "Who the hell knows? What do you want? A written guarantee?"

Purchase of the lease had wiped out Clay's available cash. They agreed that while Pierson remained in Wichita Falls to find equipment, Clay would head back to Fort Worth to raise more money.

Never stopping to consider any other course, he went to Durwood at the bank. Despite their differences, he had always looked upon Durwood as the banker. In recent years Durwood had edged upward on the bank totem pole. Clay had heard Travis bragging about Durwood's sharp investments in lots around Niles City and the packing plants. He had made a bit of money. He now handled all real estate and business loans at the bank.

"What can you offer as collateral?" Durwood asked.

Clay looked at his brother and shrugged. "My two hands," he said. "Look, you know I'm good for the money."

Durwood examined the lease papers, Clay's figures. "Your honesty isn't in question. We're talking about standard business practice."

Clay hesitated, stymied. He felt uncomfortable. Without thinking, he had entered the bank in his field clothes. Durwood sat at a large, neatly polished desk. His office was carpeted. Durwood wore a dark, well-cut suit and a high starched collar.

"Couldn't I put up the lease, the well itself?"

"Neither has any value until proved," Durwood explained. "Since you're leasing the equipment, you've nothing of actual cash value. The bank can't lend money to drill a hole in the ground that'll probably be worthless."

"Seems to me the bank will have to change that practice. There'll be a few dry holes. But if the bank takes the long view, and finances a wildcatter through several wells, they're bound to make money."

Durwood raised his eyebrows. "The bank can't gamble with its money. And that's all this is. A gamble, pure and simple. I could never justify making such a loan. It'd surely be questioned by the bank examiners. I must have collateral."

"What about the estate?" Clay asked.

Durwood frowned. "What estate?"

"Papa still has some money. We both share in the will. There'll be money from our inheritance someday."

Durwood placed both arms on his desk and sniffed. "Clay, I've never heard of anything so callous in my life. For your information, our father is only sixty-six years old. As far as I know, he's in perfect health. He well may live another thirty years. And I hope he does. I wasn't aware you were sitting around waiting for him to die."

Clay was furious with himself for not being better prepared. "God damn it, I'm only pointing out that I'm a Spurlock, not a pauper coming in here for a handout."

"The bank can't lend money solely on the strength of a family name." Durwood raised an eyebrow. "Sometimes there are black sheep."

Clay glared at his brother. "Are you saying I'm a black sheep?"

"If the shoe fits, you might consider wearing it. I've heard stories of drunken sprees, fistfights over women, and three-day poker games. That hardly lends stature to a family name." He shoved Clay's papers back across the desk. "And this is nothing but a fly-by-night gamble. If you can show me a sound business proposition, I'll be happy to lend you money."

Clay snatched up the papers. "I don't want your goddamned money. I wouldn't take it if you gave it to me. But remember this. There'll come a day when you'll wish you'd made this loan."

He strode angrily out of the bank and stood on the sidewalk, uncertain where to turn.

Thanks to Vern, he had been barred from his own home.

He went into the nearest bar, ordered a drink, and started thinking.

Somewhere he had to raise ten thousand dollars.

18

In the hours after midnight the wind turned colder. Toward dawn frozen sleet began falling on the raw plank floor of the rig. Turning up the collar of his mackinaw, Clay fought to keep his footing as he wrestled with the icy chains and heavy machinery. Overhead the Yellow Dog lanterns attached to the eighty-four-foot wooden derrick cast eerily dancing shadows across the surrounding mesquite. They dimmed and brightened in response to each blast from the fresh norther.

Standing with his back to the wind, Clay used his full weight to guide a string of drill pipe as it was lowered. He felt the jolt as the connection was made a heart-stopping split second after he jerked his gloved hands clear. Working smoothly, he and Pete adjusted the drive chain, rotated the pipe home, then released the block. With a roar the donkey engine took the strain of more than eleven hundred feet of drill stem. The derrick floor shuddered. Then the brake drum squealed as the operator slowly lowered the drill bit deeper into the hole.

Breathing heavily, Clay backed to the corner of the derrick, once again amazed that he had managed the intricate manipulation of pipe, chains, and blocks and emerged with all fingers and toes intact. His face was numb with cold. Across the derrick floor Pete Pierson grinned and held up his left hand, palm outward, signaling that they had only five more lengths to lower before the bit reached bottom and they could return to the fire.

Around the rig, at the edge of the circle of light, the swaying sage and stunted mesquite were sheathed in ice. On the horizon the sky glowed red from burning gas, vented through towering flares as waste.

Exhausted, and half out of his mind with worry, Clay yet found himself strangely content. His aching muscles and the constant pain in his lower back intensified his sense of life and infused him with restless energy. The last five weeks had been an invigorating experience, an introduction to a complete new world. He liked the rough, give-and-take camaraderie and teamwork of the rig, the solid satisfaction of accomplishment.

They now were past twelve hundred feet. In early evening they had struck a thick layer of limestone that quickly blunted drill bits. During the night they had made two trips to change the bit. Now they were on the third.

Thus far they had not seen the slightest sign of oil.

His anxiety had long since settled into a constant queasiness in the pit of his stomach. He had borrowed heavily from friends, even sold portions of his share in the well to raise drilling cash.

Everything he owned was in hock.

Movement, a shout from above jarred him from his reverie. Another length of drill stem lifted from the derrick floor. The end swung clear. Clay stepped forward to meet it. Pete came from the opposite corner. They resumed their intricate dance amidst the moving, clashing tons of metal.

An hour later the trip was completed. They attached the grief stem, and the rotary table resumed its work, driving the bit deeper. Clay followed the crew into the tool shed.

Shivering, Pete spread his hands over the oil drum stove. "Where's that fucking whiskey?"

Clay went to the corner, reached into his bedroll, and pulled out a bottle. He handed it across the fire.

Pete tried to read the label in the dim light. "What the shit is this?"

"Only the best Scotch ever made," Clay said.

Pete rolled his eyes. "Scotch!" he yelled. "Scotch? For a bunch of roughnecks? Wait till this gets around!"

Pete freed the cap with a thumbnail. After several long swallows he wiped his mouth with a sleeve. "You're sure right, partner. This is either piss-poor bourbon or damned fine Scotch!"

Clay walked back to the corner of the shed, kicked his bedroll full-length, and sank onto it completely clothed, content with the faint warmth of the oil drum stove. Strong gusts of wind howled under the eaves above him and rattled a loose section of the sheet-iron roof. He could hear the sleet hitting the tin sides of the building. Pete handed him the bottle. He drank and felt the heat spread through his stomach, into his limbs.

"How much deeper you figure?" he asked.

Pete sank down beside him. All night Pete had smelled tailings from the well. Now he seemed reluctant to talk about it. "Hard to tell. Most of this field found production at a thousand to twelve hundred. But the deeper sands, seventeen to nineteen hundred, have been the best."

Clay tried to keep concern from his voice. "Shouldn't we have some sign by now?"

Pete took another drink before he answered. "Not necessarily. Sometimes you get plenty of sign and still end up with a dry hole. On the other hand, I've seen gushers blow in without the slightest hint." He shrugged. "Quit worrying. It's either there or it isn't, and there isn't a fucking thing we can do about it."

Clay remained silent. The payment on the leased machinery was more than two weeks overdue. Clay had telephoned the owner, promising money he did not have.

Fortunately he had made a "mistake" in setting down the location for the well. He assumed that, at best, only four or five more days of grace remained before the sheriff could track them down.

Pete drifted off to sleep. Clay remained awake, worrying. Not until daylight did he fall into a troubled sleep.

Late that afternoon they broke through the limestone and entered a bed of soft chert.

Pete examined samples from the new formation. "I don't understand this. We ought to be into pay sand. Maybe it's pinched out this far south."

At least the chert was softer and less wearing on the bit. The drilling went faster. Pete spent most of his time examining the tailings. He walked Clay a few paces away from the well. He held up a small piece of chert he had retrieved from the circulating ditch. "We may be in trouble, partner. I've talked to drillers and roughnecks all over this oil patch. I've never heard of anything like this shit."

"What'll we do? Drill deeper?"

"What the hell else is there to do?"

That night the wind died to a whisper. The temperature plunged to near zero. Pete and Clay sent the men to bed and pulled the midnight tour alone.

Daylight was breaking in the east when Pete checked another batch of tailings. He signaled for Clay to shut off the engine. He came across the rig floor holding a handful of mud. "Sniff that," he said. "Tell me it doesn't smell better than pussy."

Clay stared at the dark stain on Pete's glove. "Oil?" he asked.

"We've been getting a trace for the last hour. I didn't want to say anything until I was sure."

"A good show?"

Pete shook his head. "So far, just a whiff. But it's down there. Damn it, I feel it."

Clay roused the morning tour. Within an hour they were into soft sand and the bit was sinking rapidly.

By late afternoon oil was flowing gently out of the well and into the slush tank.

Pete was ecstatic. "Unless I miss my guess, we've got a producer. Not a big one. Probably no more than two or three hundred barrels a day. Not much pressure behind it. But we've got a good commercial location. With a little outlay for pipe, we can lease lines and pump right into a Fort Worth and Denver tank car."

Clay laughed, wondering if his father had ever dreamed that his son some day might ship oil over a railroad he had founded. "How much would a well like this be worth?"

"Too soon to tell. A lot depends on the quality—specific gravity, hydrocarbons, sulfur content, paraffin wax. Porosity of the formation. We'll know more in a day or two. We've got a long way to go yet, completing the well. Hell, the real work's just started."

Clay peeled off his gloves and walked away. Pete followed him to his car. "Where in hell you think you're going?"

"To make a telephone call."

Pete grabbed him by a shoulder and turned him around. "Wait just a minute! We've got to keep this quiet! We've still got leases to buy!"

Clay pointed to the rig and lowered his voice so the crew could not hear. "Pete, the payment on that equipment is almost three weeks overdue. The only reason the law hasn't been out here is because they haven't been able to find us. I lied about the location."

Pete's mouth hung open. He worked his jaw a few times before words came. "Holy shit, Clay. We could go to jail!"

"That thought has occurred to me. I'll keep our discovery quiet, if I can. But I've got to raise some more money. We're flat broke."

"You son of a bitch, you've been lying to me."

Clay shook his head. "I didn't lie. I just didn't tell you everything."

"We owe the crew," Pete whispered.

Clay nodded. "Stall them. Keep them busy. I'll be back in a day or two."

The nearest telephone was at a country crossroads store twenty miles away. After several attempts Clay managed to get the oil equipment firm on the line. "Mr. Johnston?" he shouted. "This is Clayton Spurlock."

He heard the old man's agitation loud and clear above the hum of the rural line. "Spurlock? Clayton Spurlock? Boy, where's my machinery? You promised you were sending me some money!"

"Yes, sir," Clay said. "That's exactly what I'm calling you about. I've been extremely busy, Mr. Johnston, completing the well and putting it into production. I've just now found time to catch up on some things I let slide. I'm calling to let you know you'll have your money in another day or two."

"That's what you told me before! You lied to me, boy! Your well is not where you said it was. Where's my machinery? I've got a warrant!"

Clay gripped the phone, aware that everyone in the country store was listening to his end of it. Up and down the party line, others could hear every word. "Mr. Johnston, that wasn't necessary. I regret that mistake about the location. You see, at the last minute we changed our minds on where to drill. I'm sure you can appreciate why I can't tell you the location over the phone. We're still negotiating a few offset leases. My partner and I will be needing a great deal of equipment during the next few months, drilling those offsets. I hope this present misunderstanding won't jeopardize our future relationship."

Clay listened to the hum as Johnston reassessed his position. "Don't lie to me now, young man. You have the money? You're sending me the money?"

"Within two days at the outside," Clay said. "I promise."

"I still have the warrant!"

"Mr. Johnston, that won't be necessary," Clay said again. "I apologize for any inconvenience I may have caused, and I'll assume any expense you've incurred. It's just that I have so many things to do."

"Two days!" Johnston shouted. "That rotary's my best rig!"

"Yes, sir," Clay shouted back. "Two days."

Limp with relief, he hung up the receiver and rang off.

Jail was no longer an immediate prospect.

But he had to raise considerable money—and fast.

He had only the barest sketch of a plan in mind.

He remembered a story Travis often told, of borrowing money solely on the strength of his hole card, to play out a winning hand of poker.

Now, with a potential producer, he had the hole card.

He returned to his car.

After six hours of hard driving over the rutted, washboard roads, he passed the stockyards and arrived in Fort Worth.

He went straight to Washer Bros., the town's finest male emporium. "I want two dark, conservative suits of the finest quality," he told Jacob Washer. "Shoes of English leather. A homburg. Spats. The whole works."

Washer's eyebrows raised in barely concealed amusement. Travis Spurlock's two younger sons had hardly been known as fashion plates.

When the selections were made and fitted, Clay waved a hand. "Just put everything on my account. We can settle at the end of the month."

As an afterthought he added a gold-headed cane to his ensemble.

Again he drove all night. He arrived in Wichita Falls just after dawn. He checked into a hotel and slept three hours. Early in the afternoon, freshly bathed, attired in his finery, and swinging his gold-headed cane, he strolled casually into Wichita Falls National and asked for the bank president. A lesser executive took only brief measure of the cut of Clay's clothes before ushering him into the august presence of Mr. Stone, a tall, lean, gray-haired man who wore a dark pinstripe suit and a perpetual frown.

Clay shook hands and began talking as if he did not have a moment to waste. "Mr. Stone, I have a crew completing a well that will expand the Electra pool more than six miles. If I'm to take full advantage of my discovery, I must move rapidly. Unfortunately, most of my capital is otherwise engaged at the moment. I need cash to secure additional leases, to obtain the necessary equipment to drill offsets, and to place the well in full production. I thought that since I apparently will be operating in this area in the future, I might do well to secure the services of your bank."

Stone was listening. But another thought seemed to be intruding. "Spurlock. Are you related to . . ."

"Senator Travis Spurlock is my father."

The banker remained impassive. But Clay felt he had gained a foothold. He pushed the advantage. "I think the most feasible route would be for us to work out a line of credit, possibly secured by the discovery well. That would provide my partner and me with the necessary flexibility."

Stone's professional frown deepened. "The value of the discovery well will have to be determined, of course."

Clay spoke quickly, knowing that if he hesitated all would be lost. "There's no time for that. The remaining offset leases must be secured before word spreads. Why couldn't we do it this way? If the bank will grant me a minimum line of credit, with the upper ranges yet to be determined, I'll go ahead and secure the additional leases. Afterward, when we come to you for more capital to expand our drilling operations, your experts can make a careful examination of our well and determine its exact worth."

Stone arched his fingers against the bridge of his nose and studied the proposal, weighing the risk against future profits. Clay waited, hiding the emotional turmoil raging within him.

The banker's gaze flicked to the cut of Clay's suit, the cravat, the gold-headed cane. He sighed. "I see your point, Mr. Spurlock. You understand, of course, that your request is highly unorthodox. Ordinarily, we wouldn't even consider such a thing. But we've learned in the last few months that the oil business is like no other. Incidentally, I once met your father, and have always held him in highest regard. I'm glad you've chosen our bank. I think we can do business."

"One more thing," Clay said. "I'd appreciate it if the mortgage lein doesn't show up at the courthouse for another forty-eight hours. I need that much time to secure the offset leases. We might as well run an ad in the newspaper as to send those papers over to the courthouse."

Stone almost smiled. "Mr. Spurlock, I can hold them on my desk until day after tomorrow. Then I'll have to turn them loose."

Clay rose and shook hands. "It's a deal."

Two hours later, again comfortable in his greasy work clothes, Clay was on his way back to the oil patch, his new finery safely stored in the hotel basement.

He spent the next four days tracking down landowners, negotiating, and closing deals. At night he slept in the car. He shaved in creek bottoms and, whenever he remembered, ate in whatever roadhouse happened to be handy. At last he closed the blank spaces on the survey map and turned back toward the well.

He arrived after dark on a Friday evening. A line of thunderstorms was rolling in from the High Plains. Lightning played amidst the derricks to the north.

Pete came down from the rig. "Shit, I was hoping you'd skipped the country. The crew was just remarking how long it'd been since they'd seen your ugly face."

Clay waved the checkbook. "Line them up. We'll pay them up to date. And the offsets are secured. We can let the crew off the reservation."

The men shut down the well and gathered in the shed. While the storm raged, Clay lit a gasoline lantern, figured their wages, and wrote the checks.

"You've stuck with us through thick and thin," he told them. "Pete and I appreciate it. We've still got a lot of work here. Those of you who want to stay, fine. If you want to move on, or take some time off, we'll understand. If I find any of you assholes in Pearl's tonight, we'll have us a party. Pete and I have some business to discuss. We'll be along after a while."

The men piled into the tarpaulin-covered truck and drove off in a blinding rainstorm.

Clay spread his bedroll and opened a fifth of whiskey. Pete sat on a toolbox, facing him. The light from the oil drum stove made patterns on the ceiling. The constant thunder, wind, and rain made the sheet-tin shanty seem almost cozy.

"What I wanted to tell you, I talked to the stud duck at Majestic Oil," Clay said. "He's sending some of his experts over to look at the well, to see if they want to make us an offer."

Pete did not answer for a moment. "Kind of taking a lot on yourself, aren't you partner?"

Clay was confused. He looked at Pete, trying to read his expression in the dim light. "Aren't we going to sell the whole package? Wasn't that the point of everything?"

Pete rose from the toolbox, stood with his feet spread, and pushed his hat to the back of his head. "Sure, we could sell. But we'd better consider this very carefully. We probably wouldn't get half as much as we would if we drilled the offsets ourselves."

Clay blew out a sigh of exasperation. "Pete, I thought I knew your fucking mind! Don't you remember the plan you explained on how to make a fortune in this game? You said the way you'd do it was get a good stake, wait for someone else to make the big strike, then move in fast, expand the discovery. Pete, this is our stake!"

"You don't understand how lucky you've been," Pete said. "Most wildcatters drill at least two or three dusters before they hit. I know one poor son of a bitch who has drilled ten and has yet to complete a producer. We could take the money from this well and piss it away on a dozen dry holes without the smell of oil. The offsets here are damned near a sure thing. By the time we prove out our strike, we'll have eight or ten wells for sure, maybe more, some probably better than this one."

"Maybe," Clay argued. "But we'd be at the mercy of Majestic. If they refuse to grant us a pass-through on their gathering lines, we're out in the cold. They could rob us blind on rates. I don't want to get boxed in!"

"Clay, God damn it, look what we've got here! If we get into the war in Europe, oil will go sky high—a dollar a barrel, maybe two dollars. The value of this strike would double, quadruple overnight! We'd be double-damned foolish to turn loose of it now."

"And if war doesn't come, if a half dozen other big pools are discovered, oil could drop back to ten cents a barrel. You know that. Anything you do in this business is a gamble. Let's take the money! Let's use it to get really rich!"

Pete sat in silence for a time. "Clay, I never said I wanted to be big-rich. Hell, I've got a wife and two kids waiting for me, if I can remember where I left them. They hardly know me. I've been working seven days a week, twelve-hour shifts, for five years or more, and that includes Christmas, New Year's, and Thanksgiving. I've dragged them over six states. We've lived in places a dog wouldn't call a home. This is my way out. And God damn it, Clay, I'm taking it."

Clay sat trying to find words to tell Pete how he felt. Drilling the offsets would be dull, unimaginative work. The excitement lay in finding oil. Any idiot could pump it out of the ground. "Maybe you could buy me out," he said.

"Don't talk foolish. Could you buy me out?"

Clay shook his head.

"Then it looks like we've got a problem. We're stuck with each other. And we can't agree. I don't know what to do."

"How about this?" Clay said. "Let's let Majestic examine the well, and make us an offer. Then we can talk about it. Okay?"

Pete hesitated for a long moment. "I guess it wouldn't do any harm."

"Of course not," Clay said. "It'd help us put a dollar figure on what we've got, no matter what we decide. Come on. Let's go into town, get drunk, and forget about it for a while. Who knows? Maybe we'll both change our minds."

Across the smoke-filled dance hall Clay saw something interesting. She wore her dark hair long, with bangs covering most of her forehead. Her full, crimson mouth was fixed in a sarcastic smile. She was small and well rounded. The plunging neckline on her scarlet dress revealed a full figure. For an interminable moment she challenged his gaze.

Clay knew he had scored. Only the maneuvering remained.

He rose and put a hand on Pete's shoulder. "Excuse me. There's something I have to do."

He crossed the crowded dance floor and stood for a moment beside a steel roof support. Again their eyes met.

She was seated at a table of a half dozen couples. Clay tried to guess which was her husband but could not. He approached the table and leaned close to her ear, raising his voice above the music from the band. "Would you care to dance?"

She gathered her skirts. "Thank you," she said. "I'm glad there's one gentleman in this place."

Clay ignored the hostile stares from her table and guided her onto the dance floor. She clung to his waist and moved lightly, following his lead without effort. She lay a cheek on his chest and looked up at him. "What's your name? Galahad?"

"Clay Spurlock. Galahad will do. Yours?"

"Leota Reeves. Everybody calls me Chippy. You can if you want. What do you do? You don't look like you belong here."

"Who does?" Clay said. He carefully moved to the opposite side of the dance floor. "Which one of those fellows you with?"

Chippy seemed surprised. "I thought you knew. Skeeter's my husband. You don't know Skeeter Reeves? You *are* new around here. He's the big squarehead over there that's looking right now like he wants to mop up the floor with both of us."

Clay turned her so he faced the table. Skeeter Reeves was wide through the shoulders, and huge. He outweighed Clay by fifteen or twenty pounds, maybe more.

"He's a driller," Chippy went on. "Mean as a junkyard dog. Don't know why I married him. That's part of his crew. All they want to do is set on their asses and get drunk. Not a live one in the bunch."

The dance ended. Only a few couples left the floor. Clay stood with his back to Skeeter Reeves and waited for the band to start the next selection. The fiddler swung into "Bingden on the Rhine."

Chippy's breasts pressed against him. Her firm body, her womanly scent, her nearness filled him with reckless thoughts. He would not have been able to stop his erection even if he had so desired. Chippy ground her stomach against him and they danced for a time in silence.

She looked up at him and smiled. "That's some problem you've got there, Galahad."

Clay glanced at her table. Skeeter was watching them.

"If you'll meet me in my car on the northeast corner of the parking lot in fifteen minutes, we'll talk about it," he said.

Chippy laughed. "Don't waste any time, do you?"

"Time's something nobody's got enough of," Clay said. "How about it?"

She hesitated. "God, we'd freeze! It's ten below Karo out there."

"I've got a heater in the car."

The dance ended.

"All right," Chippy said.

Clay walked her back to the table. Skeeter glared but said nothing as Clay pulled out her chair and waited until she was seated. "I enjoyed the dance, ma'am," he said. "Thank you."

She smiled up at him. "My pleasure, mister."

Clay ignored Skeeter and made his way back to his crew.

Pete was upset. He reached for Clay's arm and pulled him close. "Goddamn, Clay, that's Skeeter Reeves's woman! Don't you know who he is? He's supposed to have killed two or three men with his bare fists. That wife of his is a four-wheeled bitch. You're playing with dynamite!"

"She'd be worth a little risk."

"No woman's worth getting killed over."

Clay watched the clock over the bandstand. After ten minutes he rose and walked out the back door to the three-hole privy. He then circled the building to his car, started the engine, and turned up the heat.

Chippy came out a few minutes later and slid into the front seat. She glanced back at the dance hall. "I can't stay long. Skeeter thinks I've gone to powder my nose."

Clay and Chippy remained coupled more than half an hour. The windows fogged. The car became a warm cocoon, shutting out the world.

At last, half-clad, Chippy raised into a sitting position and wiped a peephole clear. "Oh goody-goody-grandma! There's Skeeter! He's looking for me!"

Clay fixed his trousers and leaned to the peephole. Skeeter was standing on the steps of the dance hall, staring out into the night.

"We could just drive off," Clay whispered.

"Oh, shit no," Chippy breathed. "Skeeter would kill me. He really would!"

"I'll circle the block and let you out at the back. You can go inside while he's out here freezing his balls off."

Clay hurriedly wiped the fogged windshield, put the car in gear, and drove out the end of the lot. Chippy rearranged her clothes while he drove around the block to the back door.

He reached across and pushed her door open. "I'll park again, wait a little bit, then come in through the front door."

Chippy scooted toward the back door. Clay drove on around the block and parked at the curb. Skeeter was no longer in sight. Watching the parking lot, Clay lit a cigarette and waited until the interior of the car cooled. He then walked back into the dance hall, showing the reentry stamp on his hand to the doorman.

He crossed the floor to his crew, casually ignoring Skeeter's table.

Pete shook his head sadly. "Good God, Clay. You think everybody in this place is stone blind? Skeeter's climbing the walls."

Clay felt alive with the familiar sensation of power and excitement. He did not turn to look. "What's he doing now?"

"He's raising hell with her. Good God! He's batting the shit out of her!"

Clay turned. Although the band continued to play, the dancers had stopped to watch the domestic drama. Holding Chippy with one hand, Skeeter was slapping her face with the other.

Two bouncers, armed with nightsticks, pushed their way across the dance floor. The short, rotund owner of the dance hall trotted after them, shouting.

Skeeter gave Chippy a violent shove, turned, and started toward Clay. Chippy fell backward over a chair.

Pete reached for Clay's arm. "He's crazy drunk! Let's get out of here!"

"Sit still!" Clay said. "I can handle him."

Skeeter stopped several feet away. His fists were clinched, poised. "You son of a bitch," he said. "Where'd you go with my wife?"

Clay looked up at him and smiled. "She wanted to know what a real man was like. I took her out to my car and showed her."

Bellowing with rage, Skeeter charged.

In a continuous, smooth motion, Clay rose from his chair and swung it into Skeeter's head.

The blow diverted Skeeter's charge. The two heavyweight bouncers seized his arms. As Skeeter struggled, the three lurched into the table, knocking drinks to the floor.

The dance hall owner held out his arms. "I can't have any trouble in here!" he shouted. "I'll lose my license! Take your fight outside!"

"Suits me," Clay said.

They walked out into the cold, crisp night, taking most of the crowd with them. Clay led the way to the bright circle under a lightpole. The crowd gathered around and moved back to shouts of "Give them room!" Chippy stood in the front row, her right eye black and closing, her mouth and nose now matching her crimson dress. Clay peeled off his jacket and tossed it to Pete.

As Clay expected, Skeeter came in a rush, swinging a roundhouse right. Clay ducked under it and rained four quick chops to Skeeter's ribs.

Eyes wide in pain and surprise, Skeeter hesitated, then charged, again leading with his right. Clay rolled under it and drove his right fist into Skeeter's solar plexus with all his strength.

Skeeter backed away, fighting for breath, arms low to guard his aching torso. Clay followed swiftly, delivering straight punches to Skeeter's unprotected face, using the full power of his arms, shoulders, and body.

Shifting his attack from face to body and back again, Clay hammered away.

Larger and stronger than Clay, Skeeter never succeeded in using his advantage. Clay received only two serious blows—a right cross that clipped the top of his head, and a left that bounced off his right cheekbone.

As Clay continued to punch, Skeeter's swings became slower and more erratic. At last he staggered and dropped to one knee. One of his crew stepped in front of him and held up a hand. "All right! He's had enough!"

Clay backed away, assessing damage to his knuckles, his cheek.

Pete handed him his coat. "Godamighty! Talk about running into a buzz saw! That beats anything I've ever seen."

Chippy still stood at the edge of the crowd. She looked at Clay in indecision.

Clay gestured toward Skeeter. "Better take your husband home before you both bleed to death."

Pete put a hand around Clay's shoulder. "Let's get in out of the cold. You need a drink."

As they returned to their table, Clay basked in the covert but intense attention of the crowd. Fistfights were a dime a dozen in the oil fields. But Skeeter Reeves had been the bull of the woods.

Shouting and whooping, Clay's crew drank to his victory. They knew that, overnight, Clay's reputation was established in the oil fields. For a time, Pete joined in.

Later he sobered. "Goddamn, Clay. That's living on the ragged edge. Skeeter keeps a Colt forty-five in the toolbox on his car. Don't you realize that if he'd caught you humping his wife he could have blown both your heads off and gone scot free? This is Texas! The land of the unwritten law! They wouldn't even have bothered the grand jury with it."

Clay nodded. "I thought about that. But you know something, Pete? When my time comes, that's the way I want to go."

"He could come back. What would you do if he came through that door, right now, with his forty-five?"

Clay glanced at the wall behind him. "I'd make a new door for this place."

Pete laughed.

"But I'd only run as far as my car," Clay added. "You see, I've got a forty-five too."

Majestic Oil sent three geologists to evaluate the well. They stayed two days, examining cores, bailing crude, and running tests.

The next week, Clay and Pete met with Majestic executives at a hotel in Wichita Falls. The firm made an offer of a hundred and fifty thousand dollars for the well and surrounding leases. Clay and Pete said they would take it under consideration.

Clay was moderately pleased. After all his debts were paid, he still would have a profit of more than fifty thousand.

"Let's take it," he said as he drove back toward the well. "It'll give us enough of a stake to jump into the next big strike and make us a fortune."

"Or lose our shirts," Pete said.

Clay drove several miles in silence, searching for a compromise. "We could checkerboard the leases and sell half. Majestic probably would go for it."

Pete shook his head. "No. They'd drill four wells to our one, and take the oil right out from under us. Either we sell all, or nothing. It's one ball of wax."

They argued through the night, poring over maps and charts, figuring probable profits from various market fluctuations.

At dawn Clay brought the discussion to a halt. "Pete, we'll never see it the same. Why don't we flip a coin? If you win, we'll do it your way. If I win, we'll sell and go for broke on the next turn of the wheel."

Pete frowned, turned, and walked to the centerpole of the shed. He stood for several minutes with his head lowered in thought. At last he kicked the pole and turned with a slow grin.

"Clay, your craziness is catching." He reached into a pocket, pulled out a silver dollar, and held it in a palm. "Call it."

"Heads," Clay said.

They watched the coin arc and land in the dirt. Both leaned to look. It was heads.

"Come on, let's go sell it," Clay said. "Maybe we can talk them up to one sixty, maybe one seventy-five."

Pete hesitated. "Don't you want to sleep some first?"

Clay grabbed his coat and started for the car. "We can sleep when we're dead."

The negotiations continued four days. Majestic held firm at one fifty, but eventually sweetened the deal by allowing Clay and Pete a one-sixteenth cut of the producer's seven-eighths.

Clay and Pete banked the money. They then began preparations to leap into the next big oil boom. Cautiously, they set up a network of scouts so they would be among the first to receive word.

Pete bought a house in Wichita Falls and prepared to move his family.

Clay returned to Fort Worth. When he arrived, he heard news that made him roll on the floor with laughter.

Van Emden, Amon Carter, and other civic leaders had convinced the Canadian government that the Texas weather was far better for training pilots than Canadian winters. Three airfields were under construction on the outskirts of Fort Worth, for lease to the Royal Flying Force.

And Vern had received orders to return to Fort Worth as an instructor.

19

The grasslands far below, lush green from abundant spring rains, were interwoven with the silver threads of meandering streams and darker clumps of mesquite and post oak. In the distance towering white clouds drifted slowly across the fathomless blue of the Texas sky. The ninety-horsepower OX-5 engine of the Curtiss JN-4D Canuck droned monotonously. Through the maze of piano wires bracing the wings, Fort Worth slowly came into view on the northern horizon.

Vern watched patiently as the student in the front cockpit maneuvered his way into the landing pattern at Carruthers Field. A herd of Herefords grazed south of the runway, undisturbed by the aerial traffic overhead.

"Nose up!" Vern yelled into the slipstream. "More throttle!"

The student pilot, a first-generation Swede from Manitoba, nodded his head and put the plane into a flat left turn, skidding across the sky in the approved manner. He lined up with the field, then again dropped the nose for a better view of the runway.

"Up! Up!" Vern shouted. "You're undershooting!"

The plane—the Canadian version of the Jenny—settled gently toward the runway, responding erratically to a strong crosswind. At the last possible moment, Vern eased the dual control throttle open, helping the student to overcome his dangerous penchant for caution.

The lecture could wait until they were safely on the ground.

A sudden gust of crosswind lifted the left wing, dropping the right. In panic, the student overcorrected, giving Vern another brief moment of terror.

Then the wheels touched, bounced high, and settled back onto the grass.

The student taxied the plane to the hangar ramp and cut the engine. Vern climbed out and waited until the student stepped down from the lower wing.

"Lidgard, you would've plowed into that herd of cattle if I hadn't advanced the throttle and kept us in the air. How many times do I have to tell you? Bring it in fast! Don't let up on the throttle until you're almost to the edge of the runway."

Lidgard peeled off his helmet and ran trembling fingers through his blond mane. "Isn't that stunting?"

Vern hesitated. It was a valid question—one to be answered carefully. Official regulations called for all flying to be done low and slow. Banked turns, rapid descents, and sudden maneuvers were termed "stunting."

Several pilots had been court-martialed for the offense.

Vern walked to the end of the lower wing. "Look at this airfoil. Flat on the bottom, curved on top. Remember your preflight training? Do you know why it was designed that way?"

Lidgard frowned in his effort to find the elusive information amidst the mass of strange material jammed into his brain in recent weeks. "Something to do with airspeed, isn't it?"

"Right. You see, if two particles of air are divided right here at the leading edge of the wing, the one at the top has farther to travel—up over the curve of the wing—than the one across the bottom. The faster air moves, the less the pressure. Bernoulli's Law. A vacuum is formed on the top of the wings. Now, what happens when you go too slow?"

Lidgard hesitated. "A stall."

"Right," Vern said again. "The vacuum is destroyed. There's nothing to hold you up. You lose control, because there's no pressure on the control surfaces. That's why it's essential to maintain airspeed. The faster you fly, the more your lift, and the better your control in case anything happens."

Lidgard vividly remembered one fact from preflight. "They told us that fast flying could tear the wings off."

Vern stood for a moment in frustration. It was a vicious circle: because the students had no confidence in their planes, at least two or three were killed each week. And the more killed, the more confidence dwindled among the survivors.

Vern yanked his leather helmet back on his head, adjusted his ears, and snapped the chin strap. "Climb in. We're going for a ride."

He took off in routine fashion, climbing slowly toward the south. Once clear of the field he advanced the throttle, turned westward, and continued to climb.

Five thousand feet over the barren ranch country thirty miles to the west, Vern gave the OX-5 full throttle, put the Canuck into a steep dive, and allowed the airspeed to build. He kept the nose down until the piano wires were shrieking in relentless discord. He pulled out of the dive, dropping the left wing as he put the plane into a gut-wrenching tight turn.

Back at five thousand, he sent the plane into a nose-down spin.

Students were told in preflight that spins were invariably fatal.

Again Vern waited until the earth was plummeting toward them at terrifying speed. He then whipped the plane through a series of sharp, S-shaped turns.

Lidgard vomited over the side of the cockpit. Vern kicked the Canuck into a skid just in time to avoid the slipstream.

He dropped to treetop height and hedgehopped, roaring down valleys and streams, zooming up over hilltops, banking sharply to avoid windmills and barns.

As they again approached Carruthers Field, Vern throttled back and sedately entered the traffic pattern. He settled the Canuck onto the runway without a bounce and taxied to the hangar ramp. Jumping from the plane, he waited until Lidgard made a shaky descent from the front cockpit.

Lidgard was green but smiled gamely.

Vern peeled off his helmet. "That's what a Curtiss can do. If you ever go into combat, that's the way you'll fly. While you're here, obey the regulations. But your first consideration is to stay alive. That means maintaining airspeed and keeping your nose up. Understand?"

"Yes, sir," Lidgard said.

Vern walked away. As he crossed the gravel parking area, heading toward the officers' quarters, the sickening thought came to him that his military career rested in Lidgard's hands.

If word of his "stunting" reached the wrong ears, he would face a court-martial.

The worry was quickly forgotten. He stripped off his flight suit and hurried for the showers, hoping to squeeze in ahead of the rush.

"Make way for the Master of Ceremonies!" someone yelled.

Vern laughed. The title was apt.

His return to Fort Worth had provided him with unusual supplementary duties. He spent virtually all of his spare time as an unofficial ambassador between the Canadian military and his hometown.

Fort Worth had gone all out in efforts to make the Canadians feel welcome. Parties, dances, and balls proliferated. Vern was the first person each local host or hostess contacted. Young women he barely remembered called, begging him to round up various numbers of Canadian pilots for lawn parties and dances. Civic leaders used him as a connection to the Canadian commanders, seeking their attendance at business luncheons, banquets, and bond rallies.

And the man everyone wanted most to meet was the commander of

Vern's own squadron, Captain Vernon Castle of the Vernon and Irene Castle dance team. The step the couple had created, the Castle Walk, was the rage throughout the country. The most fashionable hairstyle at the moment in Europe and America was the Irene Castle bob. While her husband conducted training, Irene Castle resided at the Westbrook Hotel.

Vern's wide acquaintance with the young ladies of Fort Worth did not go unnoticed among his fellow officers. Vern found himself one of the most popular officers on the field.

The situation left him with mixed emotions. He still yearned for combat, the glory of the war in the skies over Europe. And his demand as a social broker left him little time for himself. After pairing dozens of couples, Vern often attended and left parties alone.

It was a state of affairs he intended to remedy.

Carefully, he dressed in the resplendent Royal Flying Force uniform, with its jodhpurs, cavalry boots, leather belt with saber, high-collared blouse, and wide-brimmed, rakish campaign hat.

He hurried to his Rambler and pulled into the line exiting the field, his mind filled with the problems of his latest off-duty assignment.

The higher-ranking Canadian officers wished to demonstrate their appreciation for Fort Worth's generosity. They had engaged the ballroom at the Westbrook for a Saturday night dance. Invitations had gone out, and Vern had been asked to coordinate the entertainment for the evening.

He had not yet completed the program. Time was growing short.

As he left the field, dark thunderheads gathered southwest of town. Vern briefly considered stopping the car and buttoning the window flaps. But as he watched, the clouds disintegrated, yielding only dust. The sunset blossomed into a spectacular, rose-hued display.

He arrived at the Westbrook a few minutes early for his appointment. On a whim he took the elevator up to Clay's room. He had tried repeatedly during the last few weeks but never managed to catch Clay in.

He knocked and heard movement within. "The door's open," Clay called.

As Vern entered, Clay was on the telephone. The room was in shambles. Maps, charts, drawings, and sketches covered every flat surface, including most of the floor. The telephone rested amidst a sunburst of numbers hurriedly scrawled on the wall with pens and pencils of varied colors.

"Put it on the chest of drawers," Clay said without glancing around.

"Put what on the chest of drawers?" Vern asked.

Clay rose from the chair, turned, grasped Vern in a bear hug, and put a palm across the telephone mouthpiece. "I'll be off in a minute. God-damn, I thought you were room service. Get yourself a drink. I'll be off in a minute."

Vern found a reasonably clean glass and poured two fingers of bourbon. He pushed maps aside and sat on the bed. From what he could hear of the conversation, he gathered that Clay was attempting to obtain secret information on someone else's oil well.

"Goddamn, I *know* it's a tight hole," Clay shouted. "But surely somebody'll talk. We've got to find out, Pete. Those silly sons o' bitches sunk every cent they own into that well. They don't have anything around them under lease. I checked. That site is bracketed by *three* oil-bearing sands. They sure as shit ought to hit something."

Vern listened with amusement to Clay's wheeling and dealing and studied the vast changes in his brother.

Oil field work had left him rawhide lean. He seemed filled with even more energy. But Vern sensed a new quality of harshness about Clay that left him vaguely troubled.

The waiter arrived with more ice and whiskey. Clay tossed a bill onto the tray. With a brief nod to Vern, the waiter pocketed the money, picked up the depleted ice bucket, and backed out the door.

"I'm leaving tonight for Graham," Clay said into the phone. "If anything comes up, you can reach me there."

He rang off and turned to face Vern. "Goddamn, if it ain't my little brother, back down out of the clouds. Let's go downstairs and I'll buy you a steak."

"I wish I could, but I can't," Vern said. "I'm supposed to meet some people to make arrangements for a dance Saturday. The governor, everyone will be there. Why don't you come?"

Clay was restlessly roaming the room. "Somebody's got to find the gas and oil to keep you flying." He dumped more whiskey and ice in Vern's glass and poured a drink for himself. "I went by home this morning. Mama keeps hearing about the plane crashes. She's worried to death about you."

For a fleeting instant Vern relived the terror of two hours before, when Lidgard almost lost control in the crosswind.

He sipped his whiskey for a moment without answering. "They're students," he said. "They don't know any better. How's Papa doing?"

Clay shrugged. "All right, I guess."

"He's changed," Vern insisted. "It seems to me he's suddenly showing his age."

"Maybe he's losing a little of his piss and vinegar," Clay conceded. "He never really bounced back after that whorehouse uproar. He keeps the office open but just goes through the motions. His heart isn't in it."

Vern hesitated, uncertain how to put his real concern into words. "Durwood seems to spend a lot of time with him."

"I've quit giving a shit about anything Durwood does."

"It just strikes me strange," Vern insisted. "They never got along before. Now they're inseparable. Zetta says Durwood takes his wife over to Bluebonnet almost every evening."

Much to everyone's surprise, Durwood had recently married a young widow, LaFon Odom. Her first husband had been killed in an electrical accident.

Clay pushed some papers aside and sank into a chair. "It figures, though. Durwood always wanted the old man's approval. Maybe you're too young to remember. It was an obsession with him. The old man used to come down hard on Zetta and Durwood both. They could never measure up to what he wanted. Every time he raised hell, Durwood shook in his boots. Now he wants to show he's a man of the world, with a wife and all."

Vern felt driven to put his premonition into words. "Clay, listen to me. Durwood's after something."

Clay shrugged. "What could he want? Hell, let him have it. There's nothing at Bluebonnet either of us needs. I'm right on the edge of making a fucking fortune. When the war's over, I'll cut you in."

Vern shook his head. "I don't know anything about oil."

"Who does?" Clay gestured toward the maps and charts. "Right now, most of this is total bullshit. Nothing but theories. What I've been thinking, anyone should be able to see more from the air—fault lines, anticlines, structural outcrops. We'll buy a plane. You can fly me all over West Texas, and we'll map it from the air. How about that?"

Vern had not planned that far ahead. He only knew he wanted to keep flying. "We'll see," he said.

Clay slapped him on the back. "Just stay alive, and we'll both get rich."

By the time Vern reached the ballroom, the entertainers had already arrived. He walked through the milling, noisy group toward the stage and the discordant sounds of the tuning orchestra. No one seemed to be in charge. A young man danced by, leaping in repeated entrechats. Vern grabbed him by the arm.

"I'm looking for Miss Cawley. Do you know her?"

The dancer pointed to a slim girl standing on the stage, penciling notes on a clipboard. Vern thanked him and climbed onto the stage, doubtful. The girl seemed far too young to be a college instructor.

But as he approached, Ann Leigh Cawley began issuing a rapid-fire string of directions, positioning dancers and singers about the stage. She signaled to the conductor, and the orchestra began playing a Strauss waltz. Vern stopped and watched the girl, mesmerized.

A small dynamo, she moved with the authority of a drill sergeant, guiding one performer back into place bodily, another with a gesture. Her wild tumble of blond hair swung in marvelous disarray as she side-stepped the dancers. She complimented one with a dazzling smile, cautioned the next with a frown. She stopped one and effortlessly demonstrated the correct step. Noticing Vern, she waved him back, out of the path of the dancers.

Vern retreated to the edge of the stage. He waited until the orchestra brought the number to a resounding finale.

Ann Leigh Cawley went down the line of performers, issuing comments and corrections to each. As she came near, Vern called to her. "Miss Cawley? I'm Lieutenant Spurlock."

She glanced at him, signaled an assistant, and issued more instructions. She crossed the stage to Vern. "You were supposed to be here at seven."

The sharpness of her words were belied by her smiling eyes, the flirtatious tilt of her head.

Vern did not smile back. "I'm sorry I kept you waiting. I had to meet someone."

"No harm done. It's only that we were asked to provide entertainment Saturday evening, and at the moment we've no idea what's expected of us."

Vern took her arm. "Let's go where we can talk."

He escorted her to a table at the far end of the ballroom. As he pulled out her chair, he was rewarded with the subtle scent of perfume. He sat down and waited until she arranged her clipboard. "I think, with dinner and dancing, we're talking of a program of no more than forty or forty-five minutes," he said.

Ann Leigh nodded agreement. She was following his words with an intensity he found disturbing.

"I've corraled only three prospects," he said. "An Irish tenor from Toronto, with a well-trained, marvelous voice. He can do anything from the operatic to a 'Danny Boy' guaranteed not to leave a dry eye in the house. The flying cadets have organized a barbershop quartet. But their repertoire is limited, and they lost their baritone last week. We believe we've found a replacement."

Ann Leigh's lips parted in an unasked question.

Vern explained. "His plane went down near Waxahachie."

"I'm sorry. Did you know him?"

"I'm an instructor. He was one of my cadets."

Ann Leigh looked away for a moment. "And the third number?"

"Captain and Mrs. Castle have graciously consented to perform."

Ann Leigh beamed with pleasure. She clapped her hands and brought them to her chin. "Oh, I can't wait to tell everyone. What will they do?"

"The Castle Walk, I suppose."

Ann Leigh jotted on her clipboard, then frowned. "That would be an exciting curtain closer. They're bound to be asked for an encore. I wonder. Do you think they would mind doing something else, and save the Castle Walk for the encore?"

"How about the Hesitation Waltz?"

Ann Leigh agreed that the selection would be perfect. As she quickly ran down her list of numbers, Vern basked in her nearness. Nothing like her had ever happened to him before. And with the staging of the Saturday night performance, their brief association would end, unless he took steps.

He waited until she had completed a tentative program, interspersing the song and dance numbers to achieve the proper pace. With feigned solemnity, he examined the results. "This looks good. But to be certain, perhaps we should discuss it at greater length. After rehearsal, perhaps we could go somewhere for a drink."

Her gaze turned cool. "I'm with my fiancé. However, I have a friend. Perhaps we could make it a foursome."

Vern glanced at the performers to hide his disappointment. But the fact that he would be in her company was consoling. "That would be nice."

"See the young lady seated by the piano? Black dress with the white lace collar? She's the newspaper writer I mentioned, who sings Scottish ballads."

The girl was strikingly pretty, with lush black hair, an unusually pale complexion, dark features, high cheekbones, and thin but sensuous lips.

"I think you'll find her most interesting," Ann Leigh said. "She's from a Brown County ranch family. But she was reared in New Orleans and San Antonio boarding schools. She has written for newspapers in New York and Chicago, and she once had a role in a Mack Sennett one-reeler. She received an offer of a contract to go to Hollywood, but she turned it down."

Despite his preoccupation with Ann Leigh, Vern was intrigued. The girl seemed young for so much experience.

"If I were a man, I think I would set my cap for her," Ann Leigh went on, with the hint of a teasing lilt to her voice. "She's my best friend. We share the name of Ann, so everybody uses our double names. Come on. I'll introduce you."

Vern followed her across the room to the young woman.

"Katherine Anne, this is Lieutenant Vern Spurlock. Lieutenant Spurlock, Katherine Anne Porter."

From the moment they were seated in the lounge, Ann Leigh knew that the impromptu foursome was a mistake. Vern and Lester were barely polite to each other. Already Katherine Anne was taking advantage of the situation. She kept prodding both men, and even Ann Leigh, with her sharp wit.

And Ann Leigh could not keep her eyes off Vern Spurlock.

Worst of all, Lester had noticed.

The waiter took their order. As he walked away, Katherine Anne looked up at Vern with a flirtatious flutter to her eyelids. "I've always wanted to fly. Couldn't you smuggle me into your plane some day and take off while no one was looking?"

Vern smiled, and his eyes crinkled in a way Ann Leigh found enchanting. "I've a better idea," he said. "Why don't you enlist? I'll teach you to fly. I'm sure you'd be much better than some of my students."

Katherine Anne put a palm to her chin and leaned closer. "What's it like up there?"

"It's a different world," Vern said softly. "Peaceful. Incredibly colorful—the vegetation, the sky, the clouds."

"Peaceful! What a strange word for those roaring machines," Katherine Anne said.

Vern shifted slightly in his chair. Ann Leigh wondered if Katherine Anne were truly interested in Vern or merely toying with him. She found no clue.

"You have the feeling you've left all your troubles on the ground," Vern said slowly. "The world below seems so remote. There's a feeling of timelessness about it." He shook his head. "It's difficult to put into words."

"I think you express it very well," Ann Leigh said, hating the condescension she heard in her own voice.

Katherine Anne ignored her. "Aren't you ever frightened?"

Ann Leigh wanted to kick her.

Vern laughed. "At least a hundred times a day. But it's nothing to what the pilots in France face in combat."

Ann Leigh saw her opening. "I wish this terrible war would end. It must be awful over there. Look how it's already changed our lives, thousands of miles away."

"We can't keep up with the orders for tinned beef," Lester said. "We're now shipping almost a trainload a week."

Ann Leigh cringed. As usual, Lester had missed the point. "Lester is an executive at the packing plant," she explained to Vern.

She felt that everyone at the table was reading her like a book. Yet she could not take her eyes off Vern.

Effortlessly Vern turned attention back to her remark. "I think the biggest changes are yet to come," he said gently. "Whether America enters the war or not, nothing will ever be the same again."

Vern looked directly at her. For a moment, it was as if she and Vern were alone. A strained silence fell.

"I hate to leave such good company, but I must face a typewriter in the morning at seven," Katherine Anne said.

Vern stirred. He seemed confused for a moment. "I'll see you home," he said.

The men argued briefly over the check before Lester allowed Vern to pay. As they left the hotel, Vern again turned to Ann Leigh. "We still have some details of the program to discuss," he said. "May I call you?"

"Of course," she said. She watched him walk away with Katherine Anne, disturbed by a tug of jealousy.

Lester took her arm. "I'll run you right home," he said. "I've got to be at the plant early in the morning."

Ann Leigh was preparing for bed when her aunt summoned her to the phone. She slipped into a robe and went down to the landing.

"You certainly made a conquest tonight," Katherine Anne said. "I don't think I've ever seen a male so stricken."

Ann Leigh felt her heart racing. She waited until her breathing was under control. "Katherine Anne! He knows I'm engaged!"

Katherine Anne laughed. "Somehow, I don't think he gives a continental. You'd better prepare for a siege."

"You really think so?"

"You don't fool me for a minute. You're quite taken with him, aren't you?"

Ann Leigh sidestepped the question. "What did you think of him?"

"That doesn't really matter. He hasn't noticed I'm alive."

"Please," Ann Leigh insisted. "I want to know."

The line was silent for a moment. "It's my considered opinion that he's a perfect dreamboat. Intelligent, gentlemanly, poetic, handsomer than any man has a right to be, wearing the best-looking uniform ever made. If I were you, I'd give him more than a second glance."

"Don't be foolish! Lester and I are discussing the date."

"I'm only saying that if you're looking for a way out, you've found one. Take it from me. Marriage isn't everything."

It was the second time Katherine Anne had alluded to some dark experience in her past. Ann Leigh spoke firmly. "Lester and I will be married sometime this fall. If you're trying to ascertain the exact date for your scandal sheet, I can't tell you, because it hasn't been chosen. But I'll let you know as soon as we decide, and you can spread it to the four winds."

Katherine Anne laughed. "My! Aren't we touchy? I only know that tonight I saw the heavenly constellations in collision. And I know an undone woman when I see one. Good night. We'll talk tomorrow. Pleasant dreams."

Ann Leigh hung up the receiver, shaken and irritated. Sometimes Katherine Anne presumed too much.

She returned to her room, slipped into bed, and turned out the light. But sleep would not come. She kept seeing Vern Spurlock's face, with its firm, statuesque nose, solid jawline, and mystical eyes.

The vision would not go away.

She knew almost nothing about him. Her father had talked about the legendary lawyer and orator Travis Spurlock since her childhood. Someone—she could not remember who—had told her that Clay Spurlock and his younger brother had been absolute hellions, riding motorcycles and performing wild stunts with the Locklear brothers.

Ann Leigh sighed in the darkness. So many young men of her acquaintance seemed intent on destroying themselves.

Fortunately, Lester Wilson was not among them. He represented the stability she had learned to prize. During her childhood on her father's Shackelford County ranch, survival had been measured by harsh winters, summer drought, the cattle market, conditions on the range. Ann Leigh and her mother repeatedly had begged her father to build a comfortable home in Fort Worth as the other successful ranchers were doing. But he had resisted. She had settled for a compromise—living with Aunt Polly. The arrangement had its compensations. A widow more than four years, Aunt Polly was lonely and welcomed companionship. And she seemed to be acquainted with everyone in town that mattered. She said the younger Spurlock boys were "wild," but "descended from good stock."

Ann Leigh could not deny that she was intrigued with Vern.

But she had planned her life with care—a college degree, a year or two of teaching, marriage to a successful young man, children, security, and all the comforts of modern urban life.

One only had to look at Vern Spurlock to see that he never planned beyond tomorrow.

She certainly had no intention of allowing him to wreck her life.

20

"At ease, Lieutenant," Captain Castle said.

Vern stood before the captain's desk, filled with vague foreboding. When Captain Castle dropped his warm, friendly smile, he usually had serious matters to discuss.

Castle hesitated, as if uncertain where to begin. He leaned back in his chair and looked up at Vern. "Colonel Bosworth was hunting Monday afternoon in the ranch country southwest of town. He saw a plane stunting in the distance, performing banked turns, stalls, power dives, and spins. He said the pilot was handling the plane so violently he thought the wings would tear off at any moment."

Vern knew he faced disaster. Colonel Bosworth was commander of the airfield. But he saw a glimmer of hope in Castle's phraseology. "Did the colonel get a close look at the plane, sir?"

"Yes, I'm afraid he did. In fact, it flew right down the ravine where Colonel Bosworth was hunting, at full throttle, and at treetop height. Colonel Bosworth said he saw the plane clip foliage with the undercarriage. The pilot narrowly averted collision with a windmill. Colonel Bosworth was not able to see the number. But he had the impression that it was your plane."

Outside, on the runway, a Canuck was fighting its way into the air. Vern waited until the roar faded away. He decided that his only hope might lie in a personal appeal. "Captain—"

"I checked your log for that day," Castle interrupted. "You were flying with Cadet Lidgard. I talked with Cadet Lidgard. He recalls that, to the contrary, you were flying well to the southeast, down near Mansfield. He remembers using the town as a pilon while practicing turns."

Vern took a deep breath. "I really don't recall, sir."

Castle nodded. "Colonel Bosworth checked your plane. He found no foliage clinging to the undercarriage. The only indication he found that your plane had suffered hard use was some excess oil seepage around the exhaust ports. I convinced him that full throttle on repeated takeoffs can produce that effect."

"Yes, sir," Vern said.

"So it appears Colonel Bosworth may have been mistaken."

Vern hardly dared breathe. "It would appear so, sir."

Castle looked at Vern for a long moment. "However, a serious breach of discipline clearly has occurred in our training sector. We must assume it was committed by a pilot from this field. And we can have no further infractions such as this. Is that understood?"

"Yes, sir."

"Please inform all of your students, especially those in advanced training. No stunting will be tolerated. That will be all."

"Yes, sir," Vern said. He took a step backward, and hesitated. "Captain, by your leave, sir . . ."

"Yes, Lieutenant?"

"I wished to say, sir, that I can understand why some pilots may wish to perform maneuvers that may be interpreted in some quarters as stunting. The cadets arrive here with the belief that the Canuck is a fragile airplane. I truly believe, sir, that their caution is killing them. When they get into trouble, they don't have the experience, or the airspeed, to extricate themselves."

Castle stared at Vern before answering. "Do you have some suggestion, Lieutenant?"

"If we could liberalize training a bit, to the extent of banked turns, full-powered flight, and simple combat maneuvers, the cadets would have much more confidence in their aircraft. Also, we might present demonstrations over the field, to show the Canuck's full capabilities."

"Are you volunteering to perform that demonstration, Spurlock?"

Vern felt the warmth of blood rushing to his face. "I would be willing to do it, sir."

"What you suggest is out of the question. Surely you're aware that our training procedures are prescribed by our commanding general, and carefully administered by Colonel Bosworth."

"That's just my point, sir. No one on the commandant staff is a pilot. None knows the capabilities of the Canuck, or what will be required of our cadets once they arrive in France."

Castle turned and gazed out the window. For a full thirty seconds he did not speak. At last he rose from his desk and walked closer to Vern. He spoke in a low voice.

"Spurlock, I'm telling you this in confidence, only because I believe it may keep you from getting into serious trouble. What you say is true. But I also know that your approach is not the way to solve the problem."

He put a hand on Vern's shoulder. "I have some influence. Since my

return from France, I and others have let it be known that our precombat
training is insufficient. We have been assured that more pilots with combat experience will be returned home as instructors, as commanders of
training facilities. When that happens, what we now call stunting will
become routine training. But until then we must obey the rules. Is that
understood?"

"Yes, sir."

"Then that will be all."

He returned Vern's salute, then stopped him at the door.

"One more thing. I believe we should find Cadet Lidgard an attractive young lady from among the local crop and provide him with two
tickets to the dance Saturday. He's a fine young man. Good head on his
shoulders. We need more like him."

On the Thursday afternoon before the dance Vern managed to take
Ann Leigh to Bluebonnet for tea, ostensibly to make final plans for the
program.

Vern was proud of his family. In his later years Travis was clothed in
dignity. With his mane of silvery hair, erect bearing, deep, melodious
voice, and calm air of authority, he wore his accomplishments easily.
Reva remained energetic and petite, forever gracious, constantly exud-
ing Southern charm. Even Zetta was remarkable. In the final irony of her
life, maturity had softened her features, and at forty she had become a
handsome woman.

Ann Leigh seemed impressed by Vern's family, and made compli-
mentary comments on them. But he managed only two dances with her
on Saturday evening, and she declined to accept his calls the following
week.

Gradually, in want of anything else to do, he fell in with Katherine
Anne's crowd. They were a lively group, meeting almost every night to
drink wine, listen to jazz, and discuss Nietzsche, Bertrand Russell, William James, Karl Marx, and Huxley. Most had seen *The Birth of a Nation*
several times. They were excited about the future of film. They had
formed a little theater group, and performed Shaw's *Pygmalion* and *Man
and Superman*, Chekhov's *The Cherry Orchard*, and various plays by
Ibsen. Often they argued over Marcel Proust, D. H. Lawrence, Thomas
Mann, Upton Sinclair, and James Joyce until dawn, and went to breakfast
in a group before dispersing for classes.

Vern often flew without having slept.

He saw Ann Leigh frequently. She remained polite but distant.

Vern liked Katherine Anne, but she possessed traits he found disturbing. For one thing, he came to believe she was considerably older

than she appeared, or admitted. She spoke knowledgeably of life in New York's Greenwich Village, of the speakeasies and theaters in Chicago. She claimed to have been reared in convents in New Orleans and San Antonio, yet seemed well acclimated to the West Texas ranch country. She was completely feminine. But she seemed to share few of the ambitions of most women. Vern enjoyed her friendship, secure in the knowledge that their relationship would never go beyond that. When Katherine Anne became acquainted with a lieutenant from Calgary, and seemed to prefer his company, Vern was not disappointed.

He heard from Katherine Anne's crowd that Ann Leigh and Lester had set their wedding for late June. With sinking heart he noticed that she now took pains to avoid him.

Again, Vern formally requested transfer to combat. This time his application was endorsed and forwarded.

He made one last effort to call Ann Leigh at her aunt's home. She declined to accept his call. Her marriage was now only weeks away.

In desperation he turned to Katherine Anne.

Ann Leigh awoke every day feeling as if the world were enveloped by a dark, omnipresent pall. She would lie awake sometimes for several seconds, wondering why she felt so terrible.

Then she would remember: the terrible war in Europe was growing ever closer. So far, President Wilson had kept the United States out of it. But newspaper columnists were saying that American participation was inevitable. And every day, all around her, she saw fine young men training to march off to be killed.

During the last few weeks Fort Worth had been transformed. The war had created a tremendous demand for oil. Fort Worth had become the unofficial headquarters. Each day hundreds of speculators lined the sidewalks to buy leases and to close deals for drilling. At the Westbrook all the elegant furniture had been removed from the lobby so it could be used as an oil mart, filled with loud men and their cigars. Every hotel, rooming house, and restaurant in town was jammed.

More Canadian pilots and ground crews arrived for training. The familiar drone of aircraft increased on the fringes of town. More than a hundred pilots already had been killed in crashes on the outskirts of town.

Hell's Half Acre had been reborn. Ann Leigh heard dark rumors of knifings and shootings in the section near the rail stations. To prevent the young soldiers from spending their leisure time in the saloons and gambling parlors the Red Cross had opened a large canteen downtown and asked for volunteers.

Ann Leigh had signed up for three nights a week. With the added burden of her classes, the hours were taxing. But she felt she could do no less.

She enjoyed dancing and talking with the young men. Lester usually came to pick her up at the end of the evening. Busy with war contracts, he now worked twelve or fourteen hours a day. Katherine Anne frequently dropped by after completing her day at the newspaper. Often they would join a group and go to someone's home for an impromptu party.

On a sultry, warm evening in late May, Ann Leigh spent most of her shift on the dance floor. By closing time she was exhausted. She moved to the chairs along one wall and sat for a moment to catch her breath. Katherine Anne approached with Lieutenant Lidgard in tow. She gave Ann Leigh a rueful smile. "If these flyers can survive this, they can survive the war. Where's your beau?"

"He left this morning for Washington," Ann Leigh explained. "Something about a government contract."

"Top secret, I'm sure."

Lidgard touched the brim of his hat. "Could we give you a lift, Miss Cawley?"

The soldiers were spilling out into the night, rushing for the streetcars that would take them back to the airfields. Taxis were at a premium. The offer was tempting.

"I shouldn't impose," she said.

"No imposition." Lidgard took her arm and guided her and Katherine Anne to the door. They walked around the building to his car. From the moment he began grinding on the starter, Ann Leigh knew something was wrong. The engine did not make a sound.

"Don't tell me," Katherine Anne said.

"Must be the distributor," Lidgard said. He went to the front of the car and raised the hood. He jiggled something inside, then tried the starter again. The engine remained lifeless. Lidgard went back to working beneath the hood.

Another car approached on the deserted street. It pulled in beside them. To her dismay, Ann Leigh saw that it was Vern Spurlock. He shouted to Lidgard over the rattle of his engine. "Something wrong, Lieutenant?"

"Won't fire," Lidgard said. "I don't know what to think."

Vern cut his engine. "I've never trusted those self-starters. Tried the spark?"

"Dead as a doornail," Lidgard said. "I can't fathom it."

As Vern approached the disabled engine, he seemed to notice for the first time that Lidgard had passengers. He saluted a greeting, then turned to help Lidgard.

They hand-cranked the engine several times without success.

"I guess it's hopeless," Lidgard said.

"I would be happy to give you and the ladies a lift," Vern said.

"If the ladies don't mind," Lidgard said. "We can fix this thing later."

A faint hint of suspicion nagged at Ann Leigh. Vern Spurlock had persisted with his telephone calls and invitations long past the realms of reason. He came often to the canteen. Although he seldom danced with her, she often felt his hungry gaze upon her. But the possibility that he had staged the present elaborate situation seemed preposterous. And she was too well-bred to reject a gracious offer.

Lidgard held a rear door of Vern's car open for Katherine Anne. Vern opened the front door. Before Ann Leigh realized what was happening, Lidgard followed Katherine Anne into the back seat, leaving her to sit in front with Vern Spurlock.

Vern pulled on the crank to start his car. The engine roared to life. "So much for self-starters," he teased Lidgard.

Vern drove the big car with total control. Ann Leigh watched his large, strong hands on the wheel. She thought of Lester and his hesitant driving habits.

"Why don't we go to my place for a nightcap?" Katherine Anne asked abruptly.

Ann Leigh was stunned into a momentary silence. Although she agreed in principle with the recent abandonment of many social customs, Katherine Anne sometimes went too far.

Lidgard and Vern welcomed the offer with enthusiasm.

"I really must get home," Ann Leigh said.

Katherine Anne reached forward to slap her arm. "Don't be a spoil-sport."

Ann Leigh *was* in the mood for company. Until she had fallen into Lester's conventional habits she had been a creature of impulse. She now missed that freedom. "Just for a little while," she said.

Katherine Anne lived in three rooms at the second floor front of a large old house on the South Side. Vern coasted to a stop at the curb, and they tiptoed up the stairs at the side of the building.

Lidgard helped Katherine Anne mix gin fizzes.

Vern remained quiet, but Ann Leigh felt his gaze heavily upon her. Katherine Anne was chattering about the Abbey Players' production of Synge's *Playboy of the Western World,* which she had seen before leaving Chicago. Ann Leigh had heard Katherine Anne describe the play several times. She hardly listened. Vern seemed preoccupied. He smiled occasionally at some remark but made no effort to enter into the talk.

Again Ann Leigh was struck by his magnetism. Beside him other men paled.

"Damn, I'm out of ice," Katherine Anne said. "I'll have to sneak down to the basement. And it's dark down there. Gives me the creeps."

"I'll go with you," Lidgard said.

Katherine Anne brought two drinks and set them down before Ann Leigh and Vern. "You two go ahead and get started. We'll be back in a minute."

The ruse was so obvious that Ann Leigh no longer had doubts. But she did not wish to make a scene. She did not want to suggest for a minute that she did not trust Vern Spurlock.

Even more importantly, she did not want to suggest that she did not trust herself.

Vern waited until the footsteps faded on the stairway. He looked at Ann Leigh a moment before speaking. "Miss Cawley, I have the impression that you've been avoiding me. Have I done something to offend you?"

Ann Leigh felt her heart racing. She made every effort to appear calm. "Not at all, Lieutenant. It's merely that you've chosen to ignore the fact that I'm engaged to be married. Your persistence has made it awkward for us both."

"I can't help the way I feel," he said softly. "Since the first time I saw you, I've known we belong together, either in this life or perhaps some other."

Ann Leigh felt heat flush her face. Vern was gazing at her so intently, with such hunger, that she felt faint. "Lieutenant, you presume too much," she managed to say.

Vern seized her hand. "Don't tell me you have no feelings toward me. Surely I can't be that mistaken."

Ann Leigh felt helpless. She made no effort to remove her hand. "Lieutenant Spurlock, I have high regard for you, as a friend. But I'm to be married within a month. This conversation is improper."

Vern leaned forward, gripping her hand. "I don't believe we should deny what's meant to be."

Ann Leigh was rescued by a rush of anger. "Are you telling me I shouldn't marry Lester Wilson?"

Vern nodded. "I have no doubt he's a fine man. But he's wrong for you."

"You're insufferable!" Ann Leigh said.

Vern recoiled as if he had been struck. He released her hand. In the soft light his face was pale beneath his summer tan. He remained silent for a moment.

"It seems I've made a mistake," he said. "Obviously I've misinterpreted what I thought were clear-cut signals that to some degree you shared my feelings."

"I'm not aware of sending any signals," Ann Leigh said. "I can only tell you how I feel. I'm in love with Lester Wilson."

Vern shook his head. "I won't bother you any more. I'll avoid being around you. My orders overseas should arrive soon, and I'll be out of your life." He smiled weakly. "If I'm demented, please bear with me. Lord knows you're ample reason for any man to go stark raving crazy."

Ann Leigh wanted to apologize, to tell him that perhaps she had overreacted. But she was afraid the apology might also be misinterpreted. She remained silent.

She heard footsteps on the stairs. Katherine Anne and Lidgard returned. They apparently read the full story on Vern's face. Forcing small talk, they mixed the drinks and brought them into the sitting room.

Everyone tried, but the atmosphere was different. After an interminable half hour, Ann Leigh glanced at her watch. "I really must go home. I'm only half prepared for an eight o'clock class."

The relief seemed general. They tiptoed back down the stairs and out to Vern's car. When they reached her house, Vern walked her to the door.

"Good-bye," he said.

He turned away before she could answer.

Ann Leigh went up to her room and cried herself to sleep.

When Katherine Anne arrived at the canteen the following Monday, Ann Leigh took her aside. "I just want you to know I didn't appreciate your little charade the other night. I was forced to be very curt with Vern Spurlock—something I had not intended to do."

Katherine Anne sighed. "Ann Leigh, you're an idiot. Vern Spurlock is a prince. He adores you. Any other girl in town would gladly slash her wrists and die happy if Vern Spurlock merely looked her way. I don't understand you."

"Are you saying he's a better man than Lester Wilson?"

"I'm saying he's a better man for *you* than Lester Wilson."

"I'll forget you said that."

"Please don't. I'm only saying what everyone knows. You're a free spirit. You're no more suited to a conventional marriage than I. You and Lester are like oil and water. He's devoid of imagination. He lacks humor. You'll be bored to distraction within six months."

Again without knowing exactly why, Ann Leigh burst into tears. "I thought you were a friend I could trust."

Katherine Anne spoke quietly. "Only a good friend would say the things I've just said. Only a good friend would do the things I've done, to try to keep you from making the mistake of your life."

Ann Leigh felt overwhelmed by a flood of wildly conflicting emotions. She did not understand them. She only knew that Katherine Anne was to blame.

"I'll thank you to mind your own business!" she snapped.

Katherine Anne stared at her for a long moment. "In the future, I shall." She turned abruptly and walked away.

The next weekend, Ann Leigh's mother arrived to begin final preparations for the wedding.

During the busy daylight hours Ann Leigh managed to put Vern Spurlock and the unpleasant episode from her mind.

But at night sleep eluded her. She lay awake through the sultry nights, reliving her brief moments with Vern Spurlock, wondering how she could have acted otherwise.

Often she did not get to sleep until the first gray streaks of dawn.

21

This is it!" Pete shouted over the phone. "Get your ass up here pronto!"

Clay rolled over in bed and looked at his watch. It was not yet five in the morning. "Where are you?" he asked.

"Cushing, just west of Tulsa. I worked this field years ago, till it played out. Now they've hit good pay in deeper sand. All hell's breaking loose."

Clay hesitated. He knew little about Oklahoma geology. But if Pete was excited, the discovery must be valid. "How deep?"

"About three thousand, from what I hear. The Bartlesville runs about twenty-six hundred. This is even deeper."

Clay ran a quick calculation. At three-fifty a foot the drilling alone would cost more than ten thousand dollars. Adding twenty-four thousand for pipe, three thousand for a wooden derrick, and five thousand for fuel and water, a test well would cost about fifty thousand. "What's the lease situation?"

"Chancy. Most is already under lease from the earlier play. But the new discovery well is to the north and east. I've tied up six hundred and forty acres. I may find more."

"Kind of taking a lot on yourself, aren't you partner?"

Pete laughed. "Stop in Wichita Falls and buy pipe. Lumber's no problem here yet, but there's not enough pipe to plumb a kitchen. I'll leave word at the Sooner Café where I'll be."

Fifteen minutes later Clay was on the road. He reached Wichita Falls by the time the supply houses were opening. He bought the equipment, arranged for rail shipment, and drove on north. Beyond Oklahoma City the narrow rural roads were crowded with heavy wagons loaded with oil field equipment. From Chandler northward traffic was almost at a standstill. Clay did not reach Cushing until after midnight.

He found Pete sleeping in a tarpaper flophouse on the north edge of town. Cots were at a premium. Clay slept in his car the remainder of the night.

Ten days later they had the derrick completed and were spudded in, making hole. By the time they reached a thousand feet, oil sign was strong. Working almost incessantly, they kept the bit turning night and day.

One by one, they reached the pay sands—the Layton at fourteen hundred, Jones at eighteen, Wheeler at twenty-three, Skinner at twenty-four, and Bartlesville at twenty-six.

All showed oil, but not in productive amounts.

Pete grew worried. "I thought sure we'd have a producer from the Bartlesville. The formation must slope to the south. I guess it's already been pumped out from under us."

They drilled on to thirty-two hundred feet without finding the new Tucker sand. Pete finally admitted that they had a dry hole. "If this ain't a piss-cutter! Six oil-bearing formations. We did everything exactly right. People all around us hitting it big. And we come up with a duster. Just goes to show you what kind of business we're in."

They debated what to do. Most of their capital was gone. Pete suggested they sell their Oklahoma leases and try again in Texas.

"I hadn't thought it worth mentioning," he said. "But I know a spot down southeast of Breckenridge where there's been consistent production. Nothing spectacular enough to get anyone excited. There's still some land available. We'll have to run a poor-boy operation, but we might make some money."

They drove back to Texas, leased ranch land near Caddo, and spudded in a new well. Before the bit reached a thousand feet they were in trouble.

"Soft formation," Pete said. "It's caving in on us. If we don't run casing as we go, we're going to lose this fucking hole. And that puts us between a rock and the hard place. If we buy casing, we won't have money to keep on drilling."

"Maybe we could steal some," Clay said. Theft—or at least borrowing—had become a way of life in the oil fields.

"I haven't stooped that low yet. But there's a way that's just a shade this side of stealing." Pete stopped and shook his head. "This is like handing a loaded gun to a baby."

"Go on. Tell me."

"Have you ever heard of jarring?"

Clay shook his head.

"Not many people around here have. But it used to be done on the Gulf Coast. After Spindletop, hundreds of wildcat wells were sunk without rhyme or reason. Most of them were dusters. No one knew much about salt dome structures back then. Anyway, there were hundreds of abandoned wells around with the casing still in them."

Clay waited, not understanding. Once the earth closed around pipe, it was considered lost. Every abandoned well had casing in it.

"What people around here don't know, sometimes you can jar a few hundred feet of it loose," Pete said. "I've seen it done. You simply lower a bundle of dynamite down the pipe, with wires attached. You put a collar on the top of the casing and put it under a good strain with a hydraulic jack. Then you hook your detonator to the coil on your truck. The blast blows the casing apart. If you're lucky, the upper part of the pipe is jarred loose. You can pull it up with a block and sheave. If the casing has been in the ground a long time, the joints may be welded with rust. But you can use a hacksaw or torch. The pipe can be rethreaded."

"That's too much work to be called stealing," Clay said.

"With a sympathetic judge, you probably could get it knocked down to trespassing," Pete agreed. "If you drew a real son of a bitch, he might call it stealing. It's a gray area."

"How come?"

"You see, with an old abandoned well, the mineral rights probably have reverted to the landowners. They don't own the pipe. And the people who *do* own it abandoned it. So in a way, a case could be made that it's a matter of finders keepers. A real good talker like you could probably worm your way out of a jail term."

"I hate to nitpick, but my experience has been that dynamite tends to attract a lot of attention. Won't someone call the sheriff?"

"I know of some old wells over toward Strawn that are in pretty remote country. But there's where your special talent comes into play. If anyone comes nosing around, you can just shoot them a line of shit, act like you're from the oil company that owns it."

Clay approached Koonman, one of the roughnecks on the rig. He was a big bruiser, with the reputation of a hellraiser. "Koon, would you go for a little extra work, for extra pay?"

"What kind?"

Clay studied him for a moment. At least six feet three, Koonman no doubt topped the scales at two forty or more. His huge hands were hardened by years of oil field work. His weathered face and frequently broken nose plainly had all the resilience of granite. Clay strongly suspected that Koonman might not be insulted by his offer.

"Ever hear of jarring?"

Koonman scowled and looked up at the crown block, where the derrickman was making a connection. "I heard of it once. Can't say I relish hearing of it again."

"We need casing," Clay said. "There's a ten-dollar-a-day bonus in it."

"I've got a cousin in Huntsville. He says the guards down there beat up on the convicts just for sport. I don't want to become no convict."

"You'd be working for me," Clay said. "I'll take the heat."

Koonman tugged at his hat. "All right. But only because if we don't sink some casing pretty damned quick, we're going to lose this hole."

Clay nodded. "Pick two men you can trust. Don't mention it to anyone else. We'll leave about first light tomorrow morning."

That afternoon Clay drove into Breckenridge and bought the dynamite. That night he loaded the equipment into Pete's Model T Ford truck.

The next morning he drove his crew to an isolated well several miles northwest of Strawn. It was only a quarter of a mile from a county road, but out of sight behind a ridge.

Only a section of two-by-twelve plank covered the old well. Clay examined the rotting wooden derrick. He determined that with a little work it would support his makeshift draw works.

The day was heavily overcast with gray scud. The air was cool, with little wind. Koonman went to work without comment, securing a block and tackle to the wooden derrick, directing his two helpers as they fitted a collar to the top of the casing. They then put two heavy hydraulic bridge jacks under the collar and placed the casing under a strain.

While his men prepared the well, Clay unreeled two hundred and fifty feet of telephone wire. He removed three sticks of dynamite from the box, wrapped them into a bundle, and inserted a blasting cap.

Koonman approached and stood watching apprehensively. "Ever worked with that stuff before?"

"A few times," Clay lied.

"Makes me nervous. Mind if I have one of the men take the rest of that shit about two hundred yards away?"

"Suit yourself," Clay said.

After the remainder of the dynamite was unloaded at a safe distance, Clay cautiously lowered the charge into the well, a few feet at a time. He had heard of dynamite exploding from static electricity.

With the charge in place, he signaled for Koonman to start the truck. After the men took cover behind the vehicle, Clay touched the wires to the coil.

The explosion was subdued, hardly more than the rumble of distant thunder. But one of the hydraulic jacks leaped six feet into the air.

"I think that did it," Koonman said.

Within two hours they had two hundred feet of pipe out of the hole, unsectioned, and stacked on the truck. They reloaded the dynamite and equipment. Koonman cut clumps of sagebrush and tied them to the back of the truck.

"Every Arkansas moonshiner knows how to cover his tracks," he said.

They hit four more wells that day and returned with more than eight hundred feet of pipe.

Pete was jubilant but concerned. "Anyone see you?"

"Not a soul," Clay said. "That's lonesome country."

But the following day he became too greedy. On the second well he lowered the charge three hundred feet.

The casing did not break loose from the soil.

"We'll have to try again, higher up," Clay said.

While his crew repositioned the hydraulic jacks, Clay prepared the second charge. He was seating the blasting cap when Koonman spoke quietly at his side. "We've got company."

Clay looked up. A woman was sitting on a horse at the top of the ridge, watching them. She was less than a hundred yards away.

Clay handed the dynamite to Koonman. "Go ahead and set it off. I'll talk to her, keep her away from the well."

He waved to her and started toward the ridge. She turned the sorrel gelding down the slope, standing in the stirrups to ease the strain on the horse.

She stopped a few feet away from Clay and nodded a greeting. Probably in her midtwenties, she was dressed in faded Levi's pants, plaid shirt, and a heavy mackinaw. Her trousers were stuffed into a pair of black, high-topped, hand-tooled boots. She wore no spurs but carried a black leather quirt, looped around her right wrist. She shoved back a shapeless, wide-brimmed hat, allowing it to dangle from its throat latch, and regarded Clay with an unblinking gaze. Her eyes were green. Her body seemed supple, tending toward pudginess. Lightly tanned, her face was wide, with a firm, strong jaw. There was a peasant sturdiness about her. The wind rippled her hair, golden light brown, hacked off short around her ears with careless elegance. Her hands were covered by black gloves. Clay had never seen a woman in trousers before. He found the idea slightly erotic.

"I thought you folks were through with that old well," she said. Her voice was strong and melodious. He thought he detected a faint trace of mockery.

"Just salvaging some old pipe," Clay said. "My men are about to set off another charge. Will your horse spook?"

She shook her head and put a gloved hand on the stock of a rifle Clay had not seen, tucked almost out of sight in its scabbard beneath her left leg. Clay recognized it as a Winchester .30/30. "I shoot off him all the time," she said.

At the well, Koonman shouted a warning. A moment later the dynamite exploded. The hydraulic jacks tumbled, and Clay knew that the second blast had succeeded.

"You taking the derrick, too?" the woman asked.

Something in her tone put Clay on guard. "No ma'am, I don't need the derrick. Just the pipe."

She gave Clay a long, lingering appraisal, starting at his feet, and traveling upward. "You don't know who the hell I am, or who owns this well, do you? Furthermore, you don't give a damn."

"I didn't. I do now."

"I think you're stealing that pipe."

She was deadly serious.

Clay grinned up at her. "You've got a gun. Be apprised that I'm unarmed. I've got a pistol somewhere, but right now I can't remember where I left it."

She hesitated. "I wouldn't shoot someone over a few feet of rusty old pipe."

"I'm banking very strongly on that," Clay said.

She laughed, spontaneously and with complete abandon. Clay joined in.

"What's your name?" she asked.

For reasons he could not fathom, Clay did not lie. "Clayton," he said. "I'm called Clay. I didn't catch your name."

"Elise," she said.

"Elsie?"

"No, Elise. Like in French."

"I'm happy to make your acquaintance, Elise."

She turned the sorrel away. "Just leave the derrick," she said. "That's where we hang horse thieves."

"I hope we meet again, Elise," he said.

She reined in and glanced at him, then looked at the well significantly. "It might lead to trouble."

"Lady, I thrive on trouble."

Again there came that appraising study. Clay usually knew what it meant, but this time he was not sure.

"What did you say your last name was?" she asked.

Clay grinned at her. "I didn't say. What's yours?"

"I didn't say either." She quirted her horse. It broke into a fast trot. She did not look back, and soon disappeared into the mesquite and post oak.

Clay walked back to the well. Koonman and his helpers were uncoupling the first section of pipe.

"Are you really interested in that, or do you always walk around with a hard on?" Koonman asked. His helpers laughed.

"She's enough to start a man thinking in that direction," Clay said.

"She going to turn us in?"

Clay considered the question. "I doubt it. But I don't really know."

Koonman gave him a puzzled glance. "Maybe we'd better get cracking."

They loaded the pipe and drove away. On the heavily rutted dirt road to the next well, Clay kept watching in the direction Elise had been headed. As he topped a hill, he saw the roof of a ranch house in the distance.

He fixed the location firmly in his memory.

22

Within days of Lester's return from Washington, Ann Leigh knew that something was wrong. While plans for the wedding continued, he remained oddly distant. The weekend before the ceremony, he at last let her know what was on his mind.

"I heard you went out with Vern Spurlock while I was gone. Is that true?"

The accusation and his superior tone made her furious. "I don't know where you got your information. But it's wrong. I did *not* go out with Vern Spurlock. And I resent your implication."

"You didn't dance with him? You didn't go with him to a party at Katherine Anne's apartment?"

Ann Leigh gave him a cool, measured stare. "Lester, I'm not on trial."

"I have it on good authority that you did."

They were seated in his car, parked in front of her aunt's house. Tears of frustration swam into her eyes. "Lester, I won't be put in this position!"

"I certainly think I have a right to know what happened."

Ann Leigh fought to keep her voice from trembling. "I won't forget this. But since you demand an answer, of course I've danced with Vern Spurlock. Just as I've danced with dozens of military men at the canteen."

"What about the party at Katherine Anne's place?"

Ann Leigh hated herself for honoring the question with an answer. But she wanted to put Lester in his place. "There *was* no party. Lieutenant Lidgard and Katherine Anne kindly offered me a ride home one evening. The lieutenant's car wouldn't start. Vern Spurlock happened by and gave us a lift. Katherine Anne suggested we stop for a drink. I was a guest. Under the circumstances, I didn't feel I could refuse. That's all there is to your nasty accusations."

Lester's lower lip protruded in a boyish pout. "If it was all so innocent, why didn't you tell me about it? What else did you do behind my
back?"

Ann Leigh was momentarily speechless. "Well, Lester Wilson. You're
sure showing your true colors!" she managed to say.

"How do you think I feel?" he lashed back. "I'm only gone a week,
and when I come home, it's all over town that you've been out with
someone else. How do I know what you'll do after we're married?"

Ann Leigh tugged at her engagement ring. It pulled free. Amazed at
her self-control, she calmly handed it to him. "You'll never know," she
said.

Blindly she pushed her way out of the car and walked into the house.

She stayed at home for more than a week, begging illness. She
remained heedless of everything around her, not even taking interest
when her mother arrived from Shackelford County to disassemble the
wedding preparations. She slept little. Most of the time she lay awake,
miserable, reviewing the mess she had made of her life.

She had insulted Katherine Anne, who had never been able to abide
Lester, and she had hurt Vern Spurlock, undoubtedly the handsomest,
most ardent admirer she would have in her lifetime. And all because of
Lester Wilson.

On an afternoon in early December she awoke from a fitful nap and
found Katherine Anne sitting beside the bed.

"You look like death warmed over," Katherine Anne said. "What are
you doing to yourself?"

Unable to speak, Ann Leigh began to cry. She reached for Katherine
Anne and they embraced.

"I would have come sooner, but I've been ill too," Katherine Anne
said. "The doctors think it's tuberculosis. But so far they've found no
trace of the germ."

Ann Leigh momentarily forgot her own concerns. She squeezed
Katherine Anne's hand. "I'm so sorry. I feel terrible I didn't know."

Katherine Anne dismissed the subject with a toss of her head. "It's a
chronic condition I've had to contend with most of my life. But there's no
excuse for your being in bed. It's nice out today. Do you feel like going for
a walk?"

Ann Leigh compromised. "Why don't we go down and sit on the
riverbank? We can talk there."

By the time they reached the foot of the bluff Ann Leigh's knees
were trembling. She sank to the dry grass gratefully. In the distance, six
airplanes flew in formation.

Ann Leigh thought of Vern. "I'm so ashamed," she said. "I've made
such a fool of myself."

Katherine Anne was following her train of thought. "If I were you, I wouldn't stop at half measures. I'd tell Vern Spurlock exactly how I felt."

Ann Leigh glanced at her. Katherine Anne's expression was solemn. Her violet-tinged eyes were without guile. Ann Leigh watched the planes bank into a turn toward the south, still maintaining formation. "I *did* treat him badly, didn't I? And I do feel awful about it. Have you seen him?"

"He sent flowers while I was ill. But I haven't seen him."

Ann Leigh spoke on impulse. "Could you possibly hint to him, in some way, that I've regained my senses and might act more kindly toward him now?"

Katherine Anne shook her head. "Absolutely not. Matters are far beyond matchmaking. If I were you, I'd send him a formal note of apology. And if Vern is one hundredth the man I think he is, he'll take it from there."

Ann Leigh considered the suggestion. "I couldn't possibly do that. It would be so obvious."

"So what!" Katherine Anne said. "Just because you're a woman, does that mean you're not a member of the human race?"

Through the next several days, Ann Leigh agonized over the suggestion. She started dozens of notes but ripped them to shreds in disgust. Phrases of explanation and rationalization flowered like weeds. She filled an entire writing tablet. At last she settled on a simple, unadorned note:

Dear Lieutenant Spurlock:

I wish to apologize for my inexcusable behavior toward you during the last few months. I want you to know that, contrary to anything I said, I have always held you in the highest esteem. My hope is that despite my unpardonable actions, we again some day may be friends.

Sincerely,

Ann Leigh Cawley

Days crept by with no answer. A dozen times each hour Ann Leigh blushed with embarrassment at her own forwardness. Yet the note gave her a strong feeling of satisfaction, of righteousness. Finally a thick letter arrived.

In his opening paragraph Vern confessed that he had started many letters and abandoned them because he could not put his feelings into words. He said that, emboldened by her note, he would simply allow his thoughts to pour onto paper. He apologized for the charade he had performed with Katherine Anne and Lidgard. He said he did not blame her for being so angry.

Only toward the end of the long letter did he broach his desire for a renewal of their friendship. "On Saturday next, a full-dress ball is scheduled at the Fort Worth Club. If you have no other plans, and are agreeable, I would be most proud to serve as your escort."

In panic Ann Leigh pulled her formal gowns from the closet. She had lost so much weight that each hung on her like a croker sack. And she was appalled as she looked at herself in the full-length mirror. Her hair was lifeless and her skin appeared sallow. She looked positively gaunt.

Clearly something had to be done.

She set to work with a passion. Determining that her gown must be dramatic and different, she summoned her dressmaker. Since current fashion tended toward multilayered skirts and fussy accessories, she designed a simple, loose-fitting gown of white lawn, with a tiered yoke collar of the same material. For color she attached a wide scarlet sash, caught up just below the breast in the Empire style, and a matching red ribbon bow over her heart. For added drama she decided upon a shawl of black Spanish lace, worn off the shoulder, gathered over her arms above the elbows. After much experimentation she selected a pair of dangling, teardrop pearl earrings. Defying the current fashion of elaborate, artificial hair styles, she determined to wear hers loose, with its natural curl intact. She also placed herself under a laborious regimen to restore life to her poor, neglected body.

Saturday evening she dressed carefully. When her maid brought the announcement of Vern Spurlock's arrival downstairs, she gave herself one last, penetrating inspection in the full-length mirror.

She felt that she had succeeded as well as could be expected.

Vern stood at the foot of the grand staircase and watched Ann Leigh descend. She was totally different, and yet the same. Thin from her illness, she seemed strong and cheerful, smiling at him all the way down the stairs. Her dress was elegantly simple, unlike those most ladies wore. Vern knew instinctively that it was classic.

He took her hands and held her at arm's length. "You are absolutely stunning," he said.

She seemed pleased with his reaction. He guided her to the door and out to his car.

At the Fort Worth Club, Vern surrendered his car to an attendant and escorted her inside. As they were announced and made their entrance into the ballroom, Vern felt hundreds of eyes upon them.

Rumors had been flying over her breakup with Lester Wilson, and

Vern knew that a few of the stories making the rounds were malicious. He felt a moment of anger over the unguarded stares, but common sense told him that the curiosity was natural. Also, he knew that much of the attention was centered on Ann Leigh's startlingly original gown.

They joined Lidgard and Katherine Anne at a table. The orchestra began playing the jazz numbers sweeping the country. Vern led her onto the floor. For a time they danced, content with the music, the champagne, and the lavish atmosphere.

Ann Leigh seemed to be enjoying herself. Each time someone cut in, she gave him a brief, secret look of regret.

Late in the evening, as they danced to the slow numbers, they shared whispered confidences.

Afterward, in the car, they felt animated. Vern drove for miles as they talked. Then he parked on Inspiration Point to the west of town.

The moon was full and the war seemed far away. Not speaking, they kissed, gently at first, then with growing passion. At last Vern drew back. He fumbled for a cigarette. Ann Leigh straightened her dress and snuggled against him.

"I don't know when I'll receive my orders for France," he said. "I'm expecting them any day. Now I don't want to go. I want us to have more time together."

"Couldn't you withdraw your request?"

"That'd be like trying to recall a bullet once it's fired. The only reason I've been kept here until now is that instructors are still in such short supply. But experienced pilots are returning from France. They're in training to become instructors. When they're ready, I'm certain to be ordered to combat. It's inevitable."

"I'll write to you," she said. "Every day."

"I want to put what time we have to good use," he said. "I'd like to see you every night I can get off the field, every weekend I don't have the duty."

"We'll spend every minute together," she promised.

During the next few weeks they constructed barriers between themselves and the rest of the world. They attended occasional parties and dances but always left early, preferring to be alone. Repeatedly their hunger reached the point that consummation seemed inevitable. But each time they drew back from the brink.

Vern assumed Ann Leigh was a virgin. The possibility that Vern would think otherwise never entered her head.

On a dry, windy day in early August, Vern returned from a formation flight and found a staff orderly waiting for him.

"Sir, you are to report to the colonel, immediately."

His mind numb, Vern walked across the field to the headquarters building.

The colonel did not keep him waiting. "Spurlock, your orders have arrived. You and a squadron to be composed of pilots from this field are to report to the Meuse-Argonne sector for further assignment."

Vern did not answer. He could not trust himself to speak. The colonel did not seem to notice. He smiled and rose from his desk. "It is also my pleasant duty to inform you that your appointment to the permanent rank of captain has been approved. You will lead your own squadron into combat."

Vern found his voice. "Thank you, sir. I'll do my best to justify your faith in me, sir."

"I'm sure you will." The colonel shook hands. "We'll talk again before you leave."

Vern walked away from headquarters with conflicting emotions. Miserable over leaving Ann Leigh, he also felt wild elation.

If only he could endure the anguish of his separation from her for a while, everything he had worked toward could still be realized.

Ann Leigh knew from the moment she saw Vern's face. He was pale, solemn, and more purposeful. He waited until they were in the car, parked before their favorite pond.

"My orders came," he said. "I leave Friday morning."

Ann Leigh felt as if she might faint.

Friday was three days away.

Then came irrational anger. "How can they do this to us?"

"It'll be happening to everyone before long," Vern pointed out. "We have to face it."

"Can't you get it delayed? Your father knows important people. Couldn't he have your orders changed?"

Vern smiled. "Nobody has a stronger sense of duty than Travis Spurlock. He didn't want me to go. But now that I'm into it, he'd give me holy hell if I didn't measure up."

Ann Leigh started to cry. "What are we going to do?"

He put an arm around her and held her close. "We could get married," he said. "We have two days."

Ann Leigh thought of the elaborate preparations for her marriage to Lester Wilson. "How could we possibly get married in two days?"

"We could go before a justice of the peace in Weatherford. Under the circumstances, I'm sure we could get around any silly rules."

Ann Leigh thought of all the stories she had heard of cheap, runaway marriages. If she married Vern, so soon after her breakup with Lester

Wilson, everyone would assume something disgraceful *had* occurred. She could not do that to Vern, to herself.

"I wanted everything to be so perfect for us."

Vern did not answer for a moment. When he spoke, his voice was heavy with emotion. "Two days isn't much time. But it would be something to remember."

Ann Leigh knew she wanted Vern completely, totally. But she also knew she wanted him on proper terms. Anything less would not be fair to him, or to her.

"I'll be waiting for you," she said. "Wouldn't it be better to have so much ahead of us? We have our whole lives to think about. I don't want our marriage built on two frantic days. Surely we're above that."

Vern sat looking into the distance. "I suppose you're right. The war can't last forever."

The subject was not mentioned again. During the next two nights they clung together for hours, engulfed in their own emotions.

On Friday morning Ann Leigh went to the rail depot with Vern.

Travis, Reva, Durwood, and Zetta also came to see him off. Clay was somewhere in West Texas. He could not be reached.

Vern's entire squadron was leaving. The platform was decorated with American and Canadian flags. The band played lively marches, and an effort was made to infuse the squadron's departure with gaiety. No one was deceived. Everyone knew that some of the men would not return from Europe.

Vern attempted to make light banter, and Ann Leigh understood. She was determined not to cry.

When the conductor called all aboard, Vern embraced his father, his mother, and then his sister. He shook hands with his brother. And last, he turned to Ann Leigh.

"I'll be thinking of you every minute," he said. "I'll be counting the hours. I'll write every day."

He kissed her, holding her for a long moment.

And then he was gone.

Ann Leigh stood, bravely waving, until the train disappeared.

She kept her promise to herself.

She did not cry until she was home, locked in the privacy of her room.

23

The day dawned hot and clear. By midmorning the men were sweating heavily. Koon jumped off the rig floor and came to where Clay was monitoring the jury-rigged shale shaker. "Lookit that son of a bitch," Koon said. "Don't have enough sense to find some shade."

Clay followed his gaze. A jackrabbit was grazing in an open space less than thirty yards from the well.

"Anything new?" Koon asked.

Clay nodded. "I think we're into something. You'd better go wake Pete."

Koon went toward the tool shed. Clay moved on down to the tanks. Dark strings were interlaced through the drilling mud. Clay stood watching it until Pete arrived.

"Goddamn, but that's looking good," Pete said. He ran a hand through it and sniffed. "I think we'd better shut her down and see what we've got."

They pulled the string, spelling each other every thirty minutes because of the heat. By early afternoon they had a gentle stream of oil flowing into the slush tank.

"About what I expected," Pete said. "Quiet as a fucking mill pond. But this formation is usually good for long-term production. I think we've got us a well."

"How much you figure?" Clay asked.

"Hundred, maybe hundred fifty barrels a day. Probably not much more. We'll put a choke on it and run a test. Then we'll know where we stand."

Afterward, Clay and Pete walked a distance away from the well. "We're not rich," Pete said. "But then on the other hand, we're not broke."

"You think Texas Pacific would be interested in it?"

Pete sighed, took off his hat, and wiped the sweatband with his handkerchief. "Not a hell of a lot. I think we'd do best to skid the rig, spud in a new well, and prove out what we've got here. We know it's down there. We can have four or five wells making money, no matter what happens."

"At forty cents a barrel, it'd take about two years for a hundred-and-fifty-barrel well to pump itself into the black," Clay pointed out.

"The price is down only because the booms at Cushing and Healdton have flooded the market. That condition can't last. If we get into the war, oil will go to two dollars. Maybe three."

"I think we ought to look around for a good wildcat venture," Clay said.

Pete wiped his forehead and replaced his hat. "Clay, God damn it, I'm going to tell you something. Nobody wants to lay up a pile of money more than me. But what you're proposing is the dumb way to go about it. You could drill a hundred wildcats away from all known production, and you'd be damned lucky if one of them hit. Just be patient. I've always said Texas has more oil than Oklahoma and I still believe it. We've got good show from the Red River to the Gulf. Outside of Spindletop, nobody's hit the big fields yet. But it's going to happen any day. We've got to be ready to jump in and get our share."

Clay stood for a time without answering. "I guess it won't do any harm to skid the rig. But I think I'll get out and look around a little."

Pete wiped the grime from his hands. "Why don't you just do that."

He strode off with his peculiar rocking gait.

Clay turned and walked toward his car.

He stopped on the hilltop and sat for a moment, orienting himself, before he saw the top of the ranch house in the distance. He drove on, searching until he found a cattleguard and a road that wound through the low hills to the house.

He parked in the yard. Two hounds came from the direction of the barn and corrals, baying, yet swinging their tails in a friendly fashion. The house was of white-painted wood, two stories high, with gingerbread trim and a wide gallery around the lower floor. Clay saw no sign of movement at the house. He stroked the dogs and waited.

A man emerged from the barn. He was tall, lanky, and wore boots, Levi's, a faded blue shirt, and a soiled wide-brimmed white hat. As he approached, he gave Clay a brief nod. "Howdy. What can I do for you?"

"Spurlock's the name," Clay said. "I'm an oilman. Saw an interesting structure back down the road a piece. This your place?"

"What there is of it." They shook hands. "Jim Davenport."

His hands were callused, his face weathered and heavily lined. Clay guessed that he was in his early thirties. "Your place under lease?"

"Leased and drilled. They put down a test well about a mile over that way three, maybe four years ago." He shook his head and grinned. "Dry hole."

"How deep did they go?"

He frowned. "Twenty-six hundred feet, I think it was."

"Rights revert to you?"

He hesitated. Apparently it was a new thought. "I don't know for sure."

"They usually do, after a period of time, with a dry hole and no further drilling. I could tell by looking at your papers."

"Come on up to the house," Davenport said. "I'll see if I can find them."

Davenport shoved open the front door and allowed Clay to enter first. "Elise!" he yelled. "Company!"

Clay was standing, hat in hand, as she entered the room. She was wearing a simple housedress, pale green, flocked with tiny yellow flowers. Her face first registered shock, then restrained amusement, with a hint of that mocking smile. She was much smaller off the horse than he thought. Her green eyes never left his face.

"This is Mr. Spurlock," Davenport said. "My wife. Honey, we have any coffee made?"

"Maybe Mr. Spurlock would like a good cold beer," she said. "The ice truck came today."

"I'd love one," Clay said.

"Have a seat," Davenport said. "If you'll excuse me, I'll get those papers." He went up the stairs.

Clay turned and examined the room. The furniture was pecan and leather. Mexican serapes decorated the walls. On the mantel over the fireplace were a wedding picture, a photograph of an older couple, and snapshots of Elise with various horses. There were none of children.

Elise returned with three bottles of beer and three glasses. She put the tray on the coffee table, leaned close, and whispered. "You don't have a lick of sense, do you?"

"Depends on what you call sense."

Davenport called from the second floor. "Elise? Do you know where those oil company papers are?"

Elise walked to the banister and called up the stairs. "I think they're in that tin box in the bottom drawer on the right-hand side of the desk."

She came back to Clay. "I thought you stole all the pipe we had."

Clay shrugged. "I might find something else around here worth stealing."

Davenport came back downstairs. He handed Clay a bulky envelope. "This is all I have on it. I haven't heard anything out of them in two, maybe three years."

Davenport and Elise sat in chairs facing him. Clay poured his beer and sipped while he leafed through the papers. He found the notarized lease agreement. It was a boilerplate form he recognized. No amendments had been made. He skipped to the operative paragraph and read the key phrases aloud.

" 'Should the first well drilled on the above described land be a dry hole, then, and in that event, if a second well is not commenced on said land within twelve months . . . this lease shall terminate as to both parties . . . unless lessor shall resume payment of rentals.' You haven't received any more payments?"

"Nothing."

"I'd check this with a lawyer, if I were you, but it looks to me like you're clear to lease your land again."

Elise was sitting with head lowered, gazing up at Clay, rubbing the rim of her glass back and forth along her lower lip. "What about you, Mr. Spurlock? Are you really interested?"

Clay looked at her for a moment. The atmosphere was charged with her sexuality. He found it difficult to believe that Davenport remained unaware. Davenport was studying the lease agreement.

"Let's just say I've seen some surface structure I find very interesting," Clay said. "I'm here to explore it further."

She gave him that knowing smile. "How can you tell what's there, only from the surface structure?"

"Sometimes there are signs," Clay said. "But usually it's a strong feeling you have, a sort of intuition."

She obviously was enjoying the game. "Aren't you often disappointed?"

"Not often," Clay said. "I've only drilled one dry hole so far. And no gassers."

Elise giggled. Davenport glanced at her, realizing he had missed something.

"It all sounds risky to me," Elise said.

Clay grinned at Davenport, to include him in the conversation. But he spoke to Elise. "Anything worth having usually involves risk."

Elise opened her mouth with a ready rejoinder. Apparently she had second thoughts. She remained silent.

Clay turned back to Davenport. "It's too close to dark now. But I'd like to come back when it's convenient and look things over. You have a phone?"

Davenport nodded. "Three longs, a short, and a long."

"Party line," Elise said. "Other people listen in, so you have to talk around what you're saying to keep them from knowing what you're doing."

"Maybe I can learn to do that," Clay said.

He thanked Elise for the beer. Davenport walked him back to the car.

As Clay drove away, Elise was perched on the gallery rail, watching him.

Clay wandered for six days. He drove through the Breckenridge, Petrolia, and Electra fields, stopping in the cafés and bars to listen to the talk of the roughnecks and drillers. He spent a night in Wichita Falls, then headed south again. He could not forget the two or three days he had spent walking along Hog Creek, so many months ago. He remembered the uncanny feeling, some sixth sense, that told him he was walking on a pool of oil.

Beyond Ranger, he drove southward on bone-grinding dirt roads that were little more than cattle trails. With more experience in the oil fields, he now looked at the terrain with a practiced eye. Several times he stopped and examined outcroppings of rock formations, seeking the slant that might reveal an anticline where oil could be trapped far beneath the surface.

Again he walked Hog Creek, tasting the traces of sludge floating on fetid pools. He found nothing encouraging.

In midafternoon he arrived at Hog Town, a half dozen ramshackle houses clustered around a combination country store and service station. He left his car in front of the gas pump, walked inside, and asked the gray-haired old man behind the counter if he had soda pop.

"In the box there," the old man said, pointing. "No ice, though. Truck only comes Mondays and Thursdays."

"Long as it's wet," Clay said. He selected an orange drink and uncapped it on the side of the box.

His eyes slowly adjusted to the gloom. The store was stocked with a wide variety of staples, from flour to saddles and harness. Flies buzzed around the candy case. The old man's wide face was as gnarled as a cottonwood stump. His eyes were filmed over with a rheumy glaze.

"You own any of the land around here?" Clay asked.

The old man spat expertly into the coffee can at his feet. "Who wants to know?"

Clay introduced himself. "I'm an oilman. I might be interested in buying some mineral rights."

"How much you paying?"

"Depends."

"We already had our oil boom around here," the old man said. "One of the dry holes is on my property."

"How deep did they go?"

The old man shook his head. "Don't rightly remember."

Clay reached into his hip pocket and spread a map. "Whereabouts is your place?"

The old man did not bother with the map. He pointed. "I've got six forty back that way. From the top of that hill running back west. Under lease, though."

"Exploration has been abandoned," Clay pointed out. "Don't you have a reversion clause?"

"I suppose. Hadn't thought about it."

"I'll give you two dollars an acre, with a one-sixteenth override on your lease, if you'll help me locate some more land around here."

"One-sixteenth override? What the hell does that mean?"

"Probably not a damned thing. But if I drill, and we find oil, it could mean hundreds of thousands of dollars."

The old man laughed. "I like the way you do business, young fella. I get tired of these salesmen coming in here high-pressuring me. Yankees, most of them. Always giving something for nothing, to hear them tell it."

Clay ascertained that the property was clear, then signed a simple lease agreement.

He then spent the remainder of the afternoon walking the hill, searching for signs of an anticline.

The next morning he drove northward. Shortly after noon he stopped in Strawn, found a telephone in a feed store, and rang three longs, a short, and a long.

As he expected, Elise answered.

"Mrs. Davenport, this is Detective O'Shaunessey," he said. "I've definitely determined that your husband is seeing that Ferguson woman, like you figured."

Clay heard Elise giggle over the hum of the rural line. "I've been waiting six weeks for that report," she shouted. "What kept you?"

"Ma'am, for the last six weeks I've given your case my complete attention. It's been a troublesome matter that has taken me into every bar and whorehouse in West Texas. It's just about driven me completely crazy. I've got a bill of particulars here a foot long, all hard fact. I think you'll be mighty pleased. You want me to keep on searching for clues?"

Elise laughed aloud. Clay stood grinning, waiting for her to recover.

Every rural line had at least two or three nosy subscribers who eavesdropped.

"My husband claims he's at the first Monday livestock sale in Abilene this afternoon," she said. "You better get on the road. You might be missing something."

"Yes ma'am," Clay said. "I'll sure do that."

When he arrived at the Davenport place less than a half hour later, Elise was standing on the gallery, still consumed with laughter, her eyes alive with excitement. Again she was wearing Levi's trousers tucked into boots, and a man's shirt, open at the neck. She came out to the car.

"You don't know what you've done!" she said. "It'll be all over this countryside by dark that Jim's running around on me!" She burst into giggles. "I'll never live it down!"

The wind riffled her close-cropped, soft brown hair. "Jim looked like he could use a little notoriety," Clay said.

She shook her head in exasperation. "You are a total rapscallion! I don't know what to do with you!"

Clay stepped out of the car. "You might start by offering me a drink. I brought some liquor. All we need is ice."

Elise led the way into the house. She walked on through and into the kitchen.

Clay placed the bottle on the cabinet. Elise reached for two glasses and filled them with chipped ice from the box. She set the glasses on the counter and looked up at Clay.

"There's one thing that bothers me," she said. "You have too much confidence in yourself. You're assuming too much. I don't like that."

"I don't have confidence in myself," Clay said quietly. "I have confidence in you."

Her gaze did not waver. "How do you mean that?"

Clay hesitated, not certain how far he should go. "Elise, from the first moment I saw you, I knew you were ten times more woman than any other I've ever met, bottled up in a life that would bore a fencepost. You seemed ready to explode. And believe me, I know that feeling."

Elise turned to pour the drinks. Her hand trembled. She set the whiskey back on the counter. Her eyes filled with tears. "Is it that obvious?"

Clay wanted to hold her, but his intuition told him to wait. "Other people probably don't bother to notice. I just see a lot in you I understand."

She did not move or look at him. "What, for instance?"

He hesitated, wondering where to begin. "I see that you're a fish out of water. No woman wears pants in public, at least not in this part of the country. Most women around here are wearing their hair long, so you've whacked yours off. You've been kicking over the traces for years and don't even know it."

She remained silent for a time. "What you say may be true. But I've never cheated on my husband."

"I know that too. If you had, it would've taken some of the edge off."

She looked up at him. Tears rolled down her cheeks. "Damn you."

Clay took her by the shoulders and gently kissed away her tears. "We won't do anything until you make up your mind about me, about yourself. This is too important."

Elise searched his face. "I think I can best decide upstairs. But I warn you. I don't know how this will turn out. I may want to kill you afterward."

Clay grinned. "At least I'll die happy."

She led him up the stairs to a front bedroom and a four-poster brass bed. A pair of her husband's high-topped boots stood against the wall. The rough work clothes he had pulled off were draped across a chair. A briar pipe lay on an end stand beside the bed. Everywhere he looked, Clay saw signs of Davenport's presence.

"This isn't exactly a boudoir," Elise said. "You want to go somewhere else?"

Clay grinned at her. "I wouldn't have it any other way."

They kissed gently, exploring. Elise was not aggressive, but neither did she retreat. Standing beside the bed, holding each other, they took pleasure in prolonging the inevitable. Gradually their clothing fell away. As they moved onto the bed, Clay held her, moving with knowledge beyond his own understanding. He held his own passion in check, taking her to ever-climbing plateaus. At last they writhed together with an intensity and fury that was more like combat than love. Clay arched in a shattering climax and fell away. Elise followed, her face pinioned to his chest, her arms encircling his waist. They lay, gasping for breath, until a semblance of sanity returned.

"Maybe we've just invented something," Clay said.

Elise rolled onto her back and looked at the ceiling. "Damn you. What's going to happen to me now?"

Clay raised on one elbow so he could see her face. "What do you want to happen?"

She turned to look at him. "I don't know. One minute I want you to go away. The next I don't want you ever to go away. You've sure made a mess out of my life."

"Maybe it was already a mess. Maybe I just made you aware of it. Frankly, I don't understand how you ever came to be the wife of Jim Davenport. He needs a fat, loudmouthed wife that waddles."

Elise giggled. "He wasn't always that way. I've changed, too. We married young. Everybody was getting married. We did what was expected of us. He's worked hard. He really has. I should be happy. But sometimes I think I'd like to take off and never come back."

"A restless soul," Clay said. "It takes one to know one. Why don't you take off and come along with me?"

Elise studied his face, trying to determine if he was joking. "I couldn't do that. No matter what, I've never hated Jim. I've never wanted to hurt him."

"You could leave him a real nice note."

Elise hesitated. "Are you serious?"

"I've never been more serious in my life."

"I don't know anything about you! I don't even know for sure if you're really an oilman."

Clay laughed. "Come along and I'll show you."

"I don't think you know what you're doing. If Jim caught us, he'd shoot us both. I mean that!"

"I know," Clay said. "I've always thought that having a jealous husband around enlivened things."

"You'd better go."

"Not yet," Clay said. "Let's make it a little more interesting."

They lingered in bed throughout the long afternoon, drifting from frantic lovemaking to idyllic intervals and back again.

As shadows lengthened, Elise again begged him to go. "He'll be home for sure before dark."

"All right, I'll go," Clay said, rolling out of bed to get dressed. "But I'll be back. You can count on that."

24

Climbing, Vern turned toward the rising sun. To the north lay the Somme, a faint silver ribbon on the horizon. Occasional red winks of artillery blossomed far below, interspersed with black pinpoints of shell and mortar. His wingmen were locked in tight. Lidgard and his second flight were stairstepped below and to the right. Ahead, dawn was breaking, with shafts of brilliant sunlight playing along the tops of distant clouds. The night had been hot and sultry. Now, at six thousand feet, speeding along at a hundred miles an hour, the air was crisp, cold, and clear. The eighty-horsepower Le Rhone rotary engine of his new Sopwith Pup droned steadily. Looking ahead, Vern thought he saw something glint against a cloud. He blinked and wiped his goggles with his silk scarf. The glint appeared again, followed by others.

German planes were rising to meet them at the front.

Vern felt a familiar rush of excitement. He now understood Clay's penchant for fighting. He never felt more alive than in the moments before combat.

Turning in the cockpit, he gestured to Lidgard and pointed. Lidgard nodded, acknowledging that he also had seen the enemy. Vern held the course three minutes, banked into a ninety-degree turn to the left; and the deadly dance began.

Each morning the Germans attempted to lure them across the front to fight over enemy territory. Unconfirmed kills behind enemy lines did not "count." For the same reason, the British tried to draw the Germans over Allied lines.

Usually they met over no-man's-land, with the fates of the wind deciding the official score.

As Vern had anticipated, the Germans turned on a parallel course no more than six kilometers away—a squadron of Fokker Eindekkers, another of the new Albatros. Each had two fixed Spandaus, almost a perfect match for Vern's two fixed Vickers.

A red-winged Fokker peeled off from the flight and approached the lines, signaling a challenge to single combat. Vern could see the pilot plainly rocking his wings and fishtailing to simulate a dogfight.

Vern wanted to accept. But his orders were plain. He was to avoid the German fighters if possible and concentrate on the heavier Albatros bombing machines that had been doing so much damage recently behind the lines.

Vern led his flight into a climbing turn toward the front, still watching the Fokker, still tempted. A quick pass would be sufficient. Although highly maneuverable, the single-winged Fokker was slower than his new Pup.

With eight kills to his credit, Vern now needed only two more to qualify as an ace.

Lidgard gestured. Vern looked in the direction he was pointing. Far below, five Albatros bombers were crossing the front, perhaps two kilometers toward the Somme. Vern nodded and raised his hand in a signal for an attack.

Calculating speed and distance, he waited until the appropriate moment, then led his squadron into a slanting dive, approaching the bombers out of the sun. He glanced back. The Fokkers had broken their patrol pattern and were diving in pursuit.

Lidgard had seen them. He gave Vern a quick salute and pulled out of his dive in a sweeping turn. He and his wingmen would engage the Fokkers, protecting Vern and his wingmen while they attacked the bombers.

Using the speed of the dive, Vern approached the flight from the rear. He signaled his wingmen to spread for attack, and selected his own target—the bomber at the rear of the flight. He angled in low so the rear gunner would have a poor target with his flexible Parabellum. Pulling up under the bomber, closing rapidly, he managed a five-second burst from his Vickers before he had to swing away to avoid collision. Debris spewed from the Albatros tail section. The rear gunner toppled to the floor of his cockpit. The Parabellum swung free on its circular track.

Vern made his second pass high from the rear, confident that the rear gunner was incapacitated. He fired another five-second burst. The Albatros dived toward the ground, trailing a black plume of smoke.

Breaking off the attack, Vern looked back. His wingmen were engaged with individual targets. Above, Lidgard and his wingmen were swirling in a dogfight.

Climbing, Vern concentrated on the leading Albatros. He opened fire from a distance, squeezing off short bursts as he closed. He was less than a hundred yards away when the bomber disintegrated in a ball of flame. Vern pulled back on his stick. Debris thudded into the underside of his Pup.

After ascertaining that his controls still worked, Vern turned back to resume the attack. But no targets remained. His wingmen were polishing off the last Albatros.

Climbing under full power, Vern rushed to join the dogfight. A Fokker was plunging to earth in flames. Beyond, a Sopwith was going down, trailing smoke. Vern could not identify the machine.

Two Fokkers were pounding a damaged Sopwith. Even as Vern went to its aid, a portion of the tail section fell away. Taking the nearest Fokker by surprise, Vern fired a long, sustained burst. He saw the pilot slump in his seat. The Fokker began spinning toward the battlefield below, well inside Allied lines.

The second Fokker turned toward him and succeeded in getting on his tail. Vern rolled and dived, trying to twist away. The Fokker stayed with him. Vern went into a series of barrel rolls in an effort to take advantage of the Pup's superior strength and speed. Aware that he had crossed the front and was now dangerously far over German-held territory, he pulled out into a sweeping turn that would take him back to the Allied line. The maneuver was a mistake. The Fokker turned inside his circle and opened fire. Machine gun slugs ripped through the Sopwith's wings. Vern took evasive action and escaped the field of fire. Glancing back, he saw a white, misty vapor trailing behind him and realized that his gasoline tanks had been punctured. He switched off the ignition to prevent an explosion and went into a shallow glide.

The Sopwith he had attempted to save was far below, still spinning to earth. He saw it slam into a shell crater.

He had recognized the markings. The pilot was a young Scot named Campbell from Montreal. Vern remembered seeing Lidgard's other wingman, McCudden, in the dogfight. With anguish that almost took precedence over his own plight, he realized that the pilot he had seen going down earlier was Lidgard.

For the moment he had lost the Fokker. He wiped his goggles and tried to determine his location. He was too low to see the Somme. But familiar terrain revealed he was still behind enemy lines. An unfavorable wind, aided by German ingenuity, had taken the dogfight eastward. Vern stretched his glide to the limit, hoping to reach the Allied line.

The whistling stillness of his descent was broken by the sound of an approaching engine. The red-winged Fokker came up beside him. The pilot throttled back and flew wingtip to wingtip. The German wore goggles. Vern could not read the expression on his face. He seemed to be inspecting Vern's plane carefully, as if assessing Vern's chances.

The German signaled toward the ground and pointed. At first Vern thought the German was ordering him to land behind the lines. But far ahead was a patch of level ground, comparatively free of shell holes and tree stumps.

The German was showing him a safe landing spot.

Vern turned his full attention to the dead-stick landing. Slipping and fishtailing to adjust speed and descent, he guided the Sopwith to earth. His wheels hit hard, bounced over a shell hole, and sank into a tank track. The right wing dipped and the Pup almost ground-looped. The plane teetered for a heart-stopping moment, then fell back onto the wheels and tail strut.

Assuming that he might be within range of enemy snipers, Vern scrambled out of the plane and ran to a shell hole. But the only gunfire was some distance away—mostly machine guns and mortar. From the pattern of firing he inferred that he was in no-man's-land—a kilometer or more of ground claimed by neither side.

Again he heard the Fokker. The German came over low, leaning out of the cockpit for a better view. He circled for another pass. Vern ducked low in the shell crater, presuming he was about to be strafed. But to his surprise the German cut his engine. The Fokker settled to a rough but safe landing less than twenty yards away. The pilot jumped from the plane and began walking toward him.

Not knowing what to expect, Vern climbed out of the crater and brushed off his flying suit. The German did not appear to be armed. Vern carried a Webley revolver in an armpit holster.

The German wore a black leather jacket, boots, and jodhpurs. At his throat hung the Pour le Mérite. Vern wished he were wearing his own medals. The British considered the wearing of decorations on other than dress uniforms bad form.

The German was tall and blond, of ruddy complexion. He saluted, and examined Vern with Nordic blue eyes. "Oberleutnant Karl Billik, at your service," he said in lightly accented English. "You made a very skilled landing. My congratulations."

Vern returned the salute. "Captain Malvern Spurlock. Thank you for pointing the way."

The German turned his attention to the Sopwith. "I was wondering whether your plane is damaged sufficiently for me to claim a victory. I now have twenty-four. It would be nice to raise my total to twenty-five."

The Sopwith's wings were shredded. A section was gone from the vertical stabilizer. The fuselage was riddled. No doubt the frame was damaged. The engine was pocked with bullet scars. Dripping oil indicated a shattered block.

"It certainly will never fly again," Vern said. "I believe you have your victory."

Oberleutnant Billik beamed with pleasure. "Captain Spurlock, would you be so kind as to sign a statement to that effect? You see, you are my only witness."

Scribbling on the back of an envelope, Vern attested to the fact that his Sopwith Pup had been damaged beyond repair by Oberleutnant Billik. He signed his name, rank, and serial number.

Billik took the note and examined it. "The airplane you shot down was piloted by Leutnant Franz Dostler," he said. "I saw him fall. Would you like for me to be your witness?"

Vern hesitated only a moment. The month before, two kills had not been credited to him for lack of witnesses.

"I would appreciate it," he said.

"We fliers must cooperate," Billik said. "We are probably the last honorable combatants. War has become . . . how do you say . . . *dreck?*"

"Shit."

"Exactly." Billik wrote his statement on the back of an oft-read letter from Ann Leigh. He signed it, brought the paper close to his nose, and sniffed. "Your girl friend?"

"My fiancée."

Billik smiled and saluted. "Perhaps we shall meet again, up there." He pointed toward the sky.

"Perhaps," Vern said.

Billik strode to his plane, started the engine, and took off into the wind. In a moment he was gone.

Vern walked westward. A few minutes later he encountered a squad of Australian soldiers, sent to investigate the downed plane.

That afternoon he was taken to a division command post on the back of a motorcycle. A British brigadier dispatched his car and driver to return him to his aerodrome.

After a brief medical examination and a stiff shot of cognac at the infirmary, Vern reported to his wing commander. "We lost Lidgard and Campbell. I saw them go down."

"And the tally?"

Already the dogfight seemed days in the past. Vern added silently— the flight of five bombers, three Fokkers. "Eight," he said.

"Your count confirms other reports," the colonel said. "We were most concerned that we had lost you. One of your pilots last saw you at some distance, your plane damaged, with a Boche chasing you. What happened?"

Vern grinned. "That Boche was a true officer and gentleman. After he ripped up my plane, he followed me down, and we had a nice chat before an Aussie patrol came along."

The colonel raised an eyebrow. "Extraordinary. Give me his name. I'll commend his gallantry to his commanding officer."

Vern wrote down Billik's name and handed it to the colonel.

"You're scheduled to lead an evening flight," the colonel said. "Do you feel up to it?"

"Yes, sir."

Vern saluted and turned to go, but hesitated.

"Something else, Captain?"

Ordinarily, Vern might not have spoken. But fatigue and cognac had left him lightheaded. "Sir, we lost two men this morning because we divided our forces, leaving three planes to engage six. If we had engaged the fighters first, I'm sure we would have given a better account of ourselves."

"And the bombers would have escaped." The colonel removed his spectacles and rubbed the bridge of his nose. "Captain, I understand your feelings. But until further notice, the bombers will be our primary targets. Is that understood?"

Vern was too exhausted to argue. "Yes, sir."

"That'll be all then. You'd better go get some rest. By the way, they brought in the body from the Fokker you shot down. I thought you might like to take a look at the chap."

Driven by morbid curiosity, Vern crossed the aerodrome to the infirmary. An orderly pointed the way to a screened corner at the far end of a ward. Vern entered alone. The corpse of Leutnant Franz Dostler lay unsheeted on a metal table, the feet arranged close together, the hands folded on his chest.

Vern first was struck by the flyer's extreme youth. Dostler seemed no more than eighteen, with a small, delicate build, the clear, smooth skin of a child. His boots were polished to perfection, the feet slender, almost feminine. His flying helmet had been removed. He had brownish, silk-soft hair, feathered across a broad, high forehead. He seemed asleep, his expression gentle, peaceful.

Vern stood for several minutes, staring at the corpse, overwhelmed by a profound sadness. Somewhere across no-man's-land Lidgard also lay dead, and here was his counterpart. With futile regret, Vern remembered the exhilaration he had felt at the moment he closed in for the kill. He felt none now, only vague shame, anger, and frustration.

He returned to his barracks and flung himself on his bunk, but he could not sleep. Restless, he wrote a long letter to Ann Leigh, trying to capture his conflicting emotions after an especially difficult day.

That evening he led his patrol, climbing high over the front to search for night bombers. Enemy fighters came aloft, but they remained well to the east. The mission was completed without engagement.

After midnight, German bombers attacked. Vern awoke to explosions around the aerodrome, the clatter of antiaircraft machine guns. The other pilots evacuated the barracks and took refuge in sandbag shelters. Vern remained in his bunk. Before the attack ended, he again was asleep.

At dawn he was back in the air with his reorganized squadron, climbing over the front. Green replacements filled the vacant positions.

A high, thin overcast caught the first rays of the sun, coloring the morning blood red. The German fighters rose across no-man's-land like a swarm of gnats in the still air. When the Fokkers reached the front they did not take up station but continued their approach. Vern signaled his squadron to engage.

He climbed for advantage and dove on the first flight. He fired at a Fokker on the first pass but was unable to see the results. Another German crossed his gunsights. Firing, Vern pulled in behind him, pouring a stream of tracers into the fuselage as the Fokker desperately twisted and turned. The Fokker exploded.

Vern pulled up sharply to avoid the debris and flew right into the path of an oncoming Fokker.

The collision was over in an instant. Vern's lower left wing was gone, the upper sheared off to a stump. The shattered Pup fell, out of control.

Vern watched the earth approach with strange detachment. He felt peaceful, even content. He only had a brief moment of sorrow for all the pain his death would cause, the life he might have lived. He had a moment of desperate yearning for Ann Leigh, his family. His last thought was one of regret that his final vision was of a muddy, shell-pocked battlefield in France and not the lush green hills of home.

25

When the terrible news arrived at Bluebonnet it was as if the world had ended. Reva was put to bed under strong medication. Though ministers and friends came, she was beyond consolation. The nights were filled with her weeping.

Travis sat in his rocking chair in the parlor, his gnarled hands gripping the armrests, his gaze relentlessly fixed on the far wall. He nodded politely to visitors who came to offer condolences and answered in monosyllables. He reminded Zetta of a powerful locomotive after its fires had gone out. Only the shell remained.

Zetta renewed her mourning with a vengeance. Again she lived through the agonies of that distant day when word came that Auggie had died of yellow fever. For years she had kept a small shrine in her room—a photograph of Auggie in his uniform, a Bible with his name inscribed, a lock of his hair, his letters, a faded, crushed rose she had worn to a dance. The tiny shrine was her secret, long kept from the rest of the family. In her anguish and confusion she now added bits and pieces of her brother's memorabilia to the shrine—a childhood photograph, letters, grade school report cards, a whistle, a windup toy he had favored. She changed to her most severe black dresses, pulled the drapes throughout the house, and hung a funeral wreath on the front door. She chastened the servants until they crept around like ghosts.

Durwood came and sat, but he could think of nothing to say. The fact that he had resented Vern in life did not enhance his mourning. His new rapport with his father seemed lost. After a few uncomfortable minutes he left quietly.

At last Clay was reached. He rushed home and in his own way attempted to console the family, but disagreements flared. Reva felt that the funeral should await Vern's body and interment. Travis nodded agreement. Clay insisted that months might pass before the body was returned and that Vern would be the last person to wish to inflict a long ordeal on the family. Durwood lectured Clay, insisting that he should respect his parents' wishes.

After lingering a few days, Clay fled back to the oil fields.

Bluebonnet settled into a grim routine. Three times a day the servants prepared and delivered individual servings. Invariably Reva left hers virtually untouched. Travis waved his away with an impatient gesture. Zetta ate as if her mind were elsewhere.

In the mornings the leaves of the cottonwood tree outside Ann Leigh's window were the color of golden apples. As each day wore on, the shadows of the house lengthened and the tree turned dark and somber, matching the mood in her heart.

She wept for Vern Spurlock intermittently and thought of him constantly.

His final letter had arrived ten days after the news of his death. The shock of his last written words was almost more than Ann Leigh could bear. The letter was filled with grim premonitions, anguish over the senselessness of war, and a lengthy assessment of his love for her. Portions of the letter slipped into the past tense. She could not shake the feeling that it came from beyond the grave.

She remained in bed most of each day, rising only occasionally to go to a back window to watch the birds gathering along the Trinity in the late afternoon. Her aunt had summoned a doctor, but he said her illness was beyond medicine. She slept little and was awakened often by vivid, terrifying dreams. She did not go out. Her mother and aunt came often to sit and talk. She could not help snapping at them over trifles. Afterward she was angry with herself. She knew she was being selfish and childish but was powerless to do anything about it.

In time she began to think about how Vern would expect her to behave. She grew disgusted with herself for being such a weakling. Vern had died a hero's death. At least she could live with courage.

She dressed, cleaned her room, and went down to the riverbank for a long walk. She called the university and said she was ready to resume her classes. That night she answered sympathy notes and phoned Katherine Anne.

"I just wanted you to know I'm feeling better," she said. "I'll be coming back to the canteen. I'll see you there."

"Do you feel you're able?"

"Katherine Anne, I have to get out again to preserve my sanity. I know Vern would have wanted me to go on."

Her aunt seemed pleased with her change of attitude, but worried.

"Honey, you've been ill. I don't think you should try to do too much for a while."

"I've not been ill," Ann Leigh said. "I've been indulging myself. I've been selfish. I haven't even told the Spurlocks about the last letter."

The next morning she called at Bluebonnet. The maid silently admitted her to the tomblike house. After a few minutes Zetta came into the parlor to greet her. She wore solid black. Her hair was pulled back into a severe bun.

Ann Leigh felt chastised. She had chosen a conservative dark blue dress. But at the last moment she had added a dash of color with a belt and scarf. Zetta's gaze lingered on the scarf in obvious disapproval.

"So good of you to come," Zetta said. "Unfortunately, Mother is ill. She still hasn't recovered from the shock. Father is taking it hard. We've canceled all our engagements." She paused. "How are you? We heard you were ill. I would have come to see you, but I've been so worried about Mother. The doctors say she's going into a slow decline."

Ann Leigh hesitated. She wondered what Vern would say if he were alive and saw the situation. "I'm sorry to hear about Mrs. Spurlock," she said. "I haven't been ill, exactly. Inconsolable would be the appropriate word, I suppose. And then one morning I woke up, and I thought about what Vern would have wanted. I knew he would have been very disappointed in me. That knowledge has made me thoroughly ashamed. I've volunteered to return to canteen work. I'm resuming my classes. I think that's what Vern would have wanted me to do."

"That's very commendable of you. But do you think it proper?"

Ann Leigh could not restrain a hint of indignation in her voice. "Miss Spurlock, if I can help divert those young men from their worries for an hour or two before they go overseas, I know that Vern would want me to be there."

Zetta did not retreat. "But it's so soon. After all, you *were* betrothed."

Ann Leigh could not fight back her anger. "Perhaps I've already paid too much attention to convention. Vern wanted to marry before he left. I failed him. I thought it was too soon. I worried about what people would think. I talked him into waiting until he returned, and I'll regret that till my dying day. I wish I had given myself to him, totally and completely. I know I'll never find a better man."

A blush rose to Zetta's pale face. Too late, Ann Leigh remembered that Zetta had once been engaged and had lost her fiancé in the Spanish-American War. She wondered if Zetta's grief, too, was mingled with the regret of a virginity preserved.

"These are difficult times," Zetta said. "Perhaps you're right. Let's have tea. Then we'll go talk with Father for a few minutes. I know he'll want to see you."

When they entered the study a half hour later, Travis rose and greeted Ann Leigh with great courtesy and warmth. He took her hand. "You beautiful child, how good of you to come see us. We miss having young people about."

He seemed to falter. "Sit here and let's talk," he said after a moment. "Would you like some coffee or tea?"

"We've had tea," Zetta said. "We didn't wish to tire you."

Again Travis seemed lost in confusion. Ann Leigh was stricken with pity for the magnificent old man. With his Romanesque nose, sharply chiseled features, and erect posture, he still offered a most distinguished appearance.

Confronted by Zetta's deep mourning, and the shattered father's grief, Ann Leigh realized that she could not reveal the true purpose of her visit. Vern's last letter, with its aura of reflections after death, would be too much for them to bear. "You're looking well, Senator," she lied.

Travis smiled and shook his head. "I'm growing old. It seems that I have no"—he fished for the word—"stamina."

Zetta intervened. "Ann Leigh is volunteering to work in the canteen again, as a memorial to Vern. Isn't that commendable?"

Travis seemed not to hear. "Such a terrible waste," he said. "The South lost a whole generation, you know. It hasn't recovered to this day. After Sharpsburg, we stacked the bodies along the fence rows for the death wagons to pick up. We carried them out of the fields, the creeks . . ."

His eyes glazed. He was lost for a moment in the memory.

"Papa, you're growing tired," Zetta said. "We'll leave you to rest for a while."

"No," Travis said, stirring. "I'm fine." He turned his gaze on Ann Leigh. "Have you ever listened to the wind in the trees?"

"Yes. I love the sound," she said.

"They know about the hawk," Travis said. "They'll tell you, if you'll listen. The Indians knew all about these things. Have you studied Latin and Greek?"

"Papa," Zetta interrupted. "Ann Leigh just dropped by to say hello. We mustn't impose."

Again Travis Spurlock's expressive eyes showed puzzlement. "Of course," he said. He rose from his chair with great dignity and took her hand. "You must come again when we can talk."

Zetta walked her the length of the hall and apologized. "Vern's death seems to have affected his mind. Sometimes all he says doesn't make sense."

Ann Leigh could not resist a word in his defense. "Maybe it makes sense to him."

"Perhaps," Zetta said.

The strange visit bothered Ann Leigh. That night she searched through her Latin and Greek textbooks. She felt that somewhere in the writings of Plato, Epicurus, Euclid, Cicero, or Catullus she would find a magic phrase concerning wind, hawks, and death.

She fell asleep amidst Juvenal.

Ann Leigh's life returned to routine so quickly that soon her time with Vern seemed only a magical dream. With the familiar burden of her classes and long nights at the canteen, it seemed only natural when Lester again appeared on the scene. He seemed older, more mature, and he helped to restore her sense of reality.

When he again proposed, Ann Leigh accepted, feeling that order had returned to her life.

After the ceremony, Ann Leigh and Lester departed for a week-long honeymoon in New Orleans.

Lester said he could not spare more time.

He had to get back to his war contracts.

Vern's body at last was returned and buried with military honors. Travis embraced old friends and endured their platitudes. Zetta guided him through the ordeal, often treating him as a child. He did not object, for he no longer felt in control of his life.

He had only one vivid moment. After they returned to Bluebonnet from the cemetery, he saw Clay moving about the house and thought of the day at the Fort Worth Club when Clay admitted helping Vern leave to enlist.

"You killed him," he told Clay as the family and well-wishers stood in shocked silence. "If you had come to me, I could have talked him out of going off to war. But you don't care about anybody. I never want to lay eyes on you again."

Clay turned and left the room without answering.

During the weeks that followed, Travis's numbness faded. He was overwhelmed by anguish.

Occasionally he was able to see his entire life with startling clarity. At other times his memory seemed to blur. In his more lucid intervals, he was frightened by the inconsistency of his mind. Distinctions between Reva and Jeanette tended to fuse, until he no longer could trust memory. He forgot which son was dead and grieved for all three. His daughter assumed the role of his mother. Often when he awoke in the morning he lay motionless, scarcely breathing, attempting to put his existence into time and place. Sometimes he dressed and left the house for urgent appointments, only to stop in the street in complete bafflement, suddenly aware that he was on his way to a meeting that had taken place decades before.

In time he came to view life as a tragedy.

He worried over his dwindling fortune. He no longer had income from his law office, his real estate. Fortunately, Durwood came to see him often. Durwood talked familiarly of the huge sums of money he handled at the bank, and offered to make lucrative investments for Travis. Relieved of the burden, Travis signed over his final railroad stocks, his few remaining pieces of real estate in the acre.

Durwood confided that soon Travis would have his first grandchild. Somehow, that knowledge helped to ease the pain of Vern's death.

Travis wandered through his days like a sleepwalker, lost in his erratic reveries. Often he strolled downtown, stood on the streetcorners, looked at the city, and remembered the men who had helped him build it. He thought of Otto Kretchmeir, Captain Tackett, John Peter Smith, and the others so free with their generosity in aiding an impoverished orphan of war. In his mind he frequently retraced that long-ago journey of a boy, walking westward from Dallas into his own future. He remembered the hawk and the rabbit, and his resolution.

Now, weary with years, he felt more like the rabbit.

After the papers were signed and notarized, Clay revealed to Pete that he had leased mineral rights on twenty-five hundred acres south of Ranger, near Hog Town.

"You dumb shithead! Every oil company in the country has given up on that old seep."

Clay refused to back down. "You've always said you can feel oil. Well, I can feel it along that creek. I *know* it's there."

"It was probably something you ate. Hell, Texas Pacific has drilled test wells all over down there."

"They didn't go deep enough," Clay said. "If you don't want a piece of it, let's call it my play."

Pete considered the matter before answering. "No, we can share our mistakes too." He looked up at the derrick over their new well. "This sure as shit looks like one."

They had completed two more low-production wells, testing out somewhere between fifty and eighty barrels a day. The fourth had been nothing but trouble. With most of the string lowered, the draw works had parted, creating a mess that required days to fix. Not a week later they lost a bit in the hole and were shut down several days on the fishing job.

Today they had lost circulation. Some subterranean cavern or porous formation was swallowing the drilling mud as fast as they could pump it into the well.

"I've a good mind to send down some fucking concrete," Pete said.

Running more casing, they managed to solve the problem late the next day.

Clay was disgusted by the delays. He cornered Pete in the tool shed. "We're wasting our time here, busting a gut for nothing. Look in the *Star-Telegram*. Wildcat wells are being completed all over West Texas. People are making money right and left while we're sitting here drilling fifty-barrel wonders."

"A lot of people are losing their asses, too," Pete said. "You only see headlines about the wildcats that hit. You have to look in the agate type to find the poor sons of bitches that went broke."

"There's new play up by Iowa Park."

"Nothing big. Keep your shirt on. There's some boom times coming one of these days."

"When we complete this one, I think we ought to move."

Pete held his hands out to the fire and did not answer for several minutes. "Clay, we're making money. We're building a stake. With another well, we'll have enough established reserve to talk Texas Pacific into running a pipeline down here. Then maybe we can sell out. But if you want out now, maybe we better think about it."

"I don't want out," Clay said. "I want *in*."

During the next few days Clay attempted to work out his frustrations on the well. He drove the men, bursting into profanity over each mistake, every delay.

Finally Pete interceded. "I've had it with you, Clay. If things go on like this, someone's going to crown you with a pipe wrench. Why don't you take a few days off and cool off a little? Then we'll talk and see where we stand."

Clay stalked away without answering.

He got into his car and roared off through the mesquite toward the distant road.

26

Ann Leigh tried to catch Lester's eye. The band was playing "La Golondrina" and she wanted to dance. Lester sat across the table, talking business with two other men from the plant. She had heard the same discussion many times and was sick of it. Lester and his friends were convinced that President Wilson was taking the nation into the war. Already the draft had started. The army was expanding, placing more orders for tinned beef every day. Lester and his colleagues were debating whether to buy new equipment to meet the increased demand.

Light-headed from the wine, Ann Leigh turned and glanced over the ballroom. Lester and his fellow executives seemed to be the only men in sight talking business.

"Care to dance?" said a voice at her elbow.

She glanced up. Lawyer Binkley Carothers had spotted her distress and was being gentlemanly.

Binkley escorted her onto the crowded floor. He was a smooth dancer, if a trifle stiff in his movements. "How do you like married life?" he asked in her ear.

"Lester is married to a packing plant," she said, and regretted it instantly. The wine had lowered her guard. She could not think of a quick way to recover.

Carothers hesitated before he found a suitable reply. "The war work is catching up with everyone."

"And we're not even into it yet," Ann Leigh said, grateful for the opening. "What will it be like when the war really starts?"

"There'll be a lot of changes," Binkley agreed.

Ann Leigh was tempted to say she would welcome almost anything to break the monotony of her life.

She had been married less than two months. And as Katherine Anne had predicted, already she was bored.

Again she told herself she should be happy. Usually Lester was attentive and considerate. She had every comfort. Lester was well established. She had prestige, a fine home.

The band brought "La Golondrina" to a close. Binkley escorted her toward her table. As they left the dance floor, she felt an annoying stare upon her. She glanced in that direction.

Her knees seemed to turn to water. She feared for a moment that she would faint. The man staring at her strongly resembled Vern. His face remained expressionless as he continued to stare at her.

Shaken, she thanked Binkley. She attempted to concentrate on the conversation at her end of the table. The women were discussing their problems with their dressmakers. Cautiously, Ann Leigh allowed her gaze to sweep across the ballroom.

The man was still looking at her.

The resemblance was uncanny. He was larger than Vern. His features were more pronounced—almost as if he were an older, more mature version.

With that thought, she realized who he was. Although she had never met Clayton Spurlock, Vern had often talked about him, and she had seen him once, riding by in a car. Now he seemed leaner, more weathered than she remembered from that brief glimpse.

She turned back to her table and tried to ignore him. It was natural that he would be curious about her.

The topic at the table shifted to the current Broadway plays. She became engrossed and for the next few minutes forgot about Clay Spurlock. She was startled when he appeared beside her chair.

"Mrs. Wilson, may I have the pleasure of this dance?"

At close range the resemblance was even more unsettling.

Ann Leigh hesitated. She glanced at Lester. She was surprised by the anger in his eyes.

Clay was looking at Lester. "With your permission," he said.

"Of course," Lester said, unsmiling.

Ann Leigh walked ahead of Clay to the dance floor. She had never felt so uncertain of herself.

The band was playing "Let Me Call You Sweetheart." Clay danced smoothly, effortlessly, holding her at a discreet distance. "Vern always appreciated the finer things in life," he said softly. "But in your case he outdid himself."

His voice, so reminiscent of Vern's, sent a chill through her body. She felt goose bumps. "Please, let's don't talk of Vern," she managed to say. "It upsets me."

Clay held her at arm's length and looked at her. He gestured with his head toward Lester. "You seem to have recovered quickly enough."

Ann Leigh almost slapped him before regaining control. She pushed away from him and stopped dancing. "Take me back to my table," she said quietly, her voice trembling.

Clay stood looking at her, as if confronted by a piece of machinery he did not understand. Ann Leigh turned and walked alone through the dancing couples.

Lester had been watching. As she approached, he walked the length of the table to pull out her chair. "What happened?"

Ann Leigh knew Lester's temper. She did not want to cause a scene. "Nothing," she said. "I just didn't like his attitude."

"He make a pass at you?"

"No. Nothing like that."

Their friends were watching, aware that an incident had occurred. Lester returned to his chair.

When Ann Leigh checked a few minutes later, Clay was sitting alone at a distant table, watching her.

Throughout the evening she felt his gaze on her. On her way to and from the dance floor, she casually glanced in his direction, careful never to offer him a challenge. His eyes never wavered.

Acutely conscious of the awkward situation, she tried to divert Lester's attention. But he noticed. "I've a damned good notion to go over there and ask him what he's staring at," he said.

Ann Leigh placed her hand on his arm. "Please, Lester. The best thing we can do is ignore him."

Toward midnight, when she saw that he had gone, her relief was strangely intermingled with disappointment.

The following Monday morning she was passing through the hall when the phone rang. Her downstairs maid was sweeping in the pantry. Ann Leigh picked up the phone.

"Mrs. Wilson, this is Clayton Spurlock. Please don't hang up."

Ann Leigh hesitated. She did not intend to condone his rudeness. "Mr. Spurlock, I've nothing to say to you."

"The point is, I have something to say to you. I want to apologize for my behavior, and to explain, if I may."

Ann Leigh waited in silence. When he spoke, she was reminded of the celebrated eloquence of his father.

"You see, I haven't recovered from the shock of Vern's death. As you probably know, we were very close. When I saw you, it was through Vern's eyes—searching for the things he saw in you. I found them. I was jealous that, through circumstances, you were lost to Vern, to us, that I was denied knowing you as a sister, perhaps a good friend. I also resented that you've succeeded where I've failed—in adjusting. I had no right to

make judgments. Vern would have wished you to go on, make a life for
yourself. I know that. So I apologize."

His voice conveyed complete sincerity. Ann Leigh was totally disarmed. She certainly wanted no lingering ill feelings where Vern and his
family were concerned.

"Your apology is accepted," she said.

"I'm glad. Perhaps we shall see each other again, under more pleasant circumstances."

He hung up before she could reply. She lowered the telephone to its
stand with a bewildering mixture of emotions—relief, curiosity, satisfaction. Overriding all was a lingering hint of excitement.

She decided that she would not mention Clay's telephone call to
Lester.

The following Friday, trying on hats in Meacham's, she had narrowed the choice to two, and was deep in a quandary when a male voice
spoke behind her.

"Take the blue one. It matches your eyes."

Ann Leigh glanced in the mirror, annoyed. Clay stood a few feet
away. He was carrying an armload of packages. She handed the hat to the
salesclerk. "I'll take it," she said.

She turned to Clay. "As it happened, I had decided, anyway, because
it goes with a dress, not my eyes."

"The blue dress with white trim," Clay said with obvious approval.
"The one you wore to church last Sunday."

She did not know how to respond. She had not seen Clay Spurlock in
church.

"Look," Clay said abruptly. "I'm leaving for the oil fields. I was on my
way to treat myself to a big chocolate milk shake. I'm addicted to them.
My only vice. Would you join me?"

It was the sort of impulsive thing she had always liked to do. And she
did want to show Clay she held no animosity toward him. The drugstore
was near. No one could criticize her for a casual conversation with a man
in broad daylight. She accepted.

The drugstore was almost deserted in midafternoon. Ann Leigh
loved the bright, cool interior with its spicy smells, white tile floor, long
fountain, and heavy, mahogany breakfront. Clay escorted her to a white
marble-topped table in the rear of the store.

He pulled out a chair for her and stacked his packages on another.
He ordered, then smiled at her. "How are things in Niles City?"

It was a good-natured gibe. The owners and managers of the packing
plants had incorporated their own municipality to remove themselves
from Fort Worth jurisdiction and taxation. Niles City claimed to be the
richest little town in America.

"Dull," she said, more truthful than she had intended.

He studied her for a moment, apparently lost in thought. "We'll probably have more excitement around here than we can handle before long."

"The war?" Ann Leigh asked. She was tired of talk about the coming war.

"Partly," he said. "But this country would boom, even without the war. You see, everyone will soon have his own car. Every car will need gas and oil, roads and bridges. When people start motoring around the country, they'll go where the trains don't. We'll need more hotels, restaurants, gasoline stations. The cars will break down. Every little town will need mechanics. Someday, automobiles will have a far greater influence on this country's economy than agriculture."

Again Ann Leigh was struck by how articulate he was. Clearly he had inherited his father's silver tongue. Not even Vern had been so glib. Watching him in his unguarded moments, Ann Leigh was confirmed in her first impression of him as an older, more mature version of Vern.

"Then why don't you go into the automobile business?" she asked, half teasing, as she often had with Vern.

He grinned. "Not as much fun. Searching for oil is the ultimate gamble. You back your luck with your money and unbelievable hard work. It's big win or big lose. There's no in-between."

Casually, effortlessly, he began talking. He described his theory of a vast pool of oil, stretching from eastern Kansas down through Oklahoma and deep into Texas. Ann Leigh was entranced.

Prompted by her questions, he explained the emerging science of petroleum geology. He talked long after they had finished with their milk shakes.

The chimes of the drugstore clock brought her out of her trance. "Oh, goodness, I must go. I was due home an hour ago."

Clay rose and left a generous tip. "And I'm due in West Texas." He looked at her and grinned. "That oil has waited long enough."

Ann Leigh returned home feeling invigorated. It had been the type of discussion she had loved with Katherine Anne and her crowd, when talk might range over all kinds of fascinating subjects. Clay's depiction of the mysteries of the earth reminded her of the poetic side of Vern.

That evening she was tempted to tell Lester of her chance encounter with Clay. But the situation had grown too complicated. She would have to describe the incident on the dance floor, his telephone call of apology, and explain why she neglected to mention it. She did not have satisfactory answers.

During the following days the strange euphoria lingered. Images of

Clay's face, his hands, his smile, his expressive eyes intruded at the most unexpected times. And at night she dreamed about him.

One night Lester seemed unusually quiet at dinner. He did not reveal what was on his mind until the servants retired to the back portion of the house. "I heard that you talked with Clay Spurlock the other day," he said.

They were seated in the parlor, Lester with his after-dinner brandy and cigar, Ann Leigh with Booth Tarkington's new novel, *Penrod.* Seated beside the reading lamp, she felt exposed and vulnerable. She wondered who had seen them and placed enough importance on it to tell Lester. She spoke calmly.

"Yes, I met him while I was out shopping. He bought me a milk shake."

Lester was watching her closely. Ann Leigh knew he was thinking of the abrupt way she had broken their engagement for Vern.

"I thought you didn't like his attitude."

Ann Leigh felt her face grow warm. "He apologized most sincerely and earnestly. I accepted his apology. The milk shake was a peacemaking gesture, I suppose."

Lester sipped his brandy and did not answer. Ann Leigh wondered if she had explained too profusely.

"I think it would be better if you didn't see him anymore."

Ann Leigh fought down anger. "Why?"

For a moment she thought Lester was not going to answer. "He has something of a reputation as a womanizer," he said reluctantly. "As far back as high school there was talk about his affair with a much older woman. He was a drinker and a brawler, even then. He was always getting into fistfights."

Ann Leigh felt she should offer at least one line of defense, for herself as well as Clay. "Perhaps he has reformed. He seemed sober enough the other day."

Lester regarded her solemnly. "I've made my feelings plain concerning the Spurlocks. Do as you wish."

The subject was not mentioned again. But Ann Leigh's preoccupation with Clay continued through the last days of the year.

On New Year's Eve they were to attend a dance with the Duboses and the Thompsons. As the time for departure approached, Ann Leigh had trouble dressing. Her hair would not conform to the upsweep wrap she had envisioned. Disgusted, she decided at the last minute to wear it down, gathered in a jade barrette. Then she discovered that she had mislaid the matching belt to her gown. She spent several minutes hunting before she found it on the back of the closet door. Because of her delays, they arrived forty-five minutes late to pick up their guests. At the club, the maître d' had already relinquished their reservations. Lester called the manager and angry words were exchanged. The manager cited the rules but condescended to seat them in a corner remote from the bandstand.

Lester began drinking heavily. "It's your fault," he told her in front of their guests. "Why can't you ever be on time for anything?"

He said it in a joking way, but their guests recognized the viciousness. They discreetly looked elsewhere and ignored the remark. Ann Leigh felt miserable. When Dubose invited her to dance, she welcomed the chance to escape from the table.

The floor was jammed. Normal dancing was impossible. The couples merely went through the motions and attempted to keep from bumping into each other. The crowd was so noisy that she could hardly hear the orchestra. Conversation was impossible.

When she returned to the table, Lester and Thompson were telling dirty jokes. Blanche Thompson rolled her eyes at Ann Leigh and made a helpless gesture. Both Lester and Thompson were drunk. In defiance, Ann Leigh switched from gin and tonic to straight gin. Soon the noise, the shouted punch lines, the disastrous evening seemed to matter less and less.

Some time later Lester stood and grinned crookedly at her. "You girls entertain yourselves for a while. I'm taking the boys to the game room."

"Enjoy yourselves," Ann Leigh answered, more sarcastically than she intended. She had heard that Lester sometimes lost hundreds of dollars a night at craps.

A few minutes later she saw Clay Spurlock standing against the wall a few feet away, watching her. Apparently he had witnessed the whole sordid evening. She was not surprised when he approached her table.

"I believe I owe you a dance," he said close to her ear. "I hope you'll allow me to repay the obligation."

Ann Leigh hesitated. She remembered that Lester had warned her to stay away from Clay. But she also recalled the chance encounter, the enchanted hour in the drugstore, and the exhilaration that had lingered for days. She felt she should show Lester he could not pick her friends.

She walked with Clay to the dance floor. If he noticed that she was unsteady on her feet, he gave no sign. He held her close in a firm embrace, guiding her through the milling throng. She could hear the beat of the orchestra, but not until they had danced several minutes did she recognize the most popular current tune, "Keep the Home Fires Burning."

In his arms, Ann Leigh felt safe, contented. She knew she was half pie-eyed, and surrendered to a delicious wave of wantonness. She buried her cheek against his shoulder. His chin rested gently on her hair. They danced smoothly, effortlessly, their bodies melded into one. Ann Leigh forgot Lester, her guests. Nothing else in the world seemed to matter.

The floor became even more crowded. After they were bumped repeatedly by other couples, Clay broke their embrace and took her by the hand. "Come on. Let's get away from this."

He led her toward the large hall just beyond the ballroom. Ann Leigh had no idea where he was taking her, nor cared.

With a glance in each direction he pulled her into a window niche. Now curtained, the recessed windows offered a view of the street. Clay drew her close, tilted her chin, and kissed her, his large, gentle hands caressing her familiarly and knowledgeably. Ann Leigh melted against him, seeking her own pleasures in the comfort of his strong arms, his kisses. At that moment he seemed to be Vern, yet more than Vern. She felt helpless. Their unspoken tryst seemed preordained, and beyond her control.

Hidden from the hall by the drapes, shielded from all but the most inquisitive passer-by, they remained lost to the world for an interminable length of time.

At last Clay raised his head and looked down at her. "I knew you were mine from the first moment I saw you. We've got to do something about this mistake."

"Mistake?" she asked, not comprehending.

"Your marriage. You don't belong with that simpleton. You belong with me."

Ann Leigh remained silent. Katherine Anne and Vern had warned her that she would be unhappy with Lester. They had been right. It was plain for all the world to see. She knew to the depth of her soul that what Clay said was true. She did not belong with that dull, dictatorial prig.

From the ballroom came a loud cacophony of hornblowing, shouting, and whistles.

"Oh my God! It's midnight!" Ann Leigh said.

Reality returned with a rush. She had been gone for hours. No doubt Lester had returned and was hunting for her. She had guests!

The orchestra was playing "Auld Lang Syne." The crowd had joined in, discordant, loud.

"I must get back," she said.

Clay still held her. "What about us?"

Ann Leigh shook her head. "I don't know. It's impossible."

"It's not only possible," Clay said quietly. "It was meant to be."

Ann Leigh pushed away. "Give me time to think. I must get back!"

"All right," Clay said. "But I'll call you."

Ann Leigh knew she did not have time to argue.

They left the high-arched niche and hurried down the hall toward the ballroom. Ann Leigh attempted to smooth her hair, straighten her dress. She knew that her lips were swollen, her lipstick smeared. But she was more worried over being gone so long.

They entered the ballroom just as "Auld Lang Syne" ended. Another din of shouting and hornblowing erupted. The noise was just dying away when Lester came toward them from out of the crowd. His face was twisted with fury. He grabbed her by the arm, almost jerking her from her feet. "Look at you!" he shouted. "You look like the whore you are!"

Clay put a hand on Lester's chest and shoved, sending him backward several steps. "Keep your pansy hands off of her!"

Lester turned to face Clay. "You son of a bitch," he shouted. "I told you to stay away from my wife!"

"You're not man enough to make me," Clay said quietly.

Horrified, Ann Leigh watched as Lester and Clay closed the distance between them.

With shouts and screams, the crowd fell back, giving them room.

Lester missed Clay with his first swing. Taller and heavier, he almost succeeded in knocking Clay over as they collided. While Clay was off balance, Lester connected with two blows. Clay backed away, laughing, his mouth bloody from a smashed lip.

Lester stalked him. Clay ducked and weaved, still laughing as if he were having the time of his life. Lester lowered his head and charged. He landed a blow on the side of Clay's head. Clay hit Lester twice in the face. Blood sprayed through the air from Lester's smashed nose. Again, the crowd retreated.

"Stop them!" Ann Leigh pleaded.

No one would listen.

Clay advanced, dodging Lester's wild swings, and struck Lester's face time after time with the sickening sound of a meat-ax. Lester grappled, and caught Clay's head in the crook of his elbow. Twisting, he swung Clay in a circle and slammed him onto the hardwood dance floor. Clay rolled and jumped to his feet, still laughing.

Helpless, Ann Leigh watched them circle each other cautiously. Clay feinted with his left hand, then punched with his right. Lester reeled backward. Clay followed, hammering at him furiously with both fists. Something skittered across the polished floor. Ann Leigh realized it was a broken tooth.

"Clay! Stop it!" she yelled.

Lester dropped to his knees. The crowd grew quiet. With deliberate precision, Clay struck Lester on the side of the head and knocked him sprawling. Lester did not move.

Clay stood over him. "Come on, big man. Get up!" He prodded Lester's ribs with the toe of his shoe.

Dubose stepped out of the crowd. "Clay, don't you think you've proved your point?"

Clay grinned. Blood dripped from his chin to the front of his white shirt. "I suppose so," he said. He looked at the silent crowd. "Happy New Year, everybody!"

No one answered.

On the floor, Lester stirred. Dubose knelt and helped him sit up. Lester's eyes were open, but dazed. Dark bruises and crimson cuts covered his face. His nose and mouth were smeared with blood.

Ann Leigh stood frozen. Lester needed her. But she could not set aside the fact that he had just called her a whore in front of half of Fort Worth society. She was not inclined to go to him.

Clay was studying her. He seemed to know her thoughts. Calmly he came to her and took her by the wrist. "Come on," he said. "You belong with me."

Not until they were in Clay's car, on the road to Dallas, did she fully realize the enormity of what she had done.

Virtually every affluent person in Fort Worth had seen her leave with the man who had beaten her husband senseless.

The uproar would be of monstrous proportions.

"What will happen now?" she asked.

Clay was leaning forward over the wheel, straining to see beyond the reach of the headlights as they sped down the gravel road. He chuckled. "There'll be hell to pay. But you know something? As long as I've got you, I don't especially give a damn."

Exhausted, Ann Leigh went to sleep with her head against his shoulder. She did not awake until he carried her into a small hotel on the outskirts of Dallas.

"There's a warrant out for your arrest," Binkley Carothers said. "Assault and battery, intent to do bodily harm, and every legal way you can think of to say wife stealing. They're not exactly shy on witnesses. They have a dentist working up some charts to show the full extent of Lester's new bridgework. It must be fairly complicated. Also, there's the little matter of alienation of affections. They really dusted off some old law books on that one. I have it on good authority that Lester has been closeted with his attorneys for the last three days."

Clay went to Binkley's liquor cabinet and helped himself to another Scotch and soda. "Bink, what kind of a lawyer are you if you can't get me out of a pissant little thing like this?"

Binkley snorted. "Hell, they may subpoena *me!* I saw the whole goddamn thing." He rocked back in his chair and put his boots on his desktop. "And you better not be rousting me. I may be the only friend you've got right now."

Clay sprawled in the chair opposite Binkley's desk. "What can we do, friend?"

Binkley frowned and studied his glass of whiskey.

They were seated in Binkley's downtown office, the lights low, in case the police came snooping around. Outside, a January snowstorm had glazed the streets. Only an occasional car passed, wheels spinning.

"First, you'd better stay hid out another week or so, to be on the safe side. We'll give Lester a little more time to cool off before any confrontation. Keep Ann Leigh out of sight. Don't even tell *me* where she is. I don't want to know."

Clay nodded.

"We have a few things going for us," Binkley went on, meditating aloud. "First, I doubt Lester wants her back. He'd be feeling better about it if you'd just taken out your Barlow and cut his nuts off, right there in public. That's the sticky part. A man that's been ridiculed before the whole town is difficult to deal with. Lester's too civilized for his own good. Most of the men I know would've taken a shotgun and blown your head off."

"What exactly does he want?"

"Something you can't give him. Self-respect. But in lieu of that, he might settle for cash. How much, I don't know. Let's let the matter simmer down a bit. Then I'll talk with his attorneys and see if we can't arrive at some understanding. It'll help if we can make Lester see that if we go to court, he'll come out looking like an even bigger lump of shit."

"Should Ann Leigh file for divorce now?"

"Hell no! We've got to take care of the actions against you first. I imagine Lester will be inclined to let the both of you sweat for a while. In fact, it'd be better to wait until he thinks you don't give a damn and the divorce is his idea."

Clay did not answer. Ann Leigh would be inconsolable. She did not feel she could return to Fort Worth until she had obtained her divorce and was free to marry. She even refused to leave her Dallas hotel room for fear she might encounter someone she knew.

"Push for the divorce," Clay said. "I don't care if it costs a bundle."

Binkley's eyebrows raised. "I didn't know you had a bundle."

"I don't," Clay said. "But I know where I can get it."

In the face of serious scandal Fort Worth society tended to close ranks. Although Ann Leigh's conduct was generally deplored from the parlors on Silk Stocking Row to the bar at the Fort Worth Club and afternoon teas throughout town, the subject was carefully screened from servants and employees. Not a hint of the matter appeared in the newspapers. Whatever their shortcomings, the Spurlocks were among the bedrock of Fort Worth society. Travis Spurlock's accomplishments were beyond question. Zetta's contributions to Fort Worth culture were generally acknowledged. The fact that the Spurlocks once owned whorehouses, saloons, and gambling halls was irrelevant. The closets of several first families housed similar skeletons. Many respected fortunes had been founded on such diversions as mavericked calves, a winning poker hand, land deals that fell amidst the cracks of law, or range rights established with guns. Membership in Fort Worth society was not acquired through impressive money or breeding but by horny-handed, shared experience. The key to membership was a mutual you-be-damned attitude instantly recognized among that closed enclave.

In truth Clay's escapades were related with chuckles of approval in some quarters. The scions of Fort Worth society were expected to be full of piss and vinegar.

The Wilsons simply did not belong, not because they were Midwest Yankees who had not been in Fort Worth much over a decade but because they lacked the taciturn traits, the native gift for hard-nosed understatement. Like most new arrivals the Wilsons were relegated to the Niles City fringes of social affairs. Little sympathy was wasted on Lester. While Ann Leigh's conduct was not condoned, the consensus was that she came from a "good ranching family" and thus should be protected from her own transgressions.

When Clay bought a two-story brick home for Ann Leigh in the new Forest Park section, the community approved, and watched and waited.

By late March another delicious bit of gossip was making the rounds.

Ann Leigh was pregnant.

Lester Wilson still refused to give her a divorce.

Neighbors reported that Clay spent little time in the house, occasionally arriving on a weekend, leaving late Sunday night. Ann Leigh never ventured out. A live-in maid did all the shopping. Ann Leigh's parents visited her twice, but the Spurlocks had yet to call.

In late June came the rumor that Clay and Lester had reached a settlement. For a large cash consideration—some said two hundred thousand, others said a quarter of a million—Lester agreed to drop all charges and to grant Ann Leigh an uncontested divorce.

A two-paragraph item in an early September issue of the *Star-Tele-*

gram confirmed that Clayton Spurlock and Ann Leigh Cawley Wilson had exchanged vows in a private ceremony.

Among the vital statistics carried in the October 16 issue of the *Star-Telegram* was the announcement of a son, Broderick Barclay Spurlock, born to Mr. and Mrs. Clayton B. Spurlock.

27

The baby had been cranky all morning. He had just drifted off to sleep when the phone rang. Ann Leigh hurried to answer it.

"Have you heard?" Katherine Anne asked. "It's finally happened."

"What?"

"We're at war. The *Star-Telegram* is already on the street with an extra."

After the months of waiting the news now seemed anticlimactic. President Wilson had armed the merchant fleet the month before, in the wake of the Zimmerman note offering Mexico a deal to side with Germany in a war against the United States.

Ann Leigh thought of Vern, and his conviction that the United States eventually would enter the war. His death now seemed so long ago. So much had happened in the sixteen months since that terrible night at the New Year's ball. Sometimes Ann Leigh felt she was a different person entirely.

"Well, that sure makes my news small potatoes," she said. "I'm pregnant again."

The line was silent a moment. "Are you glad?"

"Do I have a choice?"

They both laughed.

"I suppose I'm pleased," Ann Leigh said, thinking aloud. "Before, I couldn't work up much enthusiasm until he arrived. Then it seemed like the greatest thing that ever happened. Maybe that's the way it is."

"When will I get to meet this husband of yours, anyway?"

"God knows. He comes in without warning, completely exhausted, and sleeps like a log for twelve hours. We have a few hours together and then he's gone."

"You sound happy, though."

"I am. I wish Clay were home more. But he seems to be enjoying what he's doing."

Katherine Anne said she had to go, that she wanted to be sure Ann Leigh had heard the news.

After they rang off, Ann Leigh again went to check on the baby, wondering what made everyone so eager to say that they were happy.

Actually, except for the few brief hours when Clay was home, she was miserable.

Her parents and her aunt had been devastated by her bizarre behavior. She eventually managed to convince them that although she had acted impulsively some measure of logic was involved. They did not like Clay. They knew his reputation and considered his oil prospecting marginal. Aunt Polly had even hinted that his continual absence proved he did not love her.

But her family had been less of a problem than the Spurlocks. Thus far none of them had expressed interest in seeing Ann Leigh or the baby. Clay would not talk about it. He seemed to take their attitude as a matter of course.

Travis, in his confused mind, apparently considered her a fallen woman and the baby illegitimate. Zetta's opinion apparently had not been much better. Word had reached Ann Leigh that Zetta had called their marriage disgraceful.

Reva had sent the baby a silver spoon, without an accompanying note.

Ann Leigh still had not penetrated Clay's mystery, and she now doubted that she ever would. His abrupt changes of mood often frightened her. One moment he could be outgoing, charming, considerate, and in the next withdraw into a brooding silence that might last for hours.

He seemed driven by an ambition that exceeded all human reason. He talked little of his hopes, his fears. She only knew that he and his partner had completed five marginal wells in Stephens County and were drilling test wells farther westward.

The condemnation of their marriage by the community—and that she had become a virtual recluse—did not seem to concern him in the least.

The first months of the war brought swift changes Ann Leigh could see and hear without leaving the house. The U.S. Army assumed command of the three Canadian airfields on the fringes of town. U.S. fliers soon joined the Canadians in training. The drone of aircraft became almost constant.

In June plans were announced for a huge army training camp across the Trinity, immediately west of town. Trucks groaned through the streets night and day, building Camp Bowie. Acres of barracks rose within sight of Ann Leigh's upstairs bedroom.

In July thirty thousand troops arrived to begin training. As she sat in the back yard reading on summer afternoons, with Brod sunning on his pallet nearby, she plainly could hear the shouted commands and bugle calls, the sound of marching men. Often she heard the dull boom of artillery on the firing range farther to the west.

As the birth of the new baby grew near in late September, Ann Leigh reluctantly sent for her mother.

In many ways she had grown accustomed to the lonely tranquillity of her life and did not wish it disrupted.

But the interruption would not be denied.

He was born just after midnight on September 28, and named Loren Malvern Spurlock.

Clay was on the rotary platform, stabbing pipe. "Lookee yonder!" the derrickman yelled from the top of the rig. "Somebody's really helling it."

In the distance a car came at breakneck speed, trailing a large spume of dust. Clay's first thought was that the driver was drunk. No one in his right mind drove that fast on a gravel road.

"It's Pete!" the derrickman yelled.

As the driver slowed for the turnoff, Clay recognized Pete's 1915 Cadillac. The car skidded almost completely around at the gate, then came bouncing over the rough trail through the cactus and mesquite. Pete pounded the horn in a constant tattoo. The car cleared the ground on the larger bumps.

"Has the son of a bitch gone crazy?" Koon asked.

Clay jumped off the rig and walked down to meet him. Pete came out of the car with a string of cowboy yells. He danced a jig until he was out of breath. He grabbed Clay by the shoulders.

"The McCleskey just blew in! Over the top of the derrick. What'd I tell you, Clay? I knew it was going to happen! Goddamn, this is it! *Ranger!* Who would've thought it'd be Ranger? Dry holes all over the fucking place."

Clay felt a shiver run up his spine. Every oilman dreamed of another Spindletop. "How big is it?"

"Seventeen hundred barrels if it's a drop. It's still blowing wild. Come on, partner. We've got to get moving. Just about every oilman in six states is on his way to Ranger right this minute."

The well was not of monstrous size, but Clay understood Pete's excitement. Many oil speculators had been convinced for years that Eastland County had tremendous potential. But no one had found anything of significance.

Now their faith had been proved justified.

He followed Pete into the tool shed. They spread a map on the workbench and consulted their notes on the activity around Ranger. The Texas Pacific Coal Company had drilled to thirty-four hundred feet at the Nannie Walker test well on the northern edge of town before losing a bit in spewing gas. Unable to retrieve it, they had abandoned the hole and spudded in another two miles southwest.

That was the McCleskey discovery well.

"What's the formation?" Clay asked.

"Our man says they hit black limestone just below thirty-four hundred. He figures that's the pay formation. But nobody knows for sure. It came in before any coring or bailing was done."

"They may have been close to production on the Nannie Walker. My notes say they went to thirty-four hundred on it."

"It's still spewing gas. Could be coming from the same formation."

Clay was still studying his map. "Damn, Texas Pacific's just about got all that country sewed up."

"That's why we've got to move fast. I've already located two more rigs and most of the equipment. But I'm not putting my trust in old friendships. If some son of a bitch comes along and offers twice as much, we're out in the cold unless I'm right there to take delivery. Clay, you get down to Ranger and buy every lease in sight. At this point we can't lose money on it. Prices will double, triple in a week. Take my word for it. Ranger's going to be one hell of a crap shoot."

Clay pointed to his map. "I'll try to lease to the north and west of town. I think the Nannie Walker site proves the zone."

"Good a guess as any. What I want to impress on you is what it'll be like. I was at Cushing, Drumright, and Healdton. But this may be the granddaddy of them all. There'll be two thousand oilmen in Ranger within a week, five thousand within a month, and by that time they'll be charging fifty dollars for a place to shit. The time to get anything done is right now. Most boom towns are as lawless as the jungle. You can get murdered for your boots. I'm not kidding. I've seen it happen."

Quickly they made plans. While Clay drove to Ranger to buy leases, Pete would go to Wichita Falls and start the rigs and equipment moving toward Ranger as soon as possible. Koon would stay and finish the uncompleted well.

Pete trotted back to his car and roared off. Clay lingered only long enough to change out of his work clothes.

Four hours later Clay drove into Ranger. He remembered it as a sleepy little town of less than a thousand people. But he saw that the pace already had quickened. The streets were jammed with cars, trucks, and wagons. Half the men hurrying along the sidewalks wore the telltale boots of oilmen.

He found a place to park and sat in the car for a few minutes, fighting a rising panic. He was on the ground floor, with at least a twenty-four hour head start on most of the oilmen in the country.

He did not know which way to turn, and sunset was only minutes away.

He pulled out his map. A large portion around Ranger was shaded red—land already acquired by Texas Pacific. He selected several choice locations, based on the two-mile interval between the McCleskey and the Nannie Walker.

He then folded his map, stuck it in his pocket, and left the car. He walked along the sidewalk, dodging the pedestrian traffic.

He found a hardware store and introduced himself to the owner. Explaining that he and his partner no doubt would be needing considerable hardware during the next few months, he asked the owner if he could tell him who owned the land he had chosen and if it were leased.

"I can tell you who owns it," the man said. "I don't know anything about the leases."

Clay penciled in the names of the landowners and asked who might be the most receptive to leasing.

"I can't help you there," the man said. "But I can give you a tip. People around here go to bed with the chickens. You won't do any good out there tonight. Best thing would be to get out before daylight. That's when you'll catch most of them."

Clay thanked him and walked on up the street. Lines of men waited outside Ranger's two restaurants. Clay decided he could go hungry. The first thing he needed was sleep. With Pete on the road he had pulled a double tour, working sixteen hours straight. He had not slept for twenty-four.

The only hotel in town was a large residence, converted into a commercial house for visiting drummers. Clay went in and asked for a room.

"You're in luck," said the landlady. "A fellow just checked out not five minutes ago. Said he won't be back till Friday."

Clay paid, and quickly learned that the term "room" was a misnomer. Fresh beaverboard and a two-by-four framework had converted each small room into three sections, each with barely enough space for a cot.

Too tired to argue, he lay down in his clothes and dropped into a deep sleep.

He was awakened after midnight by low voices on the other side of the thin partition. Lying quietly, Clay gathered from the talk that the three men had just arrived and were assimilating secret information obtained from their scouts in Ranger.

"There's no doubt about it," a deep bass voice rumbled softly. "The McCleskey formation goes north and west. Too many shallow wells have found the same, consistent overstructure, here, here, and here. I say we ought to get out first thing in the morning and sew up this area right here. It's still up for grabs."

Clay lay wide awake. What the man said made sense and confirmed his own thinking. If shallow dry holes had encountered the same layers of strata as the McCleskey discovery to a depth of fifteen hundred or two thousand feet, then odds were good that they simply had not drilled deep enough.

But his theory was only guesswork.

These men seemed to have the facts.

The information could have come only from drillers, or someone intimately acquainted with the details of each dry hole.

"Let's divide up the work," said a man with a thin, high voice. "It'll go a lot quicker."

Clay heard the rustle of paper. He fished in his pocket, found a pencil stub, and retrieved his checkbook from his coat pocket. Moving to a tiny portion of the window left to him by the partition, he shoved back the curtain and was rewarded by a sliver of moonlight. As the men in the next room divided their work, Clay made notes.

Their scouting had been thorough. Clay wondered how much the information had cost them. They had the complete legal description of each parcel, the name of the owner, and the directions to the homestead.

Clay scribbled frantically, erratically, in the near darkness. But as the men doublechecked their lists aloud, he went back over his notes in the moonlight and found them accurate.

The men continued to talk for more than an hour, discussing the rigs and machinery they were bringing in and the difficulties of transportation to Ranger. At last they said good night, and two left.

Clay waited patiently until he heard snores from the other side of the partition.

Taking care to make no sound, he slipped from his cot, dressed, picked up his boots, and tiptoed out of the room.

He pushed his car a half block down the street before starting the engine.

Well out from town, he examined his map in the car's headlights. Painstakingly he conveyed the information from his notes to the map.

Ten owners were listed, for a total of more than four thousand acres.

He parked on the road some distance from his first prospect. A few minutes after four thirty a lamp blossomed in the house. He waited until a man carrying a Coleman lantern walked toward the barn.

Clay found the farmer and two young sons milking. Within a half hour he had the man's signature and was on his way to the next stop.

By eleven o'clock he had placed the ten parcels under lease. He locked the papers in the bottom of the toolbox on the running board of his car and returned to Ranger. He was standing in line for breakfast when he heard the rumble of a deep bass voice among a group of men leaving the restaurant.

"Last goddamn time I'll wait in line. We can get some bacon and eggs at a grocery and cook out somewhere. We're getting a late start, and we've got a lot to get done today. There'll be a mob of people in here by tomorrow."

Clay did not turn to look.

He never learned the names of the men or who they represented.

Pete arrived the next morning. Clay drove him a few miles from town, stopped, and retrieved the papers from the bottom of the toolbox.

Pete was stunned by the scope of Clay's coup. He hurried through the stack of papers, checking them against the map. "God, Clay, this is one hell of a start! How'd you manage this in one day?"

Clay told what had happened in the hotel. "If those three guys find us, we may get our asses whipped."

Pete laughed. "Two rigs are on the way. We should have the other one down here within the month. We'd better pick some sites to spud in."

Thinking ahead to the inflated wages and high costs of drilling, Clay was worried about being overextended. "The McCleskey better prove out. If it's a fluke, we're flat broke again."

Pete pulled a whiskey bottle from beneath the seat and passed it to Clay. "Just think. This morning we're either millionaires or paupers. And we don't know which. What a crazy fucking business. Ain't it wonderful?"

Abandoned more than six months, the Nannie Walker test well on the northern outskirts of Ranger stirred in the predawn hours of New Year's Day, 1918. Burps and gurgles rumbled in subterranean formations more than three thousand feet below the wellhead. Then, with a tremendous roar that awakened the whole town, the Nannie Walker spewed rocks, dirt, and millions of cubic feet of natural gas high into the air.

By midmorning the blowout showed no signs of abating. Clay and Pete stood braced against the icy wind, assessing the importance of the well's impromptu performance. A large crowd stood at a respectful distance, retreating each time a shower of rock and gravel clattered against the wooden derrick. Acrid fumes hung heavily in the air.

"This puts the frosting on the cake," Pete said. "If anybody had any doubts, they're gone. Texas Pacific may never get a nickel out of this well, but it'll make Ranger the biggest boom town that's ever been."

"It proves the black limestone runs from the McCleskey this far north and east," Clay said. "I think we ought to spud in as close to that line as we can get."

"Sounds reasonable," Pete said. "Let's put two rigs in the York Survey, and one to the south and west."

"What about the Hog Town lease?" Clay asked. "Why don't we put one rig down there? That old seep may be coming from this same formation."

"Goddamn, Clay, that's eighteen, twenty miles away," Pete protested. "That's too big a gamble. This may be a narrow anticline trap, not a field. We just don't know enough yet."

"We're putting all our eggs in one basket here," Clay argued. "It's dumb to put three tests in one block. Besides, I promised that old man a test well within a year."

The issue was crucial. They had battled for six weeks to get the necessary equipment into Ranger. At first Pete had attempted to ship by rail. The Texas & Pacific was swamped. Switchmen and freight handlers expected hundred-dollar tips and guaranteed nothing. After the equipment sat idle on a siding in Fort Worth for ten days, Clay and Pete had loaded it onto six-mule-team freight wagons and set out on the seventy-mile haul to Ranger.

The trip had been a nightmare. The roads were either gumbo mud or frozen over with ice and snow. Mules died in harness and had to be replaced from whatever source could be found. Rural bridges collapsed under the weight of the equipment, causing delays, fines, threats of lawsuits. But they now had three rigs, boilers, pipe, and enough lumber for three derricks parked on a sidestreet under guard. If they moved fast, they would be among the first to spud into the Ranger field. They had good equipment. Pete believed in using only the best that could be obtained.

"I'll flip you for a rig," Clay said. "Just one. I'll take it on to Hog Town myself."

Pete considered the matter, frowning. "I guess it's the only way to shut you up." He reached into his pocket for a silver dollar. "Call it."

"Heads."

Pete flipped the coin high. It landed flat in the soft mud at their feet, showing tails. Clay felt a wave of disappointment, mingled with a vague sense of relief.

He was not totally confident of his intuition.

"Let's get cracking," Pete said.

They returned to Clay's Cadillac and drove toward the center of town, slipping and sliding through the mud, winding their way through the seething swarm of humanity walking out to see the runaway gasser.

In two months Ranger had grown from a population of less than a thousand to at least six thousand. More people arrived every day. Not all were oilmen. Speculators and fly-by-night operators stood on every streetcorner, peddling leases, shares, and stocks. Much of it was bogus. Tents and shacks had sprung up on the edges of town. Shanties of rough boards, sheet iron, tar paper, and flattened tin cans served as flophouses and restaurants. Gambling halls, whorehouses, and bars were far more plentiful than stores.

With his wheels spinning in the deep mud, Clay forced his way through the downtown section, circling around mired wagons and teams. The streets were bedlam. For twenty-five cents, husky men in hip boots carried passengers across the mire piggyback. Other pedestrians were ferried across in sleds or boats pulled by horses.

In the carnival atmosphere robberies were common, even in broad daylight. Most every morning bodies were found in alleys. The week before, five murders had been recorded in one day.

Clay and Pete reached the wagons, checked the load, rounded up the men, and began the trek out to the leases. They had found only skeleton crews, despite offers of bonuses. Wages had soared. Common mule skinners drew seven dollars a day, roughnecks fifteen. Experienced drillers and rig builders were almost beyond price.

Leaving Ranger, they joined a long train of freight wagons and groaning trucks on the way out to the new field. Some of the wagons, loaded with huge boilers, were pulled by teams of oxen. The churned road was impassable in some spots, forcing them to cut through fences and go across open country, paying the farmers and ranchers for the damage.

Two days later the equipment was in place. Clay and Pete each took charge of a well on the York Survey. They placed Koon to the southwest, bracketing their lease.

For Clay the following months took on the aura of a dream. With the shortage of experienced men he worked double tours wherever needed, sometimes spending long hours aloft as a derrickman, or stabbing pipe as a roughneck. He often slept only a few hours in the warmth of the boiler shed before returning to another double tour.

As the drill string bore deeper into the earth, the derrick trembling under the weight, Clay came to believe that he had divined the rhythm of the earth itself. At last he had found release for his restless energy, his insatiable sense of wonder. He often went without sleep to monitor the mysterious formations beneath his feet as drilling mud and test cores came up from the depths.

The pervasive atmosphere of excitement that hung over the Ranger field continued to grow. In mid-February the erratic Nannie Walker gasser emitted several thunderous belches, then gushed oil. It became a solid producer.

On the first day of March, the first McCleskey offset was brought in, laying any lingering doubts to rest. A few days later a Texas Pacific test well a mile and a half north of town blew in, flowing over the top of the derrick.

On a night in early April, Clay woke to thunder in the earth. By the time he reached the wellhead, gas was spewing up through the derrick, rattling the crown block. Clay and his crew quickly doused the boiler fires and backed away from the well. Hearing the ruckus, Pete drove over. He arrived just as the blowout settled into a steady roar.

They kept watch for hours, waiting to see if the stream of gas would turn into oil.

Unless it did, the well was worthless.

No market existed for gas.

At dawn Pete gave Clay a rueful smile. "Just think. Today we could've been millionaires. But let's face it. We may be broke."

"Broke, hell," Clay said. "We're so far in debt we'll never get out. We're in hock to our eyeballs."

"One down, two to go," Pete said. He walked to his car and returned to his own well.

Clay vented the gasser and allowed it to spew, on the remote chance it might switch to oil.

Pete's well approached the pay zone. For two days and nights Clay and Pete hovered over every sign brought to the surface.

On the third morning the bit drilled into the McCleskey black lime. Gas and sand roared to the surface. The drilling mud could not hold it.

For an agonizing five minutes, there was nothing but gas.

Then, abruptly, heavy green-black crude shot to the top of the derrick and rained down upon them.

Pete danced a jig in the shower of oil. Clay stood, emotionally spent, content that his dreams had been brought to reality.

They had extended the Ranger field by more than a mile, and their offset holdings probably were worth a fortune.

With a borrowed slip-scraper they built an earthen dam across a ravine to capture the oil until they could bring the well under control. A line of cars drove out from Ranger, and soon a crowd stood watching the gusher.

"Five thousand barrels a day, at least," Pete predicted. "Maybe seven."

In a choke test, they found it closer to ten.

Two nights later, Koon's well blew in.

They worked night and day for weeks, completing the wells and putting them into production, and skidding their rigs to new sites. For a time they freighted the oil into Ranger by wagon and team. After extended negotiations, Clay made a deal for the extension of Texas Pacific gathering lines, with arrangement for pass-through to tanks and rail tank cars in Ranger.

With the war raging in Europe, the price of oil soared to four dollars a barrel.

In late June they brought in three more producers, and the John York Survey was being touted as the "golden block" of the Ranger field. Derricks were springing up all around them.

One afternoon, when Pete returned from a trip into Ranger for some hardware, he motioned Clay aside.

"Never rains but it pours," he said. "Guess what. W. D. Cline and his partners brought in a gusher on the Fowler place on the north edge of Burkburnett. It's flowing twenty-two hundred barrels a day from a sand just below seventeen hundred feet. Know what that means?"

Clay had lost interest in the Wichita Falls area. No one had been able to extend the Electra field that far eastward.

"There's good production on the Knauth farm, a mile and a half southwest of Burk," Pete said. He looked at Clay. "You dumb shit, you don't know what that means yet, do you? It means Burkburnett is sitting right on top of the oil! Town lot leases! Biggest fucking poker game ever invented. And we're out of it!"

Clay gave Pete a long hard stare. "Okay, smartass, tell me. Why are we out of it?"

Pete hesitated, grasping what was in Clay's mind. "No! For God's sake, Clay. We can't get into it. Open your eyes! Texas Pacific, Prairie Oil, and the big boys here are drilling ten holes to our one. Unless we keep after it, they'll suck the oil right out from under us."

"We can leave Koonman in charge here."

Pete shook his head. "Koon's a good man. But the way things are, we've got to keep close supervision."

"Then *one* of us can go," Clay said. "Let's flip."

"What would we use for cash? We're still overextended. We won't see anything like big money for weeks, maybe months."

Clay remembered the banker in Wichita Falls, his suits stashed in a hotel. "I can borrow it. We've defined our pool here. The maps, leases, and production charts will show our assets."

Pete studied Clay for a long moment. "Goddamn, you really want to do it, don't you? You've made your pile, and you want to shoot the whole works all over again."

"Why not?"

Pete did not answer. He reached into the truck and pulled out a pint of whiskey. After a minute of thoughtful sipping, he passed the bottle to Clay. "I knew you had a screw loose the first time I ever saw you. Nothing I've seen since has convinced me otherwise. But I can't complain. I knew what I was letting myself in for. I guess my mama raised me to be an idiot. All right. You go on up there. You're much better at wheeling and dealing. I'll stay here and drill our offsets."

They made plans. Pete told him as much as he could remember about the formations in the Red River Uplift. He offered other advice.

"With town lot leases there'll be a well in every back yard. Don't buy leases for the future. They'll drain that pool dry in no time. With the play down here, rigs and equipment will be at a premium. Go up to Oklahoma. Some of those fields are playing out. You may have to make do with some old cable-and-tool outfits. They'll get you down to seventeen hundred feet without much trouble in that redlands shit."

Clay had been working all day, but his fatigue had disappeared. He went into the bunkhouse and returned with his bedroll.

Pete followed him out to his car. "You'd better sleep a few hours. Get a fresh start in the morning."

"I'm all right," Clay said. "If I start now, I can make it in there by night."

Clay climbed into the car, and they shook hands through the open window. "I'll make us another shitpot full," Clay said.

Pete did not smile. "Just stay out of jail," he said.

The Burkburnett boom was much like Ranger, but more frantic, and crammed into a few square blocks with no elbow room. In the first three weeks after Clay arrived, fifty-six wells were spudded in. The entire town became a forest of oil wells. Drilling was done in back yards, gardens, even through front porches. The derricks were so close together that workers often had to pass through walkways on several other rigs in order to reach their own. A boiler explosion on one well easily could injure workers on a half dozen crews.

Clay managed to obtain eight rigs. Two were rotary, but the other six were cable tool models of ancient vintage. Of the hundred and more producing oil wells completed in the first few months, eight were drilled by Spurlock and Pierson.

On a day in late September, Clay was attempting to fix a broken

Pittman on one of the old rigs when word arrived that Pete was trying to reach him by phone. Abandoning his project for the moment, he crossed the walkways to the street and hurried to his favorite blind tiger. After a few minutes of delay, he managed to get through to Pete on a moderately good connection.

"Heard about the Maples Oil discovery down at Hog Town?" Pete asked.

"Discovery hell," Clay said. "I've been trying to tell you there's oil down there for two goddamn years."

"Okay, so you were right. Everything around here that can walk or crawl is headed in that direction. Looks like Hog Town will be bigger than Ranger and Burk put together."

"How big?" Clay asked.

"The Maples well blew in as a gasser and lit from the tool dresser's forge. They brought in four boilers and snuffed the fire with live steam. Now they've got a producer, but they haven't run a test yet. Two more holes just came in, one eight thousand barrels, the other fifteen thousand. A monster gasser just blew in four hundred yards from the original well. Can you believe this? They claim it's blowing forty million cubic feet a day! You can hear the son of a bitch from our lease, almost twenty-five miles away! The people down here are going crazy."

Clay thought of the twenty-five hundred acres he and Pete had under lease at Hog Town. They sure as hell should be getting their share. "You got anything you can move down there?"

"Koon should be completed in a day or two. We can move him. That'll give us a start. I'll try to get another loose as soon as I can. I thought you might ought to come down and fix it up with the landowner, since you're the one that dealt with him."

"I'm on my way," Clay said.

They made arrangements to meet at the Ranger lease. Clay rang off, feeling the now familiar surge of excitement.

Ranger, Burkburnett, and now Hog Town.

All within a year.

Where would the next boom hit?

He drove all day and arrived late in the evening. On the outskirts of Ranger, hunting the road out to the lease, he lost his way for a time in a sea of board shacks and shanties. In eight months Ranger had gone from a thousand to more than twenty thousand people. The odor of oil now hung heavy over the entire field.

The next morning Clay and Pete left for Hog Town to select the drilling site. The road was jammed with wagons and equipment. The summer had been dry, and the many hooves and wheels had churned the roadbed into an alkaline powder. A choking cloud hung over the road for miles. The leaves of the surrounding mesquite and post oak were covered with a white, powdery film.

The twenty-five mile trip took four hours. As they approached Hog Town, the roar of the runaway Payne gasser grew louder, hampering conversation. Hog Town already had mushroomed into a tent city. Thousands of people milled about, making deals, discussing prospects. Heavy equipment moved through the throng, headed in various directions.

Clay made his way to the general store. The old man sprang up from his chair and shouted over the roar of the Payne gasser. "I've been looking for you! Where in hell's that oil well you promised me?"

"The equipment is on its way to Hog Town now," Clay said. "We'll be spudded in within the week."

"This ain't Hog Town no more," the old man said. "This here's Desdemona. We done changed the name."

Clay and Pete walked the leases and selected the most feasible sites. They then toured the new field. They learned that unlike Ranger, where the oil was high-grade, Desdemona production contained considerable paraffin that tended to plug the wells. Speculation was rampant that drillers would have to keep a string of tools hanging in the completed wells for agitation every three or four days.

"That's a hell of a note," Pete said. "That means that after the expense of drilling we'll have to keep a crew, at fifteen dollars a day per man, just to pump the oil. Not to mention all the equipment."

No gathering lines or railroad existed. Tank storage, or hauling the oil to market by wagon and team, would be expensive.

Clay and Pete decided that their venture into Desdemona would be limited.

That night Clay raced back to Burkburnett, where a Spurlock and Pierson well had ruptured a faulty valve and was flowing out of control.

During the next few months Clay shuttled back and forth among the three boom towns, solving problems as they arose.

It was during this time that the legend of Clay Spurlock took shape and thrived.

He seemed to possess the uncanny knowledge of exactly when and where he was needed. He usually arrived unannounced at some remote drill site, eyes red-rimmed from lack of sleep and many miles of hard driving, a woman asleep in the front seat of his car. After checking the core tests and logs, he would guide the well through the final phase of drilling, when fast judgments were crucial. On completion of the well he would give a new set of instructions to the driller and drive away. Sometimes, when the drill bit had not yet reached the pay zone, he would park behind the toolshed and party all night with the woman, emerging every hour or so, half drunk, to check the progress of the drill stem and to complain to the driller, "Hell, I'm making hole faster than that."

The stories became legion. It was said he once brought in an eight-hundred barrel well in Burkburnett one afternoon, drove to Brecken-ridge and danced for hours, whipped two men in a fistfight at three in the morning, and left for Desdemona, where he brought in a two-thousand barrel gusher a few hours after dawn.

Soon Spurlock and Pierson were receiving income from wells scat-tered across a hundred and fifty miles of West Texas, but their financial affairs were in chaos. When Clay felt himself overburdened with paper-work, he would stop in the nearest town, find a bookkeeper, and dump a grocery sack full of accumulated bills, invoices, and checks.

Finally Pete lost his temper.

"Clay, God damn it, this whole thing is getting out of hand. You've made deals all over West Texas without a word in writing. We have wells in production with royalty split sixty ways from Sunday, and some of the checks are months in arrears. You've probably got millions of dollars worth of paper riding around in the bottom of your toolbox. We have six accountants in five towns working on our books, and not one of them has the slightest suspicion that the others exist. I haven't any idea what our bank balances are, and I'll bet you don't either. We've got drillers, lands-men, and God knows who out there writing checks on us, with no control whatsoever. It's got to stop!"

"If you want to take care of the books, have at it," Clay said.

"That's not the goddamn point. It's time we started acting like what we are—an oil company. We need to set up a headquarters, hire a good money man, secretaries, the whole works. Production reports will go into the office. They'll split up the income and write the checks. We'll never have to worry about all this shit. We'll send in bills from the field. They'll write and mail the checks for us. That's the way the big boys do it."

Just thinking about it, Clay felt relief. Even with hired help the paperwork had been consuming a disproportionate amount of his time. The suggestion also appealed to him for other reasons.

"Where you want to put our headquarters?" he asked.

"I don't care."

Clay did.

Immediately, he envisioned an impressive building in downtown Fort Worth, visible every day to everyone who had ever ridiculed the Spurlocks.

28

The Spanish influenza epidemic came early in the fall of 1918 like a bolt from the blue. The newspapers reported that thousands were ill in various portions of the country. At first Zetta was too engrossed in her own problems for immediate concern. Reva's heart was simply wearing out, the doctor said. Travis had grown so absent-minded he had to be watched constantly. Zetta spent her days tending to their needs. But with the first intemperate weather influenza swept through Fort Worth overnight, leaving hardly a family untouched. Although she knew several who were seriously ill, Zetta did not realize the full extent of the epidemic until the mayor banned all public meetings.

Life in Fort Worth came to a standstill. The lavish entertainments for the soldiers were brought to an abrupt halt. The Red Cross canteen, theaters, and movie houses were closed. Plans for the dinners, parties, and balls that ordinarily opened the social season were abandoned. The meetings of Zetta's art and music groups were postponed. All fall concerts and artistic performances were canceled.

And with the epidemic came fear. Speculation spread that the deadly plague was a last-ditch weapon unleashed on the world by the Germans. A blackout was placed on the exact number of casualties, to withhold aid and comfort to the enemy. But plainly the toll was staggering. Everyone had friends, relatives, and neighbors who were suffering and dying.

Although the thirty thousand soldiers at Camp Bowie were restricted to the post, word soon drifted into town that under the crowded conditions of tents and barracks, more than one third of the soldiers were sick. It was said that as many as a dozen died every day.

The thousands of suffering soldiers so near to Bluebonnet weighed constantly on Zetta's mind.

Suspecting that the community was too burdened with its own troubles to help, Zetta was determined to do what she could.

Fortunately, she was accustomed to plowing her way through obstacles. For years she had successfully extracted large contributions for the arts from reluctant businessmen, riding roughshod over their protective shield of secretaries and underlings. So when she presented herself one morning at the Camp Bowie main gate, she was not intimidated in the least by the armed sentry who informed her that unauthorized civilians were not allowed on the post. She stood fast and demanded to see his commanding officer. When the captain of the guard arrived, she demanded to see *his* commanding officer.

In this way she made her way into the office of the harried major in charge of the camp's medical facilities.

"I'm here to do whatever needs to be done," she explained. "How can I help?"

Major James Garrett was exhausted. He had spent most of the night converting yet another barracks into a hospital ward. Until a few short months ago he had managed a small factory in Elkhart, Indiana. Now he was inundated by awesome responsibilities. Not the least of his problems was that he was outranked by most of the doctors ostensibly under his command. They viewed him as a supply bureaucrat failing in his duties.

The last thing he needed was a bunch of sob sisters descending upon him from town. "We have a group of Red Cross volunteers who are giving us valuable assistance," he said. "If you will talk to the lady in charge . . ."

"You misunderstand," Zetta interrupted. "I'm not talking about emptying bedpans. I've heard you have a shortage of medicine and medical equipment. My father is a former senator. I have connections. I won't stand by idly and see these young men suffer. I don't care if I have to go to Congress or to President Wilson."

Garrett reassessed his visitor. In her dark eyes he saw determination, intelligence, perhaps anger. She was impressively dressed and carried herself with a dignity that brooked no nonsense.

Garrett had depleted his own resources. He had filed complaints with the War Department, appealed to his commanding general. Nothing had been done. He was disgusted and desperate. If the remotest chance existed that the woman could help, he could not afford to ignore it. "What you've heard is true," he said. "We don't have enough blankets, bedding, or medicines. Shipments have been made, but apparently lost in transit."

"More likely appropriated by those who need them less," Zetta said. "If you'll give me what information you have, I'll find them or have them replaced."

Tired, sick at heart, and badly in need of sympathy, Garrett poured out specifics he normally would not have mentioned even to his commanding general. Aside from the missing shipments, the nursing staff was overworked. He did not have enough medical doctors. The Red Cross volunteers were inadequate to meet the demands of the epidemic. Chaplains were overburdened. Young soldiers who knew that they were dying did not have a comforting presence, or help with their last letters.

Zetta took charge. She set up a command post in the library at Bluebonnet and dispatched a blizzard of telegrams conveying implications of congressional investigations, presidential intervention. She learned what chains to pull at the War Department. The long-awaited supplies were forwarded.

Without the formalities of seeking permission, she toured the wards of the barracks-hospitals and discerned with practiced eye the needs of the patients. She spent hours on her telephone, swelling the ranks of the Red Cross volunteers, freeing the professional nurses from mundane tasks so they could spend more time assisting the overworked doctors.

After the administrative tasks were done, she spent long hours in the wards. She sat beside the beds, wrote last letters, bathed the fevered, and listened to death rales until they ceased. As she moved through the wards like a presiding archangel, she suffered with every patient. The constant wheezing of labored breath, wracking coughs, fevered mumbling, and telltale death pallors tormented her. Each morning empty beds gaped like fresh graves. Her nights were filled with dreams of the newly dead.

Engrossed in its own troubles, Camp Bowie hardly noticed the signing of the Armistice, and the end of the war.

In late December, awakened before dawn one morning by Reva's desperate coughing, Zetta hurried down the hall and found her feverish.

Zetta had no doubt that it was influenza.

With so many ill, the doctor did not come until midmorning. By then Reva was wracked by long spells of coughing, and her temperature continued to climb.

The doctor left medicines and offered hopeful words. But Zetta was not deceived. She had seen too many flu victims.

Travis went up to sit at Reva's bedside. Zetta reached Durwood at the bank and informed him that their mother was seriously ill. She then called Clay's home. Ann Leigh answered. Declining to identify herself, Zetta asked to speak with Clay. In a moment he came on the line.

"Clay, we've had our differences," she said. "But if you want to see your mother alive again, you'd better come over this afternoon. She's dying."

"You didn't bring the children?" Reva asked.

"Not this time," Clay said.

She lay against a bank of pillows, her shoulders covered with a blue woolen shawl. At first Clay did not think she was as ill as Zetta feared. But as they talked he saw the feverish intensity of her eyes, the weakness in her movements.

"I've been wrong," she said. "So terribly wrong. I shouldn't have blamed the children for what you and that woman did. After all, they're my grandchildren."

It was not the time to refight that old battle. But Clay could not remain silent. "You shouldn't blame Ann Leigh either. Blame me, if you have to blame someone."

The air was laden with the smell of medicines. A brief rattle of pans came from the kitchen below, followed by the scolding voice of Zetta setting matters straight. On his way upstairs, Clay had caught a glimpse of Travis, seated in the parlor, staring at the wall.

Nothing had changed at Bluebonnet in the three years he had been away.

Reva cleared her throat. "What are the children like? Who do they favor?"

Still resenting his long banishment from Bluebonnet, Clay found himself reluctant to answer. "Except for their size, they look enough alike to be twins," he said. "They have the Spurlock nose, the ears. No one would mistake them for anything else."

Reva smiled. "You were so solemn as a baby. We could never make you laugh. And Vern always had the sweetest smile."

Clay felt uncomfortable talking of himself as a baby. "Brod, the older one, is serious-minded," he said. "Loren is more easygoing, like Vern."

Reva was seized by a spell of coughing. She reached for a jar of menthol and camphor and inhaled for a moment. A wave of fatigue crossed her face.

"I promised Zetta I wouldn't stay long," Clay said. "I'll be back to see you soon."

She did not protest. "Bring the children," she said. "Please."

Clay evaded a direct answer. The children could not be exposed to the flu. "As soon as you're feeling better," he said again.

He moved to the door.

"Clay," she said softly. "If anything should happen to me, look after Papa. He's not at all well, you know."

"Mama, don't worry. You're going to be all right. The doctor said so."

Reva would not be put off. "Promise!"

"I promise," Clay said.

He walked down the long staircase where he and Vern had played so many rainy afternoons. The steps now creaked under his weight. The dark wood of the banisters remained polished to perfection under Zetta's watchful eye.

Clay entered the parlor. Travis looked up at him but did not speak. They had not seen each other since the day of Vern's funeral.

Travis had allowed his white beard to grow longer. He seemed much older. His gnarled hands gripped the edges of his rocker, his arms tensed as if he might spring to his feet at any moment. "How is your Mama?" he asked, as if the bitter words, the long separation had not occurred.

Clay dropped into a chair. "She seems tired. The doctor says she's responding."

"Zetta thinks she's dying."

Clay did not answer.

Travis rocked for a moment, his eyes fixed on the wall. "Sickness always comes with war, you know. Happened as far back as Roman times, through the Middle Ages. Someone told me they caught a German woman putting germs in the food out at the camp. You hear that?"

"I heard it," Clay said. Such rumors were rampant.

"Durwood says you're spending money as fast as you're making it."

Clay fought down anger. "I don't know where Durwood gets his information. But that's not true."

"He says you're putting up a big building downtown."

"Not a big one. Six stories."

"Lots of fancy stuff on it, Durwood says. More space than you need."

"If Durwood will mind his own business, I'll manage mine," Clay said.

Travis turned and looked at him. "You've brought this family a lot of grief. First Vern. Then that woman and her children."

"Papa, I didn't come here to listen to this kind of shit," Clay said quietly. "That woman is my wife. Her children are my children, your grandchildren."

Travis seemed not to have heard. "You've embarrassed your mother. You've embarrassed Durwood and his family. What are you going to do next?"

Furious, Clay leaped to his feet. He started for the hall. He stopped only to deliver a line he could not hold back. "It wasn't me that built a string of whorehouses."

He strode out of the house, convinced that he would never return.

The quiet vigil in Reva's bedroom continued far into the night. Zetta sat by the door so she could hear if the doctor came. Durwood was seated in the corner, leaning forward with his head lowered, his elbows braced against his knees. Travis sat beside the bed, holding Reva's hand.

She had been in a deep coma for more than two hours. Her breathing was shallow and labored, the death rales unnaturally loud in the stillness of the room.

Just after midnight the sound ceased. Travis and Durwood sat listening, unable to accept the terrible truth.

Zetta rose and gripped Travis by the shoulders. "She's gone. Her suffering is over."

"No!" he shouted. He paced up and down the room, his arms jerking as if they had a volition all their own. Tears streamed down his face. His mouth worked, but no further sound came. Zetta was frightened. She had never seen him in such a state.

Durwood came to help. They managed to guide him down the stairs and into the parlor. Zetta summoned the maid and cook. Working together, they managed to talk Travis into sitting in his rocking chair.

Leaving him in the care of the servants, she again called the doctor.

An hour later the doctor arrived and gave Travis a sedative.

At first light she called Clay and told him that their mother had died.

"How's Papa taking it?" he asked after a moment.

"I think his mind has come unhinged. He went into a kind of panic. The doctor gave him a shot. Now he just sits in the parlor, and won't talk to anyone."

Clay remained silent for a moment. "Zetta, I don't know what I can do," he said. "My being there would just upset him even more. Durwood has told him things to set him against me. I think it would be best if I don't come to the funeral."

Zetta began to weep, not for Reva but for her family, wondering how the Spurlocks had become so estranged that they could not bear each other even long enough to attend a funeral.

"Of course you're coming!" she said through her tears. "With the ban on gatherings, it won't be a regular funeral anyway. Just the immediate family."

"No," Clay said. "My seeing him the other day was a mistake."

Zetta cried for a time before she could bring her voice under control. "Clay, if you won't do it for me, do it for Mama."

Clay did not answer immediately. "All right," he said. "I'll come to the funeral, but not to the house."

The brief service was conducted in the church sanctuary. The ban on public gatherings was still in force. Only the family attended.

LaFon sat at the left end of the front pew, with Durwood next to her, tending to his father. Zetta sat to the right of Travis, providing a buffer between Clay and the remainder of the family.

Zetta hardly heard the preacher's eulogy. Her mother seemed tiny in the large rosewood coffin she and Durwood had selected.

Afterward they rode to the cemetery in two cars. Travis, Durwood, and his wife followed immediately behind the hearse. Zetta rode with Clay.

At the graveside her father stood as if in a trance as the minister and the funeral home attendants did their work. Twice his arms flew up in a gesture of helplessness, but he did not speak. He did not seem to notice Clay's presence.

Travis spent much of the days that followed in his rocking chair, staring at the wall. Durwood came often, but Travis no longer seemed interested in events around him. He ate whatever was set before him. He was docile and did not protest each night when Zetta sent him to bed.

Gradually the flu epidemic abated. Many remained ill, but the worst appeared to be over.

On a day in late February, Zetta summoned Dulcie's son Sam and drove downtown for some long-delayed shopping. After Dulcie's death, Sam had become the Bluebonnet live-in handyman and chauffeur. Travis seemed to like him, and they spent much time together.

The day was deceptively warm, offering promise of an early spring. Foolishly, Zetta left her coat behind. In midafternoon a blue norther struck, and by five o'clock the temperature had dropped forty degrees.

Zetta returned home. As she approached Bluebonnet she grew increasingly apprehensive. She was not surprised when she found the house deserted.

At first she was concerned only that Travis had gone on a walk downtown and neglected to take a coat. She feared he might become chilled on his way back.

Again, she summoned Sam. "Go to every place Mr. Spurlock might visit. The Fort Worth Club, his brokerage—you know his habits better than I. Take this coat to him. Bring him home."

She remained worried. But she really did not grow alarmed until an hour had passed. By the time Sam returned, well after seven, she was frantic. She saw fear in Sam's eyes.

"I've looked just about everywhere, Miss Zetta. No one has seen him all day."

Zetta tried to reach Clay at his office. His secretary said he was on the road and would not be back for several days. In desperation she asked for Pete Pierson. Although they had never met, she explained the situation.

"Clay was in Breckenridge last I heard, Miss Spurlock," he said. "Don't worry, I'll track him down. Then I'll be right over. I think we should organize a search party."

Zetta called Durwood. Predictably, he flew into a rage. "Papa's been gone for hours? In this weather? And you haven't done anything? Call the police!"

"Do you really think we should?" she asked, fighting back panic, seeking solid logic. "If he only stopped to visit with someone, he'd be furious. You know how he just lets time get away from him."

"Call the police!" Durwood insisted.

The desk sergeant handled the matter routinely until Zetta gave him the name. Immediately he took charge. "We'll have a car right out, Miss Spurlock. I'll notify the chief at home. Don't you worry, Miss Spurlock. We'll find him."

The possibility of tragedy sent Zetta into a trancelike state that persisted even after the house filled with people who came to help. She heard all that transpired around her, but as from a distance.

Two plainclothes detectives arrived and solicitously asked scores of questions concerning her father's habits. Pete Pierson brought a group of employees from the oil company and organized a search. Pierson said he had reached Clay in Burkburnett.

Durwood roamed the house, making continual complaints, first that Zetta had not sounded the alarm before darkness, then that the search was being conducted in the wrong places. He kept repeating the phrase "He's got to be somewhere!" until Zetta at last told him to hush.

Clay arrived a few minutes after two in the morning. He seemed tired, and Zetta smelled whiskey as they embraced. He quickly reviewed what had been done, and he and Pierson made plans for an exhaustive search to start at daylight.

Help came from every direction. Boy Scout troops were dismissed from school to conduct an organized sweep of pastures and fields around the city. Railroad men volunteered to walk the tracks and rights-of-way. Masonic lodges, churches, and civic groups responded, asking how they could help. The governor phoned, offering to call out a National Guard unit if the police chief felt they were needed. Zetta was assured repeatedly that with thousands of volunteers searching, Travis would soon be found.

But in the hours before dawn, as the temperatures dropped to a low of twenty-two degrees and sleet began to fall, driven by a strong north wind, Zetta lost all hope.

She was certain that if he were exposed to the elements all night, little chance remained that he would be found alive.

Travis turned his back to the wind and curled his long body into a ball in the lee of a tree trunk. It was a trick he had learned long ago. He no longer felt the cold. He had seen much worse. He remembered the frozen rain that fell during Burnside's attempt to cross the Rappahannock in his march on Fredericksburg. It seemed only yesterday.

He could not see the stars, but he knew morning was not far away. His fire had gone out. He no longer had the strength to find dry wood to keep it fed. Besides, he was now convinced that Jim Courtright had missed their rendezvous.

He put Courtright's sack of provisions under his coat to protect it from the sleet. He had been waiting in the brush behind the cemetery since dark, listening for three hoots of an owl, Courtright's signal. From time to time, random thoughts intruded. Once it seemed he could recall that Courtright was buried somewhere in the cemetery. He looked for the tombstone, but the elusive fog of recollection kept fading. For long intervals he stood, uncertain where he was, what he had planned to do.

Dawn came, cold and dreary. Travis sat leaning against the tree trunk, watching the sparrows as they searched for food among the fallen leaves. Occasional thoughts tugged at the corner of his mind. He felt that someone was expecting him, somewhere, and that he should make an effort to be there. But the details eluded him. He opened his sack of provisions and fed breadcrumbs to the birds.

Two Boy Scouts found Travis late in the morning. Conscious, but feverish and lost in delirium, he was rushed by ambulance to City-County Hospital.

Zetta waited silently in the hall with Clay and Durwood while he was examined. A doctor emerged and led them to a quiet alcove.

"Frankly, I have little hope. His lungs are filled with fluid. His temperature is soaring. I'm afraid his condition is irreversible."

Zetta had not anticipated anything different. "May we see him?"

The doctor hesitated. "One at a time, and only for a moment. We should keep him quiet. He's hallucinating. He wants to talk. But I should warn you. Little he says makes sense."

Clay touched her arm. "You go first."

Zetta walked into the darkened room. As her eyes adjusted, she saw that her father's head and shoulders were under a heavy canvas tent, with only his face visible through a small isinglass window. The room was filled with the sound of his breathing, the hiss of oxygen. Zetta approached the bed and took his hand in hers.

His eyes opened. "Jeanette?" he said.

Zetta froze. She remembered once, long ago, seeing him board a train with a woman. She had heard rumors of others. She saw confusion in his eyes.

"It's Zetta," she said calmly. "You're supposed to rest. Clay, Durwood, and I are right here if you need us."

His head moved in a slight nod. He smiled and squeezed her hand. Zetta backed away, fighting back tears.

She walked to the end of the hall and gazed out the window. The sleet had changed to snow. Automobiles were slipping and sliding along the streets. Zetta shut out the hospital sounds behind her and prayed.

Clay came out a few minutes later. "Who in hell's Jeanette?" he asked.

"I don't know," Zetta answered.

"He's out of his head. He told the doctor the headless major was about to catch up with him. You know what he's talking about?"

Zetta shook her head.

"Durwood wants to call in a specialist from Temple, or maybe Houston. You have any objection?"

Zetta had watched, helpless, when her mother and so many young men died. She recognized the symptoms. "I don't think it would do any good. He has been going downhill since Vern was killed." She turned from the window. "This is my fault. I shouldn't have left him alone for a moment."

"No one could have known it would happen." Clay put an arm around her. "Why don't you go home for a while and rest? This'll probably be a long siege. We can take turns."

"You must be worn out," Zetta said. "I can stay. Or Durwood."

"I won't ask him. You'd better not place us together much. I may clobber him before this is over."

Zetta sighed. "Clay, he can't help being Durwood, any more than you can help being you."

The schedule was arranged. Clay took the first watch, until midnight. He was relieved by Durwood, who stayed until eight.

The days crept by. Travis remained comatose. Only an occasional, slight smile or faint nod acknowledged the presence of the nurses.

From time to time he stirred and cried out in delirium. The words he spoke were muffled beneath the oxygen tent.

Durwood was at the hospital when the change came. Travis slipped into a coma, hardly breathing. Durwood telephoned Zetta and Clay. They arrived within minutes. The doctor met them in the hall.

"He has put up a grand fight," he said. "But now I believe you should be prepared for the worst. He is weakening rapidly."

Zetta, Clay, and Durwood gathered at the bedside. A night lamp cast a soft light on Travis. The doctor and two nurses stood unobtrusively in the shadows. Travis lay motionless, eyes closed, his breathing slight, almost obscured by the hiss of oxygen.

For an interminable time, they waited.

Then Travis lay still. Zetta heard only the sibilant sound of the oxygen.

The doctor moved to the bedside. He felt for a pulse. He listened with his stethoscope. Slowly he removed the earpieces.

"He's gone," he said. He turned off the oxygen and lifted the canvas tent.

Travis lay magnificent and distinguished in death, his monumental nose, prominent cheekbones, and sculpted chin undiminished by his beard. Zetta rose from her chair, overwhelmed for a moment by a rush of memories of her father's kindness and goodness. She turned, buried her face in Clay's shoulder, and wept. Clay held her in a firm embrace. When she recovered and wiped her eyes, Durwood had left the room. The doctor escorted them into the hall.

"What happens now?" Clay asked. "Are we to notify the mortician?"

The doctor hesitated awkwardly. "I believe your brother has already made arrangements."

Zetta's grief was swept aside by anger. She glanced at Clay. His face was cold, devoid of emotion, but she saw fury in his eyes.

"Where's my brother now?" Clay asked the doctor.

"He went downstairs to talk to the news reporters. Several have been keeping vigil in the lobby."

Zetta opened her mouth for an angry retort. Clay stopped her with a squeeze of her hand. "Let's go home and let Durwood have his day," he said. "It doesn't matter."

Zetta phoned the mortuary from Bluebonnet and learned that Durwood already had scheduled services for Friday, three days away.

She could not find words to express her humiliation and rage. "Why couldn't he have consulted with us?" she asked Clay.

Clay stood looking at his father's favorite rocking chair. He crossed to the fireplace, rested his elbow on the mantel, and watched the flickering flames. "Do you have any strong objections to holding the funeral Friday?"

Zetta shook her head. "Only I don't think we should have to wait three days."

"Durwood's right about the delay. A number of people will travel long distances to attend."

"But he shouldn't have presumed—"

"Of course not," Clay interrupted. "And I'll tell him so, in no uncertain terms. But after all this family has been through, I'll not allow Durwood to cause more unhappiness."

"So many groups will want to be represented," Zetta said. "The Masons. Confederate Veterans. Elks. . . . ."

"Durwood will talk with us before he does anything else," Clay said. "I guarantee it."

He went to the phone and called Durwood at home. Within a few minutes Durwood arrived. Clay ushered him and Zetta into the study and closed the doors against the servants.

"Durwood, I'm not going to mince words," Clay said. "From now on, anything done concerning the funeral will be a three-way decision. No one—not even Vern—was closer to Papa than Zetta. She knows what he would want."

Durwood glanced at Zetta. His face was pale, but as he turned back to Clay, his tone was firm. "I'm the eldest son. It's my place to make the decisions."

"And I'm beginning to think it just may be my place to beat the living shit out of you," Clay said.

Zetta's protest sounded more like a sob than a word. "Clay!"

Clay stood glaring at Durwood. "Don't worry, Zetta," he said. "I won't do anything now. But I promise you, if Durwood doesn't act civil to us through the rest of this, I'll make goddamn sure he lives to regret it."

He wheeled and strode from the room. Durwood remained silent. Zetta waited.

Durwood walked over and again closed the door. "I don't understand Clay," he said. "I've tried to be decent to him. He came to me once for a loan and I had to turn him down. It was bank policy. But he has never forgiven me."

"He's right about this," Zetta said. "We should act as a family—at least this one last time."

Durwood shrugged. "I thought I was taking burdens off of you two. I certainly didn't expect anyone to take offense. All right. You two can take care of the funeral."

"I'm not asking for that!" Zetta said, her voice rising in exasperation. "I'm only asking for a little peace and harmony."

Durwood laughed. "Clay doesn't know the meaning of those words."

The next morning hundreds of telegrams of condolence arrived.

"I'll answer every one," Zetta vowed.

"My secretaries are efficient," Clay said. "They can write in longhand and sign your name. No one will know the difference."

"I'd know," Zetta said. "I'll do it."

After the mortician completed his work, Travis lay in state in the parlor, and once again Bluebonnet was host to the famous. From noon until dark each day the crowds filed through. Zetta, Clay, and Durwood sat in straight-backed chairs and received the guests.

Each evening members of the Masonic lodge came to keep watch over the coffin through the night.

The day of the funeral dawned cold and gray, but by the time of the services a warm winter sun was shining. The church was filled. The windows were opened, and the overflow crowd heard the service from the lawn. With all the eulogies, the funeral lasted more than an hour.

The procession to the cemetery, more than a mile in length, was said to be the largest in the history of Fort Worth. Graveside rituals by fraternal and military organizations required another hour. The winter sun had set and cold dusk was approaching when at last Travis's body was lowered into the grave. As spades of earth fell on the coffin, Zetta shuddered with apprehension.

She knew she would hear that hollow sound the rest of her life.

Exhausted from the long ordeal, Zetta slept late the day after the funeral. She was awakened when Binkley Carothers telephoned early in the afternoon.

"Zetta, I'm sorry to bother you so soon. But I need to talk to you. Are you familiar with the terms of your father's will?"

Zetta had been expecting the call. Binkley had handled her father's legal work since his retirement. She had been anticipating—and dreading—the legal machinery that inevitably would follow the funeral.

"Only in a general way," she said.

The line was silent for a moment. "What did he tell you about it?"

"He said he was naming you as executor and that his holdings would be split three ways. Also, the boys would get what's left of his downtown property, but he was leaving Bluebonnet to me. Doesn't that cover the main points?"

"There's a later will," Binkley said gently. "You didn't know about it?"

Zetta felt a constriction around her heart. For a moment she could not answer. She sensed that Binkley was walking an ethical tightrope. "What does it say?"

"It's considerably different. It now reposes in my safe. I wouldn't bother you, but Durwood called this morning. He wants to file it for probate. I've made a true copy. I think you should read it before anything else is done."

"Should I come down to your office?"

"I believe it would be better if I just dropped by."

A few minutes later he arrived, unsmiling. Zetta led him into the study.

Not much past thirty, Binkley seemed older, with his tall, gaunt build and thick, graying hair. Without comment he opened his briefcase and handed her a legal-sized document.

Through the first few sentences, Zetta was confused by the legal language, but the meaning became clearer as she read with a mounting premonition.

Under the terms of the new will, Durwood was named executor. A few items were bequeathed to her, to Clay, and to Durwood. The downtown property was not mentioned—nor were the railroad stocks or other investments.

Bluebonnet was left to Durwood. The will specifically cited the historical custom of primogeniture. A sizable trust fund was established for Durwood's son, Troy. Much of the will consisted of legal language concerning the administration of the trust fund until Troy's twenty-first birthday.

Zetta did not know what to say. "Has Clay seen this?" she asked.

"I've tried to reach him. He left town early this morning."

For once in her life Zetta felt helpless. "What does this mean? Why is so little property mentioned?"

"I didn't draw up this will, Miss Zetta. You'll note it was written and notarized elsewhere. A sealed copy was left with me, to be opened in the event of his death. I'm certainly not in a position to advise you. But if I were in your shoes, I would turn this house upside down and try to determine exactly what has happened to your father's property."

"Then this is a valid document?"

Binkley sidestepped the question. "It'll be filed for probate. That's inevitable. And it'll be adjudged valid unless it's successfully challenged in court."

Zetta understood that Binkley had said as much as he could, ethically. She rose and offered her hand. "Thank you, Binkley. You've been a friend. I'll have to reach Clay. I don't know what we'll do."

She saw him to the door, then walked straight to her father's desk. First she looked at his checkbook and bank savings accounts. She was appalled by what she found.

Her dismay grew as she dug deeper into the desk. She uncovered letter contracts, quit-claim deeds, documents delegating power of attorney.

The facts were plain: at the time of his death, Travis Spurlock was practically destitute. His real and monetary property had been signed away to Durwood Spurlock, piece by piece.

Zetta phoned Pete Pierson and asked him to reach Clay. She waited more than two hours before Clay returned her call.

"What is it?" he asked.

Zetta thought of the telephone operators, who sometimes listened to conversations. "It's too complicated to go into. Just get back here as soon as you can."

"Durwood?" he asked.

"Yes."

"I'll start back right now."

By the time he arrived she had the incriminating evidence piled on her father's ironwood table in the study. She first showed him the strange will. Then she handed over the other papers, one by one.

Clay scanned through them without comment, his huge hands tossing each aside and reaching for the next. When he had finished, he slammed a fist into the heavy table.

"I ought to go over there right now and shoot him."

"Clay, please! I've had some time to think. We must calmly decide what we're going to do about it."

"I knew he was a bastard. But I really didn't think he had the guts for anything like this. Trust fund for Troy! What about *my* sons?"

"We can contest it. I think Binkley was suggesting that we should."

Clay shook his head. "We'd never win, even if the decision went our way. What little is left would be eaten up by lawyers."

"Papa wasn't in his right mind. Everyone knows that. We could prove Durwood simply took advantage of a senile old man."

Clay sat at the table and went back through the papers more carefully. After several minutes he tossed them back in a heap. "We can sue, if you want. But you'd better understand what's involved. We'd have to call the laundress to the stand to testify that Papa sometimes lost control of his bowels, that he dribbled pee in his drawers. We'd have to call Sam to testify that he often had to go out and hunt his employer, that he was a watchdog as well as a chauffeur. He'd have to describe some of the places he found Papa, and God knows what they would be. I think he was still seeing Eunice Gray. The whole world would know that Papa was confused, and didn't know where he was half the time. The doctors, the nurses would be placed on the stand. There'd be speculation about Jeanette, the headless major, all that wild talk."

Zetta fought back tears. She knew for a fact that Travis had continued to see Eunice Gray, who had acquired widespread notoriety as a well-paid courtesan. No doubt other embarrassing things would come to light.

"I couldn't do that," she said. "We can't destroy Papa's reputation."

"His reputation would survive. I'm just thinking of another way to handle it. Why don't we just walk away from it and leave him everything! I'll build you a house. I'll make it up to you."

"And let him get away with it?"

Clay shook his head. "No. That's my point. I'll take care of that worthless son of a bitch in my own way."

Zetta hesitated. She did not know what to do. The money was not important. But she knew she could never forgive herself if she did not put up a fight.

Papa had always told her that Bluebonnet would be hers as long as she lived.

She simply could not give up Bluebonnet.

"First thing tomorrow I'm instructing Binkley to draw up the papers to contest the will," she said. "You don't have to be a party to it."

Clay shook his head. "Zetta, I don't think you know what you're getting into. Every parcel of property Papa ever owned will be examined in detail. The whorehouses, the saloons, the gambling halls will all be aired again. It'll be a three-ring circus."

"I know that," Zetta said. "You're not talking to an idiot."

"Our hands will be tied," Clay went on. "As long as we're involved in litigation, the entire estate will be in limbo. The time away from my work will cost me a fortune. Why don't you let me do it my way?"

"I'm contesting the will," Zetta said again. "You don't have to support me."

Clay rose and paced the room. He stopped in front of Zetta and spread his hands in surrender. "Without me you wouldn't have any case at all. The judge, every juror would wonder why the other surviving brother didn't protest. I can't put you in that position. Tell Binkley to call me when the papers are ready to sign."

He paused at the door to give her a grim smile. "But I still intend to take care of Durwood in my own way."

29

While their own building was under construction, Clay and Pete leased the top floor of another in downtown Fort Worth. As the months passed, Clay watched in warm satisfaction as their headquarters building gradually took shape.

By September it was completed. The ground floor was leased to a prestigious men's clothing store. The next three floors were allocated mostly to lawyers, insurance companies, and other oilmen. Clay and Pete reserved the upper two floors. They installed twin executive suites just off the sprawling lobby on the top floor. Down the hall, space was assigned to the office manager, bookkeepers, and the secretarial pool. The fifth floor was occupied by the exploration and production department, staffed by geologists, landsmen, and production engineers.

Pete plunged into the life of an executive as though born to it. He blossomed into checked three-piece suits and long cigars. Each noon he strolled to the Fort Worth Club for lunch and seldom returned to the office before two. Within months he acquired a paunch.

As office manager they hired a tall, graying man named Hiram Spears. He had been head bookkeeper at an Alabama steel plant before moving west because of his wife's health. In marathon sessions with him, Pete and Clay outlined the work the office would perform. Spears quickly grasped the details but seemed appalled by the firm's lax business practices.

After the novelty wore off, Clay found the office routine monotonous. He felt confined, hamstrung. Ann Leigh entered into a troubled pregnancy, and for a time he had to remain close to home. But their first baby girl, Crystelle, was born without complications, and Ann Leigh quickly recovered.

When word came of an ongoing production problem in the Desdemona field, Clay welcomed the chance to flee back to the oil patch.

Gradually Clay and Pete drifted into a working arrangement more through habit than conscious decision. Pete directed the office. Clay took charge of the field operations.

In the summer of 1919, Clay and Zetta's suit against Durwood at last came to trial. As Clay had foreseen, the issues were embarrassing. Zetta was on the stand for three days, describing her father's mental lapses, his constant dependence on others. Binkley Carothers called the Bluebonnet servants to the stand one by one to describe the eccentric habits of their employer during his final years. Almost every word of the testimony was carried in the newspapers.

Durwood countered with a portrait of himself as a dutiful eldest son, solely trusted with his father's affairs. Summoning Clay to the stand, Durwood's attorney established that Clay usually was out of town, had not visited Bluebonnet during his father's last three years, and in fact had been banished from the family home. Under questioning, Clay was forced to admit that he had no knowledge of his father's financial affairs during the years immediately prior to his death.

"It doesn't look good," Binkley said. "We've managed to throw doubt on your father's mental competence at the time the will was made. But Durwood's story holds water. We haven't been able to shake him."

Still, the court's decision came as a shock.

The will was ruled valid.

A Dallas newspaper was moved to print an editorial, lamenting that the good name of Travis Spurlock had been dragged through such an unsavory legal battle. In various ways many people in the community let Clay and Zetta know that they disapproved of the public family squabble.

"We can appeal," Binkley said. "The court has made assumptions that conceivably could be in error. There's a chance we might at least win a new trial."

"Are you sure you want to go through all this again?" Clay asked Zetta.

"If it's necessary."

"I think we ought to drop it," Clay said.

Zetta spoke sharply in anger. "And let Durwood get away with what he's done?"

"Zetta, I've told you that I'll take care of Durwood in my own way. I just think you're whipping a dead horse."

"I want to appeal," Zetta told Binkley.

They both looked at Clay. "I'm opposed," he said to Zetta. "But if you feel so strongly about it, I'll go along."

"There's one benefit in an appeal," Binkley said. "As long as the case remains in the courts, you'll retain possession of Bluebonnet."

During the first years of her marriage Ann Leigh learned the full meaning of the phrase "oil field widow." Clay remained away almost constantly. She was left to face the community alone.

She went out seldom and chose each occasion with care. Twice she endured incidents when drunken men—apparently inspired by rumors and stories—assumed she was of weak character and ripe for conquest. But the worst were the women, who simply stared with benign smiles. In time, Ann Leigh decided she did not have to accommodate such rudeness. She went out less and less. Solitude became a comfortable habit.

She had lost contact with most of her friends. Katherine Anne again had become ill and was sent to the tubercular sanitarium at San Angelo. Ann Leigh had received a wry, whimsical postcard, and later another from Denver. Years had passed. She heard no more.

Her hours were spent reading, sewing, listening to the Victrola and radio, and playing with the children.

Clay seldom talked about his work. Most of Ann Leigh's knowledge of the oil fields came from newspapers. She followed reports of the strikes at Ranger, Burkburnett, Desdemona, and Breckenridge. Occasionally her husband's firm was mentioned.

As the children came of school age, she became increasingly concerned that they had no sense of family. Their classmates had grandfathers, grandmothers, aunts, uncles, and fathers who came home at night.

Ann Leigh spent many hours thinking about the problem.

On an afternoon in the fall of 1927, she set aside her pride and phoned Zetta.

"Miss Spurlock, I don't think you should make your niece and nephews suffer because of your opinion of me. They're growing up without any sense of their fine heritage. When Clay is home again, I wonder if you would see fit to accept them into your home for a visit. I would like for them to see Bluebonnet before . . ."

She was unable to complete the sentence tactfully. Litigation had climbed higher and higher in the courts over the Spurlock estate. The outcome did not look favorable.

"Before it's lost forever, you mean."

"I certainly hope it doesn't come to that."

"I've lost count. How old are the children?"

"Brod's nine, Loren eight, and Crystelle six."

The line remained silent for what seemed an interminable time. When Zetta announced her decision, she spoke brusquely.

"I would be happy to receive the children Sunday afternoon. If you like, you can bring them yourself. You will be welcome."

"That was your grandfather's favorite rocking chair," Zetta said. "He spent many hours there, reading the newspapers, working on his speeches."

Brod, Loren, and Crystelle stood subdued, awed by the vast expanse and heavy, ornate furnishings of Bluebonnet. Zetta watched them, carefully seeking clues to their personalities, disturbed that she had allowed Clay's children to grow up as complete strangers. With that terrible lawsuit, the years had gone by so quickly. Perhaps she had been wrong to condemn Ann Leigh so arbitrarily. Apparently she had done a good job rearing the children. They seemed well behaved.

She saw that Brod was much like Clay at that age, solemn and self-contained. Loren had Vern's stamp of a daydreamer, the same indefinable aura of vulnerability. Crystelle had inherited her mother's beauty and more than a dash of her father's brashness.

"Let's go into the library," Zetta said. "Many of your grandfather's things are in there."

She opened the large mahogany doors and led them in. As she expected, the mounted animal heads immediately seized their complete attention. Ann Leigh trailed along behind them.

Zetta was impressed with the changes in Ann Leigh. Maturity had deepened her beauty. She seemed composed and more serene, and she carried herself with dignity.

"Those are animals your grandfather killed in Africa. The lion, gazelle, springbok, zebra. That's an elephant's tusk over in the corner. The tiger I believe he killed in India."

The children wandered about the room, gazing up at the animal heads. Zetta waited until she thought she again could gain their attention.

She ushered them to the display of photographs. "When you're further along in school, you'll learn about President Theodore Roosevelt. That's his picture. He was your grandfather's close friend. They went hunting together, and he once visited in this house. See the writing on the picture? It's a dedication to your grandfather, in the President's own hand."

The children moved forward to study the inscription. Zetta pointed to the next photograph.

"This is Chief Quanah Parker, one of the last of the wild Indians to surrender. Your grandfather was his friend and attorney. They also were partners in a railroad venture, I believe. The Comanches gave your grandfather an Indian name. I forget exactly what it was."

"Why would an Indian need a lawyer?" Brod asked.

Zetta was reminded of the way Clay used to ask probing questions. "Under the surrender treaties, the Indians were given a great deal of land. They leased it to the big Texas ranches, who herded cattle on it. There were legal matters involved. Quanah had several wives. The government didn't care for that."

The children giggled. Zetta moved on. "That's King Edward the Seventh. He also was a friend of your grandfather. The framed letter underneath the picture is in the king's own handwriting, inviting your grandfather over to his castle for a game of cards. The king died not long after. He was a rather tragic man."

"Your Aunt Zetta is being modest," Ann Leigh said behind them. "She also knew these people."

"I only met them," Zetta said crisply. "Your grandfather was on intimate terms with them, was their advisor. He was a great man. Never let anyone tell you otherwise."

Crystelle had wandered a few feet away. "I know who that is. That's Uncle Vern. We have pictures of him."

After her father's death, Zetta had moved her shrine into the library. "Yes, that's your Uncle Vern, killed in the war. I find I tend to remember him as he was about your age. He and your father were practically inseparable when they were young."

"Who's that?" Crystelle asked.

Zetta's hesitation was brief. She found she wanted to talk about Auggie. "That was a dear friend of mine. In fact, we were to be married. He died in the Spanish-American War."

"Was he with Uncle Vern?" Loren asked.

"No, child," Zetta said. "That was a different time, a different war."

Brod was staring at the gun cabinet.

"Those are your grandfather's guns," Zetta said. "I know little about them, except for that big pistol there in the center. It was carried by your great-grandfather, who was killed in the War Between the States. Your grandfather brought it west with him. It was his most prized possession."

"May I look at it?" Brod asked.

"We'd better not touch it. It's loaded and dangerous. Your grandfather always kept his guns loaded. He said that way no one would ever be injured by mistaking it for an unloaded gun. I suppose there's some logic in that."

Zetta led them on through the house, pointing out the various mementoes. When the children grew bored, she took them into the kitchen for ice cream and cake.

Afterward Ann Leigh was effusive in her thanks for the visit.

"It's been my pleasure," Zetta said. "Not until I saw Bluebonnet through the eyes of the children did I fully realize all we stand to lose."

Each working day Durwood Spurlock walked the two blocks to the
Fort Worth Club for lunch. Going and coming, he passed the imposing
black marble entrance to the Spurlock and Pierson Oil Company. Each
glimpse of the building filled him with unbounded envy.

His career at the bank had not gone according to plan. Although he
carried the title of senior vice president, the higher rungs had eluded
him. The president and the chairman of the board were doddering old
men who seemed destined to live forever. Durwood had not achieved
real wealth. His investments in blue chip stocks were growing steadily
but not rapidly. Daily he heard talk of the huge profits to be made in oil
speculation and yearned to participate. But he also knew the risks. He
had seen many knowledgeable oilmen go broke. Fraud was widespread.
Durwood wanted to gamble for big stakes but only if it was a sure thing.

In the fall of 1927 oil speculation was much on his mind as he
attended the state banking convention in Houston. Mingling with the
banking executives, he listened for any clue to a sound, high-return
investment. He heard of none.

On the final day, an Odessa banker invited Durwood to lunch at the
Petroleum Club. "My brother's a member," he said. "We'll dine on him.
He'll never miss it. He's a fucking millionaire several times over."

The Odessa banker had been especially friendly throughout the
convention. Durwood quickly rearranged his schedule. He felt that no
harm could come from being on good terms with the brother of a Houston multimillionaire.

Durwood arrived at the Petroleum Club on time and identified
himself to the maître d', who turned especially solicitous when he heard
Durwood's name.

"Mr. Burkart phoned to apologize, and to say he would be a few
minutes late. I'll show you to your table. Perhaps you'll have a drink while
you're waiting."

Durwood did not mind the delay. He welcomed the opportunity to
savor the affluent atmosphere. He followed the maître d' to a corner table
and ordered a drink.

He would have paid no attention to the conversation at the next
table if the two men had not been talking in an undertone. Their backs
were toward him. Apparently they had not noticed him.

"I shouldn't be telling you this," the first man said. "It's strictly inside
stuff. I could get my tail in the crack if it gets out. But I figure I owe you
for your help in that Mexia deal."

Durwood casually glanced in their direction. One wore a gray suit, the other a blue pinstripe, both well cut and tailored. Their bearing and general appearance exuded wealth.

"Tom, you don't owe me a thing," said the man in the gray suit. "I just hated to see you throw good money after bad. I just happened to hear information I thought you could use."

"Well, anyway, I'm returning the favor," the man called Tom insisted. "This bit of information won't be known generally for weeks. If you get in right now, you'll make a killing. You ever hear of Texas Group Unlimited?"

"Carl Newton's baby, isn't it?"

"Right. A spinoff. Now, the thing nobody knows is, he's gradually moving all of his assets into Texas Group. He's in big trouble, so he's putting everything he has into this raft called Texas Group. He plans to let everything else sink. Get the picture?"

"Where's the killing? I thought that was a private company."

"It is. But Carl's hurting for flexible cash. Next week he's going public with twenty percent of Texas Group. What's not generally known is that his untapped reserves are fantastic. The initial price probably will be about twenty-three cents a share. But wait till Carl starts moving his assets. I'll bet my bottom dollar it'll be twenty-three dollars within two or three years."

"You're sure about this?"

"I told you! I have a pipeline right into his office. If you don't believe me, have your broker request a prospectus. You'll have to read the fine print, but it'll all be there."

Durwood's host arrived. He waved and made his way through the tables to Durwood. He glanced at the next table and spoke casually to the two men.

Afterward Durwood asked about them.

"Tom Shannon and Arlo Williamson," Burkart said. "Big oil operators. They practically own Houston. I played golf with them once in a foursome with my brother."

On his return home Durwood asked his secretary to telephone Houston and request the stock prospectus.

Two days later the packet arrived. Durwood examined it with a practiced eye. Tom Shannon's information seemed valid. Considerable assets were buried in the small type.

That afternoon Durwood used the bank facilities to run routine financial studies on Tom Shannon and Arlo Williamson. The replies confirmed everything Burkart had said. Confidential queries also upheld the information in the prospectus.

When the stock came on the market, Durwood bought a hundred thousand shares. In ten days the price doubled. Emboldened, Durwood sold his relatively inactive blue chip stocks and plunged all available money into Texas Group.

He had visions that as a major stockholder and successful banker he might some day be asked to serve on the board of Texas Group.

If the company's stock soared to twenty-three dollars, as Tom Shannon had predicted, Durwood Spurlock would be as wealthy as his smartass brother.

When that day arrived, he could buy the bank and boot the president and board chairman out the back door.

"Pete? This is Koon. Listen, we've got one hell of a problem down here. The drill stem's stuck tight as a drum. We've lost circulation. Looks to me like we may lose the hole."

Pete unbuttoned his shirt collar, loosened his tie, and turned to catch the full effect of the air from his office fan. He held the receiver against his ear and raised his voice, rather than lean forward to speak closer to the mouthpiece. "How far down does it seem to be binding?"

"Offhand, I'd say about two thousand feet. I think it's key-seated. I've got a numbnut kid on the midnight tour. He may have been riding the bit. I've tried everything. I don't know what else to do."

Pete thought about the problem. Key-seating was something every driller feared. Normally the entire weight of the drill stem was suspended from the derrick and gravity kept the hole straight. But if too much pressure were placed on the bit, the hole could go astray for a few feet. Later the weight of the drill string hanging from the curve would cause it to bind.

"I haven't heard from Clay in three days," he said. "I don't know where he is. I've got an all-points out for him."

"You tried to reach any of his women?"

"What womon?"

Koon laughed.

Pete was still thinking about the key-seated drill string. Sometimes he felt like getting back out into the field himself. He once had freed a stuck drill stem in Oklahoma after everyone else had given up on it. He knew a few tricks. "If I can't find Clay, I'll be on down there this afternoon."

"I'll appreciate it," Koon said. "I think I know what'll happen if we put any more strain on it. I just don't want the fucking responsibility."

Pete called several of Clay's favorite haunts without success. No one had seen him.

Pete abandoned the search. He called his wife to let her know he was leaving town. He left word for Clay, serviced his car, changed into his field clothes, and set out on the ninety-mile drive to the Corsicana well.

He arrived just after dark. Koon was in the tool shed, studying a layout of subsurface strata.

"It's a bitch," Koon said.

"When did you lose circulation?"

"Yesterday afternoon. We hit some porous shale that isn't on this chart. Took the mud as fast as we pumped it in. Then the pipe froze."

Pete studied the chart. He examined the most recent cuttings brought to the surface by the drilling mud. He found no reason for the difficulty. A few good jolts might jar it loose. He was stirred by the challenge.

"Let's try it," he said.

He followed Koon to the derrick floor. Koon gave the signal, and a strain was taken on the draw works. The cables popped and creaked, but nothing moved. Koon raised his hand and the strain eased.

For the next several hours they tried every trick Pete knew, risking snapped cables or—the ultimate disaster—pipe broken off in the well. Eventually they succeeded in pouring some oil down the casing. On the next attempt the pipe rose a few feet, then stuck again.

"Come on!" Pete yelled. "Jerk it! Put the pressure to it!"

The motor roared. The draw works sang with the tension. Again the pipe string moved.

Encouraged, the operator let out on the clutch and gave the engine full throttle.

Pete was the first to see the danger.

"Careful!" he yelled.

He was too late. The drill stem again jammed in the hole. With the motor running wide open, its power multiplied immensely by the draw works, and the pipe frozen in the well, something had to give.

What gave was the derrick. With the suddenness of a thunderclap, the metal tower collapsed, raining huge steel beams, the traveling block, cable, and the crown block to the drilling floor.

Pete tried to run. He saw Koon and the remainder of the crew fleeing. But Pete's legs seemed bogged in the timeless, molasses terror of a nightmare.

He had just reached the edge of the derrick floor when the crown block struck him, driving his head into his chest cavity.

The rest of the derrick fell upon him in a twisted heap.

Koon and the crew worked the remainder of the night with cutting torches. Pete's body was not removed from the wreckage until after daylight.

"It was poor planning," Clay said to Betty Pierson. "But neither Pete nor I ever dreamed that something like this might happen. I still can't believe it."

"Nor I," Betty said.

Clay, Pete's widow, and Binkley Carothers were seated in Clay's office. On the other side of the glass partition the staff continued work, quiet and subdued, aware of Betty's presence and of the discussion going on. Although Pete's funeral was a week in the past, his office still stood empty, a constant reminder.

"We had no agreement as to what would happen in this eventuality," Clay went on. "Obviously, Pete's share was half of the company. But then the question follows of how much that half is worth. I know of no way to put a value on it."

"Whatever you want to do is fine with me," Betty said. "Pete once told me that if anything happened to him, I should come to you for help, that I could trust you."

"Maybe he didn't know me as well as I thought," Clay said.

Betty smiled. "For the last few years he was truly happy for the first time in his life. You gave him that."

Clay glanced at Bink. They had argued for two days over the best solution for all concerned. Bink had pointed out that, legally, Betty now had an equal voice in every company decision. He felt that whatever the cost Betty should be eased out of the company. Speaking as Clay's attorney, he warned him that no matter how amicable the arrangement at the moment, the situation could change in future years.

In some ways Betty was sharper than Pete. The negotiations would be delicate.

"I see two ways for us to go," Clay said. "Both have merits. Both have shortcomings. We could put an arbitrary price on Pete's share, and I could buy you out. It would be enough money to see you and the children through the rest of your lives. The drawback is setting the price and suitable terms of payment. The other way would be a restructure of the company, with you receiving an equal share of company profits in the future."

"That wouldn't be fair to you," Betty said. "All the work would be on you, now that Pete's gone."

"It might not be fair to you or the children, either," Clay said. "As you well know, this is a risky business. The bottom might fall out of oil prices tomorrow. Some years, there might not *be* any income."

Again Betty smiled. "Then I believe I prefer the first alternative. It seems more fair to us both."

"I agree," Clay said. "But as I said, we still must come to terms."

Bink cleared his throat. "Clay, I believe we've gone about as far as advisable for the moment. Mrs. Pierson should have her own legal counsel present for the actual negotiations."

"Mr. Carothers, I'm dealing with my husband's dearest friend," Betty said. "I see no need to have my own lawyers."

"You misunderstand me," Bink said. "I not only recommend it. I insist on it. The *worst* legal problems occur between close friends. None of us wants that to happen. We should take every precaution."

"Very well," Betty said. "I see your point. What's the next step?"

"Have your attorneys contact me," Bink said. "We'll select a knowledgeable third party to establish an arbitrary price. Once that's established and agreed upon, we'll negotiate a mutually satisfactory payout."

"Then that's settled," Betty said, rising. She gave Clay her hand. "And thank you, Clay. You've been a rock through all of this. I don't know what I would have done without you."

Clay escorted her out the door and to the elevator.

When he returned, Bink was staring gloomily at the floor. "I still can't imagine you two stupid bastards running this company without a single word of writing between you. I just hope there's not hell to pay."

"You heard her," Clay said. "Everything's fine."

"Sure it is. Don't you realize that every oil well, every lease, every dollar of production this company owns has just been thrown into a legal swamp? Don't breathe this to a soul, but every Spurlock-Pierson title is clouded. Every agreement you two ever made is in jeopardy."

"Betty's a good girl," Clay said. "And I intend to treat her right. I don't see how we can have a falling out."

"Oh, we'll probably work it out between you and Betty," Bink said. "What's really in question is the agreement that was never effected between you and Pete. If the issue is ever raised, that one could haunt us till doomsday."

Negotiations continued for several months. In January of 1928 terms were reached. Clay was to pay an initial three million, with one million due each year for the next five years, payable at six-month intervals.

"You're boxing yourself in," Bink warned before papers were signed. "We should insist on an escape clause, maybe an option to delay payment a certain length of time, with penalty and interest."

"It's complicated enough," Clay said. "Let's not fuck things up even worse."

The agreement was signed.

After a decent interval Clay installed new signs, and changed the company letterhead to read *Spurlock Oil Company.*

He missed Pete.

But there were compensations.

He now had his own oil company.

In spring of the following year Bink phoned Clay with the bad news. "I've just received a wire," he said. "We lost."

Clay was not surprised. Every appellate bench thus far had upheld the lower courts. "Could we take it any further?"

"We could," Bink said. "But I've got to tell you. It would do no good."

Clay sighed. "All right. I'll break the news to Zetta."

He drove out to Bluebonnet. Zetta was in the kitchen, preparing a lunch for her garden club. Clay took her into the library.

"The Supreme Court has ruled," he said. "Durwood has won."

Zetta sank into a library chair. She looked at the bookcases, the pictures, the paintings. "How will I ever move all of this?"

"You won't," Clay said. "The terms of the estate says house and furnishings. I don't want any further dealings with Durwood. Walk out of here with nothing but the clothes on your back. Let him have it all."

At the moment Zetta seemed much older than her fifty-one years. Her shoulders sagged. "Where will I go?"

Clay had made plans. In the postwar years miles of new residences had spread across the land once occupied by Camp Bowie. Fine homes were being built even farther to the west.

"I'll buy you a home in Rivercrest," Clay said. "Nothing will have changed. You'll see."

Zetta turned tear-filled eyes toward him. "How can you say that?" she demanded. "I've spent my entire life in this house. Every memory I have is buried in these walls."

Clay did not answer for a moment. "Get a good night's sleep," he said. "Tomorrow, after your party, we'll go look at houses. If we can't find one, we'll build one."

The following day they found an imposing two-story house overlooking the golf course. Zetta liked the white fluted Southern columns, the modern amenities in kitchen and bath. In the evenings she could sit on the veranda and watch the sun set through the tall trees across the fairway.

She moved in the following week, not missing a single engagement in her busy schedule of operas, art committee meetings, concerts, church activities, Eastern Star, bridge sessions, and garden club luncheons.

Durwood moved his family into Bluebonnet the day after Zetta left it. As befitted his new station in life, he hired a chauffeur to drive him to the bank each morning. He justified the expense by keeping the chauffeur busy, driving Troy to school, then awaiting LaFon's bidding until late afternoon, when he returned to pick up Durwood at the bank.

The following few months were the happiest period of Durwood's life. He basked in the attention he received each morning as he arrived at the bank, always a trifle late to be certain of an audience.

On reaching his desk, his first act was to open the morning paper to the financial section, to check the most recent price of Texas Group stock.

As the Houston millionaire Tom Shannon had predicted, Texas Group had soared. By the early fall of 1929 it had reached fifteen and three eighths.

Durwood was a millionaire, and he felt like one. Other stocks were rising spectacularly in the strong bull market, but Texas Group was in a class by itself. Durwood sincerely believed that his rise to wealth was a tribute to his financial acumen. As he went about his business each day he dispensed financial advice freely. At every opportunity he implied that his wealth had grown beyond measure. When asked if he was connected with Spurlock Oil, Durwood smiled enigmatically and changed the subject.

Once, while awaiting an elevator, he heard a man refer to him as "a prick." But Durwood merely considered the source. A few weeks later he had the satisfaction of vetoing a sizable loan to the man.

On a day in late September of 1929, after making his daily check and learning that the Texas Group was up to sixteen and seven eighths, Durwood was about to close his newspaper when a headline caught his eye. He reopened the paper, and his heart seemed to stop.

Carl Newton, president of Texas Group Unlimited, and two associates had been charged with fraud in Houston.

His head swimming, Durwood read further. The three Texas Group officials were accused of misrepresenting company assets and hiding liabilities. Each also had taken large, unsecured loans from the company. The newspaper story implied that something was fishy about the loans.

Durwood called his broker.

"If you read the piece in the morning paper, you know as much as I do, Mr. Spurlock," his broker said. "Trading on Texas Group was suspended at the opening. I'll phone you if I hear anything."

Durwood cradled the receiver, pushed the phone across the desktop, and sat frozen, trying to decide what to do.

Oil speculation frauds were rampant. Both federal and state agencies were cracking down. Judges were promising no leniency. He could expect the worst. When trading reopened on Texas Group—if it resumed at all—the price could drop to pennies a share.

Durwood had bought heavily on margin.

Even if he sacrificed his bank stocks, he still might not have enough to cover.

Durwood buzzed his secretary. "Please locate a Mr. Tom Shannon in Houston. I believe he has an oil company in his own name."

Within a few minutes she buzzed back. "Mr. Shannon is on the line."

Durwood picked up the receiver and positioned the mouthpiece. "Mr. Shannon? We have several customers at our bank who are affected by the Texas Group situation down there. I was wondering if you could enlighten me as to the firm's prospects."

"Just heard about it myself," Shannon said. "I don't know why you'd be calling me for information."

Durwood hesitated. Something was not quite right. "I've been told you were a principal stockholder."

Shannon laughed. "Good Lord, no! I've known Newton for years. I can assure you that anything he's connected with I wouldn't touch with a ten-foot pole. I don't have a single share of Texas Group. Not only that, I don't know anyone who does. Most everybody around here knows him."

Durwood cradled the receiver, puzzled and frightened.

If he started selling large blocks of his bank stock, word would get around fast. He would have to make explanations.

But he would soon face a sizable margin call.

Durwood moved through the next several hours in a daze. He did not go to lunch. In early afternoon he ascertained that Texas Group had been placed in receivership, pending a determination of its financial situation.

Before the end of the working day he managed to reach the court-appointed receiver, a Mr. Van Laningham. Durwood identified himself as a major stockholder and begged for information.

The line was silent for a moment. "Mr. Spurlock, I can understand your concern," Van Laningham said. "But surely you know I can't discuss the matter until I complete my investigation and report back to the court."

"When will that be?"

"I don't know. A week, at least, perhaps longer." He hesitated. "I can tell you, Mr. Spurlock, that I wouldn't be optimistic if I were you. At this point I believe the news accounts may have understated the seriousness of the situation."

Durwood thanked him and broke the connection with a sigh of relief.

He had at least a week before trading resumed.

For years Durwood had handled the accounts of some of the bank's most affluent customers. As a young man on the floor he had exuded an efficient, polite confidence that elderly customers found comforting.

Even after he moved into the executive suite, they continued to come to him.

He knew their banking habits.

He now could put that knowledge to good use.

During the next several days he quietly removed considerable sums from those savings accounts. Since he usually took care of the transactions himself, no one questioned his activities.

When the margin call came the following week, he was able to meet it. He even managed to joke with the broker about the shellacking and to imply that his loss was small potatoes.

Through several brokers he sold his bank stock a few shares at a time and began restoring the savings accounts to their original levels.

It was tedious work. By the last week in October he had managed to replace only a third of the money.

Friday of that week dawned cold and overcast. A light mist fell in early morning but had ended when the bank opened its doors for business.

An hour later a bank cashier came running up the stairs, ignored Durwood's secretary and entered Durwood's office without knocking. Durwood saw the fear in his eyes.

"Something bad is happening," he said. "There's a panic on Wall Street. It's on the radio. Our depositors are coming in for their money."

Durwood walked out to the head of the stairs and looked down into the lobby. Long lines had formed at each teller's window. He hurried back to his desk and called a broker. Several minutes were required to complete the connection.

"It's unbelievable, Mr. Spurlock," the broker said. "The ticker is way behind. Prices are dropping like rocks. I've never seen anything like it."

By the time Durwood returned to the head of the stairs the lobby was full. The crowd was overflowing into the street.

Durwood felt his pulse racing. He had trouble catching his breath.

Withdrawals were being made wholesale.

Discovery of the shortages was inevitable. He had to stop the run on the bank.

Strieber, the bank president, was away from his desk, probably out on the golf course. Durwood remembered the plan formulated long ago for a run on the bank.

"Call the Federal Reserve in Dallas," he instructed his cashier. "Have them send over all the cash they can spare. Bring all of the cash out of the vaults. Put it where the crowd can see it. Tell the cashiers to be calm, cheerful, confident."

He summoned the janitor and ordered large signs painted, using whatever material was at hand.

He then went down to the lobby and climbed onto the top of the cashiers' counter.

"Your attention, please!" he shouted. The crowd quieted. Durwood waited until he had full attention.

"This bank is prepared to pay out every penny you have on deposit." He pointed to the stacks of money behind him. "We have sufficient cash to serve you. And more is on the way from Dallas. All of this is an unnecessary inconvenience to you, and to us. But it is your privilege to obtain your money on demand. It is our obligation, and we will meet it. Please be orderly. The bank will remain open as long as necessary for your demands to be met. Thank you."

He stepped down and directed the posting of the signs in the windows. They read:

THIS BANK IS SOLVENT
Every Cent on Desposit Will Be Honored
Please Be Orderly
The Bank Will Remain Open as Long as Necessary

As he turned from the windows, Durwood was confronted by Mrs. Whitley Stone, a widow who owned a large block of bank stock.

Durwood felt his heart lurch.

Mrs. Stone had more than a quarter of a million on deposit in various savings accounts. Durwood had borrowed heavily from her. He had not yet returned the money.

"Are you sure our money's safe, Mr. Spurlock?" she asked.

Durwood felt like reaching out and wrestling her away from the teller's cage.

He forced himself to smile. He spoke with all the confidence he could muster.

"Of course it's safe, Mrs. Stone. The panic is on Wall Street in New York, not Fort Worth. This is a sound institution. Every cent you have is in your account."

Mrs. Stone smiled. "Thank you, Mr. Spurlock. I heard the news on the radio, and I didn't know what to make of it. My neighbor said I should rush down here and get my money. But if you say so, I'll just leave it on deposit."

"It's safe, Mrs. Stone," Durwood said again.

The exchange had been overheard. Mrs. Stone's confidence began to spread.

The incident gave Durwood an idea. He roamed through the crowd, greeting everyone he knew by name and assuring them that their money was not in the slightest danger.

He kept a sharp watch for other depositors whose accounts were short. He saw none. But he knew he could have overlooked one in the crowd.

By four o'clock the panic had faded. The bank lobby was nearly empty. Durwood walked to the front door. The intersection was blocked by a milling crowd. Small groups stood in worried discussions. Durwood stood for several minutes, trying to devise some way to cover any missing funds that might have been discovered during the run.

He could find no possible solution.

He went back up the stairs to his desk. Strieber had just returned. He caught sight of Durwood. "I heard about your speech in the lobby. It looks like you saved the day."

Durwood did not answer. The bank routine had been thrown into disarray. Even now, someone in the platoon of bookkeepers down the hall might be discovering a shortage as the blizzard of transactions was posted.

"Come on into my office," Strieber said. "I want to talk to you."

Durwood followed him, suddenly terror-stricken. Irregularities were always discussed privately in Strieber's office. The crime may have been discovered but not yet solved.

Strieber closed the door and glanced through the glass partitions, making sure no one was close enough to overhear.

"We lost a bundle today," he said softly.

Durwood's mind was locked on the missing funds. "How much?" he managed to say.

"No way to know until the market reopens. We may not be hurt as badly as it seems."

With a rush of relief so great he almost fainted, Durwood understood that Strieber was referring to the bank's own investments in the market.

"Somehow we must bolster the confidence of our shareholders," Strieber went on. "Our own stock was down to four and five eighths before I got sick and stopped watching the tape. I don't know what it is now. You have any suggestions?"

Calamities were coming faster than Durwood could assimilate. Not once throughout the long, terrible day had he seriously considered that the bank itself might be in danger. The idea seemed preposterous. To his mind the bank had always been the epitome of stability. He had spoken his sincere belief when he told the crowd that the bank was a sound institution.

His own concerns had kept him from realizing the truth. The bank had taken a beating from three directions. With millions of dollars invested in the market, the bank no doubt had lost a large portion of its assets. With the prospect of an extended economic downturn came the threat of massive defaults on loans. And during the day, frightened depositors had taken much-needed cash out the front door.

But the most devastating news of all to Durwood was the plummeting of the bank's own stock.

Since morning he himself had lost almost all the reserve he had left—money he had planned to use to cover the shortages.

He shook his head. "I think we'll have to wait and see where we stand. Much will depend on what the market does Monday."

Strieber nodded. "I agree. We mustn't panic yet."

He put a hand on Durwood's shoulder and guided him to the door. "You've had a tough day, and it shows. Go home, get a good rest over the weekend. Don't worry about it. First thing Monday morning we'll do a thorough internal audit. With all the financial panic, there's bound to be some hanky-pank here and there in the business world. Always happens in hard times. We'll want to watch our p's and q's, and keep our books above reproach." He slapped Durwood affectionately on the back. "Our integrity may yet be our salvation."

Durwood numbly left the bank and rode home in silence.

When he arrived at Bluebonnet, he went upstairs to his private study and bolted the door. On a scratchpad he assessed his situation.

With mounting horror he slowly understood that he was virtually broke. At the lowered price of the bank stock, he could not possibly sell enough to cover the shortages.

And the missing money had to be restored the first thing Monday, before the internal audit started.

He lowered his head into his hands and searched for some way out.

At last he realized that he had only one asset of any value—Bluebonnet.

Fortunately, he knew of two people who might want to buy it.

He went down to the stair landing and telephoned Zetta. "I've got to talk with you and Clay right away."

Zetta did not answer for a moment. "I doubt that Clay would want to see *you*. I'm not sure I do either."

"It's a matter of life and death."

"Whose?"

"Call Clay!" Durwood begged. "I have a proposition for him."

"Why tell me?"

"It involves you too. Look, call him! I'll be over in an hour."

Again Zetta hesitated. "I'll see if he's in town."

Clay was working late in his office when Zetta reached him. He listened in silence to her description of Durwood's call.

"He's beside himself," Zetta concluded. "I think we should listen to what he has to say."

Clay could imagine the reasons behind Durwood's call. "Why didn't the son of a bitch come to me with it?"

"He said it involves both of us."

Clay was intrigued. He was about to leave the office anyway. "I'll be over in a few minutes."

When he arrived, Durwood's chauffeur was parked in the drive. Clay walked in the front door without knocking. Durwood and Zetta were seated in the living room. As Clay entered, Durwood rose and offered his hand. Clay ignored it. "What the hell do you want?" he asked.

Durwood was pale and nervous. He kept fingering the temples of his steel-rimmed spectacles. He seemed on the verge of bursting into tears. "I'm willing to sell you Bluebonnet," he said. "Make me an offer."

The idea of Durwood wanting to sell Bluebonnet, after years of bitter court battles, struck Clay as funny. He could not help bursting into laughter.

"What the hell would we do with Bluebonnet now?" he asked. "I don't need it. Zetta's happy here. You sold or threw away most of Papa's stuff, I hear. What makes you think either one of us would want Bluebonnet now?"

Durwood seemed at a loss for words. He turned to Zetta. "But you always wanted it!"

Zetta opened her mouth, but her reply seemed to stick in her throat. She shook her head helplessly.

"Are you that broke?" Clay demanded.

The answer was plain from Durwood's pallid face, the fright in his eyes.

"Broke?" Zetta said, aghast. Durwood had always been the conservative one in the family, clinging relentlessly to every dollar he made. "How on earth . . ."

"Our brilliant brother made a bad investment," Clay said. "You remember the Texas Group oil swindle that broke into the news in Houston a few weeks ago? Our financial genius here was suckered into it up to his eyeballs."

Durwood stared at Clay. "How did you know that?"

Again Clay could not help laughing. "You stupid son of a bitch. Who do you think set you up? Who do you think gave that bastard Newton the idea for the whole scam, and set the ball rolling? Who do you think blew the whistle on him?"

Durwood could not believe what he was hearing. "You?"

Clay did not attempt to keep the anger out of his voice. "It cost me a half million dollars to suck you in, big brother. And you know what? It was worth every fucking penny just to see your shit-green face crawling in here tonight."

Durwood could not absorb it. "But Tom Shannon . . ."

"You didn't eavesdrop on Tom Shannon and Arlo Williams at the Petroleum Club. You overheard two actors I hired to play the part. You were taken there by another actor, not an Odessa banker. The prospectus you received was printed just for you."

"But why?" Durwood breathed.

Clay loomed over him. "Remember what I told you when Papa died and you cut us out? If you want to play hard-nosed poker with me, you better bring a sack lunch. I wouldn't have Bluebonnet if you gave it to me. I'd never get the fucking smell of you out of it. Try being broke for a while. Try starting out from scratch, like I did. It might make a man out of you."

"It's not only that I'm broke," Durwood said, pleading. "I also owe money."

Seeing the panic in Durwood's eyes, Clay suddenly understood.

He stared at Durwood in disbelief. "You stupid shithead. You've embezzled from the bank, haven't you?"

Durwood shook his head. When he spoke, his voice was barely audible. "I've borrowed . . ."

He trailed off. A long silence filled the room.

"It'll be interesting to see the label the grand jury puts on it," Clay said.

"How much did you take?" Zetta asked. "Maybe Clay could lend you enough . . ."

Clay turned on her, furious. "You'd bail this weakling son of a bitch out? After what he has done to you? After what he has done to Papa? Me? My children? Hell no! Let the bastard rot in jail!"

"Please!" Durwood said, breaking into tears. He reached for a handkerchief.

"I'd help him if I could," Zetta said. "For the Spurlock name, if for no other reason. Surely this family has had enough!"

Clay saw a way to twist the knife. "I'll tell you what I *will* do. I'll buy your bank stock, at the price on today's close. This stock market collapse you financial geniuses didn't see coming is going to be a lulu. I double-guarantee you won't get a better offer for five years. Maybe ten."

"That wouldn't be enough."

"Then I can't help you." Clay rose and started for the door.

"Clay, I'm begging you . . ." Durwood called.

Clay paused in the door. "Don't be a sniveling pansy all of your life.

It's about time you got a little backbone. Until you do, don't bother to call me as a character witness."

Clay drove away, reflecting on the vast difference between Durwood's values and his own.

He had known for years that Durwood's wealth was nothing but paper.

His own wealth was real. If a depression lay ahead, as he believed, he could simply wait it out. Most of his own money was under ground in oil reserves, waiting for him to bring it to the surface.

Durwood rode home to Bluebonnet and dismissed his chauffeur for the night. He did not speak to LaFon but went up to his study.

Toward midnight, LaFon came to the foot of the last flight of stairs and called to him, but he did not respond.

Shortly after three o'clock in the morning, he walked down to the first floor and opened his father's gun cabinet. He removed the ancient pistol his father had carried into the West sixty-four years before. He cocked the hammer, placed the barrel above his right ear, and pulled the trigger.

The ensuing explosion, and the disposition of Durwood's brains on the opposite wall, proved beyond doubt that the .44 caliber, 1847 Whitneyville Walker Colt was one of the most powerful handguns ever made.

BOOK FOUR

A Goose's Dream

Broadway and the wild west are jointly producing what probably is the biggest and most original show ever seen in the United States.

> Damon Runyon
> Fort Worth, 1936

So gargantuan. So fantastic. So incredible. They have merged the dreams of Buffalo Bill with Broadway Billy.

> Robert Garland
> New York World-Telegram

REPORTER: What will you do to top this?
BILLY ROSE: I'll get one of those little Balkan wars and go on tour with it.

30

Brod stretched to his full height of six feet three, tossed the tennis ball into the air, and followed through with his standard stiff-armed, overhead swing. His serve cleared the net with less than an inch to spare and landed just inside the line. Loren moved gracefully to meet it with a solid forehand.

Scrambling, Brod managed to get the ball back across the net, but his desperate move took him to the edge of the court. With an effortless backhand, Loren sent the ball to the far side, beyond reach.

Loren yelled in triumph. "I can beat an Okie any day of the week. How about another set?"

Sunburned, exhausted, and covered with sweat, Brod shook his head. He walked off the court, reached for a towel, and stretched out on a bench to catch his breath.

He had been back from the University of Oklahoma two weeks, and he could not yet absorb the fact that his long academic battle was over. His head was still stuffed with geological time tables, chemical formulas, theories of hydraulics and pressures, the intricacies of logarithms, qualitative and quantitative analysis, and the myriad other subjects paraded before him as he completed the four-year course in three years, compiling the highest marks ever accorded in the engineering school.

Loren sank to the grass beside him. "That degree hasn't made you any smarter. I really suckered you out on that last shot."

Brod turned his head to look at his brother. Tall, gangling, and awkward off the tennis court, Loren was driven by a restless, nervous energy. He seemed unable to sit still. He kept spinning his tennis racquet, bouncing the strings against his knuckles.

"Heads up!" Loren said.

Brod followed his gaze. Two girls had emerged from the locker rooms and were selecting a court. Tanned, their blond hair pulled back into chignons, they moved with studied grace, their bare legs lean and lithe. As they tossed for first serve, they cast long glances toward Brod and Loren.

"Who are they?" Brod asked.

"The Gardner girls. I don't know their names. The older one is a senior at Heights. Want to go check them out?"

"Too young," Brod said.

Loren shrugged. "Then what do you want to do?"

"I'm happy right here," Brod said.

Loren sighed and flopped full-length on the grass. He began flipping his racquet into the air with one hand, catching it with the other.

Brod closed his eyes. What he really wanted to do was start his career. He had broached the subject twice with his father in the last three weeks. Both times Clay had slapped him on the back and said, "There's plenty of time for that. Get some rest. Enjoy that new car. You've earned it."

Ever since he could remember, Brod had wanted nothing more than to go to work with his father. He had returned home with high anticipation of taking his place in Spurlock Oil. Instead he had been given a convertible as a graduation present and told to go joyriding.

He wondered if there were other reasons his father did not want him around—reasons he did not understand.

All through his formative years there had seemed to be a portion of Clay's life that remained secret. He was forever dashing off to tame a wild well, explore a new oil field, or solve some drilling crisis. As Brod grew up, he had always assumed that some day he would participate in the excitement, the glamour, the danger. He had worked long and hard, qualifying himself for the role.

Now it seemed that nothing had changed. Clay still breezed through town, traveling from here to there. He spoke vaguely of a fishing tool job he had to supervise near Kilgore, or a production problem in the Borger field. But he would never speak of specifics.

And he never invited Brod to go on the road with him.

"He wants you to have an easier life than he has had," his mother had told him. "He tends to think of you as still a boy. Give him time."

Brod felt he had no time to spare. He was almost twenty. During the three years he had traveled back and forth to OU on the *Santa Fe Chief,* he had seen the Hoovervilles along the rights-of-way, the heavily laden jalopies of the destitute Arkies and Okies on the highways, headed for Oregon and California. He knew it was a tough, cutthroat world out there in 1936. He wanted to earn his place in it.

He did not intend to spend his entire life at River Crest Country Club.

Loren stopped flipping his racquet. "Brod? Have you noticed any change in Crystelle lately?"

Brod considered the question. He had not seen much of his sister since he had been home. "Nothing except she sure reached frying size in a hurry."

Loren seemed to be struggling to get something said. Brod remained silent. Away at college for a full year during his accelerated course of study, he had not been able to keep up with the undercurrents at home. Loren was attending Texas Christian University, only a few blocks away, and living at home. An inveterate eavesdropper, Loren usually knew everything that happened in the house.

"Crystelle and Moon Belford are getting pretty thick," Loren said. "I think they're about to do something."

Brod looked at him. "What do you mean, 'do something'?"

Loren shrugged. "Hell, I don't know. I just don't think they'll wait for everybody's approval."

Brod considered the information. He had no objections to Moon, except that he seemed young for anything serious. Both Moon and Crystelle would be high school seniors in the coming school year.

Loren rolled to his feet and poked Brod in the stomach with the handle of his tennis racquet. "Come on. Let's shower, go drag Casa, and try out that new car. We might just latch onto something."

Reluctantly, Brod nodded agreement. He did not especially want to go.

But he could think of nothing better to do. He followed Loren toward the showers, warming to the idea of driving over to Casa Mañana.

Loren was right.

They might just latch onto something.

The two-million dollar Casa Mañana, born of anger, was rapidly turning into a giddy extravaganza.

When the governor named a committee to select the host city for the centennial celebration of Texas independence, competition was keen. As the members of the committee studied each municipal presentation, excitement grew.

Would they pick San Antonio, the home of the Alamo, the cradle of Texas liberty, with its soil forever enriched with the blood of one hundred and eighty-seven martyrs to the cause of Texas independence? Or would they pick Houston, only a stone's throw from the San Jacinto battlefield where, in one of the most decisive, spectacular, and courageous battles ever fought on the American continent, Texas independence was won?

When the gubernatorial committee in its infinite wisdom selected *Dallas* as the centennial host city, indignation knew no limits—especially in Fort Worth.

On the verge of apoplexy, Fort Worth boosters pointed out that Dallas had not even *existed* during the Texas Revolution! John Neely Bryan's log cabin—the first habitation Dallas could claim—was not built until 1840, *four years* after the fall of the Alamo, the Battle of San Jacinto!

Fort Worth leaders called an emergency meeting.

The heated session concluded with an announcement to the world that Fort Worth would conduct its *own* centennial celebration and the governor's committee could go to hell.

The times were auspicious. For six long years the nation had wallowed in the doldrums of the Depression. Texans were bored, and in a mood to kick over the traces.

Major Van Emden had died in 1930 at the age of ninety-four. He long since had surrendered the reins of civic leadership to others. Most notable was *Star-Telegram* publisher Amon G. Carter, who took charge of planning for the Fort Worth version of the centennial celebration.

On occasion, Amon Carter was a one-man celebration unto himself. He had been known to don a Tom Mix-style cowboy outfit, stand up in Washington restaurants and New York theaters and yell, "Hoo-ray for Fort Worth and West Texas!"

Goaded by the devils of showmanship, Carter could be loud, flamboyant, beyond ignoring. But he had quieter, redeeming moments. He mingled his own ambitions with those of Fort Worth and West Texas. He was a relentless friend and a remorseless enemy.

And he could not abide Dallas.

Polling his show business friends in New York and Hollywood, he determined that the most up-and-coming showman in America was an unlikely, bantam-rooster-sized New Yorker named Billy Rose, who had just closed a curious, gargantuan production in the New York Hippodrome starring a long-nosed comedian named Jimmy Durante and a long-nosed elephant named Jumbo.

Carter also learned that Rose was in Hollywood, desperately seeking gainful employment. Married to a popular Broadway singer, Rose was sometimes referred to as "Mr. Fanny Brice."

Carter boarded a plane, flew to the West Coast, and cornered Rose. Curious, Rose came to Fort Worth, looked over the proposed site, and saw nothing but a vacant field filled with nettles that stuck in his socks.

Rose shook his head and declined the proposition. He pointed out that Dallas was spending twenty-five million dollars on its centennial celebration only thirty-five miles away. Too much competition, he said.

When Rose boarded a plane, Carter seized the adjoining seat and talked all the way to New York. By the time they landed, the Fort Worth production did not seem nearly so preposterous.

Rose was not exactly flush. He liked the sound of Texas money. He saw possibilities.

Rose was told he could design and build his own theater—and the bigger the better. He was assured that the restrictive Texas liquor laws would be all but suspended during the celebration. He was informed that reasonable nudity would pose no problem, that Fort Worth wanted a *fun* show. Moreover, he would be expected to sign the best talent in the country.

For this he would receive a thousand dollars a day for one hundred days.

Rose had long harbored dreams. He saw the chance of turning them into reality. He moved to Fort Worth and put two thousand construction workers to building a theater-restaurant named Casa Mañana. It was designed to seat forty-five hundred diners.

Intriguing news stories soon started flowing out of Fort Worth and into the nation's press. Rose said he planned to hire the controversial friend of the king of England, Mrs. Wallis Simpson, to appear in his centennial celebration. He wired Germany, seeking to hire the airship *Hindenburg* to transport one hundred showgirls from Broadway to Fort Worth. He offered Ethiopian Emperor Haile Selassie a hundred thousand dollars to appear in a lion act. He announced that nude dancer Sally Rand would be one of his stars, and that he was negotiating for that darling of the movies, Shirley Temple. He said actor Clark Gable had been selected to choose the Texas Sweetheart for the centennial celebration. He revealed plans to restage the Battle of San Jacinto. He said he had hired two thousand Indians, one thousand cowboys, and a genuine two-headed snake. He also auditioned a sixteen-piece, all-monkey band, a mind-reading dog, and a frog circus.

Most of the news in 1936 was grim. Newspaper editors doted on Rose's bizarre hoopla. Sensing that something at least peculiar, if not substantial, was transpiring in Fort Worth, they dispatched their top writers. Rose kept his constant retinue of columnists and reporters supplied with fresh stories.

As the sprawling dinner theater took shape, and exotic performers arrived with every train and plane, Rose reassured Fort Worth promoters their money would be well spent.

"You people stick with me and I'll make a big state out of Texas," he promised.

When billboards portraying naked women were erected, Fort Worth ministers protested vociferously.

Amon Carter went straight to the font of self-righteousness with a phone call to the Reverend Mr. J. Frank Norris.

"You going out of town this summer?"

"I might," Norris said. "Why do you ask?"

"We've got this centennial show and some nude girls. And we're going to sell liquor . . ."

A deal was struck, the exact terms never recorded. Norris left on a twenty-seven thousand mile tent-revival tour and saved souls in distant states while members of his hometown congregation bayed at the moon.

In Dallas a sign was erected, second in size only to a chewing gum advertisement in New York's Times Square, informing visitors to the Dallas Centennial:

FORTY-FIVE MINUTES WEST TO WHOOPEE!

But as the official, twenty-five-million-dollar Dallas Centennial got under way, the Fort Worth production remained in shambles.

The opening was delayed time after time.

By late June even Rose's most ardent supporters were anxious. Only a few positive signs were evident.

Paul Whiteman and his orchestra were in rehearsal. Everett Marshall and Faye Cotton were preparing to introduce Rose's new songs. Sally Rand had arrived with her feathers and balloons, and the eighteen beauties who would staff her Nude Ranch.

Fort Worth—and the nation—was waiting to see what Billy Rose had wrought.

Joanna Mitchell pranced along the edge of the stage under the broiling Texas sun, rocked back, kicked twice, and retreated, kicking every step of the way. Director James Bryan Nicholson walked around the circular stage, shouting in time with the music "Higher! Higher!"

Joanna pivoted, bumped hard into Stuttering Sam, recovered, and linked up with the chorus line as it assembled. Kicking, the line wheeled, broke into rotating segments, re-formed, and slid abruptly to left knees as the music ended.

Nicholson draped his head over the edge of the stage and buried his face in his arms. Joanna sneaked her right foot forward for balance. Her drop to one knee had come dangerously close to a split. The bright sun pouring into the open-air theater was devastating. She wiped away perspiration with a bandana she had learned to keep handy.

Nicholson raised his head. The chorus line tensed, awaiting the inevitable critique.

"Chigger, God only knows where that small mind of yours wanders," Nicholson thundered. "Four steps back, turn, four kicks left, turn, then the finish. Surely any halfwit can remember that! Try!"

The beads of sweat on Chigger's flushed face masked tears. Nicholson had not bothered to learn the girls' names, inventing his own. For reasons she could not fathom, Joanna's was "Ice Cream."

"Stuttering Sam," Nicholson yelled. "You almost knocked Ice Cream off the stage. Remember! Those stepladder legs of yours cover twice as much ground. Shorter steps! Please!"

Nothing fazed Stuttering Sam. "I c-c-c-can't while I'm k-k-k-kicking," she yelled back.

The chorus line collapsed in laughter. Nicholson did not smile. He jumped onto the stage, pulled a high stool into position, and perched on it, facing them.

"Listen to me, you wretched girls. Press night is two weeks away. And you know what the Big Chief has cooked up for you?"

The chorus girls waited. Everyone knew that "the Big Chief" was Nicholson's nickname for Amon Carter.

"One thousand newspapermen, that's what. Think about it! Every columnist, every critic in the country. He'll first entertain them at his ranch with champagne, and some ghastly concoction called chili. He then will bring them *here* to watch you dance. And if his chili doesn't turn their stomachs, you will! Every newspaper in the country will report that Stuttering Sam knocked Ice Cream into the water, that Chigger can't count, and that Mutton Chop fondly scratched her fanny during every two-beat rest."

He pointed toward the dressing rooms. "Now, please get out of my sight. I've had enough of you. *Think* about what you are supposed to be doing out here. Tonight we'll do the St. Louis segment. Maybe it'll go better. God knows, it can't be worse."

Joanna followed Stuttering Sam off the stage. "We'll never be ready," she said.

"Aw, he's just k-k-k-kidding," Sam said. "We'll do f-f-f-fine."

Sam probably would, Joanna thought. Standing six feet tall in her stockings, Sam possessed an arrestingly pretty face, a beaming smile, and bright red hair that made her a standout. She walked like a queen, and projected a confident stage presence. Joanna knew that despite Nicholson's ranting, Stuttering Sam was already a favorite and a natural-born showgirl.

Of herself Joanna was not so sure. Until the last year, she had never considered a career in show business. She liked to dance, but her training had been fleeting and haphazard. She had tried for a small part in her college musical. Much to her surprise, she won the leading role. She reveled in the acclaim she received, the fun, and the deep satisfaction.

Her tryout for Casa Mañana had been on a dare. She accompanied a friend who was too frightened to go alone. Her friend was rejected, and Joanna won a part. She had welcomed the chance to see Texas, with its wide-open spaces.

She had been in Fort Worth three weeks and had seen nothing but the inside of a hotel room and Casa Mañana—both stifling in the hundred-plus degree heat.

"H-h-h-hurry!" Sam called, striding on ahead. "We'll miss the b-b-b-bus!"

"I don't care," Joanna said. "I'm taking a shower if I have to walk back to the hotel."

She showered and changed. When she emerged, Sam was waiting, hands on hips.

"Now we *will* have to w-w-w-walk," she said. "The b-b-b-bus just left."

"We can call a taxi," Joanna said. "I'll pay."

"You don't know F-F-F-Fort Worth. We'll have to w-w-w-wait forever."

They walked out into the glare of the driveway. Overhead, workmen were putting the finishing touches on the blue-and-white circular front. Joanna glanced out through the numerous high arches to the parking area. No taxis were in sight. She was aware of the admiring glances from the workmen, from the small crowd of locals who gathered in the afternoons to catch glimpses of the Billy Rose showgirls.

"I'll go back inside and call a taxi," she said.

"W-W-W-Wait!" Sam said. "I think I see us a r-r-r-ride!" She raised a long arm and shouted. "Loren!"

Embarrassed, Joanna pulled at her arm. "Sam! Please!"

"It's Loren Spurlock," Sam explained, waving. "I've known him since h-h-h-high school."

Sam was such a professional that Joanna tended to forget she had been selected in local auditions. Sam was a Fort Worth native. Her father was chief of police.

A Cadillac convertible purred to life and pulled into the drive. Joanna glanced at the two young men in the front seat. Both were dark-haired, strikingly handsome, and dressed like film stars in elegant open-necked shirts with contrasting cravats, cream-colored trousers, and sunglasses. The car eased to a stop. One of the young men stepped out. Joanna noticed that he stood well over six feet.

A girl five feet eleven tended to notice that detail.

"This is L-L-L-Loren," Sam said. "My good friend Joanna M-M-M-Mitchell."

"Pleased to meet you," Loren said. "This is my brother, B-B-B-Broderick."

"Loren!" Sam said. "Now q-q-q-quit that!"

Loren's teasing seemed good-natured. He turned to Broderick. "You remember Mary Dowell, don't you?"

Brod nodded. "It's been a long time. You've grown up. And then some."

Sam laughed, taking the remark as a compliment.

"Could we offer you ladies a lift?" Loren asked.

"We'd appreciate it," Sam said. "We got left by the b-b-b-bus."

Loren had an open face, and a wide, infectious smile.

Broderick stepped out of the car and instantly captured Joanna's full attention. He was even taller. On first glance he could be mistaken for Loren's twin. But he seemed older, more mature. His eyes were placid, controlled. He did not smile.

The rust-colored Fleetwood Cadillac seemed brand-new. Broderick came around the car and opened the doors. Loren followed Sam into the back seat. Joanna stepped into the front. Broderick closed the doors and returned to the driver's side.

He did not speak until they were on the street, headed toward the Trinity River bridge and the downtown skyline.

"Where's your home?" he asked quietly.

"Upstate New York," Joanna said. "Ithaca."

The sun scorched her bare neck and arms. The wind was dry and hot on her face. She had tied her hair back to shower. Now she wished she had taken the time to comb it out. Sam and Loren were chattering away in the back seat. Broderick glanced at her.

"You making show business a career?"

"I'll be a junior in college next fall," she said. "Music major. A summer on the stage sounded like fun. I didn't know it would be such hard work." She paused. "What do you do?"

Broderick attended to his driving for a moment, as if undecided how to answer. "I just graduated from the University of Oklahoma. Right now I'm on a sabbatical summer. Next fall I'll go into the oil game, I guess. I'm a petroleum engineer."

Joanna made the connection. She remembered the small, impressive building not far from the hotel, with a black-marble, well-designed entrance, and the gold-lettered brass plate, Spurlock Oil Company. The name had caught her eye as a bit of Texana. One did not see local oil firms in Ithaca.

Broderick remained silent until they were parked in front of the hotel. He turned to her. "Now that we've been introduced, could I take you to dinner some evening, show you what passes for local attractions?"

Joanna hesitated. "I'm sorry, but we're practically being held prisoners until the opening. Rehearsals twice, three times a day. All we do is dance and sleep."

"Surely there'll be a celebration opening night," Broderick said. "Maybe we could go out later. Fort Worth does have some good night spots."

Joanna did want to see him again. "Perhaps," she said.

"Good," he said. "I'll call you."

Later, Sam asked her what she thought of the Spurlock brothers.

"I liked them well enough," she said.

Sam laughed. "Watch your s-s-s-step," she said. "I hear they're h-h-h-hell among the women."

The store had long since closed. The babble of departing employees had ceased. And still Herman Lutz hunched over his ledgers, questioning Troy Spurlock item by item.

"Bow ties!" he said. "A gross! Whatever possessed you? When have we ever sold that many bow ties?"

"Sir, Casa Mañana will soon have a grand opening. There'll be a number of black-tie parties. In fact, I wondered if I should have ordered more."

The naked bulb over the old man's desk cast a yellow sheen across his bald head and highlighted the heavy wrinkles on his face and neck. Lutz poked a stubby forefinger at another entry. "Three-quarter length kid gloves? What is that?"

"A popular item at the spring showings in New York, Mr. Lutz. I've found that our customers are very aware of such fashion trends, even if you're not."

Troy knew he had gone too far, but he did not care. His apprenticeship was near an end.

Lutz removed his spectacles and placed them carefully on the ledger. He turned his sad eyes on Troy. "Young man, I've tried to teach you the principles of merchandising. And you refuse to listen. You have to watch every penny! Staple items are your bread and butter." He waved a hand at the ledgers. "These frills will put us in the poorhouse!"

Troy did not feel like arguing. "Yes, sir," he said.

Lutz warmed to his theme. "Most of our customers are working people. They need practical clothing. They don't go out to parties, like your rich friends. They stay at home and listen to Jack Benny, Edgar

Bergen and Charlie McCarthy, George Burns and Gracie Allen. What do they know of fashion?"

"Yes, sir," Troy said again. Thank God, he soon would be selling his last pair of Oshkosh-by-Gosh overalls.

"You simply must be more careful," Lutz said. "The department supervisors always have whims. Don't listen to them! Stick with the staples!"

"I understand," Troy said.

Lutz pulled out his pocket watch. "Enough for now. Don't be late tomorrow. Remember, we have a supervisors' meeting scheduled at seven!"

"I remember," Troy said.

He said good night and walked away before Lutz could think of another complaint. He ducked into the cubicle set aside as his office, retrieved his hat and cane, and fled the store.

He emerged on the street just as his cousins Broderick and Loren drove by in a new Cadillac convertible. Laughing, engrossed in their own conversation, they did not see him. He stood for a moment, gazing after them, immobilized by the old, familiar mixture of emotions.

Again he wondered what his life would have been if Clay Spurlock had helped his father on that terrible night, so long ago. He still did not understand his uncle's refusal. Clay would not have missed the money.

The scandal, the shame could have been averted, his father's life saved.

He had asked his mother.

"Clay was hurt when your grandfather favored your father, and you, in his will," she said. "Clay sued over this house. He tried to break the trust your grandfather set up for you."

"But this was his brother! In trouble!"

His mother turned her face, as she did when she avoided unpleasant matters. "Clay and your father never liked each other," she said. "Not from the time they were children."

Troy could still remember the thunderclap that awoke him from sound sleep. He had sat bolt upright in bed, frightened because he knew it was not thunder. A moment later came his mother's screams. He found her at the door of the library. Past her, he saw his father's body on the floor, the top of the head gone, spectacles askew, one eye dangling on the cheek.

If he lived to be a hundred, Troy would never forgive Clay Spurlock.

The news of the shortages at the bank came on the day of his father's funeral. Troy overheard gossip among the pallbearers. The next day, bank officials came with a deputy sheriff and a court order to seize his father's papers.

"We know he was speculating in oil stocks," the bank president told his mother. "From what we can reconstruct, he lost heavily. He took cash from the bank but was gradually making restitution. Apparently he thought he could restore the stolen money, with no one the wiser. Then the crash wiped him out."

They learned of Durwood's visit to Clay from the chauffeur. Reluctantly, he admitted that with the windows open he had overheard enough loud talk between the two brothers to understand that Durwood was trying to borrow money and that Clay was refusing.

Overnight, life had changed for Troy and his mother. They dismissed the maids, the chauffeur. At fourteen Troy became the breadwinner, working long hours after school, through weekends.

In those Depression years, no job was too small. He delivered newspapers, painted houses, mowed yards, cleaned septic tanks. His mother took in sewing, and in time established a clientele as a dressmaker.

She refused to give up Bluebonnet. "Your father fought for this home. It's yours by right."

The house was too costly to heat in winter. On cold nights they retreated to the kitchen, LaFon with her sewing, Troy with his school books.

His mother would not hear of his quitting school. "You'll come into your inheritance on your twenty-first birthday," she kept reminding him. "You must know exactly what you want to do with the money, and how to use it wisely."

When he was sixteen, Old Man Lutz hired him as a stockboy. Lutz said he remembered Troy's father. "Durwood always took personal care of my accounts," he said. "Perhaps I can repay him now. Plenty of grown men would like to have this job. You mustn't let me or your father down."

At eighteen, after his graduation from high school, he was promoted to men's underwear and socks. The following year he was selling men's suits. At twenty he became department supervisor.

During the last six months he had served as director of special promotions and specialty buyer, understudying Old Man Lutz, talking with customers, salesclerks, and supervisors throughout the store.

In two weeks he would be twenty-one and would receive the trust fund his grandfather had set aside for him.

And he knew exactly what he would do with it.

For five long years he had studied the art of running a department store. Not only had he absorbed valuable lessons from Old Man Lutz, he also had learned from his mistakes. He had listened to the complaints of salesclerks, supervisors, customers, and the suppliers.

Troy knew he could open a competing store, selling exactly what affluent Fort Worth customers wanted, using streamlined merchandising methods Old Man Lutz did not know existed. Fort Worth had changed, and Old Man Lutz had not noticed. A larger segment of the community now traveled. They wanted the fashions they saw in the East, in Europe. Old Man Lutz sold practical clothing, not fashions. Troy saw a vast, burgeoning market that remained untapped.

He had examined a site across the street from Lutz. The long-term lease papers were to be signed next week. He had explored financing. With the money from his trust fund, and fixture-secured loans, he would have sufficient capital to open his new store with a splash. He had spent two years carefully devising the promotional campaign for the new store.

It would be based on the new persona of Troy Spurlock.

Within a month everyone in Fort Worth would be aware of Troy Spurlock and his new store.

Troy's ambition did not end there.

He planned to put every cent of his profits into real estate. He had studied economic history. He was convinced that with the country emerging from the Depression, expansion and soaring prices lay ahead.

In ten years, perhaps twenty, he would be wealthy.

From that point on Troy's plans were vague.

He knew only that when the opportunity came he would see to it that Clay Spurlock and his family suffered as he had suffered for so many years.

Watching Broderick, Loren, and their Cadillac disappear into the traffic, Troy renewed his determination.

He then walked toward the streetcar stop, and his ride home to Bluebonnet.

In the open-air auditorium, most of the forty-five hundred first-nighters had finished dinner. The tables were almost cleared. Brod and Loren lounged at their table, only a few feet from the circular stage, sipping sour mash bourbon. As the orchestra sounded the first tentative, tuning notes, a hush fell over the crowd.

The press preview the evening before had been a resounding success. Fanny Brice had attended. "It's a goose's dream!" she told Billy. Excerpts from nationally known critics, all effusive in their praise, had been reprinted in the local press.

"My God, look!" Loren said. "Isn't that Cousin Troy?"

Brod turned casually. Troy was escorting a tall blonde to a front-row table, creating quite a stir in the process. As accessories to his white tie and tails, Troy wore a long black cape, lined in scarlet silk, and carried a gold-headed cane. The blonde wore a white, filmy, full-length dress, with layers that fluttered behind her with each step.

"Is he in the show?" Brod asked.

"Maybe he *is* the show," Loren said. "What an entrance!"

"Who's the girl?" Brod asked.

"Never saw her before. What in the world brought Cousin Troy out of the woodwork?"

Brod recalled the long-ago talk, the scandal, the animosities. "If I remember right, Troy turned twenty-one last week. Apparently he came into his inheritance—from our grandfather."

Loren's frozen expression eloquently conveyed his memory of that childhood injury. Brod still wondered why Grandfather Spurlock singled out Troy in his will. Sometimes, if he allowed himself to think about it, the rank favoritism still hurt.

"I guess he's blowing it," Loren said.

Troy continued to stand as the waiter rushed a liquor-law-defying setup of ice and soda to his table. Troy poured from a silver flask with a theatrical flourish. His performance was perfectly timed. He and his companion touched glasses at the instant the orchestra opened the overture, as if on cue from Troy.

"Prick," Loren said under his breath.

The vast change in Troy's manner vaguely disturbed Brod. He could not remember seeing Troy at a public performance before. The contrived entrance seemed to constitute some sort of an announcement to the world. For a moment he wondered what Troy thought he was doing.

Brod pushed the thought aside as Billy Rose's fabulous Cavalcade of World Fairs opened.

The plot of the show was thin, merely providing an excuse for the stunning costumes, outrageously elaborate sets, stirring music, and overwhelming spectacle. Singers Everett Marshall and Faye Cotton honeymooned at the St. Louis World Fair and were inspired to continue the bliss through fairs in Paris, Chicago, and Fort Worth.

The most awesome aspect of the production was the revolving stage, proudly proclaimed in the program notes as "three and a half times bigger than the one in New York's Radio City Music Hall," floating "on six hundred and seventeen thousand gallons of real water."

"Only in West Texas would they claim 'real' water," Loren had said.

The revolving stage allowed the massive sets to be trundled into place for each act. Towering two and three stories high, each was greeted by gasps and applause from the audience.

The mood of the evening was set early in the St. Louis segment when Everett Marshall sang to his stage bride "The Night Is Young and You're So Beautiful," a tune hurriedly scribbled by Rose in his Worth Hotel room to fill a blank spot.

Brod searched for, and found, Joanna in every number. In the St.

Louis segment she paraded around the stage with a male dancer, as part of a large ensemble, poised and elegant in a long, sweeping gown topped with a long boa and cartwheel hat. A few minutes later, with a costume change into a simpler dress of the period, she returned on a bicycle built for two. In the dance numbers she held Brod's eye throughout.

By the time the Eiffel Tower soared onstage, outlined with five thousand sparkling lights, the audience was totally enthralled. Sally Rand stole the show with her nude dance in the Chicago segment. The evening breeze cooperated, whisking away two of her protective balloons.

The finale arrived with the entire cast onstage. As Marshall sang "Lone Star," eighty-five fountains lofted rainbow-hued water high into the air, the six flags of Texas waved, and gondoliers poled gondolas across the lagoon.

On recovering, the audience gave Billy Rose a resounding ovation for the magic he had created under the open Texas sky.

Brod and Joanna circled the stage of Casa Mañana to the strains of "Red Sails in the Sunset." Joanna moved with the poise and elegance she had shown all evening. Brod wondered if he was being selfish. "Are you tired?" he asked.

She laughed softly in his ear. "I came to Texas because I love to dance." She glanced at the bandstand. "Look at those musicians. They spent yesterday afternoon in rehearsal, played for the press preview, rehearsal this afternoon, the opening tonight, now this. And when the dance breaks up, they'll probably go out somewhere and jam. Show people are crazy."

"And you're show people?"

She looked up at him a moment before answering. "I don't think so. It's fun. But it isn't me."

The dance ended with "Take Me Back to My Boots and Saddle" and, appropriately, "Three O'Clock in the Morning."

"I'm sorry it's over," Joanna said.

"The Casino out at Lake Worth will just be warming up about now," Brod said. "We can take a run out there."

Loren was dating Luella Lucas, a showgirl from Cleveland. Loren and Luella agreed the remainder of the night should not be wasted.

But when they arrived at the Casino, a large pavilion built over the lake, it was jammed to its capacity of twelve hundred dancers.

"I know a fun thing to do," Loren said. "Let's go for a boat ride."

"At night?" Joanna asked doubtfully.

"The moon is full," Loren said. "Know a better time for it?"

So they spent the remainder of the night cruising the lake in a speedboat under a full moon.

With the first hint of dawn they docked and drove into town for breakfast before returning the girls to their hotel.

"I thank you again for the flowers," Joanna said to Brod. "I'll keep them always. My first professional opening night."

She said it had been a perfect evening.

Brod agreed.

There were others during the next several weeks as Brod and Joanna fell into a pleasant routine. Sometimes he would sit through the show, but more often he would arrive late and pick her up at the door. They danced at Casa or the Casino, or at such night spots as the Crown, the State, and the Buccaneer. Often musicians from the Whiteman and Joe Venuti bands were jamming at the State. On occasion, Brod and Joanna drove to the black neighborhood at Lake Como, where Fats Waller was playing at the Humming Bird. Some nights, when Loren and Luella were along, they went to Dante's Inferno on the West Side to watch the homosexuals dance.

In the afternoons they played tennis or lounged around the club pool. When he became bored with the Cavalcade of World Fairs, Brod visited Billy Rose's other Fort Worth Centennial productions. The Last Frontier offered a Buffalo Bill type show with cowboys, Indians, buffalo, Longhorns, and the inevitable stage robbery and Indian-cavalry clash. *Jumbo* had been brought from New York virtually intact, with Eddie Foy, Jr., replacing Jimmy Durante as Brainy Bowers. Sally Rand's Nude Ranch, billed as the only educational show in the Frontier Centennial, featured an occasional glimpse of a partially bare breast as the eighteen performers tossed beach balls, practiced archery, or sat on horses. The girls were protected from their audience by a wire screen.

For twenty-five cents extra spectators could watch Florence undress and take a milk bath.

The Pioneer Palace was a honky-tonk featuring ten-cent beer, pig races, and the Rosebuds, a chorus line of outsized dancers. The smallest weighed two hundred and fifteen pounds, the largest three hundred and forty.

Brod fell into the leisurely, pleasurable life so completely that he no longer asked Clay when he could go to work. He hardly noticed when his cousin Troy announced the opening of his new department store and started attracting attention with his speeches before civic and political groups, offering pungent views on local issues.

Brod drifted through the summer, blithely unaware that the leisurely interlude in his life would soon be brought to an abrupt end.

With the coming of daylight the crew stabbed pipe. After a marathon effort the derrick floor was depleted of the ninety-foot stands of pipe. The kelly was lifted out of the rathole and reconnected. The four-hundred-and-fifty-horsepower diesel engine resumed rotation, and again the bit was making hole more than eleven thousand feet below the surface.

On hearing the engine, Clay left the driller's shack and climbed to the derrick floor. He was curious to see what the circulating mud returned from almost two miles down.

Never before had he drilled to such depths, and no one had drilled in these formations.

Each foot was exploration into the unknown.

From the moment his boots touched the long flight of steps leading up to the floor of the rig, he felt the constant, sensual quiver from the eleven-thousand-foot drill stem, snaking its way into the earth. Since the tremendous weight of the pipe was suspended from the derrick itself, every variance in the rhythm of the drill stem was felt throughout the rig.

Clay looked up to the top of the one-hundred-and-twenty-two-foot derrick that made deeper drilling possible. Constructed of heavier, sturdier steel, the derrick was far better designed than the rig that killed Pete. The drill pipe they were now using had greater tensile strength, capable of rotating the bit far deeper without twisting off. Heavier muds —containing barite, hematite and similar compounds—helped to cool the bit, clear debris, and combat the pressures of lower depths. The floor, all exposed machinery, and the roughnecks were covered with the light brown mud that stuck like glue.

Koon saw Clay and called from the far side of the twenty-four-foot-square drilling floor. "Come here! I want to show you something."

Clay followed Koon down the catwalk to the shale shaker, where the circulating mud was cleaned of debris. Koon reached into the mud, pulled out a cutting, and handed it to him. "What do you think?" he asked.

The sample was heavy limestone, with chalk and sand streaks. Clay held it close to his nose and sniffed. He could detect no significant odor. He touched his tongue to the gritty rock and tasted mild salt. He turned his head and spat into the sand. "We may be close to something. That could be a caprock."

Clay was keeping a careful log, confident now that the well would be a producer. Twice he had cased off modest but promising shows of oil. If he found nothing better at greater depths, he would plug back to the earlier formations and perforate the casing.

"I'll play around with this," he said. "Let me know if there's any change."

He scooped out a half dozen new cuttings, took them to the driller's shack, and placed them at the bottom of the latest row of samples.

The mystery of subsurface geology had never relinquished its hold on his imagination. He picked up one of the samples and placed it under a low-powered microscope. The limestone seemed well metamorphosed. It had been formed under monstrous pressure. The sand in the streaks was pitted—miniature golf balls, similar to the Wilcox. The chalk was light, revealed only in spider-web streaks that defied his crude analysis. He pulled up a stool and applied various new tests that had been introduced into the oil game. He soon abandoned the effort.

He would leave such toys to Brod and his college degree.

Bouncing the rock in his open palm, he thrilled to its presence. It had lain in the earth for millions of years, waiting for him to bring it to the surface. He wished he could have had Brod with him, to instill in him something of the way he felt about exploration. The professors had filled Brod full of facts. Clay wished he could make him understand the need for risky, wildcat ventures such as this.

The well was his most expensive gamble. Even moderate production from the proven oil bearing formations might not pay out. But as test cores and cuttings came from unknown and uncharted strata, he had found himself swept into the old, familiar excitement.

The oil game had become too safe—and dull—in recent years. He had continued to make money through the worst of the Depression, but only through careful planning.

When the East Texas field sent production totals soaring in 1930, he had seen the inevitable. After a few months of runaway production, the price of oil dropped to ten cents a barrel. Clay virtually ceased operation, secure in the knowledge that his wealth remained underground and that decent prices would return. When the governor sent troops into the oil fields to enforce proration, Clay complied—for a time. As the price rose, Clay quietly replumbed his producing wells, installing secret and gateless valves, underground pipes, bypasses, and mine valves that appeared to be closed when they were in fact open. Assembling a fleet of oil trucks, he continued to ship oil to the smaller refineries.

The traffic in hot oil had carried his company through the roughest times.

In recent months conditions had changed. With the outbreak of the war in Spain and in the Far East, fears of a possible global conflict were mounting. The federal administration had voiced concern over the nation's dwindling oil reserves. Again exploration was encouraged, and the price of oil was edging upward.

If this well brought in deep production, Clay would have the one thing that had always eluded him—a discovery well.

He had extended pools, found new pay zones, and invented new drilling techniques. But he had yet to bring in his own field—an accomplishment that would place him in the hallowed company of Captain Lucas at Spindletop, "Dad" Joiner in East Texas, and S. L. Fowler at Burkburnett.

His every intuition told him he was close.

He had been on his feet thirty-six hours. Exhausted, he walked to a bunk and stretched out full-length, without bothering to remove his boots.

In moments he was asleep.

Koon watched the bit clear the wellhead and swing high into the air. He caught it and swung it to one side. "Goddamn," he said to his roughnecks. "Look at this!"

The teeth were worn almost smooth. He had seldom seen a bit wear out so fast. He wondered what kind of rock they were into now. The last time he had looked, the cuttings were still heavy limestone. Koon stepped back. "Come on!" he said to the men. "You're not doing any good with your thumb up your ass."

Routinely he checked the condition of the rig. The stands of pipe were tucked neatly into the far corner of the derrick, the kelly lowered into the rathole. As the bit was changed, Koon walked over to examine it closer. It had worn smoothly, indicating no serious problems at the bottom of the well. The metal was still hot.

Koon looked up. The new bit was already in place. "Okay!" he yelled. "Let's stab some pipe!"

The engine raised the drill collar and attached bit. Suddenly, a roughneck threw up an arm and yelled, "Hold it!"

Koon was walking away toward the shale shakers. He turned back. "What the hell now?" he asked.

The roughneck stood frozen, staring at the hole. Koon hurried across the derrick floor.

The heavy drilling mud was boiling up in the casing. Bubbles of gas popped to the surface. Koon watched in disbelief. The column of heavy mud two miles high was exerting unimagined weight on the bottom of the hole.

But something down there was fighting back with even greater strength. The derrick began to tremble.

Koon put his hand to the casing. He could feel vibrations traveling up through more than eleven thousand feet of pipe.

"Get off this fucking rig!" he yelled. "She's going to blow!"

The roughnecks ran to the edge of the floor and jumped. A rumble came from deep within the earth. Koon glanced up. The derrickman was sliding down his safety line.

The drilling mud gurgled and spat a solid stream several feet into the air. Another rumble came from the earth. The derrick floor shook.

Koon needed no further warning. He ran to the edge of the floor and jumped. He landed with a painful jolt and fell sprawling. Behind him he heard the torturous scrape of ripping metal. Gas roared out of the hole, spewing mud and sand into the dangling draw works.

Koon struggled to his feet and ran. The roughnecks had stopped some distance away and stood gawking back at the well.

"Run!" Koon yelled. "Get your asses out of here!"

Mud, sand, and salt water were now shooting out of the hole in intermittent, roaring bursts.

Clay came hurtling out of the driller's shack. He seemed to take everything in at a glance. He grabbed Koon by the arm.

"Did you close the blowout preventers?"

"Wasn't enough time!" Koon shouted back. "Won't do any good! They won't hold it!"

The ground shook beneath their feet. A grumbling like distant cannons tore through the bowels of the earth. The roar at the wellhead dwindled to a penetrating hiss.

Clay started for the well.

He had survived Ranger, Burkburnett, Desdemona, Mexia, Kilgore. He did not intend to lose a well just because no one had the sense to close the blowout preventers.

Koon grappled with him. "Clay, don't be a fool! It isn't over yet."

Clay pushed him away with clenched fists. "Get out of my fucking way!"

Koon tried to wrestle him to the ground. He saw Clay's fist coming. He could not avoid it. The blow landed solidly on his cheekbone. Stunned, he fell.

When his head cleared, Clay was circling through the pipes and machinery under the derrick floor to reach the Christmas tree with its stacks of blowout preventers.

Clay was turning the metal valve wheel when the thunderous rumbling in the earth resumed, increasing, traveling upward. Lying flat more than fifty yards away, Koon was jolted into the air. He had a glimpse of a scene that was seared into his brain forever. Struggling with the valve wheel, Clay suddenly was enveloped in an exploding sheet of flame. The derrick, draw works, ninety-foot stands of pipe, all the ponderous machinery were sent hurtling skyward. Twisted steel and drill pipe fell like metal hail.

The roaring column of gas snorted and screamed as it hurled mud, sand, and rocks out of the crater where the derrick had stood. With another convulsive roar, hundreds of feet of casing soared into the air, followed by a pillar of fire.

Koon put his arms across his face to shield his bare skin from the heat. Staggering to his feet, he glanced back at the boiling crater. He saw no sign of Clay.

Again the underground rumbling built to a crescendo as it rocketed to the surface. A short distance from Koon, the ground humped like a cat arching its back, and a column of sand and gravel shot into the air. Farther away, another geyser spouted.

Koon turned and ran. Freed of the upper reaches of casing, the hole no longer could contain the monstrous pressures. The gas was bursting through the walls of the hole, hundreds of feet down, and finding its own way to the surface through the light sand. Koon struggled on, panting for breath, fearing that at any moment he would be caught in a blast of exploding gas.

He found his men behind a clump of creosote in the lee of a sand dune, more than a quarter of a mile from the well. He fell down beside them, gasping for breath. He then turned and vomited into the sand.

When he recovered, the runaway well had settled into a roaring tower of fire. He checked his men. Remarkably, none had been injured. He remembered a blowout and fire in East Texas that had killed an entire crew of eight.

He climbed to the top of the dune. In the distance, cars and trucks raced toward him. Help was on the way.

He knew he held no authority for the many decisions that now had to be made. But with Pete dead—and now Clay—no one else was left, except those numbnut accountants at headquarters.

All he could expect from them was panic.

Stepping off the dune, he organized his men for the job ahead. He assigned some to go into town to telephone for supplies and assistance, others to circle the well from a distance, to assess the extent of the disaster.

As darkness fell, the soaring flames lit the night sky. The burning well could be seen from fifty miles away, and its constant roar could be heard from twenty-five. Twelve miles to the east, a rancher sat on his front porch that evening and read a newspaper by its light.

In the days that followed, Koon drove his men relentlessly. Tons upon tons of cement were dropped into the smaller holes pocking the sand dunes. Eventually the small craters were subdued. Only then did Koon turn his attention to the well itself.

With Caterpillar tractors, every scrap of metal was snaked away from the crater with draglines. Wrapped in wet rags, shielded by a makeshift portable barrier, Koon and his men placed a charge of nitro and blew out the flames.

Over a period of days the pressure decreased. Koon and his crew set up a small rig and whipstocked into the hole several hundred feet below the surface.

For six days they dumped wet cement into the well, ever fearful the gas would reignite.

Slowly the well was tamed, the hole plugged.

No trace of Clay Spurlock was ever found.

As you may know, Clay had an abiding aver-
sion to anything written on paper," Binkley Carothers said. "I warned
him. But it didn't do any good. He died intestate. In short, he didn't leave
a will."

From the large wing chair by the fireplace, Brod listened with a
curious detachment, his emotions depleted. Ann Leigh, Crystelle, and
Loren sat on the couch opposite him, intently following Binkley's every
word. Crystelle's eyes were red-rimmed and swollen. Loren for once was
quiet and subdued. Ann Leigh seemed tense, apprehensive.

Outside, beyond the French doors leading onto the patio, the leaves
of the oak trees were shriveling under the August heat. The lawn was
brown and brittle despite constant watering. The family had just returned from the memorial service, where the pastor had spoken of death
and rebirth. The thought weighed on Brod's mind.

Binkley shifted uncomfortably in the straight chair. He leaned forward, elbows on knees, and frowned at the carpet. With a growing
premonition, Brod saw that he was deeply worried. Ann Leigh sat alert,
watching him carefully. Her nervous smile was frozen.

"Ordinarily, I'd expect no trouble," Binkley went on. "Texas law is
clear. Unless so designated by a valid will, the surviving spouse retains
half interest in community property. The remaining estate goes direct to
the issue of that marriage. Each of you children is designated by law to
inherit one third of the remaining one half of the estate. There'll be
inheritance taxes, but they're negligible."

"What will we do about the company?" Ann Leigh asked.

Binkley raised his head. "This would be a poor time to liquidate. My
advice would be to form a family corporation and to muddle along until
the economy gets better."

"We *do* have a petroleum engineer in the family," Loren said. "I can
quit college and take over the business end."

"You'll stay in school," Brod said. "That comes first."

Binkley continued as if he had not heard the interruption. "I know that you," he gestured toward the four of them, "are close. In normal circumstances I'd anticipate no undue delay or complications, despite Clay's carelessness."

He paused for a moment, then struck the side of his chair with the heel of his hand. "Damn it! I warned him a dozen times . . ."

Brod glanced at his mother. Ann Leigh was listening with her rigid smile. Loren was frowning, puzzled. Crystelle again was on the verge of tears.

Ann Leigh quietly broke the silence. "Go ahead and say it, Bink."

Again gazing at the carpet, Binkley did not answer.

"Say what?" Brod asked.

"He's trying to tell us that your father had another woman stashed out in the sticks, and she's apt to cause us trouble."

Brod remembered talk from long ago, conversations overheard, half understood. He glanced at his brother and sister. Jarred from his reverie, Loren sat bolt upright, staring at Bink. Crystelle's face had drained of color.

Ann Leigh waved a hand. "You children shouldn't be so shocked. I've known for years there was another woman."

"Not just a woman," Binkley said quietly, not looking up. "We're talking of another family. And not one, but two."

Ann Leigh's voice trembled. "Clay had *two* other women?"

Binkley inhaled deeply before answering. "Two other *families*, Ann Leigh. They've both contacted me since he was killed, demanding to know what provisions he made for them. Thus far, I've managed to put them off. They can't be ignored much longer. We must decide what course to take."

"Who are they?" Ann Leigh asked.

"The woman in Eastland is white," Binkley said. Crystelle gasped. Ann Leigh's body jerked as if she had been struck. Binkley did not seem to notice. "She calls herself Elise Sterling, which I understand is her maiden name, restored after a divorce. I haven't met her. On the phone she talks like an intelligent person." He glanced at Brod. "There are two sons. Grover, twenty-one, and Archie Scott, sixteen."

Brod's mind was swimming. For twenty years, he had only one brother, one sister. And now?

"What about the other family?" Ann Leigh asked.

"A Mexican woman. Three or four children, all fairly young. I couldn't understand much of what she said on the phone. She was upset."

"How do we *know* they're his children?" Ann Leigh asked. "Can they prove it?"

"I'm hoping nobody will have to prove anything," Binkley said.

Ann Leigh opened her mouth to ask another question. Brod interrupted.

"Bink, where do we stand, legally?"

Binkley gave him a grateful glance. "That's the main issue, of course. First, let's look at the bright side. This is the only family of record. By that, I mean Clay's marriage to your mother was his only registered marital contract."

Ann Leigh raised her hands to her face. Binkley, facing Brod and engrossed in his legal terminology, did not notice. "The only validity that could be placed on his other relationships would lie under the concept of common law marriage, which we inherited from English jurisprudence. Back in the times when clergy and record keeping were minimal, the English declared that a marital partnership without benefit of clergy or ceremony could be accorded legal status, in certain situations. The English abolished common law marriage in 1823. But in America, where similar conditions prevailed . . ."

Brod interrupted. "Are you saying Dad was a bigamist?"

"No! Thunderation! I'm saying no such thing. I'm only pointing out that, legally, it's open to question."

"How open?"

Binkley sighed. "Brod, I've spent the last two nights researching precedents. Here's what I found. Under various interpretations of the Supreme Court of Texas, the parties must have a present and continuing intention and agreement to be husband and wife. They may have us there, on both counts. Clay bought them houses and provided for their upkeep. The court says the parties must live together and cohabit as husband and wife. Again, they can make a case. Clay probably spent as much time with them as he did at home. The third requisite is a gray area. The court says the parties must hold themselves out to the public as husband and wife. Both women claim Clay as their husband. We don't know what Clay has done."

Loren attempted to laugh, but his voice broke. "Are you sure there's only two?"

Binkley looked at him for a moment. "Since you've raised the question, the answer is no. These are all that have come forward. I think we can assume that even Clay had limitations."

"What can we do?" Brod asked.

"Settle out of court. There's no doubt in my mind they'll seek legal recourse. They could tie up the estate for years. They probably won't wish that any more than we do. In the case of the Mexican family, I believe a generous cash settlement would be welcomed."

"Wouldn't that be recognizing their legitimacy?" Brod asked.

"No! We'd only be recognizing the hazards of their claim. There's a difference!" Binkley turned to Ann Leigh. "I'm in an uncomfortable position here. I can be either a good lawyer or a good friend. I can't be both. I only hope you'll forgive me for saying this. Despite his faults, Clay was a generous man. I believe he'd want us to take care of those families."

"What about the white family?" Brod asked. "What do they want?"

"At the moment they're an unknown factor," Binkley said. "Elise Sterling strikes me as strong and independent-minded. And they say the boy Grover is a real pistol."

Brod was growing more angry with each passing minute. At last, so much was explained. Clay had kept him away from the company and the oil fields to prevent him from learning about the other families. Clay's long absences and vague destinations had been by design. And now, because of Clay's infidelities, his own dreams were being shunted aside.

"What do you propose for Spurlock Oil?" he asked.

Clearly Bink had given the matter much thought. He answered without hesitation. "We can hire an administrator, hold it together until such time as we can effect a suitable sale."

"No!" Brod said. "Loren was right. I can run it."

Bink glanced at Ann Leigh. She did not respond. Bink turned back to Brod. "I'm not minimizing your potential, Brod. I've heard Clay brag about your accelerated schoolwork, the honors you won at OU. But you lack practical experience. You're not yet of age. You couldn't even make contracts. It's out of the question."

"I can hire the experience. Isn't there a provision in law for the underaged to be accorded the status of an adult?"

"Well, yes," Bink admitted.

"Then do it. And I'll run the company."

Again Bink looked to Ann Leigh for support and found none. "I don't think you understand the situation. Most of the people at Spurlock Oil have been there a long time. They'd resent someone without a day's experience coming in and telling them what to do. You'd meet resistance at every turn. You couldn't just walk in and take over. It's impossible."

"Just watch me," Brod said. "And let's get one thing straight right now, Bink. We're not retaining you to tell us we can't do what we want to do. We're retaining you to tell us *how* to do what we want to do."

Bink studied Brod for a moment. "Have it your way. But don't forget. I warned you."

Brod went into the office the following Monday and took his place at Clay's desk. He summoned the company's four department heads—general manager Osborne Griggs, senior landsman Ramsey Sullivan, geologist Clyde McGowan, and production chief Tyndall Ryan. He asked Margaret Banning, his father's secretary for more than a decade, to take notes.

The atmosphere was charged with tension. Out on the floor the secretaries and accountants cast anxious glances toward the glass partitions that separated them from the office where their fates were being decided. Most had known Brod as a boy and as an adolescent. Now the boy in a business suit was presiding over a meeting of their bosses. That fact had a disquieting effect.

Clay's office was too small. Only Miss Banning was seated. The men stood, leaning awkwardly against the furniture. The supervisors seemed ill at ease.

Brod waited a moment until all found a perch. "First I want to put to rest any possible rumors," he said. "Spurlock Oil will continue to operate. Everyone presently employed will be retained."

The supervisors remained poker faced, but Brod felt some of the strain ease. Casual glances were exchanged.

Brod paused. He was walking a tightrope. The employees should be reassured but not to the point of complacency.

"Inevitably, there'll be changes," he said. "My father had his methods. They'll not necessarily be mine. The company will be restructured. Already this has begun. Our attorneys are realigning ownership as a family corporation. My title will be president and chairman of the board. Also serving as trustees will be my mother, my brother, our attorney Binkley Carothers, and other individuals as yet undesignated. Any questions so far?"

No one spoke. But the tension had returned.

"For the moment all departments will continue their duties as before. No changes will be made until after a thorough study. During the next several weeks I'll be spending considerable time with each of you. Is there anything else?"

Again the only response was silence.

"Very well, that'll be all. Miss Banning, would you please stay a moment?"

The supervisors filed out quietly. Brod waited until they had closed the door.

"Miss Banning, please make a note to yourself to provide me with these items: all of my father's correspondence for the last year. All the itemized long-distance telephone billing for that period. A list of all realty owned by the company. A complete roster of employees, with an explanation of their duties. Any appointment book, expense account log, or journal you may have maintained on my father's activities."

Margaret Banning was jotting in shorthand. A tall, skinny spinster of thirty-five or forty, she habitually wrapped her long hair in a bun. Her lips were thin, and she wore no makeup. But her hazel eyes betrayed an inner hunger. As he waited for her to complete the notes, it occurred to him to wonder if his father had ever liberated her long-confined passions. She looked up, her face expressionless. "Anything else, Mr. Spurlock?"

"Only this. I'd like for you to describe your working relationship with my father—how he handled routine business. Can you do that for me?"

Margaret Banning blushed. Brod knew then that she had been in love with his father. He wondered if Clay had ever noticed.

"He was in the field most of the time," she began hesitantly. "Usually he'd call every two or three days. Sometimes it'd be a week or more. He'd ask about the mail, and I'd read him the most important letters. He wouldn't exactly dictate a reply. He'd just say, write a letter and tell them so and so, and I would do it." She blushed again. "I usually knew what he wanted to say."

"I see," Brod said. "Suppose something came up unexpectedly. Did you know how to reach him in the field? The hotels, residences where he might be found?"

Margaret hesitated, flustered. She was a poor actress. Brod was convinced that she had long known about the other families.

"I kept a list," she said. "But lots of times we couldn't find him. Apparently he had some hideouts we didn't know about."

"I'd like to see that list," Brod said. "That'll be all for now."

Margaret returned to her desk. Brod set to work cleaning out Clay's desk. Most of the material was junk—bills and invoices a decade or more old, drilling reports on wells long completed, production reports, yellowed newspaper clippings.

Absorbed, Brod assessed each item. Most he tossed into the trash. Once, when he glanced up, three employees were watching him from their desks on the other side of the glass partition. Brod buzzed Margaret Banning.

"One more thing," he said. "Find out who's the best architect in town. Get him over here."

He found a bundle of keys with no clue to what they fitted. In a bottom drawer he encountered a loaded .45 revolver and a box of ammunition. Unlatching the cylinder, he found the cartridges covered with a soft green mold. Beneath the pistol were two boxes of 12-gauge, double-ought buckshot, the cases dried and discolored with age. Digging deeper, he found a locked tin box.

None of the keys was small enough. With a penknife, he prized the lid open.

On top were a number of mortgages for loans, each marked paid in full. Pitched carelessly among them was the deed to the family home. Brod put it aside for safekeeping. Next he found a complex series of buy-and-sell confirmations from a broker, beginning in 1926 and ending in 1929. All were for shares of a stock called Texas Group Unlimited. Brittle newspaper clippings described the company's demise in bankruptcy, with the top management indicted for fraud. Curious, Brod put the material aside for further study.

He found his parents' marriage certificate. Near the bottom of the stack was a legal packet wrapped in brown twine. He unfolded the papers and stared at the citations in disbelief.

The papers concerned the divorce of his mother from a man named Lester Wilson.

Brod had never known—never even suspected—that his mother's marriage to his father was her second.

He turned back to the marriage certificate.

The date of his parents' marriage was only four months before his birth.

Brod leaned back in his father's chair and shook his head in bewilderment.

Was there a chance that Clay was not his father?

He quickly rejected the thought. The family resemblance was unmistakable. He read on.

Apparently his mother had been married to Lester Wilson at the time he was conceived.

Was there another batch of half brothers and half sisters waiting to be discovered?

Brod laughed aloud. He understood Bink's complaints about Clay's carelessness. The private papers had been lying unprotected in an ordinary desk drawer, fully accessible to janitors and more than a hundred employees. On further reflection, he assumed that the information probably was widely known anyway. Fort Worth was not large enough to hide juicy gossip of this scope.

He slipped the papers into his briefcase. He would rent a safe-deposit box for them.

Margaret Banning entered with the material he had requested. He scanned through it. Most was irrelevant, but he began to see a pattern. He became adept at distinguishing letters written by his father and those drafted by Miss Banning to be sent out over his signature. His father's letters were abrupt and to the point. Miss Banning's were couched in the polite amenities of formal business correspondence.

In midafternoon the architect arrived. He was a small, elfish man named Martin.

Brod pointed to the glass partitions. "I want a wall built there. Heavy

paneling on the inside." He picked up an envelope and sketched. "Knock
out this wall and expand into the next office. I want a reception area here,
with plenty of room for a couch and chairs, files, and my secretary's desk.
Are you familiar with the Fort Worth Club?"

"Of course."

"That's the idea—lots of dark wood paneling, comfortable leather
furniture, crystal lighting, and good-looking carpets."

Martin arched his pale eyebrows. "Sounds to me as if you need an
interior decorator."

"Then get one. Work with him on it. Let me see some sketches and
we'll start moving."

By the time the working day ended, Brod had successfully jarred the
headquarters staff to its foundations. Word of his meeting with the department heads, the hiring of an architect had filtered down to the lowest
secretary. Brod saw the change on the employees' faces. They seemed
alert, even excited.

During the next few days he called in the department heads, one by
one. The more he questioned and probed, the more the mystery grew.
He could find no sense of direction anywhere in the company. Each
segment simply drifted along, routinely performing only what had to be
done.

No records of ownership existed on many of the wells under production. A rough profile could be reconstructed from the royalty payments.
But the accountants who compiled them had no use for the drilling logs,
which had been either discarded or stored away before the production
department came into existence. Brod could not determine the pay
formation on some of the company's best producers. Nor could he find
evidence of offset leases he felt must exist.

"Pete used to take care of all that," said production chief Tyndall
Ryan. "Clay had no need for records. It was all in his head. He could rattle
off the strata on every well. Most of my department's operation has
dwindled to maintaining pumps, cleaning wells, and keeping a log on
proration. In the final analysis we *have* no exploration department. Clay
was it."

Ryan's view was later seconded by geologist Clyde McGowan. "The
only thing Clay wanted from me was confirmation on a decision he'd
already made. A geologist's report didn't mean a damned thing to him.
Usually he only wanted something to show to a banker or investor. He
was a creek-ologist if there ever was one. He had a sixth sense about what
was below the surface. If you have that, it's better than all the geology."

But it was general manager Osborne Griggs who best put the situation into words. "Clay didn't want to be bothered with running the
company. As long as we kept things moving smoothly, he was happy. If

something went wrong, he would come back, raise hell for two or three days, then disappear again. All he wanted to do was drill for oil. Anything else irritated him."

As the weeks went by, Brod became totally engrossed in the problem of achieving control of the company. The life he had led through the summer now seemed frivolous and childish. For a while he continued to see Joanna. But with increasing regularity he phoned her to explain that he was tied up for the evening. After a time he no longer called.

As he plowed through the fragmented material, he began to see his father in a new light.

He understood Clay's singular quest for oil, his disdain for offices and pallid-faced, soft-handed men. To a degree Brod shared those feelings. But he could see beyond Clay's limited world. Brod's college training had included courses on oil refining, marketing, and distribution—the interlocking economy of the industry. Reading the production reports, he could envision Spurlock Oil's small place in the whole process, from exploration and drilling to the gas pump, to tankers plying the oceans, to diesel trains and aircraft fuel. In estimating Spurlock Oil reserves, he saw them not as an entity but as part of the worldwide energy pool from Venezuela and Mexico to Persia, from Rumania to Indonesia.

Sifting through the debris of his father's life, Brod gradually acquired habits he was to maintain the rest of his life. He grew impatient with small talk. If his mind was concentrating on the remote problems of a well drilled and plugged two decades ago, he did not want to be interrupted, even for impending crises. He became curt to the point of rudeness. When he felt a conversation exhausted, he either hung up the phone, turned on his heel and walked away, or shifted his attention to some other matter at hand. Employees became accustomed to his habit of dismissing them in midsentence as effectively as if he had closed a door in their faces.

He spent long hours at the office. Most evenings he brought work home.

One night as he worked in his room Ann Leigh came to his door and knocked.

"It's two o'clock," she said. "Crystelle isn't home yet."

Brod got out of bed, pulled on a robe, and fished for a cigarette. Ann Leigh sank into the couch by the windows.

"Have you called anyone?"

Ann Leigh shook her head. "She's out with Moon. I've been intending to talk to you. Have you noticed the change in her since your father's death? She seems to be rebelling against something. I can't do anything with her anymore."

Brod remembered Loren's warning earlier in the summer. "Maybe it's just a phase," he said.

Ann Leigh shook her head. "There's a sulkiness, a resentment I don't understand. I thought you might talk to her."

"Why me?"

"She looks up to you. She rebels against everything I say. Maybe you can make her understand the kind of trouble she could get into. Young people don't know how one foolish moment can affect their whole lives."

Brod remembered the divorce papers he had put away in a bank vault. He had decided he would never mention them.

"Mom, I don't think I'm the right person. I'm not that much older. She'd resent my trying to put her in her place."

Ann Leigh placed her hand on his arm. "Brod, I don't think you realize how much you influence people. I was afraid Loren wouldn't return to school. I knew he felt left out of this dramatic change in our lives. He wouldn't have listened to me. But you convinced him with a few short words. Look how they've turned to you at the company! Bink didn't think you could do it, but you have. You're a natural-born leader. Perhaps even more so than your father."

Brod wondered what his mother would say if she knew the extent of the disorganization in the company. He had not brought his worries home. "Even if what you say is true, it doesn't make me an ideal counselor for a sixteen-year-old girl."

"Sixteen, going on thirty. I do wish you'd talk to her."

Brod thought of his sister and the hazards she faced. "I'll try," he promised.

But during the next few weeks no suitable opportunity arose. When Brod returned home each evening, Crystelle would be out with Moon. He usually fell asleep before she returned. In the mornings he left before the household stirred.

Complications occurred at the office, diverting his attention. One afternoon Binkley Carothers phoned and said he had to see Brod. He arrived a few minutes later, his expression drawn and worried. "We've got troubles," he said. "It looks like we may be thrown into court supervision after all."

Brod had hoped the impending legal battle over the estate could be settled amicably. "I thought you were near an agreement with the Mexican family."

Bink nodded. "I am. No problem there. And I've had a few sessions with Elise Sterling. Hell, I *like* her, Brod. She's an intelligent woman, independent as a hog on ice. Just between us, she's got a good case, and she knows it. I get the feeling she doesn't want to drag things through the courts any more than we do. We'll probably come to terms."

"Then what's the problem?"

"Remember Betty, Pete's wife?"

A tall, willowy blonde came to mind. Brod had seen her several times during his childhood. "I thought she was out of the picture."

"So did I. But she remarried about a year ago. A lawyer. One of the sorriest sons o' bitches I've ever known. He has now convinced her that Clay robbed her blind. They've hired some jackleg to compile an estimate of Spurlock Oil holdings. They're preparing to file suit."

During his study of company records, Brod had reviewed the settlement with Betty. The terms had seemed generous. "How serious is their claim?"

"We probably could whip their ass in court. Those several million dollars your daddy paid out to her, the fact that she signed a witnessed agreement, the estimates made of the company's worth—that's all in our favor. But some aspects worry me. Texas courts traditionally are overzealous in protecting women. Texas statutes assume a woman doesn't have the brains God gave a goose, and that it's the duty of male jurors to look after them. If their attorneys could find implication that Clay took advantage of her, we'd be in big trouble."

"Could they?"

"I doubt it. My own belief is that he paid her more than Pete's share was worth at the time. It's true that some reserves proved out far larger than anyone dreamed. But I believe we could wipe up the floor with them in court."

"Then what's the problem?" Brod asked again.

"Timing," Bink said. "This fucks us royally. I personally would see these people in hell before I'd pay them another nickel. But any impending litigation, whatever its merits, could tie our hands for months, maybe years. And there's another aspect. Clay and Pete never had a scrap of paper designating the terms of their partnership or the ownership of the company. If that fact is ever trotted out in court, we could face nuisance suits till doomsday over every contract they ever signed."

Brod thought through the possibilities. "What can we do?"

"Sit tight for the moment, and see what they come up with. In the meantime, we might call in a team of auditors under the auspices of the court, to show the difference between the company then and now."

"Not yet," Brod said. "Give me a few more weeks."

Bink frowned in puzzlement. "Why?"

Brod sighed. "What would your auditors say if they found royalty payments going out in every direction, with no apparent rhyme or reason? What if they couldn't find any evidence of lease agreements on some of the best producers? What if they found wells shut down, with no records of when they were taken off pump, or why? What if they found yellowed checkbooks in the bottom of desk drawers, with stubs showing a quarter of a million dollars on deposit, called the bank, and ascertained the money was there, in an account six years dormant?"

Bink had almost stopped breathing. "Is it that bad?"

"Worse. Just for example, I've now heard from five hotels, wanting to know what to do about Dad's rooms and the stuff he stored in them. Wichita Falls, Houston, Amarillo, Austin, and New York. God only knows how many more, or what I'll find."

"You'd better wrap it up soon. We can't go before the judge with a pending civil suit, three squabbling families, and a washtub full of unanswered questions. At the moment that's exactly what we have."

Billy Rose's production continued to play to packed houses into the fall months. The audiences came from throughout the country. Hardly an evening passed without at least one famous person at the front-row tables. Earl Carroll, Jake Shubert, and George White came to assess their competition. Politicians, corporate executives, playwrights, athletes, and film stars visited in dizzying succession, each greeted at the airport, presented with a Stetson, and duly photographed for newspapers and newsreels.

Joanna could not bring herself to quit the show. She knew she should return to college. For weeks she was torn by indecision. She could not determine how much her judgment was impaired by the fading hope that something might yet come of her summer romance with Brod Spurlock. Since his father's death he had been distant and preoccupied. He seemed to have retreated into his own world, closing all doors, pulling all blinds.

She had not heard from him in more than two weeks.

After much thought, she had decided to stay with the show until the end of the season, partly out of loyalty, partly because she was meeting so many interesting people. She had never seen such lavish entertainment as that offered in Fort Worth homes. There were parties almost every night, with Billy Rose's long-stemmed beauties as decorative ornaments. Joanna found herself chatting with such diverse fellow guests as J. Edgar Hoover, Ernest Hemingway, Max Baer, Patrick J. Hurley, William Knudson, Barney Oldfield.

Members of the cast frequently drove out to Lake Worth Casino after the show for drinks, relaxation, and breakfast before returning to the hotel.

One evening after an unusually successful performance Joanna joined them. They danced and performed impromptu skits. Spirits were high. Joanna and Stuttering Sam had just completed an extemporaneous

burlesque routine and collapsed into their chairs when a tall, immacu-
lately groomed young man approached their table. He gripped Stuttering Sam by the arm. "Vice squad," he said. "You two'll have to come
along with me."

Stuttering Sam stared at him, then burst into laughter. "T-T-Troy! I
d-d-didn't recognize you! You scared the s-s-s-shit out of me!" She turned
to Joanna, and made introductions. "This is T-T-Troy Spurlock. I haven't
s-s-seen him since the s-s-sixth grade."

Joanna saw the strong family resemblance. "Are you related to Brod
and Loren?"

The question seemed to amuse him. "In a manner of speaking. By
the rules of consanguinity, we're first cousins." He gestured toward a
distant table. "I just dropped in for breakfast. Why don't you two join
me?"

"Here, s-s-sit with us," Stuttering Sam said. "We're just about to
order."

Troy accepted. A place was made for him at the table. Joanna noted
he quickly fitted into the group.

He lacked Brod's firm manner, but he also seemed confident and
self-possessed. Thinner than Brod, but almost as tall, he obviously was
much more conscious of fashion. His three-piece navy blue pinstripe was
perfectly tailored, and his dark hair was combed straight back, with
every lock in place. On anyone else, his red and gold striped tie might
have seemed flashy, but Troy managed to give it flair.

Two or three times he looked at her with a quiet smile. But he only
stayed long enough to finish his breakfast.

Later, Stuttering Sam told her that Troy had just opened a new
department store downtown. "He was a s-s-strange kid," she said. "And
don't t-t-talk to him about Brod. There's some kind of b-b-bad blood
between them."

When Troy called her two days later and asked for a date, Joanna was
not surprised. In fact, she had made her decision beforehand. She still
had not heard from Brod. Their romance had lasted only two months.
Nothing was ever said about an engagement or marriage. She felt used,
and angry. She wanted to send Brod a message. She could think of no
better way than to date his estranged cousin.

Besides, Joanna was enough of a realist to admit to herself that she
was intrigued with Troy.

On their first date he picked her up after the show and took her to a
small, *intime* party in Westover Hills, an enclave of homes for the affluent. Troy was on first-name basis with everyone.

Joanna later remarked on the sophistication of the group.

Troy studied her a moment before answering. "You've just had a glimpse of a side of Texas most people never know. For every loud Texas millionaire there are dozens who avoid the spotlight with a passion. Unless you're well informed in the financial world, you never even hear their names."

"They seem close-knit," Joanna said. "If there were any undercurrents, I didn't notice."

"Oh, there's infighting," Troy said. "But you're right. It's a closed group. And the only way to crack it is to be born into it. Money isn't what it's all about. In fact, some of those people out there tonight lost their shirts in the crash. For them, being broke is like a summer cold, mildly embarrassing, something you simply endure until it's over. But new money doesn't stand a chance. You have to have a grandfather who came west without a spare shirt and took the country away from the Indians."

"You must have an interesting grandfather," Joanna said. "They seem to think a lot of you."

Troy laughed. "I have the requisite grandfather, in spades. In fact, I still live in the house he built. I hope you'll come see it before it falls down. But aside from my obvious charms, I'm accepted mostly because I represent something to them. They need me, and I need them."

He said he had noticed that Fort Worth merchants, nurtured in a practical, frontier environment, paid little attention to fashion. Many women, and some of the men, were forced to buy their clothing in St. Louis, Chicago, New York, and Europe. Troy believed these merchants were ignoring a growing market.

"These people have lawyers, doctors, accountants to advise them on other matters. I'm their consultant on fashion. I have practical, no-nonsense merchandise for those who want it. But I also carry top-of-the-line labels for those who care."

In the nights that followed, Joanna led Troy into discussing his ideas. He said most merchants simply stuck samples of their merchandise in the windows. He planned themes of window decoration, presenting each carefully calculated array of merchandise like a stage set. He drove her to the store and they walked around the building, discussing his Halloween window displays.

He said most Fort Worth merchants simply listed bargains in their advertisements. He was striving to imbue his newspaper ads with an element of sophistication, allure.

"I want to appeal to the imagination," he explained. "I believe there is creative ability in most everyone. I only want to suggest, and let my customers fill in the rest with their own personalities."

Joanna found Troy exciting and fun. He was a superb dancer. He was handsome, knew everyone, and made her feel glamorous. At times she did wish he were more ardent. He was circumspect to the point of exasperation, and his occasional kisses were more dutiful than passionate.

Not until Joanna visited Bluebonnet did she form serious doubts about Troy. She found the huge old house enchanting beyond words, with its stained-glass and leaded windows, gingerbread trim, high ceilings, and ornate woodwork. Troy showed her through the ground floor. Joanna was most taken with the library and its signed photographs. She learned for the first time that Troy's grandfather—and Brod's—had been a special friend of President Theodore Roosevelt, several Indian chiefs, and King Edward VII.

Troy's mother served tea. Joanna found her charming and without pretense. But Joanna saw an abrupt change come over Troy in the presence of his mother. He was ingratiating to her, like a little boy overly eager to please. Joanna felt as if she were a prize object brought home for approval.

Later she mentioned her impression to Stuttering Sam.

"Oh, he's a m-m-momma's boy," Stuttering Sam said. "I c-c-could have told you that."

Joanna was unable to dismiss Troy's finer qualities. She knew he was ambitious and caring. She could envision a life with him. She knew that she had much more in common with Troy than with Brod. Yet in her idle moments she longed for Brod to solve his personal problems and renew his courtship.

The carpenters completed their work, the carpet was laid, and at last Brod moved into his new office. It was suitably imposing. It achieved the psychological effect Brod had envisioned. The ghost of his father was banished. The new office clearly informed every employee that the son was now in charge.

By keeping the door to his new office closed, and dealing only through Miss Banning, Brod kept his distance from the employees. He also managed to get more work done.

On a day in late September, he had just returned from lunch and was studying a list of untested leases when his intercom buzzed. "Mr. Spurlock? Mr. Grover Sterling is here to see you."

Brod reached for the talk switch, intending to ask Miss Banning to inform Grover Sterling he had nothing to say to him. But with his hand on the button, he paused, his emotions confused. Common sense told him he should avoid a confrontation.

If they had a row, a settlement might be jeopardized.

But curiosity crowded out his better judgment.

What kind of man was his half brother?

And what did he want?

Brod punched the button. "Send him in."

He rose from his chair as Grover Sterling walked into the room. Brod did not invite him to be seated, nor did he offer to shake hands. They stood for a long moment, studying each other.

For Brod, the shock of seeing his half brother was even greater than first learning of his existence.

He was almost as tall as Brod, and lankier. But his shoulders were broader. He wore scuffed boots, soiled and faded Levi's, a battered leather jacket, and a broadbrimmed Stetson pulled low over his forehead. As if in defiance of his surroundings, he did not remove his hat. A pair of work gloves dangled from a hip pocket.

There was no mistaking the Spurlock face. Brod even saw something of himself there.

It was a disturbing moment.

A jury would have to be blind not to see the resemblance.

"Yes?" Brod said.

When Grover spoke, his voice was so much like Clay's that it gave Brod a momentary start. "You and your family have made me an offer," he said slowly, drawling each word to the edge of sarcasm. "I'm here to make you a counter offer. I propose that you leave my money in the company, in the form of shares, and put me in charge of all drilling and production."

Brod said the first thing that came to mind. "Get the fuck out of here."

Grover grinned—a carbon copy of Clay's slow, go-to-hell smile. He put his hands in his hip pockets and rocked forward on his boots, flexing his legs for a moment as he stared at his toes. He looked up at Brod from beneath the brim of his hat. "Brod, if you let me walk out that door, it'll be the biggest mistake you ever made. If I leave now, I promise I'll give you more trouble than you ever dreamed existed. I really don't want to do that. I'm here to tell you that you need me, and in the worst way."

"You don't have a low opinion of yourself, do you?"

"Nor of you. I don't think you're that big a fool. I know you're smart. I know you've got a head full of subsurface geology, hydrology, a thousand and one things Pop never knew. You've got something Pop never had, the scientific approach. That's worth a lot. But I also know that you don't know doodly shit about fieldwork. And I do."

Brod's third shock was in hearing Grover call Clay "Pop." He, Loren, and Crystelle had always called Clay "Dad."

Brod gave him a cool stare and did not answer.

"From the time I was in rompers, Pop took me with him around the patch," Grover went on. "We'd sit around a well night after night, and he'd show me everything. When we were traveling, he talked. During the summers, when I got old enough, he put my ass to work with the crews. It was tough, but I learned. You see, I've got the other side of the coin. You know the things I don't. I know the things you don't. No matter what our feelings are, we should be working together, not against each other."

Brod felt mixed emotions. In one sense, he felt superior. He had legitimacy and control of the company. Yet he burned with envy over the time Grover had spent with Clay—a companionship he himself had never known. He wanted to reach across the desk, seize Grover by the throat, and choke him to the floor.

"I'm not after the Spurlock name, a place at the family table," Grover went on. "It's too late for that. I'm Grover Sterling, an oil patch bastard. That's the way it's always been. Nothing will ever change it." A sweep of his hand encompassed the lavish office and furnishings. "I don't want all this. I only want to do the job I was born to do. If you have a shred of fairness, you won't deny me that."

Brod knew he should turn the matter over to Binkley Carothers. He was too disturbed to make a decision. But he was swayed by Grover Sterling's argument. During the last few weeks he had regretted his inadequacy on so many facets of field operations. In college he had learned how work in the field should be done. But Clay had never heard of the right way to do things. He had invented his own.

Yet there was something about Grover Sterling that put Brod on guard. Underneath that rough exterior was a manner a bit too smooth. His disarming directness seemed to mask a cunning mind.

Brod made a decision of sorts. He returned to his desk and gestured Grover toward a chair. "I can hire people who know drilling and production."

"Not people who know Pop's way of doing it." Grover hunched forward in the chair. "You must know by now that he was totally ignorant of common business practice. He still ran things from his hip pocket, the way he did when he started. The real headquarters of this company was wherever he happened to be. This building was set up as an extension of the toolbox on the running board of his car, of the leather wallet in his hip pocket. And there toward the end, the company was getting far too big, too complex, even for him."

Brod acknowledged the point with a brief nod. Grover Sterling had just stated what Brod had spent weeks learning.

"I've thought a lot about it," Grover went on. "I've talked to people who knew him, people who know the oil game. You and I ought to be putting this oil company back together instead of fucking around with a bunch of lawyers. If you read the newspapers, or listen to the radio, you know there's one hell of a war about to break out in Europe. I don't see any way we can keep out of it, no matter what Roosevelt says. The government will need all the oil they can get. Proration will be lifted. We ought to be getting ready."

"And just how would you go about that?" Brod asked.

"First, I'd block out and confirm our reserves. Pop had no patience. He'd ten times rather wildcat a new field than drill a surefire offset. If production dropped on a well, he'd quit pumping rather than milk it for a little extra profit. I've seen some mighty sick wells come to life after a dose of acid or nitro. God knows how many of those wells, shut down now, are crying for secondary recovery. New workover methods are coming along all the time. But I guess you know about that."

Brod nodded. Much experimentation had been done with various acids on different types of oil-bearing formations. Fracturing of the formations had been achieved with shaped charges. Sometimes a combination of methods had proved even more effective.

"And when war comes, equipment will be at a premium," Grover went on. "The company ought to be hocking everything to buy rigs and tools right now. I don't know how that's done. That's your department. I only know it should be done."

Brod sat lost in thought. He was impressed with Grover Sterling. What he said was true. The company needed him. Brod did not know how much his suspicions and resentments were affecting his judgment. But something did not seem right.

"You've made your point," he said. "Obviously, many other considerations enter into it. I'm in no position to make any commitments now, one way or the other. But I'll see to it that your proposal is cranked into the machinery."

Again came Grover's disturbing smile, so reminiscent of Clay. "That's all I ask." He rose from his chair and stood for an awkward moment.

Neither wanted to shake hands.

Grover backed away. "I'll be at the Worth for a few days. You can reach me there. I'm taking in the sights at the Centennial."

With one last, lingering glance around the office, he turned and strode out the door, closing it behind him.

Brod sat shaken. He knew he should call Bink immediately and inform him of Grover's visit.

But he wanted time to think it through and to talk with the family.

He knew instinctively that his decision on Grover Sterling's proposition would be one of the most important he would ever make for Spurlock Oil.

32

No!" Ann Leigh said. "Are you crazy? We won't have *anything* to do with those people! Do you hear me? I absolutely forbid it!"

Brod toyed with his dessert spoon. He had waited until after dinner to broach the subject. Ann Leigh's reaction did not surprise him. "Mom, we'll have to make some kind of a settlement with them eventually," he said quietly. "I'm just exploring our options."

"He's trying to get his head in the tent," Aunt Zetta said. "Mark my words."

Brod and Loren exchanged a covert glance of amusement. Aunt Zetta often visited now. She could be depended upon to voice the negative viewpoint.

"What do you think, Loren?" Brod asked.

Loren frowned at his plate. Ann Leigh, Zetta, and Crystelle watched him, waiting. Loren looked up at Brod. "The way you explained the situation, it sounds like we need him. The name's different. Maybe not many people would know."

"They'll know," Aunt Zetta snapped. "It's all over town by now. You can bet your bottom dollar on that."

"What do you think, Crystelle?" Brod asked.

Crystelle laughed in surprise. "Why ask me? This is a problem for you adults."

"Don't be a smart aleck," Brod said. "This may concern you more than any of us."

Crystelle stared at him in puzzlement. "Me? Why?"

Brod smiled at her. "I think Loren and I can survive with an illegitimate half brother running around town. But a girl has to think of her reputation."

"So I keep hearing," Crystelle said, with a sarcastic glance at her mother.

"Well?" Brod insisted.

Crystelle shrugged. "I don't care. What does he look like?"

Brod started to turn the question aside. Then he saw that Ann Leigh also seemed interested. "He's about my height," he told Crystelle. "Skinnier. Big nose, big ears. You'd never mistake him for anything but a Spurlock."

"Jeepers!" Crystelle said.

"I don't want to hear any more about him," Ann Leigh said.

"I haven't mentioned his proposal yet to Bink," Brod said. "Probably nothing will come of it."

Afterward, Loren came to Brod's room and made a point of raising the issue again. Brod was lounging on the daybed, boning up on the newest methods of secondary recovery. Loren sprawled in a wing chair and braced his house slippers against the coffee table. "Look, don't let Mom's attitude keep you from working out a peaceful settlement with the Sterlings," he said. "You're the one with the problems down there. It seems to me we need all the help we can get, no matter who or what."

Brod tossed his books aside. "I didn't tell Mom. But I was really impressed with him. He's rough as a cob. Looks like something you'd find in a bar out around the stockyards. But he has good ideas. And he seems to have a lot of Dad's piss and vinegar."

Loren laughed. "Not too much, I hope."

"I haven't made up my mind about him," Brod confided. "He might be invaluable. He knows the drillers, the roughnecks, the production crews, people who are just names to me. He could fill in a lot of gaps."

"Then I think you ought to accept his offer."

"You wouldn't mind?"

"Why in hell should I?"

Brod hesitated, choosing his words carefully. "I talked you into staying in school instead of coming to work. I thought you might feel he was taking your job."

Loren shook his head. "Hey, I'm going to run the business end someday, remember? Finding and pumping the oil is your department. I don't care who you hire."

Loren's support resolved the matter for Brod. "If it works out, I'll probably accept his offer," he said.

But Binkley Carothers was furious when Brod phoned to inform him of Grover Sterling's visit.

"God damn it, Brod! Anytime two principals are any way near litigation, they should never talk, except through their attorneys. Remember that! For God's sake, remember that!"

Brod ignored Bink's anger. "I want to explore this, Bink. He might make a real contribution, as long as his position is made clear."

"Meaning that he keeps it firmly in mind that he's oil patch trash?"

"Exactly. He more or less put that promise into words."

Brod heard only Bink's breathing for a time. "Brod, I think we'd better talk about this. He may be sincere at the moment. But we know what kind of blood is in his veins. I wonder if he'll be content, later on."

"We'd just see to it."

Again, Bink remained silent. When he spoke, his tone was thoughtful. "If you're inclined to accept his proposal, we may have the lever to effect the final settlement. We're close now. I'd like to have you over here at two o'clock Friday. Elise Sterling, Grover, and Archie are coming in with their lawyer. I think you should be here."

"What about Mother and Loren?"

"I don't think we need to subject Ann Leigh to this. It would be awkward. You can bring Loren, if you want. I hope to hammer out something everybody can live with. Then both sides can talk it over before drawing up the papers."

"You sound optimistic."

"I am. Elise Sterling is sensible. She knows she has a claim, but she also knows it's limited. She doesn't want to get bogged down in litigation or cause any more suffering. Damn it, the more I see of her, the better I like her."

"What about the Mexican family?"

"I talked to their attorney for about an hour this afternoon. We're working out the details of the trusts. I'll have the papers ready for your signatures next week."

"Sounds like we're out of the woods."

"Not quite. There's still Betty. But I've researched the law. I believe I can convince the court that her claim is a separate matter and not properly in the purview of probate. We'll see."

Twice during the next three days Brod called Joanna Mitchell at her hotel and suggested that they go out for an evening. She was cool and distant and made excuses. Brod did not take the third rejection lightly.

"Look, you have every right to be angry with me. Since Dad died, I've been faced with circumstances beyond my control. I hope you'll allow me to make amends."

"I'm not angry," Joanna said. "No amends are needed."

"If you're not angry, why won't you go out with me?"

"I told you. We have rehearsals for some replacements."

"What about the weekend?"

The line was silent for a moment. "I don't know what my schedule will be. Call me if you wish."

Brod cradled the phone, mystified. One of Joanna's most appealing qualities had been her honesty. She had never used the common feminine ploys. She had sounded as if she really did not give a damn whether he called.

Annoyed, Brod decided he would not call before the weekend.

Playing hard to get could work both ways.

Crystelle sat on the bottom row of bleachers, tucked her skirt, and arranged her notebooks on her lap. The afternoon sun had dropped below the rim of the stadium. An uncomfortable chill rose from the concrete. Across the field the cheerleaders were practicing, their yells bouncing hollowly throughout the empty stadium. At the south end, near the goal posts, the A and B teams were squared off in scrimmage. The A team was about to score.

She watched Moon as he broke from the huddle. He trotted to his position and bent over, one hand to the turf. While the quarterback called signals, Crystelle mentally confirmed her carefully considered opinion that Moon possessed the best-looking rump on the team. The ball was snapped. The quarterback handed off to the tailback, who faked to the outside, then cut into the hole Moon had cleared through the line. The tailback went into the end zone untouched. The coach blew his whistle, and scrimmage was over.

Moon got up slowly, roughhoused for a moment with his B-team opponent, then trotted across the field to Crystelle. He pulled off his helmet, leaned against the concrete barrier separating the field from the bleachers, and wiped sweat from his face with his sleeve. His golden curls had fallen across his forehead. A vicious bruise marred his left cheek. Crystelle wanted to inspect it, but some of his teammates had lingered. They yelled teasing catcalls. Moon ignored them.

"You didn't have to come down here," he said. "I could've picked you up later."

"I wanted to," she said. "We have to talk about you know what."

Moon glanced back at his teammates. "I've got to go shower."

"I'll wait for you in the car."

He trotted away, his head lowered in a shy-athlete shuffle, grotesque shoulder pads bouncing, hip pads flaring from his waist like stubby, misplaced wings. Crystelle often fantasized about making it with Moon still in uniform, fresh from a hard-fought game. She had never considered turning the daydream into reality. She would have died before mentioning it.

Gathering her books, she walked toward the parking lot.

Moon's battered Model A Ford was parked carelessly at the edge of the blacktop, the rear wheels on the grass. Crystelle climbed into the front seat, slid down to rest her knees on the dash, and thought about her growing problem with Moon.

They had never made it. Twice they had come close—so close that her stomach turned over each time she remembered. She had barely succeeded in fighting Moon off, while wanting him more than anything else in the world. She knew herself, and she knew Moon. Next time she would probably give in. She might yet become the school joke, like her former friend, Effie Lassiter.

Effie had sworn to Crystelle that she only did it one time, and that the boy had used one of those things. Yet she became pregnant. Effie's family said she had gone to St. Louis to visit an aunt, but everyone knew she was over in the Edna Gladney Home and had signed papers to put the baby out for adoption.

Moon came trotting across the grass, head down, arms pumping. He slid into the car behind the wheel, reached for Crystelle, and they kissed until he put a hand to her breast. She pushed away. "Moon! I told you!"

He grimaced, retreated, and started the car. "I thought about you all through scrimmage," he said. "You see me drop that pass in the end zone? No concentration."

"I can't concentrate either," Crystelle said. "I'm flunking algebra. We've got to do something. You think about what we talked about?"

Moon frowned and focused his attention on maneuvering the Ford through the parking lot. His hair was still wet from the shower, the blond curls darker. Crystelle smoothed them with her fingers and inspected the bruise on his cheek.

"There'd sure be hell to pay," Moon said, lowering his face and squinting against the glare of the sun on the pavement. "My folks, your family. I don't know what would happen."

"I'll tell you what would happen," Crystelle said, nibbling at his ear. "We could do it, then. Anytime we wanted. All the time. No one could say anything!"

Moon's face relaxed into a slow grin, and Crystelle knew he was envisioning the possibilities. Then a troubled thought rippled across his countenance. "They'd probably kick me off the team."

"They won't. You're too valuable. Moon, you're just hunting excuses. You've been lying to me about the way you feel."

He looked at her, anguish in his eyes. "No I haven't! Honest! It's just that this is a big step!"

"Of course it is. That's why I want to get it behind us."

They clattered out the Weatherford Highway and into the rolling hills west of town. Moon turned off on a ranch road and drove to a creek bottom. He stopped under the trees.

Moon sat watching horses graze in a pasture across the creek. "I think we ought to wait until I graduate," he said.

Crystelle moved away from him, knowing that Moon could be driven only so far. He had to make up his own mind. She leaned against the door on the passenger side. "That's almost a year away."

"Just eight months."

"This is our last chance," Crystelle said quietly. "This weekend, no one will miss us. I checked the calendar in the principal's office. No more school holidays until Thanksgiving. Then we'll be stuck with family stuff all through the holidays. If we don't go now, we never will. I'm scared. I don't know what may happen."

Moon turned and looked at her. Crystelle did not attempt to hide her torment. Unbidden tears surfaced and trickled down her cheeks.

Moon reached for her. "All right. We'll do it!"

Overcome by relief, and the light-headedness of love and adventure, Crystelle laughed and wept simultaneously, wiped at her tears, and covered Moon's face with kisses.

Gradually they quieted, and made plans.

"We'll take off first thing in the morning," Moon said. "You sure your brothers won't come after us?"

Crystelle scoffed. "They don't know I exist. Believe me, I won't be missed until Sunday, at least. Maybe not then, if Mom has anyone else around to gripe at."

Moon sobered. "My folks will have the troops out by Saturday."

"Make up a story."

Moon considered the problem. "I'll tell them I'm spending the night with Dwayne. It'll be a while before they check."

The next morning they each cut two classes and drove across the county line to Weatherford. Crystelle wore her long navy blue tweed skirt, matching jacket, and the dark blue blouse with a mandarin collar. She applied mascara and a heavy layer of makeup, and examined the results in her compact mirror. "I look positively middle-aged," she said.

"You look different," Moon conceded.

Moon wore his dark gray suit. Accustomed to seeing him in plain trousers and a pullover, Crystelle thought he looked like a little boy masquerading as an adult.

"I hope we get away with this," she said.

Moon laughed nervously. "They can't put us in jail for trying."

After all their preparations the brief routine in the county clerk's office was anticlimactic. Moon showed his driver's license, with the birthdate artfully altered. Crystelle merely swore she was over eighteen.

In less then ten minutes they emerged with a marriage license.

Then they sped back to Fort Worth in time for their eleven o'clock

classes, each with an explanation for the tardy arrival. Moon told his
teacher he'd had car trouble. Crystelle implied that she was experiencing
one of those days every young woman could expect. She was not questioned further.

On Friday, with school dismissed for the annual teachers' meeting,
they again drove to Weatherford and were married by an aged justice of
the peace. Clerks from the tax office across the hall served as witnesses.
Moon kissed the bride, and received handshakes and congratulations.

In a daze they walked out into the soft sunshine of October, husband
and wife.

Moon stopped and looked at her. "I've got news for you. I can't wait
till we get to San Antonio."

"We can't do it here on the courthouse steps," Crystelle said. "Take
me somewhere, Moon."

With his first glimpse of Elise Sterling, Brod knew beyond doubt that
his father had loved her passionately. Not even Bink's effusive praise had
prepared him for her unusual beauty and singular charm. She strode into
Bink's conference room poised, petite, quietly dominating the moment.
Her gray-tinged brown hair was close-cropped and feathered, framing
her delicate but strong features. Her skin was tanned, making her pale
green eyes even more striking. They conveyed deep intelligence.

Her two sons and a lawyer trailed in her wake. Grover accorded
Brod a brief nod. Archie glanced at Brod, then looked away. At sixteen,
Archie had not reached his full height. He was thin and lanky.

Bink greeted them and took his place at the end of the conference
table. The Sterling family lawyer was introduced as Donald Benton. He
was rotund and prematurely bald. He did not offer to shake hands.

The Sterlings and their lawyer sat on Bink's left, Brod on his right.
"I'm hoping we can come to an understanding today, Don," Bink said. "I
believe we're close on all the essentials."

Grover spoke directly to Brod. "What about my proposal?"

Brod glanced at Bink for a cue, found none, and fielded the question
himself. "Under the terms you outlined, I'm inclined to accept."

Grover smiled. "You can put the bar sinister on my office stationery."

Brod did not answer.

Bink cleared his throat. "Grover, if that bothers you to the point of
conflict, perhaps the arrangement would not work out."

"Of course it bothers me," Grover said. "Why in hell wouldn't it? But
I accept it. There'll be no conflict."

Brod saw that Elise had ignored the exchange. She was looking at him with a faint smile. She seemed amused, as if she and Brod shared some secret.

"I'll speak frankly," Benton said. "Aside from some questions of payout, we can live with your offer. But Grover insists on receiving his portion in company shares and his employment in a position such as he discussed the other day."

"Not *a* position. *The* position," Grover said.

"I'll be just as frank," Brod said. "Most of my family is firmly opposed to Grover's proposal. But I'm president and chief executive officer. As long as he does his job, fine. But I must protect the company. I insist on an escape clause."

"Such as?" Benton asked.

"The right to dismiss him for cause, should the occasion arise, and to convert his shares to cash."

"Wait a minute," Grover said. "I've got to have some protection, too."

"Perhaps we could effect the clause, with penalties if exercised," said Benton.

The negotiations continued for three hours on this and other issues. Eventually all details were worked out. Brod was pleased with the results. Grover would be brought into the company as an employee, with enough shares to spur his extra efforts. Archie would have a college trust fund, plus an unencumbered trust on his twenty-first birthday. Elise would receive a cash settlement that should see her through the remainder of her life.

When the session ended, Elise came around the table to Brod. "I would have known you anywhere. You're so much like your father when he was about your age."

Brod did not know what to say. He did not want to talk with the woman who had caused his father to betray his family. Yet he was drawn by the mystery she posed. "You knew him then?"

She smiled and infused a single word with infinite meaning. "Yes."

The others were filing out the door. Brod sought a lighter topic. "Will you be in town long?"

"We're driving back in the morning. We've been taking in the Centennial celebration. It's been fun, but I'm exhausted. I don't much care for city life."

Brod studied the woman his father had loved for more than twenty years.

He felt mingled curiosity and aversion.

Her hand went tentatively to his arm. "Brod?" She searched his face. "I see something in your eyes that disturbs me. You mustn't hate your father because of me, because of this." She gestured to the lawyers' table, her departing sons.

Brod remained silent, irritated that she had read him so accurately.

She frowned up at him. "Clay used to say I'm a witch. Maybe he was right. But I knew his mind, and I think I know yours. It's natural for you to resent me, even to hate me. But you shouldn't blame Clay. I wish I could make you understand how it was. I owe you that. I owe it to Clay."

Brod hesitated. He knew his mother was right. He should have nothing to do with this woman. But he was driven to explore all the unknown aspects of his father's life. "Perhaps we could have dinner at the Fort Worth Club. Just the two of us."

Elise laughed. "You don't do things by half measures, do you? Full speed ahead and the devil take the hindmost. That's exactly the way Clay would have handled it. All right. I'd love to have dinner with you. We'll set this town on its ear. Broderick Spurlock and his father's kept woman, having a good time together."

As they moved toward the door, she added, almost under her breath, "I hope Clay is watching."

Elise talked through dinner, giving Brod a clearer picture of her life. She revealed that Clay had bought her a small ranch early in their relationship. Raising purebred cattle and registered quarter horses, she had expanded the ranch to almost three thousand acres.

As she talked, Brod could envision her strong hands tending newborn calves, her soft, authoritative voice dispersing her Mexican hands to various portions of the ranch. Everything about her was practical. She was as natural as the cactus flowers in her own pastures.

The dinner dishes were cleared away. Elise declined dessert. Brod ordered coffee and brandy.

Elise toyed with her snifter, as if trying to determine how much to tell. She looked up at Brod and smiled. "I was married to someone else when I met your father. Did you know that?"

"No," Brod lied.

"He stopped to steal some pipe from a well on a corner of our ranch." She saw Brod's expression and laughed. "Yes, steal! He was broke. He needed the pipe. So he lowered some dynamite into that old well, blew the casing apart, and pulled out the sections he had jarred loose."

Brod had never heard of the trick. He was fascinated by the sheer simplicity of it.

"I heard the explosion," Elise went on. "I was hunting a colt I was treating for an infected leg. I rode over the hill to see what the hell was going on, and there was Clay."

Her eyes glazed with memory. "God, but he was handsome. High boots, whipcord britches, and that go-to-hell grin. I knew right then I had met somebody. He lied like a dog trotting, that grin daring me to call him a liar. And I thought what the hell, that old pipe wasn't doing anyone any good, in the ground rotting. So I just joked, and let him take it. From the way he was looking at me, I figured I hadn't seen the last of him. I was right. A few weeks later, he came back and stole *me.*"

Brod laughed. He liked Elise's humor.

"That was the way your father was. What he wanted, he took. And he always hoped that someone would give him enough of a fight to make things interesting."

She cocked her head to one side in reflection. "I never knew how he realized I was ripe for stealing. I was bored with my life. But I didn't even know it. I guess he saw that. Hooking up with Clay was like grabbing a live wire. Sometimes it was more than I could stand. But I couldn't turn loose."

Again Brod laughed. "Someone once told me that meeting Dad was like getting picked up by a tornado."

Elise nodded agreement. "He picked you up and whirled you around and around. And when he set you down you were somewhere else." She paused. "Where he set me down was on the ranch. And I was pregnant."

Elise leaned forward, her eyes pleading. "It's very important that you understand this. I knew from the first that I could never have all of him. So I never made any demands. I knew that if I did, I'd lose him. He had too much energy to be corralled. Nothing would hold him. But I understood him well enough to know that if I gave him independence, and preserved my own, I would always have that part of him. And that's the way it was. He had a drive for respectability, family ties, convention. Your mother gave him that. But he chafed against the restraints. I gave him independence. It hurt, but I never asked him where he was going, when he would be back. I heard about his other women, but I ignored them. I just preserved what we had. Can you understand that?"

Brod hesitated. He thought of his own yearnings for his father's attention. "I've never understood how he could take so much from so many, and give so little of himself."

Elise reached for his hand. "Oh, Brod, you mustn't think that! Clay was a giver, not a taker. I know most people think he was cold and unfeeling. But he wasn't. That was his problem. He truly loved your mother, me, the Mexican woman, and probably about two dozen others we don't even know about. He wanted to spend time with you, Loren, Grover, Archie, the Mexican kids, and all the little bastards he probably left scattered around the oil patch. He loved life, people, every moment he breathed more than anyone I've ever known. There simply wasn't enough of him to go around. You *must* understand that."

Brod had revealed far more of himself than he had intended. Clay had been right. Elise was a witch. He was under her spell. "I certainly can understand why he was attracted to you," he said.

Tears sprang to her eyes. "Oh, Brod, thank you for saying that." She fought for control. "Do you see why I'm telling you all this?"

He thought he knew, but he wanted her to spell it out. He shook his head.

"Grover also has deep resentments. You're both so much like Clay. His energy, strength, determination. If you two can work together, I promise you the world will sit up and take notice. But if you two ever fight, please let me know, so I can sell tickets. Someone should make a little money out of it. Because you'll destroy each other, as sure as God made little green apples."

Crystelle was not missed until Saturday afternoon, and then only because Moon Belford's parents became alarmed.

Brod was in his office, studying the logs on an old well, when Harvey Belford phoned. Belford had been a middle-level bank executive under Durwood Spurlock at the time of the embezzlement. He was now president and board chairman. He did not hold a high opinion of the Spurlock family.

"Moon's missing," he said. "Have you seen Crystelle lately?"

Brod had not seen her at breakfast. But that was not unusual. He recalled that she was not at dinner the previous evening. She had left word that she had a date. Brod thought of her growing sullenness, her secrecy.

He gripped the phone, alarmed at the possibilities. "I'll find out and call you back," he said.

He phoned Ann Leigh. After a search she determined that no one had seen Crystelle since early Friday. The maid said her bed had not been slept in. Some of her clothes were missing.

Brod returned Harvey Belford's call. "Crystelle isn't at home. Her mother is searching for her. But it seems obvious they're probably together."

"Damn it, they've eloped. I'll tell you right now. I'm not going to allow that boy's life ruined. I won't stand for it!"

Brod checked a quick flash of anger. Moon was almost eighteen, Crystelle not yet seventeen. "Let's find them before we make any decisions. Something else may have happened to them. Can you come over to the house?"

Brod drove home. The Belfords had already arrived. Ann Leigh and Estelle Belford were barely civil to each other, and Brod gathered that a remark already had been made expressing concern for Moon's ruined life. Loren was in the study, phoning Crystelle's friends, probing for information.

Brod called Bink and asked his recommendation for a private detective.

"The best is Wells, a retired policeman," Bink said. "I don't remember his first name, but everyone calls him Apache. That's the way it's listed in the telephone book."

Apache Wells listened to Brod Spurlock's explanation with professional detachment. The young man seemed completely composed. Wells was impressed. Usually the family was too upset to make good sense.

"Don't worry," he said. "We'll find them. This happens all the time. I'll need some information."

Within fifteen minutes he had filled three pages of a five-cent Red Chief tablet with facts. He thanked Spurlock and promised to call him back as soon as he had the couple located.

He scanned back over his notes, absorbing the material. The situation seemed routine. Long ago he had established a basic procedure in such cases.

First, he always checked the public records in neighboring counties. If that failed to produce clues, he then checked the second tier of counties. Couples of high school age seldom traveled any great distance for the wedding ceremony.

All county offices were closed for the weekend, but he was on a first-name basis with county clerks and peace justices. Within an hour he learned that Moon Belford and Crystelle Spurlock had exchanged vows in Weatherford.

He systematically telephoned tourist courts and service stations along the highways leading out of Weatherford and found that Moon and Crystelle spent their first wedded night at the Alamo Courts on U.S. 80.

"A lovely couple," said the owner of the Courts, a woman Wells estimated to be in her late sixties, from the sound of her voice. "They seemed a little young, but very much in love."

Experience had taught him that young couples tended to follow a pattern. If they did not go to the Crazy Water Hotel in Mineral Wells for their honeymoon, they invariably traveled to San Antonio, Galveston, or New Orleans, if they had the money. He gathered that money was no problem for Moon Belford.

He phoned the Crazy Water Hotel, a health spa elevated into a well-known resort. He drew a blank.

Next he turned to San Antonio, simply because it was more likely and less complicated than Galveston or New Orleans.

By midnight he had found them. He phoned Brod.

"They're at the Menger Hotel, registered as Mr. and Mrs. Montgomery B. Belford. They've reserved the room for three nights. So unless they're planning to skip without paying the bill, they'll be there a while."

Brod repeated the detective's findings for Ann Leigh, Loren, and the Belfords.

Estelle Belford was inconsolable. "Moon still has a year of high school and at least four years of college before he can even think about supporting a wife. We must put a stop to it."

"That won't be difficult," Brod told her. "Crystelle is underage. We can obtain an annulment. If Mr. Belford and I left now, we could be in San Antonio before noon tomorrow. I think we should drive down there and bring them back."

Belford agreed. Estelle wanted to go, but her husband vetoed the idea. "We'll drive straight through," he explained. "It'll be a hard trip."

Belford spoke little on the seven-hour dash to San Antonio. Brod drove steadily, stopping only once for gasoline. They arrived a few minutes after nine on Sunday morning. Brod pulled into a parking lot across from the Alamo. They left the car and walked into the white marble lobby of the Menger Hotel. Brod asked for the supervising manager and demanded a key to the room.

The manager checked the registration card and call slips. "Our guests have asked not to be disturbed," he said.

Brod loomed over him. "Mister, I'm the brother of the young girl in that room. She's underage. This gentleman is the father of the boy. If you wish to avoid legal complications, I advise you to give us a key to that room."

The manager's hesitation was brief. He summoned the house detective, who led the way. Brod rapped on the door.

"Who is it?" Moon called.

"Brod Spurlock. Moon, I'm with your father. We're coming in."

Through the open transom Brod heard frantic whispering.

"Just a minute!" Moon called.

Brod, Belford, and the house detective waited. Moon opened the door.

Brod strode into the room. Crystelle was wearing a white negligee and wrap. Brod saw both fear and anger in her eyes. "We're married, Brod!" she said, raising her voice. "There's nothing you can do about it."

"Get dressed," he said. "Get your things together. We're going home."

Belford took Moon into the hall, out of earshot. The house detective left.

"I'm probably pregnant," Crystelle said. "What'll you do about that?"

Brod thought she sounded more hopeful than certain. "We'll cross that bridge when we get to it."

"I'm not going to let you do this to me. We love each other. We belong together."

"Crystelle, you're legally a child. The marriage will be annulled, as if it never happened."

Crystelle began to cry. "But it *did* happen. You can't change that!"

"No," Brod said. "I can't change that. I wish to God I could."

"Don't do this to me!" Crystelle begged. "Please!"

"It's for your own good."

Moon and Belford came back into the room. Moon seemed dazed. He stared at the floor. He would not look at Brod or Crystelle.

"Moon and I will drive back in his car," Belford said. "I trust we can accomplish the legal work Monday."

Brod nodded agreement. Belford walked to the phone and called his wife in Fort Worth. He talked for a few minutes in low tones, then turned the phone over to Moon.

Brod could hear Estelle Belford's strident voice as she lectured her son. For the most part, Moon only listened, his body slumping. "I'm sorry, Momma," he kept repeating.

Moon signed off after promising his mother he would be home soon. He stood for a moment, tears coursing down his cheeks. Belford gestured impatiently. Moon hurriedly picked up scattered clothing and stuffed it into a suitcase.

Moon and Belford left without looking back. Brod walked over and closed the door behind them.

Crystelle burst into wracking sobs. "Oh, God, I hate you! I'll never forgive you. You've ruined my life!"

"Shut up and get dressed. Someday you'll thank me. You've just seen what a gutless wonder you tried to marry. A momma's boy if there ever was one."

"I'm not going back. It'll be all over school Monday."

"It'll be forgotten in six weeks. I'll give you thirty minutes to get dressed and pack your things."

He walked down to the lobby, bought a newspaper, and strolled into a dark-paneled bar. A plaque on the wall said that Teddy Roosevelt had used the bar as headquarters while enlisting his Rough Riders for the Spanish-American War. Brod scanned through the paper, finished a drink, and returned to the room.

Crystelle did not answer his knock. The silence behind the door suddenly filled him with dread premonition. He fished for the key, and entered the room.

Her clothing still lay scattered. The suitcase rested on the rack in the corner, untouched. The bathroom door was closed. Brod hurried to it and knocked. "Crystelle?" She did not answer. He tried the knob. The door was locked.

"Crystelle! Answer me!" he yelled, rattling the knob.

He could hear the hum of the distant elevators, cars passing below on the streets. From behind the door came only deadly silence.

Frantic, Brod slammed his shoulder into the door. On his third try, the wood frame split and the door swung open.

Crystelle lay in a crimson pool, her eyes staring sightless as her life's blood slowly spread across the white tile floor. Totally gripped in the horror of the moment, Brod knelt and touched her face. Her skin was cold and drained of color.

He hurried to the phone and rang the hotel desk. "Call an ambulance! Get a doctor to this room! My sister is bleeding to death!"

He returned to the bathroom, lifted Crystelle from the floor, and carried her to the bed. He was standing over her, trying to find a pulse, when the house detective entered the room. He pushed Brod aside.

"A doctor is on the way," he said. He examined Crystelle's arms, then seized her by the elbows, blocking circulation with his thumbs. "See if you can find something to use as a tourniquet."

With his pocket knife, Brod cut two lengths of cord from the window blinds. He maintained pressure on one of Crystelle's arms while the detective applied a tourniquet to the other.

They had just finished with the second tourniquet when the doctor arrived. Registered for a medical conference, he had been paged from the dining room. He hurriedly examined Crystelle and gave her a shot of Adrenalin.

"Will she live?" Brod asked.

"Too early to tell," the doctor said. "The essential thing is to get her to a hospital for a transfusion."

The ambulance arrived. Crystelle was placed on a stretcher. Brod followed as she was taken to the waiting ambulance.

At the hospital he was asked to wait in a lounge outside the emergency room. As hospital attendants passed through a swinging door he caught glimpses of a medical team working over her. A policeman arrived, asked a few questions, and made notes. More than an hour passed before a doctor came out to talk to Brod.

"Officially, she's still in critical condition," he said. "But unless further complications develop, I have hope for her."

"What kind of complications?"

"She went into shock. We almost lost her. At the moment she's stabilized. But reactions are difficult to predict, especially in such massive transfusions. If all continues well, we'll move her to intensive care. We can worry about repairs to the wrists later."

"What kind of repairs?"

"The cuts are deep. Especially on the left wrist. Nerves, tendons severed."

"Will there be permanent damage?"

The doctor hedged. "It's too early to tell."

Brod called home and told Loren what had happened.

"Try not to alarm Mom. But I think you should bring her down here."

That evening Crystelle regained consciousness and seemed much better. Brod was allowed to see her. She was tucked away in one corner of intensive care, her bed curtained off from the traffic.

"You should have let me die," she said. "I'm going to make you sorry you didn't."

He ignored the threat. "Mom's on the way down here to take care of you."

"Birds of a feather," Crystelle said softly. She laughed. "We can both hole up in the house and keep each other company."

Brod wondered if she was hallucinating. Her eyes were glazed, and she seemed animated. "What are you talking about?"

"Don't you know? Mom was married to somebody else when she met Dad. There was one hell of an uproar. Mucho scandal. That's why she seldom goes out."

Brod thought of the papers he had found in Clay's desk. "What makes you think so?"

"Suggie Donnalson overheard her mother telling someone about it. Suggie told me. That's why she's always lecturing me. That's why Granddad wouldn't have anything to do with us, why he left all his money to Troy. We were all born in scandal. I'm a chip off the old block."

"All that was a long time ago."

"People remember," Crystelle insisted. "Suggie's mother remembered."

With the arrival of cool nights in late October, attendance in the open-air Casa Mañana declined. The production was still playing to better than eighty-percent capacity. But rumors spread that the show would soon close.

Joanna Mitchell faced the inevitable with mixed emotions. She had not heard from Brod Spurlock in more than three weeks. Her dalliance with Troy had been diverting but in many ways disappointing. Witty and charming, he seemed incapable of strong feeling. He had given no evidence that their relationship ever would progress beyond friendship.

One rainy morning she overslept. Stuttering Sam and Bojangles had gone shopping. Joanna prepared to go down to the coffee shop alone for breakfast.

When the elevator door opened on her floor, she thought for a moment that the tall, solitary passenger was Brod Spurlock. She opened her mouth to speak, then realized her mistake. The man was slimmer, more rugged-looking. The elevator operator held the door and looked at her askance. Hurriedly, Joanna stepped into the car. The moment had been so awkward she felt an explanation was in order.

"I thought you were someone else," she said to the man as they descended.

He smiled at her. "Now, why would you think that?" he drawled. "I gave up a long time ago on trying to be someone else. Looks like I'm stuck with being me. Grover Sterling, at your service, ma'am."

His resemblance to the Spurlocks—Brod, Loren, Troy—was uncanny. He had a rural look about him. His West Texas accent was more pronounced. She liked his relaxed, offhand humor, his slow, easy smile.

"Joanna Mitchell," she said.

"I know. I've attended Casa the last four nights. I looked you up on the playbill the moment you came on stage."

They reached the ground floor. As they stepped out into the lobby, Sterling gestured toward the coffee shop. "I'm going in for breakfast. Would you care to join me?"

Joanna did not like to dine alone, especially in public. She had found that quick, impromptu friendships were common in Texas. She saw no harm in it. "That'd be nice," she said.

He was adept with small talk and kept her occupied through breakfast. Nor was his engaging manner reserved for her alone. He deftly handled the waitress with such skill that the poor girl was completely undone and hovered over his every bite.

He was not handsome—not in the dark way of Brod, Loren, or even Troy. But he possessed a wiry, rawhide strength, and his face had character. He was not impressively dressed. His boots were scuffed. He wore ordinary work trousers, a well-worn suede leather jacket, and a white shirt open at the neck.

"What kind of work do you do?" she asked.

He pondered the question for a moment, as if there might be alternative answers. "I'm in oil."

Joanna had to know. "Your own company?"

He hesitated. "I'm with Spurlock Oil."

Now she was sure of the resemblance. It dawned on her that he could be a cousin, through the distaff side. "I know Brod, Loren, and Troy," she said. "Are you related?"

He laughed. "Not close enough to claim."

Remembering Stuttering Sam's warning of the rift between Brod and Troy, Joanna changed the subject, assuming that Grover Sterling was somehow involved.

He talked about his experiences in the oil fields. "We'll have to fly out and look at an oil well while you're here," he said. "In the meantime, let's go honky-tonking."

"Go where?" Joanna had not heard the term before.

"Honky-tonking. I'm sure the good people of Fort Worth have shown you the best they have to offer, the finest restaurants, the best night clubs, the most lavish homes. I therefore believe it my solemn duty to show you the other side—the dirty saloons, filthy beer joints, and unadulterated dives where all true Texans really live. I promise you, if you can endure hearing W. Lee O'Daniel's 'Beautiful Texas' a hundred times, you'll see sights you'll remember the rest of your life."

Joanna laughed. She had heard that song repeatedly. Raucous, yet appealing, it was on every jukebox.

She hesitated.

"If the rain keeps up, there won't be a show this evening," Sterling said. "We can make a night of it."

Joanna was intrigued. Never before had she been enticed with promises of touring dirty dives. "All right," she said.

Sterling gave her his slow, devastating smile. "Good. Wear the cruddiest clothes you can find. We may have to fight our way out of a place or two."

He first took her to a saloon near the stockyards. Despite Grover's warning, Joanna was appalled. Beer signs over the bar provided the only illumination. The rough concrete floor was filthy. The only furniture was cane-bottom chairs and tables of unfinished wood. The place was jammed. A loud string band made conversation almost impossible.

Grover led her close to the bandstand. He stopped at a table, talked with two seated men, and slipped them some money. They rose and moved to the bar, leaving the table for Grover and Joanna.

A male vocalist sang in a flat, nasal tone, wailing something about an empty cot in the bunkhouse. On the dance floor, couples shuffled in time to the music. Grover was smiling, watching her reaction.

Most of the men around her wore Levi's, bright-colored shirts, and wide-brimmed hats. The Levi's were dirty, the shirts faded, and the hats greasy and soiled.

Suddenly Joanna understood. These men were true cattlemen, as authentic as the cow manure on their boots. She leaned close to Grover's ear to talk above the noise.

"Are all of these men cowboys?"

"More or less," he said. "Some are truckers who brought a load in to the slaughterhouse. Most are here to sell cattle in the auction ring, or to buy. A few of them work in the stockyards."

The singer ended the number to enthusiastic applause. After a lead-in, he began singing a ballad about a great speckled bird. The melody was plaintive, appealing, a timeless lament. Guitars and a violin filled in the background. Joanna listened, mesmerized. The vocalist, a small, earnest young man with dark, wavy hair, sang with feeling. When the number ended, Joanna joined the applause.

"I've never heard anything like it," she said.

"I was wondering if you'd pick up on it," Grover said. "You either love it or you hate it."

"What kind of music is it?"

Grover spoke close to her ear. "It's so new it hasn't even been named yet. It's something that's happening now, and it's happening right here. There must be at least a hundred bands like this, maybe two hundred, playing all over Texas tonight, shaping what this music is going to be. People who don't know any better call it hillbilly. But it isn't. It's different. Someday it'll have a name, and it'll be an American phenomenon, like jazz."

They bar-hopped to other places, similar, but different. Grover expanded on his theme. Joanna found he was an authority on what he called "the beer-joint sound."

"It's a blending of Southern hillbilly, English and Scot folk songs, Negro spirituals, cowboy lament, Mexican heroic ballads, fiddlers' tunes, Cajun love songs, church hymns. All of these musicians grew up hearing the phonograph records of Jimmie Rodgers, the Carter family, Vernon Dalhart. Most of them learned to yodel like Rodgers, until their voices changed. Now they're evolving their own styles."

They ended the night in a large, barnlike dance hall. Grover taught her dances called the Bob Wills Two-step, the Cotton-eyed Joe, and Put Your Little Foot.

By the time they returned to the hotel at three in the morning,

Joanna was exhausted. Grover simply said good night and left her at her door.

Stuttering Sam was already asleep. Joanna dressed for bed and lay awake, reflecting on her adventures in Texas. She had just had the most unusual date of her whole life—and one of the most enjoyable. She thought of the men she had met in Texas. By comparison those she had known in college seemed half alive. She found herself reluctant to return to the East.

With cool calculation, she evaluated her chances for remaining in Texas as a bride. She had dated a dozen men. She narrowed the possibilities to three—Troy, Brod, and—after tonight—Grover Sterling.

She was attracted to all three.

Not until the next morning did she discover the irony in her thinking.

When she mentioned her adventures with Grover Sterling, Stuttering Sam burst into peals of laughter.

"You're s-s-sure going through the S-S-Spurlocks," she said.

"What do you mean?"

Stuttering Sam hesitated. Joanna had noticed that Fort Worth residents were reluctant to confide local gossip to outsiders.

"Please tell me," Joanna pleaded. "I can keep a secret."

"Brod and S-S-Sterling are half b-b-brothers," Sam said. "They say Brod's d-d-daddy scattered his s-s-seed all over West Texas. Sterling's an oil patch b-b-bastard."

Joanna felt her face glow with embarrassment as she remembered Grover's amusement and deliberate hesitation at her mention of the Spurlocks.

Somehow, the knowledge that Grover was an illegitimate Spurlock made him even more intriguing.

33

"Y ou've got to understand how it was in those days," Grover said. "The waste was tremendous. Apparently they just didn't give a shit. With a good workover, some of those old wells could still make money."

Brod sat silent for a moment, thinking the problem through, trying to imagine the huge gas wells his father and others had allowed to blow, taking pressure off entire oil fields. "It wasn't that they didn't care," he said. "They just didn't know better. The professors told us half the potential was lost at Desdemona alone. Gone forever."

For two weeks Brod and Grover had been drafting a sound production program, aimed at revitalizing old wells and drilling offsets to known reserves. It was long after midnight. Maps, seismographic reports, production records, and lease agreements lay scattered around them in Brod's office. Brod was exhausted. He had been working steadily eighteen hours. Grover had proposed twenty-two potential secondary recovery operations, sixteen offsets, and three dry holes he felt might merit reentry for deeper exploration.

Brod was pleased with most of the proposals, even though he wondered if the overall plans were not too ambitious. Grover was an intelligent, conscientious hard worker, with sound knowledge of field operations.

Thus far they had functioned well together. Brod's early reservations had eased. He no longer listened to his mother, who remained strongly opposed to Grover, or to Aunt Zetta, who as usual predicted disaster. Grover had been invaluable. The headquarters staff seemed to like him, and if any resentment existed over his appointment as production chief, Brod was unable to detect it. In fact Grover had most of the staff fawning over him.

Brod turned through the list. Even with expanded operations the work should keep them busy for the better part of a year.

He now had to decide if the list should be trimmed. Also, he remained uncertain of how best to put the plan into effect. Two courses of action were open. He could lease the equipment and hire the work done through drilling contractors and service companies or he could expand Spurlock Oil's own production department, borrowing money to purchase the equipment.

Grover wanted to expand.

Brod was doubtful.

They had been debating the matter for the last two days.

"Can't you see, Brod? We're doing what Pop always wanted to do but didn't know how," Grover said, summing up his argument. "Other early wildcatters cashed in on their big strikes and spent the rest of their lives behind a desk. Some never looked at a drill bit again. They milked everything out of their reserves and piled up the money. All Pop knew was wildcatting. He didn't have the patience to follow through. He left that to Pete. After Pete was gone, that part of the company went to hell. Pop was flush when he hit, broke when he didn't. He knew there was money in workovers. He just didn't want to be bothered with it."

"And you do?"

Grover pointed to the material scattered around them. "I double fucking guarantee you that if we follow up on this, we'll double the proven assets of this company in five years."

"Maybe," Brod conceded. "But there are risks I can't ignore. We'd have to take on a heavy debt. If prices drop again, the company would be in serious trouble."

"And if there's a war, the lid will be lifted on production. Prices will go up, like they did during the Great War. Right now good men can be hired dirt cheap. We can use them now at low wages to prove out the company's reserves. The Depression isn't going to last forever. Some economists think we're pulling out of it now. If there *is* a war, Spurlock Oil can become a big corporation, not just one more pissant little oil company. I'm gambling everything I've got that within five years, my part of it will be worth ten times what it is now. If I didn't think so, I'd go out and wildcat on my own."

"You might make more on the commodities market," Brod said. "This is the same thing. High-risk gambling on the future."

"Sure! But how can we lose? We're on the upward curve from the worst depression in history. Equipment, manpower will never be cheaper, at least not for the next twenty years. If we lose, we can just start over. Pop did it a dozen times."

Brod gave the thought one of his rare smiles. In many ways he would relish the challenge of building a company from scratch. He fully understood his father's drive to keep moving on, leaving the duller work to others.

He sighed and rubbed his tired eyes. He had delayed his decision long enough. Expansion would not be easy. But Grover was right. The rewards might be spectacular.

"All right," he said. "We'll go for expansion. I'll take these figures and meet with the bankers today. When will you have the bid specifications?"

Grover glanced at his watch. "I'll get on it the first thing today. I should have them by tonight. When do you want to start the grand tour?"

Brod hesitated. They planned to make an on-site inspection of old holes, producing wells, and potential drilling sites. Unless problems developed, he should finish with the bankers during the day. Crystelle had been brought home by ambulance. The doctors said she was now out of danger. Her mother was keeping a close watch on her.

"I could leave tomorrow," he said. "You?"

Grover nodded agreement. "I'll set things up."

"Good. I'd like to go over the details of the equipment purchase tonight."

Grover frowned. "One problem. I have a heavy date. I'd hate to break it."

Brod was thrown off guard. He had devoted himself completely to the company during the last few weeks. He assumed that Grover was doing the same.

"No need," he said. "You can leave the material on my desk. We can discuss it on the road."

"Will do," Grover said. He stuffed papers into his briefcase, rose, and started for the door. He paused. "By the way, the girl I'm dating said she knew you. Joanna Mitchell."

Brod saw that Grover was watching him carefully. He fought down an irrational pang of jealousy. Allowing nothing to show on his face, he nodded. "I dated her a few times."

If Grover was disappointed in Brod's response, he gave no indication. He left, letting himself out of the building with his own key.

Brod returned to work. During the next hour and a half he assembled all of the figures on equipment and payroll. When he finished, he was too tired to move. He poured a shot of brandy, hoping it would give him enough energy to drive home to bed.

Waiting for the alcohol to take effect, he leaned back in his chair and closed his eyes.

Grover's calculated mention of Joanna Mitchell had been a jolt. He thought back and was amazed to find that almost a month had passed since he had called her. Of course, much had happened—the legal matters, company problems, and Crystelle's elopement and suicide attempt.

He should have telephoned and made some explanations.

He thought of those summer nights they had spent dancing at the Casino, kissing in his convertible under the trees beside the moonlit lake. Those leisurely days of tennis at the country club, long drives in the country, and dusk-to-dawn parties now seemed of a different world. Examining his feelings with the same thoroughness he applied to cost-and-revenue statements, he emerged with a fact that he had been denying to himself: he was far more attracted to Joanna Mitchell than to any other girl he had ever known.

He wondered if he unconsciously had fled from that attraction.

There was something within him that would not allow him to admit that he needed anyone. He was driven constantly to present himself to the world as self-sufficient.

Now time was short. Casa would be closing soon. Joanna would be returning to the East.

For once in his life he should face facts about his emotions.

He wanted her. He probably would never find a better wife.

Leaving a note to himself to call her later in the day, and to send flowers, he staggered to his feet, turned out the lights, and headed home for a few brief hours of sleep.

"You can put out the word, Koon. We'll be hiring," Grover said. "Good men who aren't afraid of work."

Koon spat off his front porch, glanced at Brod, then regarded Grover with narrowed eyes. "How many?"

"We haven't worked it out yet. That's the purpose of this trip. We'd like for you to travel with us for a few days to look things over. We figure there's nobody who knows more about Spurlock holes than you."

Koon's gaze flicked back to Brod. "So you're taking over the company. Going to reorganize things, top to bottom."

Aware he was being baited, Brod gave Koon a flat, expressionless stare. "There's a lot I need to get acquainted with," he said impassionately. "We'd appreciate it if you could come along with us. If you can't, we can make other arrangements."

Koon grinned. "Well, if you've got a single drop of your old man's piss in your bloodstream, maybe you'll do. I was with him before Ranger, you know. I stuck with him through Burk, Desdemona, Mexia, Kilgore, Corsicana, the whole shoot. Clay always had a wild hair up his ass. But a better man never lived. I can tell you that. I've never known anyone else like him."

Brod did not answer. Apparently he had just passed some sort of test.

He realized for the first time that with these drillers and roughnecks he would have to learn new ways of communication.

He and Grover had driven into a dust storm all the way from Fort Worth. The air still hung heavy with grit, the sky brown-tinged, the sun merely a red poker chip. They were standing on the porch of Koon's one-story clapboard house on the edge of Breckenridge. Wind-driven tumbleweeds bounced across the graveled street and piled against Koon's cowlot.

"You took me by surprise," Koon said. "I thought I'd get my walking papers after that blowout. I was given the idea there was some unhappy people in your accounting office when all the bills came in."

"They don't pay the bills. I do," Brod said. "From now on, you'll deal through Grover. He'll take care of complaints from the accounting department. And in case no one else has told you, we're grateful you took charge that day. There was no one else who could have done it."

Koon studied him for a moment. "That was the way I figured it. I tell you, though. I wish I'd of had a Stillson wrench in my hands. I might of been able to keep your daddy from getting hisself killed. I just couldn't stop him with my bare hands."

"Someone said he hit you."

Koon grinned. "I saw stars. Knocked me flat." He pointed to his mouth. "Lost a tooth and didn't even know it for two days. That's how busy we was."

He turned to Grover. "I reckon I can tear myself away for a few days. Let me talk to my secretary. I'll ask her to cancel all my appointments."

He walked into the house. The screen door slammed behind him. Brod could hear him talking with his wife. In a few minutes he emerged, carrying a denim jacket and a pair of heavy work gloves.

As they began their tour in the Breckenridge field, Brod soon found that they formed an effective team. Grover tackled every problem with enthusiasm and a string of innovations. Koon brought caution from the depths of experience, warning of all that could go wrong. Brod introduced newer methods and scientific reasoning. He also refereed and made the decisions.

Production in the Breckenridge field had declined dramatically after the early twenties, when the price of oil dropped to a dollar a barrel. Only a few Spurlock wells remained in production.

Grover wanted to buy equipment for extensive secondary recovery operations, acidizing each well. Koon recalled the hazards, the many difficulties he had encountered in treating wells with hydrochloric acid. Brod recalled studies showing that two or three thousand gallons of acid usually doubled the production of any well blocked by calcareous material. He felt that Grover and Koon were both right. He ruled that the

Breckenridge wells should be farmed out to a stripper-well operator who specialized in the work.

"The equipment wouldn't pay for itself in just this one field," he explained to Grover. "We'd have to hire people qualified to handle that stuff. With a service company we'll still turn a profit and we're rid of the problem."

During the next two weeks they toured Electra, Burkburnett, Ranger, Desdemona, Mexia, and Kilgore. Each field posed new challenges. They selected new drilling sites, set up poor-boy shacklerod systems, laid out new gathering lines, and estimated the potential for offset wells.

They worked through each day and late into each night, digesting their figures in tourist courts, cafés, and beer joints.

Gradually they worked their way through the Spurlock holdings until only one major unsolved problem remained—the blowout that had killed Clay.

They arrived at the well site late in the afternoon. Stepping out of the car, Brod was unprepared for the emotional impact. Since no sign of Clay's body had been found, it was the same as visiting his grave.

The terrain was not what Brod had envisioned. In every direction only low, rolling sandhills were visible, the dunes held in place by scrubby greasewood and occasional yucca. The day was cold and overcast. An icy wind blew out of the north, driving dead yucca leaves across the bare ground.

"There's where the well was," Koon said, pointing to a deep crater in the sand. "Two or three hundred feet of casing blew out. After that the whole ground heaved. It was like being on the fucking ocean."

Brod walked to the top of a dune and looked down into the crater. The cement that plugged the well was now partially covered with sand.

"Any chance of reworking the hole?" he asked.

"Not a prayer," Koon said. "We whipstocked in from about a hundred yards over that way and bled off some of the pressure. It'd dropped to about a third of what it had been. Still it took a hell of a lot of wet cement to shut her down."

Brod walked into the crater and examined the debris. He found himself looking for any trace of his father. He saw only bits of twisted, blackened metal. Grover had followed him into the pit and had walked around to the other side of the cement plug without speaking.

"I looked at the logs," Brod said to Koon. "I gather you had a show of oil before it blew out."

"Just a whiff. I can't say for sure how much. Clay did say we might plug back and perforate if we didn't find deep pay."

"What's your gut feeling?"

Koon did not answer for a moment. "I've got nothing to go on, but I'd say gas is the only real play. Maybe not a hell of a lot, considering the way the pressure dropped. I think we hit a freak pocket."

"Bullshit," Grover said, returning from the far side of the well. "What're you talking about, Koon? No little pocket could tear up a rig, blow out casing. There must be enough gas down there to run the whole state for ten years."

"There's gas," Koon conceded. "I'm not denying that. I'm only saying we don't know how much." Koon did not seem to want to talk about it.

Brod shared Koon's reluctance. His every inclination was to walk away from the well, to have nothing more to do with it. But a decision had to be made.

"We're a hell of a long way from any gathering lines," he said. "We'd have to find a lot of gas for it to be commercial."

"We can spud in a few yards to one side and drill a new hole," Grover said. "This time we'd know what to expect."

"It'd still be hellishly deep exploration," Brod said. "We could drill six normal wells with the same money."

"I still think we ought to do it," Grover said.

"Koon?" Brod asked.

The old driller would not meet his gaze. "I don't think there's enough oil down there. And I'm not sure about the gas."

Brod weighed his decision. He felt that Grover wanted to drill a new well and develop a new field as a monument to Clay. Koon's judgment seemed to be influenced by his dark memories. Again Brod shared both views to some extent. But logic should prevail.

"We can put these leases on the back burner," he said.

Grover wheeled abruptly and strode angrily toward the car.

Koon watched with an amused grin. "I still can't decide which one of you two reminds me most of Clay," he said.

Ahead, the running horses splashed across the creek, climbed the opposite bank, and disappeared into the trees. Close behind, Brod spurred his dun stallion for the run up the creek bank. With her heart racing, Joanna put the rowels to her sorrel mare and followed, leaning forward in the saddle. She grabbed wildly for the saddlehorn as they plunged across the shallow shoals and left the creek bottom. Dodging tree limbs, she again reached level ground. Brod galloped on across the pasture, circling around the herd of horses, turning them toward the open gates of the corral a quarter of a mile away. Joanna saw that some would pass the gate and escape. She spurred her horse again and, standing in the stirrups, raced at a dead run to head them off. They saw her, turned, and went meekly into the corral.

Brod closed the gate, laughing. "We'll make a cowgirl out of you yet," he called.

Beyond him, four of the ranch hands were leaning against the wooden rails of the corral, grinning. Joanna waved, and their grins widened.

Not every day did a Billy Rose showgirl do their work for them.

Joanna reined in and absorbed the spectacular view of the vast sweep of rangeland to the west. Brod said the ranch had been in his mother's family from the time of the Texas Republic.

Brod swung down from the saddle and came to hold her horse while she dismounted. After two hours of riding, the ground seemed strange, different. Joanna walked a few experimental steps, feeling stiffness in her thighs and back. The November chill had penetrated her jeans.

"I hope no one expects high kicks in the cancan tomorrow night," she said.

"You've used some muscles you didn't know you had," Brod said. "We can walk out some of the soreness."

She followed as he led the horses into the corral and shut the gate. A ranch hand came to strip off the saddles. Joanna gave the sorrel's nose one last affectionate rub. She backed away, then turned and followed Brod through the barn and out the front door to his convertible.

"I've got to talk with the ranch manager for a minute," Brod said. "I'll start the heater for you."

While she waited in the car, Joanna removed her ten-gallon hat and brushed her hair. The car warmed quickly, and within minutes she felt comfortable again. She waited quietly, watching Brod as he talked with the ranch manager.

He had reentered her life with such single-minded concentration that she felt overwhelmed. He first had called her, most apologetic, blaming the crush of business affairs after his father's death. "I simply lost my perspective for a while," he said. "But I want you to know that you have always been on my mind."

Flowers came, and gifts, ranging from a pet horned toad to a small, exquisitely fashioned diamond-and-gold necklace.

He had taken her to dinner and dancing at the River Crest Country Club, introducing her to influential persons whose names she recognized.

Stuttering Sam had smiled knowingly when Joanna told her of the new turn of events. "Brod w-w-wouldn't be introducing you to that c-c-crowd if he d-d-didn't have p-p-plans," she said.

Sam's observation seemed prophetic. Tonight Joanna was to meet Brod's family.

She could not make up her mind about her feelings. She continued to date Grover Sterling, who made no secret that his intentions were serious. She had found Grover more fun and much easier to know. His charm was on the surface, always in evidence. Brod seldom revealed his true thoughts. He often remained preoccupied for hours at a time, in the grip of some dark mood. Yet he could be most attentive and endearing.

Brod shook hands abruptly with the ranch manager and strode back to the car. Stepping in, he tested the air from the heater.

"Too warm?"

"Comfortable," Joanna said.

He wheeled the car around the graveled drive and they sped down the long lane toward the ranch road. Brod glanced at his watch. "We should be back by three," he said. "I'll pick you up again at seven. That be all right?"

"I think so," she said. She had been concerned that she might not have enough time to dress.

"I wanted you to see the ranch before you met Mom," Brod said. "She was raised here. And this is where Loren and I spent our childhood summers. That was Loren's saddle you used today."

"I'll remember to thank him," Joanna said, watching the rugged, starkly beautiful countryside as it passed.

"Some day I want to build a house on the ranch and spend a lot of time out here," Brod said.

Joanna recognized the admission as significant. But she did not answer. The ranch country seemed as far from upstate New York as the mountains of the moon. She was enchanted. But she did not know if she wanted to spend the major portion of her life in Texas.

"Have they set the date to close the show?" Brod asked.

"I hear only rumors," Joanna said. "But I'm sure it'll be soon. The audience sat frozen the last three nights."

Brod drove for a few minutes in silence, smoothly swerving to avoid the occasional carcasses of opossums, rabbits, and armadillos on the gravel road. "What do you plan to do?"

"Billy Rose is opening another Casa in New York. He said that if I'm interested he'd find a spot for me. I may accept. But I really should go back to college."

"The new Casa sounds like a great opportunity," Brod said.

Joanna was aware that Brod was probing the depth of her commitment.

"With Rose you never know what'll happen," she said. "He literally has a brainstorm a minute. Our floating stage has given him an idea for a swimming chorus line. He's now trying to find pier space on the East River. He's negotiating with that swimmer who was kicked off the Olympic team for drinking a bottle of champagne with Helen Hayes's husband."

"Eleanor Holm," Brod said. "And Charles MacArthur."

"It's an open secret that Rose and Fanny Brice are separated. He's apt to go off in any direction. I want something more permanent in my life than show business."

This time Brod did not answer. He drove on to Fort Worth, apparently engrossed in his own thoughts.

Joanna did not intrude. She gazed at the fall-tinged scenery, wondering if she had been too forward.

That evening Brod drove her to his home. Aware of the Spurlock wealth, Joanna anticipated the large, mansionlike home, the lavish, tasteful furnishings. But she was not prepared for the forceful, disparate personalities of Ann Leigh, Crystelle, and Zetta Spurlock.

The home itself was English Tudor, sprawling in its immensity. Ann Leigh received them in the sumptuous living room. Behind Ann Leigh, Joanna glimpsed a rosewood sidechair that would grace a museum, and a marble-topped side table, carved and gilded, no doubt worth a king's ransom. She suppressed a moment of amusement, remembering that some of her New York friends thought she was leaving civilization for the land of cowboys and Indians.

"I'm so glad you could come," Ann Leigh said. "The boys have talked so much about you. They said you were beautiful, but my dear, the word simply doesn't do you justice."

The reticence of Brod and Loren also had shortchanged Ann Leigh, Joanna thought. Apparently in her early forties, she remained slim and petite, even doll-like. Her light blond hair was fashionably arranged, and she wore an off-the-shoulder, burgundy-colored dress with casual aplomb.

"And this is my Aunt Zetta," Brod said.

As Zetta Spurlock strode majestically into the room, Joanna hoped she was successful in hiding her astonishment. Dressed entirely in black, Brod's Aunt Zetta resembled a large blackbird. The feathered folds of her layered gown added to the illusion. Her head was cocked to one side, favoring her good ear. Brod had warned Joanna that she was hard of hearing. Her hawkish eyes remained fixed on Joanna as she solemnly spoke a greeting. Joanna was glad that she had worn her most conservative dress, a basic navy blue, with buttons slanting to the left shoulder in an asymmetrical closing.

"And my sister Crystelle . . ."

A younger, more substantial version of her mother, Crystelle nodded without speaking. Joanna could see resentment in her eyes. Joanna knew from the first that Crystelle meant trouble.

"My brother Loren you know."

Loren came forward and kissed her on the cheek. He seemed amused.

A servant brought sherry. While they sat in the living room and made small talk about Casa Mañana and her part in it, Joanna felt Aunt Zetta's eyes upon her. She noticed that the family habitually talked loud around Aunt Zetta, out of consideration.

In for a penny, in for a pound, Joanna thought. "Isn't that a Heade?" she asked, gazing at the landscape over the mantelpiece.

Aunt Zetta jumped as if she had been stabbed in the brisket. She tended to talk in shouts. "Yes. Martin Heade. That's a Pennsylvania landscape. Are you interested in art?"

"Interested, but not an expert by any means," Joanna said, raising her voice. "I've always admired Heade's work, his unusual sense of light."

"Aunt Zetta gave us that painting one Christmas," Ann Leigh said. "We've enjoyed it so much."

Joanna was careful not to overplay her hand. At dinner she complimented Ann Leigh on the Limoges service, confident of the rarity of the pattern. Calculatedly, she made no more display of her background.

"Mother used to be in show business," Brod said after a lull in the conversation.

Ann Leigh actually blushed. "Brod! Really!"

"She trod the boards, to coin a phrase," Loren drawled.

"Boys!" Ann Leigh said. She turned to Joanna. "I taught drama at the college level. But I assure you there was nothing professional about it."

"My true interest lies in music," Joanna said. "But my minor is serious drama. I never dreamed I ever would play in a musical."

"We overreached dreadfully," Ann Leigh said. "Shakespeare. John Webster. We even played *Tartuffe.*" She laughed. "But I did think we once presented a passable version of Shaw's *Joan.*"

Joanna and Ann Leigh fell to discussing plays. Joanna was aware of Brod's quiet approval, Aunt Zetta's incessant inspection, Loren's mild amusement, Crystelle's sulky silence.

At one point Joanna mentioned Billy Rose. Suddenly Aunt Zetta's deep voice boomed out. "He came to the Woman's Club to raise money. He looked like an overwound toy."

Joanna was consumed by laughter. The family seemed amused by her helpless mirth. Even Crystelle lost her bored look.

Joanna tried to apologize. "Forgive me. It's just that your description was so apt."

Later, relating an anecdote, Joanna addressed Ann Leigh as "Mrs. Spurlock."

Ann Leigh put a hand on her arm. "Call me Ann Leigh, please."

Joanna had long been intrigued by the western fad for double names. "Have you always used the double name?" she asked.

"Not until I came to Fort Worth. As a child, I was simply 'Ann.' But my best friend here was named Anne, with an *e*. Katherine Anne Porter. We were practically inseparable. So she became Katherine Anne, and I was Ann Leigh. The names stuck."

"Katherine Anne Porter, the writer?"

Ann Leigh grew animated. "Yes, do you know her?"

"I know *of* her. My professor in American literature called her 'Flowering Judas' the best short story ever written in this country. I didn't know she lived in Fort Worth."

"Oh, honey, that was way back before the war. She was quite a gadabout. She went on to Mexico, Chicago, New York, all over. And when she came back here, in the twenties, I was married, and she was running with a different crowd. I didn't see much of her. I did read one short story in manuscript, called 'Maria Concepcion.' Did she ever publish it?"

Joanna remembered the story, concerning a Mexican Indian woman who murdered her husband's lover and took the woman's baby as her own. "It's one of the stories in the *Flowering Judas* collection," she said.

"A strange story. I found it rather frightening. She said she actually met the person she wrote about. Katherine Anne was quite adventurous."

Afterward, in the car on the way back to her hotel, Brod reached for her hand. "You were wonderful. The whole family adored you. Even Aunt Zetta. I don't think she found a thing to criticize. And that means I'm right. You're perfect! I've never seen Mother so taken. She started calling you 'honey.' That's always a dead giveaway. You had them eating out of your hand."

Joanna felt she should put all the problems up front. "Not everyone. I had the feeling Crystelle doesn't like me at all."

Brod spoke as if carefully choosing his words. "Crystelle is going through a difficult time. She's not herself."

Two nights later Grover Sterling and Joanna spent the evening at a small private club near Arlington Downs. Grover said it had been a speakeasy during Prohibition. Afterward he drove through Trinity Park, stopped at the Botanic Gardens, and talked awhile. Then he turned in the car seat to face her.

"Joanna, I love you," he said quietly. "I don't want you to go back east. I want you to marry me."

For a moment Joanna could not bring herself to speak. "Grover, you hardly know me," she said.

He took her hands in his. "I know you well enough. I knew the first moment I saw you on that stage. I wanted to ask you the first time I spoke to you, in the elevator."

Joanna met his gaze. "Grover, it's too soon."

"And next week will be too late. Look, I know Brod is after you too. I don't know if he has popped the question yet, but he probably will. I want you to think about your answer carefully. I can make you happy. Brod never could, not with that screwed-up family of his. And I promise you, some day I'll be ten times richer than Brod."

Joanna could not ignore the implicit offensiveness of the remark. "Grover, surely you know money isn't important to me."

"I want to give you everything. Money is a part of it."

He waited, leaving his proposal hanging. Joanna resorted to the truth. "Grover, I'm terribly confused. This whole, wonderful Texas experience has left me bewildered. I no longer know my own mind. I *need* to go back east to recover my equilibrium. I need time."

Grover nodded without speaking. He sat watching the moonlight through the trees. "At least that isn't a no. I guess I can live with that for a while."

Joanna endured the following week in a daze. On Tuesday the closing of the show was announced. Only three more evenings remained. She telephoned her parents. They said they would expect her home for Thanksgiving. Billy Rose sent her a note, asking her decision on performing in his New York Casa. She stuck the note into the frame of her makeup mirror and stared at it for hours, trying to make up her mind. A letter came from the director of her college drama school, urging her to return for the start of second-semester classes. He said she could obtain college credits for her professional experience—perhaps enough to catch up with her class and graduate on schedule.

She felt increasingly disoriented. Each performance was exhausting.

On the final night of the Casa season Brod took her to early dinner in the elegant, crystal-chandeliered dining room at River Crest Country Club, then drove her to the theater. He met her after the performance and drove to Lake Worth. Parking under the trees beside the beach, where they had spent so many summer nights, he asked her to marry him.

Joanna had already made her decision.

After many hours of thought, she had closed all doors, one by one.

She liked Grover, even admired him for rising above his background. But she felt his ambition contained a ruthlessness she did not trust.

Before the closing at Casa she had sent Billy Rose a polite note, thanking him for his consideration, saying she had other plans. After sampling the relaxed, comfortable life in Texas, she did not want to return to the pressure cooker of New York City.

Nor could she envision her return to the theories of the classroom after so much practical experience on stage.

Intrinsic in these decisions was her knowledge that she could not leave Brod. Not if he truly wanted her.

She did not delude herself. In his family she sensed undercurrents and passions that could bring unhappiness, even tragedy.

She sensed that Crystelle's animosity was deep-seated and ingrained. Joanna knew intuitively that Crystelle was her enemy—and a dangerous one.

She also recognized that Brod contained mysteries that might never be revealed. She wondered if she would ever be able to penetrate his habitual reserve. She doubted that he had ever been truly intimate with anyone.

But she loved him. She could not deny that fact.

"Brod, I'll marry you on one condition," she told him. "Let me return home for Thanksgiving, to convince my parents that their daughter hasn't gone stark, raving crazy. I'll break the news. Then you can come up and meet them and put their minds at ease. You have to understand that in their world, Texas is on the fringes of creation. They think of this as the wild frontier."

Brod grinned. "What makes you think it isn't?"

34

Brod and Joanna were married the following
April, sailed aboard the French liner *Normandie*, and spent three glorious weeks at the Ritz in Paris. As they visited the museums, walked the
boulevards, and dined in the sumptuous restaurants, they began to hear
serious talk of general war.

Europe was gripped in an eerie atmosphere of suspended anticipation. Fighting continued in Spain. Italy had annexed Abyssinia. The Nazis
were totally in power in Germany, rapidly building a military colossus.

"*Alors*, what does the world expect?" their waiter exclaimed one
night. "I was at Verdun. The Germans are preparing for war because it is
their nature. They have occupied the Rhineland. They have given Adolf
Hitler ninety-nine percent of the vote. Hitler has repudiated the Ver-
sailles treaty. He has made a pact with Mussolini. We are living on borrowed time!"

From Paris they traveled into Austria. But not until they arrived in
Germany did they become convinced that war was inevitable. In Berlin,
uniforms were everywhere. The whole country seemed to be swept up in
a national hysteria. Almost everyone they met attempted to tell them of
the glories of Nazi Germany. They saw Hitler leading a parade of goose-
stepping soldiers through the streets—thousands of them—followed by
tanks, artillery pieces, and uniformed children waving Nazi banners.
That evening, while Brod and Joanna were at dinner, Hitler spoke in the
Sportspalast. His emotional tirade was piped into the hotel dining room
by radio. Abandoned by the waiters, appalled by the frenetic cheering,
Brod and Joanna at last left their table and returned to their room.

"It would be funny if it weren't so frightening," Joanna said.

Cutting their Berlin visit short, they traveled on to Italy. There they
found conditions slightly better only because the people were less fervent. They spent time in Rome, Naples, and Athens, then cruised the
Mediterranean on a hired yacht, landing at Monaco. After a quick visit to

Switzerland they took the boat train to London. They found the English almost traumatized after King Edward's abdication.

After they toured Scotland, Joanna confessed she was tired, and ready to go home. "We can save a little of it for later," she said. "Russia, for instance."

They again boarded the *Normandie* at Le Havre and sailed for home. Brod arranged for Pullman rooms on the *Twentieth-Century Limited* to Chicago, the *Santa Fe Chief* into Fort Worth.

Loren met them at the station, tanned and lean. He obviously had put in plenty of time on the tennis courts and in the swimming pools. As Brod was attending to the luggage, Loren approached and spoke quietly. "I'd better warn you. Everything is in an uproar at home. Crystelle has flown the coop again. She sent a note from Mexico City, saying she was married."

Brod thought back to his desperate trip to San Antonio, his revulsion and fear over Crystelle's attempted suicide. He did not want to go through that again. "Moon?" he asked.

"Oh hell no!" Loren said. "Last I heard, Moon's parents had practically made a castrato out of him. This is a new guy. Doyle Galloway, a lush if there ever was one."

Brod moved away from the redcaps as they finished stowing the luggage in the trunk of the car. "Who in hell is he?"

"Surely you remember the Galloways, insurance and real estate. Doyle's their youngest son. About twenty-five. Flunked out of college, if I remember right."

Brod vaguely recalled a Galloway, a year or two ahead of him in high school. "Have you located them?"

Loren shrugged. "Brod, what's the use? She's eighteen. You can't haul her back this time. Not unless you want to declare her *non compos mentis.*"

Brod checked the stowage of the luggage and tipped the redcaps. He stood for a moment, absorbing the news. Crystelle now *was* legally an adult. "How's Mom taking it?"

"She blames herself. Of course Aunt Zetta has been doing her Greek chorus bit. I'm glad you're back."

"They give you your sheepskin?"

Loren grinned. "Already framed."

"Ready to go to work?"

Loren's grin widened. "Ready as I'll ever be."

Brod drove straight home. He found Ann Leigh inconsolable.

"Brod, I've talked to the Galloways. They're upset. They think Doyle has only a few hundred dollars with him. Crystelle cleaned out her checking account. They're living on her money!"

"Don't worry," Brod said. "Maybe it'll work out."

The next day he located them through private detectives in Mexico City. Crystelle came to the phone reluctantly.

"Brod, I'm not going to take any more of your shit."

"I'm not going to give you any," he told her. "You've made your choice. I wish you well. But Crystelle, don't do this to your mother. Call her, or at least write to her. Let her know you're all right."

The line was silent for a moment. "You're not going to try to bring me back?"

"You're an adult, Crystelle. I hope you're acting like one."

"Part of that goddamned company is mine, you know."

"I know. It'll be there when you need it."

"I want Doyle in the company, Brod. I need somebody there to look after my interests."

Brod hesitated. He wondered whether it was her idea or Doyle's. "When you come back, we'll talk about it."

"And we're going to talk about my money too."

"Anytime you want."

Brod disconnected, then called his mother and told her he had located Crystelle.

"Is she all right?"

"Sassy is the word. She wants to bring Doyle into the company to look after her interests. I imagine she'll hold out for a vice presidency."

"Oh, Brod! Can you do that?"

"Sure. We can give him a desk and a title. I'll make him Loren's assistant."

Ann Leigh laughed. "Don't be mean."

"I'm not worried about Doyle," Brod told her. "Crystelle is the one that's going to be the problem."

He called Loren into his office and closed the door. He poured two snifters of brandy, handed one to Loren, and raised the other in a toast.

"Here's to us," he said. "To the Spurlock brothers, who are going to build this company beyond their old man's wildest dreams."

Loren laughed. "I'll drink to that."

Brod motioned Loren into a leather wing chair and sat facing him. "I'm not just making a place for you, Loren. I really need you. How does the title of senior vice president strike you? That'd make you number two around here."

Loren shook his head in embarrassment. "Brod, for Christ's sake! I'm just a kid right out of college. I'd be resented!"

Brod looked at him for a moment. "Of course you'll be resented. What in hell do you think I faced when I came in as president and board chairman? I was a kid right out of college. Some of these people around here worked with Dad for twenty years. He gave them complete control. Then I came in and took it away from them. They hated my guts. Maybe they still do. But there's one thing everybody respects, and that's competence. You're a Spurlock, and you're part owner. That counts for a lot. Don't you worry one minute about resentment. That's *their* problem."

Loren hesitated. "Brod, I know myself. I'm just not as forceful as you. I don't have your drive. I'm not saying I can't make a contribution. I can. But please don't expect too much of me."

Brod remembered that Loren had always been reluctant to put himself forward. Brod did not know the reason. He suspected it might stem from living in the shadow of an older brother, the constant absence of a father figure while growing up. He believed that all Loren needed was confidence.

"You just need to get your feet wet," he said. "In a month you'll be right into the swing of things. Eventually I want you to take over the whole business operation—accounting, records, taxation. You'll run that end, I'll run this end—exploration, production. But at the moment we'll bring you in to head a special project. By the time you wrap it up, everybody will know you're a whiz, the man in charge. How much did they teach you about oil royalties?"

Again Loren hesitated. "Not much."

"Good. Anything they taught you would probably only confuse you." He pointed to the stacks of folders on a side table. "I'm sure no one in the academic community ever dreamed of a mess like this. We send out hundreds of royalty checks each month. Almost every one is figured differently. The bookkeeping load is tremendous. But it's always been done that way, and it'll be hard to change. You're familiar with the standard royalty contract, aren't you?"

Loren frowned. "One eighth of gross production?"

"Right. We have damned few of those. Some are on an acre basis, figuring in the number of acres in the lease. Some are royalty-additional, with an override clause inserted to sweeten the deal. Some are written with the original landowner, who is the lessor. Those can get pretty complex, especially if the owner's dead and it's split among heirs. Some are under royalty-minimum, figured on production rate, quality of the oil, market price, and God knows what. Some are participating royalty, where the cost of production is factored in, and payment is based on the net profit. Some you wouldn't believe. Dad and Pete made all kinds of verbal deals. I had a devil of a time tracking down the paperwork. You'll find that in some cases we don't even have the original contract, only a copy I've managed to obtain. When you look over the material, you'll see the situation."

Loren shifted uneasily in his chair. "What can be done about it?"

"I want you to place an arbitrary value on each agreement, add a healthy bonus, and offer the royalty holders simple participating shares in Spurlock Oil. We could cut our paperwork by a third, maybe half. They would benefit. We would benefit."

Loren finished his brandy and set the snifter on a lowboy. "Won't they be suspicious of the deal?"

"Not if it's presented right. We can tell them the truth, that it's a cost-cutting measure for us, that we're willing to pass some of the money on to them for their participation. At the moment they have shares in a well that some day will be pumped dry. We're giving them shares in a growing company. The advantages speak for themselves."

"How soon do you want it done?"

"It'll probably take you all summer. As you complete each deal, pass the information on to bookkeeping. By fall everyone in the company will know you've reorganized the whole department. Then we'll restructure the organizational chart, to conform with an obvious fact—Loren Spurlock is running the business end of the company."

Loren grinned. "You make it sound easy."

"It will be, aside from one hell of a lot of hard work. There'll be a lot of correspondence. I'll assign you a couple of secretaries. Let me know if you need more. You'll be off to yourself for a while. Don't discuss what you're doing with anyone on the staff. Just do it. If you need any help on the legal aspects, call Bink. He's the best oil attorney in town, maybe in the state. Everything understood?"

Loren shrugged. "I guess."

"Good. As of now, you're senior vice president of Spurlock Oil Company, engaged in a special project. That's all anyone needs to know."

They shook hands, both constrained by the emotion of the moment. Loren turned at the door. "I wonder what my professors would say at my rapid elevation. They'd probably shit."

Brod gave his brother a long, searching look. "Loren, you're a better man than any of those professors. Remember that. They're theorists. We turn those theories into reality. We grow. Twenty years from now they'll still be there teaching the same courses. There isn't one of them that could do what you'll do in the next six months. I don't want to hear one more word of poor-mouthing out of you. You're a Spurlock. Act like one."

Brod and Joanna drove their mothers to the site of their new home in Westover Hills. The foundations had been poured. The carpenters were starting on the framework.

"We bought two lots," Brod explained to Faye Mitchell. "With the house situated like this, we'll have more privacy."

"What a lovely setting," Mrs. Mitchell said. "I hadn't expected Texas to be so green."

"A blessing of spring," Ann Leigh said. "Unfortunately, in August and September this part of Texas sometimes bakes to a consistent brown."

Mrs. Mitchell had arrived by train two days earlier. She and Ann Leigh had taken an immediate liking to each other. Brod had heard them up talking long after he had gone to bed.

Brod parked the car in the street and led the women down the slope to the house. Joanna explained the layout, detailing her problems with the architect.

Walking to the corner of his property, Brod determined by estimate what he hoped would soon be proved by survey. With careful shifting of the soil, good drainage might be achieved.

He watched Joanna scamper over the scattered lumber, pausing to point out the entryway, the living room, the fireplace. He loved her more every day, constantly finding marvelous new aspects to her personality. She was a treasure.

His life had fallen into place even more wondrously than he had thought possible. The expansion of the company had gone well during the time he was in Europe. Already new profits were flowing in from long-neglected sources.

He had been concerned that Grover Sterling might harbor some resentment over Joanna. But after the announcement of their engagement Grover had extended his hand.

"I was raised to tell the truth," Grover said. "So I'm not going to say the best man won. But congratulations."

Brod knew that much of the profit increase could be attributed to Grover's unflagging efforts. Grover had remained on top of every project, driving the field crews to completions in record time. Now, with Loren taking over the business end, the company should soon be functioning like a fine piece of machinery.

Somehow he would find a way to keep Crystelle happy.

The women came back up the slope. Brod walked over to the car and opened the doors.

The women entered the car, talking of drapes, color schemes, and furnishings.

Brod drove by reflex, enveloped in his own thoughts. An idea that had been growing in his mind began to shape itself into an enormously detailed plan.

He said nothing to the women. Patiently, he waited until he returned them to the house.

Then he returned to the office to put his plan into motion.

"War's inevitable," Brod told Grover Sterling. "We don't get the full impact through our newspapers and newsreels. Germany's an armed camp. Even the children are marching. The whole country's gone crazy. In France, England, there's such a feeling of gloom. *Everyone* knows it's coming."

Grover nodded. "Spurlock Oil is ready."

"Not ready enough," Brod said. "I want to set up a refinery, a distribution system."

Grover laughed. "Good God, I thought I was the gambler!"

"There's some risk," Brod admitted. "But with our own refinery and retail outlets, we'd be in position to pull out all the stops, once the allocations are lifted. We'd be in total control of the situation, from oil in the ground to the gasoline pumps. We wouldn't have to depend on anyone."

Grover drew a deep breath and held it for a moment. "Brod, you have any idea what that would cost? The problems? The experienced men we'd need? This company's already in hock up to its balls. Where would you get the money?"

"Borrow it. Right now the move might not be as expensive as it seems. There's a small refinery in trouble down on the Gulf. I checked into it. They give various reasons for the shape they're in, but it all adds up to bad management. We can get it for a song. I'm flying to Houston tomorrow to see what I can do."

Grover sat for a moment, contemplating the enormity of it. "Distribution. That will involve trucks, rolling rail stock, holding tanks . . ."

"And ocean tankers," Brod said.

Grover looked at the ceiling.

"When war comes, the government probably will help us buy the tankers. But we've got to be in position, ready to move."

Grover sat and thought the plan through. Excitement showed in his eyes. "It might be done."

"Of course it can be done. Any time you have a good idea, you can always find the money. Here's what I want from you. Get me an estimate of our full production capacity. Every well. This country can sit around with its thumb up its ass. But when war comes, Spurlock Oil is going to be ready."

Slowly the house took shape. Each day Joanna spent more and more time with tape measure and drawings, figuring the furnishings to the most minute detail. At last she summoned the architect.

"Mr. Hodges, I thought we had planned these closets off the upstairs hall differently. See here? In the blueprints they're forty-eight inches deep. I now measure them less than thirty-two. And under the stairs we had projected a walk-in closet. Now it's barely big enough for brooms!"

She went on, listing the shortcomings she had found. The architect listened patiently, nodding, nervously fidgeting with the Phi Beta Kappa key on his vest.

When Joanna finished, he began a series of explanations. Brod had insisted on more air vents. Compromises had to be made, reducing the size of the closets. Under the stairs, support beams were needed, making the large walk-in closet she had planned impractical. The contractor had been unable to obtain some of the materials he had worked into the design, making alterations necessary. His toneless voice droned in her ears, piling complication on complication.

Joanna felt beleaguered. She had been determined that for once she would live in a house with adequate closet space, with doors and bathrooms that did not make her feel like Gulliver in the land of the Lilliputians. For a moment she was furious, on the point of tears. She had assumed that the job of an architect was to solve such problems.

"Mr. Hodges, I'll not have my plans ignored! Why wasn't I consulted before these changes were made? Sixteen inches off those closets may not sound like much to you, but that space is needed for storage chests and deep drawers. I must have it!"

The architect stood for a moment, looking up at the framework of the house, his gray hair rippling in the wind. "Mrs. Spurlock, I don't know what we could do at this point."

"I'll show you what we can do!" Joanna said. She charged over the foundations and up the raw framework of the stairs, so angry she did not wait for the carpenters to get out of her way. She stepped over boards, across open spaces in the flooring. Hodges followed in her wake.

"We can move this wall over two feet," she said. "It's only a partition, not a bearing wall, and . . ."

Joanna suddenly felt dizzy. Her stomach heaved. She was overwhelmed with nausea. She grabbed a doorframe for support. Alarmed, Hodges came to her aid, seizing her by the elbow.

Joanna had a sudden, irrational vision of the frail little man attempting to cope as one of Billy Rose's long-stemmed American Beauties collapsed on him. She laughed.

"I'm sorry," she said. "I just had a dizzy spell. I don't know what happened."

Hodges remained uncertain. "Are you sure you're all right? You seem pale."

"I'm fine," she insisted. "I guess I just went up that flight of steps too fast. It's over now. But you will see to moving that wall?"

He nodded. "It can be done without much difficulty. Of course it will take some dimension from the next room. And under the stairs I suppose I could use side posts and a truss beam support."

"Then please do," Joanna said. "I'll call you later, and we can discuss the other problems."

He followed her down to the car. "Are you sure you're able to drive? I could run you home."

Joanna reassured him.

When she arrived back at the Spurlock home she did not mention her fainting spell to her mother or Ann Leigh. But the incident nagged. She did not believe for a moment that a girl who had kicked her way through eight cancans a week could be fazed by a flight of stairs.

She suspected she knew the cause.

Turning through the phone book, she selected a physician and arranged an appointment. That afternoon she made excuses to her mother that she wanted to examine some bathroom fixtures the architect was considering.

The doctor said he could not say conclusively, but he also believed that she was pregnant.

That evening Joanna and Brod dined at River Crest. After the dessert, moved by the wine and the romantic ambiance, she told Brod. He shouted with joy, attracting the attention of the entire dining room. Embarrassed, laughing, Joanna shushed him. "Brod! All precincts haven't been heard from. I shouldn't have told you. We may be disappointed."

He ignored her and summoned a waiter. "This calls for another bottle of wine."

Joanna was hesitant. "If I'm right, I should start thinking about the baby."

Brod filled her glass.

"He'll thrive on it," he said. "He's a Spurlock."

Joanna sipped her champagne, not speaking what was on her mind.

The baby would be a Mitchell too.

Acquisition of the refinery went smoother than Brod anticipated. He spent ten days examining the plant's records, looking over the facilities. At night he reviewed his college textbooks, refreshing his memory on the details of operations. Most of the equipment seemed to be in good shape. Talking with the foremen and supervisors, Brod determined that the plant was adequately staffed with experienced men. The owners simply had put their tail in the crack through slow sales, too little attention to profit and loss.

His bankers actually seemed eager to finance the deal. In the midst of the Depression the rejuvenation of Spurlock Oil had attracted attention. "Nothing against Clay," said one of the bankers. "But I've been familiar with Spurlock Oil's books for twenty years. This is the first time the company has been on a solid footing."

Slowly, Brod began buying a few independent service stations, leasing others. He ordered six new tank trucks. He hired an artist to design a logo—a gusher spouting oil over the top of the derrick. By late August the first truckloads of Spurlock gasoline were leaving the refinery for the service stations. The remainder of the production was either shipped east or sold to independent distributors.

Engrossed in the expansion, out of town much of the time, concerned over Joanna's pregnancy, he did not realize until late August that Loren's project was in trouble. He returned from a trip to Houston and found several call-back slips on his desk. The first person he reached was Otis Nippert, an Odessa independent oil operator.

"Brod, what the hell are you trying to pull on me?" Nippert shouted. "I was doing business with your daddy when you were in rompers. We had a deal. I let Clay checkerboard my leases up by Graham, free and clear, with the understanding he'd assume all exploration risks and give me a sixteenth override. The lucky son of a bitch hit on the first test at thirty-seven hundred feet. I was happy with the deal. Clay was happy. Now what's this shit about trading the contract for shares in your company?"

"It's a take-it-or-leave-it offer, Otis," Brod said. "If I were you, I'd take it. But that's entirely up to you."

"Well, what's behind it? I've been trying to get ahold of your brother for a week."

"It's simple," Brod said. "We're buried under paperwork. We pay accountants more to figure, write, and send some royalty checks each month than those checks are worth. We figure we can give you a good bonus and still be ahead. The cash value of your holdings would be growing instead of depleting."

The line was silent for a moment. "That makes sense. Why in hell didn't you say that in the first place?"

"I thought we did," Brod said.

After two similar calls Brod rang Loren's office. Loren's secretary said he had left for the day.

The next morning Brod called Loren and asked him to bring in some of his correspondence. After glancing over the letters, he quickly understood why the project was in confusion. "Good God, Loren, this reads like a come-on for a fly-by-night used-car lot! You're dealing with plain-talking, busy men. They don't waste words. All you have to do is put the situation into simple English. Your figures seem about right. But they probably never even looked at them."

Loren was leaning forward in his chair. As he reached for a letter, his hand trembled. "This is the approach we learned in marketing."

"Hard sell won't work with these men!" Brod knew his voice was rising, but he was so angry he did not care. "Most of these deals Dad sealed with a handshake. The contracts weren't drawn till years later. And you send out something like this! No wonder they're shying away from it."

Loren spread his hands. He seemed close to tears. "Brod, that wasn't explained to me."

"And where were you yesterday afternoon?"

"I went out to the club for a round of golf."

"Otis Nippert said he'd been trying to reach you for a week. You been playing golf every fucking day?"

Loren rose to his feet. He stood, furious. "Brod, if you want to put in eighty-hour weeks, fine. Just don't expect me to cheer. I told you to begin with. I'm not you. I want to get a little enjoyment out of life. I'm not going to kill myself working in this goddamned place."

"From what I can see, I don't think there's any danger of that."

Loren wheeled and walked out. Brod sat at his desk for several minutes, his anger slowly fading to regret. In all the time they were growing up, he and Loren had seldom exchanged a cross word.

He picked up the phone and reached Loren in his office. "Loren, come back. Please."

Loren returned, hesitantly. His lips were still trembling with anger.

Brod gestured. "I'm sorry. Sit down. Please."

Slowly, Loren returned to his chair.

"All right, it's partially my fault," Brod said. "You didn't know. I should have looked over your letters. A year ago I might have done the same thing."

"I should have brought them to you," Loren said quietly. "I thought for once I knew what I was doing."

"No great harm done," Brod said. "We can send out another letter. And about your taking the afternoon off, I don't blame you for wanting to enjoy life. But we *do* have a responsibility to this company."

"Why?" Loren asked.

Brod stared at his brother, momentarily speechless. "Loren, surely we owe something to Dad's memory. And maybe Granddad's. They built everything we have."

Loren shook his head. "Brod, I can't even remember too well what

Dad looked like. That's how much I saw of him. And if we want to honor Granddad's memory, maybe we ought to build a whorehouse or two. People still remember that, you know."

Brod did not answer for a moment. Loren was showing a cynical streak he did not know existed. "At least we owe something to Mother," he said. "And to our children, when we have them."

Loren smiled. "That's the difference between us, Brod. You've got to prove yourself, show the world that nothing can beat a Spurlock. I just don't feel that way. I can enjoy golf without trying to be Ben Hogan. I'm content that we don't own the biggest oil company in Texas. You're not."

Brod thought Loren's statement through before he spoke. "Maybe we'd better talk this over," he said. "If you don't want to pull your weight, perhaps we ought to make some arrangements."

Loren sat deathly still. "Like what?"

"Like my buying you out."

Slowly, Loren shook his head. "Never! You've misunderstood everything. I didn't say I'm not devoted to the company. I only object to your ambitions for it."

"You mean the refinery?"

"I'm supposed to be senior vice president, an equal owner. Did you consult me before you left for Houston to buy that refinery? Did you consult any of the other owners? Mom? Crystelle?"

"As president and board chairman, I have discretionary powers," Brod said. "Surely you know that."

Loren picked up his papers and walked to the door. He paused, his hand on the knob. "I also know that you'd better keep the board happy. If you don't, you can be brought to heel just as fast as the lowest secretary in this building. Bear that in mind."

Loren went out, closing the door behind him.

Brod sat motionless, pondering the perplexing new insight he had gained into his younger brother.

35

They drove northward from Monterrey during the night, cleared customs at Laredo early in the morning, and soon were on the highway to San Antonio. Doyle drove fast, constantly passing diesel trucks and slow-moving pickups with reckless ease. Crystelle dozed most of the way, bored by the flat, brush-covered landscape.

She was counting the miles, eager to get home. Mexico had been fun while it lasted. They had explored Mexico City, Cuernavaca, Taxco, and the fishing villages along the west coast.

Now they were broke.

Doyle bypassed downtown San Antonio. Crystelle stirred and looked at the distant buildings, remembering that there was where it all had almost ended. She felt a shiver up her spine, thinking of the blood on the bathroom floor. She had never told Doyle about it. And she had lied to him about the scars on her wrists, saying she had fallen through a plate glass window as a child, almost severing her hands.

Doyle had kissed her wrists.

In so many ways he reminded her of Moon.

She dozed again. When she awoke, they were passing through a small town south of New Braunfels. Crystelle only caught a glimpse of the sign in front of a service station. Doyle already was accelerating at the end of the speed zone.

"Stop!" Crystelle said, instantly awake. "Go back!"

Jarred out of his own reverie, Doyle slowed, looking at her in confusion.

"That sign back there on the service station. I think it said Spurlock Oil."

Doyle glanced at the gasoline gauge. "We can make it to Austin, easy," he said.

"Damn it, I want to see that sign!"

Doyle made a U-turn, drove back to the station, and with another U circled into the gravel driveway of the station.

The sign bore stylized script spelling out Spurlock Oil, with a logo of a gushing oil well.

"Daddy never had service stations," Crystelle said. "And I don't think there's another Spurlock Oil Company. What the hell is Brod doing?"

"It looks like a cheap-gas place," Doyle said. "The prices are two or three cents less than most of the signs posted up and down the road."

"Fill up," Crystelle said. "I want to find out about this."

Doyle parked beside the pumps. A boy of about eighteen came from the car rack, wiping his hands on a red grease rag. He stopped, apparently overwhelmed by the abundance of attractions in his driveway. He seemed unable to decide which to ogle first, Doyle's fire engine red Lincoln-Zephyr or Crystelle.

Doyle told him to fill the gas tank and walked around the station to the rest room.

Crystelle slid out of the car. The pump jockey fitted the nozzle into the tank, watching her nervously. She slouched against a rear fender and studied him. One more peek down her blouse and his tongue would be hanging out.

"We've been in Mexico a while," she said conversationally. "I've never seen this brand of gas before. Is it new?"

"Yes, ma'am," he said, nodding in his eagerness to talk. "We've been open about a month now."

"Cheap gas?"

"Costs less. But the trucker that brings it says we get the same gas as other stations that sell it higher."

"How can they do that?"

"I asked him. He said Spurlock Oil has their own crackin' plant. They truck it straight from the refinery. No middleman."

Doyle returned from the rest room, his hair neatly combed, his clothing readjusted. The pump jockey immediately became more attentive to his duties. Crystelle sauntered into the station, ostensibly to the chewing gum machine. She found what she sought. The posted permits identified the proprietor as Spurlock Oil Company of Fort Worth. She walked back to the car.

"Big Brother now has an oil refinery," she told Doyle. "I think it's about time Little Sister had a talk with him."

They arrived back in Fort Worth after dark and drove straight to the house. Doyle parked in the driveway behind Brod's car. Crystelle led him up the walk to the front porch and peeked through the front windows. Everyone was seated at the dining room table.

"The family's at dinner," she said. "How quaint."

They entered through the unlocked front door. Ann Leigh was the first to see them. She gave a little cry, leaped up, and came to take Crystelle into her arms.

"Why didn't you let us know you were coming? I've been so worried! Oh, I'm so surprised!" She released Crystelle. "Doyle? You must forgive my manners. Welcome to the family."

Doyle bent and gave her a peck on the cheek. The others came trooping in from the dining room. Brod wore a slight frown of disapproval. Loren was grinning, as if the whole performance were staged for his entertainment. Brod's amazon stood to one side, as usual looking as if she had a cob up her ass. Crystelle saw that something was different about her, then realized that she was pregnant, beginning to show. Crystelle had momentary visions of a huge child tumbling out, half grown, and staggering to its feet like a newborn colt.

"My, but you make such a handsome couple!" Ann Leigh said.

Doyle beamed, willing to take full credit.

"A little the worse for wear, I'm afraid," Crystelle said. "We drove straight through from Monterrey." She was tempted to add that they had no money for a tourist court, not to mention a hotel room.

She introduced Doyle. Brod and Loren came forward to shake hands. Even Joanna unbent enough to hug Crystelle and wish them well.

That night she and Doyle slept in her old bedroom.

Two days later Brod and Joanna moved into their unfinished house. Crystelle knew her precipitous return was the reason. She was not chagrined.

"They've had the use of the house all summer and fall," she told Doyle. "Now it's our turn."

Ann Leigh remained superficial but pleasant, as long as Doyle was in the house. She waited until he had gone to visit his parents one afternoon before speaking her mind. "I do wish you'd waited until we could have given you a real wedding," she said, tears coming to her eyes.

They were seated in Crystelle's room, Crystelle on the sofa, her mother on a footstool.

"I had what I considered a real wedding once," Crystelle said. "And a wonderful honeymoon in San Antonio. This is what I have to show for it."

She turned her scarred wrists to the light.

"Oh, honey, don't be bitter! We did it for your own good! You were so young!"

"It was for everybody's good *but* mine," Crystelle said. "Brod got to show what a big man he is. You thought you were scotching one more Spurlock scandal. Moon was sentenced to a year of hard labor at Groton, and four to six at Harvard, straight time. I'll probably never see him again. So why shouldn't I have Doyle as a sort of consolation prize?"

Ann Leigh put a hand on her knee. "Honey, Doyle's a fine young man. He . . ."

Crystelle pulled away. "Don't be condescending. I know exactly what Doyle is—a hell of a good lover, a man everybody likes simply because there's not enough there to dislike."

Ann Leigh again sat erect on the footstool, her back straight, her mouth prim. "Since you brought it up, what exactly is Doyle planning to do?"

"I doubt if Doyle ever planned to do anything. *I'm* planning for him to go into business. My business. Spurlock Oil."

"Honey, please don't force him on Brod," Ann Leigh said. "There's so much potential for animosity to develop in a family-owned enterprise."

Crystelle laughed. "Animosity? Tell me about it! You know what happened to me on the way back from Mexico? We didn't have enough money for a room. We stopped for gas at a Spurlock Oil station. I stood in that fine new service station, broke, and suddenly realized that I owned one sixth of it. One sixth of the profits should be coming to me. One sixth of all the profits of Spurlock Oil. And where are they?"

For once Ann Leigh seemed helpless. She spread her hands. "Crystelle, I don't know what arrangements have been made. But surely you know that Brod wouldn't cheat you. Talk to him about it."

"You bet your boots I will. I'm sure Brod is looking after Brod. Loren is down there looking after Loren. And I'm going to have Doyle down there, looking out for me."

Brod did not want her to bring Doyle. He said it was a family matter, between the two of them. She finally relented.

Brod met her at the door of his office and ushered her to a leather sofa.

Crystelle was impressed—and angered—by the office. From the few times she had visited with her father, she remembered the headquarters building as drywall drab, with plain furniture and boxlike, glass-partitioned offices. Brod had built a private office suitable for royalty, with dark wood paneling, cut-glass chandeliers, leather-covered furniture, and heavy carpeting.

"You've managed to do well for yourself," she said. "Where's *my* office?"

Brod smiled but did not answer.

"You know why I'm here," she said. "I want an accounting."

Brod reached for a folder. "It's all here, sis. I had this prepared for you. Dividends from your shares have been deposited to a special account. Here are the papers. All you have to do is go to the bank and complete the signature forms."

Crystelle examined the figures. They meant nothing to her. "What about the profits? Don't tell me this big oil company isn't making money hand over fist."

Brod sighed. "It isn't that simple. I'll try to explain. The company is in expansion. If war comes, there'll be shortages of drilling rigs, pipe, everything. We're preparing. All profits are being plowed back into the company, along with a lot of borrowed money. You're a lot richer than you were six months ago. But your money is in equipment and oil reserves. It's not in a form you can spend right now."

"Don't I have any say-so at all?"

"We've had two board meetings." He reached for another folder. "Here are the minutes of both. You'll note that your absences were duly recorded."

"I want more than a board meeting every six months. You and Loren are executives in the firm. I demand that Doyle be given equal footing."

Brod hesitated. "What contributions do you think he can make to the company?"

"What the hell do you mean, contributions? It's my money in the company. That's a contribution!"

Brod remained silent for a moment. "Sis, I'm working at least twelve hours a day, six days a week, overseeing this company that stretches over two thirds of Texas. Loren is completing a special project that will cut our bookkeeping costs by a third. We're earning our salaries."

"What makes you think Doyle won't?"

Again Brod hesitated. "You really want me to tell you?"

Crystelle braced herself. "Go ahead."

"Doyle graduated high school by the skin of his teeth. He enrolled at A and M and was kicked out within two months. They said he was bright enough. He just never bothered to go to class. A 'disruptive influence,' they said. He wrecked three cars in five month's time. He can drink eleven vodka double martinis and remain on his feet. He has the reputation of a womanizer. They say he can meet almost any young woman and disappear with her in five minutes. His own father fired him from the family firm when he was found *in flagrante delicto* by a mixed group touring the model homes during Real Estate Week. He has never held any other job. And you want me to make him an executive of Spurlock Oil."

"I not only want you to make him an executive, I want you to make him vice president with access to all company books."

"You're asking the impossible."

"You have any alternative way I can protect my money?"

"I could buy you out."

They exchanged stares.

"You'd love that, wouldn't you? Not only no, but hell no, brother!"

"Then we're at an impasse."

"Not quite. You've been playing fast and loose with this company. I understand Loren well enough to know that deep down he probably resents it. Mom is gullible. You don't have the corner on conning her. I can trot out lawyers, demand that they have access to your books. I can send accountants in for audits under court auspices. And if I know you, some things you're doing won't bear close scrutiny. In short, dear brother, I can make one hell of a stink and foul up your little playpen."

Brod looked at her as if he had never seen her before. "I'm beginning to suspect I don't even know you. You've turned out to be one tough little cookie. You know that?"

"I turned tough one night in San Antonio when you took away the only thing I ever wanted. You wouldn't even let me die. Well, now you'll pay for it. Go ahead. *Don't* hire Doyle. I'd love to take you on."

She rose from the couch and started for the door.

Brod spoke from behind her. "You win, sis. I'll make a place for Doyle."

She turned. "How much?"

"Loren is drawing nine-five. I'll start Doyle at eight-five. Fair enough?"

"Nine."

Brod sighed. "All right. Nine thousand." He walked toward her. "But you're wrong about San Antonio. We honestly felt it was the right thing to do."

Crystelle had been waiting for a year to tell Brod what she thought of him. She made no effort to hold back her anger.

"I know exactly what was in your mind. You wanted to show off, the eldest son taking over the family and all that shit. Mom couldn't stand to see me happy because she's never been happy. So she denied me my chance. You call me tough. Well, tough titty makes strong baby."

Brod's hand shot out and slapped her, knocking her backward into the door. Her cheek stung and her ears rang. She looked up at him with a smile of satisfaction.

"Thank you for that, Big Brother," she said. "Now we know exactly where we stand."

She walked out, slamming the door behind her, raising heads throughout the floor. She walked toward the elevator, hoping that Brod's handprint was emblazoned on her face plain enough for all to see.

36

By the beginning of 1938 war seemed much closer. Hitler had annexed Austria, uniting the German-speaking nations under the Nazi flag. The Japanese had seized Peking, Tientsin, Shanghai, Nanking. The civil war continued in Spain, where Stuka dive bombers leveled city after city.

But in Washington the isolationists still talked as if the United States could remain neutral. The newspapers and newsreels devoted most of their attention to the almost constant peace talks in Europe.

"Of course Hitler is talking peace!" Brod fumed to anyone who would listen. "He's building his war machine while we do nothing!"

In early February, Joanna delivered a nine-pound, two-ounce baby boy. Brod and Joanna had picked the name Weldon, simply because they liked it.

Their house was completed except for a few odds and ends of furnishing. Ann Leigh had been of marvelous help, coming over almost every day to relieve Joanna of many chores during the last stages of her pregnancy. Brod was pleased that Joanna and Ann Leigh seemed to grow ever closer. Crystelle and Doyle had moved into a house in Rivercrest. Now only Loren was left at home with Ann Leigh.

Doyle Galloway fitted in better at the office than Brod expected. As handsome as a movie star, and as gregarious as a sheep, Doyle easily won instant acceptance. Brod put him to work setting up a distributorship program, thinking that the project at least would keep him out of office traffic. To Brod's surprise, Doyle began submitting reports on excellent potential sites, complete with rundowns on probable costs and the levels of competition.

Loren at last completed his special project with some measure of success. Brod restructured the organizational charts, placing all business operations under him. Brod sensed some resentment among the older department heads, but nothing of an extent that might undermine morale.

In early June, Grover came to him with a bundle of maps and figures. "Brod, we're paying too goddamn much to use other people's oil lines," he said. "We're being bled white by rail costs. We could run a six-inch line from about here to the refinery, and cut our freight costs to a fraction."

Brod examined the map. "I've often considered something like that. But the payout would be too long. Right now we can't afford it."

"We could if we brought other independents into it," Grover argued. "Look here. We could spread gathering lines to hell and gone. On the Gulf end we could tie on with other refineries, port facilities. We'd have more oil than we could handle."

Brod was impressed. He took Grover's survey home and spent two nights absorbing the details. It was an excellent piece of work. Grover had figured production levels, port tonnage, refinery capacities, and the competition. He had concluded with an argument that with war, rail and freight cargo space would be available only at a premium. The line would relieve the company of that worry.

"Let's do it," Brod told him. "Go ahead and talk to the other independents. Then we'll decide whether we want to go six- or eight-inch."

Grover looked at him with his calculating grin. "You mean you want *me* to do it?"

Brod knew he was jeopardizing his own position by allowing Grover to represent the company among other independents. The question might arise as to who was running things over at Spurlock Oil. But Grover deserved the recognition. "You thought it up," he said. "It's your baby. While you obtain the commitments, I'll go ahead with the planning. I wrote a term paper in college on oil line design and pumping. I'll see if I can find it."

Within a month Grover had obtained the commitments. Brod arranged financing, ordered the pipe and pumps, and signed with a contractor to start the ditching.

The months seemed to fly. Brod no longer could complete his work at the office. Each night he took reports home and sat up late, absorbing all the details of his burgeoning company. Joanna complained, but only mildly.

Engrossed in his work, Brod tended to overlook tensions on the staff.

On a day in June of 1939, Loren came into his office unannounced and closed the door. "I guess I'll have to be the one to tell you," he said. "We have a problem. Did you know that Doyle is going through the secretarial pool like a fox in a henhouse?"

Brod removed his reading glasses and rubbed his eyes. "Oh, shit. How long has it been going on?"

"Months. I'm sure you're the last person in the building to know."

"Why in hell didn't you tell me?"

Loren shrugged. "I've been trying to learn how he does it. Office gossip says he's hung like a stud horse, but I put that down to false advertising. Maybe it's the way he keeps his hair combed so perfectly, or that little hairline moustache. I also have a theory it's the heavy taps on those black-and-white wingtips. The sound alerts them. When he walks through the office, they look up, and he rolls his eyes at them."

"You have any suggestions?"

"Three options. One, we could hire uglier secretaries. Two, we could hire secretaries of higher moral character. Neither appeals to me. I think you ought to fire the son of a bitch."

Brod remembered Crystelle, her threats. He wanted to avoid unpleasantness if possible.

"I'll talk to him," he said.

After thinking the problem through, he summoned Doyle into his office. He did not bother with preliminaries. "Doyle, I'm going to cut through the shit. I hear you're screwing my secretaries blind. Is that true?"

Doyle lately had affected a gold cigarette holder. He toyed with it for a moment, lighting a cigarette. He looked up at Brod and smiled. "Sounds like you've got the goods on me. I guess the question is what you're going to do about it."

"No," Brod said quietly. "The question is what *you're* going to do about it."

Doyle's smile wavered. "I understood that my job here is more or less protected."

"Your job is, to some extent. But you're not. You're two-timing my sister, and disrupting my office staff. Can you think of any good reason why I shouldn't beat the living piss out of you?"

"You might try," Doyle said, his voice weak with tension. "I'm not so sure you could."

"You know damned well I could. But I'm hoping it won't be necessary. I'll make you a deal. You keep your screwing away from this building and the people in it, and I'll forget my inclinations."

Doyle studied his cigarette holder for a moment. He looked up and smiled. "It's a deal," he said.

"You can begin by taking those taps off your shoes," Brod said.

When the war began in September of 1939, Spurlock Oil was prepared. As the allowables were lifted, the company went into full production. Brod opened new areas to exploration, confident that further expansion was justified. He followed the news as the Nazi blitzkrieg overwhelmed Poland, Norway, Denmark, the Netherlands, Belgium, Luxembourg, and France, the British retreated from the beaches at Dunkirk, and the Battle of Britain began.

Although President Roosevelt had declared the United States neutral, the Gulf ports were operating at capacity, loading fuel, arms, and food for the European countries fighting the Nazis.

That spring Brod was visited by Harold Bennett, a vice president of Shell Oil. Bennett went right to the point. "We were impressed by the innovations in the oil supply line you organized and enterprised. We'd like to cut you in on a deal, in exchange for your help."

He spread a map on Brod's desk. A red line ran from Baton Rouge in Louisiana to Greensboro in North Carolina.

"We're thinking about laying a twelve-inch line across these six states. It'll supply eighteen army camps, thirty military airfields. Twenty percent of the Army Air Corps fuel use lies in these six states."

Brod examined the route. The project was daring in scope. He counted fourteen major rivers that would have to be crossed. Baton Rouge was only a few feet above sea level. Greensboro was near a thousand feet. Pumping would be an interesting problem.

"Where do I fit into it?" he asked.

Bennett leaned back in his chair. "As I say, we admired the new wrinkles you used in your line. We can get the men and equipment. But we need all the expertise we can find. We'd like to retain you on a consulting basis, with side benefits to your company."

"Who's we?"

"Standard of New Jersey, Standard of Kentucky, and Shell Union. We've been approached by the government in the planning of the defense program."

"I have my own company to run," Brod said.

Bennett nodded. "I know that. And I also happen to know that when U-boat warfare moves to the East Coast and the Gulf, you'll have market problems. Rail will be able to carry only a fraction of the demand. Existing pipelines will be inadequate."

"Still, I'm an oil man, not a pipeline engineer," Brod insisted. "I think I can make my best contribution right here."

Bennett again pointed to the map. "Those six states also use fuel to supply much of the nation's iron and steel, paper pulp, cotton, turpentine, resin, timber, fertilizer, foodstuffs. I needn't tell you what a load this pipeline will take off the railroads and highways."

Brod was moved by the argument. The contribution to national defense would be significant. And Bennett had confirmed some of his own worries. If the Gulf ports were closed by U-boats, much of the

Southwest's oil production would be unable to reach markets in the rest of the country and Spurlock Oil would suffer. If he were to join the big oil companies in this venture, a steady market would be assured.

"I'll be glad to do what I can," he said.

In the press of work during the next few weeks, Brod almost forgot about Bennett's visit.

Spurlock Oil's new exploration program resulted in one lucrative new pool and several disappointing failures. Brod spent many nights poring over the drilling logs, assembling information on strata, seeking new sites.

One afternoon Binkley Carothers called with disturbing news. "Betty Pierson and her husband have made us an offer. I think we'd better grab it."

Bink had delayed the case for two years. But it had remained a constant worry. "I thought you wanted to fight it out," Brod said.

"I did. But things have changed. With every expansion of Spurlock Oil, the more logical Betty's contention sounds that Clay swindled her out of a fortune. We could probably beat the case. But as I told you, we're vulnerable in other areas."

"What're her terms?"

"A hundred thousand shares of Spurlock stock, a seat on the board."

"Out of the question," Brod said. "To begin with, there's not enough company-owned stock."

"We could generate some. You'd better think about this, Brod. This way, she's only one voice on the board. If she should win her suit, she would be half owner of Spurlock Oil. Surely you see the danger."

Brod agonized over the decision for days. But he could see no other way out. Bink convinced him that the lack of a partnership agreement, as well as other foggy matters, would be made public record once the case went to trial.

Brod called a meeting of the board and explained the situation, and Betty Pierson Adcock became a director and a principal shareholder of Spurlock Oil.

Other concerns intervened. Joanna was again pregnant. In his second year Weldon had to be watched every minute. Ann Leigh helped, but Weldon often was beyond her capabilities as he charged headlong about the house. Joanna had complications, and for a time the doctor feared she might miscarry. But in January of 1941 she gave birth to a seven-pound, eight-ounce boy. They named him Kelly to honor her mother's family.

In May, newspapers and newsreels told of U-boat sinkings off the East Coast. The survivors were landed at Norfolk, Boston, and New York. President Roosevelt proclaimed an unlimited national emergency.

A few days later Bennett again visited Brod. "We've got the go-ahead on the Plantation Pipeline. When can you start work?"

For the next six months Brod literally worked day and night, catching only a few hours of troubled sleep when he could. He and his fellow engineers determined that fourteen pump stations fifty-six miles apart could do the job, each run by six hundred horsepower engines. An elaborate switching arrangement was designed, connected by teletype. Brod had determined from his own experience that the water slug commonly used to divide shipments of the different petroleum products was not needed and only caused complications. But old ideas died hard. He at last talked some executives into flying to Texas, and he demonstrated with the Spurlock line that kerosene could be sent behind gasoline, or gasoline behind crude, with minimal mixing.

During his long trips Brod left Loren in charge of the Fort Worth office, with instructions to call him if any major decision was needed. But he often was in the air, flying over the route of the pipeline, consulting with chemists over the electrolytic action of various soils, or searching for leaks in sections of the pipeline with pressure tests.

He called Loren often. But Loren usually was away from his desk. Worried, Brod flew back to Fort Worth.

"God damn it, you're in charge," he told Loren. "You should always be available."

"Brod, I only work here," Loren said. "I didn't marry the fucking place. There's no need for me to live in the building. Don't worry. Everything's fine!"

Loren's lack of responsibility remained a rift between them. Brod never felt completely safe leaving the company in his hands.

The pipeline was completed in seven months.

On Sunday, December seventh, Brod was home. After lunch he stretched out on a couch for a nap. An hour later Joanna awakened him.

"An announcer just broke in on the radio with a bulletin. The Japanese have bombed Pearl Harbor."

They listened to the confused bulletins throughout the remainder of the afternoon and evening. Information was scant. The White House announced that President Roosevelt would appear before the joint houses of Congress the next day.

The next morning Brod took a table model radio to the office. The entire staff gathered around it with sober faces and listened to President Roosevelt's historic "Day of Infamy" speech and the polling of the Congress on a declaration of war.

Brod plunged back to work, seeking to protect Spurlock Oil from the shortages he knew were to come.

A few days later Brod was visited by a man from the War Production

Board who explained that the government wished Spurlock Oil to convert a portion of its refinery operation to the production of toluol, needed for explosives. He said that scientists had determined that tuluol could be made by a simple rearrangement of hydrocarbons.

"It used to be made from coke ovens," he said. "But all the coke ovens in the world couldn't make enough for this war."

Brod went to work on the problem. He flew to the Gulf, visited pilot plants, talked with chemists, and directed the conversion. A separate plant was quickly erected to accommodate the new facility.

A few weeks later the man returned. "We also need another hydrocarbon, butadiene," he said.

He explained that the war had cut off all supplies of natural rubber. Liquefied butadiene, mixed with styrene, was used in the production of synthetic rubber. Brod worked marathon hours, effecting the second conversion process.

On the third visit the War Production representative seemed embarrassed. "We'd like to set up a laboratory in connection with your refinery."

This time he explained that with the likelihood that much of the war would be fought in the tropics, insecticides were needed. "For instance, dimethyl phthalate is an effective mosquito repellant. We need to put it into production. And we want to experiment with other hydrocarbons."

Brod listened in dismay as the new program was described. Mosquitoes, flies, and cockroaches would be bred under laboratory conditions and subjected to various oil derivatives. In addition to its other expansions, Spurlock Oil set up facilities to produce flies, mosquitoes, and cockroaches.

In early January, Brod was summoned to Washington. The letter requesting his presence was signed by the secretary of the interior, Harold L. Ickes, over his secondary title of Petroleum Coordinator for War. Military air transportation was arranged.

Not knowing what to expect, Brod reported to the designated room in the Interior building on C Street. He found himself waiting in a lobby with eight oil company executives asked to report to the same place at the same hour.

Brod was acquainted with three of the men. He knew the others by reputation.

An aide ushered them into a small conference room. "The secretary will be with you in a moment," he said as he left, closing the door behind him. Brod and the other executives waited in silence, aware that speculation would be futile.

After a few minutes the door opened and Secretary Ickes strode into the room. Brod would have recognized him from newspaper photographs but he was not prepared for the sheer dynamism of the man. Short and stocky, his blond hair blending into gray, Ickes had a direct, no-nonsense manner Brod liked. Carrying no papers, accompanied by no aides, he effectively conveyed the impression that he contained within himself everything that would be required.

"I'm Harold Ickes," he said. "In the following day or two I'll have the opportunity to get to know each of you personally. Today I'm sure you'd rather know why you're here. First let me say I'm grateful that each of you could come on such short notice. I appreciate the spirit in which you responded."

He readjusted his rimless glasses, setting them more firmly on the bridge of his nose.

"Most of you may have guessed our situation, but it is far more serious than any of you may have dreamed. I needn't tell you the importance of oil. Two thirds of the tonnage we will send overseas during this war will be oil and oil products. Oil is essential. Thanks to you, and other companies like yours, we have—or will have—the oil. Transporting it to where it's needed is another matter."

He glanced at the closed door. "I tell you this in confidence. The U-boat menace along our East Coast has been far more devastating than we have admitted to the public. Fuel for the northeastern sector of the United States—homes, factories, automobiles—is far below even minimum requirements. Crude for our eastern refineries is inadequate."

He paused. "This also is in confidence. I hereby swear you to secrecy, until such time as it is announced. We are now committed to the building of a twenty-four-inch oil pipeline from Longview, Texas, to the port terminals of New York City. It will be fourteen hundred miles long and capable of transporting more than twelve million gallons a day from Texas to New York and Philadelphia."

Brod sat stunned, trying to grasp the immensity of the project. The line would cross mountain ranges, the nation's largest rivers. The link over the forest-covered Appalachian chain alone was enough to stagger the imagination.

"We must have oil flowing through this line within a year."

The announcement of the time limitation broke the tension. A murmur of astonishment came from the group.

Ickes acknowledged it with a brief smile. "For purposes of construction the line will be broken into fifty segments. There are ten thousand experienced pipeline construction workers in this country. We intend to put each to work, but they will not be enough. You gentlemen will be the administrators, coordinating the whole effort. Later I'll go over your proposed responsibilities with each of you, individually. Right now I must move along."

He rose and left the room. Brod and his fellow executives looked at each other silently for a moment.

"I don't know about you boys," said Red Lewis of Houston. "But I feel like I've just been hit in the face with a shovel."

The aide reentered the room and passed out sheets of paper.

"Here is the schedule of conferences for the next two days," he said. "Please note that each of you will meet for an hour with the secretary."

Brod returned to his hotel with mixed emotions. Before his arrival in Washington, Spurlock Oil had seemed all-important. He had shoved all other thoughts of war aside. But the atmosphere in the capital changed his mind. Uniforms were everywhere. Faces were grim, resolute. The whole city vibrated with energy. As he passed through the crowded lobby of the Mayflower, a line waited at the registration desk. The town was jammed. Everywhere, talk was of the war. To Brod, it was amazing that despite Pearl Harbor, the loss of Wake Island, and the desperate situation in the Philippines, attention already had returned to the European front. The South Pacific seemed remote. The war in Europe, brought to within a few miles of the American coasts, appeared far more threatening.

He was now twenty-six, with a wife and two sons, and head of a company in an industry already declared essential to the war effort. The chances of his being drafted were remote. But he wanted to be a part of this grand adventure.

Slowly he began to entertain the idea of enlisting. He had connections. He was certain he could obtain a commission, perhaps at a moderately high rank.

Through the following day of conferences, the desire grew. The vast array of charts and detailed plans for the pipeline spread before him by the Interior people suggested that the project had long been on the shelf, awaiting the propitious moment. The extensive commitment of equipment and the sweeping movements of workmen indicated the magnitude of a military operation. His imagination was stirred. But he wanted the real thing. He thought of his soldier-grandfather, his Uncle Vern, who had died in France before he was born.

By the time he was ushered into Secretary Ickes's office for his private interview, his decision had been made. With the expansion program completed, Spurlock Oil was now functioning like a precision machine. He could turn the company over to Loren for the duration. Single, with no dependents, and not a trained oilman, Loren was vulnerable to the draft.

The maneuver probably would make Loren exempt.

He sat facing Secretary Ickes, wondering how to broach the subject. The Interior Department had invested two days in him. Ickes probably would be nettled that he had not informed them from the first moment. He was taken by surprise with the secretary's first question.

"Are you by any chance related to Travis Barclay Spurlock?"

"He was my grandfather."

The secretary frankly studied Brod's face. "I see a strong family resemblance. I knew him. Not well, but we were Bull Moosers together. He came to Illinois to help us. Brilliant orator, in the old-fashioned sense. All off the cuff, too. I don't recall ever seeing him use a prepared speech. I always thought of him as a mystic." He paused at the memory. "One evening he invited me to his hotel room and we talked. My God, the scope of that man's mind! We don't have men around like that anymore, self-created, who dreamed, and became exactly what they wanted to be. I believe they were a singularly American institution. Men like Benjamin Franklin, Abraham Lincoln, Theodore Roosevelt."

Ickes smiled in reflection. But before Brod could voice one of the thousands of questions he would have liked to ask about his illustrious grandfather, the moment passed. Ickes abruptly flipped open the folder on his desk. "Well, we'd better get on with the matter at hand. I think we've outlined, in a general way, what we hope you'll be able to do for us, and the arrangements. Can you see your way clear to take the job?"

He misinterpreted Brod's hesitation.

"Surely there's someone in your company who could fill in while we use you."

"Frankly, sir, I've been thinking of applying for a commission in the army."

Ickes sighed and placed his pen on his desk with great deliberation. "Brod, I think we all feel the same way on that. But the question is, where can we serve best? Technically, you're frozen in an industry essential to the war effort."

"If I understand the rules, I have the right of appeal," Brod pointed out. "I believe a request for combat status might take precedence."

Ickes nodded. "You're probably right. But the moment you were in uniform I could go to the commander in chief and have you assigned to this project on temporary duty. But that would take weeks, perhaps months. And we need you now."

Sobered by the threat of intervention by the President, Brod did not answer.

"Brod, I don't believe you yet realize the importance placed on this pipeline. Think of the amount of steel alone we're putting into it, when every ounce is desperately needed for arms production. The millions of dollars we'll spend on it would buy a fleet of destroyers for the navy. The hundreds of thousands of man-hours we're committing would put ten shipyards into production. But if we're to achieve full war production, and send millions of men overseas, this pipeline *must* be built."

"Sir, I'm not even a pipeline engineer," Brod said.

Ickes pointed to the folder on his desk. "When we went to the University of Oklahoma for recommendations on who we wanted, your name came back at the head of the list. The dean remembered a paper you wrote on the subject some years ago. His word for it was 'brilliant.' When we went to the people who built the Plantation Pipeline, again your name was at the head of the list. I'm not saying you're essential. Who is? But we certainly consider you among a very small handful."

Brod was taken aback. Until Spurlock Oil built its own line, he had almost forgotten that long-ago paper, written in a lab course.

Under Ickes's relentless logic, Brod's earlier resolve faded into confusion. He was awed by the reality of the situation—that a member of the Cabinet was terming him almost essential to the war effort, and threatening to go to the President to secure his services.

And he was dawdling like a reluctant schoolboy.

"In that case, sir, I suppose I can only say I'll contribute what I can to the project," he said.

"I'm pleased more than you know," Ickes said. "I welcome the pleasure of working with you. Perhaps some day we'll have a chance to reminisce about your grandfather."

"I'd like that, sir."

Ickes turned slowly through the folder until he found the page he sought. "They tell me that one of your innovations is your claim that water slugs are not needed between liquids of unlike material moving through a pipeline. Are you absolutely certain of this?"

"There's no doubt at all, sir. We've never used water slugs. I understand the Plantation Pipeline has abandoned them, with good results."

"Our operational plan calls for total separation of liquids. That complicates schedules considerably. Do you think your plan might be feasible for a twenty-four inch line?"

"Essentially the same thing," Brod explained. "You see, the theory is that the liquid tends to move as a solid. Mixing is minimal—no more than a few barrels at most. As long as you give the less volatile fuel preference, there's no problem."

"What do you mean?"

"A few gallons of kerosene mixed with thousands of barrels of gasoline wouldn't harm the finest engine. Even a good lab test probably wouldn't detect the difference. But a few gallons of gasoline mixed with kerosene conceivably could be dangerous, if fed into a boiler, home furnace, or cookstove."

They moved on, discussing various problems of pumping and switching. Brod was amazed by Ickes's grasp of the subject.

An hour later Brod was back on the street. The five o'clock crush had started. Rain was falling. Lines had formed for taxis.

Brod walked north, past the Ellipse and White House, to the Mayflower, savoring the wartime atmosphere of Washington.

It no longer distracted him.

Now he felt a part of it.

"You should have checked with me," Loren said. "I told you I thought I'd have some news when you got back. Remember? I applied for a commission in December. I was notified yesterday. I've been accepted."

Brod's first rush of anger was followed quickly by recognition that only three days earlier he himself had been on the verge of seeking a commission. Still he could not hide his concern and irritation. "Why didn't you tell me?"

"Hell, Brod, I didn't know if it would work out. Besides, you were all wrapped up in your trips. I thought it best not to add another worry, over something that might not happen."

"When do you leave?"

"I've been granted sixteen days' delay in reporting, to wind up my affairs. They'll give us ninety days of training, then a commission. Maybe this is going to be a speedier war."

"I wouldn't bet on it. What the hell am I going to do with the company for the year I'm gone?"

Loren smiled. "Don't count on Doyle. His father's pulling strings to get him a commission."

"On what grounds? His two months at A and M?"

"Maybe the army wants him to pose for recruiting posters."

Brod sat wondering who could run Spurlock Oil while he was gone. Most of the department heads were old hands, but few were acquainted with the overall operation, especially in the field.

He could think of only one man who could step in and do a competent job.

Loren had already come to the same conclusion. He spoke quietly. "Grover has been wanting to run this company for six years. I suppose he'll now get his chance."

Brod remained silent, reluctant to commit himself to the decision.

He worried over the problem for several days. He could find no other solution.

With deep misgivings he summoned Grover from a drill site in West Texas.

"Loren's going into the army," he explained. "I've been asked to undertake a project for the government that is, for the moment, secret. I'll be gone most of the time for the next year. I'd like for you to look after things."

Grover grinned at him, an amused glint in his eyes. "What's in it for me?"

Grover was slouched in the leather wing chair, his long legs thrust out straight, his rough field boots resting on their heels.

Brod considered the question, its hidden implications. "A ten percent raise. Possibly a bonus."

"Not good enough. If I'm qualified to run this place while you go off and play spy, or whatever, it seems to me I should have a more responsible position, permanently."

"I thought you weren't after a plate at the family table."

Grover's grin widened. "I didn't say I wouldn't accept a seat on the board."

"That'll never happen," Brod said. "You can get that idea out of your mind."

Grover's grin did not waver. "Right now, I'd settle for the raise, bonus, and the title of senior vice president."

"Loren's the senior vice president."

"There can be two," Grover said. "Hell, some banks have dozens. How else can I boss these old-timers, especially those you've kissed off with titles?"

Grover had a point. Brod could see no alternative. "If it means that much to you," he said.

During the next few days Loren shifted his duties to others and vacated his office in the far corner of the building.

Brod decided to move Grover into that office and not relinquish his own.

"I'll be doing some of the government work here," he told Grover. "How much, I don't know."

He saw Grover's eyes narrow. Grover opened his mouth, then closed it again, his protest unspoken.

The day before Loren left for camp, he voiced a thought that had already crossed Brod's mind.

"Remember what Aunt Zetta said about Grover? I think the camel has just stuck his head in the tent."

37

For years Joanna worried over the long hours Brod devoted to Spurlock Oil. He kept assuring her that eventually his work would become easier. But with the war, and his secret project, he seldom came home at all.

On his rare visits she was alarmed at his thinness. His prominent Spurlock cheekbones had become even more pronounced. He slept fitfully, rising every few hours to return to his work in the study. He spent many hours on the telephone, conferring with officials in Washington, other engineers in the field.

Joanna worried that the boys were growing up without him. She knew Brod's deep resentment over the absence of his own father during his formative years. Now family history was being repeated. The boys spent much of their time in the back yard, watching airplanes. The walls of their rooms were covered with photographs of warplanes, and models hung from the ceilings.

Around Joanna life changed with startling swiftness.

Consolidated-Vultee constructed a monstrous bomber plant on the edge of the city, almost within sight of her home in Westover Hills. Within months thirty-five thousand workers were rolling B-24 Liberator bombers off the mile-long assembly line. The Army Air Corps built an airfield adjacent to the plant for pilot training, and the roar of the four-engined bombers continued day and night, robbing her of sleep. With people dying all over the world in the horrendous war, it seemed little enough to endure.

The sleepy little villages in the Fort Worth-Dallas corridor sprang to life overnight, producing fighter planes and other war matériel. Great masses of people were constantly on the move, military men to new posts, workers to new jobs, families to be near husbands and fathers.

Life took on a curious temporary quality. And without permanence, nothing seemed to matter. Appalling prefabricated houses sprang up overnight. The workers who came to live in them were very different. They drove ancient cars, wore overalls and print dresses. They were taciturn. Their faces were weathered, their eyes solemn with an enduring patience. The native Texans called them Okies, but they came from everywhere—the swamps of Louisiana, the hills of Arkansas, the Piney Woods of East Texas, the dirt farms of Oklahoma, the farthest reaches of the Texas Panhandle. Descendants of the Indians driven out of Texas in the nineteenth century returned in force to work in the war plants.

Joanna recognized a prevailing irony: those who had suffered most during the Depression now had money and nowhere to spend it. Luxury items were unobtainable. The automobile factories had converted to military production. Shortages extended to candy, soft drinks, clothing, and cigarettes. Liquor was at a premium.

Everywhere Joanna looked she saw a sort of gallows gaiety. Under the guise of entertaining the swing shifts, night clubs and dance halls persisted until dawn. Theater box offices remained open until midnight.

Joanna contributed her time to various causes. She sorted and packed clothing in the Bundles for Britain campaign, and helped in the various scrap drives. Domestic help became impossible to find. More in a spirit of adventure than practicality, Joanna planted a victory garden. Her harvest was so profuse that she kept Ann Leigh and neighbors inundated with vegetables each summer.

Gradually the war years settled into a grind. Ann Leigh heard regularly from Loren, now overseas. He could not reveal his exact location, but Ann Leigh was convinced he was in North Africa. Doyle Galloway had been accepted for flight training and was stationed on the West Coast. Crystelle had gone to join him there.

The veil of secrecy was lifted from the Big Inch pipeline, and at last Brod was able to tell her what he was doing. Mostly she heard from him only in hurriedly scribbled notes, mailed from some remote mountain crossroads.

One evening she had just put the boys to bed when the phone rang. She had not heard from Brod in more than a week. She dashed to answer it.

"Joanna?" said the vaguely familiar voice. "This is Doyle Galloway. Is Brod in?"

Joanna explained the situation. "I know he would want to see you. Is Crystelle with you?"

Doyle hesitated. "No, I'm just passing through. I only stopped by to see my parents. I'm leaving in the morning. But I was hoping to talk to Brod while I was here."

Joanna gathered from his manner that something was wrong. "Can't you come out, if only for a few minutes? I know Brod would insist."

The line was silent for a long moment. "If you're sure it's not too late."

"I'll put the coffee on."

Doyle had always been indecently handsome, in a boyish way, but Joanna was totally unprepared for the tall, lean aviator who walked into her living room. He had lost considerable weight. His babyfaced delicacy was gone, replaced by firm, well-tanned flesh and hard muscle. He seemed quieter, more composed.

"You look terrific," Joanna said, offering her cheek. "A uniform couldn't make that much change."

Doyle smiled. "Credit several hundred hours of running around a grinder with full pack. I set records for demerits."

Joanna waited until they were seated. "Crystelle couldn't come with you?"

Again Doyle hesitated. "Crystelle and I are separated. That was what I wanted to see Brod about."

"I'm sorry," Joanna said.

They talked for a while of other things—Doyle's training, Loren, Brod's work, the changes in Fort Worth, the war itself. Inevitably the conversation circled back to Crystelle.

"I'm very concerned about her," Doyle said. "I do love her. But the situation became impossible. Someone should save her from herself. My hands are tied. It's all over between us."

"Is there anything we can do?"

Doyle seemed to be considering how much he should reveal. He looked at Joanna for a long moment. "Perhaps. I know Brod didn't think much of me." He smiled. "He once threatened to whip me. Did you know that?"

Joanna was mildly shocked, and fascinated. Brod had never mentioned it. She shook her head.

"I was playing around some with the girls in the office. Brod told me to quit or he'd pound me to a pulp. I knew he'd do it too." He studied his coffee for a moment. "I thought a lot of Brod, even if he didn't think much of me."

"I'm sure you're too hard on yourself," Joanna said.

"No, I know what I was. Maybe it's a terrible thing to say, but this war has helped a lot of people, including me. These wings represent the only real accomplishment in my whole life. I worked and sweated blood to get them."

"I'm sure you did," Joanna said.

"But Crystelle has gone the other way. I knew from the first that she had self-destructive tendencies. Back when I first met her, she made up a story about the scars on her wrists. She said she fell through a plate glass window. But I'd heard gossip, rumors."

Joanna did not answer. Brod had told her the story of Crystelle's first marriage in confidence.

Doyle stared at his coffee cup. "To put it bluntly, she started running around on me. I wasn't exactly in a position for outraged indignation. But she fed me the details." He spread his hands in a helpless gesture. "Maybe part of it can be blamed on the times. Life out there around the airfields and camps is unbelievable. Casual affairs are as common as palm trees. And it's true I was concentrating on pilot training at the expense of spending time with her."

He was silent for a moment, reflecting. Joanna remained quiet, assuming he needed a good listener.

"The last I saw of her, she was running off with a marine corps captain. He had a two-week leave and they were headed for San Francisco. I don't think there's anything permanent in it. I found out he has a wife and four children back in Ohio. I told her I wouldn't be there when she got back." He smiled ruefully. "The army cooperated. I'm in the process of reassignment. I expect to be sent overseas." He met Joanna's gaze. "I still love her, even though I never want to see her again. Tell Brod that if he can pull her out of the gutter, I'll be grateful. Even if I hated her, I wouldn't want to see her like she is now."

Joanna kept the secret of Doyle's visit for the next several days. She could not tell Ann Leigh about Crystelle, even if it were her place to do so. She loved Ann Leigh too much, and she knew the pain the situation would cause.

Nor did she want to tell Brod. He was overworked to the point of constant exhaustion. She worried about subjecting him to the additional emotional strain.

Yet she could not keep the secret forever. If in later years the facts emerged, neither Brod nor Ann Leigh would forgive her.

Reluctantly, Joanna determined that she would have to tell Brod, as soon as possible.

The artillery barrage began at 0400. When it lifted at first light, Loren saw the German Mark IV's moving up the road toward Sidi Bou Zid. With his spotting scope on maximum range he counted twenty. Beyond he saw the dust of more. A shiver of excitement gathered at the short hairs at the back of his neck. Clearly, Rommel's Afrika Korps was on the move. He reached for the field phone.

"Twenty tanks, heading west. Looks to me like they're trying to break out toward Kasserine and Tebessa. They're definitely advancing in force."

The major's voice crackled in the handset. "Just report what you see, Spurlock. You say twenty tanks confirmed?"

"Correction. Twenty-six," Loren said, adjusting the scope. "Single file. Fifty-yard intervals. Another dust cloud in the distance."

"Confirmed. You have any casualties?"

"Two dead, three wounded."

"Hold as long as you can, then fall back. We'll move out under cover of darkness to regroup."

Loren acknowledged by reflex, leaving the obvious unstated. The German thrusts up from Bir El Hafey and Faid had left them encircled. If they were to retreat through the Kasserine Pass to regroup beyond the Western Dorsale, they would have to fight their way out through Rommel's best.

Loren summoned his squad leaders. "We're to hold until dark, then join up on Djebel Lessouda. I think we can expect more incoming artillery before we're engaged. I don't want to see any moving around. Let's keep our heads down."

The noncoms moved away without comment, their estimates of the situation recorded on their faces. Loren shared their view. Rommel's armor was passing them by, cutting them off from Corps, but the Desert Fox would not be content to leave even a small force at his back. They could expect a mopping-up operation sometime during the day.

Loren and his men were dug in at the peak of a low string of hills called Djebel Ksaira. The dust, the flat, barren terrain reminded Loren of Far West Texas. His was one of a string of observation posts along the Eastern Dorsale. From every clue he could gather, the main body of Allied armor was at least fifty kilometers behind them.

Lieutenant Anderson completed his check of the perimeter and came to hunker down beside Loren.

"Fischer died," he said. "Martin may not make it."

Loren grunted an acknowledgment. After two months of combat, the artillery barrage had cost them their first casualties. Psychologically they were unprepared.

The Torch operations had gone too easily. They had landed at Safi in Morocco, and moved through Casablanca and Port Lyautey without serious trouble. They had traversed the northern coast of Africa, encountering no serious opposition until they arrived in Tunisia. Now they were up against Rommel's best.

"Why are we waiting until dark?" Anderson asked. "Why don't we pull back now?"

"It'll be safer tonight," Loren said.

He knew his answer would be recognized for the lie it was. Corps badly needed intelligence. He and his men were at high risk, perhaps expendable.

German trucks and personnel carriers were now dispersing along the desert floor behind the tanks. Loren rang the major and reported.

"They could be laying mines. But it looks to me like they're preparing for a sweep."

The major did not answer for a moment. "If we're separated, try to make it to Kasserine. The First Armored will be moving up to engage somewhere. That's as good a guess as any."

Loren heard the peculiar sigh of incoming artillery. The round landed forty yards away. For a moment he had trouble with his bowels as the barrage was renewed with even greater intensity. He lay in the bottom of the slit trench, the metallic taste of fear rising in his mouth as the ground shook under each explosion.

The shelling lasted thirty minutes by his watch. As soon as it lifted, he moved among the men, counting casualties, reorganizing the mortars. Four more were dead, six wounded.

The German troops had left the personnel carriers. They were now less than a mile away, spreading out as they moved into the foothills.

Loren repositioned two mortars to cover a gap in the field of fire.

Then there was nothing to do but wait.

The first assault came just after noon. Advancing under the cover of heavy mortar fire, the Germans moved up the ravines, taking positions for a three-pronged attack. Loren held his fire, preserving his ammunition, until the Germans left the partial protection of the foothills and moved onto the open slopes.

With machine guns, rifles, and mortars, Loren and his men held off the first assault. The Germans took cover in the ravines. For more than an hour the battle was a mortar duel.

By 1600 only a few mortar rounds remained. Other ammunition was running low.

Loren was certain the Germans would try at least one more daylight assault.

"Pass the word," he said to Anderson. "We're pulling out. Mortars will provide cover. We'll move south until dark, then turn west. Maybe we can fool them."

Anderson hurried away. Loren was reaching for the field telephone when he was lifted high into the air. He remained fully conscious as he turned a graceful flip and landed back in the slit trench.

He tried to get to his feet, but he seemed to have no feet. His pants were bloody. His right leg lay at a peculiar angle. He was surrounded by an awesome silence.

Then Anderson was beside him, his mouth working as he shouted for a medic. But Loren heard no sound. The medic came and, after a quick glance at Loren, gave him a shot of morphine. Loren tried to protest. Hurriedly the medic applied tourniquets.

A blackness descended.

When he awoke, his men were gone. He had been left among the dead.

He pulled his .45 Colt automatic, chambered a round, and placed the pistol in his lap. He reached for a Garand M1 rifle, checked the bore to be sure it was clear, and inserted a fresh clip.

He then sat in the slit trench and waited patiently for the Germans to arrive.

High over the Appalachians, Brod kept his eyes on the thin shimmer of metal far below, snaking its way through the trees, across the creeks, over ridges and hollows. It was the last link of the Big Inch, waiting to be lowered into its trench. Brod gave the signal. The light plane turned, its steady drone altering pitch as they lost altitude.

With the spring rains he had been unable to get bulldozers into the mountains for the backfilling. Now the equipment was on the way.

For a time Brod sat and enjoyed the mountain scenery, thinking back over the incredible year.

At first some of the problems had seemed insurmountable. The digging of the fourteen-hundred-mile trench from Longview, Texas, to New York Harbor had been assigned to nineteen contractors. The trucking and stringing of the forty-foot lengths of pipe had to be contracted. Soils all along the route had to be tested for excessive acidity or alkalinity. Where corrosion was a danger, the pipe was tarred and wrapped.

The welding of each joint had to be perfect—smooth on the inside, yet strong enough to prevent leaks. For a time, expansion and contraction under heat and cold had seemed an insurmountable problem. Eventually they learned the trick of lowering pipe in the morning and backfilling before the heat of the sun could reach it.

Frozen ground had delayed them in winter, heavy rains and floods in the spring. They had crossed thirty rivers and two hundred streams and lakes. They had designed and built twenty-six pumping stations.

All this they had done within a year. Yet only forty minor leaks had been found in the fourteen-hundred-mile length. Each had now been repaired.

The job had taken its toll. Brod missed Joanna and his sons more each passing day. He worried about Spurlock Oil. Although Grover was more than competent, he had taken the company in directions Brod questioned.

And if he had been home, he might have been able to do something about Crystelle. He also might have helped to ease Ann Leigh's anguish over the news about Loren.

Officially, Loren was listed as "missing in action and presumed dead." Brod had appealed to his connections in Washington. He had been unable to learn anything further.

The plane went into a shallow glide. Ahead lay the small airport. Brod braced himself as the pilot throttled back and side-slipped through a mountain pass, lining up with the runway. The wheels touched gently. The pilot taxied toward the hangars. Brod's assistant was waiting.

Short, heavy-set, and prematurely balding, Jerry Hamilton was a recent graduate of the Colorado School of Mines, temporarily detained on his way to service in the U.S. Army Engineers. He approached as soon as the plane stopped rolling.

"The dozers are in place," he said. "Weather Bureau says we'll have two or three days before rain moves in."

"That should give us time enough," Brod said. "Send word to the crew boss that we'll start at first light."

Hamilton nodded. "There was a phone call for you from Washington. It was from Secretary Ickes. He said it was personal. He asked that you come to see him as soon as you're free."

Brod stood for a moment, examining the possibilities. A personal message from Ickes could mean only one thing: He had finally obtained information about Loren.

"I'll leave this afternoon," Brod said. "You can supervise that final link-up in the morning."

Hamilton did not answer. His hesitation conveyed his doubts.

"You know what to do," Brod said. "Just get the pipe in fast, with the dozers working right behind the cradles. As soon as it's in the ground, put it under hydrostatic squeeze. A thousand pounds pressure for twenty-four hours. Let me know the results as soon as you can."

He followed Hamilton to the waiting car, and a ride into the nearest town.

He did not yet know how he would get to Washington. But he was prepared to travel all night.

"The line is virtually completed, Mr. Secretary," Brod said. "Only one section remains to be tested under pressure. The first oil should be in New York within the week."

Ickes removed his glasses and polished them with a white handkerchief. "Brod, I can tell you that the President is most pleased. This project has served as a model for the whole war effort."

He paused. "The reason I asked you here, I've been able to obtain a little information on your brother. It isn't good."

Brod waited, preparing himself for the worst.

"Captain Spurlock was badly wounded in the preliminary stages of the Battle of Kasserine. His observation post was overrun. Almost his entire command was lost. A soldier who escaped reported that your brother received an almost direct hit from a mortar round, and his legs were shattered. He said Captain Spurlock was still alive when he last saw him."

For a moment Brod did not trust himself to speak. He knew that his face conveyed his anguish. "Still nothing on the POW lists?" he managed to ask.

Ickes shook his head. "Nothing. But that may not be significant. Conditions in that sector were chaotic. This I tell you in strictest confidence. In all, twenty-four hundred American soldiers were surrounded and captured before a counterattack could be mounted. The effect has been traumatic on the army. Several generals have been replaced."

Brod waited until he felt he could keep his voice under control. "Sir, I thank you for your efforts. This is the first real word we've had."

Ickes was silent for a moment. "Brod, I know what this job has cost you, in money and in self-sacrifice. I'm now put into the position of asking even more of you. I didn't intend to bring it up this morning, thinking it'd be a poor time. But I now believe there might not be a better time."

He gestured to a world map on the wall. "We still have such a long way to go. Landings in Europe. Dozens in the Pacific. Planes, tanks, armored columns, ships and submarines, millions of gallons of fuel. Fortunately, we have the oil. We have the refineries. Distribution will be our problem."

He rose and pointed on the map. "When we invade Europe, supply and distribution will be taxed to the limits. Two key factors have emerged as essential in this war, airpower and fast-moving armored forces. Already they are consuming fuel at a rate undreamed of only a year ago. Our estimates of the requirements for a two-ocean navy have tripled. We can't have armored columns halted because the gas isn't there. We can't have bombing missions scrubbed because the fuel hasn't arrived. The navy can't delay intricate sea operations to wait for delivery of oil. In short, I need a troubleshooter, to see that oil and gasoline get from the source of supply to the point where they are needed."

He paused. "Brod, you have a remarkable talent for organization. I need that talent. I know we requisitioned you from your company only for the duration of the Big Inch. But this new job is even more essential to the war effort. Could you see your way clear to accepting it?"

Brod had been living for the day he could return home to Joanna, Weldon, and Kelly. He felt driven to resume control of Spurlock Oil.

But his work on the Big Inch had enlarged his perspective. He now had a global view. He did not need Ickes's explanation. He knew that the invasion of Europe would require months of saturation bombing, several large-scale landings in both the Mediterranean and the Atlantic. The advancing armies would require long lines of supply as they rolled across Europe. In the Pacific, the strategy of island hopping all the way to the Japanese homeland would require myriad air strikes, extensive sea battles, and dozens of bombardment and assault operations.

No military plan should be hampered—the men endangered—because the essential fuel was sitting in the wrong place.

Ickes was right on another point: he could not have picked a better time to make his plea.

Compared with the sacrifices made by Loren and thousands of other men, Brod knew that his own were insignificant.

"Mr. Secretary, I see no way to refuse," he said.

38

nn Leigh never wavered in her belief that Loren was still alive. From the day she received the first telegram, she never relented in her efforts to locate him. She remained in constant communication with the International Red Cross. She used her political contacts in Washington shamelessly. House Speaker Sam Rayburn, Senator W. Lee O'Daniel, Congressman Fritz Lanham, and an aide to President Roosevelt wrote, reassuring her everything possible was being done.

She talked with *Fort Worth Star-Telegram* publisher Amon Carter, whose own son also had been captured in North Africa. Amon Junior was a POW in Poland. Carter and his son had established a clandestine link through Portugal and were smuggling out the names of American POW's. Carter inquired about Loren without results.

Belatedly Ann Leigh learned that Brod had obtained additional information through his Washington sources, and had withheld it to protect her. She was furious with him for a time. The fact that Loren was badly wounded did not alter her conviction that he was alive. She was certain that if he were dead she would have *known*.

She followed the horrible news from day to day, through the landings in Sicily, Anzio, and Salerno, and the long-awaited invasion of Normandy. As the Allies moved across France and into Germany, she awoke every morning with a prayer that the day had arrived when Loren would be found.

Crystelle came through town, once with a navy flier from New Jersey, and once with a merchant marine captain from Corpus Christi. She said she was divorced from Doyle Galloway, but she was vague on details. She introduced each boyfriend as "the man I'm going to marry."

"Don't waste your time with her," Aunt Zetta said. "She has chosen her life. Let her live it. There's nothing else you can do."

Ann Leigh found the advice difficult to follow, even though she recognized its worth. She worried about all her children: Loren, wherever he was; Crystelle, lured into wanton dissipation by a generation that was living too fast, too desperately; and Brod, who came home each time from his travels more gaunt and pale than the last.

At last the war in Europe ground toward a close. After a few heart-stopping weeks in December, when the German counterattacks pushed the Allies back, the advance moved steadily into Germany. By April the newspapers were predicting that the end was only weeks away.

At last the long-expected telegram arrived. Loren had been found. Through direct appeal to the White House, Ann Leigh learned that he would be sent to the States as soon as his health permitted.

Brod had just returned from Washington. That night Brod and Joanna brought the children over for a celebration. Joanna could not stop crying. It was the first time Ann Leigh realized the depth of Joanna's love for the family.

But now she was worried about Brod. His grayish pallor was deeper. In a certain light his lips seemed blue.

"Brod's not well at all," Aunt Zetta said to Joanna. "Why don't you get him to go to a doctor?"

"Aunt Zetta, I've tried. He insists that all he needs is rest."

A few weeks later Loren was transferred to Brooke Army Hospital at Fort Sam Houston in San Antonio. En route through Washington, he and five other long-time POW's, also convalescents, were decorated by President Truman. A photograph of the ceremony appeared in *Life* magazine.

Brod and Joanna drove Ann Leigh to San Antonio to see him.

He was wheeled into a sunny day room by an orderly. His left leg was gone above the knee and his right was in a cast. But he seemed to be in good spirits. He was wearing the same carefree grin she had first seen on him as a baby.

His face was thin, but tanned and firm. As he hugged her, his arms were strong.

Loren tried to put them at ease by describing his capture. He said he had loaded his guns and prepared to fight, assuming he would be killed anyway.

He laughed. "Just think, if I hadn't passed out, I might have killed the man who saved my life. There may be a moral there somewhere."

He said that after the German medic tended to his wounds, he was sent to a hospital in Italy, where his leg was amputated. He was too weak to be sent north with the other prisoners, and apparently for a time was forgotten. He wasn't sent to Germany until just before the fall of Rome. In the confusion his name simply had not cropped up on the lists.

Advancing Allied troops had only recently encountered the death camps. The full horror of the Holocaust had just been revealed to the

American public. The hospital day room was filled with newspapers and magazines containing photographic evidence of the Nazi atrocities—the ovens, mass graves, bodies stacked like cordwood. The nation was stunned. Not even the worst of the wartime propaganda had prepared Americans for the grim realities.

When the subject was mentioned, Loren shook his head. "I don't understand it. Everywhere, I was given royal treatment. Rommel's soldiers went to a great deal of trouble to save my life. After my leg was taken off, Italian women came to my room and prayed. In the camp in Poland, the Polish people smuggled food to us when there wasn't enough for themselves. And now this! It's beyond comprehension."

Loren said his right leg had not mended properly. The army surgeons had rebroken the bones so it would heal straight.

He grinned. "If they'd just give me a pegleg, I think I could walk all the way to Fort Worth right now."

Ann Leigh, Joanna, and Brod spent three days in San Antonio, visiting Loren at every opportunity. They had agreed beforehand to lie to Loren about Crystelle until he was stronger. They only told him that she was on the East Coast, where her husband was stationed, and unable to come.

Throughout their stay at the Menger, Brod was restless. He spent much time on the telephone and was even interrupted twice at dinner with messages.

"It has something to do with redeployment," Joanna explained to Ann Leigh. "With the end of the war in Europe they're preparing to move everything to the Pacific. Brod said it means tearing down the distribution system they've spent four years building, and erecting it all over again."

On the drive back to Fort Worth, Ann Leigh saw lines of fatigue around Brod's eyes and mouth. But he would not allow her or Joanna to drive.

They arrived home shortly after ten. Ann Leigh took a quick shower and went straight to bed.

Hours later she was awakened by the persistent ringing of the phone.

"Ann Leigh, this is Joanna. It's Brod's heart! I'm at John Peter Smith. In the emergency room! Oh, Mama Spurlock, I'm so scared! I think he's dying!"

Ann Leigh dressed hurriedly and drove to John Peter Smith Hospital. She found Joanna in the corridor outside the emergency rooms. They clung together in paralytic dread until a doctor emerged, hours later. His face was grim.

"He has had a massive coronary. He's now stabilized, and I can offer you hope. But you should prepare yourselves. If he survives, he may be an invalid for the remainder of his life."

After leaving Pensacola, Grover Sterling found himself on a narrow, two-lane blacktop that skirted the snow white beaches for the ninety miles to Panama City. Aside from an occasional fisherman he encountered little traffic during the long stretches from one small seaside hamlet to the next. The day was hot and humid. Huge thunderheads hung a few miles off shore, threatening rain.

The blue waters of the Gulf, the lonely, immaculate beaches, the waving mounds of wild oats offered a view of immeasurable beauty. Grover hardly noticed. His mind was on what he had come to Florida to do.

His private detectives had spent two months tracing Crystelle Spurlock. According to their report she seemed to have a predilection for pilots. She now was living with an air corps pilot stationed at Tyndall Field near Panama City.

Grover had spent months planning his elaborate maneuver to assume complete control of Spurlock Oil.

Crystelle was the key to the whole game.

He would have to play his cards exactly right.

He crossed the long bridge over St. Andrews Bay and stopped at a shrimp stand to ask for directions. Grover had removed his coat and tie in deference to the heat, but the natives still seemed to regard him with curiosity.

Following directions, he drove to a small red brick house situated on a sandy street a few blocks from the bay. He parked in the sandy drive beside a battered yellow Lincoln convertible.

He walked up to the house. The front door was open, the screen door hooked. Flies were buzzing around the screen. At his knock he heard movement in the back, then silence. He knocked again.

A woman came padding into the tiny living room. She was barefoot, wearing only shorts and halter. Her tousled blond hair was piled carelessly on the top of her head. She spoke with a voice that seemed accustomed to discouraging door-to-door salesmen and other unwanted intruders.

"Yes?"

Grover was not completely certain of her identity. She seemed older than he had imagined her. "Crystelle Spurlock?"

She looked at him for a long moment. "Who wants to know?"

"I'm Grover Sterling."

Crystelle moved closer to the screen, her hand poised on the latch. "Holy shit. What are you doing here?"

"I came to talk to you. May I come in?"

Crystelle's hesitation was brief. "Sure." She unlatched the screen. "If you won't pay any attention to the mess. We had a party last night. I haven't got around to cleaning up."

With an adept wave of her hand she warded off the flies as he entered. The floors were bare wood. A tired couch, two chairs, and a scarred coffee table were the only furnishings. The walls were undecorated.

"Have a seat," Crystelle said. "Can I get you a drink? I think there's some bourbon left."

Grover studied her as she went into the kitchenette. She wore no makeup, but her skin was tanned to a deep brown. Love handles rippled at her waist. Her face bore a look of dissipated fleshiness. He heard the movement of someone in the back rooms of the house.

As Crystelle returned with the drinks, a tall, rangy lieutenant emerged in a crisp, open-necked uniform. He stopped and glanced at Grover uncertainly. Crystelle padded over and took him by the arm.

"Honey, you're not going to believe me, but I'll tell you anyway. This is my half brother. And this is the first time I've ever laid eyes on him in my entire life." She turned to Grover. "You don't mind my calling you my half brother, do you?"

"I can live with it if you can."

Grover rose and shook hands with the lieutenant, whose mind seemed to be elsewhere. He was a strikingly handsome man, with curly blond hair and perfect teeth. He turned away and picked up a small bag.

"He's running late," Crystelle said. "He's got a date with a tow-target out over the Gulf."

With apologies, the lieutenant left. Crystelle sat in one of the stuffed chairs and tucked her bare feet beneath her. Rivulets of sweat ran from her neck into the halter top.

"You still haven't said why you're here."

Grover was not sure how to begin. "You've heard about Brod's heart attack?"

She nodded. "I manage to keep informed. I hear he's going to be all right."

"As long as he takes it easy. But you know Brod. He won't take a back seat unless someone makes him."

Crystelle studied him for a long moment. "And you're going to make him?"

"Crystelle, I've been running the company for four years with both hands tied behind me. Now Brod is out of it, but he won't relinquish control. Loren will be in and out of hospitals for the next five years, maybe for the rest of his life. Your mother has never had any real interest in the company, and she's vague on what's going on. That leaves you, me, and Betty Pierson."

Crystelle finished her drink and almost missed the coffee table with the glass. Grover realized it was not her first drink of the day.

"Exactly where do I fit in?"

"I need your proxy. I intend to reorganize the company, generate capital with a public offering, and reserve controlling blocks of shares for ourselves. I have an angel who will bankroll us, if we cut him in on the deal. He has access to unlimited money."

"Who's your angel?"

"I'm not at liberty to say."

"Then count me out. I'm not about to play poker with half a deck."

Grover sighed. He had been warned that Crystelle would drive a hard bargain.

"All right, I'll tell you. It's Troy Spurlock."

Crystelle burst out laughing. She threw her head back and cackled at the ceiling. "Boy, when you shaft somebody, you don't do it by half measures, do you? There's nobody on the face of the earth Brod would hate worse to see in Spurlock Oil. What's Troy's price?"

"He'll be chairman of the board."

"And you?"

"President."

"And what's in it for me?"

Grover hesitated. "Money. Prestige. Power."

"How about a little revenge? Why don't you try that on for size?"

Grover grinned. "You know, I came here with the thought that we might have more in common than the same father."

With the back of her hand, Crystelle wiped away beads of sweat from her lip and forehead. "God, I'm slowly dying in this heat. Let's drive out to the beach. It's the only place you can breathe around here. I'll find you a pair of shorts. You look like an undertaker in that outfit. Nobody wears clothes around here."

An hour later they lay under an umbrella on the white sand, the waters of the Gulf only a few feet away. Behind them, Doris Day was singing "Sentimental Journey" over a raucous radio at a Sno-Kone stand. Crystelle had not mentioned Spurlock Oil again. She lay with her eyes closed. Like most of the Spurlocks she seemed given to long silences. Grover did not want to press her.

At last she rolled over and looked at him. "My family has always treated me like dirt. I guess you know that, or you wouldn't be here. Brod took away the only thing I ever wanted, with my mother's blessing. My daddy screwed himself silly all of his life, and it was supposed to have made him a great man. And if I have a little fun, it's a big-assed tragedy. At least I'm not scattering kids all over the place."

Grover did not respond. He wanted her to convince herself.

Crystelle sat up and rubbed more suntan oil onto her shoulders and arms. Then she stared for a long time at the storm clouds out over the Gulf.

"You can count me in," she said. "I have some money stashed away. I'll put that into it. But I'm not giving you or anybody my proxy. I'll be there to speak for myself."

Behind them, an announcer broke into Bing Crosby's "Accentuate the Positive" with a news bulletin. In the wake of the second atomic bomb over Nagasaki, the Empire of Japan had surrendered.

"Well, I might as well go back to Fort Worth anyway," Crystelle said. "It sounds like the party's over."

"Mama, can't you see what he's doing?" Loren demanded. "He'll buy up that stock himself and gain control!"

"But he doesn't have that kind of money," Ann Leigh protested. "Brod said that everything Grover has is already invested in the company."

"For a piece of Spurlock Oil he can find the money. Why didn't you come to me?"

Loren regretted upsetting his mother, but Grover's ploy was so transparent she should have seen through it.

"I didn't want to bother you," Ann Leigh said, on the verge of tears. "And what he said seemed so logical. He had charts showing the need for recapitalization and expansion. I didn't think I should worry Brod . . ."

"We *won't* worry Brod. I can take care of it before I have to go back to Fort Sam. We can rescind your approval. But I've got to find out exactly what he's doing. We could be squeezed out of the company."

"You're not well enough yet!"

Loren did not answer. He laboriously climbed the stairs to his room. Collapsing on the daybed, he fished in his jacket pocket for the painkillers. He swallowed a capsule dry. It was a trick he had learned in recent weeks.

The last operation had not gone well. The surgeons had found evidence of deterioration in the bone. Further surgery was now scheduled to insert steel rods.

Loren waited until the heavy dose of morphine took effect. He then rolled to the phone, called Spurlock Oil, and demanded to be put through to Grover Sterling.

"Grover, I'm just calling to inform you that my mother is withdrawing her support of the stock issue. None of the family will approve."

Loren had almost forgotten how smoothly Grover could hand out a line of bull. "Loren, you don't know the situation down here. You've been away from the business too long. With the end of the war we've got to switch back to the civilian market fast. That means expansion of our retail outlets. If we don't do it now, the opportunity will be lost forever. And we need capital to do it."

"Then we can borrow the money. We've never sold part of the company before. We don't need to do it now."

"Loren, we haven't had a board meeting in years. I can demonstrate dereliction. Under the articles of incorporation I have certain discretionary powers as executive vice president. I can exercise them."

"Grover, you're talking nonsense. That's a family-owned business. You're a hired hand with a piddling amount of stock. Don't let it go to your head."

"And you haven't been inside this place in four years. Loren, I sympathize with your situation, but I've got to face facts. You've got a long way to go before you'll be well enough to return to work. Brod probably never will. I've got to protect what you call my piddling little investment. I've been running this company for four years. This reorganizational plan has been in the works for twenty-four months. I've obtained the permission of the majority of the board. That's all I'm required to do. I have your mother's signature."

With a jolt, Loren realized how far along the plan had progressed. A majority of the board would include Crystelle and Betty Pierson, leaving out only himself and Brod. His mother's signature was crucial.

"Grover, listen to me. I'm going downtown this afternoon and obtain a temporary restraining order. When it comes down to a show-cause hearing for a permanent restraining order, you know as well as I who'll win."

The line was silent so long that Loren began to wonder if they had been disconnected. When Grover spoke, his voice was more subdued.

"Loren, we need to talk about this. I think I can convince you that what I'm doing is right. For the good of the company, we should be working together on this, not against each other."

"I'll be right down," Loren said.

"No, I'd rather keep our disagreement out of the office. There's no need to air it here. I'll meet you somewhere. How about the drive in front of Will Rogers Memorial Auditorium? At four o'clock."

"I'll be there," Loren said.

Thirty minutes later, after taking another painkiller, he left the house. Ann Leigh asked where he was going. He refused to tell her.

When he did not return by early evening, Ann Leigh grew worried. A few minutes after ten, she was sitting at the telephone, wondering whether to call the police, when a detective arrived at the front door. He introduced himself as Sergeant Prescott.

"Mrs. Spurlock, do you have a son in uniform, driving a black nineteen forty-one Cadillac, Texas license . . ."

He paused, hunting for a long moment before he found and read off the number.

Ann Leigh envisioned Loren injured in a terrible wreck. "Is he hurt?"

"Mrs. Spurlock, maybe you'd like to sit. I have very bad news. If your son had one leg missing, above the knee, I'm afraid there's no doubt of the identification. He committed suicide late this afternoon. Two boys fishing found him in his car, near the river in Rockwood Park. He apparently killed himself with his service pistol."

Ann Leigh went numb in mind and body. But a conviction rose in her more powerful than any emotion she had ever experienced. It overrode her shock and grief. "No!" she said. "He wouldn't *do* that. If he's dead, he was murdered!"

Prescott hesitated. "We'll look into every possibility, Mrs. Spurlock. But at the moment the coroner's preliminary verdict is suicide." He glanced around the room. "Are you alone here? Is there anyone I could call?"

Ann Leigh's first thought was of Brod. They had to keep the news from him. "My daughter-in-law. She's with my other son, at the hospital. I'll summon her, if you'll be so kind as to wait."

Joanna came immediately. They remained awake through the long night, so emotionally devastated they could not yet feel the loss. They agreed that the shock might kill Brod.

With the cooperation of the hospital staff they took elaborate precautions that he would not hear or see the news.

Two days later Loren was buried with full military honors. Ann Leigh kept the flag from his coffin on the mantel in the living room. She could not bring herself to put it away.

During the next two weeks Brod grew stronger. He regained some of his color and developed an appetite. He began to rail against the hospital routine. Through sheer persistence he talked his doctor into allowing him to return home.

"Actually, there's little we can do for him here," the doctor told Joanna. "He has stabilized. His attitude is good. No doubt home would be the best environment. But he must be kept quiet, with minimal exertion.

From what we can determine, the damage to his heart is extensive. He must have bed rest, to allow the heart to recuperate."

Joanna explained her worries about Loren's death. "Brod has asked about him twice. I'm a poor liar."

The doctor considered the problem at length before answering. "He should be told. I won't deny there's risk. But we must preserve his trust in us. If you'd like, I can stand by while you tell him."

On the following afternoon Brod was taken home by ambulance and installed in the master bedroom on the second floor. The next morning when the doctor came, Ann Leigh and Joanna told him about Loren's death. Ann Leigh went on to explain about the situation at the company, Loren's concern over the new stock issue.

Brod listened in silence. Not until they were finished did he speak.

"Loren would never have killed himself. Get that detective up here. We'll reopen the case."

Sergeant Prescott came and sat in a straight chair beside Brod's bed. He remained adamant. "Mr. Spurlock, I know this is painful for you to accept. But the evidence at the scene was convincing—the pistol in his right hand, the angle of the bullet."

"He was in excellent spirits. He wouldn't have done it!"

Prescott nodded. "That's a familiar pattern in suicide. The victim often hides his mood. I checked on his medical condition. He was in constant pain, and he had little prospect of ever being free from it. Frankly, the autopsy showed that he was stoned on painkillers at the time of his death."

"Sergeant, my brother was practically blown apart in North Africa. He rode to Italy in the bottom of an ammunition barge loaded with German wounded. There was one doctor aboard, and very few medical supplies. His leg was amputated under primitive conditions, by an Italian surgeon who saved his life. He spent two years flat on his back, ridden by fevers and infections. He had bedsores that left scars as big as your fists. He was shipped through Germany to Poland in a cattle car, so weak he couldn't even sit up. Until the end of the war, he lived on a starvation diet. The temperature in the barracks was often below freezing. And you're telling me he survived all that, and returned to Fort Worth and the family who loved him, only to commit suicide?"

"Let me put it this way," Prescott said. "In my opinion, even if we established a motive suggesting that your brother was murdered, we would never obtain a conviction on the basis of the physical evidence."

The detective met Brod's gaze in silent communication.

"Then you *do* have doubts," Brod said, making the question into a statement.

"I didn't say that. I only have a few reservations."

"Tell me," Brod demanded.

"This wouldn't stand up two minutes under the worst defense attorney in town. And if it's brought up again, I'll deny I ever said it. But a forty-five automatic is a vicious weapon, with considerable recoil. Your brother's hand, and the gun, were tucked a little too neatly against the body, rather than flung out to one side, as usually happens. Understand, I'm not even saying it's suspicious. It could happen that way. I'm only saying it's unusual. The gun wasn't his. It traces to an armory theft in Alabama. There's no proof the gun was ever in your brother's possession. And the body was a bit too erect, as if it had been arranged in place, instead of collapsed in the rag-doll way of most gun suicides. But that isn't solid enough to stop a coroner who wants to get back to his domino game. Maybe some day we'll have a medical examiner and do a better job on this type of case. But right now I have every evidence to suggest that your brother committed suicide and a coroner's report that says he did. I have *no* evidence suggesting that he didn't. If you have anything to offer, Mr. Spurlock, just tell me. I'll go to work on it."

Brod lay for a long time staring at the ceiling. He turned back to Prescott. "No, I think not, Sergeant. I appreciate your coming by. You've been most helpful."

After the detective left, Brod summoned Joanna. "Listen to me. I want all the servants out of the house for two hours. Send them shopping, give them the rest of the day off, whatever you have to do. Take the boys and go to a movie. Lock the front door when you leave."

Joanna moved to take his hand. "Brod, I can't leave you alone! What if . . ."

He gave her a grim smile. "I promise you, I'll be all right. I only have to make a few telephone calls."

Emerging from Sardi's a few minutes after midnight, Grover Sterling raised his arm to signal an approaching taxi. Bobbi grabbed his sleeve. "I feel stuffed. Come on. Let's walk."

Grover allowed the taxi to pass. He also felt like walking. The Algonquin was not far away, and straight down Forty-fourth Street.

As they crossed Broadway, Bobbi began humming "Oh, What a Beautiful Morning," performing light dance steps to her own music. Grover watched, eager to get her on to the Algonquin and into bed.

It had been a wonderful day. The talks with the financiers in Rockefeller Center had gone well. The money men had been especially impressed with Spurlock Oil assets and the potential for extensive profits. The signed agreement was now in his coat pocket. He had phoned Troy

the results, and taken Bobbi to the long-running musical *Oklahoma!*
They had topped the evening at Sardi's.

Bobbi turned to face him, took his hands, and danced backward.
Grover laughed. He liked her whimsical, kooky humor.

She had said she was a high-fashion buyer for a Chicago department
store. They had met on his arrival in New York, sharing a taxi from La
Guardia. They learned they were booked into the same hotel. One thing
led to another. They had now spent three nights together. Her hair was
black, her mouth warm and sensuous, and her dark eyes full of impish
mischief. She had taken considerable interest in his stock negotiations,
asking many questions. He had felt expansive and told her about his
financial coup.

Ahead, toward Sixth and Fifth Avenues, Forty-fourth was darker
than he remembered. Visitors to New York were now warned to be wary
of sidestreets and not to wander from the lighted paths in Central Park.
Muggings were on the increase. But he and Bobbi seemed to have the
street to themselves.

"Come on," Bobbi said. "Let's dance all the way into bed!"

Caught up in her high mood, he held her, turning as she made circles
around him.

Concentrating on Bobbi, Grover did not see the short, squat man
step out of a doorway. He seemed to materialize on the sidewalk. He was
holding a snub-nosed revolver.

"Get your hands up, away from your body," the man said.

Grover stopped in his tracks and complied. Bobbi moved away from
him and stood watching. Grover glanced at her, puzzled.

"Don't forget the papers," she said to the gunman. "They're in his
coat pocket."

Grover stared at her, confused. Then a second man stepped from the
shadows and drove a knife into his back.

Grover tried to stay on his feet, but the paralyzing pain drove him to
the sidewalk.

The gunman knelt and reached into his coat for his wallet and papers. Grover lay with his face to the cold concrete, wondering who had
set him up.

He was still making connections as he sank into oblivion.

Troy Spurlock awoke to the ringing of his bedside phone.

"Mr. Spurlock?" the caller said. "Your store's on fire!"

The caller giggled and hung up. Troy recognized the voice of his
head window decorator. The man sounded drunk.

Pulling on a robe, Troy walked down the hall to the front windows of

Bluebonnet. A rosy glow hung over the downtown section. In the distance he heard sirens.

He returned to his room and dressed hurriedly, fumbling with the buttons of his shirt. As he backed his car out and drove toward town, he watched the growing red pall of smoke, mesmerized.

Fire engines, intertwined snakes of hose blocked the street two blocks from the store. Abandoning his car, Troy walked on until stopped by a policeman.

"You'll have to get back, mister," the officer said, taking his arm.

Troy jerked free. "I'm the owner! Why don't they stop it!"

The policeman motioned to a helmeted fireman.

"Get the fire marshal. This guy says he's the owner."

Troy could not take his eyes from the fire. Although hoses were playing on the first four floors, flames were shooting out the windows, the blackish gray smoke curling upward, eerily lit by spotlights on the trucks.

The fire marshal introduced himself. "I'm afraid it'll be a total loss, Mr. Spurlock. It was totally engulfed when the first units arrived. There's so much smoke we can't get at the fire itself. You have any idea how it started?"

Troy shook his head. A section of brick cornice fell from the third floor and shattered on the sidewalk.

"The hot spot seems to be in the basement, near the elevator shafts. Do you have anything combustible stored there?"

Troy envisioned the basement storeroom. He remembered the merchandise that had just arrived. "Furs. We just received our fall furs."

"I doubt furs would cause that much heat. It must be from something else."

Troy could not get his mind off the fur coats, alone worth more than a half million dollars, wholesale.

They were uninsured. He only had a blanket policy on the stock. The amount was woefully inadequate.

Slowly, branching out from the furs, he began to absorb the scope of the tragedy.

The building, furnishings, and merchandise were covered for only a fraction of their true worth. He had protected himself against small hazards, never dreaming such a catastrophe could possibly occur.

The bills had not yet arrived for the fall merchandise.

Not until daylight, with the store a hollow shell of ashes, did Troy realize the full scope of the disaster.

He was broke.

He would even have to sell Bluebonnet to survive.

Each morning promptly at nine the bright young men arrived at the Spurlock home in Westover Hills, stood respectfully in the upstairs hall, and came in to see Brod one at a time. He listened to their reports, asked quiet questions, made a few suggestions, and signed whatever was required. By ten they were gone, and Brod had the remainder of the day to himself.

His days had fallen into a peaceful routine. After the morning business he had a light lunch with Joanna, usually on the terrace, weather permitting. During the early afternoons he slept, preserving his strength. When the boys returned from school, he would sit on the terrace and listen to them at play. In the evenings, after the boys were in bed, he and Joanna talked or enjoyed a quiet game of cards.

At first he had railed against the restrictions of his illness. But he soon saw his situation in a different light.

He had now learned what Loren had always known, that the true riches of life are the small pleasures, the gentle touch of a hand, the shared solitude of love, the laughter of children, the gold of a summer day.

Each hour had become precious.

He had to live for his sons.

They were his future.

He had to live to preserve Spurlock Oil.

That was their future.

Most of the time, Brod remained at peace with himself. Only at random, dark moments did moral burdens intrude. He quickly shoved them aside. He would have to endure them, as long as he lived.

But what he had done, he had done for his sons, for his family.

He would do the same again, no matter what the price.

Long weathered to a somber gray, Bluebonnet stood vacant and forlorn for years while the growing city passed it by. Only the rare curious paused, intrigued by the persistent dignity of its rotting gingerbread, the glint of its last shards of stained glass.

Eventually the older generations died away. Few were left who knew its story, or cared.

At last progress stirred along that stretch of the Trinity bluff. The demolition began one bleak day in late fall, and by four thirty the following afternoon nothing remained of the house Travis Spurlock had built so many years before.

Only his dreams survived.

Afterword

$\mathbf{R}$eaders of historical novels deserve an explanation of the boundaries observed between fact and fiction. In Fort Worth, the delineation is simple: the Spurlocks, their activities, in-laws, and business associates are fictional. The historical events through which they live are factual. Fort Worth's past is presented with conscientious, if not complete, accuracy.

Local historians will recognize that the fictional character of Major Van Emden is based heavily upon that of Major K. M. Van Zandt, and Captain Tackett on that of Captain J. T. Terrell. Major Van Zandt and Captain Terrell were strong, reticent men. They revered privacy, and remain remote, even to their descendants. I have not presumed to reconstruct their personalities.

The nationally known personages who figure in Fort Worth's past and in the novel are fairer game.

Long Hair Jim Courtright, surely one of the most colorful of all western gunmen, died on Fort Worth's Main Street as depicted. Luke Short, the nemesis of Courtright and several other gunfighters, lived out his natural life, and died in 1893 at Geuda Springs, Kansas. His body was returned to Fort Worth for burial.

Sam Bass, who plagued stagecoaches and trains serving Fort Worth and Dallas, was fatally wounded during an aborted bank robbery at Round Rock in 1878. While dying, he earned a measure of immortality in song and legend by refusing to betray his comrades.

Eagle Ford, site of at least one Bass train robbery, boomed upon becoming the western terminal of the Texas & Pacific in 1873, and for a brief time threatened to eclipse both Fort Worth and Dallas in population. But Dallas—as ever—prevailed. Today Eagle Ford no longer exists as a geographical entity.

Readers who care about such things will be happy to know that State Representative Nicholas Henry Darnell recovered from his near-fatal *illness in the summer of 1876, and enjoyed several more years of good health.*

Editor Buckley B. Paddock retired from newspapering in 1884. He later served four terms as mayor, and two in the Texas legislature. He spent his final years writing extensive local biographies and histories, and died in 1922. His idealism as a Yankee who fought for the South, and his daring exploits during the Civil War inspired George Washington Cabell to write a novel, The Cavalier *(1901), based on his life.*

Wolf-catcher Jack Abernathy survived his subsequent adventurous career as a U.S. marshal in Oklahoma during territorial days and early statehood, and later acquired considerable wealth as a wildcatter and lease trader during the Burkburnett oil boom.

Benjamin D. Foulois, the Spanish-American War veteran who flew with Orville Wright and who took delivery of the army's first air machine, retired in 1935 as a major general. He never ceased speaking his mind. At a ceremony honoring him as "the father of the U.S. Air Force" in 1964, the 84-year-old general turned the occasion into an impromptu political rally for presidential candidate Barry Goldwater. Laden with honors, Foulois died in 1967, only two years before the first man walked on the moon. He was 87.

Arriving for a landing at Taliaferro Field on February 15, 1918, Captain Vernon Castle crashed his plane while attempting to avoid collision with a student pilot. His wife, Irene, was awaiting his arrival at Westbook Hotel for dinner when the news was brought to her. "I'm told it was a brave man's death, sacrificing his life to save another," Irene told assembled newsmen. "It's not a woman's place to complain." In the years following her husband's death, Irene Castle appeared in a series of dramatic Hollywood films. A movie, The Story of Vernon and Irene Castle, *was released in 1939, with Fred Astaire and Ginger Rogers in the title roles. Irene died in 1969, a decade after publication of her autobiography,* Castles in the Air. *A marker on Vernon Castle Avenue in Benbrook, a Fort Worth suburb, commemorates the spot where Castle died.*

Ormer Locklear enlisted as a U.S. Army pilot, but failed to reach Europe in time to see combat in World War I. Bearing an uncanny resemblance to the latter-day film star Clark Gable, he became an early stunt pilot and movie actor, starring in The Great Air Robbery *(1919) and* The Skywayman *(1920). The scene in* The Skywayman *in which he flew a Curtiss Canuck through a breakaway church steeple is now a film stunt classic. His meteoric Hollywood career ended during night shooting for a final segment of the film. In a power dive, with cameras rolling, he crashed into an oil sump just off Wilshire Boulevard. Witnesses theorized that he was blinded by searchlights.*

The fact that Butch Cassidy and the Sundance Kid made Fort Worth

*their home away from home did not come to public light until 1949,
when author James D. Horan gained access to private files of the Pinkerton Detective Agency. Horan's published findings confirm material from
Fort Worth city records. The postnuptial celebration at Maddox Flats on
Main Street, wherein Butch rode the bicycle, was later described to Pinkerton by wedding guests.*

*Evangelist J. Frank Norris, generally credited with cleaning up
Hell's Half Acre, did not rest long on his laurels. He gained national fame
in 1926 when, embroiled in Fort Worth city politics, he shot a man dead
in his church. After a lengthy, emotion-packed murder trial, he won
acquittal. He became a pioneer radio preacher and, with dual pastorship
in Fort Worth and Detroit, broadcast his highly controversial sermons
across most of the nation. Eventually he proclaimed his Christian congregation second only to that of the pope.*

*Katherine Anne Porter managed to shove her Fort Worth years aside
and, in 1966, emphatically denied to me that they ever occurred. Her by-
lined writings for the Fort Worth weekly,* The Critic, *consisted mostly of
gossip columns and light theatrical reviews, and reveal little of her later,
awesome talent. Apparently Miss Porter wished to keep her earliest published material buried. Her authorized biography,* Katherine Anne Porter: A Life, *by Joan Givner (Simon and Schuster, 1982), arrived too late to
affect this manuscript. But Miss Givner's superb book, gleaned from
letters, diaries, and other sources, supports local memory concerning the
celebrated author's activities in Fort Worth.*

*After the closing of Casa Mañana's first season, Mary "Stuttering
Sam" Dowell became a Broadway favorite, and a delight among New
York newspaper columnists, who gleefully reported her every witty, stac-
cato quip. Later she herself became a columnist. Her typewriter did not
stutter. She knew everyone who was anyone, and wrote in a light, breezy
style. In 1944 she married Sigmund Hindley, a New York broker. Newspapers reported that she did not stutter when she said "I do." After her
husband's death on their sixth wedding anniversary, she married Guild
Copeland, a New York advertising executive. At the time of her death in
1963, she resided on Park Avenue.*

Which leaves us with the tantalizing question of Etta Place.

*Pinkerton Detective Frank Dimaio, who pursued Etta, Butch, and
Sundance to South America, once said he had evidence that Etta was a
schoolteacher before Butch and Sundance met her as a Fort Worth prosti-
tute. Nothing else is known about her early years.*

*The Pinkerton files reveal that Etta Place developed chronic appen-
dicitis in South America. Harry Longbaugh returned her to Denver,
where she submitted to surgery. While she recuperated in the hospital,
Longbaugh went on a drunken spree and shot a policeman in the leg. On*

sobering, he fled back to South America. Etta Place was released from the hospital and simply disappeared.

About this time Eunice Gray arrived in Fort Worth. A remarkably attractive woman, she soon became the well-known courtesan of several prominent Fort Worth men. Stories about her are legion. Those who knew her said she often enlivened conversations with tales of her escapades in South America. (This was long before the name of Etta Place and her activities were known to the public.)

For forty years Eunice Gray operated the Waco Hotel, which in time acquired a reputation of its own. She died in a fire at the hotel on January 26, 1962. According to her own accounting, she was 77. In the walls, firemen found bank stock valued in excess of $90,000. Later, when the building was razed to make way for the Tarrant County Convention Center, more bank stock was found.

Local historians—including one close to the handling of Eunice Gray's estate—have convinced me that Eunice Gray and Etta Place were one and the same. But perhaps we will never know for certain.

On release of the movie Butch Cassidy and the Sundance Kid, I wrote a newspaper column speculating on the many known parallels between Eunice Gray and Etta Place. Afterward, I was visited by a Pinkerton detective. He wanted to know the source of some of the information. I provided it.

I asked why he was interested, so long after the fact.

His reply had the ring of an epitaph.

"The file has never been closed on Etta Place," he said.

Leonard Sanders
Fort Worth
April 24, 1984

DATE DUE

DEC 12 1984	Nov 25 8 6		
JAN 23 1985	Jan 20 8 7		
1985 13	Ap 23 1987		
MAR 8 1985	[Au 4 1987		
APR 1 1985	Se 8 1987		
MAY 6 1985	Oc 7 1987		
JUN 17 1985	De 22 1987		
JUL 1985	Se 13 1990		
AUG 16 1985	NOC 10 1990		
OCT 18 1985	[De 6] 1990		
NOV 8 1985	Ja 30 1992		
DEC 4 1985			
MAR 12 1986			
APR 4 1986			
SEP 17 1986			